'A novel brimming with imagination and execution ... The Shadows of the Apt series is quite distinct, mainly due to the insect-kinden and Tchaikovsky's fertile imagination' *SciFiNow*

'Epic fantasy at its best. Gripping, original and multi-layered storytelling from a writer bursting with lots of fascinating ideas' *WalkerofWorlds.com*

'Superb world building, great characters and extreme inventive-ness' *FantasyBookCritic* blog

'Adrian is continuing to go from strength to strength. Magic' *FalcataTimes* blog

'Reminiscent of much that's gone before from the likes of Gem-mel, Erikson, Sanderson and Cook but with its own unique and clever touch, this is another terrific outing from Mr Tchaikovsky' *Sci-Fi-London.com*

'I cannot even begin to explain how much I enjoy the Shadows of the Apt books. Their level of originality and their sheer epic-ness makes for some of the best fantasy entertainment out there' *LEC Book Reviews.com*

'Tchaikovsky's series is a pretty great one – h̶ has some classic fantasy elements and a a unique ware) twist and element to his chara ovsky has created a world that blen blog

The Air War

Adrian Tchaikovsky was born in Woodhall Spa, Lincolnshire, before heading off to Reading to study psychology and zoology. For reasons unclear even to himself he subsequently ended up in law and has worked as a legal executive in both Reading and Leeds, where he now lives. Married, he is a keen live role-player and occasional amateur actor, has trained in stage-fighting, and keeps no exotic or dangerous pets of any kind, possibly excepting his son.

Catch up with Adrian at www.shadowsoftheapt.com for further information about both himself and the insect-kinden, together with bonus material including short stories and artwork.

The Air War is the eighth novel in the Shadows of the Apt series.

BY ADRIAN TCHAIKOVSKY

Shadows of the Apt

Empire in Black and Gold
Dragonfly Falling
Blood of the Mantis
Salute the Dark
The Scarab Path
The Sea Watch
Heirs of the Blade
The Air War

SHADOWS OF THE APT
BOOK EIGHT

The
Air War

ADRIAN
TCHAIKOVSKY

TOR

First published 2012 by Tor
an imprint of Pan Macmillan, a division of Macmillan Publishers Limited
Pan Macmillan, 20 New Wharf Road, London N1 9RR
Basingstoke and Oxford
Associated companies throughout the world
www.panmacmillan.com

ISBN 978-0-230-75700-4

1 3 5 7 9 8 6 4 2

A CIP catalogue record for this book is available from
the British Library.

Typeset by SetSystems Ltd, Saffron Walden, Essex
Printed and bound by CPI Group (UK) Ltd, Croydon, CR0 4YY

Visit **www.panmacmillan.com** to read more about all our books
and to buy them. You will also find features, author interviews and
news of any author events, and you can sign up for e-newsletters
so that you're always first to hear about our new releases.

To all those people. They know who they are.

Acknowledgements

I continue to be in debt to my agent, Simon Kavanagh, to everyone at Tor, to the editing prowess of Peter Lavery, and to the constant support and assistance of my wife. I'd also like to thank everyone who has contributed to the Shadows of the Apt Wiki at http://shadowsoftheapt.wikia.com/wiki/Shadows_Of_The_Apt_Wiki, especially Jackson Cordes and Roderick Easton.

I also owe a debt to everyone at Rebis for making me so welcome in Poland, including the translator Jarek Rybski, and particularly because a fair slice of this book was conceived of or written over there. A surprising amount was also written on trains going in various directions, so possibly I owe some manner of debt to Network Rail, whose many delays gave me so much unanticipated writing time.

Thanks also to Shane McLean for information on army procedure, and explaining why sometimes the best thing an engineer can do is make sure everyone gets fed.

And finally, going far back into the mists of time, a nod to Andy Campbell, porter at the Reading University Faculty of Letters and Social Sciences, who taught me some valuable lessons about warfare in the days of Napoleon, that era when a new war was just beginning to hatch from the cracked shell of the old.

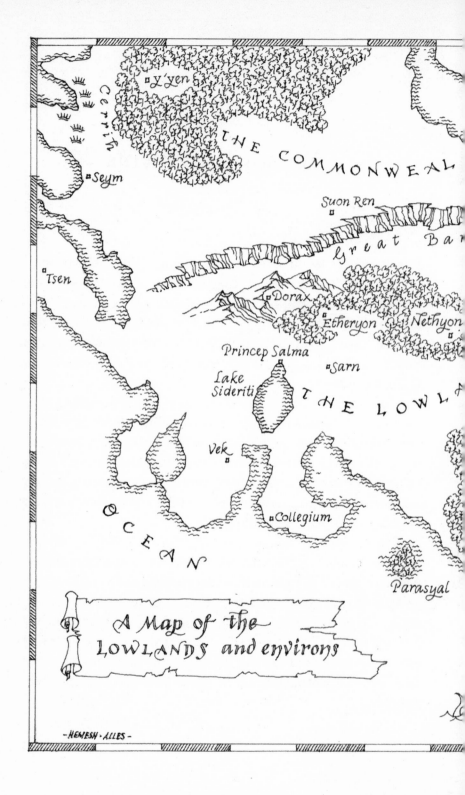

A Map of the LOWLANDS and environs

- HEMESH · ALLES -

Shon Jhor

Lake Limnia

Jerez

WASP EMPIRE

Luscoa

Sa

rier Ridge

Maynes

THREE CITY ALLIANCE

Szar

Myna

Tharn

Darakyon Forest

Helleron

Asta

N D S

Akta

Malkan's Folly

Merro

Tark

Egel

Thord

Iak

Seldis

Felyal

Silk Road

Everis

Araketka

Kes

Dryclaw Desert

Toek

SPIDERLANDS

Siennis

Mavralis

Porta Mavralis

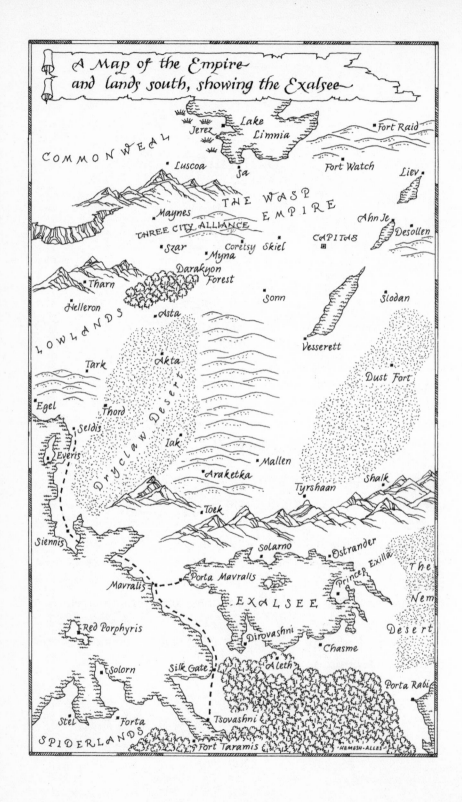

A Map of the Empire and lands south, showing the Exalsee

Summary

The last war against the Wasp-kinden ended in a draw. The demise of the Emperor, ostensibly at the hands of the Mantis Tisamon, forced a recall of the Imperial armies, and the Empress Seda has since been occupied in retaking provinces of her empire from the various traitor governors who sprang up in the wake of her brother's death.

Collegium has fallen out with its erstwhile allies in the Spiderlands, but Stenwold Maker has secret, new allies beneath the waves, having established tentative diplomatic links with the Sea-kinden, a civilization that most of his people are not even aware of.

Seda and her Empire have not been idle, though. The traitor governors are defeated now, and the Imperial engineers, men such as the aviator Varsec, have been devising new ways of making war. Seda herself has other needs. The unnatural death of her brother rendered her Inapt and gave her access to a magic fuelled by blood, and she has forced even more power out of the shadowy Masters of Khanaphes since conquering that ancient city.

The time has come for her and her Empire to look outwards to the wider world once again.

Principal Cast

In Collegium

Assemblers and City Leaders

Jodry Drillen, Speaker for the Assembly
Stenwold Maker, War Master
Corog Breaker, Master Armsman
Marteus, chief officer, Coldstone Company
Elder Padstock, chief officer, Maker's Own
Janos Outwright, chief officer, Outwright's Pike and Shot
Helmess Broiler, Assembler, alleged Imperial sympathizer

Students of the College and Associates

Straessa ('the Antspider'), duellist
Eujen Leadswell, agitator
Gerethwy, Woodlouse scholar
Averic, Wasp-kinden scholar
Sartaea te Mosca, teacher of Inapt studies
Raullo Mummers, artist
Castre Gorenn, Dragonfly exile

Imperial Embassy

Aagen, ambassador
Honory Bellowern, Aagen's adviser

Also in the City

Te Schola Taki-Amre ('Taki'), pilot
Banjacs Gripshod, master artificer
Berjek Gripshod, historian and diplomat
Praeda Rakespear, artificer and diplomat
Amnon, former First Soldier of Khanaphes
Willem Reader, artificer
Bola Stormall, artificer
Arvi, Jodry Drillen's secretary

In the Empire

Imperial Court

Seda I, Empress
Brugan, Rekef general
Harvang, Rekef colonel
Vecter, Rekef colonel
Gjegevey, Woodlouse adviser
Esmail/Ostrec, agent
Lien, general of Engineers
Knowles Bellowern, Consortium magnate

Second Army ('The Gears')

General Tynan
Colonel Mittoc, Engineers
Colonel Cherten, Army Intelligence

Imperial Air Corps

Varsec, colonel of Engineers
Aarmon, captain, pilot
Scain, pilot
Nishaana, pilot

Eighth Army

General Roder

Colonel Ferric, Engineers

Fly-kinden from the Factories

Pingge

Kiin

Gizmer

Elsewhere

In Solarno

Laszlo, agent of Stenwold Maker

Lissart ('te Liss'), agent

Te Riel, agent

'Painful' Breighl, agent

Garvan, Imperial Army Intelligence

In Myna

Kymene, Mynan leader

Edmon, pilot

Franticze, Szaren pilot

Aldanrael

Mycella of the Aldanrael, Lady-Martial

Jadis of the Melisandyr, officer of the camp

Morkaris, mercenary adjutant

Iron Glove

Dariandrephos ('Drephos'), the Colonel-Auxillian,
  master artificer

Totho, artificer

Part One

The Calm

One

Nobody built cities with aviators in mind, and that was a cursed shame, in Taki's opinion. That those cities had generally been planned before flying machines had been thought of was a poor excuse. She had taken her *Esca Magni* over to Princep Salma to have a nosy around, seeing a great blank grid of streets where the buildings themselves were still nothing but plots or foundations. A glorious opportunity, she had thought, to get the place properly designed for flight, but no, they had all sorts of ideas about how the place should look, and had set aside one dirty field on the outskirts for any luckless pilots who happened to come calling.

Backward thinking, that's the problem, she told herself. Now Solarno, her beautiful city beside the Exalsee, had at least made a game try at adapting itself to aviation. There were a dozen private airfields, and the city itself was set into a rolling hillside so that all a flier had to do to get airborne was simply pitch off the edge. The houses immediately beneath such jump-off points were always up for sale, she recalled. She couldn't imagine why.

She had flown into a lot of cities in her time, especially after the Wasp Empire's crawling tide of conquest had encompassed her home, driving her thence all the way along the western coast to Collegium. This, however, was a new experience for her, and her heart caught in her mouth at the sheer daring of it.

But she lived for daring. What else was a pilot for, after all?

The *Esca Magni* was handling beautifully today. The new clockwork was as smooth as butter, measuring out its prodigious stored power with an unprecedented ease and response. It broke her heart to admit it, but her previous machine, the nimble and much-mourned *Esca Volenti*, could not have matched her new *Magni* for speed, distance or agility in the air. If there was a machine to challenge her in any contest, she had yet to find it, though the Collegium artificers were constantly nipping at her heels to provide one.

The thought still caught in her like a hook: recalling her poor faithful *Volenti*'s brutal fate. It had been during the retaking of Solarno, her band of mercenaries and air-pirates against the Empire's new-fledged air force. She had duelled their best pilot – dragon-fighting, they called it around the Exalsee, after the fierce aerial battles the Dragonfly-kinden loved. He had been very good and, although she would not acknowledge him as her better, he had met her and met her, time and again, even though his black-and-yellow striped Spearflight had not been equal to her *Volenti*.

And at the last, with her machine torn and mauled and its rotary piercers jammed, she had taken advantage of his fixation on her, and baited him in too close, leaping from the cockpit before their two fliers crashed and tangled, removing herself from the fight. She had watched, her own wings ablur, as the conjoined machines tumbled and fell – and felt as though she had killed her best friend.

The *Esca Magni* was some consolation after that. The original design had sprung from the best of Collegium artifice and her own unparalleled understanding of the simple business of flying, and never had there been a more demanding mistress for the artificers than te Schola Taki-Amre, known as Taki to her friends. Even a month ago, she had still been making minute changes to perfect the new flier's handling. The *Esca Magni*, as originally built, had surpassed the *Volenti* by a small but measur-

4

able degree – and there had been a great deal of measuring, for the Collegium Beetles were fond of that.

Then had come the new clockwork – or the 'New Clockwork', to reflect the reverent way that the artificers talked about it. It involved some mad innovation in metallurgy from somewhere across the sea, some Spiderlands place or other, and it was not exactly common but there was a steady supply of the improved spring steel seeping into Collegium. An artificer called Gainer had begun using it for some boat he was working on, and shortly afterwards one of Taki's mechanic disciples had brought it to her attention.

The level of precision required to take full advantage of the New Clockwork was formidable, but at around the same time, and apparently from the same source, Collegium began to see machine parts crafted to a frightening exactness, perfect in every tooth no matter how small. The resulting engines were lighter, smaller and considerably more powerful than anything *anyone* had seen before, and Taki had kicked an awful lot of shins in the College – and got up the noses of a great many ground-bound Beetle-kinden – before she secured a supply for the flying machines. Thankfully, by then, she had her supporters: her students and a ragbag of Collegiates who shared her passion for the air.

She had run the *Esca Magni* through a lot of paces since then: distance trips and mock-duels, up and down the coast, hops over to Sarn and Princep, even back to her old home of Solarno to show off to those of her friends that were still among the living. *This* journey was different, though.

She had thought to make it in one long leg, gliding where she could, hitching a ride in the high air currents and testing the New Clockwork to its logical conclusion. She had made good progress at first, but eventually minute changes in the engine's ticking and a sluggishness in the controls had convinced her that reality was going to fall considerably short of her ambitions –

and that was without any hard weather or, most demanding of all, actual air combat. She resolved to try and kick her tame artificers into working on something even better.

She put down in Helleron, and paid for the use of a winding engine to re-tension her flier. She felt bitterly disappointed about having to break her journey, for all that it gave her the chance to eat something that hadn't been dried half to death.

Taki was the first recorded pilot ever to make the trip from Collegium to Helleron in a single journey in a heavier-than-air machine, but she had failed in her original plan, therefore it still seemed like second prize.

She had managed the flight from Helleron to *here* in another single bound although, had the political situation been tenser, she would have expected to have to fight her way past half the cities that had glided past below her. She had worried about her navigation as well, and whether she would even recognize her target when she saw it, but her charts and her compass were in agreement, and the view could have been nowhere else on earth.

Capitas, the heart of the Wasp Empire.

This city had not been built with aviators in mind, either, but at least it was planned out by an Apt kinden that could fly, and so she spotted a half-dozen open spaces that looked to be ideal for landing her *Esca*, and several large fields outside the city as well, mostly attended by louring barracks and presumably given over to the innumerable soldiers of the Imperial army.

She brought her flier in low as she neared, knowing that every city provided a free updraught for the canny flier. She was determined not to end up somewhere on the outskirts: *that* would be a failure of daring. Besides, the city looked rather flat and, while that detracted from its scenic value, it was a gift to a pilot coming in low.

She revised her assessment of the place very quickly, because she was still coming in low – dangerously low now – and she had not quite reached the sprawling outskirts. *Right, so it's just a little bigger than I thought.* She pulled up on the stick, inching a little more height, and then the first suburbs of Capitas were speeding beneath her, close enough that she caught the pale flash of faces peering up. *And we'll see how good that cursed invitation was, too.* The spectre of a dozen combat Spearflights lifting straight up from one of the airfields loomed large in her mind.

The sheer number of aircraft she saw was proof positive that she was not here on false pretences, however. Every airfield was cluttered with them, and the sky above Capitas was lumpy with airships and spotter balloons.

When the invitation had arrived, her fellow aviators at the College had thought it was a hoax or a trap, depending on how suspicious their minds were. None of them knew that she had been corresponding sporadically, secretly, with the Wasp capital for over a season. Not even Stenwold Maker was aware of that. In fact, he probably topped the list of people Taki had no intention of telling.

Capitas saw itself as the heart of Aptitude, and it was keenly aware of the longer pedigrees of Collegium and Helleron. Taki had a vague understanding that there had been some changes here in the Empire since that woman took over, but they had held no interest for her until now. Capitas was hosting a grand exhibition of aviation, and notables from the entire known world had been invited. After all, the war was the past, as everyone knew.

Her face abruptly set, Taki slung her *Esca Magni* past the long flank of an ascending airship, seeing the square ports all the way down the side of its hull. She knew what *they* were for. The *Starnest*, which had been the linchpin of the Solarno invasion, had been three times as long, but it had used the same method for dispersing its complement of soldiers across the city: the Wasps simply throwing themselves out of the hatches and gliding down on their Art-fed wings.

But the airships, even the great war-dreadnoughts, had a shamefaced and sheepish air: the *Starnest* had been unseamed and had fallen from the sky; the Collegiate *Triumph* had burned.

The age of the airship as a great tool of war was done. The air now belonged to the heavy fliers.

Ahead she saw one of the city's parks, which had been converted to an airstrip. There was precious little space there, but she reckoned she could touch down the *Esca* without too much jockeying.

A score of different fliers had landed in haphazard rows, most of them looking completely unfamiliar to her. Even as she slowed and banked, achieving a jittery hover over the field, she found herself facing a solid rank of black and gold. One entire edge was composed of a line of Spearflights hunched beneath their folded wings. For a moment she was inclined to touch down in front of them, just to show them how cursed daring she really was, but something in the uniform discipline of their positioning broke her resolve, and she hauled back and had the *Esca Magni* circle a little, as nonchalantly as she could manage, looking for other lodgings. Capitas was a city dominated by ziggurats, the characteristic form of Wasp architecture. Some were grand and some were squat, and all were surrounded by lower buildings with flat roofs. After a pass around the field, Taki spotted a rather inviting prospect that was probably some mid-ranking official's little kingdom, and she slid the *Esca* through the air, folding down the craft's three legs so that they ghosted across the stone, the entire flying machine poised momentarily, almost still in the air, the tilt of its wings exactly cancelling out her lateral movement, before she let herself drop, with the legs bowing to catch the strain.

Even as she hopped out, a man had already scrambled up onto the roof through a hatch, a lean Dragonfly-kinden wearing a simple tunic – a house slave, she realized. He stared at the flying machine perched on his master's roof, and she saw a very small smile twitch at his face because *here* . . . here was some-thing that he could not possible be blamed for.

She let her wings carry her down the tiered facade of the building and was immediately surrounded by soldiers. They came from all sides, and some dropped from the air onto the building behind her, between her and the *Esca*. Cursing herself for being too caught up in her daring to keep a basic watch out for trouble, she was reaching for her little knife by instinct, in the face of their stings. Or perhaps she would leap back and try for the sky, trusting that she was swifter and more nimble than they.

She stopped herself, calmed herself. Yes, they were Wasps, but she was already within their city. The protocols were somewhat different.

'Is this how you treat your guests here, sieurs?' she demanded, muscling up to the nearest of them as though they were not twice her size. It took physical effort to hold the light smile on her face, because her heart was hammering in her chest and her instincts were screaming at her.

One of the soldiers stepped forward, their sergeant or something. 'Is this how you think guests are supposed to behave?' he demanded, seeing only a lesser kinden – and a woman to boot – but a foreigner and yet not a slave, and so outside of the hierarchy he was used to.

'What?' she asked brightly. 'Don't tell me these nice flat roofs aren't meant for landing on?'

For a moment she could not read him, and she was ready for him to give his next order: it was the blessing of opposing a military group, rather than just some band of rogues, that they would considerately tip you off by having to instruct each other when to kill you. Then she marked an extremely grudging smile, fighting for purchase at the corner of his mouth – not unlike the slave's, in fact – and she guessed that whoever owned this house, he was both well known and not popular.

'You're here for the exhibition?' the soldier asked her gruffly, and yet a certain degree of tension had ebbed away.

By way of reply, Taki gestured towards the *Esca Magni*. 'I'm come from Collegium – aviation department of the Great College.'

This did not produce the sort of automatic respect that most College Masters always assumed it would. 'You have papers?' the soldier enquired.

She blinked. 'What, you mean like College accredits? Only, I'm sort of an honorary assistant scholar, and . . .'

'Papers. Visitor's papers.'

That seemed too much even for a military bureaucracy. 'I've only just arrived,' she pointed out.

He took in a deep breath and she saw, with an involuntary spark of sympathy, that the people who had organized the Imperial Air Exhibition – their merchant Consortium and engineers – were not the people who were having to put a great deal of it into practice. She wondered how many obstinate, ignorant, irreverent foreigners these soldiers had so far rounded up.

'Fly-kinden,' the soldier addressed her, 'anywhere between the Three Cities and here could have drawn up papers for you. Most of your fellows procured theirs in Sonn or Shalk.'

She folded her arms and tossed her head back, a minuscule study in pride. 'That would require me to come down to land somewhere between Helleron and Capitas.'

His expression remained wholly unimpressed, and she realized that he had little understanding of either the distances or the technical feat involved in her journey. She was just a foreigner who was making his life difficult, an invader in the Empire's heart, and yet he couldn't do anything about it. She was sure he wanted to kill her or enslave her, or take her prisoner and lock her up. His entire world view was based on that shortlist of responses towards strangers. That he was restraining himself now indicated why he had made sergeant, she suspected.

'Show me where to go to get these papers, then,' she suggested, somewhat more meekly, and at last she was behaving as he expected, and shortly thereafter some Consortium clerk had drawn up her visitor's pass, cautioning her to keep it about her person at all times or she might not be so lucky next time. She bit back a sarcastic jibe about Imperial hospitality, because the truth was that this *was* Imperial hospitality, the best there had ever been. A hundred or so aviators and several hundred more pedestrians had come from across the Apt world to their capital, absentmindedly breaking their laws, offending their sense of racial superiority and threatening their security, and the Wasps were somehow allowing them to do so without ordering a general massacre. Yet.

Her papers stuffed in the inside pocket of her tunic, Taki strode out into the city of her enemies – or at least they had been her enemies not so very long ago, and would be again soon enough, most likely. She was a striking woman of her kinden, small and slender, her chestnut hair falling past her shoulders. In her pilot's overalls of canvas, a pilot's helm of chitin over leather dangling from her belt beside her flying goggles, she would have looked foreign anywhere outside Solarno, but most especially here. Still, there were a great many foreigners being tolerated in Capitas during these few days of the exhibition. The city had gone to some lengths to accommodate them, and still it was an unwelcoming place.

Any other city, and Taki would have looked for wayhouses, tavernas, chop houses, all the necessaries that accompanied trade and travellers. The citizens of the Empire still traded and travelled, of course, although perhaps not quite so much of either as most others, but they were never out of place, not in any Imperial city. It was a humbling, disturbing thought, but everyone in the Empire had their place assigned to them, like it or not. When one of them journeyed to somewhere else within the Empress's realm they would stay at their Consortium's factora, or the local garrison barracks, or in guest chambers prepared by the governor. Their way was pre-paved, both easier and less free. Along the road there were inns, although they were regulated and administered by the civic governors. In the cities there were only homes away from home. Anyone left to wander the streets without fitting into this great pattern would soon be obligingly found a place by the Slave Corps.

There were neighbourhoods of Capitas that had been turned into impromptu inns, she found. Canvas had been stretched from roof to roof, and whole streets had been set out as common rooms furnished with simple beds. Dour slaves exchanged food and drink for coin that would only go to their masters in the Consortium. A brief but thriving temporary service economy had been created from first principles. Taki bought herself a square of floor and a pallet bed in one of the women's districts – the separation amused her – and paid a sergeant of the Imperial Engineering Corps to have her *Esca Magni* rewound, going into some detail so that he would be able to find her machine back on its rooftop. The engineer was more her sort of person than the street guards had been, and was properly impressed by her feats of long-distance flying.

After that, with dusk looking an hour away at best, she let herself wander over to the exhibition itself, a quartet of civic squares that had been given over to aviation demonstrations and contests. Two score of different models of flying machine had been parked there and anatomized, their workings laid open for public inspection. Here, a Spearflight with its guts out, four wings unfolded and poised as though caught in mid-beat. There, the great, blocky shape of the old heliopters that the Empire had once relied on almost exclusively – and not so long ago at that – which seemed laughably primitive to Taki's eyes. There was a section of the gondola from an airship dreadnought that visitors could walk through and, beyond it, an ear-jarring racket as a dozen different engines were run against each other in a competition to see which had the most staying power.

Everything was of interest, but nothing quite held her attention for long. There was so little of it that she would count as cutting-edge. It made her feel quite patronizing towards the Empire that they had proffered this display so proudly. What meant more to her was that she was surrounded by other pilots, her peers and fellows, and that was something she had missed since leaving Solarno.

She still received invitations to return to her home city for good, but she had left a crashed flier and a lot of dead friends there and, despite the time that had passed, she found such losses too recent. Besides, she was fond of Collegium – honestly, she was – it was just . . . sometimes she missed having someone on her own level of skill, someone to share the skies with as only another fighting pilot could.

Being free of the demands of the College and being amongst her own kind was all so much fun that she forgot about the Wasp soldiers for whole minutes at a time.

There was not a foreigner there not being watched – watched with the sort of paranoid suspicion normally the preserve of the most insular of Ant cities. They were all potential spies, these visiting aviators and artificers, and everywhere Taki looked were the uniforms of the Imperial army, singly and in small groups, their eyes raking the crowds, looking for the enemy. After a while she decided that at least half of them were watching the citizens of Capitas, in case being around all these foreigners gave the locals any ideas.

After dark, Taki flitted from one canvas-roofed hall to another until she found some faces she knew. Over glasses of some very acceptable brandy, she settled down beside another Collegiate, a diminutive Beetle-kinden by the name of Willem Reader, who had set off considerably earlier than she and yet arrived only the day before. He was an aviation artificer who had authored a number of texts about the New Clockwork, and was now gathering material to present to the College for its next aviation symposium. Across the round table from them was a Solarnese pilot she knew slightly: a man named Shawmair who had been a pirate and outcast for years, but was now back in the city's good graces due to his part in the liberation. Beside Shawmair was a lean, nervous-looking Ant-kinden with bluish skin, from no city Taki could name. He spent most of his time glancing over his shoulder.

'You missed a good show this morning, Bella Taki,' Shawmair declared. 'They held a contest: teams of fliers against each other. No doubt our hosts were itching to show us how grand they were.'

'I take it they didn't succeed?' she asked cautiously, aware that there would be Imperial ears listening to all of this.

'Oh, their old Spearflights held up well enough until our fliers came against them. The new Firebugs, Bella, they'll knock anything else out of the sky. I'd stake them against whatever you're flying these days, and that's knowing your exquisite taste.' He sneered a bit at Reader. 'No team from Collegium, then? Even your Helleren magnates managed a respectable entry.'

'Ah, well, organizing academics ... what can you say?' Reader replied mildly. 'Perhaps next year, if there is one.' He did not look at Taki, but they both knew that the College's aviators, the cornerstone of the city's pilots, were currently training with new machines that were Beetle-sized cousins of Taki's own orthopter.

'I remember when Solarno's strength was its pilots, as individuals,' she noted. Indeed, a few years ago it would only have been the Empire, and perhaps some plodding Ant city-states, who produced a standard model of flying machine.

'Past times,' Shawmair said dismissively. 'After the retaking of our city, everyone can see how any future war will be won or lost and, with all that riding on it, how can you trust to just some bunch of pilots, and what they may or mayn't, can or can't do?' The former rogue and criminal put on a virtuous face. 'Solarno needs to know for sure it has a force that can take on the Empire ...' Here he stopped and realized at last, even through the brandy, that he had gone too far. 'Take on the *enemy*, I mean, and give him a thrashing, without having to worry about whether our people'll feel like it, or be up to it. And the Solarnese air force has the finest pilots and machines in the world, as this morning's games have proved. The Emp— other cities may have more to put in the sky, but skill triumphs over numbers any day. We stand on the shores of the Exalsee, and our Firebugs say, "You shall not touch us."'

He was drunk and talking too loud, and the Ant beside him was growing increasingly worried about what attention Shawmair was attracting. He was a useful diversion, though, so nobody was listening to Taki when she murmured to Reader, 'You've made contact?'

'He approached me,' the Beetle whispered back, his brandy bowl close to his lips to mask them. 'He'll be here. And I'm nothing to do with it, remember. I barely know you. Some of us can't just skip off into the sky.'

She had wanted to sit and wait, but Shawmair was still expounding the virtues of Solarno's new machines, and she *was* curious. When he offered to show her, she glanced at Reader and he nodded slightly. He had been making notes, she saw, for whatever talk he was preparing to give here.

Shawmair's craft was standing close by, one of an untidy semicircle of visiting machines scattered about a garden park that was now badly in need of re-landscaping. The stocky-bodied machine was painted red, fading to darker hues towards the tail, which curved sharply down and forward, and its wings, at rest, were vertical, tips touching. She recognized parts of it: oddments of shape that mirrored elements of her *Esca*, others that had been drawn from fliers she had known or flown against. Her eyes weighed it at once, not needing Shawmair's commentary, and she felt a tinge of envy – not that she would admit it was better than her *Esca*, but nonetheless she saw a dozen little innovations she was itching to reverse-engineer.

'Fuel engine, triple-action, with halteres to balance the wings,' Shawmair was saying. 'The beat is four times what a Spearflight would give you, so it just guzzles the mineral oil, won't keep in the air for all that long, but nothing else has the speed and power. And they reckon those villains in Chasme have an improved engine design if we want to pay their price for it. Four-way rotary piercers from a central drum, and, look, this slide here stops jamming in the bolt-feed . . .'

His voice droned on, but she was aware that she was being watched: a feeling that she had been expecting for some time. From the corner of her eye she marked a dark, thin figure at the far end of the grounded fliers.

'Excuse me,' she broke into Shawmair's bragging. 'You wait here, and I'll be right back.' It was a lie, but he was a bore, so she didn't feel too bad about it.

She hopped into the night sky, her wings casting herself over the head of her watcher, knowing that he would mark her, assuming automatically that he would be able to plot her course and trajectory, to work out that she would end up with her feet on the ground a street away.

She hoped that this figure was who she thought it was, and not just some Rekef snoop clumsy enough to be spotted.

In the dark street beyond, she touched down, then shrugged back against a wall on hearing multiple footsteps. Within moments, a trio of soldiers passed by, but they did not seem to be acting as city watch, instead talking quietly amongst themselves, and passing a little metal flask from hand to hand. On their way back to barracks, perhaps, or on to some nocturnal assignment.

After they had gone she waited. And then she continued waiting beyond the point when her internal timekeeping, which had always been keen, told her that any watcher should have caught her up. At last she caught a faint shuffle and, after an unexpectedly long gap, the same figure appeared.

I should have thought. He was not as she remembered him, but then she could have predicted that, had she only put her mind to it. The newcomer was a Wasp, lean and bundled in a greatcoat that had been standard Imperial issue during the Twelve-year War with the Commonweal. For Taki the Capitas night was mild, spring already well under way, but it seemed that winter still clung to this man. Or perhaps the coat was simply to hide what was beneath, for one of his shoulders was higher than the other and there was a terrible lopsidedness to all of him, inherent in the very way he stood. His gait, as he stepped onto the street, had been an uneven limp, with one leg stiff as a stilt.

She approached cautiously because, if he was like *that*, what would his reaction to her be? Had this all been a trap, a plan for revenge? Even crippled as he was, he could still sting.

She coughed to draw his attention, ready to trust to her wings at a moment's notice.

His face, as it turned to her, was shiny with burn scars. 'Bella Taki?' came a coarse voice. There was no hatred or hostility in it.

'Sieur Axrad,' she named him, and then, 'Lieutenant Axrad, I mean.' She approached cautiously, less from fear of him than a reluctance to see what she had made of him. He had been the Empire's pre-eminent pilot in Solarno and, when she had flown during the liberation, it had been against him. His Spearflight had crashed and mangled into her *Esca Volenti*. She had assumed he had died.

It was a long time later when his first letter reached her, a halting missive reintroducing himself, stiffly offering his congratulations on her victory over him.

They had exchanged a few letters since, and she had read, between his words, that he was lonely. The Empire might be a fierce and Apt state, but it lacked the pilot's society of Solarno, that exclusive and peerless fraternity of those who *could*. Axrad had more in common with her than with his own.

His face was blank as he gazed at her, but after a while she noticed that his eyes looked as though they should be smiling, and realized that the burn had left him without much range of expression.

'Come with me,' he rasped, and went limping off without another word, leaving her to patter after him, still not convinced that it wasn't all a trap.

He took her to a Capitas drinking den – not like the place that Reader and the other foreigners had been guided into, but the real thing. It was in the cellar of a squat, square house, almost twice the size of the cramped ground floor above. Everyone else there was Wasp-kinden, and all men, some of them in uniform. All were drinking, and most of them seemed to be there for nothing else, save for one huddle playing cards on the floor. There were a few tables available, and she saw that Axrad was known because they cleared one for him. By the way he levered himself painfully into a chair it was plain that sitting on the floor would not have been possible for him.

There was no other chair. She sat on the table, close to him and keenly aware of the baleful looks she was getting: wrong kinden, wrong gender, wrong nationality. Still, nobody had bolted out of the door to tell the Rekef, just yet.

'So, how . . . ?' She could not ask the question, stupid as it was. She knew from his letters that he was bitter and frustrated. She had known he was unable to fly, although he had not been clear, in his writing, just why. Asking him how he was getting on now would be sheer insult. 'Still "lieutenant", though?'

His nod was jerky. 'Don't assume that I asked you here to catch up on old times,' he told her. 'Though I'd like to. They're all I have. But I wouldn't call Collegium and Solarno's greatest pilot all this way just to indulge me.' He sounded like an old, old man, and moved like one too. He was probably only a few years her senior. 'You wonder if I've lured you here for the Rekef?' Without needing an answer he went on, 'I wonder if you've come here as a pilot or a spy. Are you here with your Stenwold Maker's blessing?' His eyes were still mobile and young, as he probed her face.

'No, and for two reasons,' she told him. 'One, he's so twitchy about your lot he'd try to stop me coming at all. Two, if he couldn't stop me he'd give me all sorts of other rubbish to be doing here that would get me arrested or killed, or both. So, no, just me. The pilot.'

'I will tell the pilot things that the spy would kill for. I *was* a pilot, Bella Taki. I was a *pilot*.'

She stared at him: of course he had been a pilot, but she saw his hand clamp on the table rim, the fingers white and shaking with all the emotion his mute face could not show.

'No longer,' he said at last, his eyes alarmingly wide. 'This? Oh, this.' He made such an offhand gesture, dismissing the ruining of his body as though it was a shaving scar. 'But, even if I were whole, nothing for me. Men who were my equal, the best in the aviation corps – denied the new machines, sidelined, even taken from combat duty and reduced to supply runs, civilian freight or sent in old Spearflights to terrify the savages in the most backward part of the Empire. Or made to *teach*. They had me teaching.'

She didn't want to confess that she had been doing exactly the same at Collegium. Secretly she agreed that it was a poor second to actually flying, but she owed the College a great deal.

'Teaching the junior pilots I knew from before we went to Solarno, though? No,' he spat out. 'Listen, Bella Taki, we don't have much time. Listen to me. They have me teaching clerks and slavers, factory overseers, men plucked from the Consortium or the Light Airborne – oh, lots of the Light Airborne. Have they any flying experience? No, almost without exception: clueless, hopeless, and yet they are the new pilots, the next generation of combat fliers rushed through training, hours and days in Spearflights and whatever else is to hand, More training in a few months than most trainees get in a year.' His voice sank lower. 'And there's something *wrong* with them,' he whispered. 'They sit there . . . like machines. They watch, they learn. Not a twitch, not a shared joke with their classmates: men of all ages, all backgrounds, and yet . . . by the end, I had begun to fear them.' His hand was shaking again. 'Then one of their own – he had been a pilot, the only one that had been – took over the teaching. I was no longer required. I have been cast away. All the men I knew, the Empire's pilots, are being displaced by these . . . *freaks*.'

'Well, it doesn't sound as though the Lowlands or Solarno have much to worry about, then,' Taki tried, dismissively, but Axrad's eyes flared, and he had her by the wrist before she could pull away.

'I'll show you,' he threatened, lurching to his feet. In actual fact there was pitifully little strength in that grip, but there was a warmth to his palm that frightened her, because one sting and he could take her hand off.

As he hauled her out of the drinking den, the looks on the faces of the other Wasp men were mostly approving. At last she was being taught her place, apparently.

Axrad started stomping haltingly away, and he could not hold her, his fingers weakening and loosening his grip after only a few steps. 'I'll show you,' he said again, less of a threat now. He did not even look back to see if she was following.

She wanted very much to return to the other foreigners now. She wanted Axrad to come along with her and talk about old times. Her daring had abandoned her without warning. Still, to go now would be to show fear in front of another pilot, for all that he would never fly again. She was the greatest pilot that either Solarno or Collegium had ever known. She had bested the Empire's own best. This is what she told herself whenever she met life's obstacles. If she fled now, she would never quite recover that iron self-confidence.

Axrad was making surprisingly quick progress, his hoarse breath showing that he was pushing himself painfully to do it. She kept pace without difficulty, could have gone twice as fast without resorting to her wings but, even so, his grim determination scared her. Here was a different man to the earnest pilot she had met in Solarno.

Crashing in flames and becoming a burned cripple will do that.

'Axrad,' she did not want to raise the issue but it was unavoidable, 'you should hate me.'

'For Solarno?' he panted. 'You were the last person to treat me as an equal. As someone who *mattered*. I save my hate for others.'

He took a sharp turn, hissing with sudden pain, and they were at the edge of an airfield, a narrow strip easy to overlook, since the city was strewn with more inviting spots. With a start she realized that they were towards the edge of the city here. They had come further than she thought. Beyond the strip lay a rabble of small houses and two or three big sheds – no, hangars that had been storage sheds not so long ago.

This can't be a secret airstrip. We're right in the capital. We're surrounded by buildings. And yet she guessed that the locals kept their mouths shut and, besides, it was night. The Wasps were not a nocturnal people. They did things by day for preference. Night was for stealth and subterfuge.

'They call them Farsphex,' the Wasp breathed, and then stared down at her as though he had forgotten she was with him. 'Hide yourself,' he snapped. 'Just watch.'

She blinked at him, then flitted up to the roof of the nearest building, but the flat roof made her feel exposed, so she darted down again, finding a narrow alley that had been fenced off where it met the airstrip. With a little scrambling and balancing she had found a roost tucked into the shadows where the fence met the alley wall. By then, her ears had already registered the sound.

It was a familiar drone, which she had lived with all her life: the sound of a fixed-wing flier coming in to land. After a moment she had identified it as a twin-propeller vessel, small enough to be a fighting pilot's, but bigger than the *Esca Magni* even so.

She saw figures moving out on the field. Abruptly there were fires out there: bright white chemical flares in a triangle, illuminating some hurriedly retreating Wasp-kinden, throwing their shadows in long strips of night reaching all the way to the field's edge. She caught a glimpse of Axrad, his face given a fishlike pallor by the light. His expression was fixed, fatalistic.

The approaching flier was closer, but something was wrong, and Taki seized on the anomaly quickly. That triangle was a landing spot, but fixed-wing craft could not land on a point like that, not reliably. They could not manage that last-minute arresting of their momentum, that second's hovering which would allow them to drop neatly to the ground.

Her eyes – better than the Wasps' at night – caught a glimpse of the machine as it made a pass, plotting its descent, the long, low turning circle that she would have expected, but then abruptly it was upon them, dropping out of its turn sharply enough to make Taki catch her breath.

She had been wrong, she realized with annoyance more than anything else. An orthopter, not a fixed-wing. The sound of the propellers had gone, and there was a moment's silent glide before its wings were backing, thrashing at the air, tilting the whole machine back and fighting to hold its place, before dropping slightly off the mark, a few yards to Taki's side of the triangle.

Immediately the ground crew rushed forward to douse the lights, but she had a good chance to study the machine before they did.

Farsphex, Axrad had said. Bigger than the little air-duelling craft she knew, perhaps enough to carry two at a pinch, but with sleek, elegant lines for all that, its wings folded at an angle, back along the curved sweep of its body and tail. But there were the two props, whose drone she was sure she had heard, where the wings met the body and, now she looked, the styling of the hull was not quite an orthopter's, concessions being made to other design imperatives . . .

Instead of the cockpit glass hinging up, a hatch popped in the flier's side and the pilot scrambled out. Two other Wasps were coming to meet him, striding across the field in a way that suggested this clandestine exercise was over. She expected voices, but not a word was exchanged.

Taki stared at that flying machine once again, trying to appreciate what she had been brought here to see, trying to reconcile what she had heard with what she now saw.

But of course. She started with the revelation, understanding coming to her at last. Perhaps it was not quite enough to justify Axrad's manner, but still . . . the technical challenge alone was remarkable, but what could the Wasps hope to *do* with it?

Then they spotted Axrad. One of the ground crew challenged him, and the sound was all the more shocking because of the utter silence of the men up to that point. Taki saw the crippled pilot step forward.

'Lieutenant Axrad,' he threw back, 'Aviation Corps.'

The two men who had gone over to the flier were storming towards him now, and Taki saw that they were also dressed as pilots. One of them growled something, but too low for her to hear what.

Time to go. But she stayed, nonetheless, watching.

For a moment Axrad was angrily dismissing them, pulling rank, facing them down, but then their eyes, both sets, both at once, were turned on Taki.

She could not understand how she had been detected. The two of them had not even been glancing around them.

Abruptly they were moving, and Axrad tried to get in their way, stumbling forward into their path, hands reaching out for them – to grab or to sting, she would never know. She saw a fierce flash of gold, fire leaping from one of their hands, and Axrad was down the next moment, just a crumpled dark heap.

In the next moment she was standing on the ridge of the fence, wings springing from her shoulders. She had a brief glimpse of the flying machine – of its pilot, his goggles turned her way, silent but with a palm directed at her.

She kicked into the air and *flew*, and knew for sure that they were behind her.

She was faster and smaller, and their night vision was not the equal of hers, but if she had needed to head for any of the usual airfields, she was sure they would have caught her. She spotted three of them in pursuit, but she had the feeling that the city was bristling with other eyes, that there were hordes of them converging on every likely spot. She concentrated on sheer speed, zipping across the city with no clear destination: just putting distance between her and them, then doubling back, reading the web of streets with a navigator's eye, just as she would if she were piloting over the city, and getting her bearings by long-honed instinct.

There had been not a shout when they took off after her, not an alarm bell or warning cry.

She found the *Esca* and dropped straight onto it, throwing open the cockpit and almost falling into her seat. One lever disengaged the wing safeties, nudging gear trains in so that their teeth meshed. Another—

A sting blast crackled from the roof beside her craft, a long-range shot. She thought, *They've found me*, but she felt a horrible certainty that whoever was shooting at her was not one of the men from the airstrip, but some new enemy, brought down on her by . . . what?

No time to ponder that. She threw another lever and all that stored power in her *Esca*'s springs slammed the gears into motion, slapping the wings down, throwing the entire craft vertically up in the air. Then the oscillators were hammering with their comforting rhythm and the wings were ablur on either side of her, thrusting the flying machine forward between the buildings of Capitas and the stars.

It had been a short visit, she reflected, but instructive, and she had made sufficient impression that she guessed the locals did not want her to leave. She slung the *Esca* sideways in the air until her compass read south, and decided to play dodge over a swathe of the South-Empire, to lose any other machines, before turning east for Collegium and what these days counted as home.

Two

Laszlo's family had once performed a series of services for Stenwold Maker, ending in an arrangement which was continuing
to this day and which had resulted in a number of technical
advances in Collegium, including the feted New Clockwork.
Having shared some remarkable adventures with Maker, and
after his family hung up the trappings of their previous profession
to become respectable merchants and members of Collegiate
society, Laszlo had presented himself to Stenwold again, saying,
Make use of me.

It was not patriotism that had driven him, for he had no
strong attachments to anything aside from family. It was not a
nose for profit either; his instincts in that direction had been
telling him to run in the other direction. He and Stenwold
Maker had gone through a great deal together, though: privation, fear and wonder that neither would forget. Laszlo was
young, and a chancer by nature, not one to settle for the quiet
life. Becoming an agent of Collegium when rumours of war
were hanging heavy over every city in the Lowlands seemed a
good way to keep his hand in, and Solarno a better place than
most.

The early morning sun had set fire to the waters of the
Exalsee, fierce as summer even on a spring day, so that the half-
dozen ships out there were mere silhouettes, cruising in towards
Solarno docks as they took in sail and prepared to weigh anchor.

A few flying machines droned overhead: a decent-sized fixed-wing bringing in small-packet cargo, a smallish airship for heavier freight and a little spotter heliopter, off to pry into someone else's business, no doubt.

As Laszlo watched, a new shape skittered across the sky, tracing a long arc out over the water and then banking into a ridiculously sharp turn that sent it scudding back over the city. The sun painted it a deep metallic red, even at this distance, its body resembling a hook balanced between two blurred wings. One of the famous Firebugs, Solarno's new pride and joy.

Laszlo kicked off into the air himself, out of the window of his garret lodgings, down the tiered slope of the city towards the waterfront, lazily tacking to avoid other Fly-kinden or the occasional Dragonfly. It was a few hours after dawn, and the city was still sluggish, for sleeping late was a Solarnese tradition.

There was a cool breeze coming off the lake, and Laszlo leant into it, changing his course abruptly to hang out over the Exalsee and enjoy it, dipping almost low enough to reach down and trail his fingers in the water. Out further from the shoreline there were aquatic denizens that would have made him regret that, but they would never come so close to the city. The water was clear and inviting enough that he almost decided on an impromptu dip; only the reaction of the others, if he turned up drenched from head to foot, dissuaded him. Ridicule was a game they played constantly with one another here and he had no wish to hand out any free ammunition.

He changed bearings with a thought, angling back towards the land just as the Firebug had done. Even as he did so he spotted another three of the new fliers cutting across the sky, heading out over the lake in formation. Perhaps they were off pirate-hunting, or keeping an eye on one of the other city-states, but Laszlo suspected that it was all about nothing but showing off. That was another long-held Solarnese tradition.

He was still going at a fair rate as he nipped in through the open frontage of the Taverna te Remi, fast enough that he

26

needed a tight circuit of the common room to burn off speed before he could drop down into his seat, as theatrical a piece of self-promotion as any native Solarnese could wish. The other three were already there, which was good because being the last to turn up was worth extra points. It showed that you didn't need to work at the job; that you already had everything under control.

After the war, having taken advantage of the Empire's commitments elsewhere to reclaim its pawned freedom, Solarno had been left in an odd position. For those very few families deeply involved in the city's governance, this was mostly important because of the unbalancing effect it had on Solarno's party system, with the formerly dominant Crystal Standard becoming almost an irrelevance, whilst the once-marginal Path of Jade – and several other minor parties – had gained a great deal of influence. To everyone else, and to anyone with a grain of common sense, the liberation of the city had set a clock in motion. How long now until the Empire took its revenge?

Solarno was unique in its position. The Exalsee was not the Lowlands, for those cities had been forced into an uneasy union by the war, and had come out the stronger for it, ready to lock shields the moment the Empire even glanced their way. Although fighters from several Exalsee cities had assisted in the liberation – in the air and on the ground – there was no such unity to be found here. Exalsee rivalries ran deep, and any brief alliances were affairs of convenience only. Solarno was one city standing alone, on the southern border of the most powerful Apt state the world had ever known.

But the Solarnese were proud, and they were inventive. Unlike many of the cities the Empire had preyed on, they were every bit as technically adept as the Wasps and the Lowlanders, and perhaps more so. Specifically, faced with the aerial predation of hostile Dragonfly-kinden neighbours, they had pushed the science of aeronautics much further than had either Capitas or Collegium.

The old system of a rabble of individual pilots – skilled but disorganized – that had served to defeat the Imperial air force in the liberation had been seen as insufficient, and in a rare moment of cooperation the two current leading parties and over half the local Spider-kinden Aristoi families had thrown a great deal of money at Solarno's artificers, refining their techniques to produce a standing civic-defence force of flying machines. Three Crystal Standard leaders had been indicted for collaborating with the Wasps, and the grounds of their confiscated mansions – which just happened to neighbour one another – had been converted into the city's first municipal hangar. Solarnese pilots were now vying for the privilege of serving their city – not just a family or faction – by flying a Firebug. Solarno had turned to face the Empire with open defiance: *Touch us if you dare.*

The Empire itself had reasserted control of its various rebel provinces now, and everyone could feel the eyes of the Empress roving the map, looking for her next meal. Solarno's fierce little show was to demonstrate just how indigestible it had become.

The war was in abeyance, so the tools of statesmanship were the telescope, the bribe, the secret identity and the coded missive. Every key city near the Imperial borders was the rightful prey of the spymaster just now, and every nation scattered its agents there, putting out trembling feelers for the first move of the enemy. Helleron, Myna, Seldis – all of them hotbeds of espionage after their own fashion. And, of course, Solarno.

In Helleron the spies bribed magnates and hired criminals, and crept through slums. In Myna they played constant dodging games with the paranoia of the locals. Seldis had been a hotbed of Spider family politics since long before the war. Solarno, though, had gorgeous views of the lake, and a hundred eateries, theatres and fine wine. Spies must go where they were sent, but where they *wanted* to be posted was Solarno. Laszlo reckoned he had been well rewarded for saving the life of Stenwold Maker, Collegium's greatest statesman.

Spies came to Solarno to keep an eye on the government

infighting, or to wheedle secrets from its artificers, but most of all they came to spy on other spies and, soon enough, their solid tradecraft was corrupted by the slower pace and higher standard of life there. Confronted with a city in which a day spent creeping about the backstreets was a day wasted, a fragile detente had slowly formed. Hence the Taverna te Remi, which was where the spies went to watch the other spies, sitting across tables from one another, asking veiled questions, playing games of chance and skill, trading information and favours, making deals.

It was not as simple as that, of course, and there were certainly deep-cover agents in the city, especially from the Spider Aristoi houses, but if one of the te Remi regulars failed to show, it was a sure sign that they were up to something, and that in itself was valuable information. So it was that, this morning, Laszlo could cast his eyes across the taverna's common room, note who was present, who absent, who was sitting with whom, and have material enough to compose a decent report for Stenwold Maker before being served his first drink.

He waved an airy hand towards the taverner and beamed across the table at his fellows, almost daily companions for the last couple of months. Agents all, enemies and rivals, but friends of the moment. As a former pirate, Laszlo was well used to making the most of acquaintances before chance should set them at daggers drawn again.

Taking up at least a third of the table was Breaghl the halfbreed, who claimed to be a freelancer willing to spy for anyone's coin. He had Fly-kinden blood bulked out awkwardly by Solarnese Beetle heritage, and amongst themselves the others guessed that he was securely in the pay of the Chasme merchants, here to keep tabs on Solarnese innovation and steal any of it that was not securely nailed down. He had the locals' sand-coloured skin but his features were lumpy and irregular, his hair receding without grace. He was half again the size of any of his companions – although still smaller than the average Solarnese

– as well as a strong drinker, a weak gambler and a man who apparently made cowardice a matter of principle. He had let slip that the Fly in his parentage had been his mother and, reflecting on the eye-watering image of his birth, the others had taken to calling him 'Painful'.

Te Riel was neat, and looked weak and bookish when he wanted to, but Laszlo knew that inside his crisp and reserved clothes the man was solidly built enough. His manner was smooth and he was a Fly in early middle years, a seniority that he routinely tried to capitalize on. He insisted that he was an intelligencer for hire, but peculiarities of accent had led the others to conclude he was almost certainly Imperial. Laszlo considered him a prime rival, albeit not over anything so professional as espionage.

The woman, and object of their rivalry, called herself te Liss, or sometimes just Liss, and Laszlo thought that he was probably in love with her. At least, it stabbed him somewhere close to the heart whenever she smiled at te Riel. In truth, all three of them were a little besotted with her, professional agents or not. She had a heart-shaped face with sly eyes and a constant air of mockery, and her hair was an explosion of red curls that Laszlo had never seen on a Fly before. She wore dark colours that marked her out against the usual local white, and professed to be a mercenary out of the Spiderlands, but the three men were quite sure she was in the pocket of one of the local parties, if they could only agree on which one.

Laszlo himself had also claimed neutrality, but te Liss had told him, one stolen evening when he had her to himself, that they all knew he was an agent for the Aristoi, and that he should stop trying to hide it.

'Beginning to wonder if your mistress had called you up,' te Riel observed, apparently oblivious to Laszlo's aerobatic entrance. 'Hung over?'

'Perhaps he was out all night watching over the Firebug hangars,' Liss suggested. 'One of us should be getting on with some work here, after all. For myself, I can't be bothered, honestly.' It was bad form, amongst the agents of the Exalsee, to be seen to be *working*.

'As though that's worth the effort,' Breighl grunted. 'After all, they'll practically guide you around during the day, they're so proud of the place.' It was true. The Solarnese were not shy about showing off their new toys – after all, there was no point in having a deterrent if the other side remained ignorant of it.

Liss cocked her head to one side, eyes twinkling. 'I did come into possession of a little roster: flights in, flights out, day and night. Cost me dear, too.'

'Hardly, given that you *work* for them,' Breighl remarked sourly.

'Me? Why would you think such a thing?' Her smile disarmed him, as it always did. Of the three of them, the halfbreed was the unhappiest, for he was as smitten with her as the rest and yet knew he had no chance with her.

'Who do I owe, I wonder? Who do I want to owe me?' te Liss's eyes roved about the table. 'Dice for it, perhaps? Or will the Empire stump up some coin to keep me off the streets?' She raised her eyebrows at te Riel.

He controlled his momentary scowl. 'What the Empire will do, I can only guess. I'm more than happy to keep you off the streets, Bella.'

'Hover-fly. Your round, hover-fly,' Laszlo told him.

'Don't call me that.' Their needling him about the Empire was the only thing that got a rise out of te Riel, and the more he denied it, the more they believed it.

'Brandy, was it?' Laszlo kept on. 'Pick a good year.' Everyone knew the best brandy was Wasp-export.

Te Riel stood, turning the angry motion into a curt wave at one of the taverna staff. 'If you truly thought I was Rekef you'd not be so free with me.' He had said it before, and it was the unconscious stress he put on 'Rekef', that sudden passion, that had decided the others about his allegiance.

'I see Lorchis isn't in his seat by the corner yet,' Breighl observed, changing the subject as naturally as he could. 'And no sign of Raedhed either.'

A fresh bottle came, not brandy but local sweet wine, and they got to discussing their peers, presences and absences and speculation, trading gems of information that spies in other cities would have had to shadow and lurk and burgle for and still end up with nothing more reliable at the end of it.

The Empire was out there, a formless shadow on the northern horizon, a vast storm-front that could head south at any time. There were Aristoi families, just the far side of the Exalsee, that had designs on Solarno, and probably on the wider world. There were Ants whose only plan for defending their sovereignty was the systematic beating down of their neighbours. There was a Beetle spymaster who had readied himself so much for the next Wasp attack that he might just end up precipitating it. Laszlo knew it, and everyone in the Taverna te Remi knew it.

But Liss was sneaking him a grin, even though she was hanging on to te Riel's arm. Her expression seemed to say that she was forced to pander to the Imperial, with his ready money and his arrogant manner, but they both knew who she would rather be touching.

The spring was warm, the promised summer hotter. The prospect of war, always alluded to but never spoken of outright, seemed a long way away just now.

She had left on te Riel's arm that day, but two days later towards nightfall she dropped into Laszlo's lodgings, where he was keeping a desultory eye on the civic hangars. Letters of introduction from some Fly aviatrix in Collegium had secured Laszlo a small third-storey room within sight of the city's upper classes, and this place was more than most foreign agents could have boasted. Besides, small and high up only meant that it was perfect for a Fly-kinden.

'I can't stay,' she warned him, even as she flitted in through his window. He was lying on his side, stripped to the waist in the evening's muggy heat, trying to balance his telescope so that it would support itself while he looked through it.

'Top-secret orders come through at last?' he asked her drily.

'Breighl wants me to go to the theatre with him.'

'You'd rather have orders?'

'Wouldn't you?' She raised her eyebrows. 'And I'm not suggesting that Painful feels that way about you, but some *orders*, hm? From whoever you really work for?'

Laszlo shrugged. 'Nice just to take stock, sometimes.'

She had been poised in the open window all this time, and now she darted over to the bed, landing demurely beside him. Laszlo was lean and strong, for a Fly, having spent much of his life wrestling with sails and lines, and she put a hand on his arm with a mischievous expression. 'Stories, stories,' she murmured, for it was his bad arm, the one he had broken, and the mottling of injury was still to be seen.

'You've seen mine, do I get to see yours?' he asked her gamely.

A snort was all that got him, and a change of subject. 'Anything to drink? If I'm going to sit through three hours of Spider opera, I need a lining to my stomach. Brain, too, probably.'

He had a bucket of water in the lee of the window, where the sun never quite chased the shadows away, and the bottle he extracted from it was still cool. He was quite aware that this was not what Stenwold Maker had sent him here for, and that a proper spy would probably know all sorts of ways to seduce te Liss and get her talking. He could only imagine te Riel trying and – in his mind's eye – abjectly failing. With Laszlo himself, however, she seemed more than willing to be seduced, and by unspoken accord neither of them asked awkward questions. *Take good weather where you find it*, as Laszlo's old sailing master used to say.

They would talk often of te Riel and Breighl, or of other

agents, the individual personalities of the Solarnese intelligencing crowd, but nothing of the causes, the nations and powers.
*We are living in the moment between one wave and the next. Long
may it last.*

She did not make the theatre that night.

Later, close to midnight, there was a crash from outside, a
shattering of glass, and Laszlo leapt from the bed, whipping a
knife from his discarded belt without thinking. A moment's
pause and he heard drunken laughter outside, and someone else
cursing – just late revellers bound for home. He looked for Liss's
sleeping form and found her already halfway to the window.
The blade in her hand was hiltless with a weighted pommel,
perfect for throwing. For a moment they faced each other,
armed and deadly, waiting to see if something had changed.

Liss breathed out a shuddering sigh, casting her weapon
aside. She sat on the bed, looking abruptly tired and human, not
the grinning little tease who kept three men on their toes at the
Taverna te Remi. 'Laszlo . . .' she began.

He was beside her on the instant, and she leant into his
embrace gratefully, even though he only remembered to drop
his dagger a moment later.

'It wasn't—' he started, but she just shook her head. *War. It
wasn't war.*

Three

In the last days of spring, the high paths of the mountain were still treacherous with snow. When she walked, she skidded and slipped, clinging to the slick rock face with both hands for purchase. When she flew, the wind made a plaything of her, whirling her about the stone as though she was flying through a maze of knives and bludgeons.

She was Moth-kinden, though, and this was her home. The peaks around Tharn had been a stronghold of her people for thousands of years. One of the last few since the Apt had driven them from the Lowland cities.

Grey-skinned, grey-robed, her eyes featureless white, her hair a sheet of black falling past her shoulders: a monochrome woman, a shadow or a ghost, slipping silently at midday through the high passes, unnoticed.

She hoped unnoticed. She had a great deal of practice in passing unseen past living eyes, but she was no great magician – certainly as her people measured such things – and if the eyes that were seeking her belonged to her own kinden, then no amount of stealth and secrecy might suffice to hide her.

Her name was Xaraea, and she was a woman of fragmented loyalties. Loyal to her kinden, of course, or at least to those that called Tharn their home, or to their secret service, the shadowy Arcanum that could evoke the same fear as the Imperial Rekef in the right circles. But even that was not quite true, for the

Arcanum had been riven with factions and rivalries since long before some barbarian Wasp chief ever thought of building an Empire. She was loyal to a handful of Skryres – the high magicians of the Moths – who were her superiors in her chapter of the Arcanum, men and women of implacable, unquestioned authority whose names she did not even know.

There was a sudden flurry of white, not fresh but blown from above, and she crouched, drawing her cloak about her, displaying stone colours against the stone. Moth eyes could still be blinded by snow, so she remained huddled, looking over her shoulder and waiting to see if the passing of the gust revealed any untoward movement behind her.

She had done good work during the war, had contributed to the costly victory that had seen the Empire driven out of Tharn. The price had been high, though, and the architects of that freedom had found themselves under attack from their enemies within the city, and even from those who formerly had not been their enemies. Xaraea knew that her masters were on the defensive on the home front, but she knew also that their main focus had not wavered. As they wrestled with rival factions, in fierce debates that she would never be admitted to, they never lost sight of the enemy without. The Empire could come back at any time.

Xaraea had the sense that other factions were considering the Empire, too. She knew well that there was a surprisingly large Tharen diplomatic delegation at the Empress's court. Wheels were in motion, and hers was the frustration of every intelligencer: that she could not know everything all at once. Sometimes she wondered if she knew anything at all.

Her orders still rang in her ears, though: clear, simple words from a cunning old man normally given to riddles and circumlocution. *On no account must you be discovered. Nobody must know of what you have done.* Implicit in the words was the knowledge that those he was warning her about were not foreign agents but others of her own people.

The phalanstery loomed before her without warning. It had

been carved from the rock by her people long ago as a retreat, austere and understated, just a doorway and some narrow slits of windows cut into a span of rock that barely seemed the work of human hands. The door was new, though, crafted of heavy wood bound with metal, and with the look of being cut down from something larger. How the current occupants had hauled it all the way up here was beyond her, but then they were likely to feel the cold more than her mountain-loving kinden.

About to reach for the iron ring set into the door's surface, she had a sudden moment of suspicion, looking about her in every direction. But she knew that, if she had been followed here, such caution came too late, and she had failed.

The place was a well-guarded secret, its very existence buried deep within the great libraries in the heart of the mountain, lost in plain sight as only the Moths could conceal their lore. Her masters had installed the current residents here a generation ago, and helped them become self-sufficient, teaching them all that the Moths knew about growing crops in the thin soil of the high fields. Those who lived here owed a great debt to her masters, and she had come to collect on it.

The door swung open, and she looked into the face of a Wasp-kinden.

She had been properly briefed and she did not even flinch. Fully three-quarters of the phalanstery's residents were Wasps, and almost all of them former soldiers. That was essentially what this place was all about.

Perhaps he saw something in her face indicating the purpose behind her visit, for he hesitated before stepping back and letting her in. He wore a long robe, brown like a Way Brother's, belted but without the sword that must have travelled with him most of his life. The calluses on his hands were born of the rake and hoe now.

'Your name?' she demanded of him. Names had power, everyone knew, except the Apt, and therefore perhaps the names of the Apt had no power after all. Still, old habits died hard.

'Salthric,' he told her flatly, not hostile but not welcoming either. 'We were not expecting visitors.'

I should hope not. 'Never mind that. I am here to see one of your people. Who must I speak to? Who is your . . . commanding officer.' She pronounced the Wasp-kinden words precisely, and saw them strike him like a blow.

'You may speak with me,' Salthric said firmly. 'I am Father here.' In the Empire, his order organized itself into cells, brothers under the hand of a Father. She sneered inwardly at the patriarchy of it, but the Broken Sword cult was almost exclusively male. It was well known that the Empire did not tolerate societies, philosophical orders or sects within its hierarchy. No two masters: that was the Imperial creed. In reality a fair few were diplomatically overlooked, such as the Mercy's Daughters, who trailed the armies and brought succour to the injured, or the Arms Brothers duelling societies that had such clandestine popularity amongst the Imperial officers. Of all the sects that the Empire hated, however, and rooted out wherever it was found, the Broken Sword was the most reviled. Its very existence was anathema to the Empire, for it dared to speak against war, the Empire's lifeblood. Its members were mostly soldiers who had seen too much, done too much, lost too many friends, gone too long without seeing their families or homes. Most of them worked secretly within the Empire, within the very army, but one of their projects was to smuggle out those who had simply had too much of war, and this phalanstery in the mountains of Tharn was one such destination.

She faced up to Salthric, a slender, grey young woman against a strong-framed man whose very hands could kill. 'Esmail,' she said. 'I'm here for him.'

His expression told her that he had been expecting something of the sort. He took a deep breath, and said, 'No.'

'It was not a request.'

'No, he is at peace here. He does not deserve to have it taken from him,' Salthric replied, with surprising vehemence.

'You have no understanding of what he is,' she told him flatly.

'I may only be one of the Apt, but I know,' he hissed. 'I understand. I know how much he has lost – to *your* people. I will not let you have him.'

They were not alone now. Three other robed Wasps had heard their voices and drifted in: two were middle-aged, one old enough to have retired if he had still been with the army. They looked from her to Salthric warily, not sure what was going on.

'You *owe* my people,' Xaraea stated, staring Salthric in the eye. 'Who brought you here? Who gave you this place? Who let you live unmolested in the mountains? Who taught you our ways so that you could survive?'

'I know all this—' he started, but she was not done.

'And when the Empire came to Tharn with its machines and soldiers, who was it said nothing about our guests here in the phalanstery?'

Silence fell, her eyes boring into his.

'The politics of Tharn are very fluid at the moment, Salthric – especially where the Empire is concerned. Who would you want to be the next visitor knocking at your door?'

In his face was not fear for himself, but fear for everything else there, for the other exiles, his precious order.

She had no time for respect or pity. 'Take me to Esmail, if you please.'

She saw his hands twitch at his sides, fingers clawing as his stinging Art surged within him, and as he fought down generations of Wasp anger. He could kill her, without doubt, but then what? The Broken Sword's existence here was precarious enough as it was. At last, he turned, storming off into the deeper halls, and she stepped lightly after him.

There was a little light within, from shafts sunk into the rock, but mostly they relied on torches and lanterns fixed to the walls. She suspected that the older residents no longer needed them, finding their way through the buried rooms by touch and memory. That Salthric took a torch with him was, she suspected, a wretched attempt to warn her target that they were approaching.

The faces she passed were almost universally Wasp men, but not quite all. Some were women; the luckiest escapees had managed to bring their families away with them. There were a few Ants as well, a Bee-kinden, the grey-blue of a Mynan Beetle. The Broken Sword was for broken soldiers, and they made no hard distinctions as to kinden.

Esmail, the man she had come to see, was no Wasp, and – despite Salthric's words – Xaraea was unconvinced that the Broken Sword truly knew what his heritage was.

Salthric guided her to a doorway hung with a curtain, in the Moth style. For a moment he just glowered at her, then he stalked off, leaving her alone.

Perhaps he hopes Esmail will kill me, she considered. It was certainly a possibility.

She pushed aside the curtain and went in. There were two rooms beyond, square boxes of stone one after the other, and Esmail stood in the archway between them, ready to fight her if necessary.

Xaraea smiled, for she saw her path clearly now. They taught cruelty early, in the Arcanum.

He was a lean, poised man with a gaunt face and a high forehead, eyes deep as wells, dark enough to defeat even a Moth's sight. His mouth was a narrow line. Not a Wasp, and yet most would find it hard to say quite what kinden he was. Some halfbreed, perhaps, save that he bore none of the signs of crossed heredity. His hair was the colour of iron, his skin a tan that could have been inherent or just the work of the sun. His hands were empty, no weapon in sight, but he was only a moment away from killing her. He would always, she suspected, be a moment from killing her, or anyone he met, for it was his blood and his nature. Right now he was ready to kill her because he was defending something. Esmail was not alone.

There was a woman behind him, a Dragonfly-kinden from

the Commonweal, and Xaraea wondered idly what her history must have been to bring her here and in this company. At their feet clustered the children. The eldest was a girl of perhaps five, and looking very like her mother. The younger two could have been two or three, surely born together and yet how different! One boy was as much a Dragonfly as his mother, but the other had his father's features, his father's entire kinden – as unlike his siblings as a total stranger.

'Ah, look,' Xaraea said sweetly. 'One has bred true. Another generation secure, hm?'

Esmail's eyes looked loathing at her, but he was scared. Not scared of her but of what she represented, the same threat that had cowed Salthric. Esmail had lived in peace here because Xaraea's people had arranged and permitted it: not the Moths, not Tharn, nor even the Arcanum, but that small section of it that she served. Skryres loved their secrets, and some of those secrets were men.

It was a strange quirk of Esmail's kinden that their offspring were always true-bred, following one parent or the other. If not for that, they would have died out centuries ago, for they had been near-exterminated and the few survivors scattered across the world. The chances of a suitable pair of them meeting and raising children was tiny, and yet the kinden itself clung on through a precarious chain of mixed-kinden matings like Esmail's.

'We call on you,' Xaraea told him. 'The time has come for you to go out into the world once more, Assassin Bug.'

Oh, there had been a war: one of the bad old wars the Mantis bards sang of, full of blood and dark magic. Hundreds of years before the Apt arose, the Assassin Bug-kinden had launched their campaign to rule the known world by stealth and murder, and the Moths had met them and cast them down. How ironic now that this man would serve the destroyers of his own people.

And he *would* serve. He would serve because he had too much to lose if he disobeyed.

41

'Terms?' Esmail's voice was accentless, precise. Of course, his voice could be anything he wanted it to be. He was no ordinary killer. Even amongst his rare and deadly kind, he was special.

Xaraea herself did not know, of course. She drew the sealed scroll from within her robe, orders intended for Esmail's eyes only. Her masters did not want to risk some scrying enemy finding *that* knowledge inside her mind later. All that she did know, she explained to Esmail: 'You are to go into the Empire. An identity will be arranged for you. From there on, do whatever you are instructed to do.' Preparing his way had been her own hard work and that of her agents within the Imperial borders. Her masters might be the greater magicians, but she was a modern intelligencer, and she had been successful amongst the Apt, where more sorcerously gifted spies had failed.

She saw his hands twitch on the scroll. Killing hands, of course. All of his kind possessed Art that killed. On this mission, though, it would be his other talents – his arcane training – that would count. Back in the mists of history, when his kind had been common, men of his particular skills had formed a secret elite amongst his kinden, just as the Skryres were to the Moths. She suspected that he was now unique.

He did not break the seal. He did not want to expose his wife or his children to whatever task was required of him. He knew also that it would make no difference. Xaraea was not giving him a choice.

'Look after my family while I'm gone,' he told her.

Xaraea saw the Dragonfly woman's face go very still, her hand tightening on his arm. Even the children were silent, staring up at their parents, or wide-eyed at the Moth.

We all know that you might be 'gone' for good, the Moth thought. Such was the taint of his heritage that she could not think of that as a bad thing, for all that he was now her instrument.

'Now go,' Esmail told her flatly. 'If I'm to leave here, I'll make the most of what time I have.'

She took a breath, preparing to remind him of his place, of who served whom, but his eyes flashed with sudden danger.

He will do what he is told, she assured herself, but it was more than she was capable of to stay there with that threat hanging over her.

There was precious little welcome for Xaraea anywhere within the phalanstery, but she had accomplished what she had come to do, and so she took her leave of Salthric and the other deserters swiftly. If there were sorcerous eyes searching for her, then it was best they did not pinpoint her presence there.

It was a long walk to Tharn, and the wind was showing no sign of dropping. She might try to fly high, to rise above it all, but there was no guarantee she would not simply be swept miles off course and dropped somewhere hostile once she was too tired to keep to the air. Instead she took the high paths on foot again, putting her shoulder to the wind and pressing on.

Her only stroke of luck was that she had put well over an hour's progress between her and the phananstery before they found her. If they wanted to work out where she was travelling from, there were too many paths, too much of the mountain to cover. They would not be able to retrace her footsteps.

'Xaraea!'

She had not noticed them before their leader called her name. Names were power, of course, and by using hers, he was demonstrating his superiority. Needless to say, she could not have named him in return. He was a lean old Moth wrapped in the elaborate folds of his robe, the sunlight glinting on his metal skullcap. He must have been eighty years, if he was a day, but that was perhaps not so old amongst her people, and especially not for a great magician. She recognized him as a Skryre, but not one of her masters. She was willing to bet he was their fellow within the Arcanum, though. *The knife at your back is always keener than the sword before you.*

He had not come alone. Flanking him was a younger pair: a man and a woman in tunics of the same drab hue, each with an arrow nocked to their showbows. Behind them, in armour of dark leather bands, was the pale-faced figure of a Mantis-kinden, a sharp-featured man whose gauntlet sported a metal talon folded back along his arm.

'You have been missed in Tharn. I wonder where you have been in such inclement weather,' the Skryre addressed her but, when she opened her mouth for a reply, simply held up a hand. 'Save the lies. Let us assume they have been spoken and dispensed with. I will know where your masters sent you.'

Strangely, what she felt was a rush of relief. *He does not know.* Her own masters must have shielded her from this man's scrying, forcing him to quarter the mountains in search of her.

Seeing her defiance, the Skryre smiled with a touch of weariness. 'Listen to me, Xaraea. Your services to Tharn have not gone unnoticed. It is your misfortune to find yourself shackled to the wrong masters. They have cast you away. They care nothing for you save as a tool. I give you this chance to be something more. Come with us. Tell us what has been done. You shall be rewarded. You must know I would not make this offer lightly.'

She took a step back, feeling the path's edge at her heels, the yawning abyss of the mountainside beyond. The wind plucked at her clothes, as if sounding out how secure her footing was.

If they took her, they would know it all. She could keep no secrets from a skilled magician. If she held out and defied him enough, he would simply bring his strength of will and magical craft to bear on her and crush her mind like an egg in order to get at what was within. She had witnessed it. She herself had held the victim down.

There was no signal, but abruptly the two archers were airborne, the man casting his bow aside. The wind was her

44

friend now, though, as it battled with them for control of the air, and so she stepped back and let her wings catch her.

An arrow sung past her, and she had a glimpse of the Mantis rushing forward. They would catch her at any moment. She could not evade two of them in the air for long, and if the Mantis could fly . . .

She had a moment of complete understanding, as if the wind stepped back to grant it to her. She felt bitterly ill-used, and grief for what must happen.

She let her wings take her down, smashing through the wind that tried to slow her, faster and faster, as fast as falling and then faster still. The others were grasping out for her ankles, she knew. They were pushing themselves just as hard as she was. They knew she must pull up from her dive, and then they would have her, crashing into her at speed, wrestling her to a halt, willing to chance her dagger or her nails. They were as loyal and devoted as she.

But not quite so determined, she guessed.

Think well of me, masters. They had made it very clear to her indeed: *The others must not know.*

They broke away, driven to the limits of their courage. Had they been less fierce in their pursuit, she might have salvaged something, though the effort of wrenching from her breakneck descent might have crippled her in any event. They had kept their nerve to the very last moment, however. She had no time.

There was never enough time.

The rocks met her like a lover.

Elsewhere, Esmail packed what few possessions he had: a change of clothes folded with a care that made him smile painfully, dry rations, an Imperial-issue waterskin Salthric had gifted him. A bedroll likewise. Paper, ink and a few chitin pens. No weapons, but then he had little need of them.

He stowed everything in his old canvas satchel, a calming ritual recalled from his youth when he had been a man with a dozen masters, going wherever the gold might lead him but taking the work for the love of it, the craft of it. The Arcanum had found its uses for him, but so had so many others.

A stupid life. A pointless life. Did he feel the thrill of it now, calling from his memories, the faint old clarion call to war?

He did not. If he had died an old man, grandchildren at his bedside, he would have counted it a life well spent, his earlier escapades just an aberration best forgotten. But now they were calling him back to it, and could he honestly say he was surprised? The Moths would hardly have sheltered him here out of human kindness. They possessed no such thing, and certainly not towards him.

Alone and unobserved, he took the Moth woman's scroll up and cracked the seal. There was a brief summary of where he must go, who his contact would be, what passwords to use: the familiar information of any mundane spymaster. After that, however, came his orders, with a stern exhortation to memorize and then destroy them.

Infiltrate the Rekef and the Imperial court.
Investigate the nature of the Empress and her intentions.
Kill her.

Four

The Antspider was stepping into the ring of the Prowess Forum, in her first showing at a formal contest, and a murmur of interest passed through the spectators.

The Master Armsman officiating was a sour-natured Beetle-kinden named Corog Breaker, who had been souring still further throughout the proceedings. He held out the swords, wood sheathed in bronze, and she took one lightly and her opponent, a sturdy Beetle youth, took the other. Having second choice, he looked at her suspiciously, as though she had somehow tampered with the sword she had left him, but that was the price of having a reputation.

She was a lean, compact woman with snow-pale skin whose tan mottling could, with a dash of cosmetics, be formed into striking darts at her brow and cheekbones. She presented a most martial image, her features fierce, pale hair cut short as a soldier's, her stance making the blade in her hand a natural part of her, the point into which the rest of her was focused. In contrast, the Beetle opposite her held his sword first like a hammer and then, as she directed her weapon at him, like a shield.

The Prowess Forum was more popular now than ever before. The College's students had lived through war with Vek and the Empire, so that matters martial were on everyone's mind. Four new departments had been created on the back of the war, and every student was expected to be able to acquit him- or herself with a sword. The Apt had a chance to learn the crossbow and the snapbow as well, training alongside Collegium's Merchant Companies.

'Salute the book!' Corog Breaker growled, and the two of them duly raised their blades to the Forum's emblem – a brass sword within the open pages of a wooden tome – which had become the city's own martial symbol during the war.

'Distance,' the Armsman snapped. This instruction was new, born from a combination of the pastime's popularity and peace-time's renewed drive amongst the sponsoring magnates to count victories over sportsmanship. There had been, a half-year ago, a spate of unsatisfactory contests, with one duellist rushing the other in a frantic exchange of blows. The difficulty of adjudica-tion had led to the introduction of a more formal start. The Antspider and her rival touched blade points, arms extended, each out of reach of the other, each theoretically just as ready.

'Clock!' called Breaker, and in that moment's echo she struck, sword nipping past her enemy's to poke him in the upper arm. The Beetle-kinden swore, then put his hand to his mouth and looked guiltily at the Master Armsman.

Breaker's eyes flicked suspiciously between them. 'First strike to the halfbreed,' he said, with heavy disgust on that last word. 'Second pass. Distance! Clock!'

And she was in again, a seemingly impossible lunge that caught the Beetle youth in his already bruised arm, making him drop his sword with a yelp. The commentary amongst the spectators was now running rife. The Antspider had not even moved her feet, only leant in a little, weight on the front foot ready for a quick retreat.

She gave Breaker a silent count of twenty before suggesting, in a breach of manners beyond enduring, 'If you wish, I'll play the point again, Master Breaker.' She needed to win, and her two team-mates needed to win as well, because the fourth of their number was inexplicably absent. It was just possible, at that point, that she could talk Breaker into simply declaring that bout a lost match, rather than ruling that their team had forfeited, whereupon they would win the contest three–one. The four of them had worked very hard indeed even to get as far as being allowed to compete.

Corog Breaker stared at her without any love. 'Play the point again,' he directed, but now she didn't like his tone. He was sounding like a man looking out for something specific, which might be bad news. Still, retaining an unassailable confidence in the face of bad odds had got her this far, and it might get her much further if she didn't acknowledge the chasm yawning at her feet.

'Distance,' Breaker snapped, and she lined up with her opponent, their blades touching at the very tips. The Beetle youth had a look of tremendous concentration on his face, as though trying to catch out a street conjuror.

'Clock,' said the Master Armsman, and she hit her opponent on the arm, lightly this time for mercy's sake.

'Excuse me, Master Armsman!' one of her rival's team-mates piped up. 'The Antspider's cheating, Master.'

Breaker's eyes were flicking left and right like flies in a bottle. The Antspider held herself very still. Would the Armsman stoop to admitting he had not seen it? Would his dislike of her – and, she had to admit, his preference for people actually playing the idiot game properly – overcome his oft-acknowledged pride?

'Show me,' he growled, and her stomach plunged.

A minute later and it was all over.

'I have stretched the rules of the Forum and of polite society to accommodate you misfits,' Breaker was complaining, giving the word a venomous twist. 'You arrive one man short, I let you fight anyway, because you assure me he's just on his way. Your sponsor is absent but I agree to accept her letter of commendation. But now I discover that you have found a way to break the rules, despite every measure we take. The last time a team was actually disqualified from a contest, Miss Straessa, was in the early stages of the Twelve-year War, so you may have some satisfaction in knowing that you have achieved at least a footnote in the histories of our duelling society. Do you have anything you wish to say about the matter? An apology would not be amiss.'

This is where my mouth is due to get me into trouble, considered Straessa, known by all as the Antspider. But she had dug a fair-sized well of trouble so far, so she might as well keep digging till she struck something useful. 'Why, yes, Master Breaker. Take him out and bury him. That boy's three times dead by now.' She directed the wooden sword at her opponent, who started out of a conference with his friends and stared at her.

'By the rules of the contest, one must stand at full extension, blade to blade, before the clock begins,' Breaker told her sharply. 'Your little tricks—'

'Master, had I met him on the field, he'd be dead,' she pointed out. 'Do you think this game will help him if he joins the Merchant Companies? By rights I should be allowed every trick I have. I should be allowed to jump him from the rooftops on his way to the Forum. Rules, yes, but you know I won.' Her smile was feral. 'And you know what else? I killed him exactly the same way, three times. Cheating or not, what sort of swordsmanship is that?'

Corog Breaker regarded her, and she was surprised to see something other than hostility in his face: understanding, she realized, even agreement. Soldier and artificer, he had fought in the war, and against the Vekken before that when they had come to lay siege to Collegium. Of course, he knew she was right and that this anachronism would not see anyone safe through the next conflict, whenever that might be.

Neither rhetoric nor reality was going to win this contest, though. He was already shaking his head, and she turned to her fellows, Eujen and Gerethwy, holding her hands wide to show that she had done what she could, which was mostly to make a bad situation worse. *Play to your strengths, that's what I say.* Still, many of the spectators were discussing her technique, and she reckoned that she might cover the month's rent by teaching a little fencing in the evenings, after this. It was the Spider part of her nature: *Losing with flair is something better than winning without.*

They had called their team 'the Dregs', and Eujen Leadswell was their tenuous link with the general populace, being Beetle-kinden born and bred in Collegium, a young son of a brewer-turned-soldier, and a figure of notorious energy in the debating chamber. Gerethwy, on the other hand, seven feet tall, robed and hooded, had been put in the world purely to make honest halfbreeds like the Antspider feel normal.

'You!' Breaker suddenly spat out, the word shot through with loathing. 'Out!'

And then there's that: a pale young man had just appeared in the doorway, late and yet still managing to pick his moment.

'What does *that* think it's doing?' Corog Breaker, veteran and conservative, had been given a target for his temper.

Is it me again? Do I get to do my usual grand job of salvaging the situation? the Antspider was thinking. But Eujen was already standing up to receive the brunt of Corog's wrath. 'Master Breaker, this is our fourth.'

'I will not have it in the Forum.' Breaker's voice came out dangerously low.

'Master Breaker, Averic has been accepted as a student of the College,' Eujen pressed on, all formal politeness.

'I'll not have a Wasp in the Forum.'

'What authority have you?' Eujen Leadswell managed, in the face of Breaker's wrath.

'I am Master Armsman of the College,' Breaker thundered. 'If I say he's not to set *foot* on these tiles, he's banned. Bring your complaints to the Masters, do. Let's see how many of them have any cursed sympathy with you. Or don't you think they were up on the walls doing their piece when that lad's Empire came?' The last words saw Breaker's face rammed close to Eujen's. 'Just you think, boy, about what your choice of friends says about you.'

With that, Breaker had clearly had enough. He stormed out, choosing the doorway that Averic had been hovering in, forcing the young Wasp to back out quickly to avoid being knocked aside. The brief quiet that Breaker had been speaking into degenerated almost instantly into a storm of gossip, much of it derogatory and aimed at the Dregs.

Eujen looked over at Averic. The young Wasp had his fixed smile on, the one he used whenever his kinden became an issue. He had not taken one step forward.

'Leadswell!' It was one of the opposing team, a burly man named Hallend, shouldering his way through the crowd that was already breaking into clumps spread out across the fighting ring. 'What were you thinking, bringing one of *them*? You think that *they* understand any kind of fighting but the real thing?'

'You think he'd beat you to death with a wooden sword?' Eujen asked witheringly.

'I think I know his lot's temper,' Hallend spat back. 'And if not now, then later – a knife in some dark alley, or that sting of his. We all know how they like to *win*. I lost an uncle to his kind in the war,' Hallend persisted. 'My parents fought his people to keep our city free. And now their spies are walking about in daylight, students at the College.'

'My father died in the Vekken siege,' Eujen snapped, 'and now the Vekken are our new great friends and allies. How was that achieved, save that Maker's party reached out to them? Two generations ago we counted Sarn a great threat to our north, but then we went to them with open hands.' He gave Hallend the chance to draw breath for a rebuttal, and then spoke over him fiercely. 'But every Makerist agitator in the Assembly tells us there must be war with the Empire. We must not trade with the Empire. We must be on our guard against the Empire's spies. Is there some moral difference between Vek and the

Wasps? No, it is just the fact that the Empire is far away, and so the Makerists can rail at it with impunity. It is because the Empire is large, and so they see too great an effort in converting it to our philosophies, so they do not try. It is because the Empire seems set to last, and it is convenient for some men to have a strong enemy abroad. What other tyrannies are hidden at home when all eyes look over the wall for an army? What taxes, what confiscations, what laws are passed? Does the Empire hate us more than Vek has hated us? No. Is the Empire the unrelenting, irredeemable evil that the Makerists paint it? No. The distinction is not one of morality but one of convenience.'

'Eujen, quiet,' the Antspider hissed in his ear, but he was getting into his stride now.

'But I ask you this,' Eujen went on with a grand gesture. 'Is the Empire truly as vast and powerful as the Makerists say? Is it truly as warlike? Yes, of course it is. We have seen ample evidence in these last few years. What, then, do you think the wages of Makerism will be? If we daily speak of war waged by the Empire, of the threat of the Empire, of the unending hostility of the Empire, then what possible alternative do we give the Wasps, but to become the monsters we cast them as? If the only hand we show to them has a blade in it, what response will we receive? And, when that war comes, where will our moral high ground be when we have so long invited it? We are Collegium, and we have stood for ethical enlightenment for five centuries. We cannot govern our state on principles of convenience.'

'Eujen, shut up now,' the Antspider urged again; everyone else was quite silent. Hallend, sensing something was up, glanced over his shoulder and then squeaked in alarm and scrambled out of the way, exposing Eujen to the full glowering regard of the man standing there.

Eujen was not tall for a Beetle, and this man had a good few inches on him, and a good few decades too, and he was broader at the shoulder than the young student, but he had the fierce, brooding presence of a much larger man, even so. His reputation towered above him, and threatened to crush Eujen Leadswell flat.

A current of whispers danced about the Forum, speaking the name, *Stenwold Maker*.

Eujen swallowed, seeming smaller and smaller, but never quite backing down, weathering the fire of the old statesman's scorn, as though staring into the sun.

The older man said one word: '*Makerist?*'

Eujen was going to keep standing there, Straessa realized. *He's going to argue with Stenwold Maker!* She did not know if Maker, like the theoretical Wasp, would have his enemies killed in dark alleyways, but she was certain that making a scene just now would do no favours for Eujen's academic career, and so she kicked him sharply behind the knee, so Eujen found himself sitting down abruptly with the breath knocked out of him.

'Mouth shut,' she snapped.

It was as though Eujen no longer existed, but then she realized that Maker had not really been staring at him at all. It was just that Eujen had been standing between him and the Wasp, Averic.

She saw Averic's fingers twitch, the Art in his hands being kept on a tight leash. One of Maker's own hands was at his belt, she saw, and with a swooping lurch she spotted the butt of a weapon there. *Only Stenwold Maker could bring a snapbow into the Prowess Forum,* and on the back of that thought her prediction changed from *Stenwold Maker is going to beat Eujen to death with his bare hands,* to *Stenwold Maker is going to shoot Averic dead right in front of us.*

But Averic was holding very still, giving no excuse, making no trouble, and at last Stenwold Maker turned away and stomped heavily out of the Forum, sheer murder evident in every step.

★

'Since when did we have Wasp-kinden students at the College?' Stenwold demanded as his opening salvo as soon as he was through the door of Jodry's office.

Jodry Drillen, Speaker for the Assembly of Collegium, cast a tolerant eye over him. 'Since start of autumn, I think. Averic, his name is. He turned up with money and sat the entrance exams and came with a commendation from the Imperial cartel thing, the Consortium.' He had obviously been in the middle of some papers, but he leant back in his overstuffed chair, gesturing for Stenwold to sit down.

Stenwold remained standing. 'And you let him in?'

'I? I haven't been a Master of the College for more than a decade, and the right of the College to do just about whatever it pleases without interference from the Assembly is the first thing both of us learned when we were studying for our accredits, eh? I recall a certain lecturer in modern history who made considerable use of that freedom to preach all manner of truths that the Assembly would rather were kept quiet.'

Stenwold glared at him, but conceded the point by sitting down across the desk from Jodry, his fervour ebbing a little. 'Since autumn, though. Six months, then, and I never even knew. Why wasn't I told?'

'Aside from the fact that the College is similarly not obliged to run its decisions past the War Master, you *were* told,' Jodry pointed out. At that moment his Fly-kinden secretary arrived, bearing a bottle of wine and a plate of honeycakes, probably less because his master had a guest than because his master tended towards gluttony. After he had put the tray down, Jodry waved him away and then busied himself in finding a second bowl and decanting the wine. At last, under Stenwold's stare, he was forced to add, 'It may be that I didn't exactly take pains to draw it to your attention, but only because I knew you'd overreact.'

Stenwold took a bowl and stared at the dark contents. 'He's a spy.'

'Probably is.' Jodry stuffed an entire cake into his mouth and mauled it for a while. He had been an expansive man before winning the Speaker's post, and success had added a few handspans to his waist, and at least one additional chin. Stenwold was his contemporary, and not a slender man even now, but Jodry, some inches shorter, must have weighed half as much again.

Seeing that Stenwold's exasperated expression would outlast his mouthful, Jodry lost most of his geniality and added, 'Or would you rather they just put some chit of a Spider-kinden girl in under a false pretext, so we'd not know until she betrayed us?'

Stenwold put the bowl down on Jodry's desk with a click of porcelain. 'That,' he said, 'was a low blow.'

'True, though, and the boy might actually just be a student, but if he's a spy, at least he's an obvious one. The College was divided about it, but in the end what I consider to be sensible heads won out, and young Averic got his place. An adequate student, I'm told, artifice and history. And if you'd actually been to the College in the last few months, you might know about it – or even if you'd turn up in the city for longer than it took to stoke the fires in the Assembly once every few tendays.' Jodry looked sidelong at Stenwold, as if estimating how far he could push his luck. 'And he's fitted in, in a way. What about that duelling clique of his, hm? Brings back a few memories: local boy of decent family, some odd artificer, a girl who's handy with a sword, round them off with an exotic foreigner – sounds a bit like . . .'

Stenwold was half out of the chair as soon as he caught Jodry's meaning. 'You—! Don't you *dare* equate that pack of feckless conspirators with my students!'

Jodry was unruffled, barely acknowledging the outburst. 'I'm just saying, it's a rich tapestry we have here at Collegium – threads of all colours.'

Stenwold sank back into his chair, feeling that he was becoming Jodry's opposite. Two men of late middle age, the same dark skin and receding hair, both veterans of two conflicts and innumerable debates, and yet the fat man grew fatter and happier in his role, increasingly comfortable with the subtle power of his position and the material benefits that came with it. Stenwold, meanwhile, was growing leaner and more distanced from the very city he was working to save. Each time he came back here, the streets seemed a little stranger, a little less like home. When he returned, it was less to a city and more to *absences*: the memories of those that time and war had taken from him.

'Since when was I a political movement?' he seized on as another ground for complaint. 'Some student was bandying about the word "Makerist", for grief's sake.'

Jodry took a deep *you only have yourself to blame* breath. 'Stenwold, Losel Baldwen sets aside a month on Makerism in her social history class – has done since the war.'

Stenwold stared at him, but Jodry met his eyes without flinching. 'I refer you to my previous comment. If you actually spent a reasonable time in the city you'd know these things, and have a chance to do something about them. Instead of which, you're forever off about the Lowlands or to Myna, or at that retreat on the cliffs that you signed over to those pirates.'

'Sometimes it's good to get out of the city,' Stenwold replied, infuriated that he was now on the defensive, but unable to do anything about it.

'Sten, I'm fat, not dead. I know you miss that' – his voice dipped – 'Sea-kinden woman. It's a shame, I fully admit, but there it is. You need to start living like a citizen of Collegium again.' Jodry was one of the very few who knew even half of the secret alliance with the Sea-kinden that Stenwold had brokered. In fact he was one of very few who even knew that Sea-kinden existed.

'So, tell me what a citizen of Collegium does,' Stenwold snapped.

'Well, for one, he doesn't march into the office of the Speaker for the Assembly any time he likes, just to vent his spleen.' As Stenwold rose to that barb, Jodry levered himself to his feet, abruptly becoming the man who swayed the city's government, and not just a fat and idle wastrel. 'Listen to me, Sten, and look at yourself. Your actions have been instrumental in putting us where we are now. In preparing for the next war, in devoting so much time and money to the aviators and the Merchant Companies, we have committed ourselves to a particular view of the world – of the Empire most especially. You *will* see it through. You *will not* leave me to parrot your words while you mope about like a sea-master's widow.'

The words sparked a few uncomfortable memories of that student decrying 'Makerist' policies in the Forum. How earnest that young man had been, how passionate! Did Stenwold not recall another youth, not so very much older, debating in tavernas and on street corners, haranguing a hostile crowd to try and open their eyes to ideas they did not want to tolerate. Only, in Stenwold's time, that idea had been the Empire's hostility. *And I won. I opened their eyes, after near on twenty years. The boy's not the same. After all, I know the Empire, and he doesn't.*

'Jodry,' he said, a little subdued, 'I'm *right*, aren't I?'

The other man's first reaction was a shrug, as if to say that it was too late to change things now, but he plainly sensed that would not be well received, so put in hastily, 'Oh, without a doubt. Come on, Sten, they were at the gates not so long ago, and if it wasn't for your Mantis friend doing away with their Emperor, and all the chaos that caused, they'd have had us, too. And since they pulled themselves together, it's been swords drawn all along the border, little skirmishes and raids, and a war looking for an excuse to happen. Of course you're right, Sten.'

And Stenwold looked on his – what? Not quite old friend, so political ally, then – and realized that at last he could no longer read Jodry with utter certainty. He shook his head, giving up and conceding the point. 'You bring me down to business, then.'

'I thought I ought to add some structure to the debate, that being my job,' Jodry agreed gravely. 'So, speaking of skirmishes and borders, do I take it I can't dissuade you from this little jaunt?'

'The Mynan border situation is looking serious,' Stenwold said. 'It needs attention. The Three-city Alliance needs to know that we're holding to our treaty, and they know me. And the Empire knows me, too. Maybe just turning up will get everyone to back off.'

Jodry looked at him doubtfully. 'So this isn't . . . *it*, then? Only, I've seen some of the reports, the sort of numbers massing at the border there.'

'I wouldn't think so,' Stenwold assured him, with as much confidence as he could muster. 'You, I and the Empire know that the peace can't last, but we've time for a few more rolls of the dice yet.'

Five

Winter had brought fouler weather than normal, and every hand had been working day and night, slave and free, mending fences and clearing ditches ready for the growing season. Now the spring seemed to have come early, an unwanted stagnant heat that surely belonged to the depths of summer beating down oppressively on all and sundry, sapping strength and shortening tempers.

Still, the dry earth was beginning to submit to the plough. All those irrigation dykes they had so carefully re-dug were distributing the water neatly, only needing a little aid from the pumping well in order to reach every field. This was a dry land, south of Sonn, but his family had worked it for generations. They knew how to wrestle with it, to conquer and command it.

There was an hour and some left before the heat of noon drove everyone into the shade, and he pitched in as though he was nothing but a servant himself, and a young one at that. He might be old, and need a broad-brimmed hat to keep the sun from his bald head, but he took some pride in knowing there was scarcely a stronger man on the farm. Now he straightened up, ignoring the twinge in his back. Something had caught his attention, and he scanned the flat landscape, trying to work out what it was: some discontinuity, something that did not belong.

The ploughing automotive was chugging its slow way back and forth in the next field, slaves following it on foot to strew the seeds, and boys following them with slings and sticks to keep off thieving beetles and roaches that might try to plunder the furrow before it was turned back. All was as it should be, surely, and yet . . .

A man running. A simple sight, but he ordered his land well, and there was no need for anyone to run. For a moment he wondered if one of the slaves was making a break for it, and he reached inward for his wings and his sting, quite willing to go after the man personally – but, no, the man was running *towards* him.

It was his overseer, Mylus. The Ant-kinden had served him as an Auxillian for ten years, and performed well enough that he had bought the man's service from the army in order to bring him here. He had a rare gift for organization and a firm, even hand with the slaves.

If Mylus was running, something was wrong.

'Lyren!' he called out, hoping his son was within earshot. Sure enough there was a patter of feet and the boy – *boy? He's past thirty. Must stop thinking of him as the 'boy'* – was at his elbow.

'Father?'

'Get Aetha and the children into the house, son.' Mylus was skidding to a stop before him now, saluting out of unbreakable habit, but the old man's eyes were focused past him, watching the great plume of dust raised by an automotive. *Not one of mine, that's for sure.* The machine was paying precious little heed to the neat order of his farm, stilting over field and ditch on its six curved legs, gashing the ground and scattering the workers.

'But, Father—'

'*Go*,' the old man snapped, and almost everyone in earshot was at attention automatically, Lyren included.

'At ease,' he added, when his son had taken off for the house, calling out for his wife. Mylus remained impassive, but the old man knew him well enough and could read worry in the mere way that the Ant stood. 'What will be, will be. Let us hope it's only me they're here for.' The vengeance of the Imperial throne had been known to encompass entire families before. 'If that's so, and the worst happens to me, you'll have to manage the farm. Lyren will return to service soon enough, and you know the place better than he does, anyway.'

'Yes, sir.' To Mylus, everything was still an order.

The automotive was a model that the old man had seen a few other times, a good all-terrain scouting model, swift but exposed. Even as it neared, one of the occupants had kicked off into the air. They must have already picked him out at a distance, for the flier headed right for him, dropping down a few yards away to study him.

'General Tynan?' the newcomer enquired.

The old man nodded guardedly. Instinct was calling on him to fight, but he could not fight the whole Empire. He had known that the throne would send for him sooner or later. He was a loose end that must be tied up one way or another. After all, he was the general who had failed to take Collegium.

It had been hard, giving the order. Another tenday, at most, and the Second Army, his glorious Gears, would have been inside the walls. two more tendays, perhaps four, and he would have had the streets secure, or most of them. The city would have been his, for the glory of the Empire.

Except the Empire that he had left behind him had run into difficulties of its own. The Emperor had been murdered, then his sister – *A woman? Unthinkable!* – had taken power, and what seemed like half the Imperial governors had decided that they could do a better job than her. He had received orders to return home as swiftly as possible, to support the pacification of the traitor-governors. He had known a no-win position when he saw one.

Conquer the Beetle city and he was betraying the throne. Abandon the siege and he was betraying the military campaign that was the Empire's lifeblood. But even if he could have taken Collegium in a day, he would have needed the bulk of his army to hold it, at least at the start; and of course the rest of the front had been falling apart even then, had he but known. In marching the Second back home, he had made the correct choice, but history books were cruel arbiters of right and wrong.

'Your presence is required in Capitas, sir,' the messenger informed him smartly. Tynan wondered idly if his visitor was Rekef. If he himself had become a serious inconvenience, then he might even disappear conveniently without ever reaching the capital.

'Of course,' was all he said. 'May I bid farewell to my family?'

'I am sent to fetch you *urgently*, General,' said the messenger, without sympathy.

Fight! Run! But he knew he would do neither. It was not his years in themselves, but the ingrained sense of duty they had gifted him with. He would submit to his fate. He would serve the Empire, as always.

'Let's go,' he said, and began to plod towards the automotive.

Across the Empire, soldiers moved: companies on the march or travelling by automotive, airship or rail; specialist detachments from the Engineers or the Slave Corps split off from their strongholds, assigned to one army or another. Materiel was stockpiled and weapons were tested. Quartermasters and Consortium merchants shuffled commodities and supplies like decks of cards.

Outside the Empire itself, what moved was information. The spies and their handlers sent reports in, the tacticians and spymasters sent orders out across the known world. Agents who had lived a comfortable life under a secret identity received word that they should ready themselves to strike, to disappear, to begin manipulating their carefully hoarded contacts. Others, already hard at work, received definite instructions. *The time is now.*

Not everyone in Solarno was intent on living the high life. Major Garvan lived in a poor garret, a single room whose one window looked onto the wall of the building opposite. Not for Garvan the scintillating waters of the Exalsee. A bed, a rickety desk, poor meals and scraping together a few standards each week for the food and the rent. There was a surprising number of Wasps in Solarno, but the rich ones were always watched. The Solarnese could not imagine an Imperial agent of any standing not living like one of the Aristoi, if only to share in the gossip of the moneyed classes. Most of the Wasp-kinden there were poor, though, refugees from the internal troubles in the Empire, fugitives from the Empress's wrath. There were enough of them – angry, disenfranchised and sometimes violent – that the Cortas, Solarno's baffling twin engines of government, were considering making some laws about them. For now, though, they provided a perfect cover for an army intelligence officer.

Army Intelligence had always trodden a narrow line, not regular soldiery but decidedly junior to the Rekef. Before the war, they had served as the eyes and ears of each army, ostensibly more trustworthy than the Rekef Outlander, though in truth many held a rank in both services. During the Lowlands Campaign, however, the Rekef had gone berserk, tearing at itself in a series of brutal culls so that the genuine spy-work had often been left to Army Intelligence. Those officers who had distinguished themselves now found themselves with an uncertain authority, placed in command of important operations like the Solarno gambit, and yet with no assurance that some strutting Rekef man would not turn up and take it all over, the moment results started coming in.

Garvan was better than most at the espionage game. Garvan was used to living with lies and secrets, and the keystone of the major's secrets was known by not one other living soul, a situation that Garvan intended to maintain. It irked the major that the various Imperial agents in Solarno – many of them not Imperial citizens at all – lived considerably more affluent lives, and even more so when Garvan had to pay out from the

Empire's coffers to keep them that way, while living in this wretched hole. Most of the agents probably found it funny, thinking back on it as they wined and dined and made polite conversation with their opposite numbers.

Intelligence Corps codes were rugged and practical, encrypted by letter substitution and then again by reference to a memorized number sequence. Nothing fancy, and the document itself had looked like nothing but an encrypted message. The army preferred functionality to Rekef subtlety. The slip of paper had been decoded, then burned and, as the flames died, Garvan was smiling a hard smile. At last the orders were in that would wrap up this operation, and where would all those pampered agents go for their next fine meal then?

A mirror hung on one of the few vertical walls of the garret, an odd piece of vanity but a necessary one. Garvan scrutinized the reflection there, seeing that familiar, slightly weathered face with its constant faint just-shaved blue about the cheeks and chin. Not a striking face, but that made it a good face for a spy.

Garvan sighed, hands slipping under the poor much-darned Wasp's tunic to adjust the strap that flattened down her breasts. Twenty years living like this, and still it pinched. Her mother had been a camp whore with the Sixth, and she had grown up around soldiers, seen how they spoke, how they walked. She had seen, too that while they swore and complained and died, they still lived better than their enemies – or their women.

The Twelve-year War had been a good time to find spare uniforms, provided you didn't mind stripping the dead, and there were always soldiers getting separated, then joining up with other detachments. The girl her mother had called Gesa had become the soldier Garvan, a boy too young to need to shave, but who could swear with the best of them. Always she had driven herself harder, taken more soldier's risks to cover the woman's risks that nobody knew she was taking. In that way she had been promoted. In that way she had been put to use by the intelligencers. Going alone into enemy territory to spy and scout was dangerous, but the duty relieved her of the constant threat of discovery. She spent her war fighting on two fronts.

For all she knew, there were dozens of women engaged in exactly the same deception, but if she had ever met one, they had not been so poor at it for her to know it.

But now she was a major and, if she had no close friends, she had some very impressed superiors. The Solarno mission was of far greater importance to the Empire than the mere city itself would suggest. She knew there were wheels within wheels, even if she did not know quite who was spinning them. A lot of her work involved ensuring that certain missives reached her superiors in the Empire, and she was not supposed to have worked out that they all came from across the Exalsee.

She straightened her tunic, the very picture of a down-at-heels Wasp-kinden man, a little slighter of build than most, but not unusually so. Living a soldier's life had made Garvan strong and robust.

Now she would take her other tunic and wash it in a fountain somewhere, to the annoyance of the locals, and hang it out of her window to dry. Soon after that signal she would be meeting with her agents, some of them here in the garret, others elsewhere at pre-set places and times. She felt an old, familiar excitement. The Empire was on the move again, at last.

A few days later, and there were some empty tables at the Taverna te Remi. Just a couple maybe, but the place had been full to the brim all winter, each spot taken by its own band of intelligencing illuminati, the network of loyalties and hostilities drawing a political map of the world in miniature.

'Te Gressi's gone, and all that mob,' Breighl observed. 'That surprises me.'

'They were merchant factors out of Dirovashni. They were after aviation designs, but not enough to get knifed,' Liss declared with confidence.

'Well, whatever – they've gone.' He was speaking more quietly than usual. Everyone in the taverna was, as though the future might overhear them.

'That Scorpion Valek,' te Riel added. 'Valthek? Vathek, was it?'

'Back to Toek Station,' Laszlo said, a guess, although he tried to sound authoritative. 'Good work to be had keeping watch to the north, but then you'd know that.'

Te Riel stared at him flatly. 'I don't work for the Empire, Laszlo. Let it alone.'

'You're going to tell me what I *know*, now, are you?' Laszlo locked eyes with the man, and mostly because he felt that the layout of their little table had changed slightly. The space between him and te Liss was greater. She had shifted to little closer to te Riel.

'Boys,' she said, holding out her hands. 'Forget who's not *here*. Grevaris is gone, who ran that brothel west of the Venodor. Just upped sticks and left. And I hear that clothier's on Habomil is closed now, that I always – well, probably we all reckoned was a front for someone.' She looked far more serious than she usually did, glancing from one face to the next. 'Tervo's gone, too – that fishmonger, remember? Left unpaid bills and a job lot of old fish.'

'People are getting out of the game,' said te Riel stiffly. There was the echo of a tremor in his voice, though, and the same feeling was running through all of them, of thin ice, of sands running down, storms on the move.

Breighl sighed deeply. 'Te Rorvo – Tervo – was fished out of the harbour last night. I heard it from the militia. Whoever did him in didn't even bother to weight the body.' His gaze passed over the three Fly-kinden, judging them. 'But I suspect *one* of you knew that already.'

Te Riel flushed although, in all honesty, Brieghl's eyes had not especially fallen on him. 'I am *not*,' he insisted in a hushed voice, 'for the Empire. I am a freelancer.'

'Like all of us,' said Breighl. 'Like Tervo, for that matter. I reckon the freelancers are getting out of the city, those that can. For those that know too much ... Solarno isn't a city for freelancers any more.'

'And yet here we all are,' Laszlo finished for him. 'True colours yet, anyone?' He pinned te Riel with his glare. 'Hover-fly?'

The man met and matched his hostility. 'I am going to *gut* you one of these days.'

'Enough,' te Liss snapped. 'No more of this.' She pursed her lips for a moment. 'We all know what's happening. Let's not bring it on any sooner by fighting. We all know that we'll be at daggers drawn soon enough. I don't care whether te Riel's with the Empire or not. Not yet. Not now.'

Laszlo reached for her hand beneath the table, as he had sometimes before, but that extra distance between them suddenly seemed insurmountable. He felt she was drawing further away, even while sitting there before his eyes.

'What I hear,' said Breighl, in a overly casual tone, 'is that the Empire might just be the least of it.' He was watching them all carefully again, but they all did that when ostentatiously dropping a titbit of information into the ring. 'I hear about interests from across the Exalsee, instead. Chasme has been getting very bold since their Iron Glove took over. And there's the Spiderlands ...' He finished up looking directly at Laszlo.

'What? I don't work for the Spiderlands.' The reversal of fortunes made him indignant.

'Oh, no – just for some Aristoi family or other. I mean, who could work for the whole Spiderlands?' te Riel put in.

'I'm ...' *A freelancer,* but of course everyone said that, and nobody believed it, for all it must be true in many cases. 'I'm not for the Spiders,' he finished lamely. 'Believe me, out of anyone who might have eyes on Solarno, I'm not for *them*.'

There was a shout from outside, and a Fly-kinden woman

popped her head around the door, passing a quick word to someone at a nearby table. The Solarnese mob who had been drinking there bolted up immediately and were out of the door on the instant, and within moments the entire clientele of the Taverna te Remi had gone after them. Nobody knew why or what was happening, whether invasion or a militia raid or who knew what, but everyone was so jumpy that they were cramming the door in moments, clawing for the outside.

Two streets away, in a little square within sight of the Corta chambers, Laszlo and the others alit on the rooftops to watch a hanging.

Hanging was for traditional Spider-kinden executions, and Solarno was a Spider city at heart: a dozen militia in their plated white leathers had strung up a halfbreed in plain view. Spider-kinden, of course, could not fly, but it turned out that their victim could, and in the end the spectators were treated to the hideously incongruous spectacle of three soldiers hanging off the wretch's legs like men trying to wrestle a kite down in strong winds. Their weight told, though, and abruptly the man's wings were gone, and the snap of his neck was audible across the square.

Breighl was bold enough to make enquiries, trusting to his militia contacts to shield him. The dead man had been a spy, he was told. A spy for whom? Nobody seemed to know.

The crowed was dispersing rapidly, most especially those who had come out from the taverna. The square seemed an unhealthy place to be, and Laszlo looked about for te Liss, reaching for her arm. 'Come on,' he told her, envisaging a quick jaunt back to his lodgings: wine and safety and an attempt to forget.

That distance between them was still there, though, and a moment later she was inexplicably *with* te Riel: on his arm, an inseparable part of him, as the man looked smugly over at Laszlo.

The Empire, Laszlo thought numbly. *The Empire's coming.* A city-wide tragedy for Solarno, a personal tragedy for himself. Liss, like all freelancers, wanted to end up on the right side, after all.

Six

There was a wayhouse west of Skiel that was more than it seemed – not one of those disapproved-of-but-tolerated places run by the Way Brothers, but a proper army place, a regular stopover for soldiers and messengers and Imperial officials. Since the place had found its new purpose, just before the war with the Lowlands started, hundreds of Wasp-kinden had passed through and never realized that it was a trap.

The trap had remained unsprung all those years, until now.

When the Empire had mounted its invasion of the Commonweal it had gained the attention of the Moth-kinden in a distant kind of way. Most of the Skryres, the arch-magicians who ruled the Moths, cared nothing for the newly ascendant Apt race, but there had been a few concerned enough about the future to begin planning. Commonweal slaves had flowed into the Empire by the thousand, and some were recruited by the Arcanum, and some had already been agents, willing to risk the brutal life of a slave out of loyalty to their shadowy masters.

Before the war, Xaraea had worked tirelessly to prepare a few fallback places like this, taking her masters' vague mandates and making them into hard reality. It had been foreseen, for example, that the Moths might one day need to capture an Imperial officer of some standing.

Esmail had made good time from the mountains of Tharn. He had not travelled like this for many years, but the habit had not left him. He passed through the countryside – whether Lowlander or Alliance or Imperial – like a ghost, taking what he needed, sleeping unnoticed in sheds and barns and warehouses, or out under the stars. The spring was cool, but the mountains had been colder.

He rode on an army automotive for much of the way once he had crossed the Imperial border: nothing but a ghost, unseen, unsuspected, listening to the idle chatter of the Consortium merchants and their slaves. They spoke of prospects and ambitions, the fortunes of common enemies, the free men and the slaves exchanging banter with a familiarity that they would have curbed instantly had any officer come near. They spoke of home and families, too, and when they did, Esmail stopped listening.

He did not know whether the Moths would keep their promise, to preserve his wife and children. He did not even know if they were capable of it but, if they had the power, they were still a subtle and treacherous people. They would dredge up crimes of his ancestors a thousand years old and call any punishment they exacted on him mere justice.

No choice, though. Not with her turning up without warning like that. Had he known what was coming, he might have risked the cold and the hunters to try and get his family away, but he had never been a seer. His magical talents lay in other directions.

The wayhouse in question, like most of them, was owned and run by the Consortium. The Beetle-kinden lieutenant in charge never guessed that five of his slaves had been suborned. Indeed, he was daily impressed by their efficiency. They had lived to please him for years, and solely for this moment.

Three days ago, a Wasp-kinden officer had arrived to spend the night on his way to the capital, and been detained. The slaves had taken him before he had ever reached the wayhouse, ambushing him on the road, and had kept him in the storage shed ever since. The Beetle-kinden lieutenant, of course, never needed to go into the shed, such was the efficiency of his slaves.

Those same slaves would be gone on the morrow, and their master would never understand why.

It did not escape Esmail's notice that the capture of this man – this man who would be so extraordinarily important to the Assassin Bug's immediate future – had happened *after* Esmail had left the phalanstery. One thing the Moths were good at was timing, arranging for the conjunction of what should have been unpredictable events.

The slave that approached him was a lean old Grasshopper-kinden, tall and cadaverous, his grey hair just a fringe about the back of his head. The other conspirators were staying out of Esmail's way, in case the Moths had made some mistake, and he ended up helping the Rekef with their inquiries.

It was midnight now. The Beetle lieutenant and his guests were all abed, as were the rest of the staff, as Esmail was led into the storage shed. There, as promised, was a gagged and bound Wasp-kinden, his pack beside him lying open to display a sheaf of documents.

Esmail knelt next to him, seeing the Wasp's eyes flare with hatred at this newcomer – *Just some nondescript halfbreed*, was the man's first thought, no doubt. The prisoner looked to be a few years short of thirty, but his clothes were finer than mere army-issue would account for, and he had a couple of rings and a torc that all spoke of good family. It was his face that interested Esmail the most, though: high cheekbones, straight, dark hair worn a little longer than army standard, blue eyes set in that pale skin the Wasps had. Not a bad face, all told, and it could have been the setting for a great many virtues. Instead of which, of course, it was crawling with so much hate and loathing that there was no room at all for fear.

Esmail leafed through the papers, wondering what he would be taking to Capitas. They were trivial stuff, the sort of humdrum logistics reports that nobody would bother a man of the captive's rank and station with: coded messages therefore, but that would not pose a problem.

73

The captive's expression said plainly, *I will tell you nothing,* but he had not quite understood his situation or his purpose here.

Esmail took a deep breath, feeling rusty and out of practice. His training was no suitable pursuit for a family man, and he had not been sad to set it aside, either. In the back of his mind, however, he had always known that he would be calling on these hard-learned skills once again. Spies never really retired, they said, and it was true, whether talking of a Rekef man or a Lowlander agent or . . . what Esmail was.

The Wasp's was a good enough face, he reflected again, and he should be grateful for that. It would be more familiar to him than his own soon enough, seen in every mirror, distorted in every polished piece of armour. He felt its contours, the straight nose, the slightly hollow cheeks, the squared-off chin, that slight nick beneath one ear that was probably a trophy of shaving rather than a duel. The prisoner had gone very still, and when Esmail reopened his eyes – blue eyes now, not his natural dark ones – the Wasp was trading fear and shock for all the other expressions he was capable of.

But Esmail was not finished yet. Some initiates of his mystery had to resort to crude torture to perfect their guises, or perhaps they chose to do so, but he had been trained in the higher arts of the spy, and had had his education finished off by the Moths themselves.

He put his hands either side of the man's face and bent his head forward until their foreheads were almost touching.

Who? he asked, and the helpless, uncontrolled answer came back, *Ostrec.*

My name is Ostrec, Esmail told himself, knowing that he would answer to that name as swiftly as to his own – more swiftly even – as long as he wore this stolen face. *Show me all that is Ostrec. Family, friends, contacts, rank, passwords, codes, missions.*

The Wasp arched and twisted, the old Grasshopper leaning

74

on him to hold him down, and his life began to tumble into Esmail's mind in fragments and pieces, never to be quite assembled, never to be a complete whole, but with luck enough for Esmail to wear Ostrec's shoes. After the initial incredulous horror, the Wasp was fighting him, an Apt mind forced into an Inapt arena and finding what defences it could. Ostrec hid his thoughts from Esmail just as he would keep them off his face before a superior officer, forcing the spy to hunt him through the rooms of his own mind, beating down doors, creeping through keyholes.

Esmail was an old hand at this, and at last he had enough: there were gaps still, odd holes and voids in his internal picture of Ostrec, but he knew that he could scavenge nothing more from the picked-out interior of the Wasp's brain. He nodded at the Grasshopper: not a cut throat, with all the mess that would make, but a narrow stiletto rammed into the ear, neat and lethal and swift. The body would be disposed of far from here, never to be found again, if the Moths' agents were any good.

Esmail straightened up, waiting for his joints to creak, but of course he was younger now, stronger and more vital. He ran a hand across his face, and it felt entirely familiar to him, as though he had been wearing it his whole life. He had put on Ostrec as a man donned a coat, taking up the Wasp's memories, prejudices and loyalties, holding them at a slight distance so as to remain Esmail, and yet having nothing of himself showing to the world that was not Ostrec. The dead man's own mother would not have known otherwise.

They were building a railroad depot at Skiel, but it would not be finished for months, so Ostrec was travelling by horse, with Esmail letting his natural skill decline to the basic competence of the Wasp-kinden. Because he could, and because Ostrec would have done so, he imposed himself on Skiel's governor enough for a change of mount, so that he could make up for lost time on his way to Capitas. A lamed horse left behind on the road had already been concocted to explain why he was behind schedule, should anybody care to ask. Esmail lived out Ostrec's pasts and futures in his head, even waking from black and gold dreams in the morning, weaving a web of anticipation to cover whatever he should encounter in Capitas.

The Moth Skryres had chosen well with this man. They could not have known the precise details of the victim they were offering up to Esmail, but their divinations had guided their hands to someone perfectly suited to the task at hand. Outwardly he was a lieutenant in the Quartermaster Corps, but his Rekef rank was major, and he had spent the war travelling between armies and conducting purges of other Rekef men who had backed the wrong general. He had spent a lot of time in Capitas since, and been rewarded for his successes. He was returning now after digging out – and Esmail was startled to discover it – a cell of the Broken Sword that had established itself near the Mynan border. In the coded papers in his pack were confessions extracted on the artificers' tables that implicated another three Broken Sword groups, for Ostrec had been a thorough man. Esmail knew that he should leave the entire business as it was, for meddling would only endanger his role and his mission. One night out from Skiel, though, he rewrote one page of the report, in Ostrec's handwriting and using Ostrec's codes, omitting all mention of such discoveries. He owed the Sword that much, and he had his own family to think about.

He had seen Capitas in Ostrec's head, but the Wasp, a well-born native, had a very skewed picture of it: all politics and hidden rooms, brothels, clandestine meetings, the houses of the wealthy. Seeing it with his own eyes, for all they had taken on Ostrec's lighter colours, Esmail was taken aback. *So large! And so foreign.* The sky over Capitas buzzed with tiny machines, and the roads into it likewise; then he drew nearer, and the city only grew, and perhaps the machines were not so tiny, and then another shift of perspective, and yet another, until he realized that the stepped pyramids that dominated Capitas were far grander than he had thought, the surrounding crush of flat buildings far wider, everything about the place bloated and expanded beyond reason, and heaving with more human beings than he had ever seen before in one place.

Only Ostrec saved his composure, for, to the stolen Ostrec in his head, it was a sight of no great consequence: just another view of his home city which was commonplace to him. Guiding his horse between the stinking, grinding, rattling and stomping – *automotives*, Ostrec knew them to be – Esmail could only cling to his borrowed memories, using the Wasp's jaded recollections to cut the looming threat of the city down to size.

Ostrec knew his way around, too. He had superiors waiting for his reports, and even if his parents had been on their deathbeds, that duty would have come first. It had not been loyalty with him, but ambition, for Ostrec knew who his future depended on. So it was that Esmail guided his horse to the stable yard of the Quartermaster Corps, leaving it unhobbled there without a word, knowing that the slaves would scurry out to take care of everything and that he, as a Wasp of some import, did not need to spare the animal another thought.

Once Lieutenant Ostrec of the Quartermaster Corps had paid his minimal respects – to superior officers who, Esmail could see, were well aware that he lived a double life that made him dangerous to offend – it was time for him to attend his real masters. There were not so very many Rekef colonels in the world, perhaps a half-dozen at the utmost after all the infighting, and only half of those were in Capitas at one time. The hand holding Ostrec's leash belonged to a corpulent, jowl-faced monster of a man named Harvang, who had tiptoed his decaying bulk through the web of Rekef politics, taking each general's orders in turn, whilst reporting on the other two to General Brugan, the eventual victor. Now Brugan was sole general of the Rekef, and Harvang had been tentatively rewarded, becoming a kind of secretary and doorkeeper to the great man. Examining this arrangement, and how Ostrec felt about it,

Esmail found that he agreed with his borrowed identity that Brugan was keeping Harvang at arm's length and in sight, just in case the man's treachery had one more turn to it.

Harvang was at dinner, but from Ostrec's pilfered experience this was generally the case at any time of day. When he saw his protégé stride in, though, the fat man lurched to his feet.

'Where the pits have you been?' Spittle streaked the air between them. Even as Esmail opened Ostrec's mouth to reply, his words were being waved away. 'Never mind. Hungry? Sit. Eat. Brugan has me hopping to him every cu'sed moment this last tenday. All manner of stupid Outlander business. Could have used you yesterday.'

Esmail picked at a plate of crabs in wine, watching as this huge hulk of a man paced ponderously back and forth. A neutral 'Sir?' was what Ostrec's experience recommended.

'Had to bring some cu'sed tyro scribe with me. Stuff not fit for a junior's ears. Have to have them cut off, eh? Need someone taking notes who won't end up signing his own death warrant.' The light tone always suggested that Harvang was about to laugh, and yet he never did. Esmail had to force himself not to stare at the man's teeth, like black and brown grave markers cramming his cavern of a mouth.

'Need rest? You've until the fifth hour. Eat, sleep, stick one up a whore, just be here and ready for the general by then.' Without warning Harvang had turned on his heel and was retreating from the room, burrowing deeper into his offices like a beast into its hole. The meal, a fair-sized banquet by Esmail's standards, was abandoned without a second thought. Harvang's servants must eat well, and perhaps that helped make up for everything else they endured.

The fifth hour came, and Ostrec had already presented himself, early as was his custom with superiors. Harvang emerged from his rooms, wiping grease from his hands, but his uniform tunic was spotless: severe gold-edged black offset by the glitter of a few war decorations. The Rekef did not give itself medals, but Harvang had been a capable army officer before the years had so bloated him.

Their destination was the palace. Ostrec kept to Harvang's heels briskly, but behind his new face Esmail was suddenly wary. He was too much in the thick of it, too fast. Only a day in Capitas and already going before the general of the Rekef? Was he discovered, somehow? Or had the old Moths wrought better than they knew? A glance around Capitas's streets gave him some comfort, for it seemed that everyone was in the same state of agitation. There were soldiers and clerks and slave and goods wagons all around, and every one of them furthering the manifest destiny of the Empire. Esmail had passed through Helleron a few times, that churning hub of commerce, and he had not imagined that two such huge cities could be so different. Helleron was a puppet worked by a thousand different competing hands, its wheels working against themselves often as not. Capitas perhaps lacked the perfect smoothness of an Ant city-state, but it had the same unity of direction, and on a scale no Ant had ever dreamt of.

I'm here none too soon, he realized. Every single human being around him, every machine, all of it was the war effort. He was watching the little stones that brought the avalanche.

Official Consortium records listed the place as Factory Nine, Capitas, but its residents referred to it as the Colonel Valrec Street Place, after the thoroughfare that ran between their place of work and the tenements that most of them lived in. Capitas itself was not the centre of heavy industry that might be found to the west, in Sonn, but there was still a sizeable factory district: a large paperworks, the main Imperial mint, and various factory lines churning out uniforms and the sundry small items an army might need: pens, packs, boots, weighing scales, buckles, harness, all the tiny but essential pieces of a military machine.

Factory Nine made trousers mostly, although the machines there could be configured for all manner of cloth goods. Its complement per shift was eighty-seven artificers, two overseers, one foreman and five cleaning staff, the latter being Common-weal slaves and the only Inapt that the place had any use for.

Pingge and Kiin were part of the early shift, arriving every morning three hours before dawn to take over the constant motion of the machines, stepping into the weary shoes of the late shift with a fluid ease born of long practice, so that their mechanical charges need never know that the hands that tended them had changed.

They were both Fly-kinden – as were a little over half the workers, because they could get into the small spaces around the machines and hover over them, and had quick fingers, and the reflexes to avoid losing them to the teeth and shuttles of the automatic looms when things went wrong. They might not keep the army marching, as they said to one another, but they kept it from marching bare-arsed, and that was surely all the Empire could ask of them.

The pair entered the factory chattering, a constant patter of banter and gossip that kept them sane through the long stretches of tedium, and stopped only when some mischance of the machines made their job briefly and dangerously interesting. They were deft, skilled, trained hastily by their instructors and then patiently by years of experience, so that they could deal with almost any problem without having to commit the cardinal sin of shutting the machines down. They were the artificers of small things.

Pingge and Kiin had worked here together, side by side, for eight years. They were of an age, although Kiin was very pale, with hair she dyed fair like a Spider-kinden. She still had a trace of accent from the East-Empire her family had come from, having earned or bribed their way to a travel permit, and gone to seek their fortunes in the capital. Pingge was tanned and more robust, laughing louder, daring more, always a step away from drawing the ire of their overseers. There were rules of conduct in the Empire's factories: indeed they were written on the wall for all to see. That the machines should run, that the factory should be productive, Pingge and the rest held to be a sacred duty. All the rest of it, about silence and deference and proper place, could go hang as far as they were concerned. They were artificers, after all, and not just slaves or common labourers. So long as they made quota they felt it was no business of anyone's – no, not the Empress herself – how they went about their lives.

Or at least, that had been their sentiment until today. The foreman was absent, for a start, which they would have assumed meant he was sick almost to death, but then one of the overseers was missing too and, short of a city-wide plague, that was unthinkable. The remaining overseer, a stooped Beetle-kinden man a few years from retiring, was plainly worried enough that he just let them get on with matters. Had the machines been less of a inviolable trust – a symbol of the elevation of their status, however meagre – then things might have been let slide, and Consortium clerks might have been knocking on the door a tenday later, demanding to know where their trousers had got to.

The talk was slow to start up, but soon the familiar chatter of the machines soothed their nerves, and the comments began to fly, pitched over and under and beneath the constant hammering of the mechanisms, passing from ear to ear in ripples of hearsay and defamation.

'. . . and she's not been sleeping in a cold bed these last three nights, despite her man being posted to Shalk . . .'

'. . . ask me, they put something in the water, never known a man less able to . . .'

'. . . came in and stomped about the place and then had his dinner and went out, and never did look in the cupboard . . .'

'. . . all that talk about flying the length and breadth of the city to bring me a bag of flour and he . . .'

'. . . got sick, and her with three children at home, and what can you do . . . ?'

'. . . roach of a housing-master changed her to a smaller room again, all that talk of supporting the troops and it's still bribe money doing the talking . . .'

Each train of chatter came down the line to Pingge, or was started by her, and Kiin added nothing, passing it on, her mouth pressed into a careful line to hide the smile, because you never knew who might walk in, and sometimes the Consortium clerks or army quartermasters took offence, and the foreman was forced to make some show of discipline, not that he was even here . . .

Then abruptly the foreman *was* there, the broad, stomping Beetle man entering hurriedly with the missing Fly-kinden overseer, and with a stranger in tow: a Wasp-kinden, a sharp young knife of a man looking altogether too keenly down the lines of the machines. Wasps actually visiting the factory almost always meant trouble for someone, but with luck it was trouble that the foreman's bulk would absorb.

They remained near the door, which let in only a pre-dawn greyness, not enough to rival the lamps. The echoing noise all around masked what they were saying, but it was quickly evident that they had brought an argument in with them. The foreman was shaking his head until his jowls quivered, making quick, angry gestures towards the workers. They caught some notion of quotas, of penalties.

'They're going to raise us,' Pingge observed, meaning that the quota would go up. 'Bound to happen.'

Kiin nodded. Life would get harder in direct proportion to the new requirements, but they had lived through it before. The trick was to come out the other side with all your fingers still on your hands.

The foreman had made some particularly angry point, and abruptly the Wasp had a palm to the man's forehead, freezing the Beetle into immobility, face now utterly still, almost expressionless save for a slight frown of concentration, no more than the girls might show, watching the repetitive round of their machines.

Abruptly Pingge fell quiet, and a peculiar focus had come over all the workers, bent over their machines as though oblivious, dearly not wanting to become involved.

The Wasp had to ask three times, louder and louder, before they heard him. 'Stop the machines!'

It was unthinkable, unheard of, but now the Fly overseer had gone to the Big Lever, the one they never used unless the end of the world was only a yammer of the looms away, and had dragged it down with all the force of his wings and bodyweight.

One by one the great machines fell silent, stopped in mid leap, ruining an entire batch. It was a disaster. Nobody could think what the matter might be. Did the Empire no longer *need* trousers?

The silence that now fell on Factory Nine had never been known in living memory. The Wasp strode down the line unhurriedly, eyes sharp. He was not quite in uniform, or not any specific uniform, although a lieutenant's rank badge was pinned carelessly to the sleeveless robe he wore over his tunic.

'All of them women, really?' he called back to the foreman.

Pingge exchanged an uneasy glance with Kiin, because there were indeed a few men working there, Beetle-kinden and a couple of halfbreed slaves; but of the *Fly*-kinden, yes, women all.

The foreman shrugged. 'As you see, sir.' He had not quite recovered from being a second away from death.

'You, you, you.' The finger stabbed out, selecting prey. 'You, you and you, with me now.' The last two at his finger's end had been Pingge and Kiin.

For a moment nobody moved. Pingge's eyes were on the foreman, whose face was a picture of misery. *Losing his workforce* – but not just for the day, she read there. Losing a half-dozen skilled workers for good. She felt a terrible sinking feeling in her stomach, her instincts crying for her to fly, seek the sky and get out of the city. But of course that was out of the question. She had family here and, besides, where was there to go?

'Move!' the Wasp lieutenant snapped, and the half-dozen were reluctantly leaving their stations, gathering in a fearful huddle close to him, but not too close. Pingge squeezed Kiin's hand for mutual courage, as the Wasp turned on his heel and marched out.

Rekef, he must be Rekef, she thought. *What have we done?* It seemed impossible that anything anybody had done in Factory Nine could possibly have brought down the wrath of the Rekef Inlander. *Was somebody using the machines for something else? Something subversive. Or maybe it was some other factory? You hear all sorts about Factory Five down on General Malik Street.* The idea that the Rekef would just round up and shoot a few random factory girls because *someone somewhere* had done something wrong seemed entirely plausible. You heard about it happening all the time, in the next city, in the neighbouring district, on some other street.

They kept within six feet of the Wasp's heels, and not one of them made a break for it. In retrospect that was what surprised Pingge the most.

Within two streets they had picked up company, another little gaggle of Fly-kinden, mostly women still but also a couple of men. Soon there were more than a score of them, pattering behind a few striding Wasp-kinden like orphans behind a matron, the occasional straggler flying to keep up.

'But where are we going?' whispered Kiin, the first words anyone had dared utter.

Pingge frowned. There were maybe a dozen places across the city that you emphatically Did Not Go because the Rekef worked there, but they were nowhere near those. Instead, this looked like . . .

'Severn Hill,' she said abruptly, and loud enough to draw an angry frown from one of the Wasps.

The Fly-kinden milled and clustered, and slowed noticeably until the Wasps shouted at them to keep up. Severn Hill was Engineering Corps territory, and that raised an entirely different spectre: not execution or torture perhaps, but everyone knew the Engineers got through a steady supply of slaves in testing their inventions. Perhaps they had run short of slaves?

Severn Hill itself was a grand ziggurat, the outside bustling with a few hundred Wasp artificers who spared the straggling Fly-kinden not a glance. The air was loud with strange mechanisms, not the familiar patter of the looms, and the drone of flying machines was a constant background noise as they shuttled to and from a pair of nearby airfields.

'In,' snapped the lieutenant, and they entered the shadow of the ziggurat, were hustled down low-ceilinged corridors until they were disgorged into a square, windowless room over-lit by the rearing flames of gas lamps.

There was a man there, another Wasp but a strange-looking one, bearded like a Spider-kinden and with a slightly manic look in his eyes, and yet with a major's badge at his collar. He regarded them from the far side of a vast desk, the top of which was entirely invisible beneath a clutter of papers.

'As requested, Major Varsec,' the lieutenant reported. 'All the Consortium would spare us at this time. All factory artificers, and used to handling machines.'

The major regarded them coolly. 'Do you think Captain Aarmon will take to them?' he asked, smiling slightly.

Pingge saw the lieutenant twitch at the question, for all it was plainly rhetorical. Whoever 'Captain Aarmon' was, he was not well liked.

'Take them to the new machines,' Major Varsec ordered. 'Let's see who has the knack of it.' He stood abruptly, looking them over as though they had become soldiers. 'Your old work is done. They'll manage without you. You're in the Engineers now, and you're mine.'

This audience chamber was much too grand just for waiting in. Abandoned there, General Tynan stood at near attention, suspecting eyes peering at him from every wall. He was deep within the palace, some part of it beyond the known haunt of soldiers, sycophants and foreign diplomats.

The walls were hung with tapestries showing interlacing Spider-kinden arabesques, gold and red and black, that did strange things to the eye. There was daylight from shafts in the ceiling and there was a flaring white glare from chemical burners on the walls, but the tapestries ate it all and smouldered sullenly, holding on to a darkness that the room should have been rid of. The rugs beneath his feet were from Vesserett, he guessed, woven bee-fur now slightly threadbare from too many marching boots. The furniture – a long table alongside one wall, and the single seat at the far end of the room – was local work but very fine, ornate black wood with gilded highlights, some slave craftsman's masterpieces.

It put him off his stride: not a cell, but a long way from freedom. Where now for General Tynan of the inexorable Second Army?

There was the sound of bootsteps behind him, and he shifted to one side as another man was led in. They exchanged glances, reading a great deal into one another's presence.

'General Roder,' Tynan noted, and the other man nodded.

Roder had been only a colonel when Tynan had last seen him, but then the Eighth had gone up against the Spider-kinden at Seldis, and a lucky assassin had attempted to throw it into disarray by killing its leader, a practice that the Imperial rank structure was there to blunt. He made a young general, did Roder, a solid, soldierly man more than ten years Tynan's junior but showing every sign that he would be just as bald soon enough, his dark hair on the retreat from his forehead. The left side of his face was stiff and expressionless courtesy of a failed poisoning attempt.

We are two of a kind. Tynan did not need to say it. Roder had hauled the Eighth Army off the Spiders' doorstep when the Emperor had died, just as the Second had come hotfoot from investing Collegium. They were both men who had missed out on their chance to be the great heroes, failing the Empire by serving their new Empress.

Roder gathered himself to say something, but at that point everyone else trooped in, judge and jury and all.

I could have asked for some of these faces to have fallen from favour during the infighting, Tynan considered, but there was a certain class of man who never seemed to misstep, clinging to power like a leech.

He knew General Brugan, of course, and would reluctantly admit that he was glad the Rekef had ended up in that man's hands rather than those of either of his late rivals. Still, it was a rare army officer who had any love for the Rekef Inlander, and generals had as much – or more – to fear from a purge than common soldiers. Brugan, at least, could pass for a fighting man, still strong and fit even though he was greying. The lancing gaze of his piercing grey eyes was often all he needed to draw confessions from the fearful, and obedience from his underlings.

To his left was Colonel Vecter, who had served with Brugan in the East-Empire before the war: a deceptively scholarly looking man with neatly parted hair and spectacles, a skilled artificer who was a constant innovator of the interrogation machines. On Brugan's right was Colonel Harvang, as though some magician had taken two whole men, swept some small quality of discipline one way to make Vecter, and then shovelled all the fat and sloth and idleness the other. In straining tunic, the gross colonel was chewing constantly at some piece of gristle, with some smug young major at his heels – to feed him sweetmeats, no doubt.

There were more: lean, bald Colonel Lien of the Engineers had stolen a general's rank badge from somewhere, and was looking insufferably pleased about it, whilst Knowles Bellowern's dark Beetle face held an expression of mild indifference, masking the fact that the Consortium colonel was one of the richest men in the Empire and head of a powerful and ambitious dynasty. Tynan looked on them all without love.

Well, at least we know where we are. But he was wrong about that. Despite the two former generals being faced with as imposing a clique of power-mongers as they had ever seen in one place before, everyone there was still waiting. There could be only one person able to bring these dignitaries together and force them to fidget and shuffle at her pleasure.

Tynan was ready for her when she swept into the room: the Empress Seda the First, whose throne he and Roder had saved by abandoning their respective campaigns, at her command. He had never actually met the woman before. His fall from grace had been too immediate, his army disbanded, his soldiers redeployed. He had thought it merely due to his failure, at the time. In retrospect he had realized that it was simple mistrust. A general with an army, in those turbulent days of secession and civil war, might have been just a little too tempted to try for the throne himself.

Seda was absurdly young – years younger than any of them, even than Harvang's protégé. A frail and slender girl, and as beautiful as nature's gifts and Spider cosmetics could make her, and when she entered the room she held all their attention utterly captive. Tynan, older and wiser than most, saw from the corners of his eyes just how she affected them: Bellowern's moistened lips, Vecter removing his spectacles to clean them, an unnameable, hungry expression nakedly apparent on General Brugan's face. Harvang's young follower started noticeably, flinching away the moment she entered the room.

She was slim and delicate, but her presence filled every inch of space there, forcing itself on them.

'General Tynan,' she acknowledged, and his name on her lips jolted something within him, despite himself. 'General Roder.' Her smile was painful to behold, like looking at the sun.

General Brugan cleared his throat. 'It has so pleased Her Imperial Majesty Seda the First to summon you to her presence,' he began, but the Empress had taken her seat by then, and now waved him to silence with a brief gesture. Tynan had heard many theories about the precise balance of power at court, and many of them claimed that Brugan, lord of the Rekef, held the reins, and that the Empress was his puppet.

Oh, not true at all, he understood now. For a moment, examining her, he found himself locking eyes with the woman. The sense of power was palpable: the entire might of the Empire balanced on her shoulders.

'Enough formalities,' she said softly. 'You must have known this day would come. Since being removed from your commands you have waited faithfully for our call, and whatever fate it should summon you to. Unlike others with guiltier consciences, you have not gathered your riches and tried to flee our borders. Well, then, the Empire has called. It requires its heroes once again.'

'Heroes?' Roder burst out, raising angry scowls from all three Rekef men and a raised eyebrow from Bellowern of the Consortium. Even facing the Empress's cool regard, the former general could not keep the words in, though: 'But we failed!'

Tynan had not realized that the man had taken it so seriously, but his failure to capture Seldis was writ large on his half-paralysed face.

'You obeyed. In the final analysis, what else is there for a soldier?' Seda asked him, forgiving his outburst implicitly. 'Who could blame you for following orders?' Hanging in the air was the common knowledge that there were plenty who *had* been blamed for just that, at the throne's convenience, but apparently this was not one of those cases. 'No,' Seda continued, 'you are heroes, for you are the Empire's generals who were never defeated.'

Tynan risked a sidelong glance at Roder, and caught the man looking back at him. *Well, there's a novel turn of phrase.*

'You must know that our Empire is under threat,' Seda informed them earnestly. 'Collegium will not raise a flag against us directly, but their agents have worked against our reunification, their weapons flood into hands of the Three-city Alliance, our closest enemies. They would have war, if only others will fight us in their stead. We see what they mean plain enough. General Tynan.'

He snapped to attention without thinking about it, for a moment just the parade-ground lieutenant he had once been.

Seda smiled to see it. 'We are re-forming the Second Army, your beloved "Gears", along with some elements of the Fifth. You are hereby restored to your position, and we send you south to meet up with your men. You carried the war to the gates of Collegium once before, General. Now you will fulfil your destiny and make that city ours.'

'Majesty,' Roder addressed her, voice hoarse with emotion, 'I shall take Seldis for you. I shall take the whole Spiderlands, if you ask it.'

She turned her benevolent regard on him. 'No, no, General, that is in hand. General Brugan and his Rekef tell me that arrangements have already been made for the Spiders, starting with a timely resolution to the Solarno situation. I have other tasks for you. We have been gathering troops near the Mynan border for some time now, in order to fend off their raids and skirmishes. The bulk of your old Eighth is marching to join them even now, along with some new toys for the Engineers. You will return our rebellious neighbours to the Imperial fold, General Roder: first Myna, Szar and Maynes, and then on to Helleron.'

She looked about brightly. 'Colonel Bellowern has made the logistical arrangements personally, and General Lien and his associates will ensure you lack for nothing in the field of artifice, and of course the Rekef Outlander is already working to smooth your way. The Empire has too long been sick and at the mercy of its enemies. Now we look to you all to put the world to rights, to restore us to our proper place in the world.' Abruptly her eyes were steel, and there were fluttering banners of black and gold in her voice, and a thousand marching feet, and great engines. 'You know your duty, all of you, for your love of the Empire, and for me.'

Seven

'You're ready?' the Antspider asked.

'I'm watching,' confirmed Eujen Leadswell, and he was, keenly, measuring his reach against hers, sword tips even, arms parallel, shoulders almost touching.

'And lunge,' she instructed, and they took a simultaneous step and, without seeming to stretch, her blade point's lead had become the best part of a foot. 'You see it?'

'I see it but I don't see *how*,' Eujen complained, dropping from his swordsman's stance. Around them, the clear airy space of Mummers's studio picked up their every sound and murmured it about the paper-covered walls.

'She's rolling her shoulder back as she stands ready,' came Gerethwy's measured tones, the cadence of an old man behind the lighter tones of a young one. 'Her arm's longer than yours, and when she lunges, she's casting her shoulder forward as well as her arm. Her joints must be as freakish as the rest of her, in my opinion.' He moved a piece on the board in front of him, then glanced blithely at the Antspider, waiting for a challenge. He was by far the most outlandish figure in the room, and perhaps in Collegium. Most people had never so much as seen a Woodlouse-kinden before, but certainly nobody had ever seen a *young* one.

Averic, across from him, made a quick counter-move. He played chess, even this outrageously chaotic version that only he and Gerethwy knew how to play, as though he was being timed. He was a strange sight in Collegium, this lean Wasp youth: not the hulking brute that most Collegiates imagined or remembered from the war, but a quiet, studious figure who wore eyeglasses to read, with sandy hair of a conservative length for a College student, but that the Antspider had taken for the height of rebellion in an Imperial. When she had confronted him with that thought, he had patiently explained that, no, the height of rebellion for an Imperial was setting yourself up as the Emperor. That was when she had decided she liked him.

He had turned up at the city's gates in company with Gerethwy, not from the same starting point but from the same point of the compass. Averic was all the way from the Empire – where else were Wasps from? – and Gerethwy from some unimaginable place north or east even of that. The joke ran that the cartography department had offered to pay for his tuition if the Woodlouse only filled in the blank spaces on their maps. He was hairless, gaunt-faced, light grey skin marked with dark grey bands running up over his scalp and down his back. Gerethwy was the only one of their little circle who could give the Antspider an even fight. He was close on seven feet tall, even with the slight bunching of his back and shoulders, and his reach was prodigious. What he lacked in speed he made up for in precision, and he would lead her on and lead her on, defence and defence, until her temper gave out and she did something incautious, which inevitably resulted in an immediate victory for one or the other of them.

'I still can't see it,' Eujen complained, 'even if you do have trick shoulders.'

'I wish the crowd at the Forum had your eyes,' she remarked lightly. The disqualification had been a shame, but notoriety was hard currency even in Collegium, and especially amongst the students. Besides, odds were that Averic's late arrival would have seen them lose anyway, and if it was a choice between a mundane loss and a flamboyant one, then the Antspider knew which one she would take every time.

Averic had been late, it turned out, because the city militia had stopped him in the street no fewer than three times on his way to the Prowess Forum.

'Pose, please,' came the voice of Raullo Mummers, whose studio they were cluttering up. He was a stocky Beetle-kinden a few years senior to any of them, a professional artist trying to clinch some manner of deal with one of Collegium's galleries, and sketching anatomy and engineering designs for the College to pay the rent. The single long room he lived and worked in filled the entire lower storey of a ramshackle house near the College, with one wall mostly given over to a grand circular window, intricately leaded in the Spider style some decades ago, and now boasting some half a dozen missing panes covered up with wood. All the rest of Mummers's walls were covered with his sketches, the work of a decade plastered and overlapping, the inspiration from them constantly feeding back into his work.

The Antspider sighed and adopted her ready pose again, although this time Eujen decided not to join her, instead drifting over to speculate on the chess game.

'Next year, do you think, for the Forum?' she asked.

'Oh, certainly,' Eujen replied over his shoulder, but his voice carried an uncertain tone.

'It's a wise man who knows tomorrow,' said Gerethwy, making another move after some thought, and watching Averic respond with instant certainty.

'Talk, all talk. Will Collegium be here next year? Yes. Will we be students at the College? Yes,' Eujen said defensively.

'So sure?' the Antspider demanded, her straight arm beginning to tremble as she held her pose for Mummers.

'The alternative is too dire to think about, Straessa,' Eujen declared. 'Look at where everyone stood after the last war, the loss of life, the chaos and disruption, missed harvests, civil strife . . .'

'You don't have to do the grand speeches with us, Eujen. We're your friends,' she pointed out. 'You're very quiet, Averic.'

The Wasp looked up from the board for a moment, and then seemed to become utterly absorbed in the position of the pieces. Eujen had been the only student willing – or daring enough – to approach the College's new Imperial recruit, beginning an unlikely friendship born of curiosity and cultural differences. Averic avoided contradicting or arguing with Eujen whenever possible. For a Wasp he seemed remarkably tactful. Patient, too. For a long time Straessa had thought he was simply devoid of the ugly temper that three generations of his kinden had made notorious. Then, once, she had seen him off guard for a moment: not in defence of himself but when some magnate's son decided to call Eujen a coward. Averic's hands had clenched into fists – a gesture of peace amongst his violent kinden – but she had caught an expression on his face, visible only for that single moment, and she had understood. It was not patience, but sheer bloody-minded willpower. He was constantly restraining himself, every day, through every barb of provocation and frustration, holding in check that reflexive retaliation his kinden would normally resort to.

'Enough,' she told Mummers. 'Or I'm going to strain something. Do you pay me to be your model?'

'Do you pay me rent to sit around my studio?' he returned, looking sullen. Because he was, at least notionally, a productive member of society, she sometimes forgot he was only a few years older than her.

'Wasn't te Mosca coming tonight?' Gerethwy observed, staring at the board.

'Trying to pin down Mistress te Mosca is like trying to stop the sun,' Eujen observed, and then the door slammed open suddenly and a half-dozen soldiers spilled in. They were Merchant Company men and women, solid Beetle-kinden in barred helms and breastplates over buff coats, each sporting a blue sash with a gold portcullis emblazoned on it. They all carried snap-bows.

In the initial confusion, the crash of the door still echoing, the Antspider had traded her wooden sword for the narrow-bladed steel weapon that was lying by the chessboard, the move from play to real following an instinct that had come with her from her childhood in Seldis amongst the full-blooded Spider-kinden. Gerethwy had taken up his staff in a single understated gesture, the weapon and his long arms giving him an improbable amount of reach. Eujen had brought up his practice blade into line as though he was in the Forum. Only Averic had no weapon and, although he stood up immediately, he kept his arms by his side, no expression on his face.

'You,' the leader of the soldiers, a tough-faced woman, picked out Averic, 'you're wanted.'

'What is this?' Eujen demanded, advancing with his wooden blade still in hand. 'What right have you to just burst in here?'

'Civic security,' the woman told him curtly.

'Where is the law?' he demanded, and there was no admission in his face that her snapbow was now directed at him. Straessa sensed rather than saw Averic tense – not a threat to him but this one to Eujen eating away at his control.

'Officer Padstock of the Maker's Own Company,' the Ant-spider declared brightly, drawing everyone's attention. 'Every-one knows Officer Padstock wouldn't go breaking down doors without good authority.' Straessa's sword went back on the table, a plea for a moment's calm.

In truth, everyone knew nothing of the sort. Elder Padstock, chief officer of the Maker's Own, was as much Stenwold Maker's creature as the company name suggested, and she was known for enforcing his perceived wishes with utter conviction.

Padstock regarded all of them without love. 'The Speaker for the Assembly wishes to see the Wasp-kinden. Is that sufficient authority?' She tried to lock eyes with Averic but he was having none of it.

Eujen was gathering himself for another outburst, but now the Wasp stepped forward, one finger flicking over a chessman to signify surrender. 'Of course, I would be honoured to meet with Master Drillen,' he observed mildly.

'Not alone,' Eujen insisted. 'I'll go with you.'

'That's not in my brief,' Padstock snapped.

'I'm going with him to Drillen. What are you going to do?' Eujen put himself right in front of her, making himself impossible to ignore.

She put the barrel of her snapbow to his chest, finger on the trigger, and Straessa found herself thinking, *This is it. This is when Collegium went mad.* Probably Padstock had looked Eujen over and seen only a posturing academic whose wars were fought on paper, but one thing he had never lacked was courage. *Too much courage for his own good.*

Straessa could almost hear Averic winding up until he was tense as a bowstring, with fingers pressing into his palms until they were bloodless. Somewhere out of her eyeline, Gerethwy changed his grip on the staff slightly. *We're going to get into a fight with the Merchant Companies. We're going to get shot.* She now wished she had not put her sword down, especially as the move had bought her nothing. *This is the night that they started shooting students.* The thought went round and round in her head.

Then Padstock lowered the snapbow with a sound of disgust. 'Fine. come with us. See what Drillen makes of you, Wasp-lover. Just you, though. The rest of your menagerie stays here.' Her eyes flicked across Gerethwy and the Antspider, and then settled on Raullo Mummers. 'Quite the nest of dissension you keep here, Master Mummers. An artist should have a better feel for the mood of his public. Now, let's move. And you can leave the toy sword here. I doubt you'll find a use for it where we're going.'

Eujen cast the Antspider a familiar look – she knew it well from his turns in the debating circles, or stepping into the ring at the Prowess Forum. She had to tell herself, over and over, that this was Collegium, after all. People did not get *vanished* in Collegium. They did not die at the whims of their betters. That was reserved for the Spiderlands or the Empire, or for foreigners in an Ant city-state. The whole point of Collegium, which had drawn her across half the Lowlands with nothing but a haphazard education, a pocket of stolen gemstones and a cocky attitude to recommend her, was that its people lived in peace, free from fear and oppression. *Eujen must be the future, not Padstock. If Padstock is the future of this city then there will be nothing left recognizable. Like Eujen says, we can't kill all of what we are just to survive.*

Then they were gone, the soldiers, Padstock, Eujen and Averic, marching off into the night, and Gerethwy was relaxing by careful degrees, releasing all that stored power that his lanky frame hid so well, and Mummers was hunching over, muttering to himself and peering at the door to see what damage had been done to it.

Jodry Drillen was found sitting at his desk, some unfinished document of state beneath the nib of his reservoir pen, a bowl of wine half-finished at his left hand, and still wearing the creased robes that he had worn to that day's session of the Assembly. He was to be found thus so often that a number of his associates had compared notes and knew full well that it was a studied pose that he adopted quite deliberately: the elder statesman at work for the city's good at all hours. If he had a great many visitors of an evening, then the half-bowls of wine he was required to drain left him positively light-headed towards midnight.

Mere students were not privy to the higher echelons of rumour, of course, and so he cut a suitably grave figure as the Wasp boy was led in by Jodry's Fly-kinden secretary, Arvi.

There was another youth tagging along, but Jodry was hardly surprised. The student body tended to form close-knit factions at a moment's notice – good practice for a life of politics – and, in all honesty, half of Jodry's visitors arrived with some unwelcome hanger-on.

'Young Averic,' he noted, 'and I believe it's Leadswell, is it not?'

The Beetle boy nodded, and Jodry saw that, although much of him looked soft, like most Beetle lads whose families had a certain income, his eyes and the set of his jaw were solid. *Very much Assembler material,* Jodry considered, an assessment backed by what he already knew of the young man. 'Come in, both of you. Chief Officer Padstock, thank you for your assistance. Speed and discretion as standard.' The words were clearly a dismissal to the woman who loomed in the doorway behind the two students, her snapbow shouldered, but she did not go.

'Master Speaker, I must advise you, it is not safe to be in a room with one of his kinden. They are never unarmed.'

Jodry opened his mouth to wave her concerns airily away, but an odd feeling down his back stopped him. The Wasp's expression was as bland as a statue's, but of course his provenance was in question, and what if all this was some Rekef scheme after all, to get a man close enough to kill the Speaker for the Assembly?

Would they? Am I so important? He had planned to make this a comfortable, avuncular interview, a word from the wise to young Averic, a gentle sounding-out. To ask Padstock to stay would be to show weakness. To command her to go had an outside chance of being fatal.

'For your peace of mind, then, Chief Officer,' he tried, magnanimously, and she took up a post in the corner of his study, beside the comfortable chair he kept for College Masters and merchant magnates. Needless to say, neither Averic nor Leadswell took a seat there.

Eujen Leadswell looked as though he wanted to make some

angry statement, no doubt about rights, but the fact that this was the actual *Speaker* for the Assembly before him had apparently gifted him with a little uncharacteristic caution, instead yielding the floor to their host. Jodry allowed himself a grand sigh, a busy man with the presence of mind to attend to small things himself.

'Master Leadswell, I would ask you why you have honoured me with your presence but, to avoid mutual embarrassment, let us pretend that you have told me that you are so solicitous of your Wasp friend, and so doubtful of Collegiate legal procedure, that you attend as an observer. Let us pretend that I have taken this in good humour.'

Leadswell opened his mouth, one hand making a half-gesture towards Padstock, which had her twitching to bring her snapbow around. Jodry took a moment to adjust his mental picture of Padstock inviting Averic to his office. *Did she read a little more into my instructions than I meant? Yes. Did I honestly think she would not, given who she is? Hmmm.*

'Averic, I understand that you are having a difficult time adjusting to our society.' It was a neutral opening. 'Reports of your academic record are mixed,' because Jodry knew well that certain teachers at the College had war records and too many memories, 'and the College bailiff's office has a number of reports that mention your name,' notably as the victim, although some of those bailiffs were similarly partisan.

'Have you brought me here to expel me, Master Drillen?' Averic asked quietly.

'No doubt your friend Leadswell is about to insist that a vote of senior Masters is required for an expulsion, and I've not been amongst that number for a decade and more,' Jodry corrected him, and caught an expression fleeting across the Wasp's face: surprise. Of course, in the Empire, it was orders or nothing, and men lived or died by the whims of their superiors. That was what Jodry had always understood, and it was interesting to see it confirmed in these present circumstances. 'Look, boy, I admit that, since the war, the student body has never been so diverse – Solarnese, Ancient Leaguers, Tseni, all manner of curios turning up at our gates looking for their accredits. Spies, some of them – but there is a school of thought saying that showing a spy that we are a benevolent, humanistic society that believes in equality and opportunity for all is by no means a wasted practice. It worked with Sarn, after all. However, and despite the recent alliance, no Vekken youth has applied to study here, and wisely so, for the wounds are still fresh from their most recent attempt to subjugate us. Not quite so fresh as the wounds your Second Army made when they camped outside our walls.'

He looked from face to face: Leadswell's dark features, Averic's exotic pallor. Both were waiting for the strike, so that they could parry and riposte in kind.

'I know a little about how matters work within the Empire. One central authority over corps, armies, Auxilians, slaves. A place for everyone, hm? So what am I to think? That you're a renegade or you were sent? You'll appreciate how the situation out east makes the question pertinent, and I'm not surprised that you find it hard to walk down a street in this city without being called out.'

Leadswell opened his mouth again, but Averic just said, 'I was sent, sir. But I was sent by my family. Do you think nobody in the Empire looks over at Collegium and wonders, *What is their secret strength?* But I am not a spy. There are those in the Empire who believe that the future may bring us to terms with the Lowlands – with Collegium therefore. What better adviser and ambassador than one who has studied with you? Would you not have some scion of yours serve in the Imperial army, if he could?' The boy's voice was careful: not fierce with sincerity, nor hesitant with doubt.

'It's a pleasant enough thought,' Jodry allowed, bringing all his scrutiny to bear, but finding the Wasp's features impossible to read. The boy's hands were fists, he saw, clenched tight, but none of that made it to his face. 'You must admit that the future you describe seems unlikely just now.'

Averic shrugged. 'I hope for better, sir. That the war between our peoples is not finished seems unarguable, but all wars eventually end. My family have made an investment. They are soldiers, as all our people are, but they are merchants also.'

'Leadswell, I recall you from the end-of-year debates,' Jodry noted. 'You spoke very well in favour of just such a future as young Averic describes. You lost, however. The judges were unkind, perhaps.'

Eujen Leadswell took a steadying breath, neither of them feeling it necessary to mention that Jodry had been one of those judges. 'Master Drillen, you asked why I came. Do I fear for my friend under Collegium justice? No, for he has broken no laws. But any man may call him a spy, and I do not trust that the law would be swift enough to save him. You talk of our educating spies about our cultural superiority. Averic has been shown precious little of that, Master Drillen. What report do you think he would give of us if he returned home now?'

'That we were more like his people than he had thought,' Jodry snapped, nipping the oratory in the bud. 'Do you envy the lot of an Imperial's life – and I mean that of our kinden there, who do well enough as the Empire goes? Do you think it is some grand lie that suggests the Empire is a cruel regime that makes cities into slaves and slaves into corpses?'

'I think that it is our duty as Collegiate men to do all we can to change the Empire, Master Drillen,' Leadswell shot right back, and Padstock tensed, for the lad was abruptly leaning over Jodry's desk towards him, all awe at the office of Speaker forgotten. 'But I think that if we treat them as nothing but a threat, then we shall *create* our own future. Also, I know him. He is my friend. I choose to trust him. He is no spy.'

Averic's face was very set, but Jodry wondered if he detected some suppressed emotion there, even if only the eyes were a party to it. 'And when the Empire comes to us with armies and not with words?' he asked. 'How will you meet them, then?'

Leadswell stepped back, his face bitterly displaying the thought, *So, you think I'm a traitor, too.* 'As I did last time they came, Master Drillen. When Tynan's Second was at our gates, I was loading artillery on the wall.'

'And you?' Jodry's gaze swept towards Averic, meeting that lack of expression head on. Before the Wasp's silence became awkward, Arvi opened the door with another Fly accompanying him, a woman in a grey robe that was decidedly not Collegium standard.

'Mistress te Mosca,' Jodry observed. He had wanted this interview but, now it was cut short, he found that he was relieved. *For Leadswell is right, of course, from a certain point of view – right and yet too late. That ship sailed before the Wasps put us to the siege the last time.*

'Master Drillen.' Sartaea te Mosca was not a full Master of the College, but a mere associate. Still, she had been hired to head a department left vacant, and one that nobody else wanted. She taught Inapt studies, as the College preferred to refer to the mysticism and flummery that surrounded the ways of the old Moth-kinden. She was a young lecturer, but a few decades amongst the Moths at Dorax had given her a curiously ageless air, which in Jodry's experience persisted even after she had downed close on her bodyweight in imported spirits. She had also taken a keen interest in Averic and Leadswell and all their little clique, and was sociable enough to have garnered a certain fondness amongst the College Masters.

'Mistress te Mosca,' Jodry repeated. 'These two lads appear to have found their way to my study. Would you perhaps ensure they reach their lodgings?'

She studied him, testing her Moth-taught inscrutability against his professional regard, and breaking first, into a slight, submissive smile. 'I'd be delighted to, Master Speaker.'

She turned to go, the two students lagging behind, and Jodry tapped his pen on the desk for their attention. 'One more thing, young Leadswell. I know it is always a fine thing to imagine yourself the rebel, fighting for a grand cause against the ignorance and prejudice of many. Believe me, Stenwold Maker traded on that for decades, and you might want to think about *that*. However, I trust that in your social history classes they still teach the rivers hypothesis? That no society travels all one way, dances to a single tune, but there are mingled flows, so on, so forth? Did you see the play *The Officer's Mistress*?'

Leadswell frowned at him, shaking his head, knowing the trap was there, but unable to see where Jodry was going with this.

'Too late now, then. It closed after four nights. Full houses, too. A grand shame. Set during the war, don't you know? Some piece of business about the Empire in the second and fourth acts.'

'I don't understand, Master Drillen,' Leadswell admitted.

'The theatre owner brought the curtain down,' Jodry explained gently. 'Not healthy, you see, to be associated with something that's making fun of the Empire, for all that the commons rush to laugh. After all, you never know who your patrons might be next year. You never know who's making a *list* right now. You might want to think about that.'

Arvi would, left to his own devices, have escorted the two students from Drillen's chambers coldly and without ceremony, to let them know just what the establishment of the Assembly thought of them, as interpreted by himself, the Speaker's secretary. However, they were accompanied by Sartaea te Mosca, who was a Fly-kinden teaching at the College, and Arvi had an entirely intentional double standard when it came to his own people. Those who had made enough of themselves to become respectable always found a friendly reception at the Speaker's offices. Besides, Arvi was now, in his own estimation, sufficiently advanced in society to start casting around for his own dynasty, and attractive and influential Fly women were always worth keeping on the right side of.

The two youths looked shaken, as well they might, but te Mosca's admirable presence was calming them, and Arvi indicated to her, by a careful nod and a twitch of an eyebrow, that he would give them all a moment to settle themselves before turning them out of doors. Her smile, in return, was small but elegant, and Arvi made careful adjustments to the mental list of eligibility that he carried constantly in his mind. He considered whether offering a little warmed-over wine might be appropriate, but no doubt the students would want some too, in which case the only appropriate offering would have to be an insultingly poor vintage. Associating with the student body at all, in fact, seemed to indicate a flaw, in this woman's judgement. He frowned to himself and annotated his list further.

At that moment a Beetle-kinden woman burst in, the doorman actually running after her in an attempt to restrain her.

'I need to see the Speaker right now!' she snapped, heedless of the other visitors. Even as Arvi rushed at her, hands up to implore discretion, she was saying, 'No! Get out of my way, you bloody functionary. That maniac Gripshod is going to blow up the whole *city* if somebody doesn't stop him . . .'

Something in Arvi's demeanour communicated itself because the woman turned round and saw a Wasp staring at her with some interest. She stuttered to a halt.

Arvi sighed, but this sort of thing was happening all the time. One could not get efficient enough door staff, and some day he would have to speak to the artifice department and get them to automate the process somehow. He managed it all without Jodry ever knowing, shuffling the Beetle woman – a regular informant – into a side room, and then gently decanting te Mosca and her charges onto the street with a kind word, ensuring by looks and manner that the woman understood how he was going out of his way and beyond the call of duty for her. Then he returned and gave Jodry sufficient warning for him to receive his next guest in his customary fashion, even tweaking his master's robes into a suitably picturesque dishevelment.

At last the informant was ushered in with whatever alarming news she had about Gripshod – and what a name *that* was to conjure with, Arvi thought – and he could now take a moment for a sit-down and a fortifying sip of brandy from the flask he kept in a holster under his armpit.

Just as he was stowing the covert article away, another Fly-kinden burst in, this time so far ahead of the doorman that Arvi could only hear his running feet.

'Need to see the Speaker,' she got out. She was still wearing the light canvas overalls of an aviatrix, and Arvi guessed she had flown here straight from the airfield with the stink and oil of the orthopter still on her hands.

'Mistress te Schola,' he greeted her, because this woman also taught at the Assembly – and she was a beauty, too, for all that she was Solarnese and therefore somewhat eccentric of manner.

'Taki,' she corrected him absently, and only raised an eyebrow when he kissed her hand, a greeting he fervently hoped was appropriately Solarnese. 'Look, seriously, I need to see Drillen right now.'

She was still out of breath from the flight, her chestnut hair flattened by the imprint of the flying helm she had only just removed, tracking grease on to the carpets and with her clothes dirty and unchanged for too long. Arvi almost proposed there and then. However, his spine was an iron rod of duty and he could only force out the reluctant words, 'I'm afraid the Speaker is in a meeting, but if you would wait . . .'

'Get me Maker, then,' she told him. 'Stenwold Maker, the War Master.'

'Alas, Master Maker is out of the city.'

Taki stared at him. 'He's *what*?'

'He set out for Myna, I believe.' Probably that was a state

secret, but this woman was one of Maker's associates, and anyway, in that moment, Arvi would have found it hard to deny her anything.

'But I was flying *over* Myna just now!' she exclaimed. 'I've flown from Capitas to Collegium and now I have to go most of the way *back*?'

'I could perhaps inform the Speaker that you are here . . .' Arvi stretched his duty to the snapping point.

'Forget it. I need to get a night's sleep, get my *Esca* rewound and tuned up, and I need to drop some sketches into the aeronautics department just as soon as I've actually made them. Tell Drillen I've headed for Myna.' And she was gone from the room and from Arvi's life, as abruptly as she had appeared.

Eight

To anyone observing Stenwold – which meant a dozen others in the *Sontaken*'s passenger hold – he would seem to be composing a coded missive, a curiously blatant piece of espionage, as he sat there with papers spread about him. On one sheet were some sparse notes in plain script, on another a laboriously translated piece made of baffling symbols. The other pages comprised his lexicon, a book of all those familiar words that he had been able to scratch down the glyphs for. At least a couple aboard the *Sontaken* must recognize him, and several were staring and whispering, no doubt imagining the infamous War Master compiling secret orders to his minions.

In fact, he was writing a letter to a woman, as delicate and awkward a piece of wordsmithing as ever went into a student's love poem.

This was not a love letter, of course. He was too old for that sort of thing and so was she, and neither of them were in *love*. If there had been anything as fiery and fierce as love between them, then surely they would not be so utterly separated now, living amongst different kinden in different worlds. Stenwold's days as a lover had come and gone when he was a College student, and left no marks or traces behind. Even his dalliance with Arianna, the Spider-kinden girl who had deserted from the Rekef for him, had not quite been *love*, after all – her ambition, his hubris, and a passion born of war overwhelming any fear of danger. She had betrayed him, later, then died trying to save him. It had not been a happy business. He still missed her, but he knew full well it had not been love.

The *Sontaken* was a new design of airship, a streamlined canopy above, some powerful outrigger engines and a newly designed system of stabilizers meant that the little vessel could make the Collegium to Helleron run in four days of mild discomfort, when it had once been the boast of the great *Sky Without* to make the same trip in ten. Four days sitting in the same place without bureaucracy demanding his time was a luxury to Stenwold, which was why he had started abandoning the city for his clifftop refuge, where he could look out over the sea and brood, and shudder.

He had been to places few other landborn had ever seen, but he would never go back. That sunless, alien abyss offered no life for one such as him, just as his parched and dusty world was a terrible place for the woman he now wrote to.

He consulted his lexicon once again, but he had found another gap in his knowledge, another word he did not know the sigil for, nor any cognate of it. If he could have simply written to her, with all the Collegiate eloquence at his command, then things might have been different. Perhaps he could have baited the hook sufficiently to draw her up to shore again. The Sea-kinden spoke the same words that he did, but their writing was utterly different, each word a picture. Each time the sea-traders returned with more gold and more intricate clockwork, he learned another few dozen signs from them to add to his book, but even now he could write only the most halting and awkward things and, besides, what could he say? Not mawkish talk of feelings, certainly. He was Stenwold Maker, middle-aged and calloused by time and loss, and he could not open himself wide enough to admit that kind of youthful foolishness. And besides, they were both too solemn and set in their ways, and they both had responsibilities.

So instead he wrote about duty, to the wretched extent that he could. After all, he had his duty to Collegium, and she had hers to her new leader, the boy Aradocles. Perhaps even the differences of land and sea might not have sufficed to separate them had they not both been so *busy*.

Her name was Paladrya, this woman he did not love. Her letters came back to him, sometimes, infrequently, partly in her confident pictograms, partly in crude letters that he had a hard time deciphering. He could ask the Sea-kinden who brought them to translate, of course, or to write down for him what he wanted to say in return, but his words were for Paladrya alone, for all that they were of such everyday things. He did not want to share them with anybody else.

Without ever really thinking about it, he had disclosed such things to her that the Assembly might have exiled him for treason. When he thought of her, when he painstakingly fumbled out those complex glyphs, he had no secrets.

He sensed a change in the *Sontaken*'s progress, felt his stomach shift with a gradual loss of height, and knew that they were now coming in to Helleron. He would secure transport to Myna there, but first he would meet up with an old friend. The business of the world was pressing on him again. Stenwold gathered up his papers and stowed them back in the pack at his belt, ready for the next rare opportunity for contemplation.

He was far from the sea here but, as he listened to the wind whistling past the hull outside, to the drone of the engines changing pitch, he thought he heard breakers for a moment, on a distant shore.

Helleron was as he remembered it, save that perhaps there was now more of it. The city's innards sprawled in mounds and tangles of ghettos, factories, slums and tenements, all beneath the pall of smoke and soot that arose from the belching throats of a thousand chimneys. The grander houses of the magnates themselves were mostly located on higher ground, and where they could hope to remain upwind of the industry for as much of the time as possible.

Helleron to Myna was not the most reliable journey, as the newly freed Three-city Alliance was not rich enough to make a good export market, nor particularly trusting of where Helleren sympathies lay. The factory-city had rolled over quickly enough when the Empire had reached it the first time, and there was no suggestion that the magnates would put up much more of a fight should the Wasps come again. Whether this was just due to the legendary neutrality of the city, or whether there was something deeper working in those cluttered and grimy streets, was something that Stenwold was hoping to uncover.

He had secured passage on a freight fixed-wing that was making a quick round-trip to Myna, and that only because he had chartered it and paid for its cargo himself. He had a few hours, though, and furtive messages had brought him to an eating house in a moderately affluent part of town, a street of prosperous artisans and middling shopkeepers, not amongst the great and the good nor yet in the gutter. In Helleron, the distance between the heights of luxury and the depths of despair could be very small indeed.

Stenwold recognized him immediately, but then the man's bodyguards did rather draw the eye. Greenwise Artector was a man too grand for this sort of place, and it showed even though he had dressed down. Turning up with a couple of Ant-kinden at his shoulders, who pointedly took a table near the door and stared at every other patron as though they were all assassins, could not help but make an impression, and Greenwise was well known enough that word would soon spread. By that time, however, he and Stenwold would have concluded their business, and the idea was that people would remember the great and wealthy merchant but not the hooded man in the artificer's canvas whom he spoke to.

Greenwise Artector had never quite been Stenwold's friend,

but he had been a covert supporter for years. The two of them saw eye to eye on the problem of the Empire, and Artector had done a lot of good hidden work when Helleron had seen Imperial occupation. His information had been vital in fuelling the anti-Imperial resistance.

He looked thinner than Stenwold recalled, the clothes hanging off him a little, clearly tailored for more expansive days. The expensive cosmetics that smoothed out the signs of age and wear on his dark face no longer quite hid the worry around his eyes.

'Sten,' he said. 'Just like old times.'

'The wheel has rather come full circle,' Stenwold admitted. 'At least this time round, Collegium will be ready.' There had been moments, before the war, when it had seemed his home city would simply ignore the entire situation, turn its back on the Imperial advance until the Wasps had reached their very doorstep, and it was too late. 'Where will Helleron be?'

'Officially?' Greenwise grimaced. 'We are proud of our neutrality. We bow to no man. Listen to most of the magnates and you'd never realize we had an Imperial governor not that long ago, and that our factories were given over to their war effort.'

'Unofficially?'

'There are a lot of Imperial dignitaries turning up at the airfields, Consortium merchants mostly. They turn up for a desultory bit of trade, and end up staying on to dine and chat with this magnate or that. More than half the Council plays host to them, and they talk about lucrative contracts, but there's more going on. I have a few servants here and there that take my coin. Occupation terms for Helleron are already drafted, or as good as. The Empire's diplomats are getting clever, and everyone's going to end up subscribing to the same convenient lie: Helleron will get to keep its autonomy, so long as it does everything the Empire tells it.'

Stenwold nodded soberly, and then they paused while the wine arrived. The nervous waiter's insistence that it was on the house told them that they had only a short interval before all the spies caught up with them.

'Nothing there to surprise me,' the War Master noted. 'Greenwise, what do you hear from Myna in the last few days?'

'I'd not go to Myna for all the gold in the mint,' the magnate told him straight off. Seeing Stenwold's expression, he nodded grimly. 'But, as that's where you're going now, nothing good, Sten. The Empire's had troops at the border for months now, on manoeuvres if you can believe it. Myna – the whole Alliance – is strung like a bow, ready to loose at any moment. I hear there have been a dozen separate border incidents in the last two months, crossing both ways, and that's not to mention the Principalities throwing their lot in with the Empire, which means the Alliance are all over *that* border, too. The Wasp diplomats are complaining loudly that the Mynans can't let go and will keep pushing them until there's another war. Or, to translate, the Wasps will use that logic as their excuse to bring one about. It's all firepowder over that ways, Sten. One spark will set it all off.'

'But when?' Stenwold asked him, feeling the sands of their conversation running out. 'You must have sources there.'

'All I have's a pair of low-ranking Consortium men with gambling habits, and they know next to nothing. Sten, there's been most of an army at the border for a good while now, and it's kept well supplied. They could march at any time. But all the orders come from Capitas. There's no general on the ground there yet to make the decision. That means that when the call comes . . .'

'It'll come without warning,' Stenwold finished. 'Greenwise, give me your best guess, then?'

The magnate seemed to have shrunk into his robes even further since the beginning of their conversation. 'Yesterday.' He shrugged. 'Today. Now. I don't know, Sten. And . . .'

His new tone caught at Stenwold, sensing real despair in the wreckage of the pleasant, avuncular man he had known all those years ago.

'Sten, it's all up for me when the Empire gets here. I'm selling everything I can here, shunting it south and west. What I did during the war . . . I got away with it at the time, but I know some of the others have put it all together since. They know where I stand, even if they don't know all the details. If the Wasps get here, then I get out or my life's not worth a Moth's curse.'

He stood abruptly, and the two Ants were on their feet in the same instant. 'Goodbye, Sten. See you in Collegium, maybe, or Sarn. Anywhere but here.'

They were forced down before they even reached Myna, two orthopters sliding across the sky in front of the fixed-wing freighter Stenwold had chartered. There was a scattered flash of light, the heliograph signals that were slowly becoming a crude language between aviators. In this case, Stenwold's pilot had no idea of the message, but the hostile behaviour of the Mynan fliers was unmistakable, so he brought the freighter down at a dirt airstrip outside a tiny village within sight of Myna's walls.

It turned out to be something approximating a customs inspection, with a squad of Mynan soldiers muscling up to the craft with the clear intent of searching every inch of it. Stenwold showed them his papers, and just whose name was at the foot of them. It would be pleasant to say that their attitude turned at once to helpful benevolence, but the best they could manage was a kind of stand-offish annoyance.

Stenwold considered how this was what Myna seemed like coming from the *west*. Had they flown in from the Imperial east, he guessed that the freighter would have been shot down without warning.

They made the short hop to Myna, coming down over its top airfield, of persistent memory. Stepping out onto that open space, seeing the flat-roofed warehouses and merchants' offices surrounding it, Stenwold was twenty years younger for a second, fleeing here from the city itself even as the Wasp soldiers coursed overhead.

Ah, Tisamon. His friend, the Mantis Weaponsmaster, had been trying to get himself killed that day, an ambition realized only a few years ago.

He showed the same papers to the Mynan official that approached him, while his pilot supervised the unloading. There were five modest crates, each containing a dozen snapbows and ammunition. Too little, too late, but what could he do? That Myna would be first on the Empire's list was clear to anyone who cared to look at a map, whether the Wasps turned for the Lowlands or the Commonweal. The Three-city Alliance sat at the flashpoint of the known world, so Stenwold could excuse them a little paranoia.

He had almost expected to find the city under siege even as he arrived. He could fool himself that, if he concentrated very hard, he could sense the Imperial forces massing to the east, just across the nebulous and ill-defined border.

'Master Maker, you know you're finding your own way back?' It was his pilot, at his shoulder. 'I'm not staying here, you understand.' There was neither cowardice nor disloyalty in the sentiment. The man was a Helleren merchant, not some partisan.

'Fair weather to you,' Stenwold told him. 'The Mynans will get me back to Helleron.'

'Stenwold Maker in the flesh!' The hailing voice caught his attention, and the pilot took the opportunity to make himself scarce and go to start his engines.

The woman striding across the airfield, outstripping her retinue and making them run to keep up, was a striking sight. Like the other Mynan Beetles she had blue-grey skin and blue-black hair, but there was something of the Ant-kinden in her physique, leaner and more compact than Beetles usually were.

She was young, perhaps closing on thirty these days, though she looked less than that, and had she been anyone else she would have been called beautiful. As it was, the sheer fire and drive to her overrode all other assessments. Here was a woman who had raised a rebellion, endured captivity and driven out the Empire. All of it more complex than that, of course, but she was the woman the Mynans looked to, the reason that their newly liberated state had held together – indeed the reason that the entire Alliance had remained in one piece. Kymene, the Maid of Myna: Stenwold instinctively looked for the mail beneath her black and red robes, and found it, a knee-length hauberk of fine links and a breastplate over that bulking out the cloth. One hand was always close to the hilt of her shortsword, despite the fact she was in the midst of her people and that a half-dozen bodyguards were vainly trying to catch her up.

She halted, staring at him, her eyes flicking briefly to the crates. 'I told the Consensus you were coming yourself. They didn't believe me. They couldn't see why some rich, fat Collegiate Beetle would bring his hide this close to the Empire, if he didn't have to. They don't know you.'

'It's good to see you too,' Stenwold replied drily. In fact, the last time he had set eyes on her, her city had been under the Imperial boot and she had only just been freed from the governor's cells. Since the war's end, however, there had been a clandestine communication between them, through agents and go-betweens and shipments of arms.

'This is all I could raise, and it's stretched my funds to the limit,' he told her.

She shrugged. 'I'll get them distributed. More than half our forces are still using crossbows, and I don't think Maynes and Szar have much at all in the way of this kind of weaponry.'

'How do you stand with the other members of the Alliance?' he asked her, as she turned on her heel and stalked back the way she had come, trusting him to follow her.

'Solidly, for now. We have a detachment of Maynesh Ants

on our walls already, and if you thought *we* hated the Empire, you should listen to *them*. I understand that there are troops on their way from Szar, as well, although they won't be here for a while.'

'It sounds as though you think this is it, then,' Stenwold observed.

She stopped and looked back at him; her expression was a thousand years old. 'Master Maker, it's been *it* every day since the Wasps ousted the last of their traitor-governors. Today, tomorrow, next tenday. Me, I don't know what they're waiting for.'

She monopolized his attention for the next two hours, hauling him into a spartan office that had not a single fingerprint of her personality to mark it. Looked at objectively, Stenwold realized, Kymene was a frightening creation: a child of the occupation, whose every waking moment was still devoted to keeping her city free. The rebellion that had seen the Empire's garrison thrown out and governor killed had not changed her, and for her it had not changed much in the world either. She had never lost sight of the black and gold horde just over the horizon, and in that Stenwold had to admit to a kinship with her. Still, watching her as she dealt with her underlings, giving them curt orders, receiving their reports with a stern face, dismissing them with new instructions, he felt he was watching a woman on a battlefield, not one safe in her own city. She was so striking, so young, and yet he had no sense that she had any connections with another living soul other than those directly required for the continued existence of her city.

She caught his look, and held his gaze for a moment, almost hostile despite everything, meeting everything in the world as though it was just one more challenge. Then business resumed, and she was explaining what they knew of Imperial troop positions, their distances from Myna, their expected marching time and how much warning her city might receive. Myna was the most easterly of the Alliance's three cities, for all that its strength at the time had made it the last to fall in the Empire's first invasion. This time, the hammer would fall here first, and the border was not so very far away. Myna was on high alert, all the reserves called up, orthopters standing ready on the airfields, artillerists constantly manning the walls.

She introduced Stenwold to a close-faced Ant-kinden from Maynes, the officer in charge of the detachment that had already arrived. The man had little to say to Stenwold, little use for anyone except soldiers: polite enough, but it was plain that his mind was forever focused beyond the walls, watching and waiting. Stenwold understood that there were a few score Ant-kinden scattered out towards the border, forming a chain of linked minds that would relay word of any hostile move back to the city as fast as thought.

'What good is he? What is he here for?' the Ant asked, at last, having endured several minutes of strained conversation.

Stenwold sighed, thinking how Ant-kinden were the same the world over. 'If nothing else, I'm here to show the Alliance that you're not alone. Kymene has asked me to speak to the Mynan Consensus, and I'll do so. I'll show them that the Treaty of Gold means something more than just paper.' The thought took him back to that windswept day outside the gates of Collegium – the Empire, the Lowland cities, the Alliance, Solarno and the Spiderlands, all of them putting their mark to a great-worded document of peace. A hostile move by the Empire against one signatory would mean war with all, or so said the treaty. Such documents mouldered quickly, however, and Stenwold hoped – he dearly hoped – that Collegium would remember the signing of it as vividly as he did.

The hour was late when he managed to barter some time for himself, heading out into Myna to catch up with another old friend, and mostly because he had heard that his truant niece Cheerwell had passed through Myna at the start of winter, possibly heading into the Commonweal by underhand means. That meant Hokiak's Exchange, of course. Hokiak was a decrepit old Scorpion, and Stenwold had known him years ago, back before the Empire's first invasion. He was a fixture of Myna, venal and greedy, selling to both sides during the occupation and yet always walking a fine line that had avoided reprisals from either. He would know all the details of where Che Maker had gone, and Stenwold was willing to bet that he would know something new worth hearing about the Imperial forces, too. Hokiak had always been one to keep his options open.

Stenwold had known for some time that he stood on the brink of a great fall, and all the world with him. Every figure on Myna's streets seemed to be in a desperate hurry, rushing for shelter, for loved ones. There were soldiers everywhere, many of them obviously new to the uniform, and the recruiting still going on. Even back in Collegium the murmur was of war just over the horizon, casting a faint shadow over everyone, subtly changing the investments merchants made, the books the scholar read, the goods the artisan crafted. Here, though, was the true sign of the times, an omen he needed no seer to interpret for him.

Hokiak's Exchange was boarded up. The old man, who had weathered conquest, occupation and liberation with equanimity, had seen the writing on the wall, wrapped up his business of over twenty years, and gone.

The orthopter descending on the makeshift landing field was of a design none of the watching Wasps had seen, although if any of them had been posted to Solarno recently they might have found it familiar: two-winged, with a hook of a body balancing between. Almost vertical in flight, it tacked and backed as it came down, adjusting its positioning minutely, skilled pilot and well-calibrated machine working in tandem. The Imperial aviators there exchanged glances, wondering if they could have jockeyed their own Spearflights down as neatly, especially at night.

The machine's landing gear snapped out, and it came down neatly on a tripod of slender legs, leaving it upright, the round windows of its cockpit seeming to survey the other fliers there with a predatory air. Then they were hingeing upwards, and two men emerged, one clambering heavily to the ground and the other coasting awkwardly down on Art wings.

They were not exactly unexpected, but the assembling Imperial Eighth Army was in sufficient flux that they were aggressively challenged anyway, a score of the Light Airborne dropping down all around them with palms out. The duty sergeant muscled up to them, ready to demand answers; poor communications meant that he, of all people, had not been forewarned.

He saw two halfbreeds, unescorted and out of uniform, and under normal circumstances that would have been enough for him to have them arrested first, and work out what was going on later. There were certain individuals in Imperial lore who were sufficiently notorious for their description to filter down as far as sergeants, however.

One of the two newcomers was nothing much to look at: a young man who looked as though he had Beetle and Ant blood in him, solidly built and with a brooding expression on his dark face. Like his companion, he wore dark artificer's leathers, with a surcoat over that displaying a grey open gauntlet on a grey field, the device standing clear from its surrounds by some trick of the cloth. The resemblance between them ended there. The other man was taller, standing awkwardly with a curiously lopsided posture. His face was mottled, grey on pale, and his eyes were all white and pupil, with no visible iris. His features themselves were lean and severe and somehow gave the impression of deformity for no concrete reason. One of his hands was gauntleted in steel, and it was by this, more than anything else, that the sergeant knew him.

He was a bright man, that sergeant: being faced by a figure who was renowned as genius, traitor and dead, all at once, gave him pause for thought. At last he compromised on, 'You have papers, of course, sir,' as neutral a challenge as a Wasp had ever made.

The pale halfbreed smiled slightly, and his associate reached into one of a score of pouches and brought out a crumpled document with a seal on it. The Empress's seal, the sergeant noted. This dog-eared and maltreated piece of paper had once been in *her* own hands.

A moment's reading had confirmed either the best or the worst. Yes, this was the infamous Colonel-Auxillian Darian-drephos. Yes, he had never been a deserter, after all, nor dead, but had been released from his official duties by the Empress, a pleasant fiction given that he had surely abandoned his post before she had ever assumed the throne. Yes, he had every business being here. After the rest, the sergeant could have guessed that. After all, there had been a contingent of the mercenary Iron Glove artificers working alongside the reforming Eighth for the last month.

'Welcome to Malek Camp, sir.'

'You'll go far, sergeant.' Drephos, as those closest to him called him, cast his gaze about, seeing the ragged bustle of a more than usually chaotic Imperial camp: several thousand soldiers and their slaves and supporters and – most importantly – their machines. 'Two questions. Where are my men, and where is your Major . . . ?' He snapped the fingers of his armoured hand with a hollow click.

'Ferric,' the other halfbreed filled in for him.

'You'll find them both together up on the rise south of camp,' the sergeant replied, and promptly detailed a reluctant soldier to lead the way, and thereby get both halfbreeds well away from him.

Major Ferric was presiding over a grand assembly of what must have been most of Malek Camp's cooking staff, and the smell of some kind of stew came clearly to Totho as he and Drephos ascended. All around them, artificers were working, both Imperial engineers and the men of the Iron Glove, but Major Ferric was distinguishing himself by not getting in the way and instead making sure everyone got fed.

He was a heavily built, broad-shouldered Wasp with a face dominated by a broken nose that had never been reset properly. He had sharp eyes, though, spotting his visitors as soon as they stepped within the white light of the working lamps, and Totho saw his eyebrows lift.

'Colonel-Auxillian!' Ferric called, without leaving his post by the cooking fires. 'Over here.'

It was hardly proper protocol, but Drephos was an odd man in that way, sometimes making the Wasp-kinden jump through hoops for his amusement, other times heedless of any and all degrees of rank and priority. He made a quick path over to Ferric in his slightly lurching stride, Totho tagging along at his heels.

'Glad to see you made it, Colonel.' Ferric gave him a casual salute. 'You won't remember, but I was with you and the Sixth during the Twelve-year War. Pleasure to work with you again, sir.'

Drephos nodded, plainly not recalling the man at all, but then most other people were not a particularly important part of his world. 'What are you doing?' he demanded.

'Well, sir, your men and mine are working to get the great-shotters up and ready, because I have a feeling we're due to get orders to kick over the ant's nest some time soon, and these beasts of yours take a lot of calibration. As there's not a great deal I can personally contribute, and as my lads are all pulling double shifts to make up the time, I reckon the best employment for me is making sure there's hot food for everyone.'

The Colonel-Auxillian – although his continuing right to that rank was somewhat in dispute – stared at him briefly, and then nodded in grudging approval. 'These men are all engineers?'

'Two-thirds of the engineers I have,' Ferric confirmed, 'and the rest are sleeping.'

'A great deal of this work is menial. Why haven't you commandeered help from the rest of the army?'

'Ah, well, sir.' Ferric shrugged, pragmatically. 'Colonel Erveg, now, he's a traditionalist. He doesn't much hold with advances in engineering. He says they took Myna without all these toys last time, and he'll do it again just the same, soon as orders come through.'

Drephos exchanged a look with Totho, rolling his eyes at the foolishness of the world with special reference to the Imperial command. 'Well, then, we should change that.'

'He won't want to listen to you, sir. Colonel-Auxillian won't cut anything with him.'

At Drephos's impatient gesture Totho pulled out another creased paper bearing a set of seals.

'Rejoice, then,' Dariandrephos noted wryly, 'Colonel Ferric.' He handed the commission over to the startled officer. 'I have been requested to make sure that the "toys" the Empire has purchased from the Iron Glove cartel are put to their best use. To that end, the Eighth Army, which this force will soon be a part of, requires a chief engineer. You seem capable, so I bestow the honour on you. Now, *sir*, perhaps you might send a runner for this Colonel Erveg.'

Major – Colonel – Ferric took his promotion in his stride, offering just another waggle of the eyebrows to indicate this sudden jump in his fortunes. Nonetheless he had a Fly-kinden in the air a moment later, off to wake up the man who, a moment ago, had been in sole charge of Malek Camp.

In the meantime, Totho had rounded up the chief of the Iron Glove men there. 'Tell me you've got at least one of the Sentinels up and running.'

'Only one.' The artificer, a squat Bee-kinden from the far shores of the Exalsee, shrugged his powerful shoulders. 'Got it in a shed down the hill. Not had the time to get any of the others into order.'

'Take a crew, then, and go get it started up,' Totho directed.

'Bring it right here. We're about to change some priorities.' He looked up at the towering greatshotters, their brass-bound steel barrels angled as though to shoot down the moon, the metal wrapped in an intricate mesh of spider silk and wire to stop it bursting asunder. Soon, he knew, these huge weapons would speak their thunder for the first time.

Myna. But then he had no fond memories of the place, in all honesty, and even the unfond ones had been so long ago that he could not bring himself to feel any strong emotion about what would shortly happen to it.

Nine

Stenwold had sent Laszlo to Solarno because he needed an agent there, also because it was a reward for Laszlo's previous efforts, and because there was some logic to sending a man who had been on ships most of his life to a city on the shores of a vast lake. Arriving with Stenwold's orders in his mind, and the white-walled vista of the city before him, Laszlo had expected many things.

He had not expected to start to care about it all. He had not expected the spying game to get so personal, friendships and rivalries and muddied allegiances. He had not expected to become infatuated with a girl who might be working for anyone or nobody at all.

She had said she would meet him. Solarno was drawn tight as a wire. The Cortas were ordering arrests, exiling random foreigners, searching ships. Nobody went to the Taverna te Remi any more. The place had closed down three days before and its owner had either disappeared or been disappeared. The casual detente between the Solarnese agents had broken at last, like ice at the end of winter. And, of course, it could not have lasted, but Laszlo had loved it while it had. There had been a feeling there that people of his newfound trade could deal with each other in a civilized manner.

Now they were at each other's throats, and Solarno had become a dangerous place to stay. They remembered the

Imperial boot there. Before the war they had been a big fish, and the Exalsee a small pond compared to the world beyond. Now the Empire and the Spiderlands and the Lowlander powers were moving out there in the darkness: great slabs of plans grinding into place, fit to crush little cities to dust. And Solarno was not even the biggest fish around the Exalsee any more.

It was time to get out.

She had said she would meet him, had te Liss. The night after the Taverna te Remi's closing they had made their pact. To the pits with loyalties and whatever wretched, desperate espionage Solarno was still a stage for. They were getting out.

So he had chosen this place – a dockside dive that catered for sailors, and few of them native Solarnese. It was one of the first places he had made contacts, drawing on his past.

Dusk, they had agreed, but he had come early to avoid any surprises. He had thought she might do so as well. Now he sat hunched at a table with a pair of other Fly-kinden, setting down cards grimly, heedless of strategy, calling every bluff and playing every hand, and watching the door and windows always. He was winning, to the disgust and annoyance of his fellows.

He saw them immediately as they came in: not Liss, but he had been expecting them anyway. They were dressed in long coats and scarves, a grab-bag of kinden and halfbreeds, but they did not walk like sailors and too many of them looked his way straight off. Some small part of him realized he had been betrayed right then. Some other part of him knew she had been caught, and they had ripped it out of her. The rest of him was already moving. Quick exits were a common event here, and they kept all the shutters thrown back for that very reason. Why else would he frequent the place?

In a moment he was standing on the table, even as the newcomers made for him. He saw glints of metal: knives and a couple of the little crossbows that the Solarnese liked. They did not look like men with capture on their minds.

Stenwold Maker had been a grateful friend and a generous

employer. Laszlo whipped out from within his own coat the parting gifts the Beetle spymaster had given him. The cut-down little snapbows had only recently made it to the markets, and at a ruinous price, but they were already starting to be known as 'sleevebows' by criminals and spies both, although they were still a little large for any Fly's sleeves. Good models would hold their charge for hours without losing any power and, though they lacked the accuracy of a full-sized snapbow, Laszlo was unlikely to be more than five yards from anyone he intended to shoot. They were curved and elegant as spider fangs, and barely six inches long.

These men were not professionals, nor used to working together. Some of them leapt back immediately, seeking cover, a couple charged at him, and one loosed a crossbow bolt, in startled reflex, that went into the shoulder of a compatriot. Laszlo grinned and kicked off into the air, his Art wings humming about his shoulder in a flicker of light.

Someone grabbed for his ankle. He looked down at one of his fellow gamblers, already reaching towards his belt for . . . Laszlo never found out what for.

In Solarno he had played the quiet man, but his family had been pirates for generations, after all, and they would be so again. He felt a stab of reluctance, but none of it reached his reaction time as he shot the man through the chest, the harsh snap of his weapon barely registering in the commotion as the regular patrons rushed for the door or took off through the windows.

It was enough confusion. Free of the dead man's grip Laszlo dodged through the nearest window himself, darting around another fleeing drinker, one weapon now discharged and the other hunting for targets.

Have they got her? Can I rescue her? If the first answer was yes, the second would likely be no – which didn't mean he wouldn't try. *Stupid, stupid,* but her face was clear in his mind, a beacon. He could not say he loved her – was there ever a more treacherous foundation to build love on? – but she had hooks in him that he could not tear out, and the thought of her in pain, in fear, or worse, tore at parts of him he had not known he possessed.

If she was free, where would she go? If, hypothetically, she was free and she wanted to keep to their pact, and knew the dockside place was compromised, then where?

She was the only person who knew where he lodged, that place near the hangars that Maker had secured for him somehow. He was not supposed to know where *she* lodged, but some very determined shadowing had uncovered it – and he had always thought, wished, hoped, that he had done so only because she secretly wished him to know. He had confessed the spying to her later, and she had been mock-outraged yet plainly delighted, her real motivation layered into unreadability.

But, if they were hunting her, she would hardly stay home and wait for a boot to kick her door in.

He was cornering across the city even as he thought about it, heading for his own room, hoping against hope that he would find her waiting for him there. *And let her be a dozen times an enemy of Collegium if only she's still alive!*

He kept the shutters of his lodgings barred from the inside – too much of an invitation, otherwise, in a city filled with his own kinden – but there was a trick to them, one loose bar that could be prised open enough to flick the bar off its rests. He could have installed a lock, but he had worked out early on that Liss was Inapt, a rare thing in a Solarnese Fly-kinden, so he had been planning ahead in a vague and opportunistic way. He had considered that, when the game turned sour, she might come here and seek sanctuary.

He flurried down out of the darkening sky and came to sudden rest beside the window, clinging to the wall with his Art.

The bar was undisturbed, and she could not have picked the door lock. She had not been here. He almost turned away then, but the thought came that she could have left a message for him, detailing some other rendezvous, and so he hopped the bar himself and swung in, heading for the door, looking for that slip of folded paper that might give him hope.

There was nothing, but when he turned back for the window, there was a man there, a shortsword in his hand.

He was bigger than Laszlo by a foot or so, but small by most people's standards. He wore a long coat; beneath it was a white cuirass plated with steel, Solarnese militia issue. His face was bleak and hostile, and it was that, rather than the dusk, that gave Laszlo a moment's blinking pause before recognizing him.

'Breighl?' he said uncertainly. *'Painful?* What are you doing here.'

'The game's up, Laszlo, or whoever you are.' There was nothing left in the halfbreed of the man that Laszlo had drunk with, gambled with and mocked. The hand not directing a sword at him was at belt-level, half inside his coat, and Laszlo guessed at one of the little local crossbows there, already tensioned and loaded.

'What's going on, Painful?' Laszlo let himself relax, wings vanishing from his back but ready to be called at a moment's notice. He had not reloaded the spent sleevebow, but its companion was still charged, and he reckoned his reactions were better than Breighl's at a pinch. 'How did you find this place?'

Breighl gave him a disdainful smile. 'You were followed here tendays ago. You're nowhere near as good as you think you are.'

'Where's te Liss?' Laszlo demanded, because he had assumed they had got his address from the girl, but now hope flared in him again.

'So you *are* working with her, then,' Breighl noted, with infinite regret. 'We'll pick her up, don't you mind about that. You're under arrest, Laszlo. You're a foreign national working against the Cortas. The order to bring you in doesn't specify that you have to still be breathing but, for old times' sake, I'll give you a chance.'

'I'm not working against the Cortas.'

'Laszlo, you're working for the Spiderlands Aristoi, we *know* that. Don't piss me about.'

All this time and he really believed that? Laszlo felt almost hurt. 'Look, if you must know, I'm working out of Collegium, and you surely see that they, of all people, don't want the Empire in here—'

'The *Empire?*' Breighl abruptly had the crossbow out and aimed at him, and Laszlo re-evaluated just who likely had the quicker reflexes. 'You think we're worried about the *Empire* now? So they have some troops up north, past Toek? So what? They're worried about what we're worried about, Laszlo. We *know* there's a fleet of ships on the Exalsee *even now*, out of Mavralis. We know that a dozen Aristoi families have finally decided they can't let Solarno remain independent any more. Don't take us for idiots. We know your employers think this is all a game, but to us it isn't!' Abruptly he was shouting, the crossbow shaking wildly, making Laszlo flinch.

'Believe me, Breighl, I have some really poor history with the Spiderlands. I'm *not* with them!' Laszlo insisted. To his astonishment – almost his embarrassment – there were tears in the halfbreed's eyes.

'Oh, I know, the Spiders think everyone else is a fool, and so do their agents. Nobody's as smart as them. Even the Solarnese Aristoi think it's all so pissing *clever*, but we Solarnese don't *want* to end up as the toys of the Spiderlands, just another cursed satrapy city, a pawn in their games. This is *my* city, Laszlo! I'm going to do anything I can to stop your filthy scheming mistresses get their hands on it, and if the first move in that is to put a bolt through your brain, then so be it!'

He jabbed the crossbow towards Laszlo for emphasis, and it went off.

Laszlo was already lurching to one side, an Art-sense unique to Fly-kinden warning him of it even before the string slipped. The bolt ploughed into the wall behind him, then he was going for the other man, not with the sleevebow, that would take a moment to aim in which Breighl's sword could bat it aside, but with a dagger. Laszlo was the veteran of countless dockside brawls, skirmishes between pirates and the contested boardings of a score of ships, and in close quarters there was no weapon greater than a simple six–inch blade.

Breighl's sword gave him reach but it was an advantage that Laszlo countered instantly, a rush of speed from his wings getting him within knife range, in the hope that a single blow might take the man down and clear the way to the window. The halfbreed was no stranger to this sort of fight either, and he was already lunging for Laszlo's dagger wrist, his crossbow spinning away. For a moment he had a grip, sword drawn back outside the Fly's reach, ready to stab, but Laszlo's wings threw him into a backwards somersault so that he could kick Breighl in the face, the man's grip loosening before he could dislocate Laszlo's shoulder. The Fly came down at the far end of the room, for all the little space that gave him, and was already launching back at his opponent, his wings just a flickering blur.

Breighl stumbled back against the window, sword out-stretched to let Laszlo run himself through, but the Fly slipped past the blade, the point shearing through his coat, his shoulder striking the man in the chest in an attempt to send him toppling out of the window. He got the back of Breighl's other hand about the head for his trouble, before the halfbreed managed to steady himself with a flurry of his wings. The sword drove down for Laszlo again, the Fly earthbound for a moment and down on one knee with the force of the punch.

Breighl was bigger and stronger and almost as fast, and there was really no other way to do it. Laszlo slammed into the man's legs, not to knock him off balance but because Breighl could not stab straight down the line of his own body with much force. Laszlo's upflung arm got in the way of the strike, the blade slicing open the tough canvas of his coat sleeve and raking a line of red, but Laszlo was too close for proper sword work. Even as

Breighl kicked at him, he rammed the dagger into the halfbreed's groin.

The first stroke cut shallowly, deflected by the cuirass's armour plates, and Breighl jerked away desperately, forcing himself half out of the window. Laszlo was beyond regrets then – they were not a currency a pirate could spend too often – and he followed, clawing his way up the halfbreed's chest and slamming the bloodied dagger into the man's throat.

Breighl died without a cry, hanging half out over the street, his blood an explosive mist that showered down below. Laszlo hauled him in with all his strength, letting the man's last convulsive shudder tilt his body into the room.

Didn't want that. Didn't want to do that. He had been a factor for the *Bloodfly* crew, after all, their friendly merchant face at each port they traded with. He was seldom called on to kill people he knew. *Oh, waste it, Breighl, couldn't you be slow enough to let me out of the window?*

He hauled his coat off. It was torn and cut, and there was a swathe of Breighl's blood across it. The cut on his arm was, in contrast, inconsequential.

Her lodgings, and if she's not there . . . He found he was still reeling, his heart refusing to slow, his head seeming to ring to the echo of some vast, unheard sound. Numbly, his hands recharged the spent sleevebow, slipping another bolt into the breech. His shock at killing Breighl had become a crawling dread for Liss's fate. If things had gone *this* wrong *this* fast, then the list of bad things that might happen to her was endless. His only consolation was that Breighl's people had plainly not tracked her down yet.

He kicked off from the windowsill, coursing over the city for te Liss's little place out by the Venador street market, hope and fear fighting over him.

She drew on her bedroom wall. It had seemed endearing, but at the same time he knew the sketches must hold hidden meanings for her shadowy contacts. The entire bare expanse of plaster over her bed was strewn with overlapping scrawls of trees, flowers, veined wings in scholarly detail, childlike abstracts of people standing, running, fighting.

When she had finally let him in there, after his confession that he had tailed her, she had pointed out one little corner, a blank space just above her pillow. 'That's for you, just you,' she had told him. Nothing more had needed to be said. Even then they had both known how they lived in an uncertain world.

Now he hung by her window, feeling the rough wood where the shutters had been wrenched off. The room itself had been turned over, furniture broken, her mattress ripped open so that twists of rag carpeted the floor like an early crop of dying mayflies.

That small space had now been filled, a rough, hasty image: a tall building with jagged rays. He stared at it blankly for a moment before matching it to a landmark. The Solarnese coast was gentle, but to the immediate west of the city there were rocks, a jagged out-thrusting of them that was probably man-made, from distant ages past, some forgotten seawall or ancient pier.

There was a squat lighthouse there, to warn off midnight shipping.

Laszlo hurled himself back from the window, well aware that his arrival might have been noticed by any number of watchers. He led any followers a merry chase, and only a Dragonfly, or another of his own kinden, could have hoped to keep up, as he went looping about the mansions of the wealthy, darting through the warrens of the poor, circling in a far arc across the water and then inland again, and all the while with no sense of pursuit, before bolting at last for the lighthouse – and Liss.

The lamp was out. He could not guess why, but only because there were too many options, crosses and double-crosses, or even the Solarnese themselves trying to thwart the Spider fleet that Breighl had spoken of. Laszlo landed on the top rail, finding the glass of the great lamp smashed, the whole place reeking of oil. *Not good, not good at all.* He could not call out her name, however much he wanted to. Anyone might be here now and, if it was not her, then it would be nobody that wanted to see poor Laszlo.

He crouched on the very rail, the wooden gantry beneath him jagged with broken glass, listening into the quiet of the night, eyes closed so that he could make his ears his only world. The wash of the waters below, he heard, and sounds from the city close at hand: engines, shouting, the drone of an orthopter.

Someone moved, not out on the gantry itself but within the lighthouse. He heard a slow scrape, metal on wood, and a hiss of breath.

He had his dagger out again and, after a moment, he took one of the sleevebows in his other hand. Inching about the railing he found the door that would let the lighthouse custodian out to clean and refill the lamp – and found it standing open. The darkness hung heavy inside, but he trusted to his Fly eyes and let his wings glide him inside, touching down in silence at the head of the spiral stairs.

Again came that gasp of breath, ragged enough to bring back too many memories of fights gone sour, of shipmates lost despite all the surgeons could do, and now it was more than he had the willpower for not to call out, 'Liss?'

Don't be Liss. Don't be Liss. There had been death in that sound, as sure as death ever was. The stairs wound about the hollow interior, simple wooden slats pegged into the stone, each bolted to the next with steel struts. There was no guard-rail, and the central well of the lighthouse tower was a yawning abyss. Laszlo called for his wings and stepped into the void without hesitation, sleevebow trained down as he descended, knowing how vulnerable he would be but unable simply to creep down like some ground-bound Beetle.

He spotted the body halfway down: small, Fly-kinden. No

cascade of curls, nothing of Liss – a man, in fact. He was going to set down a dozen steps above, but then he recognized the casualty and ended up right beside him.

'Te Riel,'

Someone had put a long knife into te Riel's gut and left him. There were other wounds: a cut-open palm and a spread of blood across his shoulder, but the stomach blow had finished it. The man was shaking, curled about the weapon that was still buried in him, one hand on the hilt but without the strength of body or mind to pull it out and hasten his own end. The other arm was hooked about a step, keeping him from a final fall. Fly-kinden were masters of the air, but the wound had stripped all that off him at the last.

'Laszlo.' A voice so low that Laszlo had to stoop down, almost ear to mouth, to hear it. 'Liss.'

Just for you, she said. It hurt a little, knowing that she had been saving that little space on her wall for te Riel as well, but not as much as it had hurt te Riel himself.

'I don't know where she is, if she's not here.' He put a hand on the dying man's shoulder, feeling it already cold despite the man's tenacious hold on life. 'Help me. Tell me. I know you liked her too.'

The awful sound of te Riel laughing would stay with Laszlo for a long time, each bark of it echoed by an agonized indrawing of breath. 'Gone. Gone,' then something indistinct, and then, clear as day, 'the *hangars*. Going to blow up the *hangars*.'

'The Empire?' Laszlo remembered who he was speaking to. 'Your lot?'

'Not,' te Riel wheezed out. 'Not mine . . . trying to get out from under . . . Laszlo, the hangars! All the . . . Solarnese have . . . going up . . .'

'I'm going, te Riel. I'm going—' but the man snagged his arm with the blood-slick hand that had been holding on to the knife hilt.

'Not . . . please . . .' There was a shuddering moment when

Laszlo thought he had died, but the bloody grip remained. 'Die with my own name, please . . . not te Riel . . .'

There was more, but it was just a whisper, barely words, certainly not a name. Then the man was dead, taking his secrets with him.

The hangars. Even with that thought, Laszlo was soaring up the well, spitting himself out into the open air and casting back for the city. *The hangars* – within sight of his own lodgings! And the war was being started right there, while he was elsewhere.

And Liss, his Liss, was somewhere in the middle of it. Someone had her. Someone was about to strike at Solarno. It was all coming together.

He had never flown faster, the buildings of Solarno rushing past beneath him, but he knew he would be too late.

Ten

It had all been like some strange kind of game although, because all the factory workers were being constantly appraised and tested, a game that was not in the least enjoyable.

Pingge had not seen Kiin for more than two days during the last two tendays, and that was what hurt most. They were being constantly reassigned to groups, randomly switched back and forth, so that they never became confortable with whoever they were working alongside. The tasks were the same, though, or at least variations on a common theme.

There was a device that the engineers called a 'reticule', and it appeared to be all important, although Pingge could not quite understand why. Her last twenty days had been spent in intensive training with it, however, so she had to assume that their faith was justified. It was intricate but hardly complex, perhaps a step above the weaving looms. Positioned above it, she could look down towards the floor of whatever warehouse or vault they had taken her to, adjusting the lenses for focus. There was a burden, too – sometimes a lead weight but mostly just a sack of flour. Pingge would be strapped into a harness with the reticule before her face, and the harness would be attached to a wire, and the wire would be strung between the walls. At the engineer's word, she was released, to rush helter-skelter across the great vacant space, and there would always be a circle or some other symbol painted below.

It was a silly, simple game, really: release the burden so that it struck home on the symbol, allowing for momentum and using the distortion of the reticule's lenses to spy out the ground ahead. Pingge had proved one of the better Fly-kinden at this charade, but mostly because she was able to relax into the business as a game, without fretting about the purpose behind it all.

A delegation of her comrades – she had not been amongst them – had gone to the engineers to point out that, as they were *Fly*-kinden, the whole business would be easier if they could guide the descent with their wings, but this apparently was besides the point. Those who could not keep their Art in check were slapped in 'Fly-manacles': leather strapping about the back and shoulders that stifled their wings entirely.

They were trained night and day, sometimes woken out of sleep as though the world was about to end, for just another session of shuttling to and fro. They trained under bright gaslamps, in daylight, at night, in dim underground caverns. They were kept without sleep for nights at a time. They were put on short rations. None of it seemed to have a pattern – no suggestion of punishment was ever implied, nor even of simple Wasp-kinden cruelty.

Although the groupings remained random, Pingge had started to see more recurring faces in the last eight days or so. Nobody wanted to ask what had happened to those people they no longer saw. The other questions could not be bottled, though: *Why conscript Fly-kinden if you didn't want them to fly?*

Today was different. Instead of more training, with the wires overhead and the harnesses ready, Pingge found herself marched into a drill hall along with around forty other Fly-kinden, all of whose faces she recognized from her most recent sessions. She caught sight of Kiin immediately, and the pale Fly woman waved to her, entirely against Imperial protocol. At that moment there was a great deal of milling and jostling, and the guards didn't seem to care.

'I knew you'd be here,' Pingge announced, as Kiin wriggled through the throng to get to her. 'You always did have steady hands.'

'What are you talking about?'

'It's obvious. We're the best.'

Kiin looked about her, considering. 'Best at what?'

'At whatever this reticule business is,' Pingge pointed out. 'We've helped them test their new machine, whatever it is. Back to the factories for us now, I'd guess. I'm hoping for a bonus, myself. Keep the folks happy.'

The Fly beside them, a crop-haired, burly man called Gizmer, shook his head in dusgust, but Pingge ignored him blithely.

'Have they had you in the airship yet?' she pressed.

Kiin frowned at her, all the while plainly keeping a weather eye out for the authority figure that was surely on his way over. 'Airship?'

'They had us up on a pissy little airship – you remember the blow we had a few days back, the storm? We went kicking about in that, tearing about the sky fit to burst, and us in manacles, too. We took turns with the reticule, dropping stuff from way up – worked a treat, too. Those fiddly little lenses are much better when you're higher up. Makes the game a lot harder.'

'Game?' Gizmer butted in, looking even more contemptuous.

'Game, test, whatever,' Pingge waved the distinction away, but Kiin interrupted her.

'Pings, what exactly did you think they wanted you up there *for*?'

'Testing their new toy, of course. They seemed happy, anyway. Everything in working order, time to go home.' Perhaps only Kiin would notice the slight edge of tension to Pingge's voice.

Or it's top secret Engineering Corps business, and now they kill us.

Gizmer snorted. 'Don't you know *anything*?' he hissed. 'They're not testing the machines. They're training *us*.'

'A lot you know!' Pingge retorted, and at the same time Kiin said, 'Why would they want Fly-kinden, though?'

At that moment, Wasps started coming in – not a few, but tens of them, a small group of officers led by the well-remembered figure of Major Varsec first, then a squad of engineers or soldiers or . . . something. These last marched in without words, without expressions, silently forming neat ranks facing the muddle of Fly-kinden.

Gizmer leant sideways and murmured, from the corner of his mouth, 'Because we're *light*, idiot, and for no other reason.'

A few ideas connected inside Pingge's mind, but Varsec was already speaking. She had heard more about him since being co-opted for the reticule project. He had been the man to lose Solarno, most famously, but he seemed to have come out of it well, promoted and in charge of whatever was going on here – and elsewhere too. He seemed to have a dozen projects on the go and was forever being flown about the city and beyond.

'Captain Aarmon,' the major said, and the man front and centre of the Wasp formation took a step forward and saluted him. To Pingge – Imperial Fly-kinden became masters of reading Wasp attitudes at a young age – it seemed that there was a distance between these men that was more than of rank, a very complex relationship indeed.

'Major.' Aarmon's voice was soft for a Wasp officer. He seemed to respect Varsec but it was not an active respect, more like that of a man for his ageing father than for his immediate superior. 'These are the best?'

'We have others in training, but these have shown the most facility,' Varsec confirmed carefully, as if anxious not to displease his subordinate.

'I told you!' Pingge hissed.

'What makes you think,' Gizmer grated, 'that you *want* to be the best right now?'

Kiin's lips were moving silently, and Pingge realized that she was counting. After that, the conclusion was inevitable.

Forty of them, she saw, if she discounted Varsec and a couple of engineers plainly not part of Aarmon's people. *Forty of us.*

Varsec gave a nod and stepped back, giving the floor over to Aarmon. He was a pale, broad-shouldered Wasp with a shaved head and oddly flat eyes, as though he was not using them in the normal way but looking out of them as one would through a window.

'Reticule-men, attention!' one of Varsec's aides snapped, and the Fly-kinden automatically shuffled and elbowed their way into rough ranks, a mockery of the perfect Wasp grid facing them. This was part of their daily routine, and they ordered themselves without needing to think about it.

Aarmon stepped forward, casting those lifeless eyes over them, looking from face to face – and looking down, of course: in size they were like children to him and to all of his fellows. He seemed to be assessing them by some incalculable criterion. All the while, his comrades stood absolutely motionless, not a fidget, not a word, not even an expression exchanged. Pingge had seen Wasps on parade before, and she knew all the little ways soldiers had of communicating one to another under the eyes of the drill sergeant. There was none of it here. It was a display to make a disciplinarian weep, presented here in a windowless hall for an audience of one major and a rabble of Fly-kinden.

Aarmon pointed and then, when no reaction was forthcoming, he said, 'You,' like an afterthought.

He was indicating Kiin, of course.

Pingge gasped, 'No!', but there was nothing for it. If this was some example to be made, crossed pikes or a stingshot to the head or some other warning to keep silent, there was nothing she could do. Captain Aarmon was waiting, his bleak stare fixed on his victim as though it could draw her to him on its own.

Kiin took a deep breath and, none too steady, stepped forward.

No windows in the room, Pingge thought miserably. *Is that so nobody can see us here? So we can't escape?* She watched her friend weave her way through the other Flies until she was standing to attention before Aarmon, staring at his belt buckle, a delicate, fair-haired woman of three foot six before a big Wasp man topping six feet.

'With me,' he told her, and turned instantly, awaiting neither salute nor acknowledgement, leaving her to stumble mutely in his wake as he stalked from the room. Pingge saw the other Wasps stepping forwards, all at once now, selecting others from the Fly group. She cast a panicked stare back, trying to see what happened to Kiin, and caught a last glimpse of her friend as Kiin's reluctant march carried her out through the door, tripping after Aarmon's longer strides.

'What *is* she?' Esmail demanded. 'What has happened to her?'

His informant shrank away from him, babbling something about not knowing what he meant, but he slammed the man back against the cellar wall, using Ostrec's borrowed strength and violence. His life was at stake in a way that his briefing had never suggested. Someone was playing him for a fool.

The Empress was something more than a Wasp-kinden woman, more than the mere temporal ruler of a military state.

He had gone along after Colonel Harvang, dogging the obese man's greasy steps until he stood amidst the great and the good of the Empire: the Rekef's sole surviving general, another colonel, their chief artificer and some Beetle-kinden who was one of their leading merchants. Ostrec had been well placed, groomed to be Harvang's aide, to run errands and messages between the great powers of the Empire, circumstances that bore all the fingerprints of Moth foretelling and calculation, but at a level far in excess of anything Esmail had worked with before.

So why had they not told him about the Empress? Because they did not know? Because they wanted his own, unbiased assessment?

He was not sure that he could possibly give an unbiased account of *that*. As she had drawn close, he had felt a pressure inside his skull, inexplicable here in the mechanistic Empire, reminiscent of times past when great Moth-kinden Skryres had turned their arts upon him. Then she had entered the room.

He was a past master at his trade, of keeping the inner man and the outer face separate, showing nothing of who and what he was and living the life of the other. When she strode in, though, he had not been able to keep still. The sheer sight and sense of her had shocked him like a spear through the chest.

She had glanced at him then, and he had fought, physically fought, to keep his wards and masks intact, because some primal part of him had been clamouring for him to fall to his knees and confess all.

Even now he could not say whether he had escaped undetected. He did not know what senses she had inherited, or what subtlety in using them. The Rekef might come for him any moment, turning on one seemingly of their own without the least stab of conscience. Even now she might have him dragged before her.

Power had radiated from her in waves, enough to blast aside his false face and leave him naked and terrified before her splendour. She had been as difficult to look at as the sun, for those first few moments, until his inner eyes had adjusted. Above her brow there had seemed a burning brand, a diadem of invisible but inescapable authority.

What his briefing *had* given him was the name of a well-placed servant who was also an Arcanum agent – an elderly Grasshopper who had served in Capitas for over a decade, feeding information back to the Moths in shreds and pieces for all that time. Any other spy would have been uncovered by now, but the old man was subtle, and the Moths had never acted on any of it, only hoarded it against the future, as they always did.

After dark, Esmail had left his room in the extensive complex that Harvang and his Rekef adherents called their own, stalking across the rooftops with a stealth that Ostrec the Wasp had never possessed, then hunting down his informant, a shadow with a Wasp's shape, until he found the single cramped room that the Grasshopper shared with a half-dozen others.

The man's name was Shoel Jhin, and he was a magician of very minor sorts, whose powers would no doubt have eroded during his long slavery here. Esmail himself was no great conjuror – the elements of his trade relied on control and elegance of manipulation rather than raw power – but he had a few magus's tricks, and it was a simple matter to put his voice in Jhin's mind and hiss out the man's name until he awoke, starting and staring: then to call him out of the room, out of the servants' block, until he met the old man face to face within the cold walls of a wine cellar.

Now he stared down at that lined face, the sallow skin bagged and creased with care and age. 'You're a poor spy or a lax one. Don't you realize there was something missing from your reports?'

'I tell what I tell. What *they* tell you is another matter,' Jhin wheezed.

Ostrec wanted to beat him for his insubordination. Esmail could feel rage emanating from the image of the man he kept in his head, the source of his mimicry. 'I came here to spy on a Wasp, one of the Apt,' he said, in more measured tones. 'An Empress, yes, and we all know the power that attaches to such symbols, but it's not a power that she should be able to *tap*. I've never . . .' He stopped, shaking his head. 'I have never felt such a presence.'

Shoel Jhin was watching him, beady eyes nesting in wrinkles examining the spy's false face. 'Help you, they said. Educate you, no. They tell you what they tell you. Not my place, not my place at all.'

Esmail still held the man by his collar but now he let go, stepping back, suppressing Ostrec's borrowed anger. It occurred to him that the old man did not know who he was, not really –

oh, a spy, yes, and one of that very select and mercurial order, but no more than that. Just some Moth, probably, was Jhin's guess.

Esmail stepped back from him. 'Tell me,' he urged softly.

Jhin actually cackled a little. 'Not my place,' he repeated, and made to walk past him.

He stopped, for Esmail had fixed him with a look, Ostrec's pale eyes holding an expression neither Wasp nor Moth ever had. Esmail let the mask slip slightly, letting out some sense of what hid behind: the villain of ages, the murderer-kinden, the lost race.

The old Grasshopper stayed very still, on the brink of a revelation he plainly had no wish for. 'You . . . you . . .' he whispered. *The assassins, the killers of the old times, but no, but surely no – they're gone, all of them, and the Moths were ever their enemies . . .* Esmail could all but read the thoughts coursing through the old man's head.

'They send who they send,' he said, pointedly.

Shoel Jhin bared his yellowed teeth. 'You think it will help, even *that*?' he started to say, but Esmail hissed out, 'Just *tell* me!' forcing the man back with his stare until Jhin's shoulderblades were against the cold wall again.

'The Emperor . . . Alvdan . . .'

'He died, yes,' Esmail confirmed. *And the circumstances of that seem confused, as well – far more going on than some Mantis slave getting lucky but, as with every other damned thing, the Moths never tell the whole story, even to their own agents.*

'She changed, after he died.'

'She became Empress. That's liable to change you,' Esmail pointed out impatiently. 'Give me specifics.'

Jhin closed his eyes, taking a deep breath. 'The Emperor's death . . . a Mantis Weaponsmaster and a Mosquito-kinden Sarcad. You know these traditions? Shadow and blood. The Emperor died to magic, the first man in five hundred years to die in such a particular way. But it all went wrong. The power, the greatest ritual since the Days of Lore, all on *her* shoulders: the inheritrix of two traditions. Changed her? Oh it changed her all right, and she knew it full well. She must have learned too much from that Mosquito . . .' Jhin's eyes shone with an unhealthy light. 'They began disappearing, soon after the coronation. Servants, mostly, some prisoners, some of the Wasps even. Nobody knew or nobody was telling, but I could feel it through the walls sometimes. The blood, the power.'

'She's Inapt,' Esmail concluded. 'She's a magician even.' *Untutored, unskilled, newly come to some semblance of power?* 'No, that's not it.'

Now it was him who was discomfited, by Jhin's gaze. 'So last year she went to Khanaphes. You know that city?'

An old name, old enough to make the clash between the Moths and Esmail's people look like recent history. *Khanaphes.* There had been power there, but the Moths did not speak of the place much, which told Esmail volumes. *Older and more powerful than their kinden, then. Their seniors, already gone senile and into decline as the Moths were climbing up.* But not decayed quite enough, for the Empress Seda had gone there, added that backwater to her Empire, and there . . .

'What?' he demanded. 'What did she do?'

But Jhin was grinning now. 'She was *crowned*. Can you not see the mark on her? She was made their heir, and if she is crude with her power, just you wait and see! Don't you understand? She'll bring it all back, turn back the glass and give us everything we've lost.'

'You're mad,' Esmail snapped at him.

'Me? You're the one who's going to try and *stop* her!' And abruptly Shoel Jhin had a blade out, a wretched little knife that a servant might palm while passing through the kitchens. He was ancient, arthritic, no conceivable threat to Esmail or Ostrec, but he was laughing even as he lunged.

The spy slipped aside without effort, striking back barehanded along the length of the old man's arm, his fingers shearing into the slave's rib-cage, then ripping his heart apart at a touch. He could have stopped himself, but he made a considered judgement, in the fraction of a second given to him, that nothing more of value would come from Shoel Jhin.

Turned, he reflected thoughtfully. *An Arcanum agent turned, and by the woman's mere being. I am in a bad place, and I have not been told what I need to know in order to survive.*

Still, that was all a part of the profession. The mystery of his trade included all such situations as this. He would watch. He would learn. He would put himself through the paces of Ostrec's life, and await opportunity.

He disposed of the body carefully and removed every spot of Shoel Jhin's blood from himself before returning to Ostrec's rooms.

In the morning the summons came: not from the throne but the next best thing: he and Colonel Harvang were called before General Brugan.

Once upon a time there had been a princess, and she had lived in fear . . .

Seda smiled at the thought, although the expression was a little tight, a little forced. Fear of her brother, yes. Fear of the Rekef general, Maxin, who had waited with a knife, ready for the order to end Seda's life. It would be far too easy to say that her brother had been mad. He had perhaps been too sane, instead. He had seen the world very clearly indeed, and his place within it, and had recoiled from both. Most of all, he had feared death, and that was a perfectly rational thing to fear. He had lived under the shadow of the throne that he was a tenant of and a slave to, all too aware that the Empire needed the office and not the man. Indeed, her brother Alvdan had possessed few personal qualities of any real value. For that reason he had ensured that only Seda, of all his family, had survived his coronation, and that any bastards he happened to sire were put to death. He had been terrified of becoming obsolete.

He had been given a chance at immortality by the Mosquito magician, Uctebri the Sarcad, but it had been a false chance. The Mosquito had engineered his death at the hands of some magical puppet, but then Uctebri himself had been slain by the Mantis slave Tisamon, who had been hacked to death before the vacant throne by the Emperor's furious soldiers. The ritual that Uctebri had raised, which would have made Seda his creature and given him control of the Empire, had earthed in her, stolen her Aptitude, gifted her with an expanded under-standing of the world – and won her a throne.

She had been so frightened, after that, of what she had become. The world had become a distorted place where nothing worked the way she remembered. Her own mind had owned to dark cravings and lusts. Fear? She had eaten and drunk it, and slept in its company every night.

Well, we all must pass our trials. It was a part of every magical tradition, in fact. No neophyte could become a true magician without being tested, and the core of the test was to establish control over the self, without which any other form of power was but an empty shell. If only her brother had understood that.

Her chambers were as richly furnished as the Empire's vast wealth could afford, with gold and gems, silks and furs in extravagant profusion. She had a hundred servants within earshot to attend to her every need. Some had already been busy tonight.

Her bedchamber was swathed in drapes of red and gold and deep, smouldering purple, centring on the great pillared bed. She slept alone tonight, since her current partner was recuper-ating. Fear again: all the Empire feared him as much as it feared her, perhaps more, but *he* feared her like no other thing on earth – feared and yet hungered for her, with a desire he could not stem. It amused her, but some part of her was disappointed in him. He had possessed such promise. He should have been stronger. *He should have been strong enough to fight me,* some small part of her whispered, *to destroy me. Someone must . . .*

Her original consort, the renegade Thalric, had been stronger, more secure in himself. She had never quite broken him, and he had fled her before she could manage it. Her thoughts still turned to him sometimes. *One day you will be mine again.*

In the room beyond her bedchamber lay what would seem, to the uninitiated, to be a scene of torture, the victim still fresh on the slab, pale and withered. Her appetites had been born of the powers that had transformed her. Mosquito magic was rooted in blood, physically and symbolically. She sipped at her goblet now, sampling the salt liquid as though it was a vintage, its colour smearing the red of her lips.

All around her, the Empire was on the move. Her orders had seen to that. She could not claim all the credit, though. *If I went before them and preached peace, I would have another civil war on my hands.* All the magic in the world could not prevent it. Her people needed to grow, and so they needed to conquer. The Consortium demanded the wealth of the Empire's neighbours and control over their trade. Her philosophers set out their proofs that the way of the Empire was superior to that of its enemies, and that by bringing them to heel the cause of civilization would be advanced. Her armies grew sullen and restless and apt to mutiny now that the Empire's internal conflict was done. There were a thousand reasons to go to war.

And she was proud. She would not deny that she felt a fierce love for her people and their relentless energy, the strength of their will. They had come so far, and they still had so far to go. Oh, certainly, the thinkers of Collegium, the merchants of Helleron, the artificers of the Exalsee – all of these had something to contribute to the world, but they would do so beneath a black and gold banner, in time.

She had her own reasons for conquest, though. She was Inapt. She was a magician. She had gone to Khanaphes and demanded the blessing of the ancient Masters there. She had planted her flag in a new arena, on whose sands the champions of other kinden had been fighting and dying for millennia.

Magic was not the force it once had been, atrophied and wan

since the Apt revolution had overthrown or remade the old Inapt hierarchies. The Moths were now hermits in their mountain fastnesses, the Dragonflies a sprawling monarchy decaying from within, the Mantis-kinden warriors entering their twilight days, the Spiders setting aside their greater powers to rule their satrapies of slaves by manipulation and suggestion. The very Masters of Khanaphes themselves hid in the tombs they had built for themselves and there dreamt of a distant future. Only the Moths had ever sought to recreate the long-gone Days of Lore, and their attempts had ended in catastrophe.

Being reborn in blood and shadow, empowered by the might of Uctebri, by the breaking of the Shadow Box that had been the result of that failed Moth ritual, she had inherited a measure of power. Being crowned by the Masters of Khanaphes had made her a player in the old, old game of magic. Her raw strength as a magician – unearned, undeserved but undeniable – was a match for any that might challenge her, but now she found that it was not enough.

For, above and beyond the remnants of the old Inapt powers, there was always the *other*.

'Tisamon,' she called, and the faintest grating of metal announced that he was with her.

Mere strength would not bow the magical world to her will, nor would all the armed might of her armies. She could obliterate whole Inapt kinden if she wanted, and it would avail her nought if she had not exacted their recognition, their fealty, first.

He was her greatest triumph to date, Tisamon. Her court knew him only as the captain of her bodyguard – those half-dozen Mantis-kinden sent to her by the Moths of Tharn as a gift, who now served her with a selfless loyalty that the Tharen had never intended. They had originally been six, now they were seven, but it was unhealthy to comment on it, just as it was unhealthy for the overly informed to note that their new captain bore the same name as the Mantis slave that had figured so prominently in the former Emperor's death.

What the old Inapt powers had lost in strength they had preserved in skill and application. All the power in the world was useless without precision. The Moths could use the little they had with a finesse that would outmanoeuvre her brute force. As her Empire needed to grow and develop, so did she.

She had called to him, to Tisamon, using his discarded blade as a focus, spilling the blood of a bastard cousin, building him a body of ancient Mantis armour. It had been her first true ritual, the greatest exercise of her nascent authority. She had sought out his ghost and bound it inside the metal, and exacted its oath. Now that tall figure of mail stepped towards her, halting at her elbow, not quite touching, and she felt the faint, cool breath from within his helm. *And would any of those old powers have dared do what I have, to bring him back so?* She had cast down the gauntlet, in her own mind at least.

She would not live in fear again, and for that she must become greater, more fearsome, than all others. Her armies and their machines would make her so in the world of the Apt, and she would hunt down the power of the Inapt, the relics of their lost world, and take everything to herself. Only then would she be safe. Only then could she be herself, and live free, and not fear. *There will come a time when I am free and do not fear. I promise it. There will be an end to it. I am not my brother.*

She glanced over her shoulder into the visor of Tisamon's helm, into the darkness beyond. When first she had called him, there had been nothing but night within, but the more she employed him, the more blood she had given him and – most of all – the more she had *thought* of him, the more real he had become. Now, she lifted the faceplate, and saw those pale, dim features that no lamp could light: severe, handsome in a cold and arrogant way, but his eyes were for her, only for her. He was a man who had lived and died for love, but that meant other things to Mantis-kinden. Now he gave her what jagged love he had left, and it was an icy and barbed thing indeed.

But he was deadly and savage and *hers*, and sometimes she

wondered what it would feel like to kiss those dead lips. *Would I be mad then, truly, if it comes to that? Surely a woman in my position could be excused some madness.*

She passed him the goblet – there was plenty more, after all, and the future held so many exciting new vintages: Mynan, Solarnese, Collegiate . . .

'I shall have work for you soon,' she whispered, and she felt his anticipation like a tension in the air. He was death and she was his mistress, and the world would soon know all the fear that she denied in herself.

Eleven

Kymene stood on the wall at Myna, staring eastwards, and her scouts came and went in a constant flurry of arrivals and just as swift departures. She gripped the crenellations, straight as a spear shaft, her cloak of half black and half red gusting in the wind.

All around her, her city prepared for war. The walls were bustling with soldiers, and the sight was far different from when Myna had first been taken by the Empire. Then they had a little simple artillery up here and, other than that, just a host of soldiers, swords and shields and crossbowmen to face down the Wasp host. Any army marching up to Myna today would meet a more modern response. The walls themselves were essentially the same – the Empire had made no changes during the occupation, and the liberated Mynans had not had the time – but artillery emplacements were set all along the line of the wall, in fortified positions that gave cover against attack from below and above. The machines themselves included the Sarnesh-designed rackthrower ballistae and scrapshotters, designed to fill the air before them with spears or jagged metal, tearing up the Imperial Light Airborne even as it tried to gain the walls. Snapbows were much in evidence, too, swifter and more accurate than crossbows, which went some way to counterbalance the Wasp-kinden's superior mobility.

We have given them all we could, Stenwold assured himself.

'Commander.' A Fly-kinden dropped down almost at Kymene's feet, wearing the colours of Myna on a sash about his chest. 'They have completed setting up their artillery on the far side of the Antosine hill country.'

Kymene frowned. 'But that's out of sight of the city. Do they expect us to come to them?'

'The artillery is guarded, but separate to their main force. We've not been able to get a good look at what their army is bringing with it, Commander, but spyglass reports suggest there are automotives and other machines there. Perhaps the hill artillery is to cover a retreat.'

Kymene nodded briefly, dismissing him. There was a lull then, perhaps because most of Myna's scouts had already reported, or were not coming back.

'Maker,' she said, descending the stone steps from the wall, and he followed after her, almost walking into her when she stopped.

'You do not believe that the Wasps have taken such precautions to cover their retreat.' It was a statement, not a question, and he realized that she had stepped down from the wall so that her soldiers would not overhear her.

'I cannot think it,' he agreed. 'All reports suggest that they have the forces for a serious attack – and to keep an army that size on the field is costly if you don't intend to use it.'

She looked away from him, and he could almost sense the wheels turning in her mind, plots and counterplots. 'They wish us to strike the first blow, to break the treaty? Are they mounting their artillery there to provoke an attack, a sally to destroy it?'

'Possibly.' But the idea did not feel right to Stenwold. There were better, more tempting places to flaunt those siege engines, if that had been the plan.

'The Szaren relief column will be with us in a day's time. More troops are expected from Maynes. The longer the Empire waits, the greater our defending force will be. Their own reinforcements seem to have slowed to a trickle. Perhaps they have been testing our will to fight.'

'Perhaps,' Stenwold echoed, in the same doubting tone. When she rounded on him he spread his hands. 'My gut says no. My instincts tell me that the Empire came here for a fight, and intends to bring it, and soon. We both know this has been brewing since their reunification. I cannot think they would throw so much of men and materiel into simple posturing.'

She shrugged. 'We are as ready as we can be, and their forces are too far still to try and catch us off guard. If they want to invest the city in siege, they will have to commit themselves, and bring themselves within the range of our wall engines. They will find us ready for them this time.' She met his eyes again. 'They hate us, Maker. They hate us for having the temerity to demand our freedom. If this city falls a second time then they will find a hundred ways to make us suffer. We cannot let them back within our walls.'

There was a faint tremor and, in its wake, shouts were going up along the wall, bringing Stenwold and Kymene racing back to the crenellations. For a moment, Stenwold could not work out what had happened, but then he saw the plume of dust rising, five hundred yards and more outside the city. *Have they set mines, buried explosives?* he wondered. *That looks like an artillery strike!*

Kymene was already shouting for her scouts. 'You missed their main engines!' she was berating them. 'While you were watching some decoy, they must have brought their leadshotters to bear!'

'Commander, I was expecting the same thing!' a Fly-kinden protested. 'I was watching for just that. There are only the two packs of engines out past the Antosine, and the smaller engines with their main force. None of it could possibly . . .'

Stenwold leant out, staring across the uneven terrain in the direction that the Imperial artillery had apparently been set up. It was hilly, a little broken with rocks, rugged grazing land from which the farmers had fled when the black and gold flag had been sighted.

Was that a wisp of smoke there, such as a leadshotter might give out? Had he heard a distant, hollow knocking from that quarter even as he vaulted the steps?

A moment later, he heard it for sure and, watching carefully, he saw the smoke as well. Even as his mind was shouting, *Impossible!* he had already noted a new plume of dust, plain to all eyes, that fountained from the earth noticeably closer to the walls.

For a moment a grand silence fell over all the defenders of Myna, and the voice of a long-dead friend told him, *You will know first from the sound.*

He had come here to give steel to the Mynan defenders, to assure them that they did not stand alone. He had come too late, however.

The Empire's assault on the city had begun.

There were flashes of light in the sky, a spotter from the Light Airborne reporting his best guess as to the relationship between city walls and the second ranging shot. Nearby, a lieutenant of the Engineers translated calmly, 'Two hundred fifty far seventy-five left, calibrate.'

The greatshotter crews turned to their machines, which were to the familiar leadshotters what those devices were to simple catapults. Totho knew leadshotters, having seen them in action many times in the hands of both allies and enemies. Strengthened tubes, metal and bound with metal, in which a large charge of firepowder was detonated to fling a projectile in a shallow arc. The firepowder reaction, which had never produced efficient weapons on a personal scale, was still accurate enough by the standards of siege engines, and those weapons had slowly been replacing more primitive devices that derived their power from torsion engines and the like.

The greatshotters were ten times the size of their little ancestors, and their barrels tilted at a steep angle, as if they sought to
make war on the sky itself. He had heard any number of
engineers, both Imperial and Iron Glove, tell him that they could
not possibly work.

The metallurgy had been the frustrating part, as he was no
specialist, and had been forced to rely on others among Drephos's people to find the precise alloys and construction that
would survive the absurd pressures the barrel interior came
under each time the weapon was discharged. The wait had given
him plenty of time to solve the other major problem: how a
weapon able to throw its missiles at a target some miles away
could possibly be aimed.

Colonel – formerly Major – Ferric was excitedly explaining
the process to the newly arrived General Roder, and Totho was
happy to step back and let him do so. Wasps reacted to
innovation so much better when it came from their own kind.

'The thing is that, whilst most engineers can do the calculations for a regular leadshotter in their heads,' the engineer was
enthusing happily, 'the margin of error for such a distant target
is simply too great, and whilst we can, of course, simply keep
shooting and adjusting by hand, it would take most of the day
to get any useful bearing on the walls, and that's assuming they
let us alone that long.'

Roder nodded, saying nothing and simply listening, which
Totho reckoned was a rare and valuable trait in a general.

'Are you aware of what I mean by a Ratiocinator?' Ferric
asked. It became clear that Roder was not, so the enginer hurried
on. 'They've been known about for maybe fifty years – a Helleren
invention – they've been unreliable for most of that time, and
only capable of very simple tasks. Think of it like an abacus or –
no, you must have seen a merchant's reckoning wheel for currency or weights and measures – numbers in, numbers out, and
the gearing on the wheel transforms the one to the other?'

Roder glanced sidelong at Totho even as he absorbed the

existence of such devices. *What's the matter, General? Ashamed that a pair of halfbreeds has brought you such a bounty?*

'Then it's a very complicated reckoning wheel – we put our best measurements and numbers in via these dials, you see,' and Ferric was elbowing the crew aside to demonstrate, revealing an intricate arrangement of brass wheels set into the brass-and-wood box bolted to the greatshotter's mountings. 'We have seven different settings to describe the spatial relationship between our battery here – that's our cluster of engines, General – and the target. The Ratiocinator takes our measurements – our best guesses really – and adjusts elevation and angle accordingly with great precision.' Even as he said it, Totho heard steam hiss within the machine's base, driving the gear chains that rotated it slightly on its turntable, whilst pistons ground up the angle of the barrel through a careful increment.

'How can it *know?*' Roder demanded, glancing at Totho again.

'It doesn't know anything, General,' Ferric explained hastily. 'It's just numbers in, numbers out, like the reckoning wheel, only the gearing within is far more complicated and able to deal with many more variables. Think of it as though someone sat down with a book of tables and worked out every possible permutation beforehand – then it's easy to see how, when we show it what our situation is by setting the dials just so, the machinery within will automatically progress through the relevant calculations.'

'Easy,' Roder echoed, plainly finding the concept anything but. 'Carry on,' he said at last and, even as he did, one of the crew shouted, 'Loose!' and the greatshotter spoke, fully half the barrel recoiling out of sight within the other half in order to absorb some of the shock of detonation. The sound was thunderous, but less than Totho might have expected, not so much more than that of two or three leadshotters discharging at once. Even so, everyone present had clapped their hands to their ears when the warning had come.

When he looked up, Roder was staring at him, stepping over, his face unreadable in its immobility. 'You're the snapbowman, they tell me,' he grunted. 'One of the Colonel-Auxillian's original crew.'

'Original crew' was hardly true, but Totho nodded nonetheless. *I will not call you 'sir'*, he promised himself. *I save that for one man only.* He waited for whatever slight or abuse the general of the Eighth Army would have for him.

'Your weapons got me to the gates of Seldis, boy,' Roder told him flatly. 'I'd have got inside them, too, given time.' He gave the nod of a man recognizing something of merit. 'You'll get me inside Myna with your engines, too. Ferric!'

The colonel of Engineers looked round, 'Sir?'

'Why are your shells undershooting the wall? Why not overshoot and them pull back towards us?'

'It's harder to judge the adjustments needed when the shots are landing in urban terrain, General,' Ferric explained. 'On the open ground, we can make better estimates and find the wall sooner.'

Roder eyed him sternly. 'Colonel, you're a grand engineer but you have something to learn about being a soldier. Shoot past the wall, not short of it. I don't care if it takes longer to crack the city that way. It'll be time well spent.'

His face, as he glanced briefly back at Totho, was as bland and pitiless as a desert, then he was striding off towards the band of messengers awaiting his convenience, calling, 'Send word to the Aviation Corps!'

The next phase of the battle was underway already.

While Stenwold was still staring out at the hill country and the far-distant Imperial artillery positions, as though the Empire was a stage conjuror whose tricks might be unravelled by careful observation, Kymene was shouting, 'Airmen, get our flying machines readied!' and sending scouts off for the airfields.

'We need to attack their engines,' she told Stenwold shortly when he glanced over at her. 'The fliers are the only way. They're not intended to fight against ground targets, but our airmen will just have to improvise.'

The scouts had already reported a significant Air Corps presence within the Imperial army, and Kymene nodded, reading his expression. 'At least this way we're taking the battle to them,' she told him.

They both heard the echoing sound of the far-off engine loosing, again just the one but, even as they turned their eyes towards the ground before the gates, soldiers were pointing behind them, deep into the city itself. Myna was built in defensive tiers up a hillside, with the main gate the only easily approachable point. The rising dust and smoke from the missile's impact was plain to see, more than half the city away.

'Fliers!' someone shouted, and neither Stenwold nor Kymene were naive enough to think they meant the Mynan machines. Stenwold had his glass out first, quickly finding the circling dots that were rising from behind the main Wasp force. A moment later he passed it grimly to Kymene. The sleek, brutal lines of the Imperial Spearflights were hard to mistake, and he counted at least a score of them taking to the air.

'Get the air defences ready,' Kymene snapped out, but they both knew the wall engines were designed to keep off an assault by the Light Airborne, not to be pitched against swift and high-flying orthopters.

'Everyone to arms,' was her next order, quietly now, to be taken by her scouts and scattered throughout the city. Stenwold saw the Ants of the Maynesh contingent already arrayed before the gate, awaiting the traditional start of hostilities that the Wasps had already disdained. Another impact smashed into a street behind them, far closer, so that the screams and cries were clearly audible. So far all the impacts, within and without, had been solid shot, but Stenwold guessed that was only for ranging, just as he supposed that, once the first missile touched near the wall, all the engines out there would be adopting the same

trajectory, both Wasp positions beginning a sustained bombardment by way of some artifice he did not understand.

Edmon's flier was named the *Pacemark* from the white stripes
on the underside of its forewings that flashed pale with each
upbeat. It was a solid, barrel-bodied orthopter, the front wings
of light wooden slats interwoven, the rear just silk over a frame,
with a cross-sectioned tail for stability. A pair of rotary piercers
flanked and disfigured the cockpit at the fore, cramping the seat
and obscuring the view, but they were far more efficient than
the old repeating ballistae that many of his comrades still
sported.

The ground crew wheeled his machine out, and he was
already thanking his luck that he had rewound the engine himself
just an hour ago. It was a nervous habit that infuriated the
mechanics, but it meant he had a fully tensioned spring, ready
to leap into the air. All about him, across the Robannen Square
airfield, other machines of various shapes and designs were
being brought into the light, whilst the handful that had already
been out in the open air from patrol were being refuelled or
rewound.

The cockpit of the *Pacemark* was open save for a glass-paned
baffle to keep the worst of the wind off, so Edmon reached up
and hauled himself in, making the undignified struggle look
almost smooth with the ease of long experience. Every variant
of this design was built too high off the ground for comfort, but
none of the airmen wanted to be seen using steps.

'Target is the enemy artillery that is a little over two miles
beyond the walls, out towards the Antosine,' a militia officer was
calling out.

'*How* far?' called Vorses from the cockpit of his *Stonefly*, and
someone else demanded, 'What about the artillery that's actually
loosing on the city, then?'

'Two miles out towards the Antosine,' the officer repeated.
'Orders are clear and confirmed. Use your piercers and ballistae,

inflict what damage you can, then return here for reassignment.'
He had his mouth open still, more orders on the way, but at that
moment a flier screamed overhead in a blur of wings, and the
west side of the airfield became a fireball, the hangar mouth
there wreathed in instant flames, men rushing out, some burning, with others trying to drag them to the ground. A moment
later there was a sharp detonation as an open fuel barrel caught
and blew.

'Get in the air! Get in the air!' Edmon roared, hands already
reaching for his controls, letting slip the gear train that threw his
Pacemark's wings into life, wrenching the machine vertically into
the air and slapping a couple of incautious mechanics to the
ground at the same time. He had no opportunity for apologies
or regrets. There were Imperial fliers in the skies over Myna,
and they were wheeling over all three major airfields. Edmon
saw the bright flash of more incendiaries, and imagined the air
power of Myna vulnerable on the ground, at the mercy of
whatever means the Wasps were using to attack it. The artillery
would have to wait.

Beneath him, in the shadow of his wings, the other Mynan
airmen – and women – were scrambling to get their fliers off the
ground. Edmon had a moment's glimpse of the city around him
– an amalgam of wheeling streets as he hauled his *Pacemark* up
above rooftop level – distinguishing a scattered constellation of
flames from the Spearflights' incendiaries and tall pillars of dust
from the ranging shots of the siege engines. He felt his heart cry
out against it: his Myna, his city, his nation. He had lived
through the last occupation. He knew there was no way back
into slavery that would not break his people.

He backed his machine's wings, trying to wait over the field
while Vorses and the others got aloft, but the *Pacemark* would
never hover at the best of times, and he felt it slide sideways in
the air, forcing him to jerk its nose up and claw for more height.
Then a trio of Spearflights were darting across the face of the
city towards him, pulling higher as they reached the airfield.

He wrestled with the controls for a moment, hearing that vicious knocking sound the *Pacemark* always made when he tried to yank it into a sudden turn. The piercers spun up nicely, Solarnese machinery five years old shaming the Mynan machine they were set into. Even as he found a line that would intercept the Imperial fliers, flames were gouting along an adjacent street, just washing out on to the airfield. *They must be dropping grenades,* but no grenade ever lifted by man could hold such an incendiary charge.

He clenched on the trigger, cutting upwards at their bellies as they rattled overhead. The leftmost of the Wasp fliers bucked, wings stilled for a second before thundering into life again, but none of them stopped. Edmon wrenched at the stick savagely, trying to drag the *Pacemark* round so that he could attack them from behind.

Fire bloomed across the airfield. He imagined he could feel the wash of heat, high up as he was. He saw Vorses's *Stonefly* instantly ablaze, even twenty feet off the ground, its wings shedding fire in a trail of embers, matchwood and crisping silk. Its ascent became a dive, almost graceful, as though Vorses, in the midst of the inferno, had decided to quit his life in the same style that he had lived it. Another orthopter was clipped, the silk of one wing instantly charring and unravelling, tilting all the way over as its pilot fought for control, the burning wingtip gently touching the smouldering grass of the airfield and instantly flying apart, the impact whiplashing up through the machine itself. Edmon could hear a voice, no words but just a sound of horror that nobody had ever had the heart to name. It was his own, he knew. It was his, and he could not stop it.

Another two fixed-wings had caught the brunt of a second explosion, one of them still lazily taxiing for a take-off that would never come. Others of his countrymen had got into the air by the skin of their teeth, fleeing the fire, desperate for height lest another flight of Imperial machines pass overhead any moment. Then Edmon could spare his comrades no more time. He had somehow brought the *Pacemark* into a messy line behind a Spearflight, jockeying and nudging to bring the piercers to bear.

He had flown against the Empire in a few border skirmishes around the end of last year, more posturing than killing. He knew, though – and the understanding sat like lead on his stomach – that the Spearflights were faster and more nimble than his *Pacemark* and most of the mishmash that was the Mynan air force. After all, what could Myna do, liberated into a callous world so abruptly, and with so little time to prepare for this moment? The Consensus had begged and borrowed, and bought what they could with the little credit the city could raise: securing the cast-offs of Helleron and Sarn and Collegium. Edmon had spent most of his savings on the piercers the *Pacemark* was armed with. The city could not afford them.

He saw it then: there had been a little finned bulk clutched to the Spearflight's belly by stubby legs, and now they flexed open and the missile was falling, wildly at first but then stabilizing, coming down towards the government district where the Consensus was no doubt meeting to shout at one another and demand that something must be done. Even before the flames began erupting, another bulb had slipped into that exacting metal grip, ready for a new target.

Edmon found his line, feeling himself drawn into place by sheer rage and hatred and desperation, and his piercers hammered back and forth, silvering the air between him and the Wasp with a lancing train of bolts. The Spearflight was more sluggish than he recalled them being, weighed down by the load of death it was carrying, and although its pilot tried to pitch it sideways to avoid his shot, Edmon held his place beautifully, neater than he ever had in training, seeing his bolts flay the enemy orthopter's hooked tail, and then smash one of the wings to splinters, the Spearflight abruptly falling into a spin, out of control and plummeting.

He was already hauling back on the stick, forcing the *Pacemark* into a reluctant climb out of the sights of a notional enemy that turned out to be a real one. He felt a single solid impact somewhere behind him, the robust barrel of his craft's hull earning its keep, and gyred his orthopter back across the breadth of Myna, avoiding shot and seeking a new target all at the same time, hoping that one of the others would spot his pursuer and put enough pressure on so that Edmon could escape. Bolts zipped past him to the right, and then above, so that he dropped from the climb, veering steeply right and downwards, then pulling up almost immediately, hoping to fool the Wasp into overshooting.

He glimpsed brief, mad snatches of the sky over Myna, the circling dots of other machines, more trios of Spearflights trailing their fiery cargoes. Some of the machines he spotted must have been Mynan, fighting as he was fighting. He had no idea how many had even made it into the air.

Another bolt struck, feeling as if it had come from directly behind, but he was casting the *Pacemark* about randomly enough for only the odd shot to reach him, not any kind of sustained burst. Even so, the Wasp was relentless, refusing to be thrown off. Edmon swung his orthopter back towards the Robannen Square airfield, in the hope of picking up reinforcements there. Even as he did, another Spearflight crossed his view ahead, and he managed to rake a dozen bolts across its hull as he fled onwards, seeing it falter but not quite fall.

The airfield was now completely ablaze, even the stone seeming to crackle furiously. The only Mynan machines were on the ground and half consumed. Another bolt clipped him, striking splinters from the rip of the cockpit.

He threw a lever to fold the *Pacemark*'s hindwings down along the tail and dropped.

Follow me, will you, you bastard?

The wooden forewings were labouring, making heavy work of keeping the machine in the air at all. Abruptly his world was a hot glare, the air about him turned instantly to choking smoke.

The Spearflights used wood-framed silk for all four wings,

that much he knew. Wood burned, but silk practically disintegrated in a flame.

He dropped, craning back for a second, looking for his enemy.

There! The Wasp was pulling out already, not so brave now he had an enemy he could not hide behind. Edmon closed his eyes for a second against the smoke, against the thought of burning to death, and pulled back hard, the forewings' clatter reaching a new strained pitch. He was slow with just two wings, so slow he thought he might fall from the air entirely. Slow enough that the Wasp passed overhead and into his sights despite everything the Imperial pilot could do to try and prevent it.

Edmon released the *Pacemark*'s hindwings and felt the sudden leap as his flier regained full use of the air, his piercer strafing across the Spearflight's belly and tail, punching holes but striking nothing vital. Even so, the game had been turned right round, and now it was the Wasp's turn to flee across the city, with Edmon in fierce pursuit.

The *Pacemark*'s wings and body were smouldering, and it was touch and go whether the rush of wind would fan them or put them out. Then the other Spearflights were diving on him, and he had other worries.

Bolts skipped and danced all about him, as though he was flying through rain, and he tipped the *Pacemark* sideways, turning on the point of one wing just ten feet over the rooftops, then slinging the orthopter back towards the gates. The manoeuvre caught some of the Wasps off guard, or perhaps they simply had other priorities, but there were still three jostling behind him as he broke away across the city.

He felt at least two more impacts, but still the killing scythe of shot never quite found him. Had there been only two of them then he might not have lasted, but they were getting in one another's way, coming perilously close to clipping each other from the sky in their eagerness to be the one that downed him.

His mind was racing, seeing flashes in the corners of his eyes that could only mean more incendiaries falling on his city while he was harried out of the way, unable to defend his people.

He witnessed the moment that the enemy artillery found the walls.

He had lost track of the shelling, but abruptly the lone engine had found the range, and a moment later every one of the Empire's far-off weapons had loosed. As he sent the *Pacemark* scudding along the line of the wall, there was an appalling series of cracks and flashes, stone-eater acid shells alternating with wall-cracker explosives. The Mynan defences held under the first thundering salvo, but Edmon knew that there were more coming, and the walls were old, still the same stones that had failed to keep the Empire out the first time.

Three bolts punched splinter-edged holes in his right forewing and another clipped his left shoulder, the pain brief and fierce, his teeth clenching. He tried slowing to make them overshoot, but they matched him speed for speed, and they could go slower than he could without stalling and dropping from the sky. Desperately he sent his vessel over the wall, dropping into its shadow for a brief respite, expecting to see the Imperial Light Airborne and ground forces already on the move.

They were not. They still sat well out of the reach of the Mynan wall engines, letting their machines carry the fight to Myna.

The shock of no army at the gates left him numb: the utter contempt for it, and all it said about the way the Wasps saw the attack, and his people. *Not even worth drawing a sword over.* Fury seized him and shook him in its jaws, and he fought the *Pacemark* round, believing in that moment that sheer anger would overcome aerodynamics to bring him face to face with the Spearflights. They stayed nimbly behind him, though he lost them their line on him, bolts flying wide as he threw his orthopter about the sky.

Then there was another flying machine cutting across him,

not a Wasp craft, nor any he knew from Myna's airfields. He had a brief glimpse of a small hull, a solitary pair of wings blurring about the hunch of its engine housing, and then one of the pursuing Wasp Spearflights jolted in the air, shuddering under piercer bolts, before coming apart as though someone had magically removed half the screws, as fragments of wing and body became a shattered cloud beneath the pounding.

The remaining two split up, one following Edmon relentlessly, the other rising to meet this new challenger. The little two-winged flier slid sidelong in the air, deft as a rapier, and the Spearflight that had been so agile behind Edmon now seemed to lumber past it like a fat man.

Then a scatter of bolts struck about the *Pacemark*, at least one holing the main hull before bounding from the engine housing to ricochet about inside. Edmon lost a few yards of height without meaning to, his wings stuttering awkwardly before finding their rhythm, and the Spearflight was stooping on him, driving him into the city wall, not letting him get clear.

For a moment, he and his antagonist were enveloped in fire and stone shards and acrid smoke as they ran the gauntlet of the Imperial artillery's assault on the wall, cutting through it so fast that the dust scratched Edmon's goggles, scored his skin raw and blasted the paint from his orthopter's hull. Then he was out again and skimming the very top of the wall, the lancing silver lines of piercer bolts dancing back and forth as the Spearflight tried to pin him to the stones.

He saw what was ahead and yanked on the stick, feeling a juddering of new impacts, trusting to the *Pacemark*'s robust hull to weather it.

Some Mynan artillerist was awake and ready. As Edmon hauled himself out of the way the wall engine he had nearly flown into had come about and, immediately behind him, the Wasp orthopter flew into a wall of scrapshot, disintegrating instantly and utterly.

Free for a moment, Edmon turned the *Pacemark* back over

Myna, trying to encompass all that he was seeing. There were isolated fires across the city, some in strategic areas, most others simply strewn randomly by inaccurate or capricious Wasp pilots. The walls and gate were under a solid, continuous pounding, but some of the Imperial siege engines had now started throwing incendiary shells deeper into the city.

Moments, it's only been moments since the attack started. We've already lost.

He could feel the *Pacemark*'s clockwork slowing, too many tight turns meeting damaged gear trains, and he knew he would have to find somewhere to set it down that was not on fire. In that moment he saw the strange orthopter again, coming in ahead and to the right, slowing to match his speed. He caught the brief flash of a heliograph, but had to wait for the message to be repeated before he saw the pilot was signalling a need to land as well.

But the Wasps . . . He looked around him, but the skies were almost clear. The Wasp pilots had taken their craft back to camp for refuelling, he guessed. The artillery was keeping their work warm for them while they rested.

He did not want to land. He did not want to face the enormity of what was happening to his city, to find out how many of the faces he had seen only this morning were lost forever. The mechanical demands of the *Pacemark* were becoming more insistent, however, and he let the orthopter drop lower, heading for whichever airfield seemed the most intact.

Twelve

Sartaea te Mosca was someone who could not help but play hostess wherever she ended up. It seemed an odd trait to bring with her from the severe Moth-kinden who had trained her in the ways of a seer, but the Antspider wondered if that was because they had treated her like a servant while she was there. Everyone knew a great deal about the standards of equality and the social hierarchy amongst Beetle-kinden of various cities, or the Wasps of the Empire, or even the Spiders, or so they told themselves. The Moth-kinden, for all they had ruled this quarter of the world some centuries back, were a stubborn mystery, and that was perhaps the one topic that te Mosca was never open about.

They were at Mummers's studio again, and Raullo himself was having one of his bad days, meaning that it was past noon and he was still stuffed into the small alcove he slept in, sweating and twitching and turning over fitfully, a shabby curtain serving to partition his little space of despair from the rest of the room and fend off the sun's encroachment. He had been angling for a big commission, the others knew, working night and day for it, repapering his walls with preliminary sketches and part-colour studies, but his patron had abruptly turned him down, or changed his mind, or even left the city. This last month it had been hard for an artist to make any kind of living. People were clinging to their money, waiting to see which way the future would jump. Besides, there was not as much money in Collegium as there used to be, after all the rebuilding following the last war. Nobody was going hungry, but everyone's belt was just that little bit tighter these days. Art was a luxury that fewer people could afford, and Raullo was suffering from it.

It had been a few days since Eujen's meeting with Jodry Drillen, and he had carried away from it not the humility that had perhaps been intended, but a deep-seated annoyance. Most galling had been the implication – as he perceived it – that his loyalty to his city was suspect. He had composed a long speech on the subject, going into some detail about how rattling sabres in the direction of the Empire – or anybody else – did not constitute loyalty. Eujen's dedication to finding a future where there would be no *need* of war with the Empire – now *that* was loyalty, because it would provide far greater benefits for Collegium in the long term. The Makerist warmongering stance would only create a worsening spiral, a degenerating pattern of mutual hostility that would end . . . where? Where would it end? Eujen had demanded, and nobody had an answer for him. Of course, they had heard the speech twice by then.

'If only I had contacts in the Empire,' he would say sadly.

'Then they could *really* call you traitor?' Straessa needled him.

'No! Then I could talk them round, influence them . . .' Eujen's hands clutched at the air.

The Antspider was herself not at all sure of that. The idea that there was a minority within the Empire who were whipping the rest to war rang false to her. The problem was the system as a whole, or so her talks with Averic seemed to suggest. Those who might see eye to eye with Eujen were the minority – Averic's own family included, apparently – and, if the majority were to lurch into battle, those few would not be able to restrain them.

It had not been a month ago that Eujen had been claiming that war itself would not come. A tenday or so ago he had taken to stating that war would not come *soon*, that everyone's excitement about the subject was premature. Since meeting Drillen, however, he had stopped saying even that.

And he would fight it, she knew, for all the good it would do him. He was doomed, and he knew he was doomed. The weight of history was rolling down on Eujen like the studded wheels of a great automotive, but he fought his battles regardless, because it was *right*. Of all his qualities, she loved him for that one. She herself came from a culture where doing what was right was a luxury that even the rich could seldom afford. Seeing the sheer, glowing naivety of someone like Eujen Leadswell, setting out to change the world, gave her an almost vertiginous feeling.

For ten minutes Eujen had been pacing now, watched anxiously by everyone except the sleeping Mummers, and Gerethwy, who was carefully annotating a schematic. Eventually, though, Eujen's failure to conceive of some political master plan resulted in him rounding on them furiously, as though it was their fault. 'And he's not *doing* anything!' he explained. 'Jodry Drillen spends his time harassing students and listening to complaints about madmen like Gripshod, while we just slide onwards to . . .' He would not utter the word 'war'.

'But Gripshod is the ambassador to Khanaphes, isn't he?' te Mosca asked him. 'Surely that could be relevant?'

'If only! It's not even that Gripshod – it's the artificer one, his brother.'

'Banjacs Gripshod is still alive?' Gerethwy raised his head.

'*Banjacs* Gripshod?' Straessa asked incredulously. 'Unfortunate name for an artificer . . .'

'No, no,' Gerethwy waved the idea away. 'Artificers say *that* about a thing *because* of old Gripshod. Something of a legend, if you talk to the older artificing staff. I thought he must be dead, the way everyone talks about him—' Then he was cut off by a hammering on the door.

'He's not in,' the Antspider said, with a gesture towards Mummers, because they had all come to the immediate conclusion that one of the artist's creditors was trying his luck, but then came a voice calling 'Mistress te Mosca, are you within?' With a worried glance at the others, the Fly woman flitted over to the door and unbolted it.

A young Beetle-kinden man was revealed, whom they recognized vaguely as one of the College's older students researching something in such and such department. The post-accredit students often found casual employment with the College Masters and the Assembly as a way of making ends meet.

'Mistress te Mosca, you're called to the Assembly. All the Masters are,' he announced, slightly out of breath.

'But I don't even have a seat on the Assembly,' Sartaea protested. 'Really, I'm not a full Master of the College. I don't feel that I should be involved in—'

'All College staff, they said,' the student interrupted. 'Please, Mistress. The Imperial ambassador has asked for special dispensation to speak to the city.'

A dead silence fell across the studio, each and everyone there staring at the messenger. In the echo of that sudden quiet, Raullo Mummers hooked back the curtain of his alcove and looked out, blinking and unshaven, as though the news' sheer significance had been enough to slap him into immediate wakefulness.

'I see,' said Sartaea te Mosca, with considerable self-possession. 'Well, then, I suppose I should go and listen to what the ambassador has to say.'

The Imperial ambassador was named Aagen, and he was a complex man who had only ever wanted a simple life. He had been an engineer, once, just a lieutenant whose life was mostly shouting at other engineers to get things fixed and machines into the air or on the road. He had even been well liked. One of the people who had liked him had ended up sleeping with the Empress, albeit briefly, and in his brief moment of power he had got Aagen sent to Collegium as an ambassador. It had been intended as a reward.

True, Aagen had enjoyed his time here, up until now. The Beetles knew a great deal about artificing, and they were remarkably open about it, even to a Wasp, when that Wasp displayed the same childlike enthusiasm for the craft that they did. He had lived here a few years now, and had not done too badly from it.

Right now, he would take it all back to be a lowly lieutenant again, as he stood before the Assembly of Collegium, although the lowly lieutenant he had once been would have seen this task merely as a duty and blithely ignored the wider repercussions. The Aagen of today, Ambassador Aagen, could not close his eyes so easily.

He had fallen in love, that was the problem. Long before being posted here he had fallen in love with a dancing slave, and loved her enough to free her and send her out of his life. After that, nothing about the Empire or the rest of the world had ever looked quite the same to him.

He had been greeted just after dawn by Honory Bellowern, Beetle-kinden, Imperial diplomat and the man who held Aagen's leash. The portly, avuncular man had beamed at him. 'Big day today, ambassador.' Aagen's heart had sunk in direct proportion to the man's cheer.

Bellowern had held out a scroll neatly tied with black tape, his habit for official Imperial statements. It had taken a few moments of blank staring before Aagen had been able to accept it from him.

'I've made all the arrangements. Of course the Speaker will make time for the words of the Empress,' Bellowern had explained happily. 'In fact, I rather think that there will be more people there to hear you than have turned up since . . . oh, the last war, let's say.'

Now, Aagen looked out at that sea of faces and knew that Bellowern had not been exaggerating. Surely the entire Assembly had jostled its way into the great amphitheatre of the Amphiophos, and there were plenty standing at the back, too: senior scholars, Assembly clerks, servants. They were all unnaturally quiet. He had sat here before and listened to members of this politic host shout themselves hoarse, while two-score separate conversations were carried on all around them. Now they just listened gravely, finally finding the decorum and dignity that their office should have always borne, and never had until now.

All those dark faces, he thought, for they were mostly Beetles, with a scattering of other kinden thrown in, mostly at the College end. He tried to picture a similar gathering of his own people, but found that the thought only oppressed him. He felt that he had more in common, under the skin, with these mercantile, machine-minded folk than with his own warlike kinden.

He cleared his throat. They were rapt. The unspoken tension and worry in the room sang in his ears.

When he had first read his orders in Bellowern's office he had demanded of Bellowern, 'When did this happen?'

'Probably happening even as we speak, my dear ambassador,' had come the reply. 'Now just do your job. I have appointments later.'

'And what do I say to Stenwold Maker?' Aagen had demanded, as his last line of defence, for he knew that even Bellowern was leery of clashing head-on with the War Master.

But the Beetle had been unflappable. 'Why, haven't you heard? Master Maker's out of the city on some sort of clandestine business.' A chuckle. 'My agents think he's gone to Myna.'

And that had been that.

'The words of the Empress, Her Imperial Majesty Seda the First,' Aagen began, falling back on his battlefield voice despite the quiet, for the reassurance it gave him. 'Be it known that the Empire has suffered, both before and after its unification, from incursions and raids from neighbouring states thinking to take advantage of our internal division.' He was surprised at how steady his tones were. 'Be it also known that the Empire's protectorates within the Commonweal, known as the Principalities, have also come under assault by the forces of these same aggressive neighbours. After attempting every manner of reconciliation and being met only with contempt, it is the sad duty of a state to defend itself by any means. So it is that the difficult decision has been made, by the Empress acting under the advice of her court, that the Empire is henceforth at war with the self-styled Three-city Alliance, which war shall be prosecuted by all means until the borders of the Empire are secure, and the liberty of its allies is won.' He paused then, waiting for the uproar, and indeed there was a murmur building, but not the grand outcry he had half expected.

'The Empress wishes it known,' he continued more quietly, 'that this is no breach of the Treaty of Gold, but the simple need of any state to defend its own. The Empire does not consider that this conflict need involve any other city. However,' and Bellowern had actually written it that way, stage-managing the speech through the weapons of punctuation, 'should any other power declare for the Alliance, or aid them in any way, then the Empire will regard such interference as an act of war, and the perpetrators as enemies of the Empress and the Wasp people, and the Empire shall not rest until such enemies are rendered incapable of threatening the Empire's security and peace of mind.'

When he rolled the scroll up again it was the loudest sound in the entire grand chamber.

He was expected to return to the ambassadorial quarters for debriefing after that, leaving the talk to build into a panicked babble in his absence. Instead, he headed straight for an airfield, where a blocky old Imperial heliopter sat waiting for him.

Shortly thereafter he had left the city, and the post of ambassador, behind him, and Honory Bellowern would rant and storm and cuff the servants, jolted from his mild-mannered act for once by this shock desertion. Aagen did not care. He had learned too much, travelled too far from the lieutenant he had once been. With the sense that behind him the world was cracking apart, he was fleeing to the only person who really mattered to him any more.

Banjacs Gripshod knew what people said about him. He was bitterly aware that his name had passed into Collegiate legend as a byword for bad artifice, so that students characterized a catastrophically failed experiment as 'banjacsed', without really understanding where the word had come from. It had been thirty years since he had been dismissed ignominiously from the Great College, and not a day had passed without his feeling keenly just how badly he had been treated.

He was old now, probably one of the oldest Beetle-kinden in the city, and most of those who did remember that there was a man behind the myth assumed he was dead. His own family, nephews and nieces and subsequent generations, would have nothing to do with him, preferring to dote on his younger brother, Berjek, historian and now apparently some manner of diplomat.

Trivialities, Banjacs knew. None of it mattered. Only his work, his grand work.

Nobody understood artifice like he did, or at least nobody in Collegium. There were no like minds. Those engineers and mechanics to whom he had attempted to expound his theories had backed away from him as though he carried a plague. He had scoured the city for like minds, and found only technological pygmies. The journals he read were likewise a waste of wood pulp, ignorant men writing on small matters. Trivial, *trivial*! Was all of Collegiate artifice come to this?

He had once obtained a few brief papers by the Imperial artificer Dariandrephos. The man had shown promise. That was the best that Banjacs would say – more promise, anyway, than the doubting, naysaying *small minds* of his own people, who had cast him out, laughed at him, declared him mad and then mostly forgotten him.

He would show them, though. That was his maxim. There

would come a time when the whole of Collegium would sit up and acknowledge the genius of Banjacs Gripshod.

The family at least had money: being cut off from the College had not denied him his research, only freed him from its constraints. If the masters back then had been men of vision, then a little devastation could have been overlooked. So he had destroyed one of their precious workshops. Did they not understand that innovation mandated *risk*? It had cost him years of rebuilding inside his own townhouse to reconstruct the equipment that the College had denied him.

He had grown used to being alone in the world, surrounded by people who could not share his vision. His time was growing short, though. He carried more than eighty years on his spare frame, and his patchy hair and beard were white against the dark of his skin. He could no longer fetch and carry as he once had, and a succession of assistants had been hired, tried, argued with and dismissed over the last few years, each one departing to spread the word that old Banjacs was madder than ever.

His current assistant was Reyna Pullard, and she was different, he realized. He had railed at the difficulties of working alone. Now he wished to be more alone than he was. She was an efficient worker, he had to admit. Her understanding of engineering was rudimentary by his standards, perfectly acceptable by the atrophied lights of the College. She kept his workshops clean – he had three of them, two taking up the wings of the house, and the special central chamber that reached all the way from cellar to central skylight – and she obeyed instructions without all the vexing questions that most of his prior assistants were prone to. He should have been delighted.

He had made a mistake, though. He had let her into the cellar, and since then he had lived in an agony of worry because he had misjudged her. He had always been misjudging people, back when he still had much to do with the rest of humanity, but long abstinence from company had blurred the memories. He had forgotten they were not crisp and clean like machines.

The cellar laboratory had taken some ingenuity to design, mostly because it had required practically coring the old family townhouse, removing an ascending column of floors and ceilings all the way up to the special round skylight that Banjacs had designed and had had installed. The machinery he had painstakingly constructed filled almost half the available height in a great reaching flurry of bronze and leaded glass, the transparent tubes like colossal organ pipes, the globes of the capacity chargers, the awesome spinning wheels of the accumulators. Beneath the laboratory floor was still more: the differential vats, seething with corrosion, that stored his life's work.

It was all locked away, even the skylight capped, and Banjacs had made sure that his assistants could busy themselves in the other two workshops without even suspecting the house's main secret. He had thought Reyna Pullard might be different, though. She had been so accommodating, not complaining about the hours or the pay or the conditions. He had thought to find in her a kindred spirit driven by the same dreams.

Standing on the circular gantry that ran around the laboratory wall at what was ground level outside, he now looked down at her. She was cleaning the charger globes, which always attracted dust and soot from everywhere else in the room: just a solidly built Beetle woman of twenty-five or thirty, and nothing in her manner or actions should have raised his suspicions, but he knew . . . he *knew*.

She was betraying him. After she had seen the cellar laboratory, something had changed in her. He was not skilled at reading people, but he had registered it nonetheless: it was unmistakable. Then she had been absent, just once or twice, but he had not believed her excuses. Banjacs knew he had enemies. He could not have necessarily said who they were, or perhaps their identity changed from day to day, simply remembered faces and imagined fears from years before. That he had enemies, though, was a point of faith for him, and now he knew that Reyna Pullard was their servant. She was telling them his secrets. She would sabotage his machine. She was working for *them*.

And there was a storm coming, Banjacs knew. He felt it within himself, as though it was the only thing still keeping him alive. There was a storm coming, and he was the only man who understood.

He was going to show the city, he was certain, but his enemies would do their best to stop him. It was his world against theirs. What was he to do?

Reyna Pullard continued with her work brightly and efficiently, and the sight of her sickened him. *Betrayed! Betrayed!* rattled about in his head, so that he could barely think. He had to act now. Another day, another hour even, and she would act on her treacherous thoughts, and then all his years of work would have been for nothing. He would be lost – and his city would be lost. There was a storm coming, and he would be needed. All those years ago he had looked into the future as if he had been a Moth-kinden. He had known the path that history – artifice – would take, and now that moment was almost upon him. He could not *allow* anything to stand in his way.

He had seen her making notes, taking measurements. He knew she was passing his secrets on to . . . it didn't matter who. She was a spy. She was the enemy.

His hand tightened on the lever.

The machine was not ready yet. The great accumulator wheels were barely turning, and the skylight was closed off. Still, it was a very grand machine, colossal power penned into every bolt and bulb of it, the greatest lightning engine ever made. It was dangerous, he knew. The device that had destroyed the College's workshop had been a fraction of the size.

Accidents happened.

Not taking his eyes off Reyna Pullard, he threw the switch.

★

For the next few days after Aagen's speech, Collegium was foreign to itself, a place haunted by a spectre that everyone had been talking about before, but that now must not be named, lest the naming call it closer; superstition hung about the city as if the Moths were back in charge. Business deals were broken off, or hurried to a conclusion. Buyers demurred or paid over the odds, whilst sellers hoarded or let go their goods for a song. Some even spoke of leaving the city, but where was there to go? Collegium was where people *came* to in times like these.

Straessa the Antspider had just finished a one-to-one with te Mosca regarding her progress in Inapt studies. The little Fly-kinden taught a measure of the histories of the Moth-kinden – or their myths, as the two were often inseparable – and Straessa was sharp enough that she could crib during the tenday before and produce accomplished essays as a result, especially if she could confer with Gerethwy, whose facility with the subject was as notable as his prowess with artifice. What Straessa could not master was the rest of the course, the curious hints and para-doxes and platitudes that were supposed to go some way towards explaining the Moths' belief in magic. Gerethwy again could set it all down effortlessly, but this time Straessa could not follow him. Her Spider blood was mute on the subject.

Now, crossing the crumbling quad that housed te Mosca's rooms, along with some two or three other departments that nobody thought much of, she became aware of some shouting coming from the square beyond, the big Appellant's Muster quadrangle that hosted most of the modern history departments.

She was ready for anything, for there had been a great deal of shouting in parts of Collegium of late and, at the same time, a great deal of conspicuous quiet. There had been rallies pro-testing against the Empire, and the few Wasps in the city had been staying indoors – especially when the rumour surfaced that someone had murdered the Imperial ambassador after his speech and disposed of his body in the bay. Averic had turned up one day with a black eye and a cracked rib, yet not a dent in his fanatical self-control.

But Straessa remembered what Eujen had reported of the Speaker's words, representing the other side of the coin, and it was obvious to her now. Whilst they shouted, all the students and impoverished patriots and the immigrants who had given their loyalty wholehearted to their new home, there were plenty of the better-heeled quietly stepping back from the situation, withdrawing their support from those who spoke out, choosing their trading partners wisely. Those who had too much invested in Collegium just to run off and seek refuge in Sarn were quietly preparing for the worst.

The disturbance at Appellant's Muster quad was something else again, though. When she arrived there she saw a dozen Beetle-kinden, dressed in the buff coats and breastplates of the Merchant Companies, standing idle with snapbow and pike while their chief called out to a scattering of students.

'Do not think the Assembly will sit idle now that the Empire has made war on our allies!' he declared, a pale Tarkesh Ant-kinden no doubt long renegade from his original city-state. 'We've seen this before, have we not? Did not Master Maker warn of this the last time – and wasn't he *right*? The Wasps cannot stand up against all the powers of the Treaty of Gold, and so they make their excuses to divide us, as they always did. Do you think Sarn will sit idle? Or the Spiderlands? No! And when they march to relieve Myna, Collegium's brave soldiers shall go with them. We fought at Malkan's Folly and we fought them from our own very walls. We'll show them that our reach is as great as theirs. We'll fight them wherever they bring their armies.' His grey sash and those of his followers showed an Ant-kinden helm in profile and the motto, *In Our Enemies' Robes*.

'Come, then,' he was saying. 'Now the Assembly has given the Companies the right to recruit once more, who'll stand beside Collegium's allies? Who'll march to give the Empire a taste of its own fire? For if we don't stop them in their tracks they'll be at our walls again, and then *everyone* gets to fight. So who'll sign here for the Coldstone Company?'

Straessa watched the man's audience with fascination, noticing Hallend there, who had been so vociferous about Averic at the Prowess Forum, and plenty of his fellows. Many here had been amongst the worst to victimize the Wasp student, to decry the evils of the Empire. Yet they were regarding the Ant as though he had the plague, and was trying to give it away for free. When the same man held out a snapbow for anyone to come and claim, she saw many of the most normally outspoken of them flinch away.

She slipped up behind Hallend's little knot of followers, then loudly declared, 'Why, which proud duellist here would not jump at the chance finally to take action against the Wasps, eh?' They jumped, indeed, and rounded on her, facing the cruelty of her smile. 'Aren't they incurable bigots and villains, each and every man of them?' she went on. 'Why, I hear they even dare send their sons to be students here, to soil our pristine educations with their filthy minds. Sign up! Sign up, I say. Now that the liberty of the world truly is at stake, what red-blooded Collegiate would not?'

She wanted a battle, a real slanging match, as though the exchange of hot words would break the tension within the city like a storm, but instead she found Hallend's face naked and terrible. Guilt was there, and shame and fear, and she remembered then that he was not quite twenty and had never left the city, and there was a blot of horror and loss in his recent history which was the last Day the Empire Came.

'But . . .' he managed to get out, 'Eujen said . . . Eujen's always saying, peace at any cost . . .'

Her sword had cleared its scabbard before anyone had seen her reach for it. 'Wrong!' she declared, aware that the Company snapbows were now drifting her way. 'Make peace with me, Hallend. Go on, I dare you.' Her rapier point danced before his eyes, 'Can you?' She backed him up three steps, unsure why she had not been stopped yet. 'It's not peace at any price; it's a *lasting* peace. So it's true, after all, that line of yours – not that they're all evil, but that they need to be stopped. We can't reach a lasting peace while we preach war against them, but we certainly can't while they're *making* war against us. They won't ever start to change their ways until they respect us, and what they respect is strength. Come on, Hallend, you know I'm right.' By the end her voice was tense and quiet, her eyes trying to hold Hallend's, but his kept sliding away.

And Hallend followed the route of his eyes, edging back from her as though she was mad, and in the end it was just her and the recruiting officer staring at one another.

Which was why, when she arrived late for her lunch with Gerethwy and Eujen, the first thing the latter said was, 'What *is* that you're wearing?'

She could only pluck at the grey sash with its device and words and shrug, 'Somebody had to,' she said.

Thirteen

That he was unfit to be a spy was proved to Laszlo when he almost went back to his own rooms to get a look at the Solarnese city hangars they overlooked, only darting away from his window at the last moment to swing about a few streets' worth of space before finding another rooftop to perch on. Aside from the unhappy corpse of Breighl, who could know what welcome was awaiting him within those bloodied walls?

Breighl dead. Te Riel dead. The dread was mounting higher inside his chest, threatening to choke him. *Time to be gone. Time to be long gone.* He could feel death approaching like a shadow in the water, vast and swift and inexorable.

What's a spy supposed to do in this position? He knew that hanging on in this suddenly murderous city would gain vital intelligence for Sten Maker, if Laszlo could only live long enough to pass it on. So many of the familiar faces had gone already, though, and some that had lingered now plainly regretted it. *I should be gone.* It was not spycraft that kept him here, and his loyalty to Maker only went so far, despite all they'd shared. *Liss, te Liss, don't be dead. We can get out together. It's not too late.*

It hurt to think of her: each time like touching a broken tooth. He had never realized, as he drank with her or joked with her, even when he slept with her, that she had wormed her way into his heart so deeply. Only now, with no idea whether she was even still alive, did he recognize how far inside his defences she had pierced.

Then shouting broke out at the hangars, and he skipped across two rooftops to look.

There was a broad landing field before the hangar mouth, although all the Firebug orthopters were safely within caverns specially dug out of the rock by acid and engines. The lamps that gave onto this open space were harsh and uncompromising, the bright white glare of some chemical reaction that burned flamelessly with a constant hiss and crackle; open fire was not something anybody wanted close to all that fuel-powered machinery.

For some reason the great metal doors were already partly open, but there were more guards there than Laszlo had ever seen before, at least thirty of the city militia, so te Riel's warning had plainly been one among many. They were under attack.

Or not quite yet, but it looked as though the fighting would start off any moment, for a large band of Scorpion-kinden had just rolled on to the scene, a mismatched two score of hulking villains in a ragbag of armour, most of them armed with great-swords or long axes or halberds. They outnumbered the militia, though not by so very many, and they were likely the better warriors fighting one on one. As against that, the Solarnese had a fair stock of their little crossbows to hand. Alarmed challenges rang into the night.

Scorpions could mean the Empire or the Spiderlands, or pretty much anyone else, for they were inveterate mercenaries. However, getting a mob like this into the city – in twos and threes perhaps – and then organizing them was a feat in itself.

The Scorpions were shouting back, generic insults about Solarnese manhood and their mothers. They were plainly not about to commit themselves just yet, and more militia would surely be on the way even now to reinforce the defenders. *So what are they hoping to accomplish* . . . and Laszlo swore to himself because he should have thought of watching out for whoever was using this as a distraction, and he had become too absorbed in the mummery itself.

Too late now, surely – whoever it was, they must be inside. He looked anyway, though, his sharp eyes raking the darkness where the hissing lamps left off, and he was rewarded by the sight of a small figure slipping by and into the hangar, on foot and cloaked, but he knew her.

But who's she chasing? What's the Empire's plan?

Blow it sky high, came the instant thought and, try as she might, Liss could not stop that. She was Inapt. The only thing she could do with a bomb would be to set it off inadvertently.

I, however . . . and, with that thought, Laszlo was airborne, streaking down towards the hangars.

Liss had crept in, of course, because the Solarnese were more than used to airborne subterfuge. Laszlo was spotted immediately. Some of the militia loosed their crossbows at him, and he lurched sideways in the air as they did, trusting to his instincts to keep him out of the path of their bolts. Others, because they had been keeping their weapons trained, their fingers on the triggers, loosed at the Scorpions by reflex, just one or two, but it was enough.

Even as another dozen militia arrived, wondering what all the noise was about, the Scorpions charged. It was an ill-thought-out piece of theatre but one that Laszlo took full advantage of, by darting past the militia towards the hangar mouth.

The first blast came just as he dipped down to enter, and the hot breath of it caught him and tried to throw him out into the night again. He fought it furiously, seeing a lazy wash of fire roll out of the opening. He might have been screaming Liss's name.

He fell to the ground, feeling his hair and clothes on the point of smouldering. Another explosion roared at the far end of the hangar, tongues of flame licking out, and a dozen separate fires inside illuminating the compact shapes of the fliers. He saw Solarnese mechanics running past, beating at themselves. Others were helplessly trying to drag one of the machines out, loyalty to their trade taken to the point of suicide. Laszlo dashed past them, the air about him gusting hot and hotter, searching in the dark and the leaping orange light of the place for Liss.

He spotted her, for she was beyond hiding. She stood surrounded by fires, bright and alive in their glow. The picture would stay with him for all his days: Liss, the flames, the stacked barrels of mineral oil that was meant to fuel the Solarnese air force.

She stretched out a hand almost playfully and it was wreathed in fire instantly. Laszlo screamed, because he had not taken it all in, and he could not. It was beyond his understanding.

Like a hunting dragonfly flown from the wrist, the flames leapt from her to one of the Firebugs, and instantly the silk of its wings was ablaze, turning to cinders and setting the wood of its body alight. A moment later, Liss herself was engulfed, even as Laszlo tried to fight his way towards her, yelling her name until the fumes choked him.

But when the flames dispersed, she was still there, her clothes burned away from her but her skin still perfect, rosy with energy. Naked and beautiful, she turned and saw him, and smiled as the world caught fire all around.

He wanted her then, despite anything. The jolt that went through him as their eyes met was one of pure unfettered desire.

She blew him a kiss, and he felt the distinct heat of it against his face, then the barrels blew.

The force of the explosion caught up his small frame and threw him end over end out of the hangar.

Elsewhere in Solarno, Major Garvan awaited the report of her key agent. From the open window of her miserable garret she had heard the great explosions rolling across the rooftops like thunder, and she knew that the plan she had painstakingly put together had finally paid off. Yet another triumph for careful, patient Army Intelligence, and no sign yet of the Rekef swanning in to steal the glory. Oh, surely, by the time the final word had been passed by General Brugan to the Empress, no doubt the Rekef Outlander would be the ones holding the reins, but Garvan's own superiors, the army colonels who decided her future, would know the truth.

She stood and checked her appearance in the mirror on the back of her door, cautious as always. Unlike so many of her peers, victory had never been an excuse for carelessness. Far too many operations went wrong just as everything seemed to be safely in hand.

There was a flurry of wings and she went to sit behind her battered old desk, all business. Despite the pauper's life she led, compared to their own profligacy and waste, she never let her agents forget who was in control. And especially this one, whose mercurial nature almost outweighed her considerable usefulness.

Grinning from ear to ear, Lissart squeezed in through the narrow window wearing clothes made for a someone noticeably bigger. By looks just a Fly-kinden girl with unusual red hair, she was of course another kinden entirely, a vagrant visitor to the Empire from foreign lands. Intelligence work challenged her, and Garvan knew she worked for that incentive more than for pay, but she was a wild and whimsical creature, always at the fullest extent of her leash.

'You're out safely, then,' Garvan remarked, a neutral opening. 'Report.'

'Nobody's flying anything out of those hangars any time soon.' Lissart set herself down on the ramshackle desk, which creaked under even her minimal weight. 'I got a count of the machines. One missing, out on some errand or other, but your boys were making with the noisy outside, so I reckoned it was time.'

'Not *my* boys,' Garvan noted. She loathed joint operations, and this one had been more knife-edge than most, because coordinating with Intelligence's current business partner in this part of the world had been a nightmare of conflicting standards – the Empire's and Garvan's own high ones contrasted with the apparently random ones she had been forced to work within. 'How did the Scorpions get on, anyway?'

'When everything went up, they all legged it.' Lissart's grin grew even wider, if that was possible, until Garvan wondered if the top of her head was going to fall off. 'You should have got yourself over there. Was a beautiful sight, I can tell you. *Phwoosh!*' Her arms described the majesty of the explosions. Lissart was a cracked enough creature at the best of times, but once things started catching fire, she became a regular mad-woman. Garvan didn't know whether that was a personal trait or one that applied to all of her pyromaniac kinden.

'Some of us had other business to tie up.' It was true: Garvan had not been short of visitors earlier that night, enough to strain her feigned identity here, but that was not an issue any more. 'How's your cover identity?'

For just a moment, Lissart was not smiling. 'Burned,' she said shortly, but without the usual relish.

Garvan chose to ignore that. 'Solarno is just about wrapped up, so I have orders for you.' She recognized the look that came immediately to Lissart's face. 'New cover in the Spiderlands. We need agents there who can talk their talk enough to fit in, but can handle a little sabotage when the time comes – meaning your speciality.' She had assumed the chance of setting some-thing else alight would overcome that sullen, stubborn expression, but now the little woman was shaking her head.

'Send me north, send me west, Major. Not the Spiderlands. Solarno's as close as I go.' The smile was back, but it was harder. 'They're too sharp there, and there's a colony of my kinden over at Firewater. The Solarno Spiders are backward, and I didn't have to deal with them much either, but the real thing . . . not me, Major.'

Garvan nodded, all business. Inside she was unsurprised. She had not worked with Lissart before this Solarno operation, but the woman's former handler had warned Garvan that the little Firefly tended to forget she was the Empire's to command.

'We've already prepared a cover for you,' she explained patiently. 'You won't need to be hobnobbing with the Aristoi, just their servants, keeping an eye on other agents – nothing so different to here. Perhaps, in time, I can find you a place in the Lowlands. Believe me, that front will be moving fast. Maybe Collegium, when the Second takes up where it left off. For now, though, you're just what we need down south.'

'No chance.' Lissart folded her arms, leaning back on nothing at all as though there was a chair behind her.

'Lissart,' said Garvan, in her Major Garvan voice that had brought into line tougher nuts than this small firestarter, 'I have orders. I don't argue with orders, neither do you.'

'Major, let's you and me make a deal,' Lissart suggested. 'Let's put that "orders" business behind us for now. You get me a nice post in the Lowlands – somewhere there's action but not an actual war front – and I'll play coy about you.'

Nothing registered in Garvan immediately. 'Lissart, orders are orders. There's no more to it than that. I need you on the *Shifting Gerontis* before dawn.'

'I'm serious, Major. See me right, and I can be discretion itself about just how you make your face up every morning, *sister.*'

For an instant, Garvan thought she would die, her heart jumped so hard. *No, no, no,* but the Fly-looking woman was grinning full-strength again, delighted with her own cleverness. 'What?' she continued, as though it was just a game and not the sum total of Garvan's life she had just disembowelled. 'Fool all the Wasps you want, but you didn't think I wouldn't be able to *tell,* did you?'

Garvan sat there like a statue for one second more, the shock charging back and forth in her head, looking for a way out, and then her left hand flew up, a bolt of golden fire lancing from the palm.

It caught Lissart across the chest, knocking her flat onto the desk but doing nothing more than scorch her stolen clothes. She propped herself up on one elbow, actually laughing, 'You don't think that's any good against *me*?'

Garvan's dagger tore into her side savagely, raising a gratifying scream from the other woman. Not a straight death blow, but perhaps a slow death anyway. *Agent Lissart lost doing her duty at the Solarno hangars*; some part of her mind was already composing the report.

Fire exploded across the desk, Garvan's coded notes and reports catching light instantly. The major recoiled across the room, flipping the desk over to keep the flames away. She had a brief, smoke-blurred glimpse of Lissart's small form lurching at the window, not flying out so much as just rolling over the sill for the two-storey drop to the ground. The room was on fire now, leaping orange flames licking about the floor and walls, dancing about the window frame. Garvan cursed and made for the door, battering it open and stumbling down the stairs, beating at the few embers that had landed on her tunic or in her hair. *Kill Lissart, protect the secret.* It was the only thing on her mind.

Laszlo dropped from the sky, diving steeply even as the small body plunged from the window, and there was nothing in his mind at all, no plan, no opinion. Only the necessity of action consumed him.

She had been stabbed, he saw, her hands weltering red as they clutched at the wound. He was not surgeon enough to know if anything could be done, but he had seen people die from less. The sound she was making was appalling, just a wordless sobbing whimper that yanked at him repeatedly, filling his ears.

She should not have been able to move, but she kicked away from the wall of the house, even as flames crackled above and embers ghosted down over them both. She was trying to get away, still. Whoever had knifed her must be coming.

Who it was, how many there were . . . Laszlo could not risk a fight, but the alternative almost seemed worse.

He grabbed her, too panicked to be gentle, one hand about her body, under her arm, the other clasped over her mouth. She writhed away when he touched her, not a human reaction but that of an animal in pain. *She burned the hangars. She sold out Solarno, She tried to kill me.* But all he wanted to do was get her somewhere safe.

He hauled her up, and she bucked in his arms, screaming against his palm, but her own hands still clasped tightly to her rent side.

Too heavy to fly, but he gave his wings their head anyway, kicking backwards too fast across the street and down a rubbish-strewn alley with the bleeding girl in his arms, always at the point of falling, his Art catching him from moment to moment.

He dropped and froze, clutching her to him, trying to stifle her weeping. Someone was there, and he could see them clearly – a lean Wasp with sword drawn and hand ready to sting, and when had he last seen just a *single* Wasp? There might be a dozen within easy shout.

'Quiet, quiet,' he whispered in Liss's ear, and she whipped her head about to look at him, cracking him across the nose. The expression in her eyes was fractured, shards of everything in there: guilt, pain, fear of him, terror of dying, but he told himself he could read something else there that looked on him more kindly. *If the Wasps want her dead, we need her alive.* But that was a fiction for the report he would have to make some day. *I want her alive* was the whole truth.

'Lissart!' the Wasp yelled, voice surprisingly high, and then went off in the wrong direction, blind as all his kind at night. Laszlo took his chance and bundled Liss – Lissart? – up in his arms. He had to take his hand from her mouth to do it, but there was no screaming, only a gasping, retching sound that made him sick to the stomach.

She got out his name somewhere in there, he was sure of it.

He ran, wings flashing in and out as needed to keep himself on his feet. She was a dead weight in his arms, but he was pelting downhill for the docks and for an old deck surgeon whose acquaintance he had made. Halfway there, Lissart got an arm about his neck, strength enough still to hold on to him, however weakly. Her eyes were open, locked on his face.

He got into sight of the bay, and skidded to a painful halt in spite of himself. 'Oh mother,' he heard himself say.

The docks were a chaos of running and shouting – militia and Solarnese citizens dashing back and forth without plan. The waters of the Exalsee beyond held a host of sails, tall and pale in the moonlight. It was not the armada that had recently come against Collegium, but Laszlo knew a Spider-kinden fleet when he saw one.

Breighl was right; it's not the Wasps . . .

Two of the ships were already moored, with Spider soldiers spilling unopposed onto the quays with bows and spears. Laszlo had no time for any of it. His feet took up again towards the surgeon's door, even though the old Bee-kinden might already have fled. He had no other option just now. Lissart laughed then, a wrenched and strangled sound. She clutched him tight with one arm, but the other pointed up and past his shoulder. Even as she did, he registered the sound: distant engines coming closer, and that would awake Solarno far quicker than any panic at the docks.

He got to the surgeon's door and kicked at it furiously, until the squat, dark old mariner threw it open, an axe in one hand to repel boarders, To his credit, despite the fleet, despite what else was surely coming, when he saw Lissart he took her from Laszlo with practised care and carried her inside.

Only then did Laszlo turn. The Wasp orthopters were hard

to see as they scattered across the sky over Solarno, but they were escorting a handful of airships which caught the moonlight well enough. There were some Solarnese fliers up there too, the free pilots, but with the Firebugs burning there would be no unified civic response. The Solarnese government was no doubt already breaking into arguing factions even as their city was invaded from north and south. Solarno was about to become a battleground.

Fourteen

General Brugan was afraid.

The world feared the Empire, and the Empire feared the Rekef, which in turn feared its lord and master, Brugan himself. His subordinates would not have believed that he himself might twitch and turn through sleepless nights, or wake suddenly from terrible, all-too-plausible dreams. General Brugan feared, too, and what he was afraid of was the Empress.

And yet he was drawn to her – fear becoming somehow an attracting quality. She was beautiful, and she had a fire no other woman possessed, and there were moments, gazing on her in daylight, when he loved her so much that he would give himself up to that fire and burn on it, agony and ecstasy together.

He had made her, he knew. He had been the first man of any influence to cast his lot behind her treasonous campaign. When she had assumed the throne, it had been by his hand, and he had looked to be rewarded.

The Empire had never been ruled by a woman before – she had needed a man beside her to reassure the traditionalists. In the end she had taken a regent, a former Rekef man, and former traitor, Thalric by name. The wretch had taken the place that Brugan had prepared for himself, but at the time Brugan had told himself that there was nevertheless time for all things to come to pass.

Thalric had gone from puppet – token male to sit beside the

throne – to a companion of the Imperial bedchamber, and only through his own reaction to that knowledge had Brugan realized that his feelings towards Empress Seda were more than simply ambitious. He discovered that his intention to control the Empress had become one of possessing her. Then Thalric had deserted again during the Rekef operation in Khanaphes, which was a disappointment to Brugan only because of the effort he himself had invested in seeing Thalric left dead and buried under the ruin of an entire civilization. Still, with the upstart bastard out of the way, he had thought perhaps the Empress would take a more suitable partner.

By then, Seda's charm and acumen had worked sufficient wonders to ensure that she no longer needed a token regent, but her hungers were no less fierce, and Brugan could still recall the cold satisfaction he had felt when she had invited him into her bed.

Could still recall . . . or perhaps say: *Was unable to forget.*

He lived two separate lives now. He was an Apt man, rational and sensible, who during the day could look at Seda and know that all he was seeing was her extraordinary charisma, her force of personality that twisted people around to her way of thinking. What else could it be? She was simply a natural leader, gifted beyond her years, well educated and advised.

After dark, however, the dreadful certainty would grow on him that, yes, she was all these things but she was more. Then she would send for him, and his feet would walk him to the Imperial chambers, desire and hunger making a slave of him. He would drink with her, the salt red wine, and in the ante-chamber would lie the ruin of some slave or servant, or some courtier who had misspoken or plotted against the crown. He had stopped looking now, since the first time he had recognized a victim. He was a general of the Rekef, inured to death and torture, but the expressions on those exsanguinated faces, the contortions of their pale limbs, affected him somewhere subconscious and primal. There had been a time when his kinden had lived in huts and feared the dark for good reason.

But he needed her, though. It was not love any more. His loins and his heart were chained to her, leaping at her least command. The base man in him was enslaved, while the Rekef general railed. He could not live in such a manner. He needed to redress the balance in their relationship and – just as to get rid of Thalric he had engineered the sacking of a city – so, to take back the reins of his private life, he needed to recreate the Empire's hierarchy with himself at the top, the power behind the throne, just as it always should have been.

There were too many close to the throne now who were beyond his influence. The Empress chose advisers that Brugan did not know, or she bought loyalty with favour and promotions, or sought the counsel of foreigners such as all those Moths and other mystic rabble who had become so common at court recently. Brugan had been elbowed further and further away from the commanding position he had intended for himself.

He had the Rekef, though, and he had others too, who felt they were owed more for the work they had put into bringing Seda's Empire about. This would be no different from any other large-scale intrigue he had been involved in. Had he not master-minded her accession to the throne? Taking the substance of her power from her should be easier than plotting in the shadow of her paranoid brother.

Whenever he made such promises to himself, something twisted inside him and fear roamed the hinterlands of his mind, raising its jaws to the moon and rattling its wings. Seda was not just a sharp young girl, it howled. She *knew* things, *saw* things, She had a power over people – himself included – that was neither Art nor skill but something else. The fact that she drank blood, he could have put down to the casual cruelty appropriate to the Imperial throne, could perhaps even have made of it a virtue, symbolic of the Empire's own thirst for conquest. Some traitor part of his mind whispered that it was no mere whim of hers, or even a simple crazed need – a little madness did not necessarily make for a worse Empress – and that she drank blood because it gave her *power* somehow, that it fuelled her as surely as Nemean mineral oil fuelled the Air Corps' new orthopters.

But Brugan was a rational man, believing in the physical world, and when he turned the lamps up high he could banish such subversive speculation and continue drawing up his list of who must disappear, who must see the inside of an interrogation room before being politely asked to change their allegiance, or who must be awarded a key post. It was a simple thing for a man of his abilities to turn poacher and devise just the sort of treason the Rekef Inlander was supposed to guard against.

Tonight. It must start tonight. She had not called for him, and the lamps were bright, and he had sent out a summons to those that he considered his allies, men who would cling to the hem of his cloak as he elevated himself, who were wronged or ambitious or just plain greedy, but men who, most of all, were *his*.

It held an odd mirror to the gathering that the Empress had presided over earlier, such was Esmail's first impression. Many of the faces were the same: there was General Brugan, and there, as if to balance Harvang's gross physicality, was the pinpoint neatness of Colonel Vecter, who had also brought along a couple of aides. Knowles Bellowern of the Consortium was there, too, the only non-Wasp and looking wholly unsettled by the business, whatever was going on. There was no Colonel Lien of the Engineers, no army generals – they were out in the field after all – but another half-dozen had taken their place, men younger than Brugan but old enough to have chosen a side and invested their power in a particular way of life. Ostrec's memories allowed Esmail to recognize many of them by sight: Rekef mostly, but with a couple from the Consortium and one who was a steward at the palace.

They took their places soberly. Brugan had not called them to his offices within the palace, the heart of the Rekef, but to this anonymous townhouse owned by some mid-ranking Wasp family who were conveniently absent. The visitors had retired to one of the inner rooms and, at Brugan's nod, the windows had been twice covered, with shutters and then with felt, so that the room became close and uncomfortable and dark.

Esmail was not concerned about the dark. From behind Ostrec's blank face he was able to read a great deal from those around him. Harvang was chewing at something distractedly, for comfort more than sustenance. Vecter cleaned his spectacles briskly, the small, sure movements of his hands revealing his anxiety. People shuffled, glanced at the door or at each other. Knowles Bellowern had a pipe in his hand, the scent of tallum pollen fragrant from it, but he kept it unlit.

Ostrec would have felt alarmed, Esmail discovered. He would have shown none of it, but Harvang's deputy had been a sharp enough man to know that this gathering, in this place, portended nothing good. Oh, opportunity perhaps, but these men were not natural allies, and Ostrec was not a major player himself. All too easy to be crushed between the wheels.

'You know me,' Brugan began. 'My interests are the Empire's interests. I am the benchmark of loyalty, the defender of the throne. As my predecessor, Rekef himself, served the first Emperor, so I have served the third, and now I serve our first Empress.' He was not looking at any of them directly, but staring down at the floor. Esmail exhumed Ostrec's memories and saw that this was not the fierce and forthright Brugan that the man remembered.

'I have sounded you all out at one time or another,' the Rekef general continued quietly. 'You may not have realized it. A conversation, hidden watchers, an investigation into your finances or your associations. No man reaches your high stations without being vetted, and you all know people who failed that test. It is my *job*, as leader of the Rekef Inlander, to ensure the purity of purpose of those in office. The Empire must be led by those who will best serve it.'

He was skirting the point, and they all knew it. Looking covertly from face to face, Esmail saw that most of them there knew already what that point would be. The tension between the men gathered there was almost audible.

'Empress Seda, the only living kin of our beloved Emperor Alvdan the Second, is but a girl,' Brugan said softly. 'She has proved that she is fit to rule, and there is none left who denies her that. Yet still she may be misled. She may fall into undesirable company, give her ear to those who do not have her best interests at heart. We are patriots; we know full well the demands of Empire. When we see foreigners and slaves gain influence with the very crown and forget their place, then does it not befit us to act? It does.' His answer to his own rhetoric came slightly too quickly, as if fearing a dissenting voice. 'I have brought you here tonight because I trust you to do what is right. The Empress must be protected.' On that word, something almost broke in his voice, and everyone there contrived to ignore it.

What does he know? For it was evident that something had dented Brugan's Apt composure sufficiently hard that he could no longer entirely blot out the truth. This was no mere coup, therefore. This was the head of the Rekef trying to master and control something he could not understand. And yet, and yet . . . hearing Brugan talk, Esmail could sense the huge contradictions in the man, his thoughts, his feelings.

Anyone signing up on this ship will regret the voyage, he considered, and it was only a shame that he must play Ostrec's role here, and become a part of this business for mean ambition. Looking about the room he confirmed that, Brugan's lofty words aside, every man there was considering how he himself might best profit from the Empire, most especially an Empire where Seda's power was considerably curtailed.

'There are two paired weapons available to us,' Brugan elaborated. 'It is our duty to remove those close to the throne who are unfit to sully it with their touch. I have some names for the list, and I have no doubt that each of you may have more.' The first incentive to treason: a free hand to dispose of their rivals, or at least those rivals not present in this room. 'At the same time,' Brugan went on, 'we will install our own people close to the Empress: as her counsellors, in her retinue of servants, everywhere she goes. When she seeks advice and aid, it must be to us she turns, no matter whose face she finds. We are the heart of the Empire, after all. Where will she find sounder counsel than ours?'

His gaze pinpointed each of them in turn, seeing how they bore up to the weight of his plan. Esmail decided that one, perhaps two of the people in this room would be found wanting – and shortly thereafter found dead, or not found at all. The extent of Brugan's treason, however he might dress it up, was such that no faint hearts could be allowed to go on beating once they knew of his schemes.

'Go make your lists,' the Rekef general instructed them. 'Men to frighten, men to blackmail and control, men to be made to disappear. We must cut out the rot, and if a little healthy flesh goes with it, well, many a surgeon has made the same decision. Beyond that, give me names of those that I should bring into the Empress's company, as her immediate retinue. The position is not without risk, but we will need such people in place.' He paused a moment, and then looked directly at Esmail. 'She's asked after your aide, Harvang.'

Even as Brugan said it, Esmail was thinking back to that unknown Moth Skryre who had set him on this path and was wondering, *How much did you know, back then? Did you even foresee this?* The conclusion was inescapable. What surprised him more were the corpulent colonel's murmured words as he stepped forward. 'You think you're up to this, Ostrec? She's quite mad, they say. Mad, and with the power of life and death over all of us. You understand the stakes?' The almost parental concern was grotesque on the man's face.

'I'm equal to the task, sir. Don't worry about me,' said Esmail in Ostrec's voice.

'Well then, my man here will do us proud,' Harvang spoke out. 'Besides, he's a fair-looking youngster. You never know, the Empress might be looking for some companionship.' His leer was vile.

Esmail braced himself. It was impossible to tell whether Harvang had simply not registered Brugan's own conflicting feelings about Seda – which were screamingly obvious to Esmail himself – or whether the fat man might be playing Brugan deliberately, engaged in some power game of his own against his superior who, of course, could not admit his emotional position. Whatever the reason, and Esmail was alarmed that he could simply not tell, there was a moment's blank silence between Brugan and Harvang before the former nodded briefly.

'I'll see that he's sent for,' the general noted, and Esmail could only hope that Harvang's games weren't about to get him killed.

Of course, death at the hands of a jealous General Brugan might be the least of his worries. The Empress's sheer magical might had already rattled him, and now he was going to meet it head-on. His own magic was one of subterfuge only, distraction, misdirection and disguise. He had a great deal of skill but relatively little power. He would not wish to go before a Skryre of the Moths, for example, or a Spider-kinden Manipula, and ply his trade. They would quickly sniff the magic on him, and have the training and experience to unravel his little spells and look on his true face. The Empress, though: if she had a fraction of their skill then she would crack his deceptions like a snail shell. He could only hope that he could deflect and divert all that thundering strength, preserving his masks in the teeth of the gale.

There was more business, and Ostrec's ears took it all in, the anatomy of Brugan's fifth column being discussed in summary detail. Esmail himself barely registered it, storing it for later. He was more concerned with planning ahead for when he himself should meet Seda's cool stare.

He was frightened, and he would defy anyone with a little knowledge of the old ways not to be. There was something else there, too, though. The servant, Shoel Jhin, had spoken of a return to the Days of Lore, a resurgence of magic. Esmail had marked him down for mad, but if there was even the slightest chance of such a thing, if even one part in a hundred of the way the world used to be could be transplanted into the present, then what was going on here was bigger than the games of Skryres, and perhaps Esmail's instructions did not mean so much any more. After all, he was beyond scrutiny now, beyond interference. What if the Empress was better fitted to be his mistress than the Moths of Tharn were to give him orders?

'Farsphex,' was all he said, as he showed it to her.

The Wasp pilot who had been assigned to Pingge was named Scain, and he was the most cadaverous of his kinden that she had ever met: a lean, gangling creature who seemed ill-suited to be any sort of soldier, let alone someone trusted with some top-secret Imperial plan. Like his commander, Aarmon, he spoke very little, although his voice betrayed the remnants of a North-Empire accent, the suggestion of an upbringing amongst the hill tribes, which made his current technically sophisticated post even more of a mystery, of course.

The Farsphex, however, was *all* technical sophistication. Pingge was no aviatrix, but she had a grasp of technology that went a little beyond what was strictly necessary for a factory worker, and she knew she was looking at something different, even if she could not quite work out what was unusual. Before her was a long-bodied orthopter, the wings folded at an angle back along its curved body, the enclosed cockpit sitting over a pair of what she guessed were the rotary piercers she had heard of, brought into the Empire's arsenal after the original Solarno campaign. The Farsphex was a big machine, half as long again as the Spearflights that had been shoved to the back of the hangar, and its belly seemed overlarge, pregnant with some manner of machinery, or something. More, she could see that there was something odd about its wings, just by looking at it. The designers had managed to give it an air of elegance, despite all that, but it was plainly a different breed to the older orthopters standing nearby.

She took a few cautious steps closer, then glanced back at Scain.

'Go ahead,' he nodded briefly, and she let her wings flurry her up to the curving top of the machine's hull. Thoughtfully, she touched the blade of one of the twin propellers there. Pingge would be the first to admit that her knowledge of aviation was limited, but she hadn't thought orthopters needed those.

Scain stalked over to the flier's side, running his hand along it in a gesture that said far more than the words he used. She thought that he would open the cockpit, but instead he popped a hatch in the Farsphex's side.

'See,' he said, pointing. She hung her head over the opening, looking upside down into the cramped interior. There was a brief crawlspace that would take Scain to the pilot's seat, but immediately inside the hatch was room for someone else, though only someone small because there, on a hinged arm, was a reticule. It was the same toy that she had been training with all this time, but seeing it in this unfamiliar setting sent a chill down her spine.

'In,' Scain directed, and he went squirming into the orthopter's innards, all elbows and knees as he wriggled through the crawlspace, then contorted himself to get into his seat.

She hesitated at the hatch's mouth, until another preremptory 'In!' from Scain forced her hand. A moment later she was sitting before the reticule, just as she had so often before, but the walls of the Farsphex's hull crushed in on her from all sides. Below her, the machine was missing a good area of floor, enough for her to slip through if she was careless, allowing the reticule's impartial eyes to view the terrain below. At the moment, all its angles and mirrors served only to give her eyepiece a good close view of the hangar floor ahead of the machine's nose.

The hatch was shut from outside with a slam, making her jump. All at once she was enclosed by darkness, but Fly-kinden were used to that, from the interconnected underground communities they favoured, or the cramped tenements they were shunted into in the cities.

'Sir, what's going on now?' she asked, giving her voice all proper deference.

'Test flight,' Scain told her. 'Live one.' A moment later and he was reaching back down the crawlspace to tug at her sleeve, making her jump. 'Wear this.'

It was a shackle, a metal band attached to the hull by a chain. She stared at Scain wordlessly, and he clipped it about her ankle, turning the key awkwardly, one-handed in the confined space.

'What . . . ? Sir?' she got out, her voice tight.

'Stop you falling out.' It was perhaps the longest single sentence he had said to her, and all it told her was that he was a bad liar. For a moment she looked him in the eyes, under the poor light that came up from the aperture. Instead of staring her down, as a member of the superior race should do, he just shrugged and looked away, plainly feeling a little guilt.

So they don't trust us. It was a bitter thought. 'I'm an Imperial citizen, you know,' she complained, before she could stop herself. 'I know about duty. It's not as though I'll just desert through the . . . the whatever this hole's called, the moment we're in the air. I have *family* in the city.'

Scain just shrugged, twisting his way back into the cockpit. Pingge stared at the shackle unhappily, but in the back of her mind she thought of Gizmer and some of the others who were perhaps less diligent servants of the Empire.

She wondered how Kiin was getting on. She would not trade Scain for Aarmon, certainly: the leader of the new pilots scared her.

A moment later she felt the engine turn over and fire, sounding as loud as any factory machine. The Farsphex jolted and swayed as it was pushed out into the open air by the ground crew, and then Scain made a kind of hissing sound and the wings were abruptly unleashed, clapping down towards the ground and springing the machine into the air at a sickening angle.

She would get used to it all in time, save that part: every time her machine – she would grow possessive of it very soon – took to the air there would be that stomach-lurching moment when she nearly sent her lunch down through the aperture. Somewhere amidst all the trade-offs that had gone into the Farsphex's finely tuned design, a graceful takeoff had been judged expendable.

A moment later the city roofs were rushing past, and then were gone, their speed being far greater than she had anticipated; the rhythm of their flight was steady rather than the furious beat of an orthopter's wings.

'Ready!' It was Scain's voice, and she guessed she had already missed hearing the word once, against the engine's racket. For a moment she did not know what he meant, but then her training took over and she had her eye against the reticule.

They were heading out across farmland now, towards a broken-backed range of hills north-west of the city. The eye-piece showed her a magnification of the view she might have if she were clinging beneath the orthopter's sharp nose, flanked by the rotary piercers.

'What targets?' she called forward, forgetting her 'sir'. Even as she asked, she spotted a plume of smoke, a fire set out on one of the hilltops. The wheeling, unsteady view of the reticule showed her several others rising beyond it.

She fumbled the first one, failing to get the trigger switch released, despite a faultless record in training. Scain said nothing, but guided the flier towards their next target.

'Remember your navigation?' he called back, his voice sounding a little taut as he concentrated on the steering, and she realized this was as much a test for him as for her.

'Probably, sir.' She had her tongue between her lips as she focused, a habit from childhood, watching the smoking target draw nearer as Scain swung towards it.

'We'll be flying nights as well; you'll need to direct me to the target. Bear that in mind.' The words seemed to exhaust him and he hunched over the stick.

And away! And she got it right this time, and felt something solid clunk directly below her seat, something leaving the belly of the flier. *And that ought to be spot on the mark*, she decided, hoping that she would get to go back over the same ground herself to see how she'd—

There was a crack and a bang from behind them and she would have feared something onboard had exploded had the sound not been so distant. She was so rattled that she missed the next target entirely. 'What was that?'

'*Live* flight,' Scain stressed. 'Real bombs.'

Pingge missed the target following that as well, because she could not make her fingers move on the trigger, even though she had the reticule lined up on it perfectly. *Bombs*, she was thinking numbly, *but of course bombs. What else? And who but a Fly-kinden would fit in here with the reticule, and who else would have the eyes for that night-flying Scain said about. Oh, someone has been thinking long and hard about this.*

And: *What about the farmers that live down there? Did they clear them out? Did they even warn them that the air force would be blowing them up today?*

And: *They're going to make me drop bombs on people, real people.* For a moment she felt ill, thinking of all that training, when it had been a game.

But Scain shouted at her, and she flicked the trigger seconds-perfect and sent another bomb spiralling away from the under-carriage, imagining it obliterating the bonfire target that some uncomprehending slave had set out.

Her name. What he had shouted was her name. She had not realized that he actually knew it.

It changed things, somehow. The Imperial high command didn't know her name, and it thought she needed to be chained to the hull to stop her flying off in terror. Right then she didn't give a bent pin for the Empress or her generals, but she didn't want to let Scain down.

She got the next three bombs off, all within tolerance of their marks, and then the Wasp was turning them round, not heading for the city but for somewhere else.

'Good,' was all he said, but she felt a curious bond with him: who else was there, after all, but Scain and herself in this hollow shell in the upper air?

He brought them down at an airstrip a few miles outside Capitas, and there he unlocked the shackle, and showed her how to open the hatch from within. She dropped out onto the packed dirt of the strip, and the first thing she saw was another dozen Farsphex arranged in a rough line, with hers on the end. There was a scattering of the new pilots and their Fly-kinden hench-men and henchwomen around, and she could hear the drone of other machines still in the air.

A curiously proprietorial feeling came over her, regarding it all. This was more than the factory, where she had been just a small part of a humdrum machine, a tiny ball bearing helping the Empire on its way. This was *special*, and she and her fellows had become an elite. Looking about her at the busy airstrip she could feel herself and Kiin and all the others help build the future right then, right there. In that moment all of her qualms about whoever might be below the bombs she was preparing to drop were banished.

Fifteen

'I thought you should hear the news, that's all,' Taki explained. 'Didn't think I'd drop into the middle of a war. Looks like, no matter how fast I fly, the world moves faster.'

She was perched on a table in what the Mynans were now calling their War Room. It was the third set of walls to bear the name. The first had been in the Consensus building that had proved vulnerable prey to the Wasp incendiaries because the Mynans had not even finished its construction. A quarter of the ruling council had died in the blaze, but at least the rest had settled their differences and were now waiting on Kymene's word. The second War Room had taken an unlucky shell in the sporadic artillery bombardment that jumped about the city, cracking the walls enough that nobody wanted to stay inside. In the end, Kymene had repaired to a cellar to hold her deliberations. It reminded Stenwold of the places that the Mynan resistance had been driven to when the Wasps had held the city. That Kymene had been reduced to this already was a bad sign.

'Your news about the Wasp air force comes late,' the Mynan leader remarked acidly, looking up from her plans. Her face was ashen and drawn: no sleep and too many worries all at once.

'That's what I'm trying to tell you,' Taki shot back. 'Those lads out there, they're old news, Spearflights and regular pilots. The Empire's cooking up something special,though – new men, new machines.'

'How does this affect us *now*?' Kymene asked her. 'Even their current forces would suffice to keep control of the air.'

In fact, the Empire had at first seemed not to be pressing its advantage. For two days the bulk of the artillery had concentrated on the outer wall, which had cracked in three places and looked as though it would cease to provide a meaningful obstacle very shortly if this concerted and uncannily precise bombardment continued. The balance of the Imperial engines had been throwing incendiaries and explosive shells into the city itself, apparently at random, ensuring that nobody in Myna slept well or felt safe.

After its initial lightning raid over the city, the air force had been absent for a day. Enough orthopters had remained to defend the artillery from Mynan reprisals, as two costly air skirmishes had shown, but the Spearflights had not been seen in the sky since that first sortie. Edmon and the other pilots had been trying to cobble together whatever new fliers they could, co-opting and arming civilian machines and repairing anything that could be dragged largely intact from the ruin of the Mynan airfields and hangars. That the Empire would still possess resounding air superiority was a grim truth nobody wanted to talk about.

The Empire's actual army, the fighting men who had previously formed the first wave of offence in any Imperial attack, had sat out beyond the hills, far out of range of the Mynan artillery, whilst its greatshotters had inexorably chewed away at the wall. The Wasp assault had so far killed over a thousand Mynans and a handful of Imperial pilots. The Mynan soldiers had milled and gone to the walls and been driven back, and talked endlessly of sorties and counter-attacks, and their Maynesh Ant-kinden allies had very nearly taken to the field alone, unable to countenance simply sitting under the shadow of the Wasp artillery without any recourse at all. Still, the column from Szar was expected to arrive any day to bolster the city's numbers, and that was anticipated to trigger some manner of reversal in their situation.

Today, though, the remnants of the Szaren relief column had finally arrived, and with it an understanding of where the balance of the Imperial air force had been engaged. Caught in the open, in close formation, the Bee-kinden had been perfect targets for the Spearflights in an attack that nobody had even contemplated a few days ago. Flying machines fought flying machines; that had been the rule. Aside from dropping grenades, usually by hand, their effectiveness on the ground was strictly limited. It had been every tactician's understanding that only airships could carry a load sufficient to make a serious impact on the ground, and so the strategic effectiveness of orthopters was limited to how well they could attack or defend such slow-moving, vulnerable targets. Surely that was what the fight for Solarno had taught?

Apparently it had taught the Wasps more than their enemies. From destroying half the Mynan air force – such as it was – on the ground, the Wasps had gone on to locate and ruthlessly attack the Szaren infantry, who had no way of fighting back. Indeed, after the first pass of the orthopters, the Szaren response had been to pull in tighter for mutual defence, giving the Spearflights all the more attractive a target.

Thirty-seven Bee-kinden soldiers had reached the Mynan walls, out of almost fifteen hundred that had marched out from Szar. Many more were doubtless still alive, but scattered by the mad rout that had eventually destroyed all of their cohesion, with small parties of Bees fleeing in every direction. There would be no relief column, therefore, and the walls were about to give way.

We will sell our lives dearly, were the words that Kymene was not saying, but they were written plainly on her face whenever Stenwold looked at her. Her name and description would be known to the Imperial army, he was sure, on a list kept by some

Rekef agent who would be in charge of hunting down every known Mynan leader. No doubt she planned to die well before they had a chance to capture her.

And I'll just be an added bonus, if they get me, he considered. The two of them had spent two hours with a map of the city and a list of all the forces Myna could command, and had come to no conclusions save that, at some point, the walls would go down, and the Empire would then have the somewhat more onerous task of actually capturing the city. At that stage, Stenwold knew, the Light Airborne and their heavier ground-bound compatriots would have to get within range of whatever the Mynans could still field against them.

With his mind full of that, Taki's dire warnings about some new sort of flying machine seemed entirely irrelevant. *One crisis at a time . . .*

'The walls are already fallen in some parts, enough for them to get some infantry inside, if they wanted a pitched battle,' Kymene stated, a new report in her hand. 'We've done all we can to shore them up with earth and wood, to soften the impacts, but nothing is helping much. My engineers tell me that the walls are likely to suffer multiple breaches within a few hours of dusk, after which any further bombardment is unlikely to grant the Empire much more advantage in an attack. The Empire will have the choice of coming for us tonight, or tomorrow morning.' Her voice was flat, as though this was all happening to someone else.

'Then get some sleep,' Stenwold suggested. He wanted to say, *Why would they risk a night attack?* save that nothing this army had done so far had been from the rule book he was used to. 'Kymene . . .'

'Don't say it.'

She knew him too well, but then she was a born leader and used to reading people quickly, seeing them for what they were. He had tried several times to suggest that she had options other than dying in the teeth of the Wasp assault, and each time she had cut him off, not wanting to hear the words.

The time will come, though. Stenwold needed Kymene, because Myna needed Kymene. It had waited almost twenty years for a leader like her, after the first conquest. If she died for her city now, then Myna might languish in chains for another twenty years before anyone could free it.

Of course, the whole plan does rely on my being able to get out of the city with her. Muted by distance and depth, the *crump-crump-crump* of the Imperial greatshotters came to their ears still, patiently turning stretches of Mynan wall to rubble.

Stenwold managed a few hours of fitful sleep that night, before Taki was kicking at his bedroll to rouse him.

'Wall's down, Maker!' she told him. 'The Mynan foot are trying to get some sort of line together. Wasps could start for them at any moment, they say.'

Stenwold sat up, trying to place the discontinuity. *They can't have the wall down already because . . . the noise hasn't stopped.* The dull thump and rumble of the artillery sounded just as constant as before.

'They're still going,' he pointed out.

'But not at the *walls*,' Taki said with some urgency. 'The barrage is just creeping into the city, striking all over the place, regular as clockwork, but breaking up everywhere near the breach so they'll have a good clear run in. Me and the Mynan pilots, we're heading for our fliers, 'cos we reckon their Spear-flights are going to come in when their Airborne and foot do and, if we're not in the air to meet them, we'll just get fried on the ground.'

'Where's—?'

'Your woman, she's gone to the front, trying to get her people together.'

Stenwold cursed and lurched up. He had slept fully dressed,

but he hauled his artificer's leather on over his clothes, the workman's armour as old and battered as he himself felt. By the time he had stumbled out into the night air, Taki had already gone.

The damage to the Mynan wall was worse than he had imagined, two long stretches turned into what looked more like gravel than rubble. Some heaped masses of broken stone were now the only impediment that Myna could offer the invader, before its soldiers had to shed their own blood. The lone pillar of wall between the two gaping gashes was barely ten yards across, enough to grant a little cover to incoming enemy foot-soldiers as they closed with the city.

Even as Stenwold approached, the artillery was lighting up the night, dropping shrapnel and incendiary shells in a wide scatter across that third of Myna closest to the breach. All around him people were being evacuated from their homes, and the streets were scattered with fragments of their lives: aban-doned possessions, the sundered stones of their homes, and more than one corpse.

He found Kymene supervising what siege engines she had been able to save from the wall, finding sites for them facing the breach, both on the ground and on the rooftops. She had even called up a pair of automotives, simple steam-powered vehicles with heavy armour bolted to their fronts and with the stubby barrels of smallshotters mounted on pivots atop them. All about, drawn up in loose order, were the Mynan soldiers: men and women with Kymene's blue-grey colouring, wearing breast-plates and tall helms halved in red and black. In their hands were swords, shields, crossbows and snapbows, but the enemy attacking them so methodically had given them no targets on which to take out their frustration.

'Kymene—' Stenwold started as he approached her.

The look she turned on him was bleak and stern. 'We fight,' she said, brooking no argument.

Stenwold gestured to the sword at his hip, for all the good it would do him. Then a shell landed a hundred yards from them, the sheer sound of it almost throwing them from their feet, blocking out the screams of those who had been closer. Kymene's jaw was clenched, her hands knotted into fists. There were tears at the corners of her eyes.

'Are they coming?' Stenwold demanded, and she shook her head.

'Dawn is two hours away,' she told him, 'but maybe they'll come sooner. We have to be ready but . . .' The punctuation of the bombardment finished her sentence for her.

Stenwold remembered the first time the Wasps had taken Myna: how terrible that had seemed, with the sky full of flying soldiers, with the gates battered down and Imperial heliopters grinding through the sky, trailing random scatterings of grenades. *How little our world knew of war back then.*

He found some token shelter, the shell of a house that had already been staved in, a superstitious thought saying, *Surely they can't strike twice in the same place.* Inwardly, he was asking himself what he intended. He had come here as a gesture of solidarity, and now it seemed very likely that he would die in this attack – one more casualty unnamed and unremarked. The Empire would never know that they had killed their greatest detractor.

He had his sword and the little two-shot snapbow that Totho had made for him; experience had made of him a passable warrior, but it would be like spitting into the hurricane. Even with the thought, an incendiary lit up the night close by, enough for him to feel a wash of heat from it. This time the screaming was all too clear.

The Mynan soldiers kept moving, as though they could cheat the odds that way, clustering and scattering, passing on. The barrage was continuous, but spread over much of the city, and Stenwold thought that it probably claimed more non-combatants than soldiers. Beyond the rough line that Kymene had drawn up, the streets were clogged with the multitude who had become refugees in their own city.

Then, at dawn, the artillery pattern changed, slowly concentrating on the ground before the ruined walls, driving the Mynan defenders back, and forcing Stenwold along with them. Kymene dispersed her forces street by street, anticipating that the barrage would sweep westwards again when the Imperial forces had neared the city. After so many hours of noise and death the actual attack was finally beginning.

She was receiving reports even then, for a few enterprising Fly-kinden had flown up with telescopes to spy out the enemy formations. The news seemed hopeful. 'They're leading with automotives,' she noted. 'Some model shaped like a woodlouse, running on many legs.' Even as she said it, the shells began to land closer, and to spread out so as to fan a broader net of streets, and she hurried out to rally her men, to bring them back to the wall, and to man such of their own artillery as they still possessed. By the time Stenwold had caught up with her, the Mynan engines were already launching, catapult arms thudding forward and winding back, and the roar of leadshotters sending their missiles in shallow arcs through the breaches.

'They're in range already?' he demanded over the noise. Kymene, now atop a great cairn of stones that had once been a house, spared him only a brief glance. All around him the Mynan soldiers were readying their weapons – on the streets, from windows, on rooftops – and still the Imperial artillery dropped shells on them and behind them, a constant reminder that nobody was safe at any time.

They can't be ... they must still be marching ... I mean automotives, yes, but ... Stenwold was well aware of the uses and limitations of such machines in war. Wheeled automotives could have closed the distance that fast, but would have faltered against the banked rubble, and legged automotives were notoriously slow. Besides, unsupported vehicles could be easily

216

mobbed by infantry. It seemed impossible that Kymene's engines were doing anything but wasting ammunition.

All he could see through the breaches was a pall of dust, the same as hung everywhere in the air, choking in the throat and gritty enough that he pulled on his artificer's goggles to protect his eyes. There were a few enterprising Fly-kinden calling out to the Mynan artillerists, exhorting them to shoot, but he could not believe . . .

The first of the Wasp machines took the rubble at a terrible pace, scrabbling up and pausing at the crest, as though surveying its prey, as swift and fierce in its movements as a beast hunting. It presented a carapace of overlapping plates, with a high rounded peak at the front, sloping down towards the tail. A round shallow depression front and centre gave the impression of a single blind eye. Beneath that, closer to ground level, the stubby fingers of paired rotary piercers bristled like mouthparts.

A Mynan leadshotter gave voice close by, and Stenwold saw the missile ricochet off the automotive's armoured shell without leaving much of a dent, and then the machine was moving again, slithering down the rubble with frightening speed, the plates of its body flexing like a thing alive.

A second automotive loomed from the curtain of dust beyond it, and then a third. The Mynan engines were all loosing now, and many of the soldiers as well. Battle was joined.

Totho adjusted the focus of his glass single-handed from long practice, finger and thumb sliding the telescoping sections while the weight of the instrument was cupped in his palm. His other hand was tight on the rim of the basket, and the shadow of the observation balloon's canopy was a constant reminder of the penalties of a loose grip. In truth he should not be up here at all, horribly vulnerable to any Mynan pilot that somehow got behind the lines, only the gas-filled bulb of the balloon keeping him up, and only a long rope tether keeping him down. Not for the first time in his life, he wished that one of his parents could have bequeathed him the Art of flight, but it was rare in Beetles and unknown in Ants. In a disaster he would have to rely on the silk glider folded on his back – a cobbled-together piece of wishful thinking that was mostly untested.

He wanted to see, though. He wanted to see progress advanced yet another notch, as his machines clambered over the Mynan walls.

The day before, just ahead of dusk, Drephos had given a lecture to a cadre of Imperial officers, with General Roder at their head. The Empire had been making its preparations for a standard assault, using airborne and medium infantry, despite the groundwork already laid by more visionary men such as Colonel Ferric. And so the Colonel-Auxillian, as they still called him, had felt it necessary to step in and show them the future.

'We called them Sentinels,' the master artificer had explained, calling to mind the old heavy-infantry elites who had recently been retired from active service. 'They fill the same role, after all, and the name of the project has caused some confusion amongst enemy agents who think we're training infantry.' His voice, as ever, had been laced with a general contempt for the bulk of humanity. Totho could still picture him stalking before his audience, his robes of black and gold – the same pattern as when he had genuinely been an Imperial subject – fluttering in the breeze against the hastily erected storage sheds from which the Iron Glove conducted its work.

'You are faced with a routine problem of attackers, General. You must get your men past the walls.' The Light Airborne could have swarmed the city at any time, of course, but the Mynan soldiers were well protected and armed with crossbows and snapbows, and their defensive position would allow them to make the Wasps pay in blood for every inch of ground. 'You need to get your armour inside the walls, to meet them, heavies against heavies, where your superior numbers and troops can truly tell. Assaulting a broken wall in the face of respectably armed ranged defence remains a formidable problem, even with air superiority.'

At his gesture, Totho had relayed his signal to the engineers waiting in the shed, and an engine had started up with a metallic growl, closely followed by a clatter of armour plates.

'What you need,' Drephos's voice had lifted over the sound, 'is something to force the issue!'

On cue, the Sentinel had picked its way out of the shed at a careful, deliberate pace. To a man, the Imperial officers had taken a few steps back as its tall, blind-eyed prow had quested in their direction. They had never seen anything like it, Totho knew. He had watched with pride as its ten legs had moved in steady, complex patterns to haul it along the ground.

After the initial shock at the machine's appearance, there had been those amongst Roder's more traditional officers who complained that the vehicle would be easy prey for Mynan leadshotters, or that it would ground itself amidst the rubble, and how *heavy* it must be, how slow – could it even keep up with walking infantry? Roder had let them cavil and had kept his own counsel, his eyes only on Drephos.

Now Totho saw the truth of it for himself, and his heart leapt with pride: to be a member of the Iron Glove, to be an artificer, to be one of the *Apt* whose world had built this glory. Ahead of the Imperial infantry, ahead even of the Airborne, the Sentinels tore up the ground towards Myna. Enemy artillery burst about them, landing mostly behind them. They were as swift and agile as animals, the line of their armoured backs flexing and rippling as they jolted over the landscape.

'When perfecting the greatshotters, we were forced to devise a new material to withstand the concentrated forces involved,' Drephos had explained to Roder and his officers. 'We call it spun steel, and it is several times stronger than Solarnese aviation steel, at a fraction of the weight. At the same time, the

Sentinel's legs are mediated by a ratiocinator, meaning that the handler does not have to worry about adjusting each one individually. He simply tells the machine where to *go*.'

'Handler?' Roder had demanded, staring up at the great sightless eye set into the thing's peaked prow. 'Driver or pilot, surely.'

'Handler seems appropriate, somehow,' had come Drephos's dry response.

For a moment the three machines were poised on the heaped rubble of Myna's walls, a colossal triumvirate regarding its subjects. The Mynans were not so reticent. All their hoarded artillery was loosing, catapults and ballistae, leadshotters, even the scrapshotters were pelting the armoured titans with hundredweights of jagged metal. The lead Sentinel rocked from side to side under the impacts, its legs spreading wider beneath its carapace, sliding slightly on the loose stone. Stenwold watched, waiting for the barrage to tell on them, for that armour to crumple under the hammer. *They move so fast*, was all he could think. *They cannot be so strong.* And yet the machines weathered the assault with what seemed like disdain.

The leftmost Sentinel opened its eye, the lid sliding up almost sleepily, and Stenwold stared into the darkness that was revealed.

The machine braced itself, legs abruptly digging in, then it was speaking thunder back at the Mynan artillery, smashing a steam-catapult to pieces. The flash and smoke of a leadshotter were unmistakable.

Then they were moving and, to Stenwold's horror, the Mynan soldiers were rushing forward to meet them. He looked around for Kymene, spotting her standing atop a half-fallen wall, directing the assault, horribly visible, and he began to run for her, shouting her name.

He knew the theory, of course. Once a squad of soldiers had clambered on to an automotive, they could pry its armour apart, break in and kill the crew. The same books of war insisted that no automotive could be built strong enough to ward off artillery. The Empire had changed the syllabus over a winter.

'Kymene!' he yelled, and then was thrown from his feet almost casually, a leadshot smashing down close by as it angled for one of the Mynan engines. For a moment his world was nothing but dust and falling shards of stone and screaming that was not his own. Then other artillery nearby was trying to answer the assault, thundering from his left and right loud enough to rattle the air in his lungs, and a thousand other sounds, metal on metal, snapbows loosing, hopelessly shouted orders, the continuing bloody deluge of the Imperial artillery as it continued its detached dismemberment of the city street by street.

Stenwold could barely breathe. The sheer sound of it was beating down on him, the anguished composite roar of a battle being lost and won. Hands to his ears, his knees striking the jagged rubble as he tipped forward, he fought for self-possession, and lost. All around him the air was full of splinters. All three Sentinels were discharging their leadshotters: each advancing a few scuttling yards and then stopping, turning and tilting to aim, then unlidding its single metal eye. Meanwhile, the breach itself, which the Mynans had not even had the chance to contest, was not empty. Stenwold saw at least another quartet of segmented machines sliding through.

He saw a band of soldiers, twenty at least, close with the nearest machine – already only fifteen, ten yards away – ready to take the monster apart with crowbars, to get to the vulnerable flesh within. The rotary piercers spoke first, spinning up almost instantly and scything away half the attackers, chewing them into a bloody rain before Stenwold's eyes, spare bolts pattering and rebounding from the stones around him. The others tried to get out of the arc of the Sentinel's frontal weapons, and some of them were cut down almost instantly by the rotaries of the next machine along. The rest . . . to Stenwold there seemed only a brief shudder that seemed to pass down the length of the lead automotive, and the Mynans were all dead, a row of snapbow barrels loosing from between its plates, the deadly little bolts quite enough to kill through armour.

Someone was pulling at his arm, and he snapped back to full control of himself, seeing how very close the machine was now. It had turned and braced itself again, its eye seeking out some further Mynan siege engine. The soldier who clutched his arm was shouting at him, but Stenwold could hear very little of it. The import was clear, though: *We have to go!*

'Kymene!' he yelled, but she was gone from her wall, her fate unknown. The Mynans were retreating in droves now, not a rout but in a determined fall-back to some prepared position. Stenwold saw one of the defending automotives, a hopelessly outdated, patched-together thing, drive full tilt into the face of a Sentinel, slamming the invader back a few feet as its feet left jagged grooves in the ruined flagstones. Then one of the next wave had put a leadshot into the Mynan vehicle, and a moment later its steam boiler exploded, just one more sound, another rain of pieces in a broken place.

There were flying machines in the air now, wheeling and darting, with wings ablur. Imperial Spearflights were coursing against the ragbag of local fliers, the air glittering with piercer bolts. For a moment he thought he saw Taki's *Esca Magni* amidst the fray, but the air was grey with sifting dust, and he had now seen such things, so many, so swift to follow each other, that he did not want to trust his eyes.

Edmon's *Pacemark* shuddered its way across the sky, curving around towards a knot of Spearflights that had briefly formed up. A moment later they were splitting off across the city, and he could only follow the one. The Imperial pilot was good enough to slow down for him, taking his time about lining up his own target, and for once Edmon was able to stoop on one of them, textbook-perfect, dropping out of the cloudless blue in an exact line, so that his rotary shot hammered all about the enemy canopy, smashing through its glass and wood. The Spearflight heeled over almost instantly, sliding sideways from the sky. A moment later he felt a scatter of impacts on his hull, guilty of the same complacency as his victim, and saved now only by the impatience of his attacker.

He skimmed away instantly, veering left and then right to throw off his enemy's aim, ducking his *Pacemark* low, to rooftop level and further, slinging the flier down the straight boulevard of the Tradian Way, the length of which he knew by heart. The Imperial pilot behind him was game, bringing his Spearflight in close to follow, and when Edmon made the sudden turn at the Way's far end, lurching up and right to claw for the sky again, any surprise intended was countered by the Wasp machine's agility in the air.

Edmon turned for the gates once more, where the artillery around the gate might be able to help him out again, but then something blurred past him – he had a vision of beating wings and then the spark and chatter of piercers only. For a moment he was not sure whether he had been hit, or what had just happened, but then he realized that the Wasp tailing him was gone, and he hauled the *Pacemark* into the tightest turn it would make in time to see the Imperial duelling with another Mynan craft, a squat, box-bodied flier that he recognized as the *Tserinet,* flown by the Szaren renegade Franticze. The two orthopters were speeding over the city, dancing almost where the wall had once been, the Wasp nimbler, but already damaged from Franticze's first pass. Edmon brought the *Pacemark* on to a heading meant to intervene, praying that the Bee-kinden pilot would give him a clear opening to their mutual enemy.

Abuptly the sky around them was busy. Another Mynan craft fled past, smoke already trailing, with a pair of Spearflights tight behind it. Edmon had a moment to make his choice, but Franticze was one of the best pilots Myna could call on. He had to trust to her skills, as he pulled around and followed the pair of harrying enemies, blazing away wildly with his rotaries just to let them know he was there.

A moment later the damaged Mynan flier had bucked in the air – he registered only the irregularity of movement, but knew what it meant. In the next second it had dropped too low, not so much clipping as ramming the upper storey of a house already on fire, its fierce, swift flight instantly transformed into violence, wrecked chassis spinning end over end, its wings flying apart in pieces. The Spearflights split up. As ever, he could only follow the one, and then the other would have him.

Edmon bared his teeth – at the Wasps, at the world – and plunged after one even so, because he wanted another kill, another dead Imperial and wrecked machine before they caught him. Even as he did so, a third Spearflight raked past him, hammering a strip of holes in one of his forewings almost casually, in passing. The *Pacemark* pitched despite his fighting it, one wingtip coming within ten feet of a wall. He fought for height, losing track entirely of how many enemy might be behind him. Momentarily the draw of the ground seemed insuperable, the *Pacemark* limping along the rooftops like a dying fish at the water's surface, lurching and flopping and always on the point of sinking altogether. He felt gears slip, the wings losing their rhythm. In that instant he was all ice, waiting for the ground to reclaim its errant son, but then the engine somehow recovered its stroke and he was still impossibly air-borne, casting out over the city streets.

He glanced behind him, gaining only hurried, wheeling snatches of sky, pillars of smoke, the dots of other fliers out over Myna. The enemy had not come with him, and he guessed they must have believed him lost, too bloodthirsty actually to wait out his death throes. For a moment there was not a single Spearflight in sight.

He looked down.

This would be the moment to take with him, if he had any

chance to take anything anywhere. Not the aerial dragon-fighting with the Imperial air force, not the moment when the ground reached up for him, but the moment he realized that his city was being taken from beneath him.

Most of the buildings down there were now rubble and ruins, or else blazing pyres as though the Empire had marked out the path of its invasion in fire. Between these churned a great silver maggot, a segmented automotive undulating swiftly along the streets of Myna – *his* Myna – stopping only to discharge its weapons. He caught glimpses of wrecked artillery that had not been able to keep the monsters out. There were bodies down there. He saw some on the streets, and knew that for every death he marked, a hundred others must have blurred by unseen. He saw the streets he knew, the places where his mother had laboured, the markets his father had haggled in. He saw the houses of his friends, where relatives had worked. He saw his childhood and his memories in those shattered homes and broken workshops, and the corpses strewn like sticks.

There was no room left inside him, then. The pain of it was worse than being shot. He sent the *Pacemark* into a dive against one of the Imperial machines, trigger down so that the rotaries shot and shot, circling and circling until they had emptied themselves. The sparks wherever his bolts were turned by the enemy armour were like a glittering constellation.

He failed to scratch the machine, although it stopped almost quizzically under his attack, questing left and right, his efforts so trivial that it could not even work out where he was.

He pulled out of the dive and skimmed past, leaving the machine behind. There had been Imperial soldiers coming into the city behind it, and he could have used his ammunition more effectively against them, but even then it would have been throwing stones at an avalanche.

The *Pacemark* was not handling well, and Edmon needed its spring rewound and the rotaries rearmed. Feeling numb, utterly drained, he coaxed the orthopter back towards the more distant airfields, unsure whether he would even find anything to land on that had not been claimed by the fires.

The war in the air was all around him still, but he had become a mere spectator. He saw the Spearflights dart and swoop, keeping the remnants of the Mynan aviators busy while others dropped their incendiaries across the city. He saw Franticze again, chasing down another enemy – her hatred for Wasps was legendary amongst the Mynan airmen. He even saw the Fly-kinden pilot, Taki of Solarno, with her little killer machine darting and swerving, almost flying backwards to throw a Wasp off her, then slipping behind him to finish him off.

Too little, all of it. The ground battle was moving street by street, and only in one direction. If the Wasps had not been more interested in punishing the city with their bombs, they could have cleared the sky of defenders already.

There had been a fierce battle over the highest airfield, he learned later, but the enemy had yet to burn it when he touched down there, and any flier downed for repairs or refuelling was being kept in hangars, out of sight. He brought the *Pacemark* in for an untidy landing, handling it by instinct, his mind still trying to find some interpretation for the images that did not mean that Myna was being lost even as he sat there.

The ground crew ran out and began to haul his flier into the shadow of the hangars. He hinged the canopy back and began to instruct them, his voice as hoarse and ragged as if he had been shouting on a parade ground all day. 'Rewind the spring and reload the weapons. I'm going straight back up. I'm going . . .' and his voice broke, and he sat there, holding the stick, mouth open, trying to work out what it was that he was going to do, because he had not the first idea.

Someone was calling to him, but they had to say his name three or four times before he would even cast a dull gaze their way.

'Stay on the ground; change of orders. We're gathering pilots for a strike. Stay on the ground while we build up the numbers.' The ground officer's voice was almost hysterical, and he spoke the words as though they were just some meaningless babble.

An artillery shell landed three streets away, making the ground shudder.

Stenwold found himself in the midst of a constant flow of soldiers, men abandoning their positions closer to the wall, running or limping in, being given orders, being sent out again. Some were sent further back, to the field hospitals being set up in taverns and workshops and backrooms, but there were few who were able enough to present themselves but yet not able enough to be thrown back into the jaws of the Imperial advance.

Kymene stood at the centre of it with her officers. They had commandeered a covered market to evade the eyes of the enemy orthopters, the stalls shoved aside to make room for the turmoil of war.

She was swift, efficient, a map of the city before her that she barely had to refer to, allotting each new consignment of soldiers an address, a junction, a street. She ordered barricades, she assigned the little artillery that had been saved. The Wasps were in the city – not just their killer machines but their soldiers, their infantry washing through the streets of Myna, the Light Air-borne taking rooftops and dropping into the undefended city behind them.

It did not escape Stenwold that many of the men and women presenting themselves to Kymene were not wearing the red and black of the Mynan army but a mismatch of everything from civilian tunics and robes to repainted Imperial armour. The Mynans had spent a long time under the heel of the Empire before they had thrown off their shackles, but they had been a martial people once. They were not lacking in spirit.

Only in training, he thought gloomily. Only in resources.

'Kymene!' he called, but before she could even look at him, someone had run in yelling that the machines were already upon them.

The Maid of Myna looked at the remaining soldiers assembled before her, and told them simply, 'Fight!' No time for street maps and strategy: immediately they were splitting up, dashing from the marketplace by every possible route. Stenwold opened his mouth to call her name again, to try and draw some order from the madness of it all, but the east wall caved in as he did so, punched through by a Sentinel's leadshotter, the iron bulk of the machine revealing itself in the jagged gap.

He saw Kymene draw her sword, and for a moment he thought that this was where she meant to end it. In the next moment she had turned and was running, cloak streaming behind her, and he was doing his best to keep up.

They burst out into the dust-heavy air, a scatter of soldiers running on either side of them. Behind, the Sentinel lurched forward, smashing the wall down and grinding into the now-empty market, its rotaries hammering. Stray bolts zipped and danced past.

Kymene ran straight for the nearest defended position, a street-wide barricade constructed from the very stones the Wasps had brought down. Stenwold saw a score of soldiers behind it, at least as many in the flanking tenements, many of them already loosing snapbows upwards as Imperial soldiers darted in at them from the sky.

The Sentinel thundered out of the market, smashing down the near wall, and the entire building began to fold in on itself in the machine's wake, too many supports and pillars knocked away. Instantly, a pair of Mynan leadshotters boomed from Stenwold's left, their paired impact striking the machine's side hard enough that it skidded several yards. For a moment the Mynans were cheering, for there was a sizeable dent in the Sentinel's carapace, and at least one leg trailed uselessly, but then the Imperial machine shook itself and turned against the Mynan engines. Its single eye unlidded and belched flame, smashing one leadshotter off its carriage, the ton of bronze and steel that was the barrel spinning and cracking, killing at least one of the artillerists. Then the Imperial soldiers had arrived: men in black and gold armour, rushing forward with snapbows raised even as more were dropping from above. Without the Sentinel, the Mynans could have made a fight of it, trusted to their weapons and their bloody-minded determination to hold the enemy for just a little more time, but the war automotive was on the move again, slewing slightly as the damaged leg dragged.

That was the last he saw of organized Mynan resistance. For the rest, he was running through the streets with Kymene, stumbling up the tiered steps, retreating ever westwards. The terrible machines could not be stopped with any weapons the Mynans possessed, but they could not be everywhere at once. The city's defenders had spread themselves out across the whole advance of the Imperial army. Stenwold retained confused images of individual soldiers at windows, on roofs, in doorways, loosing their snapbows and crossbows at the human presence of the enemy, fleeing when confronted with the steel fist of the Sentinels. The battle became a series of jumbled, unrelated moments in his mind, seeing Wasps and Mynan Beetles trading shots at street corners, Imperial Airborne making assaults on high windows to flush out snipers, Spearflight orthopters casting a killing shadow over the ground as they coasted in to drop their incendiaries. There were no lines on that battlefield. The next street that Stenwold stumbled on to could be controlled by either side, or bitterly contested. There was so much dust and smoke in the air that it was difficult even to tell friend from foe.

Then they were at the airfield, and he saw that Kymene had managed somehow to gather some soldiers together again, not nearly so many as before, but at least a few hundred, sheltering under any cover that was available.

'Kymene!' he shouted – he seemed to have done nothing all day but chase the edge of her cloak and call her name.

She turned on him as if he was the enemy, eyes flashing, sword in hand.

'It's over,' he told her. 'You have to get clear.'

'I hear this from *you*?' she demanded. 'You, who have been saying the Wasps must be *fought* since before most of your kin had even heard of the Empire?'

'Look where we are!' Stenwold told her. 'Get your fighters out of the city, get them to Szar or Maynes or the Lowlands. Get yourself out. Today is lost.' The words were so pitiful, to describe what he had seen that day, that he almost choked on them. 'Please, Kymene. Your people need you *free*.'

She started to answer, defiance blazing in her expression, but then artillery struck within streets of them and swallowed her words with its fury. Overhead, two orthopters roared past, Imperial chasing Mynan.

'Kymene!' he shouted again, but the artillery was closing in on them, *pound-pound-pound*, a seemingly random pattern: near then far, near, then closer, in a net of calculation that was drawing tighter.

Stenwold saw her lips move, read the words, 'I can't . . .' there, but one of her own was taking her arm, shouting at the top of his voice. The Mynan airmen on the ground had already scattered to their vessels. The roar of fuel-engines sparking up obscured the whirr of clockwork, and the artillery overrode it all.

At last she nodded agreement, the gesture almost wrenched from her, and the man who had been trying to persuade her was sprinting across the airfield, still shouting. They were wheeling out a fixed-wing flier, a cargo-hauler, but it would now take passengers in lieu of crates.

'Chyses!' Kymene shouted after him. 'Gather all the soldiers you can. Gather everyone who'll go with you. Get them out of the city, as Maker said. There *will* be a tomorrow!' Her fiery gaze passed to Stenwold. 'With me, Maker. If the world can't spare me, it certainly can't spare you.'

'All pilots, into the air,' someone yelled out. 'The Maid must not be brought down!'

From nowhere, it seemed, Taki's *Esca Magni* thundered down for a hard landing, its extended legs flexing on impact. 'Rewind me!' came her high, imperious voice, as though she was on her home fields of Solarno, but the mechanics rushed to obey. She had accounted for herself memorably already, through skill and superior technology.

'We're going!' Stenwold shouted at her, but the artillery had quickened, as if sensing a kill. He pointed madly westwards, then gestured broadly at the frenzied activity about the field, and the Fly nodded. Her face, through the cockpit glass, was streaked with grime and sweat, and there were several holes in the *Esca*'s wings and bodywork.

There was no more for it, then. The soldiers were already fleeing, each officer taking the survivors of his squad and hoping to get them out of the city any which way, and for whatever destination they could reach. All across the city, the citizens of Myna who could not or would not flee would be slaves of the Empire by dusk, or dead.

Kymene was already crouching in the hatch of the fixed-wing, with the craft's civilian pilot firing up the four propeller engines. The craft had swift, sleek lines but it would not move in the air like an orthopter. As Stenwold ran across the field to join her, he knew that their fate would rest in the hands of the fighting airmen, and of Taki.

A shell landed close enough to scatter debris over the field, the blast knocking a few distant mechanics off their feet. Kymene hauled Stenwold into the fixed-wing's hold, almost pulling him on top of her. Her expression was venomous, unforgiving, taking her last look at her ravaged city before the hatch closed.

The machine shuddered around them as the fixed-wing tensed, its legs bunching as the propellers got up to speed.

Then, with an explosive snap, its landing gear had hurled it into the air, to catch the wind like a kite, a long low take-off that must have barely cleared the hangar roofs.

All across the field, every flier that had been held back was now clawing for the sky. Edmon let the battered old *Pacemark* have its head, almost immediately overtaking the fixed-wing *Sweet Fire* that was carrying Kymene, as he circled up above to search for the enemy. The Spearflights were all over the city but, in that first flush of ascent, they did not see the scale of the Mynan launch. Then there were a dozen orthopters in the air, cutting up from the airfield in all directions, making a widening spiral of winged shapes that could not be missed. Within a minute there was a score, and other surviving Mynan fliers were being drawn to join them, or retreating to them.

Their numbers, which spoiled any chance of secrecy, bought them precious moments. The Empire had split its fliers into individuals and pairs, none of which was foolish enough to simply dive straight at the burgeoning Mynan flight. Instead, they took it as a counter-attack, and regrouped to meet it.

There were more of them than of the defenders, of course. Edmon reckoned the odds were two to one already, and he guessed that minutes more would see the Empire commit some of the machines they had held back to keep their artillery safe.

He flashed the pattern to split, to attack, not knowing who would come and who would stay. The Empire had taken the city so swiftly by calling the pace, and the *Sweet Fire*'s only chance at escape would be for Myna to retake the initiative, even briefly.

He let himself get quite clear of the circling mob of defenders before he glanced back to see precisely who was coming along with him. Otherwise, he knew, his nerve might not stand an empty sky.

Eleven other fliers had answered the call. He saw Franticze's *Tserinet* at the fore, almost overtaking him with the Bee-kinden woman's lust for Wasp blood. Looking forward again, his memory found names for some of the others: Bordes's *Wanderer*, Marsene's *Fierce Lady*, the *Cranefly*, the *Red Anvil* and several others he could not immediately name. There were far too many Spearflights ahead to worry about the odds now, but they had the same difficulties in communication that Edmon himself did. He saw flashes between them, officers trying to convey a response to a situation that had already changed.

Here we go, and he had chosen a target and kicked the *Pacemark* for every ounce of speed the ailing orthopter could give him. As the rotaries burst into life, he bellowed something wordless and primal, full of the death of his city.

His target skipped in the air under the battering it received, nose turning for the ground as the hammer of his bolts smashed its engine through the wooden hull. Then he was in their midst and, although many were trying to turn to follow his line, they were in each other's way, and could not shoot for fear of hitting one another. All around him the other pilots were following his suicidal lead. Franticze smashed the port wings of one Spearflight to matchwood and was needling another even before she had cut into their formation. The *Wanderer* had taken a higher line, the lean, light flier missing with its single piercer but diving into the Wasp flock from above, bringing confusion in his wake. The *Cranefly* . . . Edmon was watching when it happened, just a moment's flick of his eyes left and the image of the angular Mynan vessel steering left just when a Wasp pilot made a mirror decision, the two craft striking shoulder to shoulder, wheeling about each other like dance partners, wings stilled and broken, then dropping, still spinning, from the air.

Then he had more to worry about, clearing the Wasp pack and forcing the *Pacemark* into a complaining turn that was tighter than anything it had tried before, feeling every joint and bolt of its protest. Piercer shot sleeted past him like foul weather, a handful of impacts shunting him sideways in the air and nearly losing him control over the machine entirely. He let his rotaries blaze away, scything back through the air that the Wasps had taken, impossible to take aim at this speed, but he saw at least one Spearflight clipped by his shot, rattled, if not brought down.

Franticze's *Tserinet* leapt up past him, absurdly close. There were Wasps on her tail, but her squat and ugly-looking flier moved through the air like a hunting insect, as though the woman's sheer murderous passion could override aerodynamics. He saw another Spearflight take the full brunt of her rotaries from below, knocked from the sky just soon enough for Franticze to skip through the space it had been occupying.

He flashed the code for *Retreat!*, without knowing who might be able to see it. He had spotted Spearflights breaking off from the pack, and there could only be one destination for them.

The *Sweet Fire* would be out past the western wall already, and a cargo fixed-wing could give a combat orthopter a run for its money on the straight, but there were already Imperial fliers harrying its escape, not an organized assault but – just as Edmon's sally had been – a pack of individual pilots who had spotted the opportunity. Edmon sent the *Pacemark* back after them, not even knowing if he could catch up.

Had the *Sweet Fire*'s pilot taken a straight line then he and his pursuers would be out of Edmon's reach, but the man was unused to other pilots trying to kill him, and was twisting left and right to try and evade pursuit, giving the Spearflights the chance to outstrip him and come at him from the front and both sides.

Edmon had no idea how many Spearflights were in his own personal retinue, or whether any of his fellows had broken off with him. The Mynan pilots who had gone with the *Sweet Fire* were taking the enemy away in ones and twos, duelling savagely in the air, with no quarter given, airman against airman to the death.

Edmon felt some shocks against his hull, but only a handful – once again he had avoided the full force of some enemy's hail of bolts, but for how much longer? If he turned to shake the pursuer off, then he would not be able to help Kymene.

He screamed again as he dived on the Wasps circling the *Sweet Fire*, trigger down and rotaries blazing. Most of them saw him coming, scattering before him, which bought more time for the fixed-wing than if he had actually taken one down. He kept to no sane line, made no plans, simply slinging the *Pacemark* around so sharply that he felt the wires of the wings strain to breaking point. Stray shots were still finding him, but he was making no serious attempt to attack, merely shooting blind and diving again and again, looping the *Sweet Fire* like an erratic satellite and throwing the Wasps off at every turn. His weapons ran out of ammunition on the third pass, but that no longer seemed to matter. He did not let it dictate his tactics.

Then one of the enemy had his line at last, and the impact almost took him down on its own, skewing his flight so that he was side-on to the ground, then falling upside down before he could complete the roll and get his craft under control again. The Spearflight was well and truly with him, though, and now the *Pacemark* was not handling at all well, abruptly incapable of the aerobatics that had saved it until now.

He tried to find a Wasp to ram, but the sky seemed mockingly clear of them, save for the pilot diligently trying to kill him.

A moment later he realized that this meant he had won. There was him, and the *Sweet Fire*, and the lone Spearflight that had not been stripped from the pursuit by his distractions or by the actions of other pilots.

He was just deciding that this represented a satisfactory end to his life, when Franticze came from out of the sun and chewed the tail off his enemy, sending the Spearflight tumbling away. The Bee then followed it down, trying to kill the pilot when he bailed out to trust his Art wings, but that was how deeply she hated the Wasps, and Edmon could hardly blame her just then.

Sixteen

Laszlo slipped into the backroom of the naval surgeon's house, after leaving a bag of bread, dried fruit and a little jerky on the old Bee-kinden's table – all that he had managed to scrape together in a day's foraging. At first he had paid the man in silver, but the city had been locked in stalemate for five days now, with no traffic coming in by land or sea. Food was worth more than coin. The Spiders held the docks and those streets nearest the water. The Wasps held the high ground, the mansions of the wealthy. Both sides seemed to be waiting for the other to make a move.

Lissart drew back as he entered, clutching the blanket close to her, on her face the same expression as every other time he had come in to see her, after she recovered consciousness. It was the tense, desperate look of a woman under a death sentence.

'Don't,' he said weakly. His day had been sufficiently frustrating, scuffling and shoving and stealing to put bread on the table. He didn't need this. 'You're looking stronger.'

Again that flinch, and he saw guilt there. He supposed she was probably looking at matters in a saner and more logical way than he was. He had left her alone so far, so as not to put more strain on her wound, which the surgeon had confirmed had come close to killing her. The old man knew his trade, though, and, even if she would not be running or flying anywhere in the immediate future, she was at least on the right side of the grave.

'Let's talk,' he said, and that was something more like she was expecting.

She almost relaxed at the prospect of a good old interrogation. Probably she expected him to get his knife out, right about now.

'Lissart, is it?' he pressed.

She nodded.

'I'm Laszlo. Well, all right, you knew that, but I really am. I didn't think I needed a joke name for this business. Nobody told me. Please smile at that. I'm not expecting a belly laugh, for obvious reasons.'

'What do you want?' Her voice was like a faint echo of the tones he remembered.

'Good question. You work for the Empire?'

'I think I'm freelance just now.' The smile, when it came, was infinitesimal, but he returned it in strength.

'I was for the Lowlands,' he said. 'Probably still am, assuming I can get out of this mess.'

'What's going on out there?' She struggled to prop herself on her elbows.

'Everyone's waiting for the Spiders and the Empire to tear each other's throats out, but nothing of the sort's happening.'

'The Solarnese aren't fighting?'

'Fighting which? If it'd been just the Empire, sure, but with the Spider navy clogging the bay, and Satrapy soldiers on every street corner from here to the Venodor? Oh, a bunch of Solarnese pilots had a crack at the airships, but they weren't working together, and the Empire shot them down, after a bit of a dance. The Cortas seem paralysed. Nobody's giving orders, and meanwhile the food supplies are running low because nobody in this city thought to lay in any surplus.' He bared his teeth in frustration, and she shrank back. 'I'm not going to hurt you.'

'Why not?' she asked flatly. 'The hangar . . .' She coughed, then hissed at the pain. 'Hurt me. At least I'd know where we stand. I'm used to that.'

Laszlo eyed her sadly for long enough that the haunted, hunted look came back to her features. 'I killed Breighl,' he said at last. 'Didn't want to, but I did.' When she made no response he added, 'I'm guessing you killed te Riel.'

'Te Berro, his name was. He was ex-Imperial and he'd pretty much worked out who I was working for. He was going to stop me. He didn't leave me much choice.' Her tone was dull, and he wondered just how true that was. He hardly needed more evidence that Lissart was a very dangerous piece of work indeed.

'And then we have the hangars,' he continued. 'And we'll never know what might have happened if the Solarnese could have got those Firebugs into the air. I reckon the Imperial airships would have had a bad time of it certainly, maybe even the Spider ships as well.'

He expected her to look away, but instead she met his eyes with a little of her old spirit returning. 'Do you expect me to say I'm sorry?'

He left that one to hang in the silence building between them, until she was moved to go on: 'This is what I do, what I am. I'm a saboteur, a spy. I won't claim it as a noble calling, but I do what I'm asked, for the craft of it. That's something you never understood, though I'll wager te Berro always did.' Her words got fainter towards the end, as she had to pause to draw breath. 'If I take back what I did at the hangars, I betray myself, and then what do I have left? But I'm sorry you were there and I'm sorry you . . . got hurt.' *That I burned you*, hung on the air like smoke. 'What are you going to do with me? Hand me over to your masters in Collegium?'

Chance'd be a fine thing, right now, but he could not muster any vitriol. That spark, that defiance, there was the Liss he remembered from the Taverna te Remi.

She was a killer, although that was probably the only commodity not in short supply in Solarno. Worse, he had the uneasy feeling that somewhere in her there was a beautiful and perfect little monster, a woman for whom the values of life and death were irrevocably skewed, or perhaps simply not given any reliable weight at all.

He reached out to take her hand and, to his surprise she did not draw it back. Of course, she was no more capable of being disarmed than was a Wasp-kinden, and her hands thronged with deadly Art. Despite all that, despite her condition, despite everything that was going on outside, holding her hand right then seemed the best thing that had happened to him in several days.

She was studying his face, and he wondered just what emotions he had allowed to roam over it, just then. 'You utter fool,' she said, but gently. 'Is that *it*? I tried to kill you.'

He shrugged. 'You said you were sorry. Besides, I'm a pirate. I'm used to that.'

'A pirate?' She did smile then. 'Well then, what now, pirate? Steal me away on your sailing ship?'

'I'm getting out of the city first chance,' he told her. 'Come with me – no obligations. Although if you promise not to try and kill me again that would be a good start.'

'Go to your masters in the Lowlands?'

'Just come with me.' He squeezed her hand gently. 'Please – or I won't go at all.'

'You are the emperor of the idiots,' she whispered. 'Let me take you away from all this? I never thought I'd fall for that one in a thousand years.'

Two days later and there was still no sign of anyone being allowed to leave the city. Operating on his own, Laszlo was confident he could have evaded the Wasps' sentries and flying patrols, trusting to his wings to get him out of the city and away.

Of course, Liss would not be able to go with him and, besides, he was out here on the Exalsee, with a long and complicated road to follow back to Collegium.

Then the great face-off between the Empire and the Spiderlands happened, which changed everything.

He had been out on the streets that day, not so much seeking food as information, because the uneasy peace between the two occupying forces had been sustained beyond reason and he wanted to know what was going on. There had been a few skirmishes between Wasp Light Airborne and Spider soldiers, it was true, but far fewer than he would have expected, given the temper of the former and the pride of the latter. Instead, it seemed that the strongest orders from above were holding both in check.

He made covert enquiries about the provenance of both forces but received no intelligence that he was happy with. The Wasps had brought in their Second Army, known as the Gears, which had previously rolled all the way to the gates of Collegium during the war. The Spider force was not such a united piece of business, of course, being a collusion of various different families, interests and mercenary units, but the name at its head was Aldanrael, the very family that had given Laszlo and Stenwold such a hard time not so long ago.

Then word came that they were tearing down some buildings at the heart of the Venodor, and the next day Laszlo went to take a look. By the time he arrived, an entire block in the centre of the street market had been razed by Mole Cricket slaves, levelling a grand uneven space in what had previously always been a cluttered and claustrophobic bazaar. Shortly after Laszlo arrived and began asking questions, the delegations turned up. First came soldiers with drawn blades, Wasps from the north, Spiders from the south, who prodded and pushed until the citizens had evacuated the new space, forming an anxious, milling crowd on all sides of it. *Whatever's going on, it's meant to be as public as possible,* Laszlo decided. He felt uncomfortable about shoving his way to the front, as though the words 'Low-lander agent' were somehow visible above his head, and he had to contend with sufficient elbowing at the back that in the end he found a roost on a rooftop overlooking the new square, as dozens of other Fly-kinden had already done. Looking around he realized that there were an awful lot of people here: anxious Solarnese and Flies and the local Spiders and foreign merchants, and all of them wanting to know what was going to happen. The prolonged and silent occupation had drawn their nerves tight, as was no doubt the intention.

There were also plenty of soldiers, for neither side was taking chances. Other rooftops played host to the Light Airborne, and Laszlo could spot a fair few groups in the crowd that were surely taking Spider-kinden pay, most notably several bands of huge Scorpions who would have no trouble shouldering their way forward if necessary.

After that, the leaders arrived. He saw the Imperial delegation coming first: a squad of armoured infantry with a handful of officers in their midst, but striding ahead of the soldiers was an old man bald enough to need a broad-brimmed hat against the Solarnese sun. He stood as straight as a spear and walked with a soldier's confidence. If he feared Spider treachery, he did not show it.

One of the other Fly-kinden hissed between his teeth, mutter-ing to his fellows. Laszlo inched over and parted with a few coins for the knowledge that this was reckoned to be none other than General Tynan, the master of the Gears.

Someone else was pointing back towards the docks, and Laszlo scuttled across the rooftop just in time to see Tynan's opponents make their entrance. The escort here were all Spider-kinden: lean, beautiful men and women in light armour, bows over their shoulders, rapiers at their hips. As they reached the cleared square, a woman emerged from their midst, stand-ing there regarding the assembled crowds as archly as any empress. She wore a cuirass of silver scales, and beneath that a copperweave hauberk, the mesh as fine as cloth, stronger than steel. For all that, Laszlo would bet she needed no better protection than her own invulnerable self-assurance. Even at this distance he could feel the faint touch of her Art, making her an object both of attraction and fear. Her hair was bright silver, richer than the jewelled torc at her neck or the glittering gilded wreath about her brow, and age had brought her only authority.

Seeing her there, and recalling descriptions given by Stenwold Maker, Laszlo was willing to wager she was the Lady Mycella of the Aldanrael, who had led an armada against Collegium only the year before.

The soldiers on either side were tense, expecting a fight or a riot. The Solarnese themselves were frightened, angry, ready for violence. There would be daggers and swords aplenty for the crowds to lay hands on. They had only cast off the Empire a couple of years ago, and now here the Wasps were again.

Laszlo was depressed to see that many were plainly looking to the Aldanrael to defend them. Solarno had been a sort of appendix to the Spiderlands for a long time, but a backwater beyond the rigours of intrigue and backstabbing that dominated the Spider-kinden cities proper.

Tynan strode forward, startling his own men. His face was professionally blank as he regarded his opposite number, who matched him, pace for pace.

He put his hand out, and they clasped.

The crowd had gone completely still and quiet, waiting for the catch: for the orders that would set the soldiers on each other, or on the people of Solarno. What they saw was a clerk scurry forward out of the Spider retinue, setting down a table. A scroll was produced that nobody there bothered to read, the real business of diplomacy already disposed of elsewhere and long before.

They signed it, Tynan and Mycella, as though they were being wed.

There was an announcement after that, but the crowd had begun to murmur and argue, so Laszlo could not catch much of it. The news became the talk of every taverna and gaming house, though, so he soon pieced it all together, the Lowlander spy coming to the table for the scraps of others.

Stenwold needs to know, he realized, but he could no longer fool himself that he was nothing more than Maker's agent. The import of what he now knew shook him through and through. His family had tied its fortunes to those of Collegium, after all.

There had been a treaty at the end of the last war, the Treaty of Gold. Collegium had been a signatory, as had the Empire, the Aldanrael and their allies, as well as the Three-city Alliance and various Lowlander cities.

Last year, conflict had flared between the Aldanrael and Collegium, arising out of Spider piracy that Stenwold had met with some steel of his own. A son and a daughter of the Aldanrael had lost their lives, and Laszlo knew that there was little that the Spider nobility took more seriously.

The Empire had signed a pact with the Spiderlands, in the face of Collegiate aggression and in the wake of Collegium's tearing up the Treaty of Gold. For too long, they said, had the world been the plaything of little powers, self-important city-states such as the Lowlands was crammed with, belligerent neighbours. Myna was mentioned, also Sarn, Collegium, the Mantis-kinden. There would never be peace or prosperity while history was at the mercy of such small thinkers. The Treaty of Gold had failed. It was time to redraw the map and, as the two greatest powers of the age, the Empire and the Spiderlands would wield the pen.

Solarno had been declared a free port, under the protection of both sides, retaining a notional independence. Already the gates had been opened, the wharves cleared for trade, the relief felt by the hungry citizens quickly blurring their memory of who had taken the bread from their mouths in the first place.

Against that, the news that the Cortas would sit under the watchful gaze of Imperial and Spider-kinden advisers went almost uncontested. Having heard the rest of the news, the Solarnese reckoned that they might just have got themselves a good deal, after all. The first rumours were seeping in about Myna, and defiance was looking like an overrated quality.

The Second Army, swelled by Mycella's own troops, would be moving west, and nobody had any doubt about their joint objective. Both General Tynan and the Aldanrael had unfinished business with Collegium.

When Laszlo got back to the surgeon's house – flying at best speed all the way – and burst into Lissart's room, he had one thought in mind.

She voiced it for him. 'We have to leave.'

His thunder stolen, he gaped at her.

She misinterpreted his surprise as reluctance, sitting up in bed with a grimace, but doing her best to show that she was fit to be moving by now. 'Listen to me – I don't care if my legs fall off, we're getting out of Solarno. I saw her.'

Laszlo blinked. 'Her who?'

'Garvan,' she told him urgently, and hissed in frustration when he didn't know who Garvan was. 'The Wasp, Laszlo. The Wasp that stabbed me. Come *on*.'

'*Her?*' he demanded, more shocked by this than almost anything else.

'Yes, *her*. Why d'you think she stabbed me?'

'Liss, this isn't making any sense—'

With a sound more of annoyance than pain she levered herself out of the bed. The bandages across her abdomen, plainly visible beneath the cut away hem of her borrowed tunic, remained unspotted with fresh blood. The old surgeon knew his craft. 'Listen, pirate, a Wasp here in Solarno will kill me if she sees me, and I am in no state to either escape or fight back. What part of "Let's get out of Solarno" isn't getting through to you?'

'They have people on all the gates, and at the docks,' Laszlo said. 'Maybe after the armies leave, it'll be easier.'

'I'm serious; I saw her from the window, on this very street, along with soldiers . . .' She trailed off. 'Hold on: "armies *leave*"?'

So he explained just why *he himself* wanted to leave the city too, which calmed her down quickly enough.

'Right,' she said, after a while. 'Looks like I picked the wrong time to change sides.' A spark came back with that thought. 'And don't think that means I've picked yours, Laszlo. When are the bastards moving out?'

'Any day now, sounds like. Looks like their supplies and all that are already in place, for Wasps and Spiders both,' Laszlo told her. 'Whatever I witnessed today, the details were worked out a long time ago, and a long way from here. Solarno just happened to be a convenient place for Empire and Spiderlands to meet – and they got to slap down an ally of Collegium at the same time.'

But Lissart was only half-listening to him. 'Fine. I've got a plan. You listening?' and, when he nodded cautiously she told him, 'We'll march out with the army.' That failed to draw any intelligible response from him, so she elaborated, 'It's perfect. Once we're out of the city, we can . . . well, we could make a break for it when I get my wings again. But if you're serious about spying for the Lowlands, where better to be?'

'You're mad. They'll spot us in an instant.'

'There're always a load of non-fighters with an army. You'd be amazed how few questions people ask – everyone assumes you're someone else's slave. You've seriously never done that? Just tagged onto an army and turned parasite?' Her enthusiasm for the idea was almost childlike. 'We'll hole up with the Spiderlands soldiers – less formal, far easier to blend in.'

'But you're running from a Wasp – and there'll be more Wasps than you know what to do with, marching out west,' Laszlo objected.

'Oh, but they'll be *soldiers*,' she stressed. 'Garvan's Rekef or something and, from her little jaunt outside, I reckon she's on counter-intelligence, rounding up troublemakers. She didn't look as though she was marching out, anyway.' Seeing his concerned expression she managed a rusty laugh. 'You have me at an advantage, Laszlo dear, and that's never a good start to any relationship. Nestling inside the army, we'll balance your sound body with my understanding of how things work.' Her smile, when she gave it, was as brilliant as ever, and made his breath catch in his throat.

The Cortas of Solarno had been reconvened, heavily supervised by both Imperial and Spider-kinden deputies who had power of veto over any decision they did not like the sound of. The Satin Trail and Crystal Standard parties listlessly argued import duty and property tax, while most of the Path of Jade, which had come to prominence on the back of the liberation, had either gone into hiding or been arrested.

General Tynan had taken over a townhouse belonging to one such departed magnate, for his brief sojourn in the city. His replacement, some lucky colonel from Capitas, had already arrived and was taking the city in hand as liaison to the Spider-kinden, who would have the greater share of the governance, Solarno being more a Spider city than anything else. Whether this peculiar arrangement between the two great powers would stand the test of time, or even work at all, was something that he was entirely uncertain about. He would have to do his best to make it work, though, because, when the Second marched west, his troops would be accompanied by several thousand Spider-kinden and their sundry hangers-on and mercenaries.

This evening Tynan would have some intimation, he hoped, of how this business was likely to work.

The rap at the door came at dusk, and one of the house slaves rushed to attend to it. Tynan had located what had presumably been the former owner's audience chamber, and had entertained the idea of receiving his guests there in full Imperial pomp, playing them at their own game. That seemed a good way to make a quick fool of himself, though, and in the end he had ordered his staff to set out a table with the logistical charts laid out neatly at one end, and a couple of couches at the other. He would have preferred chairs, but the Spider-kinden resident of the townhouse did not seem to have owned any.

He had two officers with him, who would be meeting their opposite numbers at the same time. Colonel Mittoc was one of a seemingly endless sequence of new promotions within the Engineering Corps, a lean, bony-faced man whose chief expertise in life was destroying things at a distance with great skill and enthusiasm. On Tynan's other side was Major Cherten of the Army Intelligence, who was overseeing the logistics. Intelligence men were always a mixed bag, and a disappointing number turned out to be Rekef all along, which meant that they were not only spying on their superiors, but were also usually bad at the job they were pretending to do. Tynan had worked with short, amiable Cherten before, and felt that the man could be at least cautiously relied on.

The Fly-kinden slave – one of the previous owner's fixtures that Tynan had kept on – backed into the room, bowing low. In his wake stalked the woman that Tynan had shaken hands and sealed treaties with earlier that day. She had done away with her armour and her martial persona, and stood before him now in a surprisingly plain white robe, save that a faint shimmer, as she moved, betrayed the myriad of gold threads shot through it, to complement the metal of her girdle and the torc about her neck. Her silver hair was held back by a comb of turquoise in the shape of intertwining centipedes: *Beware, for I am venomous.* She saw him notice it and smiled a little.

She should have filled the room with her presence, bringing awe and humility in her wake, but he felt that she was not trying to, but instead withholding her hand and her Art from their minds. Moreover, he had stood before the Empress Seda not so

247

very long ago. There were no great prizes for being the *second* most powerful woman that Tynan had ever met and, for all that Mycella of the Aldanrael was beautiful and dangerous and cunning, the Empress had seemed something more than merely human.

The slave was bringing the wine in early, and yet the moment was right for it, and Tynan made a mental note to take the little man with him on campaign. Efficiency was something he prized, in servants and armies both.

'Is the correct address "My lady"?' he enquired. He was aware that Mittoc and Cherten were somewhat more struck by her, while his own cool civility in the face of the Arista was no doubt adding to his military legend.

'In that case I must call you "General", I suppose. How dull.' The smile was an invitation at collusion. 'These are your officers?'

Tynan introduced the two men, bringing them back to themselves by speaking their names, just like in the old stories of magic and charms. 'It's a change in structure from the old field and camp colonels, but the engineers are shouldering more of the war, these days, and Cherten will be overseeing our side of the march. Who've you got?' He was keeping his tone businesslike, and did not intend to sprinkle his words with too many 'My ladys' either. From their formal meeting, he had gained no sense of the real Mycella behind the gilded front, and he had anticipated a woman gravid with her own self-importance. Instead, she matched him, practicality for practicality, adjusting to his manner effortlessly.

'Jadis of the Melisandyr,' she named the man to her left, broad-shouldered, fair-haired and square-jawed, a hero in waiting. 'Think of him as my colonel of the camp. He captains my bodyguard, which means he also oversees the Satrapy forces and orders our march. He will need to speak with your Major Cherten, I imagine. I suggest we let them get on with it. I have no great love for counting biscuits, myself. This,' and she indicated the cadaverous man on the other side of her, 'is Morkaris, adjutant of our mercenaries.' Some reaction must have shown on Tynan's face, despite himself, for she flashed some teeth. 'We have a great many mercenary troops, General, and someone must be given overall responsibility for them or they'll run riot. Morkaris is here to keep them in line, and to answer to me if he fails. Believe me, I envy you your soldiers' unity of purpose, but things are done differently in the Spiderlands.' A moment later she was gliding past him towards the couches. 'Shall we sit, and let our henchmen argue about rope and tents and pairs of boots, or whatever it is that makes an army go?'

'I think that your understanding of such matters is greater than you pretend,' Tynan rumbled. He gestured for Mittoc and Cherten to take up the arrangements with Mycella's underlings, and cautiously followed after her, feeling as though he should be ready for the touch of silk, the sudden triggering of a trap.

For a moment he thought that she would recline on her side, as Spider Aristoi supposedly did, languorous and impossible to speak to in a civilized manner. Instead she simply sat, like any army officer might, leaning a little against the couch's low back. 'We're doing something new, General, and therefore we set the rules. Let us do so in a way that will not have us at each other's throats before we reach Tark.'

'Fine,' Tynan said shortly. Dropping down onto the other couch, he was aware that he was still studying her blatantly, but then he was a Wasp man, and women were set to be wives and mothers of soldiers, in his culture. Having travelled more than most – admittedly with an army at his back most of the time – he was aware that this belief was not shared by the rest of the world, but then the superiority of the Empire over the rest of the world was a subject beloved of Imperial philosophers. Here, before him, was the product of the exact opposite belief.

'Colonel Cherten told me you'd be a man,' Tynan observed. 'He said men lead Spider armies because the women consider it beneath them.'

'Then perhaps we are honouring you, for I know Wasps know of no higher office,' she replied drily.

'Was the last clash between you and Collegium so personal that you had to see the business ended yourself?' he pressed.

She glanced from her wine over to their subordinates. Colonel Mittoc was explaining something to the others in his rough voice, some detail of how to transport his new artillery toys, no doubt, and the two Spiders were listening with some interest.

'General, you were closer to the mark before,' Mycella said softly.

Tynan raised an eyebrow, not committing himself, and she went on, 'To lead an army is no honour in our culture. Yes, the duty would normally devolve on some son or nephew.' When he made no comment she let her expression fragment a little, so that he could see behind it. 'There was a trade dispute, nothing greater than that. Collegium killed a niece of mine, and then a son. I led an armada against it, more ships than have sailed from the Spiderlands in generations, the grandest venture of the modern age. We turned back. Can you imagine? We were not even defeated. The defences of the Beetles were such that we had no option but to turn back or lose everything. Even now, we will be marching the long coast with you, rather than taking to the waves. What does this suggest to you?'

'That you were not well received when you returned home,' Tynan suggested. 'But you are the head of your family, are you not? Who could discipline you?'

'I am the Lady of the Aldanrael,' she confirmed, 'but I am sure that your people are no more tolerant of public weakness and failure than are mine. So it is that my house is laid low, our holdings stolen, our name a jest on every lip. So it is that, to preserve my family's very existence, I have chosen this path: the path of the Lady Martial. No great triumph amongst my kinden,

250

no great standing, and yet honour enough, and that you will understand. There is honour in taking the sword by the blade when it is presented.' At last she smiled, and he almost felt he had been holding his breath for it. 'Beware me, General, for I am a desperate woman. I have so very little left to lose.'

Seventeen

The fixed-wing *Sweet Fire* had stopped for fuel on a Helleren airfield, and Stenwold had taken the chance to sample the mood of the city, while other Mynan stragglers arrived and joined up with Kymene.

He found little to surprise him, and much to disappoint. Nobody cared about the fall of the Three-city Alliance. Indeed, many of the merchants were already rubbing their hands over simpler access to Imperial markets. There were plenty of Wasps on the streets, mostly Consortium men. The road for the Empire's return had been well and truly paved.

He returned to find Kymene taking reports. Some dozen or so pilots had dropped down onto the Helleren airfield now, with more expected, their scatter of ungainly and damaged craft drawing derisive comments from the locals.

'It sounds as though those of our soldiers who got out have headed for Maynes,' she told him.

'You'll join them?' Stenwold asked.

'I've sent word to them to get clear of Alliance lands altogether if they can. If we can't stand, Maynes won't. They were prouder than us about buying in outside weapons and machines. They have almost nothing to put in the air.'

'Come to Collegium,' he suggested.

She looked at him levelly, a half-circle of airmen watching this exchange silently. 'Will your people fight again, Maker?'

'If they will not, then I'll go with you to Sarn, or wherever else we must, until we find someone who will.'

'Satisfactory,' she agreed.

Another orthopter skimmed overhead, making the Mynan airmen jump and twitch for the safety of their machines. It was Taki's *Esca Magni*, though, looking decidedly more chipped and battered than when Stenwold had seen it last. The Fly-kinden herself looked dead on her feet as she levered herself from her cockpit.

A ragged cheer went up, for the Mynan airmen had all seen her efforts in the skies over their city, and the sound of their applause transformed Taki from a weary refugee into some shadow of her past self: the Solarnese air-duellist. She managed a grin for them, and then was striding forward to clasp hands first with Edmon, then the short Bee woman beside him, then going round the circle, dismissing Kymene almost as an irrelevance.

'Someone get me wound again,' she called out to nobody in particular. 'Or are we putting down roots here?' Stenwold could see how tired she must be, but either she was putting on a brave face or her pride would not let her acknowledge it.

They flew east next, not straight for Collegium as only Taki could have managed the journey in one leg, but navigating for Malkan's Folly, the new fortress that marked the most westerly point that the Imperial Seventh Army had reached in the last war. Stenwold needed to warn the Sarnesh.

Malkan's Folly had been the project of the Sarnesh since shortly after the war because they, like Stenwold, had known the day would come when the black and gold would look westwards once again. The Ants lacked something of Collegium's ingenuity, but they were united in a way their Beetle allies were not. When the King of Sarn and his tacticians set their minds on a project, then progress would be rapid, all hands turning to the task.

The fortress was a great slope-walled monster of black stone, rising to a jagged crown of towers. There had been some talk of raising a series of smaller edifices, as a line to cut across the path of any Wasp advance, but the cost would have been great, the utility small. The Ants knew that it would be impossible physically to stop an enemy force with fortifications, given how mobile Imperial armies were. The impediment that Malkan's Folly offered was logistical. A whole army of Ants could be stationed there, well provisioned, unassailable, sallying forth at will to disrupt enemy supply lines or to attack the Wasps in the flank or the rear, coordinating with the main Sarnesh army with that impeccable ease that only Ants, with their interlinked minds, could muster. With that plan, Malkan's Folly became an obstacle no general could afford to circumvent.

Taking the fortress was reckoned to be near-impossible, according to the Sarnesh engineers. All four faces of it were studded with leadshotter emplacements, and angled so that the weapons' arcs overlapped and covered every inch of ground. Windows were narrow – enough for a snapbowman to shoot out, but not enough to allow ingress to the Light Airborne. Beneath the building itself was a network of tunnels and cellars containing ammunition and provisions enough to last out a siege. Beyond the fortress, if an army hoped to rush past the position and leave it behind, was land watched over by the Mantids and Moth-kinden of the Ancient League, other allies from the war who were more than capable of tying down an Imperial force with skirmishing, ambush and assassination until the Ant forces closed from behind.

The welcome the Ants gave to the fugitive Mynan air force was cool and businesslike. They provided food and drink, fuel and the use of winding engines, and they listened calmly to the news of Myna's fall, making notes. None of the visitors was allowed within the fortress, however, and everything was conducted out under the sky. The Sarnesh did not want any outsider knowing the secrets of their new stronghold.

'We can expect them here within perhaps a month,' estimated the Ant commander who took their evidence.

'Much less,' Stenwold suggested. 'Their force is now far more mechanized than General Malkan's Seventh was. Even if you break up the rails leading from Helleron, I'd guess they'll have enough automotives to get their siege engines here quickly.'

'Their siege engines,' said the Ant impassively, and Stenwold experienced a sinking feeling, wondering if the man – and, by extension, all of the Ants at Malkan's Folly – actually *believed* those stories from Myna. He had met that problem before with Ant-kinden. They lived in a world of absolute veracity when it came to their own people, and by contrast they found all outsiders unreliable and duplicitous.

'There will be Mynan soldiers as well,' Kymene spoke up. 'Some may come here. Will you let them fight alongside you?'

The Ant commander made a discouraging noise. 'I am not happy about asking my men to fight here alongside people who cannot follow our orders. Malkan's Folly is a machine, efficient and carefully calibrated. Any fleeing Myna will be permitted to resupply here, then pass on westwards. Our fortress is for Sarn alone to defend.' His almost uninflected tone concealed whether he meant this as an insult or not. 'Collegium need not fear enemies from the north,' he added, for Stenwold's benefit. 'Tell your Assembly that much.' For a moment a measure of real disdain flickered across the man's face. 'We take it that you *will* fight?'

Stenwold was uncomfortably aware of Kymene's eyes fixed on him too, but all he could do was nod and hope that his people would see things the same way.

Jodry Drillen had not seen his day going like this. He was the Speaker for the Assembly, after all, and it was hard to explain to those around him why he had decided to grace the scene of a particularly unpleasant-looking murder.

Still, the College Master who ran the department of justice was obviously flattered by his presence. The task of overseeing the law and order of the city had always been undertaken by the College, on the basis that those who formulated the city's laws were best fit to enforce them, and investigating a crime was simply research in a different hat. Academically, however, it was not highly regarded, and so the Speaker's personal attention was a much appreciated sign of support.

'What's it *for*?' Jodry murmured.

They were standing in the central room of Banjacs Gripshod's townhouse, which took up all three floors and the cellar and was mostly filled with a . . . a *machine*, was as far as Jodry would commit himself.

Standing beside him was a lecturer in artifice, a mechanic of fifteen years brought in to answer this precise question, and he just shook his head, eyes as wide as Jodry's own. 'I have not the first idea, Speaker, and that's my educated opinion. I've never seen anything like it.'

'It's not just a . . . murder weapon, then?' Jodry pressed.

'Must have taken years to build. I know the Spiders say that revenge tastes better in the morning, but I reckon most people would've forgot why they wanted to kill someone by the time this thing got finished.'

The mortal remains of Reyna Pullard were still being prised off the machine itself. There was not much left of her, and what survived was charred black. A discharge of lightning from the device had practically incinerated her. The thunderous discharge, and her scream, had been loud enough to alert people outside the building, and that had led to Jodry standing here, hoping that it had been quick and mostly painless, despite the evidence of his eyes.

It might have been an accident, of course, save for Banjacs Gripshod's own reaction. When the city watch had finally had to force their way into the house, he had practically assaulted them, screaming that the dead woman had betrayed him and making threats and demands . . . When they had shouldered their way into this room, he had become hysterical, taking them as more of the 'enemies' that he was apparently obsessed with, calling them traitors to their city. With due respect for his age, he had been confined to his personal chambers under guard. It seemed very likely that his mind had turned in on itself a long time before, and this regrettable business was just the final symptom.

Except for the murderous machine, which was certainly intended for *something*, but was sufficiently complex – or possibly redundant – that a College artifice master had no idea what it was for. A little voice nagged in Jodry's mind regarding Reyna Pullard's warning: Banjacs Gripshod was going to blow up the city . . .

Jodry did not believe in machines that destroyed cities but, if he did, they would probably look something like this.

There was a small cough at his elbow and he glanced down to find his chief secretary, Arvi, attending on him. To Jodry's knowledge, he had left the Fly-kinden back at his own house, but the man's efficiency seemed not to acknowledge bounds of time or distance.

'Master Maker to see you, Master Drillen.'

Jodry stared at him. 'Stenwold Maker?' he asked, although he knew no others.

'He arrived at the airfield with some numbers less than an hour ago, and he has been tracking you down ever since,' Arvi reported smartly.

'Some numbers . . . ? You make it sound as though he's invading us.' Jodry shook himself. 'Send him in, for the world's sake. I'm in need of a pillar of sanity to lean on.'

But Stenwold, when he entered, did not look overly supportive. He was wearing somewhat tattered artificer's canvas, streaked with soot and blood: not an Assembler of Collegium, but a man back from a war.

'Jodry, I need to speak to the Assembly as soon as it's in session,' were the first words out of Stenwold's mouth, not even a greeting for his old friend.

'Granted, of course. You'll be first on the list tomorrow

257

morning.' Because Jodry could see in his face that it was important, whatever *it* was. Then a memory shot through him, as shocking and terrible as the charge that must have killed Pullard: Stenwold had returned from *Myna*.

'We've had no reliable news . . .' Jodry breathed. 'Sten . . .'

'You have no idea, Jodry.' Stenwold shook his head, his eyes haunted. 'The city's not going to like what I have to say, but it needs to listen. How's it been here?'

'Rough. Sufficiently on edge that I suspect your news is only what people have been waiting to hear for a tenday and more. What news we get . . . well, it's plain that *something's* happening in Three-city territory . . . Everyone's going armed. Everyone's looking for enemies . . .' He gestured behind him at the towering glass and bronze and steel of Banjacs's machine. 'This . . . Banjacs Gripshod, you remember? He's murdered his assistant. His reasons? He said she was a spy for the enemy. For the Empire, he said at one point. He even demanded to speak to you.'

Stenwold gazed up at the bewildering tubes and chambers of the device. 'You're so sure she wasn't?'

Jodry sighed, wanting very much to just sit down on the floor, and to the pits with the dignity of his office. 'Oh, she was a spy all right. She was *my* spy, who was telling me that our most notorious failed artificer was plotting some sort of terrible revenge on the city. If the Empire's hand is anywhere, Sten, it's probably behind this . . . thing.'

'Then have someone look at it.'

'First, don't you think I have? Second, the last person who touched it was Pullard and she's charcoal. And Banjacs Gripshod is mad enough that we'd never work out if this is an Imperial plot or not until . . .' He looked plaintively at Stenwold. 'How bad, Sten? Is there an "until"?'

Stenwold did not answer him, but kept staring up at the gleaming lines of Banjacs's killing engine.

★

258

It was a short enough speech. Men had taken up more of the Assembly's time with complaints about the duties levied on beech nuts.

'Masters, Gownsmen and Townsmen magnates of the Collegiate Assembly,' Stenwold had addressed them. Almost the full house had been there, despite the short notice. Assemblers developed a certain instinct, and Stenwold had seldom tabled a motion himself since the war. It was almost as though every man and woman who had been voted in at the last Lots, and every College Master who sat in the Amphiophos by right of academic credentials, had been waiting for today, forever keeping a note in their diaries: *Stenwold Maker to declare war.*

But, of course, Stenwold Maker could not declare war. That was not how Collegium was run. Stenwold Maker could only ask to speak to the Assembly, to propose a motion that they, in their wisdom, would accept or decline.

'I am returned from Myna,' he had told them. 'You will have heard some news, conflicting accounts, rumours that are true and rumours that are misinformed, or lies planted by the Empire. I have seen what happened in Myna with my own eyes. The armies of the Empire have taken it swiftly and brutally, and despite all that its defenders could do to keep their freedom. The Treaty of Gold has been breached. I am sure that the Imperial ambassador will say that Myna commenced the hostilities, and has been complaining stridently about the aggressive attitude of the Empire's newly freed neighbours since the war. Myna is but one city, and backed by two more, all three still rebuilding and recovering from the effects of almost two decades of occupation. The Empire has tens of cities, armies of tens of thousands. You all know the chances of Myna initiating a war that it could not possibly win.

'The Collegiate Assembly signed the Treaty of Gold, and in that treaty we agreed to raise a sword against any who breaks it by attacking another signatory state. The Empire signed. Myna and its allies signed.

'We have the option to turn away now, to believe the claims that the Empire's reconquest of its former slaves is just an isolated incident, just as they claimed when they took Tark in the last war. We will be less than we were, if we do that. The word of Collegium will never again carry quite the weight it did, our reputation will lose its shine, and our allies will look on us with a doubt that would otherwise have been unthinkable.

'I am aware that Myna is far away, that trade with Myna is not as lucrative as trade with the Empire, that we have been sapped by war ere now, have lost family and friends to it, more than we can afford. I, of all people, know this.

'But what we have never lost is what makes us ourselves: that nobility of purpose, that breadth of vision, that knowledge and understanding of the world that makes us Collegium. If we are over-proud sometimes of what we have built, then at least we have built something to take pride in. Has Helleron done so, with its weathervane loyalties? Have the Spiderlands, with their hollow promises?

'My motion is this: that the Empire has breached the Treaty of Gold and, though that treaty be nothing more than paper, we are of Collegium and paper carries a weight here that it does not amongst the armies of the Wasps. In declaring war on the Three-city Alliance, the Empire has declared its intent to bring war to us all. I ask the Assembly to vote, for we cannot let this stand unopposed. We must set ourselves against the tide. War on every tyrant who would enslave the world. War on the Empress and her armies. I call for a declaration of war against the Wasp Empire.'

There was some debate. The usual voices struck up against Stenwold's, Helmess Broiler taking the lead as he had ever done, but the ranks of the Empire's champions had thinned, and sounded hollow amidst the echoes of Stenwold's words. Honory Bellowern, speaking on behalf of the absent Aagen, rose to speak, but Stenwold had already robbed him of his arguments, and what he was left with sounded much like a threat.

At Jodry's insistence, the vote was held at the end of the morning's session, although, in truth, few enough felt moved to prolong the debate. The usual murmur and gossip that was a ubiquitous backdrop to most Assembly discussions was absent. The great majority of those present had no words to offer. Fear stalked invisibly about the chamber, stilling voices, leaving a trail of drawn, tense expressions. To speak into that silence would be to take a side publicly, to be noted down in the books of the Rekef or the Collegiate Merchant Companies for later investigation.

Almost four in ten of the Assembly did not vote, even though the ballot was a secret one. The weight of the decision was such that they did not wish themselves to be responsible for the result, whichever way it went.

Of votes against, there were barely two score. After the tally, Stenwold took the floor once more, and his few closing words would be rattling from every printing press in the city within the hour.

Before noon the criers were already out in the streets of Collegium, calling out the news. The three extant Merchant Companies put their recruiting officers at street corners, with a plan already being drawn up for more companies to be formed. Word came from the Sarnesh, by rail, that they would stand by their ally, that their own forces were already mustering.

Collegium was going to war once again.

'"Let no man say that the eyes of Collegium are turned away from the world. Let history record we take upon ourselves this responsibility. Wherever the metal meets, there we will be." Stenwold Maker has finally got what he wants.'

Eujen Leadwell's voice, familiar from so many debates, remained steady throughout the reading: the printers had copies of Stenwold Maker's speech and the Assembly's decision for public purchase by mid-afternoon the same day. Now, with evening closing in outside Raullo Mummers's studio, the little band of students listened as Eujen relayed their future to them.

Sartaea te Mosca circulated, bringing them bowls of hot Spider-kinden chocolate, an expensive luxury, but, then, she asked them, what was she saving it for?

At the last, Eujen set down the cheaply printed scroll, his shoulders slumped.

'Founder's bloody mark.' Raollo Mummers lit his pipe with slightly shaking hands, letting the sweet smell of tallum pollen seep into the room.

'Eujen,' te Mosca said softly, 'I'm sorry.'

'What was I thinking?' Eujen asked them all.

'You're going to have to be more specific,' the Antspider suggested. 'You have all sorts of mad ideas.'

'Peace with the Empire. Peace with the world. A tenyear going by without another ruinous war.' He held up a hand to forestall argument. 'And I'm *not* a traitor. I'm not even an Imperial sympathizer, and there are plenty of those in the Assembly! I just . . . must it come to this? And when we beat them back – *if* we do – what then? Do we come round to the same point a few years later? Do we carry the war past their borders? Do we end up enslaving or eradicating Averic's people so we can be safe from them? Is that all there is?'

All eyes turned to the Wasp-kinden youth, marking the distance that seemed to have grown between him and them. Averic's face was expressionless, save for a tightness at the jaw, a token of his self-control. 'Next time, or the next,' he murmured and, if there was an edge of desperation buried somewhere in his voice, it seemed more that he was desperate to console his friend Eujen rather than over any fears for his own fate or that of his kin. 'There are those in the Empire who see the world as more than just something to be conquered, or why was I sent here at all? There will come a time when those people will make their voices heard.'

'If the Empire can be driven from Myna, perhaps,' the Antspider suggested. 'A quick defeat might bring the Empress to her senses. If the Assembly can grasp the idea of being gracious in victory.' She was wearing her Company sash still, and Eujen's initial horror at it had been dulled, first by familiarity and then by recent events.

'The Coldstone Company's set to go, are they?' he asked her.

'So they tell me. First into the breach – that sort of stuff. Maker's Own are ready, as well. Outright's lads are staying home to help raise fresh companies.'

'Where do I go to sign up?' Eujen asked her.

For a moment she just stared at him in silence while, across the room, Raullo Mummers dropped his pipe, grinding hurriedly at the embers as they spilled out.

'Don't,' said Straessa the Antspider.

Eujen's expression was hurt. 'You have. Even Gerethwy has.' He indicated the lanky Woodlouse-kinden bent silently over some sort of schematic, glancing up only as his name was mentioned. He, too, wore the Coldstone Company sash.

'I don't want you to, Eujen,' she insisted.

For a long while, he stared at her. 'You think I'm a coward, too?'

'Idiot.' She was across to him quickly, laying a hand on his arm, but he flinched away angrily, then rounded on her again, his mouth open for some angry retort. In a movement like a fencer's lunge she had kissed him, once but firmly, letting his words drop into the abyss of it. 'You're brave enough to say what you believe in every day, Eujen, but if you're there when we go to Myna, I won't be able to fight, because I'll always be worrying about you. Collegium's going to need you, but later, when we really do have a chance at peace, not now when all we've got is war. Join one of the new companies, if you like. Form a student company, even. Please, not the warfront.'

He stared at her for a long, stretched moment, conflicting emotions fighting beneath his skin. 'And Gerethwy?' he said at last.

'As if she cares what happens to me,' the Woodlouse intoned, and the painfully tense mood was broken.

'Besides, Averic needs you here,' Straessa added. 'He's not exactly going to sign up to slaughter his own people.'

'Unless you're leaving?' te Mosca put in, as she passed the Wasp a fresh bowl. 'Nobody'd blame you.'

Averic regarded them all coolly and, for a long while, it seemed as if he had metamorphosed, since Eujen's reading, into something else, something foreign and hostile. The *enemy*.

Then something twitched, a muscle tugging in his throat. 'I don't know what to do,' he said softly. 'If I go . . . I'm army age. It'll be straight into the Light Airborne, and up against the snapbows of Collegium, most likely. I've had all the training before I came here. All I need's the uniform. If I stay . . . then am I a traitor? Or will your people just decide that I'm a spy?' He said the words without much emotion, but his casual arms-folded pose had tightened, hands clutching at his own flesh.

'You're a student of the Great College,' Eujen said. 'That gives you all the rights of a Collegiate citizen except the vote. You're one of us for as long as you care to be.'

Only the set of Averic's eyes showed how much he desperately wished that to be true but, despite Eujen's reassurances, everyone there was thinking how, in the final analysis, his future was unlikely to be his to choose.

The next day the first news, contradictory and unclear, began to filter into the city from Solarno.

Eighteen

'This is it,' Gizmer told them, flitting into the Fly-kinden common room at head height.

There were a dozen or so sitting about the floor, Pingge and Kiin amongst them. They had not flown in three days, the routine of their training abruptly broken without explanation. Everyone had felt change on the wind.

'How do you know?' someone asked, but Pingge's question overrode it. 'Where?'

'Myna,' one of the Flies said immediately, but Gizmer shook his head irritably.

'Myna's gone,' he told them. 'Who've you been listening to, that you don't know Myna's gone? Szar as well, by now, I'd lay money on it. Maybe we fly against Maynes. Ant-kinden are stubborn.'

'The Eighth Army has the Spearflights,' Kiin said quietly. 'That's not what we're trained for.'

'Then what are we for?' Pingge demanded. 'Sitting about and getting fat, right now? Who'd have thought life in the army would be as grand as this?' It was true, they ate well, had more time to themselves, slept better and drew more pay than they ever had in the factories. There was respect, too: they were with the army, and that meant something – even for Flies.

'When they're not chaining us inside the fliers,' Gizmer muttered darkly, dropping down close to her.

'Who's even seen a pilot these last three days?' Kiin asked.

There was a mutter of discussion: nobody had.

'Final testing,' someone put in. 'I heard talk – some other hoop they wanted to jump the machines through.'

'The machines aren't at the airfield, either. They've taken them elsewhere, or they've flown them off without us,' Gizmer put in. Of all of them, the yoke of the army chafed him the most. He was forever sneaking off and poking his nose into things, getting where he shouldn't be and gleaning scraps of information.

'Three days is a long time to be testing anything,' Pingge observed. 'Unless they failed the test and all crashed or something.'

This spurred a general ripple of laughter, but Kiin said, 'Don't.'

'What? Sentiment, for the master race?' Pingge jibed her. 'Big bald Aarmon got to you, has he?'

'Shut up, Pingge,' Gizmer hissed. A moment later and the Fly-kinden fell silent as Aarmon himself walked into the room. He was wearing his aviator's uniform, black insulated leathers with gold flashes at the shoulder, a chitin helm and goggles dangling by their straps from one hand. His clothes were creased, the tunic beneath sweat-stained where his cuirass was open down the front. Probably he had not been back in the capital for longer than it took to quit the airfield and march here.

'Up, all of you,' he ordered them. If he had heard Pingge talking, he gave no sign of it. As always – and as with all the pilots – his words were sparing, given only grudgingly. 'Sergeant Kiin, rouse the others. All bombardiers to assemble in the quad, ten minutes.' His soulless eyes raked across them, but paused on nobody. Then he ducked out of the room, leaving them to follow orders – and *trusting* them to do it. It had been a long time since the Wasps had needed to guard them.

'Sergeant now, is it?' Gizmer observed acidly.

Kiin shrugged desperately. 'It's just because I fly with him, it must be.'

Pingge smirked. 'Oh, he likes you, that one. You always did go for the emotionless, goggle-eyed type.'

'Come on, you heard him,' Kiin said. 'Up.' She was already on her feet, and there was a general mutinous mutter as most of the Flies followed suit.

'Going to make me call you "sir" now?' Pingge goaded her.

'Look, he'll take it out of my hide if we're not formed up within whatever time we have left,' Kiin pleaded. 'Come *on*, set an example.'

'Right you are, sir.' But Pingge got to her feet, and then hauled Gizmer up after her. 'Drill and parades. I could get used to all of it but the standing about.'

Kiin headed into the sleeping quarters and managed to jolly along those Fly-kinden who had been taking the chance for a lie-in, then the entire company was out in the quad just about inside Aarmon's deadline. The pilots were assembling at the same time, a good half of them plainly just out of their machines, back from whatever three-day test they had been engaged on.

'Look,' Pingge hissed. Most of the Flies had now learned the soldier's trick of whispering on parade, barely moving their lips. Pingge jerked her head to indicate direction, and one by one the Fly-kinden's eyes flicked over to the newcomers marching in.

For a moment it was as though they were looking back in time, for here they came: two score Wasp-kinden, the same number of Flies following. *Look at them*, they thought – *a bunch of clueless, untrained factory workers, clerks and servants, frightened and undisciplined and without the faintest idea of what awaits them. Like looking in a mirror.* Only it was not, not any more. The new Flies could only stare wide-eyed at Pingge, Kiin and the rest standing as straight as spears in their black tunics edged with yellow, soldiers of the Empire every bit as much as were the Light Airborne.

Then a murmur began amongst Pingge's peers, not about the

new Flies but the Wasps that had preceded them, now standing to attention across from Aarmon's people.

'Quiet!' Kiin meant to hiss, but the word turned into an order somehow, and silenced them.

The new Wasp recruits stood with the same wordless discipline that Aarmon and his fellows had possessed since the Flies had first set eyes on them. Their faces betrayed no uncertainty or fear at this new assignment – indeed they betrayed little enough emotion at all. When Aamon strode out before them, there was none of the tensing or minute adjustments to the presence of a superior officer that soldiers would normally show – and it was plain that only some of them were regular soldiers, just as only some of Aarmon's pilots had been. With these newcomers, though, the difference was considerably more marked.

Almost half of them were women.

It was unthinkable. Wasp women served and raised children, and perhaps sometimes looked after the family home and wealth while their menfolk fought. Wasp women did not stand impeccably to attention, in *uniform*. Yet here they were: eighteen women amongst twenty-two men, not standing apart, nor a step behind, but standing there as if they were *equals*.

Aarmon made eye contact with one of the new Wasps, and then the newcomers were marching into the barracks without a word, the Flies following behind them in a nervous, eddying mob. *Going to take up our old rooms?* Pingge wondered.

She knew that she should be nervous, too, but in the pit of her stomach she felt the first fluttering of excitement. All that training was finally about to come to something.

'Sergeant Kiin, we march to Armour Square. Follow my company,' Aarmon instructed, and Kiin's voice piped back, 'Yes, sir.'

'I'm still not convinced we've not been called here for our own executions,' Totho muttered as he descended the steps, carefully watched by at least half a dozen Wasp soldiers and a couple of their engineers.

Drephos turned away from the pair of Consortium men he had been talking to, brushing them aside with a wave of his gauntleted hand and ignoring their surly looks in response.

'Overly elaborate, don't you think?' They had no privacy here in Capitas – with servants spying on them in the quarters they had been assigned, while here in Armour Square, below the very balcony the Empress would use, it seemed as if someone had detailed an entire army to keep an eye on them. In such conditions, Drephos's response was simply to speak his mind and not care who heard him. To his mind, he had the Empire in a vice: the mechanical offspring of his genius were at the forefront of the war, and he considered himself irreplaceable. And, besides, he was hardly being coy with their engineers: so far they had got everything they had asked him for. If he was wrong, if he was expendable after all, then watching what he said would make no difference whatsoever, now that they were here, in the heart of Empire.

Being here in the first place was what had put Totho on edge, though. He had argued passionately against obeying the summons. 'Plenty of Wasp-kinden, even, know to make themselves scarce when the word comes to return to Capitas,' he hissed now, trying fruitlessly not to be overheard by their constant escort.

'I'm assured the purges are over.' Drephos's bleak expression belied his words, but his dry smile suggested that such matters as purges were for lesser men to worry about. 'Besides, I want a look at their new orthopters. What little I've heard is maddening . . . it sounds as though they've leapt ahead of the Solarnese models somehow . . .' One of the Consortium men coughed pointedly, but Drephos ignored him. 'You've set the similophone up?' he asked Totho.

'No thanks to everyone else. They were so worried I might

be rigging a bomb or something, it took me three times as long as it should have done.'

The similophone was one of the Iron Glove Cartel's rare peacetime inventions, a little toy that Drephos and Totho had cooked up together that was only now seeing wider use. It consisted of an ear that received sound, and a loom that transcribed the sound pattern into silk cloth, which a similo-phone drum could then decode and speak back. Totho and Drephos had used the device instead of writing letters, not so much for security but just because they were artificers, and they could.

Now their toy had been requested to bear witness to history in the making.

'You can understand their caution, surely,' Drephos said smoothly.

Totho grimaced darkly, leaning in to murmur, 'I'm serious. We shouldn't have come. You're underestimating them, and *you* never met the Empress. She's terrifying.'

Troops were marching into Armour Square now: a sample only of the might of the Empire. Totho could make out Light Airborne, infantry, Engineers, Aviation Corps, slavers, representatives from all the different machines that made the Empire run. The square was large, and there were hundreds of them standing shoulder to shoulder, all those different uniforms, all that armour, the patterns and designs, and all of it black and gold.

'Colonel-Auxillian,' one of the Consortium men put in. 'If you will – we have so little time before the address.'

Drephos rounded on him grandly. 'You have our great-shotters and you have our sentinels. What other of my wonders are you about to ask for?'

'Colonel . . .' Now it was the Consortium man's turn to lean in, as though even he feared to be overheard by the ubiquitous guards. 'The Empire would pay far more for the formula to the Bee-killer.'

'The . . .' And Drephos let the word trail off into a thoughtful pause that ended with, 'So,' and nothing more. His smile returned, and probably only Totho could tell that it was a little too fixed. 'The Bee-killer, of course,' he said smoothly, a moment later. 'The formula did not survive the war. Do you think that I would not have made more, had I the means?'

'The coffers of the Consortium—' the man went on, but Drephos held up his metal hand again, imperiously.

'It did not survive,' he said curtly, and then turned away, his attention wholly directed up towards the balcony, where generals and other dignitaries were beginning to make their appearance.

'We shouldn't have come,' Totho growled again, and this time Drephos said nothing.

From the ranks, Esmail watched a conspiracy assemble, a web being strung. He – which was to say Ostrec – was simply another soldier at this point: an officer of the Quartermaster Corps amongst his peers, and ostensibly not a sniff of the Rekef about him. All around, the other servants of the Empire marched in to form their serried ranks, all the organs of the Imperial war machine falling, unit by unit, into an expectant hush.

Esmail marked the faces: the newcomers, the absences. General Brugan was in place already, just left of centre, even now giving place to the Empress, though she had yet to appear. Further left was the bloated corpulence of Colonel Harvang, the impeccably turned-out Vecter lost in his shadow. There were a couple of new faces, too: majors in the Rekef Outlander arrived from the East-Empire, Brugan's old stamping ground. True, there were a few up there, overlooking Armour Square, who were not Brugan's, bought and sold: those who were too useful to dispose of, too doubtful to approach – engineers mostly. General Lien's bald head gleamed in the sun, whilst beside him that bearded eccentric was presumably the genius aviation Major – no, Colonel, now – Varsec. Aside from these two, and a meagre handful of others, everyone up there whom Esmail could see was firmly in Brugan's camp.

There had been a very subtle changing of the guard at certain levels of the palace, as men loyal to Brugan had been summoned in from distant posts. Others had received surprising postings – mid-ranking officers sent west to the front, Rekef men posted to the Principalities to spy on the savages. Everything had been above board, nothing irregular; in some cases reassignment had even come with a promotion attached. Only someone with a deep understanding of the hidden loyalties of Capitas would have understood that everyone coming *in* was Brugan's man, while everyone going *out* was not.

The net was drawing tight, by the most delicate of stages. Esmail almost felt that he should hold his breath for it. Brugan was manoeuvring for a time when everyone around the Empress would be loyal to the general of the Rekef first, to the throne second.

Esmail-as-Ostrec was already standing to attention, but he – and every soldier there – still managed to straighten still further, shoulders back and brimming with Imperial pride, for the Empress had made her appearance, walking into the heart of Brugan's net without seeming to notice.

To his eyes, she seemed to shine like the sun itself, the outpouring of her grand and unbridled power making him wonder that those others could simply stand so close without burning. Of course, they saw none of it: they were blindly Apt, and he must pretend to see none of it either, or else give himself away. Even so, he could not tear his gaze from her: Her Imperial Majesty Seda the First, Empress of all the Wasps, young and beautiful and commanding all eyes, all hearts. Esmail could almost hear the collective mental gasp of the soldiers all around him as Seda strode to the balcony rail and looked down on them. She wore a long gown of velvet, the sleeves loose so that they fell like wings and left her lower arms bare. Over this was buckled a cuirass and, although it was a fine piece of work, light and elegant, its resemblance to the banded mail of the Light Airborne was not by chance. She had a scabbarded sword at her side, such as no Imperial woman had ever openly worn before, and in her right hand was a slender lance, its narrow head a gilded dart. Her skin was like alabaster, her hair of gold. Esmail felt tears come to his eyes, seeing her, and did not know whether they were Ostrec's or his own.

The building she had commandeered for this address was a flat-roofed, three-storey counting house of the Quartermaster Corps, previously just an abode of clerks and their numerate slaves. After today it would be known as the Little Palace, never again to be profaned by the murky business of commerce. The clerks would have to find themselves another haunt.

'My people.' Her voice was strong and clear, and the great mass of soldiers, almost two thousand of them all told, kept silent for her. Esmail was well aware that there must be at least another thousand in the buildings all around the square, looking out from windows and lesser balconies, or listening intently from within: Consortium merchants, craftsmen, the wealthy of good family, retired officers, slaves and the women of all of the above – here was the Empire in miniature.

'I am to ask great things of you,' Seda told them, as if she was speaking to each Wasp individually. 'Our Empire has fought through many trying times, but our trials are not over; indeed, they are barely begun.

'Your blood and sweat has recaptured the Empire and returned it to its rightful ruler,' she told them. 'You have held your loyalty firm, when a dozen voices tried to prise you away from your convictions. You have marched on the traitor-governors, who fancied themselves a dozen little emperors, and who would have diluted the grandeur of our state until we had become nothing better than the Lowlands: so many little cities fighting one another. I speak to you, therefore, as heroes of the Empire, saviours of its pride and peace. Do you ask: is my work not done?'

She actually paused for an answer, and Esmail felt it well up within him, despite himself. He opened his mouth, terrified by his loss of control, about to single himself out in all this great throng.

'*No!*' The shout arose from hundreds of throats all around him.

'No,' she agreed quietly, in the echo, but every man there heard her. 'For there are those who look upon all we have built with envious eyes. There are those lesser kinden, little men, who know that they can never achieve what we have achieved, and whose only response is to try and tear down what we have made. They have worked against us, sometimes even amongst us, for many years. Perhaps there are even some here now whose loyalties are bought by the enemies of the Empire.'

Esmail quashed a sudden up-welling of panic, feeling the mood of the men around him respond to the Empress's tone, ugly and fierce. He wondered if there would be another purge soon, people dragged from their homes and workshops and barracks, branded disloyal, traitors. The men who stood here would cheer that to the echo. *Until their own time came.*

'Do you think the traitor-governors worked alone?' Seda demanded of them. 'No! For there are those beyond our borders who encouraged them, and gave them aid.' She let the words ring off the walls for a moment before continuing. 'Do you think that Myna and its allies would dare raid our borders without help? *No!* For they were armed and instructed by our enemies. And now, now that we have regained our strength despite all of their schemes and machinations, they have declared their intent to destroy us utterly. They cannot abide to live in a world where we are strong, and where we are not dependent on them, as they have made their neighbours dependent upon them. They cannot tolerate the fact that we are stronger than them, and prouder than them, that we are *better* than them. My people, Collegium and its allies have declared war.'

She left another pause there, but not for words, and the angry roar of the crowd sounded like thunder, like the leadshotters, like *war.*

'So I must call upon you once again,' Seda urged them, her clear voice cutting through the sound of their anger. 'The Empire calls on you, for the Empire is beset on all sides by its enemies, by the envy of lesser kinden. The Empire must be defended, and there is only one way to defeat the Collegiate threat once and for all!

'I call upon you, each and every one of you, to return to your armies, to your subordinates, to your fellows. Tell them that the Empress has need of them. Tell them that the *Empire* has need of them.' She thrust her spear into the air, and the sun flashed on its gilded tip. 'Either we must spread our wings over the Lowlands and bring them within our shadow, or everything we have worked for will be for nothing. Either they will destroy us, with their cunning and their lies, or we must conquer them. Every soldier must do his duty if the Empire is to survive. The Empire places its trust in each and every one of you and all your comrades. Will you stand?'

'*Yes!*' There was no hesitation. Every throat was shouting out the word.

'Will you defend the Empire?' Seda cried.

'Yes!'

'Will you take war to the very gates of Collegium?'

'Yes!'

'Then you are my heroes, and because of you the Empire shall last a thousand years!' she declared. 'Go from here now! March out and spread the word! You have a duty but, more, you have a destiny. The Empire cannot fall! The Empire will not kneel! The Empire shall prevail, and it shall prevail through you, its champions!'

The roar of approval that followed must have been heard all the way across the city, and Esmail cheered too and, in that moment, forgot that he was not one of them.

Part Two

The Storm

Nineteen

The twin-rotored heliopter had been flying high, tilted nose-down at an unlikely angle as its pilot made the best of the headwind. It was an ungainly little craft, a wooden body like a squat teardrop with an outrigger either side for the blades and a box-kite tail. Someone had known a little about aeronautics when they built it, for it was swifter in the air than heliopters normally were but, when the Collegiate orthopter clipped past its nose to investigate, the visitor's response was sluggish, lurching aside and then taking its own time to steady itself again in the air.

Taki watched from on high, in her *Esca Magni*. This was only a routine patrol, but the newcomer's approach had seemed a good opportunity to set one of her students loose, so she had flashed the order. Now a young Beetle woman was guiding her flier past the visiting heliopter, before bringing herself level with it and matching course and speed. Taki nodded, satisfied.

She had not seen this model of heliopter before and it bore no markings, but it hardly seemed like something that the Wasps would use. Even now it was dropping towards Solarno, the pilot handling the craft ably despite its leaden response, and Taki used her heliograph to send another set of instructions to her trainee: break off, return to field. She could only hope that the girl would realize that Taki wanted her to advise people of the newcomer, because there was no signal for that in the code book.

The Beetle pilot obediently let her orthopter drop, far swifter and better controlled than the heliopter. Collegium had its own standard model flier, which had gone into production after Taki herself had pitched up in the city with her Solarnese know-how and got together with the capable engineers of the College. The orthopter now vanishing down towards the city was built on the same lines as the *Esca*: a two-winged craft with balancing halteres, hunchbacked over the clockwork engine, a long, tapering tail behind, and a pair of rotary piercers before. At the start, they had not wanted to build them armed, but Taki had always been a fighting pilot, the cream of Solarnese pride, and she had held out over this until she got her way.

She really was very, very glad now that she had won that particular battle.

Collegium had a modest airfleet of these craft now, and Taki's students had gone on to become tutors themselves some time ago for, in another stroke of fortune, the Collegiate–Solarnese trade that the end of the war had sparked up had led to an upsurge of interest in flying. The fighting aviators of Solarno had been much in vogue, heroes of books and songs and a play or two. Taki had done well out of that but, given all those young men and women who had found sufficient coin for flying lessons, so had the city.

They called the Collegiate models Stormreaders.

Taki let her *Esca* slide into the view of the heliopter pilot, close enough to peer through the broad windows of his canopy. Now *his* machine was not meant for combat, or at least she sincerely hoped not. It was no cargo-hauler either. She could not tell precisely what it was good for, and she was worried that the answer might actually be nothing.

The pilot was a decent hand, though, and made a neat enough landing, after circling a few times while the ground crew wheeled a couple of Stormreaders out of the way, and she made one more circuit herself just to be sure there was no funny business, before making her own descent.

When she had got the *Esca* down, dropping neatly onto its landing legs without anyone needing to clear anything aside for her, the heliopter cockpit was open and a man was already clambering out. The ground crew, some off-duty pilots and a pair of Merchant Company soldiers watched him dubiously, but Taki felt that she owed it to a fellow pilot to take the lead.

'Hey, you there, welcome to Collegium!' At the sound of her voice the other onlookers relaxed and let her get on with it, which irritated her. True, she was de facto an Associate Master of the College, teaching aviation to packed classrooms when she could be bothered to turn up, but she was not even a Collegiate citizen, nobody had given her a rank or a title, and away from her students she should have no authority whatsoever. Still, being a legend was a hard thing to live with, and anyone who had anything to do with the Collegium airfields knew te Schola Taki-Amre, and held her in high esteem.

The heliopter pilot dropped heavily to the ground. He was a short man, which was to say he was only a foot taller than she was, wearing a flying helmet with a full-face mask, a military-looking piece of kit. He stripped it off as she approached, revealing an unappealing visage, a squat broad-mouthed face with small suspicious eyes, a flat nose and skin that was white enough to look dead. *Halfbreed,* she noted, *Fly-kinden and . . . Ant, I think. Tarkesh Ant, with that skin.*

Still, some of his unhealthy skin tone was probably weariness, she guessed. There were grey circles about his eyes, and his sag-shouldered pose suggested a man who had been on the move for some time. 'What brings you to Collegium?' she asked him brightly.

'Stenwold Maker,' he replied, his voice flat and almost tone-less, and abruptly he had everyone's attention, including that of the snapbows the soldiers were carrying.

'That's a big name to be throwing around right now. He's a busy man. Has to be him, does it?' Taki asked lightly. It seemed highly unlikely that this individual would turn out to be Rekef, as she had yet to find any crowd that he would blend in with, and his instant annoyance at being questioned would not be a good survival trait in a professional spy. Nonetheless, she had lost a few nights to dreams of Myna burning, so she was not inclined to be trusting.

'Yes,' said the halfbreed wearily, as though even that one word was too much effort. 'It really, really does. You've got him here, or do I have to walk somewhere?'

'Maybe I can take a message,' Taki suggested.

The look the man gave her was venomous. 'Is this what you *do*? Is this your *job*, to make my life difficult? Urgent top-secret message, eyes of Stenwold Maker only. How difficult is that to understand? News from Tark, all right?'

'You know that Stenwold Maker doesn't rule this city, I assume,' Taki tried. Despite herself, she was fighting down a smile at the sheer magnitude of the small man's temper. As she spoke, she had to admit that, despite everything the Beetles said about their government, she was not entirely sure that Maker did *not* run things here, but it would not be politic to say so.

'Don't care,' the halfbreed spat out. 'He could clean the privies, for all it would interest me. Now, is someone here going to do the decent thing and take me to him, or do I have to start asking people at random in the street?'

'The forgemasters are all saying that they can't do everything at once,' Jodry declared mildly. He could afford to be amiable, as he sat in the expansive chair behind his desk in the Speaker's office. Stenwold, on his feet and keen to sort matters out and be gone, found the Speaker's ease aggravating.

'Jodry, I was there,' he snapped. 'I saw these monster machines the Empire are deploying. When they come for us or we go to them, we'll need battle automotives. Since we don't actually *have* any, the only thing we can do is armour up any civilian vehicle that could do the job.'

'Yes, yes, and you have made many profligate promises

where the Assembly's purse is concerned, while confiscating private property on that account,' Jodry returned sharply. 'And – yes, requisitioning, if you must, if that makes what is basically theft sound more palatable – and, as I say, now the wretched machines are backed up all over the city like an overflowing drain, because the foundries are working on yet more orthopters. Because Mistress Taki, she *also* saw the same battle you did, and apparently came away with rather different priorities.'

'Just . . . get them to strike a balance. I'm not saying Myna didn't suffer from the air, but these Cyclops machines of theirs . . .' Stenwold shook his head. 'You weren't there.'

'For which I'm profoundly grateful. Worse luck, though, that you're already proposing to go back, along with our Merchant Companies.'

'We didn't stop the Empire early enough before,' Stenwold replied promptly. 'If we can get to them while they're consolidating in Three-city territory – or even at Helleron! – then we can win the war. If we leave them to come to us . . . the Sarnesh knew that was foolishness when they went out to meet the Wasps at Malkan's Folly, Jodry. They nearly had the city the last time we let them march up to our gates.'

'And what,' said Jodry, with infinite patience, 'do you propose to do about Solarno? You've heard the same reports as I have.'

Stenwold opened his mouth, then scowled. 'I've heard far too many reports, and all of them contradictory. I hear reports about Spiderlands troops, and mention of the Aldanrael, but other people are saying the Empire is there.'

'Yes, both at the same time,' Jodry agreed. 'We didn't think of that one when we gave the Aldanrael a bloody nose, eh?'

At that point there was a polite knock, low down on the door, and then Arvi stepped in, with a brief bow towards the desk. 'Master Drillen, I'm afraid there are visitors here for Master Maker.'

'Tell them to wait,' Stenwold growled, but Arvi, with an arch look indicating that he knew exactly who he took orders from, added, 'It is Mistress Taki, and another gentleman who seems to have come straight from the airfield. It appears to be a matter of grave urgency.'

The two Beetle statesmen exchanged glances, the tension in the room tightening by another twist.

'Send them in,' Jodry decided, and Arvi bowed again, and backed out.

'You've had no word, of course, from your fellow over Exalsee ways?' Jodry enquired lightly.

Stenwold shook his head, tight-lipped. Word from Laszlo was long overdue.

Arvi reappeared, magically bearing a tray with a fresh bottle of Jodry's favourite vintage, together with an extra pair of bowls. He nearly lost the lot when Taki pushed in past him, and behind her came the awkward figure of a short, pasty-faced halfbreed.

'This here's Master Taxus,' Taki announced to the room in general. She took a full bowl when offered it, explaining, 'He's got a message, top-secret urgent kind of business,' and then she downed the wine in one gulp, apparently washing her hands of the matter.

Stenwold eyed the newcomer, who stared balefully at him, and at practically everything else. 'Word from Tark?' he hazarded.

The halfbreed nodded, reaching into his knee-length flying coat and bringing out a creased letter, folded and sealed in black. 'All yours,' he grunted.

If you've come from Tark, tell me . . . But the letter was being thrust into Stenwold's face, and it was plain that there would be nothing further from this Taxus until it was read. *It must be some word, at least, about the Exalsee situation. Tark is not so far from them. Perhaps they're seeking our aid, for when the Empire comes . . .*

He broke the seal with his thumb and folded the out letter, revealing a missive written in an economic hand.

Master Maker

You will recall me from when we stood off the Vekken together, inside your city. You will recall that I took my men to Malkan's Stand and fought the Wasps alongside the Sarnesh and your own citizens. Later, you supported my people when we returned to our city, with the occupying forces fleeing before us.

I betray my city in writing this. You must burn it when you have read it. Only because I trust you to do so have I gone so far against my instinct as to write this report to you.

We have received an ambassador. She came from Seldis and presented our king and his Tacticians, myself included, with new developments in foreign affairs. A confederation of Spider Aristoi houses, spearheaded by the Aldanrael, has signed treaties with the Empire for mutual defence, she said. As a result of this, an Imperial army was already marching west towards my city. We were not their target, you understand. We were simply in the way, and reckoned by the Wasps as hostile. War was thus upon us.

Our own orthopter scouts confirmed all she said. The Wasps were indeed coming, and with allies not marching under the black and gold. The Spider ambassador then made us what she called an offer and what I call an ultimatum.

Master Maker, the city-state of Tark has yet to recover from the damage the Empire inflicted in its conquest during the last war. Much of our city is not even rebuilt. Our armies are under strength, and we have no stores, no resources.

I am therefore bitterly sorry to tell you that the city-state of Tark has surrendered its independence. We have sworn ourselves as a satrapy to the Spiderlands. Spider-kinden Aristoi are already within our walls, quietly taking the reins whilst assuring us that nothing will change. The army that is now marching on your city will march straight past ours, and we will not raise a single blade against them. Our need to survive makes ingrates of us, and slaves also, I fear.

I am sorry, Master Maker, that Tark has repaid you poorly for your support. My people must live. If I did not remember you so much as a friend, I could not even have gone against my people so far as to warn you. I wish that my duty was looser about my shoulders, so that I could do more.

Forgive us.

Parops.

Stenwold looked up, feeling his fingers crumple and tear at the paper. Jodry was staring at him, and he wondered what expression his own face held just then.

'Who's died?' Taki asked, not quite flippant, but not solemn either.

'The Aldanrael have taken Tark,' Stenwold said flatly. 'This was . . . an old friend sending me all the warning he could. You're right, they'll be coming up the coast like before.' He was about to say more when his eyes fell on Taxus. 'You . . . can at least take a message back to Parops?'

'Back?' the halfbreed demanded. 'What makes you think I'm going back?'

'Well, you . . .' Stenwold frowned. 'Aren't you?'

'Maker – *Master* Maker, if that's how it's done – I don't know just what you read there, but if you know we've got Spiders up where it hurts, then you know Tark's not your friend any more, and your mate that wrote that, he's not either, as soon as the ink dried. Ordering me on this fool's errand was the last thing he did before he became your enemy.'

He left a pause for what he plainly considered an obvious conclusion, and none of them there managed to leap to it.

'I see. I know how it is. Mixed blood, miscegenation, I know.' He scowled at the lot of them. 'Up *here*,' and he jabbed at his temples, 'I'm Ant-kinden. Where it counts, I'm one of them. Now, having delivered some sort of secret business into the hands of Tark's enemies, you think I can go back there?'

And Stenwold did understand. He had known other Ant-kinden, in his time, who had turned their backs on their cities for their cities' own good. Sometimes being a renegade and an exile was a badge of honour. 'Parops ordered you . . .' he murmured.

'I volunteered,' Taxus said shortly. 'I knew what he was about, so I agreed. It needed to be done.' He faced them down, the Flies, the Beetles, all of them: just under five feet of pugnacious attitude.

'So what will you do now?' Stenwold asked him.

'Depends. If you'll trust me for it, I'd rather like to fight some Wasps.'

Stenwold glanced at Taki, who was looking thoughtful.

'We need every pilot we can get, Master Maker,' she agreed. 'I'll make sure someone's keeping an eye on him, but – we have so many unblooded fliers and so few who've actually flown for real. I saw him come in. His craft's a piece of flotsam but he's good with the sticks.'

'He's your responsibility,' Stenwold told her. 'Put him with the Mynans. Get him familiar with the Stormreaders. Soon enough you'll all be shipping out to fight – although whether it's north to Myna or east down the coast is anyone's guess just now.'

Being a parasite was a precarious existence, but Lissart, even injured, was obviously well used to it.

She had the pair of them ensconced within the Spider-kinden baggage train the day before the combined army left Solarno, and since then she and Laszlo had almost been travelling in style, Liss spending the days rocking gently in a wagon, cushioned amidst the supplies, whilst Laszlo ran errands and faced off against other Fly-kinden.

'To think that the only reason I'm in this fix is that I *didn't* want to go work amongst Spiders,' Liss remarked to him one night, as they lay close together in the wagon, surrounded by the whispering breath of sleepers. Her smile, just visible in the starlight, was wistful, so Laszlo kissed it gently. When he pulled away, her expression was the usual: happy, glad to have him there, and yet her eyes demanding to know, *Are you mad? Don't you know how untrustworthy I am yet?* He knew, of course. He was in the jaws of the enemy here, a step away from exposure at every moment. Each day seemed a weird dream-run, sailing through treacherous waters without chart or compass, and yet he was alive and unrevealed each dusk, and so was she. The danger that she would betray him seemed only a small voice amongst all the clamouring perils that surrounded him.

They had been aided by the Spider army's structure, for although the lady of the Aldanrael was their leader, few of the actual soldiers were sworn to her family. Instead there seemed to be a typically piecemeal construction about the Spiderland forces: a number of mercenary bands and Satrapy forces from several different cities, together with Spider-kinden units donated by various different Aristoi houses, few of whom seemed to be actual friends of the Lady-Martial Mycella. Two figures strode through this chaos and made some kind of order from it. One was Jadis of the Melisandyr, some small family that remained closely loyal to the Aldanrael, whose force of personality and – on one occasion – lethal response to an attempted assassination, kept the other Spiders under Mycella's orders. Lissart had determined to avoid his notice at all costs. He looked, she said, like someone who remembered the names and faces of any who served under him.

Instead, they had inveigled their way into the camp of Morkaris, the mercenary adjutant. There was less discipline amongst the mercenaries, and also less jockeying for position between underlings. In their baggage train of clerks, entertainers, whores and factotums, individuals changed allegiance all the time, with few hard feelings. Everyone was in it for the money, and personal honour was less of a barrier. Laszlo had quickly identified a formidable Fly-kinden matron named Drasse as the woman to cosy up to, and after running errands for the woman for a day, he had found himself and Liss safely under her protection. Liss herself could charm the stripes off a Rekef colonel, when she wanted to, and soon Drasse had found her a berth on the wagon, and some medicine besides.

The wagon was a stroke of luck they had not known that they needed, for the army was not what either of them had expected. General Tynan and the Lady-Martial Mycella were moving *fast*.

The entire Imperial contingent travelled by automotive, as did their supplies, ammunition and the disassembled pieces of such machines that could not move under their own power, including considerable quantities of artillery. Wasp soldiers sat inside and on top of great wheeled transporters that belched smoke and steam, and ground up the miles mercilessly without ever tiring. Their Spider allies slowed them down a little, but far less than might be expected. The Apt amongst them, and the unluckier of the Inapt, were in similar conveyances, a motley fleet of various walkers, rollers and tracks dredged from every vehicle foundry from Chasme to Fort Tamaris. The rest had either brought mounts – an equally varied menagerie of horses, beetles, spiders and crickets – or travelled in wagons pulled almost universally by strong hauling beetles. Travelling alongside the supplies was a luxury, as it meant that Liss was not forever jostling elbows with dozens of others.

They had swarmed past Tark not long ago, and Laszlo had only teased out the fact of the city's surrender in retrospect: not surrender to the Empire as conquerors, but a subtler and perhaps more permanent concession. Tark had become part of the Spiderlands, its king sworn to the Aldanrael as a vassal. Already the city was crawling with Spiders taking census of Mycella's new gains.

Liss told him that Spider-kinden maps had always been ambitious, when it came to the Lowlands. Most of them marked out large sections of the coast as already being under Spider control. It seemed that Mycella was rapidly making that fiction a reality.

They had coursed on south past the hills of Merro and Egel, two interlinked Fly-kinden warrens whose loyalties in the past had been a feather for every wind. Nobody had shown any great surprise when the leading families of both had assured everyone concerned that, of course, they had *always* been part of the Spiderlands. The richly dressed little magnates had put up a very convincing display of confusion that anyone should even have to *ask*. Mycella had received their declarations of fealty and loyalty with appropriate magnanimity.

But this was different. The army had barely slowed for the Fly-kinden, but now Laszlo found himself at the coast, the dangerous forest of the Felyal at his back and looking out at the fortified island of Kes.

The Ant-kinden of Kes had a chequered history recently. The last time the Wasps had sent an army down the coast, the Ants had declared themselves uninterested, hiding behind their walls and their fleet, and saving the Empire the considerable effort of investing their island in siege. There had been much speculation amongst the followers of the current army – the Grand Army, as the Spider contingent was calling it, at least – as to whether Kes would represent the first genuine military engagement of this war.

The Ants had certainly not been keen to come out with either violence or diplomacy, but a telescope turned towards their island revealed that every artillery emplacement was manned, and the ships in the harbour were fully crewed.

General Tynan had not ordered his aviators into action, as many had anticipated. Instead he had apparently decided to take defensive measures against any Kessen attack by setting up his own artillery at the cliff edge. The engines that his engineers assembled, however, were of a scale that Laszlo had never seen before, enormous leadshotters that seemed to point more at the sky than anything else. He had surmised that they would drop rocks down on any Kessen ships that sallied forth from the Ants' harbour.

The preliminary shelling of Kes had then lasted three hours, with the greatshotters finding their precise mark after only twenty minutes, to the great exuberance of Tynan's Colonel Mittoc. After that point the dozen engines had spoken in a constant ground-shaking thunder, pounding solidly at their targets, cracking walls and sinking ships, launching flame-canisters over the docks and the city. The artillery on the Kessen walls had, of course, only a fraction of their range. There was no retaliation.

After the greatshotters had finally fallen silent, though remaining a menacing silhouette on the cliff for any Kessen observer, a small vessel had put out from the harbour.

An hour later, the entire population of Kes had understood that it, too, was become a satrapy of the Spiderlands. Spider ships were already coasting in, summoned by who knew what signal of Mycella. Soldiers and assessors were disembarking at the Kessen docks that no hostile force had ever taken.

'We will come back,' Tynan had told the Ant-kinden diplomats and, through them, their king. 'If you rise up against our allies, then our engines shall never pause until your island city is just a stump of rock in the sea. We might have bombarded you until you begged me to send over my slavers. Think on how much more fortunate you are that the Lady Mycella wants you for her own.'

Laszlo had found a place quite close to the negotiations. He had heard the words plainly.

The army was moving again the very next day. The Imperial Second was known as 'the Gears', and General Tynan was not going to let them stop turning for anything, it appeared.

That night, however, Laszlo had decided that the time had come to risk everything. He had not told Liss what he was doing, in case she tried to stop him, or in case she pointed out what a stupid thing he had resolved on. Instead, while she slept, he skipped out from the wagon and flew away.

He was a sailor by training: he knew the seas and, more, he knew how sailors thought. Kes was not just a military power: it lived on trade, and there would be those sea-traders who would want to avoid the reach of the Aldanrael, for whatever reason.

Three times he let his wings carry him off the cliff, scouring the seas for sight of a sail, battling gusting wind and sudden squalls of rain before clawing his way back to land, before his strength failed. On the third venture, pushing himself further, risking more, he was lucky. A little Beetle-kinden steamer was out there on the waves, stolidly making its way towards Kes. He dropped down on to its deck, sending its crew scrabbling for swords and crossbows, and demanded, between gasping breaths, to speak to their master.

He had only moments to explain himself, but the news that the Aldanrael held Kes soon had the Collegiate skipper's full attention. Every Beetle-kinden sailor knew how the Spiders' tame pirates had been preying on the sea trade until Stenwold Maker put a stop to it.

The ragged message Laszlo delivered was wild, out of order, everything he could dredge from his mind about Solarno, Tark, Merro, Kes. He could only hope that it was enough, and would reach Stenwold in time to do some good.

Then, after a wistful thought about simply remaining on board, he took wing again and returned, dodging sentries and searchlamps, to get back to Liss's side. He could not leave her, and there would be more to learn and to report on, before he was done.

He slept not at all that night, holding Liss close to him, feeling the terrible fragility of her and, beyond the wagon's cloth walls, the commensurate fragility of everything else.

Twenty

'You must do something to control your Mynans,' Jodry said, around a mouthful of honeybread. Although most of his face was engaged in eating, his eyebrows contrived to glare at Stenwold meaningfully.

'They're not *my* Mynans.' Stenwold had no appetite, as he stood by the window of Jodry's office and stared out at the city, trying desperately to calculate rates of advance. He had received a message by ship from Laszlo, at last, which meant that he could at least assure the man's extended family of rogues and pirates that he was still alive. The contents of the message more than offset the relief, though, for General Tynan's Second and his Spider allies were practically tearing up the coast towards Collegium.

At the same time, he had received word that the Eighth Army, which had taken Myna, was already past Helleron, meaning all chance of stoppering the bottle on the Empire was already gone while the Assembly debated and the Merchant Companies recruited. The Sarnesh had sent ambassadors to Collegium, but not to debate. Malkan's Folly was manned and ready for the Empire, with a Sarnesh army already mustering in the city to mount an attack as soon as the Eighth got bogged down in besieging the fortress. The Sarnesh had told the Assembly, somewhat patronizingly, that this was a soldier's war, and real soldiers would deal with it.

And then there were the Mynans . . .

'Well, you brought them here,' Jodry pointed out.

'Speak to Kymene.'

'*You* speak to her. She scares the sandals off me,' Jodry muttered. 'Looks at me like she's trying to work out what possible good I am. Murderer's eyes, that one.'

'Her city's back under the black and gold,' Stenwold pointed out, somewhat testily. 'It's not a situation to inspire levity.'

'But if she wants to work with us to liberate the place, she has to work *with* us, and so do that rabble of pilots you pulled in, and all their soldiers who've turned up at our gates. Little Mistress Aviator's been training our fliers to work together: formations, tactics, all that sort of thing. She seems to think that's all very important. Now your Mynans are on the scene and, yes, they have more flying experience than our lads and lasses, what with all that scrapping about on the border over the last year, but they won't do what they're told, and Mistress Taki, for reasons of her own, won't tell them either, and our own pilots are frankly scared of being in the air with them because nobody knows what they'll do next. And while we're trying to train them to work alongside our people, they're trying to wing off to hunt Wasps that, frankly, aren't even here yet. Either they're flying off without orders or authorization, or they're bullying our ground crew into keeping their personal Stormreaders wound and ready, as if the Empire's already at the gates.'

'Jodry, if you'd seen Myna, you wouldn't want to be caught unprepared either, believe me.'

'Oh, I know, but then you don't have to listen to Corog Breaker moaning about how it's impossible to get them even to march in step.'

'Why would they . . . ? What's Corog Breaker got to do with it?' Stenwold pictured the Master Armsman of the Prowess Forum. 'He's a pilot?'

'Well actually he *is* a pilot, thankfully, but mostly he's a disciplinarian,' Jodry said primly. 'And he's trying to make your Mynans part of a *team*.'

'They're not—'

'They *are*. I'm making them yours. You're now official liaison with the Mynan exiles. I, as Speaker, command this. There, it's done.'

Stenwold looked at him as mutinously, no doubt, as the Mynan pilots were even now looking at Corog Breaker. The man's logic was faultless, however. 'Do you have any idea how much else I have to do?' he complained, somewhat wretchedly. 'The committees, the engagements, the planning? I'd forgotten how this city runs its wars on bureaucracy.'

'Yes, I know,' the Speaker's calm slipped a little, 'Stenwold the martyr. You'll never know the problems of yours that I've solved without your ever hearing of them, because you were in Myna or off mooning over that Sea-kinden woman of yours. But now you're the War Master, whether you like it or not. During peacetime I could keep you on a long leash because you'd done good work for the city, sterling work, and you'd earned the right to thumb your nose at our committees and our paperwork. Now it's war again, and you yourself proposed the vote, and you will *not* simply stride about in a breastplate and leave all the organization to me. I need you, and Collegium needs you. And that means at all hours . . .' Jodry's words ground to a halt, for Stenwold was no longer listening to him. 'What?'

'Quiet,' Stenwold told him, already at the window and throwing the shutters open.

Jodry goggled at him. 'Stenwold, what—?'

'You hear it?'

'I don't . . .' Jodry lapsed into silence, and the two men waited. In the air was a distant, ever-increasing drone. 'They're training in the Stormreaders . . . ?'

'Clockwork engines don't sound like that,' Stenwold said quietly, as the sound built – still far off but not as far as it had been a moment ago. The buzz of engines on the air: many engines.

A moment later and Stenwold was bolting from the room, the door slamming open as he shouldered into it, leaving Jodry staring after him, his mouth working soundlessly.

'Advance! Advance! Forward! Form shooting lines, two . . . no . . .' Chief Officer Marteus swore under his breath, holding on to his calm by the slenderest of threads. 'Two lines, one shooting over the other. You – Fly-kinden – get to the front. What's the point of you standing there when the Beetle kneeling in front of you's still taller?'

The shooting line had dissolved into chaos, and Marteus felt that same anger rising in him that had seem him leave Tark so ignominiously, years before. It had served him well enough when the Vekken had come to Coldstone Street, or when the Wasps' Light Airborne were jumping the walls, but training his new recruits was rubbing his temper raw, and any moment now he was going to explode in a wholly unprofessional manner.

'Back to where you were!' he snapped at them, seeing the motley squad of a score and ten new-minted soldiers stumble and jostle their way across the square. People were watching, he was well aware, lolling out of windows to chuckle – people who didn't have the guts to enlist themselves, but were content simply to criticize and laugh.

'Now, forward! At the trot, come on!' This time they managed it, and stopped approximately when he ordered. 'Shooting line, loose!' he bellowed hoarsely, hearing the ragged chorus of retorts from their snapbows – charged but not loaded. 'Now charge, and loose again!'

That was hoping for too much. Half of them managed a decent turn of speed with the weapons, even miming slotting the bolt in. The others were still fumbling as the first half were shooting. 'No!' Marteus roared. 'No! Stop!' His voice was failing. Ant-kinden did not have to shout at one another. The old days of service in his home city were suddenly an unexpected source of nostalgia. 'You shoot *as one*. Individual shots kill individual soldiers. Shoot together and you stop their advance dead. Ask the Sarnesh – it's what smashed their line at the Battle of the Rails, and it's what stopped the Jaspers dead at Malkan's Folly, eh? Back to where you were.'

They ran through the exercise again, got to the same point, half the squad out of position, some fumbling, some shooting. Marteus's voice cracked under the force of his invective and he turned away to take a swig from his waterskin. His ears rang to shouting, however, and for a moment he thought it was still his, or perhaps some private drill officer within his own head.

But no: a woman's voice. He lowered the skin, looking round. One of his recruits had plainly endured as much as she could take, too. She was stalking along the line, bellowing in a high, clear voice at the others, correcting their stance, lining them up. 'Come on, you maggots!' he heard her shouting. 'You're embarrassing your city! That's it! Bows level and straight – that means you too, Lucco, no enemy down near your feet – ready to loose . . . ?' And by this time she had realized what she was saying, and that Marteus was staring at her.

She was a lean, spare woman, some Spider halfbreed sort, and she did not back down before his stare, but simply adopted a stave-straight soldier's stance. 'Chief Officer,' she said and, in those non-committal words he reckoned she'd learned more of soldiering than half the men he'd served with in the Vekken siege.

'You think you can give orders better than I can?' he demanded.

'No, Chief, but I think I can listen better than these.'

Halfbreeds, thought Marteus, but the Coldstone Company had never been choosy and, besides, only around half his recruits were Beetle-kinden. *Someone* was shaming Collegium, but it wasn't these, who at least had taken up the snapbow or the pike to defend their surrogate home. 'Go ahead,' he told the woman, 'show me.'

She nodded, surprised and abruptly nervous, but turned back to her fellows. 'Loose!' she ordered, and the bows snapped dutifully. 'Recharge – that's it, wind steady and you'll not fumble it. Gerethwy, Barstall, hold your shot – you too, Master Maldredge. When you see three in four up and pointed – now – loose!' She risked a glance at Marteus, but his face remained as impassive as only an Ant's could be. 'Ready to receive a charge!' she hazarded, and the half-dozen Inapt they had with them – Mantis-kinden mostly – were shouldering forwards. 'No, not round – cut between like we practised – *and why aren't you recharging your bows? –* and – loose! Pikes at the ready!'

She turned, still in the midst of the tableau she had created, the pikemen in the second and third ranks bracing their weapons, whilst the rows of snapbowmen were recharging now without being told, raggedly but not so far out of step with one another.

'Your name?' Marteus demanded. He heard one of the other recruits snigger – a tall grey-skinned creature of some lanky kinden he had never seen before.

'Straessa, Chief Officer – called the Antspider,' the halfbreed reported, reverting to her blank soldier's demeanour.

And she knows all their names, Marteus thought. Another knack that Ant-kinden never needed to learn. 'Right. Subordinate Officer Antspider.' He made the decision quickly, the words rushing out before he could regret them. 'You drill your friends here another dozen times, then break.' *Does this mean I need more subordinates? Probably. Does that mean I need rank badges, like the Empire has? Almost certainly.* Ant-kinden needed no rank badges, of course. Everyone knew who everyone else was.

'Right, back to where we were!' the new Subordinate Officer ordered, and cuffed the tall man as he passed. 'No bloody smirking, Gerethwy, this is war . . .'

She stopped speaking, the certainty in her voice draining away. 'Chief . . . ?'

'What is it?'

'Are they ours?'

She was looking upwards, and Marteus – and everyone else – followed her gaze.

Black shapes were passing over the city against the insistent drone of engines, low enough that they could see the flickering wings of orthopters. No strange sight perhaps, given how hard the aviators were training, but these flew in formation, and they were many.

'Clear the square!' Marteus shouted, and he heard his new junior officer seconding him. 'Make for the College.' There was no great rationale in that, save that he could think of nothing else to suggest.

'Wheel left!' Corog Breaker shouted. 'Fly straight. Wheel right – keep that distance! You're moving apart.'

He had a better voice for it than Marteus ever did, honed by bellowing across classrooms and foundries and taverns. The Master Armsman of the Prowess Forum was now teaching discipline to airmen rather than fencing to students.

His class consisted of a score of men and women, some of the local Beetle-kinden – new recruits and the graduates of Taki's aviation classes – and the others a motley pick of the Mynan newcomers. He had them jogging about the airfield at a fair pace, making formations, manoeuvring on foot, trying to instil into them a basic understanding of working together. The task was frustrating and slow, but if there was one thing that Breaker was good for, it was shouting at length.

'Back into formation!' he yelled, but two or three of the Mynans had just broken off, running about the field and obviously taking the piss, he reckoned, by miming an attack on some of the grounded aircraft. 'Form up!' he shouted. 'Everyone, ranks before me! What do you think you're doing?'

The 'ranks' his class formed were split, the Mynans clumped together at one end, and a noticeable gap between them and the Collegiate fliers, who were mostly considerably younger and somewhat scared of them. Corog Breaker was older and scared of nothing, however, and he stomped up to them, glowering.

'Why aren't we in the air, *Master* Breaker,' demanded one of them – Edmon, he thought. They always used his title, since he insisted on it, but they gave it a decidedly derisive spin.

'Because in the air you can't hear me shouting at you,' Breaker snapped back.

'We want to fight Wasps.' This was Franticze, the stocky Bee-kinden woman and his worst discipline problem. 'This is a waste of time.'

'You think we'd let you fight the Wasps, alongside our pilots?' Breaker demanded. It was his best card, when working with them, and he saw them scowl and shuffle, saw the sudden *fear* in their eyes that they might be excluded, cast aside. 'If you can't work with us, then you're liabilities, and no Stormreaders for you,' he informed them sharply.

'Flying in combat, it is not like this,' Edmon said quietly, with an almost guilty look at the Collegiate pilots, their youth and uncertainty.

'Well, in the future it will be,' Breaker told him. 'Discipline in the air, just like discipline on the ground. Armies are built on it. Ask the Ant-kinden.'

'I never saw an Ant pilot worth a curse,' Franticze muttered, but a brief gesture from Edmon silenced her.

'Try it again. Follow Pendry Goswell here: turn when she turns, keep your distance, show me you can do it,' Breaker invited, gesturing for a solid Beetle girl, one of Collegium's better fliers, to take the lead. As the airmen moved off, he retreated to lean against a grounded orthopter.

'Don't say it,' he growled from the corner of his mouth.

'They're right.' Taki was sitting atop the machine. Her *Esca* had come in an hour before and she was watching the ground crew finish winding the motor. 'Air combat's too fast.'

'They're going to end up shooting our people down, or the other way around. They way they fly, nobody knows where they'll go.'

'How do you think they got out of Myna . . . ?' Taki lifted her head abruptly, frowning. 'Corog . . . ?'

There were some startled cries from the Collegiate students. The Mynans had broken formation and were pounding across the field, shouting at one another. Breaker saw Franticze take to the air, a flash of her wings dropping her neatly into the Stormreader that she had reserved. The others were grappling their way into other machines, all those that they had chosen for themselves – against his orders – and fought off all comers for, now painted with the double red darts of Myna.

'What . . . ?' Breaker began, but some of the Mynans were already starting up their motors, shouting at the ground crew to get clear, wings folding out and lifting up with the first motion of the clockwork. 'Stop that! What do you think you're . . . ?'

But then the sound impinged on him, the drone of engines from on high. He turned to Taki, but she was already across the field and scrambling into the seat of her *Esca Magni*.

With a deep buzz of wings and fire, fixed-wing fliers began to pass overhead, a flight of a half-dozen immediately above, but there were others elsewhere over the city. From somewhere close by there was a flash, a boom immediately afterwards, as the ground shook. A moment later smoke was rising.

'Get my machine ready to take off! Now!' Breaker shouted. 'Get in the air!' He waved madly to the students, relieved to see that half of them at least were already following the Mynans' lead, orders or not.

The *Esca Magni* leapt into the air, Taki bringing the machine off the ground lopsidedly in her haste, desperate to gain the air before . . .

Myna all over again. She registered the explosion without really seeing or hearing it, some consensus of the senses simply informing her. *Where was that? That was the field over Luker Street ways.* Of course the Empire would try for the same targets: strip Collegium of its air defences: destroy the Beetle orthopters on the ground, and who could defy them? And all the while the question kept hammering away in the back of her mind: *Where did the piss-cursed bastards come from?* How had the Empire infiltrated a force of fliers within strike of the city, and nobody knew of it?

She watched as the enemy machines banked ahead of her, almost following the line of the street below as they sought their target. They were not the familiar Spearflights, she registered. These were fixed-wing fliers, and almost twice the size of the Imperial orthopters she was used to. Not strange to her, though, because . . .

For a moment, as she rammed the *Esca* into a higher gear to close with them, she was back in Capitas – her one and only visit there – watching Axrad die.

Farsphex, the name came to her. The new machines that Axrad had been so insistent that she saw. So what did she recall about the Farsphex?

She recalled that it wasn't a fixed-wing at all.

She saw it then, as she raced in towards them, eating up the sky between her and the enemy. A pair of Stormreaders was coming in from her left quarter with the same intention – some training patrol returning to the city to find it attacked in their absence. They had the right line of approach, diving from on high, practically out of the sun, but the Imperials saw them nonetheless, their close formation breaking apart into a scatter of separate machines, and abruptly those rigid wings were kicked into a blur, instantly gaining that essential agility in the air that a fixed-wing flier could never aspire to.

Taki picked her target, taking a course that would bring her between the fleeing Farsphex and its comrades, separating it out

302

in preparation for a quick kill. She tried a rapid look left and right, to see how her allies were disposed, catching a glimpse of a scatter of ascending machines from the airfield she had just quit: *The Mynans defending the field, letting the others launch.* She saw more enemy, too. She reckoned two flights of probably more than half a dozen, and the smoke from the far side of the city told of a third at least.

Then she was yanking the stick over to the right, registering the glitter of rotary bolts sleeting past her, turning the *Esca* almost on a wingtip. The Farsphex she had gone after had simply run for it – no attempt to double back or engage – but two of its comrades were right on top of her. They had underestimated how nimble her little machine was, and for a moment the three of them shared an uncomfortably small patch of sky as she bolted back between them. Then she had negotiated another turn, feeling every stay and bolt of the *Esca* thrum with it, and she was behind them, opening up with her rotaries, scoring a few desultory hits as her target – the leftmost – slid sideways in the air out of her sights. The other Wasp craft lifted away, seeking height, but Taki knew she had time to pin its friend down before it could come back for her—

Except that its *other* friend, the one she had originally marked, was already returning to the fray, its line on her imperfect but enough to put her off her attack, the flashing hail of its bolts forcing her to abandon her own assault and pull away. Craning over her shoulder, peering past the sleek flank of her machine, she saw the three of them regroup into formation, not coming after her but seeking out their ground targets—

She swore. It was a display of coordination such as she had never seen, not in Solarno nor here, certainly not amongst Imperial pilots. She was struck painfully by the way they handled their machines: not superlative skill but a purely workmanlike ability, such as any Apt artisan or footsoldier could have learned, save that they worked *together* so well that Corog Breaker would weep to see it.

Taki cut a wide arc over the city, trying to take stock of the fluid situation. The field she had lifted off from was unbombed, and she saw that the Mynans – their red-painted Stormreaders identifiable even at this distance – were sallying out over the city. Some of the Collegiate machines were still circling, waiting to stave off the next bombing run, whilst others were heading across the rooftops, not looking to engage but finding other vulnerable points to defend. Somebody had slapped some sense of tactics into them: someone equipped with a heliograph and a good grasp of the flash-codes had disseminated some useful orders.

Taki threw the *Esca* across the city. She had lost the trio that had been sparring with her, but she saw another flight moving over Collegium's centre, and for a moment she feared that they were going to drop their explosive cargo over the domes and spires of the Amphiophos. A moment's reconsideration showed her that they were moving in on one of the other fields – their targets purely practical, with no thought for symbolism. *Not yet.* Six against one, but she gave the *Esca* its head, the fastest thing in the skies as far as she was concerned, climbing as she approached them so that she could make a perfect dive on them. They would see her too late, and probably the one she was stooping on would never see her at all. Except they did – they all did.

Just like before, they were scattering. Her target kept its wings fixed and used all the speed it had, not quite outpacing her even then, but she was only able to clip it a few times before its comrades were on her, transformed from swift fixed-wings to dancing orthopters in a moment. For a moment she seemed to be surrounded by their shot as she dodged and sidestepped in the sky, five of them fighting for the privilege of bringing her down, and surely they would touch wingtips at any moment, slap each other out of the sky in their eagerness.

She was worried now. She had not felt like this since . . . She had never felt like this before, not while in the seat of a good orthopter. She lived for flight. Even facing down Axrad over Solarno, she had not felt like this. This was all wrong: enemy fliers who came from nowhere, flying with such coordination. Breaker had been right about what would win an aerial war, but neither had guessed that the Empire had been so far ahead of them.

She bared her teeth. *I am better than all of you!* The *Esca* could do things that even the Stormreaders could not, let alone these big Farsphex machines. If she fought the controls with sufficient dogged determination and contrived to ignore the insistent demands of aeronautics for just a moment, backing her wings so that their joints squealed, she could even fly backwards.

It was an innovative theory, at the speed she was going, but she felt only confidence as she rammed the stick backwards and disengaged the wing gearing for a second – the vanes beating at ten times the usual speed, for a few crazed seconds, as their gears meshed with nothing – before trying to back them.

The manoeuvre was a qualified success. She dropped like a stone for a moment, seemingly having no control whatsoever, and the Farsphex pack must have assumed that she had been hit, abandoning her immediately to go in pursuit of their next target. A moment later she had her wings working – forwards still and not backwards at all, and almost went through some-one's roof as she struggled to regain the sky, coming up behind them and catching the trailing Farsphex with a solid handful of bolts that at least made it judder in the air.

Then she was not alone. Left and right there were Storm-readers with red-painted wings. They attacked as individuals, and she joined them by instinct, not even thinking it through. That saved them, she decided later. The air discipline of the Wasps was such that their flight would have outmatched an attack by a rigid formation, but Taki and her flanking allies each had different ideas as to what they were going to do, three entirely uncoordinated strikes by skilled pilots in top-class fight-ing orthopters.

They still failed to bring one down. The Farsphex were away again, splitting up and fixing their wings for extra speed if they were pursued. They refused to engage or to fight the aerial duels that Taki had been dreaming of ever since Solarno. Those not pursued were already wheeling back to come to the aid of their comrades. Taki could almost taste the frustration of the Mynans as they did everything they could to latch onto their enemy, only to be driven off again and again.

Then the Farsphex flight was abruptly coming together – all of them, flocking from every quarter of the city to rise in a dark column of machines, massing over the very centre of Collegium.

To strike where? But there was nothing in their disposition that hinted at their target. Taki skated her *Esca* across the face of their rising formation, pulling her orthopter round in as tight a turn as she could, because they were about to break and she wanted them in front of her and not behind. In mid-wheel she did her best to locate the other Collegiate fliers, flashing a quick signal for *Form on me!* and hoping that somebody would see it. She had company even before she had finished her turn, a full half-dozen Stormreaders converging on her, cutting a wider arc in the air so as to match her when she drove back at the Imperials. She noted four Mynans – Edmon and three others she couldn't name. Keeping pace were two of Collegium's own, and she knew them, from the way they flew, as the Goswell girl and the Fly-kinden, Haldri. It hardly counted as overwhelming odds, but the other local machines were scattered all about the sky, some hanging back to defend the airfields still, others just adrift over the city, losing the thread of the fight, lost over their own home.

The Imperial formation broke up, as she knew it would, and abruptly they were all moving as one, like fish shoaling, heading for the College district.

Attack. It was a pitiful signal to be sending, but she had already decided that, whatever the Wasps were after, she was committed to opposing it. She let the *Esca* race ahead, knowing that the others were still with her, left and right. She wanted to say a great deal more, to explain that the Farsphex pack would split once she attacked, some turning to meet her while the others pressed on with their mission. The Collegiate flash-codes were a language of few words, though. She had to trust that they would predict the future as well as she did.

She had the trigger pressed even before she was in range, seeing their pattern shift into carefully orchestrated chaos, orthopters peeling off and swinging back towards her from above and from either side. At least half their force was casting itself lightly over the College now, turning in unison to find their target.

Taki swore and dived after them, still shooting, trusting to her swift flying, to the *Esca*'s nimbleness against the larger machines. A scatter of bolts sprayed past her, leaving a single finger's-width hole in one wing. Around and behind her, the handful of Stormreaders engaged, fearless by necessity.

She was closing now, watching the craft ahead of her, seeing how their attack run forced them to become predictable, killable, if just for a moment. But then, so did hers as she tunnel-visioned in on them, desperate for a kill that might make them break off. Even as the silvery trail of her shot swept in towards a flier in the midst of their formation, piercer bolts were abruptly hammering into her fuselage, the physical impact rocking her, knocking the *Esca*'s tail sideways, spoiling her aim and making her entire orthopter slew in the air. She cursed, wrestling to get back on target, close now, closer than she had wanted. She actually saw the first bombs drop.

Then another bolt cracked into the engine mounting behind her, the next shattered a pane of her cockpit window, skinning a line of pain down her shoulder as it vanished into her seat. She threw the *Esca* sideways instinctively, the city beneath her opening up in flames as the bombs struck. She had left it too long, made herself too much of a target. She was going to die.

But she lived. The *Esca* suffered a riddled wing, silk parting, wood slats fracturing as the bolts tore into it, but the expected lethal shock never came. Her machine dropped involuntarily towards the flames before she could catch it, and the Farsphex that had been after her coursed overhead, banking in the air to dodge the incoming shot of one of the Mynans, who was slinging his Stormreader through the air like a madman to keep another two Imperial machines off his tail.

The *Esca* regained its hold on the air, and she saw the sky above her turned into a madness of wheeling, duelling orthopters. Instantly she was dragging back on the stick, fighting upwards to take her place there but, even as she did, she knew she was too late.

One of the Mynans lost a wing suddenly, the Stormreader coming apart as a Farsphex ripped into it from an unexpected angle. The next second, the stricken machine was whirling past Taki, spinning like a top with its one wing still beating. Taki was shooting by then, setting up a stream of bolts and then trying to find a target to bring it to bear on. Their bombing run had been disrupted now, but the Wasps had decided to make a fight of it at last, bolstering their impeccably coordination with two-to-one odds.

She had a direct line on one of the enemy and, just for a moment, gave it a solid couple of seconds of shot and saw it lurch in the air, shuddering. The bombs that had been cascading from its undercarriage, as regular as ants from a hill, abruptly stopped though the machine flew on. Then she was dancing and dodging through the air as a couple of the enemy came for her, keeping out of the way of their aim but unable to fight back. She saw Edmon's Stormreader spiralling upwards, chasing one of the enemy even as another tried to bring him down. In the next instant, Pendry Goswell was scudding past them, scoring a couple of strikes as she did, but she was lurching in the air, her machine already damaged, the beat of her wings erratic. A moment later they simply stopped, some vital piece of clockwork slipping its train, and Taki watched her helpless and achingly graceful arc as her stalled machine fell into its final dive.

Then, and all together, the Imperial machines were on the run – or at least they were evading pursuit, taking off with wings fixed and heading east. *We've driven them away!* Taki exalted, but almost immediately she guessed that the Empire was simply heading to refuel. *So where are they going?* If they had built a nest so close to the city, then these attacks could be an hourly occurrence.

She sent the *Esca* after them without even thinking about it, and when she glanced around she saw three Stormreaders joining her in the pursuit, two with Mynan colours and one of the more ambitious local pilots, looking like Corog Breaker himself by the way he flew.

Behind them, smoke rose from a handful of points across Collegium, and Taki felt that she was escaping a report on the damage, as much as chasing the enemy. *What did we lose? What people, what machines? And if the Mynans hadn't been so paranoid as to have their machines standing by at all hours, how much more might we have lost?* It was not that the Mynans had known what was going to happen, of course. It was just that, this once, their particular breed of fearful, vengeful craziness had turned out to be entirely justified.

The chase went on for barely fifteen minutes, the Imperials pulling ahead noticeably, forcing Taki to admire the design that allowed them to switch from fixed to mobile wings – and so fluidly! She had seen it, or half-seen it, in Capitas but she had underestimated the applications of the idea.

But, still, they must have a base around here somewhere. Where's the Wasps' nest, eh? But the distance between hunters and prey only increased, and the Collegiate orthopters were beginning to tire, springs losing their strength, wings working with less of a will.

The last glimpse Taki had of the Farsphex that day showed them still heading solidly eastwards, with no suggestion at all that they were about to land.

Twenty-One

Taki had asked Corog Breaker to call all the pilots together as soon as they were back on the ground. They had met hurriedly, almost conspiratorially, before any of the great and the good of Collegium could presume to interfere.

We are the elite of the air, Taki told herself. Scanning their faces, some looking determined, some stunned, she hoped that they felt the same way.

The Mynans still clustered together, but the distance between them and the others had decreased. They had shared something now, and it was the Collegiate fliers who had drawn closer to the mindset of their guests. They took a roll-call of their losses. Thyses, one of the Mynans, was dead. Collegium had lost three, although Pendry Goswell was miraculously still among the living, the first of them to have to rely on the new glider chutes that had been developed for those whose Art did not permit them to fly.

By that time they had some representatives of the ground crew with them, listening in, and a couple of academics from the aviation department, including Willem Reader, who had furnished Collegium's orthopter model with half of its name. Technically, Corog Breaker was in charge, but he deferred to Taki without her having to ask. The man was all pomp and shouting during peacetime, but now the Empire had somehow managed to attack his city, he was purely business.

They made their plans: Taki proposed and, with a minimum of discussion, they approved. There was no suggestion of consulting the Assembly or any higher authority. In a city so bound by bureaucracy and hierarchy, this independence told Taki that they understood. *The Assembly wasn't there; they won't understand. Only us. Only we are fit to helm the course of the air war.*

Well, us and the Wasps, obviously. An unhappy thought, and she would have to talk with the better aeronautical minds about just what the Wasps had achieved in their aviation technology, and in their military practice, to pull off the attack that had just happened.

By the time a messenger had come from the Amphiophos demanding that she attend some council of war, the pilots had already held their own Assembly, passed their own motions and set their own destiny.

The council of war was remarkably restrained, although Taki guessed that it would become larger and more burdened with pointless opinions as time went on. For now she was faced only with Stenwold himself and the leaders of the three Merchant Companies: the Beetle-kinden Janos Outwright and Elder Padstock, and Marteus the Tarkesh renegade.

'What did we lose?' she asked, before Stenwold could start interrogating her.

'The Teremy Square airfield was hit hard,' Stenwold told her. 'We lost eight Stormreaders on the ground there, four elsewhere. You and yours managed to keep them from inflicting crippling damage on our air capability, anyway.'

'So what was the big bang?' Taki asked him. 'Just before they took off, they hit something near the College hard.'

'Factories,' Stenwold confirmed. 'Four of them along Read Road were gutted pretty much entirely. They're still going through the rubble, but all they're finding are bodies.'

Taki frowned, and then a sudden fear gripped her. 'The Stormreader factories?'

Stenwold managed a wan smile. 'It's strange how things work out, sometimes. If this attack had come just a tenday ago, then we'd have lost most of our ability to replenish our airforce. As it was, three of the factories were being converted to work on automotives. My project. The Stormreader facilities had been moved to the Coalway workshops, on the other side of the College. From a certain point of view, we were very lucky. Their spies are just a little out of date.'

'We need more machines, as many as we can put in the air,' Taki told him. 'Seriously – their army's still a good way down the coast from here, but *somewhere* they've got an airfield. How they managed that, I have no idea, but we need scouting patrols and, at the same time, we need a strong flight on the airfields ready to fly the moment they come back. That could be tomorrow, Master Maker. That could be later today.'

'I'm putting a proposal before the Assembly today,' Stenwold stated. 'I suspect that it will pass, in light of the attack. I don't think it would pass any other way, certainly.' He looked tired, maybe sick. 'Every workshop and factory in the city must be ready to help the war effort, from the big mercantile concerns to little family-run machine shops. It's not just your orthopters, and it's not my automotives, either. We need more snapbows, piercer bolts, spare parts, tools, artillery ammunition, explosives . . . We've seen now how fast the Empire can move, so we need to get ourselves up to the same speed. You'll have your fliers, and you'll be run off your feet training people how to use them, too. We'll have a call for volunteers across the city, and I hope that people will look at the smoke rising from Read Road and realize that it's now fight or fall.'

You're not before the Assembly now, Maker, thought Taki, because rhetoric always annoyed her. 'And if you don't get your volunteers?' she asked.

'Then I go back to the Assembly with an alternative motion,' he replied grimly.

★

Helleron had been a joke. The Eighth Army had marched in from what had recently been Three-city Alliance land, leaving behind it the shattered walls of Myna and Szar, and a battle still raging at Maynes, where elements of the Fifth had been moved in to free Roder for his advance. The Ants of Maynes were no more technologically accomplished than their allies, Roder knew, but they were certainly more stubborn. There was talk of razing the city entirely, by way of a lesson, deporting the whole population to remote corners of the Empire as slaves. It had never been done before, to even the most rebellious of cities, but times were changing. The Slave Corps had seen all the advances that real soldiers were making to the Empire's prosperity, Roder thought sourly, and were trying to introduce an innovation or two of their own.

If he had thought it would work, he would have cheered them to the echo, but he read nothing but greed in their proposition. *Now, if we had some Bee-killer handy, that might be a different matter.* That near-mythical weapon that had been deployed just the once in the last war was still a subject of heated conjecture. True, the only deaths it had caused had been the Empire's own garrison at Szar, but for connoisseurs of destruction the results had been remarkable: the entire garrison, every living thing, wiped out in a night, without struggle. *And it could so easily have been the Szaren. If we're going to teach lessons, let us teach them all a lasting one.*

Roder knew that there were some, back in the capital, who believed such a weapon was going too far. He also knew that the star of such white-livered philosophers was on the wane. *No weapon was too great,* so sang the Engineering Corps, *so long as it is in* our *hands.* Roder agreed, being a modern kind of general.

The path to Helleron had been prepared long ago by Consortium merchants and Rekef agents. Twelve of the Council of Thirteen had met Roder's delegation willingly, happy to become a protectorate of the Empire and also a free city, as Roder understood Solarno had been declared, down south. Roder himself would rather have locked the entire pack of treacherous vermin up and packed them off to the mines at Shalk, but he had no authority to do so. The job of bringing the Helleren into the Empire's fold had already been achieved, by pen and coin, long before he arrived. All he managed to do was extort some supplies from the city's stores and provide some of his soldiers a night's worth of entertainment, and even then they were kept on a short leash, allowed the bare minimum of violence and pillage, just enough to remind the Helleren of who was now in control. Everything, even the expected casualties of the night's revelry, was set out in advance by the Consortium magnates in charge. With that sort of bureaucracy tying his hands, Roder was glad to be back on the road.

Like Tynan's Second, the Eighth was mechanized, supplies and siege equipment and much of its manpower being moved by automotives and by a flight of airships in this case as Sarn's aerial capability was reckoned considerably less than Collegium's. Scout orthopters kept an eye out, day and night, for a Sarnesh army either advancing cross-country or up the rails, but all suggestion was that the Ants had not calculated on the speed of the Imperial advance, and were only just on the point of setting out from their own gates by the time Roder was in sight of Malkan's Stand.

He knew how the Lowlanders named the place Malkan's Folly, as a slap in the face of the Empire that was, he hoped, about to be redressed. The Ants had built their grandest fortress there, as impressive a defensive edifice as Roder had ever seen through a telescope, and he supposed that it said a great deal about the Sarnesh mindset – perhaps the mindset of all Ant-kinden everywhere.

We could just go round it. A single fortress could not hope actually to hold up an army that was desperate to get to Sarn. All those solid walls would necessitate only a minor detour,

Roder knew. However, the Sarnesh strategy was not quite so foolish. The point of the fortress at Malkan's Stand was to be unassailable, so that the sizeable complement of troops within could use it as a sally-point to attack any enemy force that tried to pass them. If Roder pushed on to Sarn he would find himself engaged front and rear through that peerless ability of the Ants to bring all their forces to bear at the same time. So it was that the Ants would have their wish. He would have no choice but to bring down the walls of Malkan's Stand before he marched on Sarn.

He no longer had the Colonel-Auxillian and his protégé to call upon, the pair of them having been called off for some even more urgent business at the capital, but Colonel Ferric was more than competent enough to manage the machines that they had left, and there was already a plan in place for this stage of the war.

Malkan's Stand was certainly a formidable prospect, he decided, passing the lens of his glass over the walls. The place bristled with artillery, and all of it ready manned, since the Sarnesh could hardly fail to notice their approach. He wondered what word they had received from the Three-city refugees. He had been informed that a reasonably sized force of Alliance soldiers had already passed this way heading for sanctuary in Sarn, and there would have been civilians strung out all the way from here to Myna; the Slave Corps had taken up a fair few on the road. *How well prepared are the Ants, then, eh?*

That artillery had sufficient elevation to out-range anything that General Malkan's own Seventh Army might have brought to the original battle fought on this ground. Any attempt to bring such engines to bear on the fortress walls would be doomed, the machines smashed to pieces before they could ever launch their first missile.

General Malkan had not possessed Drephos's greatshotters, of course. Nor did he have the improved stone-eater acids, the rock-breaker explosives, the pinpoint accuracy of the ratiocinators that could deliver alternating rounds of each to the same precise point over and over for as long as it took.

'Colonel?' he grunted.

'Range is extreme, but viable,' Ferric reported. Behind him the construction of the greatshotters was proceeding swiftly, the cities of the Alliance having granted the artificers sufficient practice. 'We can expect them to make a sortie, I would imagine, once they realize what we're doing, sir.'

'We're ready for them,' Roder murmured, lowering the telescope at last. The rank and file of the Eighth were already throwing up earthworks, forming their own makeshift fortress to slow any Sarnesh attack enough so that the massed snapbows could have their way with as many Ants as the enemy chose to send out. Conventional artillery, such as leadshotters, were being emplaced to take on automotives, and the Spearflight wings were ready to fly, either to take on Sarnesh air power or to bomb the fortress itself.

'The Sarnesh say this hill of theirs is unbreakable, Colonel,' Roder observed.

'Perhaps they haven't checked what the word means, sir.' Around them, the spirits of the Eighth were high, despite all the digging that needed doing. 'The Empress's words have arrived, sir,' Ferric added. 'I've readied the . . . similophone.' Even the engineer stumbled slightly over the unfamiliar word. 'The actual words of the Empress on a strip of tape, imagine it, sir.'

Roder was not a man who encouraged familiarity in his subordinates, but he and Ferric shared a look almost of complicity, two men who were bringing about a glorious future.

The airfield that the Farsphex pilots used was no real secret any more. A score of fixed-wings taking off, one after another, and people were bound to talk. Besides, the time for hiding was past. Everyone involved in this project wanted the Empire to know of their contribution to the war.

They coasted in one evening, taking turns in circling the field and touching down as well as they could, a little roughly in most cases. They were returning from a very long round trip.

For a moment they sat strewn, a little haphazardly, about the field, barely enough room for them all. Pingge herself crouched in the hold of Scain's flier, still chained to it and feeling almost unused to being back on the ground. They had spent almost three days in the air with a pitched battle at the far end. She had never imagined such a thing, and that particular capability of the Farsphex had been so very secret that nobody had thought to forewarn the Fly-kinden bombardiers. How was it done? Even with her artificer's training, she could hardly guess. The Engineering Corps had hit on something almost magical, beyond belief.

The mission itself had provided a variety of unpleasantnesses. The food had been meagre, and relieving herself out into the high, chill air had been particularly unpleasant – the only time she had appreciated being chained to the insides of the machine. Mostly the journeying part had been dull, though, enough for her to get Scain talking eventually, parcelling out small parts of his earlier life, all of which suggested that nobody in their right mind would have imagined him as a pilot until he had abruptly been snatched up for the Farsphex training. She had tried to probe that further, and it was plain he knew exactly why he had been chosen, but apparently that was just another secret that Fly-kinden were not fit to know.

After bringing their craft down into a somewhat shaky landing Scain had just sat there for some time, silent. He looked tired enough to be ill, and she knew that he had been chewing some concoction of the Engineers, just to keep himself going. She, at least, had somehow managed to snatch a little sleep in the air, the cold and the hunger and the drone of the engines eventually becoming as monotonous as a lullaby.

'Sir?' she asked, after a couple of wordless minutes. 'We getting out now, or are we about to head off again?'

Scain seemed to have forgotten that she was there. He started from his reverie, and reached out to unlock her chain, stretching a long, thin arm into her compartment to free her. 'Assemble outside with the others,' he told her. 'Someone wants to meet us.'

She could not wait to get out of the machine's interior, which seemed to hold far too many memories just then. If the travelling had been dull, their brief time over Collegium had been all too bloody interesting. People had been *shooting* at them. It had been frustrating too – getting the reticule on target, ready to drop her next package, and then Scain would go chasing off across the sky while piercer bolts sang and danced in the air around them. It was a wonder that anyone could hit anything at all. She understood, in theory, that some manner of airborne resistance might have been predicted, and that the Beetle-kinden weren't just going to stand around gaping up with their mouths open but, until the Farsphex had broken formation to evade the incoming enemy, she had not quite made the logical connection.

She had been terrified then. In that moment she had wanted more than anything to be back on the factory line gossiping with Kiin, or back with her family, anything.

But her training had smoothed over that, and soon she had been snatching her opportunities, lining the reticule up faster than she had ever done in practice, getting the bombs away during the brief moments of level flight that Scain allowed her. After that had come the unexpected: she had found within herself what she had always thought the Wasp soldiers must feel all the time: hate, exhilaration, driving determination to *win*. And if winning meant killing the enemy and destroying their cities, well, then that was *war*. This fierce little fire in her had ignited after she realized that the enemy, after all, were trying to kill *her*. The understanding had seemed to remove some blindfold that had been before her eyes every day until that moment.

Now she went over and joined Gizmer, and a few other early

escapees. They made a sloppy, weary job of parade-ground order, but were too tired to care. The Wasps were coming out, too, all of them looking as ragged as Scain. Then they were straightening up, every man of them, because they had visitors.

Pingge knew the man in the lead at once now: the bearded, slightly unkempt figure of Colonel Varsec was unmistakable. He was the father of Imperial war aviation, she knew, which made everyone assembled there his children. Behind him came an older officer, another colonel of Engineers, grey-haired and solid and scorched red by a fiercer sun than Capitas normally saw.

Varsec was casting an eye over the untidy clutter of flying machines, and Pingge realized he was counting. At the last a delighted smile spread over his face.

'All back,' he said, just loud enough for Pingge to catch. 'Captain Aarmon?'

'Here, sir.' The pale, bald flying officer stalked over.

'You reached Collegium?'

'The mission went ahead as planned, sir. Some success against the airfields, but more against the factories.'

'Resistance?'

'Strong, sir.'

'But you brought everyone back.' Varsec was grinning, maybe a little too broadly. 'They'll be onto us eventually. As soon as we lose a Farsphex over Collegium they'll be all over the wreckage. They're no fools, the Beetle-kinden, but the longer we can baffle them, the better. Angved, look at them. They've been all the way to Collegium, and fought when they were there, and brought everyone back without casualties. Nobody's done it before, *nobody*! You see what we've managed, together?'

The other officer nodded, more soberly.

'Excuse me, sir, one casualty,' Aarmon declared flatly.

The weary crews of the Farsphex were still exiting their craft, dragging their feet over to join the ranks. Pingge was suddenly looking around. Where was Kiin? Was she . . . ? But no, there she was, chivvying the last straggling Fly-kinden into place, barely a glance to spare for her old friend Pingge. But, then, who . . . ?

They were a Fly-kinden short, she realized, and she was partway through her frantic process of elimination when two of the Wasps brought out the body.

The woman's name had been Forra, and Pingge had not known her particularly well, but they had all formed a kind of family, after so long training together. Her uniform was torn and crusted with dried blood, her body small and stiff in the Wasps' hands. They handled her with care, though, Pingge noted. They bore her from the hold of her vessel as though she was one of their own.

'Ludon's flier got raked from below,' Aarmon reported dispassionately. 'Cut apart the bomb bay, destroyed the reticule and killed Bombardier Forra.'

Pingge felt a peculiar shiver go through her. *That could have been me. That could have been any of us.*

Varsec nodded, but Pingge could see that he could not quite make himself care. The success of the project was all to him, just as she had met plenty of factory overseers who only had eyes for quotas and not for working conditions. The real sympathy, the solemn solidarity, came from Aarmon and the other pilots. *One of us*, they seemed to say.

Malkan's Folly was built of sterner stuff than the walls of Myna: close-cut stone over a mortar core intended to absorb the shock of artillery, earthen banks to protect the foundations, walls angled to allow shot to glance off it. Every trick of the modern war architect had been deployed to allow an attacking force to break against the fortress, to allow any besiegers to be hammered down by the Folly's own leadshotters and catapults. None of those architects had envisaged a siege where the enemy were far enough away to remain out of range of any reprisals, and where those same distant siege engines could boom and thunder day and night, regular and precise as a clock, as they lobbed chemicals and explosives at ever-weakening stone.

Within five days the first outer shell of the fortress had cracked and fallen inwards, but the Ants had used the same construction throughout, a honeycomb of small chambers within massive-stoned interlocking walls, and the defenders simply retreated to the next level immediately around the breach, ready at their arrowslits and murder-holes for the direct attack that they were sure would come. The greatshotters did not care but, with marginal adjustments, continued their remorseless pounding.

Around that time, the Sarnesh expeditionary force arrived, later than they might have done because Roder had sent flying saboteurs to destroy the rails that could have rushed a relief force to the fortress's aid. By that time, the Eighth Army was well and truly entrenched.

Seeing the inroads the greatshotters had made, the Sarnesh lost no time in mounting an assault, with troops from the fortress itself sallying forth to assist. There was a lot of open ground to cover to reach the Imperial lines, however – the same open ground that the fortress had counted on to make any attackers' lives difficult. The regular artillery that Roder had brought up, his own leadshotters and ballistae, sent down a withering barrage of canister and shot and explosive bolts, whilst ranks of snap-bowmen waited behind earthworks for the Sarnesh to come closer.

All the while, the greatshotters continued their determined work.

The Sarnesh had brought a flight of orthopters, old Collegium designs and the products of the Ants' own artificers, workmanlike but unimaginative vessels, mostly still equipped with the repeating ballistae of yesterday's air forces. The Spear-flights outnumbered them more than two to one, but the first day of aerial duelling was not won easily nonetheless, the Ant pilots selling each broken machine dearly, taking a toll on the enemy despite the shortcomings of their technology. At the same time the Sarnesh ground forces advanced the long march towards the Imperial lines, rank upon rank of armoured Ant-kinden armed with shield, sword and snapbow, backed by the trundling of tracked automotives.

The traditional Imperial response should have been to send the Light Airborne out en masse, coursing over the marching formations to lash down on them with their stings – tactics that had failed miserably in living memory. Instead, Roder held the bulk of his force in place, taking full advantage of the cover they had built up.

The automotives formed the initial point of their charge, grinding forwards at the pace of a man running. They met the Imperial Sentinels coming the other way. The articulated machines fairly vaulted the Wasp earthworks, rushing the Ant lines with bolts and light artillery bounding from their shells, only pausing with legs braced to loose a leadshotter round that ploughed through the Ant soldiers or punched into the armour of a Sarnesh automotive. Faster and more agile and vastly better armoured, as the battle progressed they hunted down the Sar-nesh machines mercilessly, crushing any soldier luckless enough to get in their way.

When the Ants got within snapbow range they mounted their charge, breaking their solid formations into a scattered skirmish line to best avoid the incoming bolts. It was at that moment that they came closest to winning, had they only known.

The snapbows and the leadshotters tore into them, scattered or not. The Ants were still trusting to their heavy armour that would carry the day if they could only get into the close combat that they were so skilled at, but it weighed them down, and it did little to slow the incoming shot, despite the silk and felt they had lined it with.

Once the Ants were committed to their charge, Roder sent detachments of Light Airborne out – not over the enemy, where they might be picked off, but in solid groups landing to the left or right flank, shooting directly into the sides of the enemy formations.

The Ant-kinden tacticians knew all this, of course. They were able to send detachments left and right to chase off the flanking forces, although the Wasps always came down out of reach, shooting even as they landed. They were able to exhort their soldiers onwards into the flaying lash of the massed snapbows, in the knowledge that, if they could only gain the first earthworks, the Empire's soldiers would surely fold, and the Ant infantry could rush through and reach the incessant greatshotters behind. By then, though, some of the last surviving Sarnesh pilots had relayed their views of the Wasp camp: trench on bank on trench, no fit terrain for armoured soldiers to clamber over into the barrels of snapbows. And, of course, the Wasp Airborne would be able to hop from trench to trench with ease.

There was a moment, a fulcrum moment, when the casualties mounted to such a level, within mere yards of the first earthworks, that even the tacticians suffered a crisis of faith. The cost was too great. Hearts as solid and dutiful as iron broke in that same moment. They felt every death, and it was too much.

They tried again over the next few days, sometimes with reinforcements, sometimes with new orthopters, but they never came as close as on that first day. The knowledge of what awaited them blunted each successive attack, never quite able to grasp the nettle now they had felt its sting. Meanwhile, the Wasps made the best use of their undisputed ownership of the sky to send their Spearflights, and even some airships, out to bomb the Sarnesh camp and to bedevil any advance.

On the twelfth day, even as another attack was aborted before it even reached snapbow range, the inner walls of Malkan's Folly suddenly caved in, changing from impregnable fortress to stone eggshell in a minute of cracking and dust. It was enough. The Sarnesh army fell back, and continued falling back because the greatshotter artillerists were already gambling with new calculations, trying to chase them back towards Sarn.

As one of the younger armies, the Eighth had not yet earned a name for itself but, with the fortress fallen and the Ants in full retreat, Roder put out the word. From now on, the glorious Eighth Army would be 'the Hammer', just as Tynan's Second was 'the Gears' and the fallen Seventh that Malkan had commanded – that Roder had now avenged – had earned the name of 'the Winged Furies'.

The men of the Eighth were ecstatic, and Roder let them celebrate because he did not want them thinking too much about what was to come. The game only got harder, the further west they marched. Partly this was because of supply lines. Partly it was that, the closer they got to Sarn, the more the Ant-kinden themselves could complicate a day's travel. Mostly, however, it was the great brooding mass of trees that would shortly eclipse their northern horizon.

This was the joke, the limitation of the Sarnesh tactical view on the world. Ant-kinden were self-sufficient, in this case actually to a fault. Their great fortress, in which they had placed so much faith, was the least of Roder's worries, for the land beyond it was guarded by a threat he took far more seriously: the Mantis-kinden.

In the last war, the Mantids of the Felyal, on the southern coast, had essentially destroyed the Imperial Fourth Army, and when General Tynan had marched that way with his Second, he had taken a great many precautions to ensure that history did not repeat itself. His advance had been slowed by the need to fortify every night, until he actually got the Mantids where he wanted them, killed their warriors and burned their forest.

The Etheryon was the largest single forest north of the Alim, containing two separate Mantis holds and a population several times that of the Felyal, and all of them killers by nature who could walk as silently as the breeze and see in the dark. Roder had dealt with his fill of assassins when he had fought the Spiders at Seldis, but it was a matter of recent record that enough Mantis-kinden could assassinate an entire *army*. It was going to be a long road to Sarn, and that was even before he considered the surprise the Ants themselves had managed to leave for him.

After the fortress fell, the Sarnesh relief force had quit the field, but the defenders of Malkan's Folly had not. Those who had survived – an uncertain number, and Roder had no way of finding out just how many – were still there because, of course, the Ants had undermined their own creation with cellars and tunnels and subterranean barracks, and probably a living ant-colony as well, full of vicious three-foot biting insects ready to scuttle to their masters' bidding. The fortress had fallen, but its architects had the last laugh: it still fulfilled its function as a threat that Roder was unwilling to leave at his back. For all he knew, those tunnels could run all the way to Sarn itself.

He had conferred with Ferric on whether sustained great-shotter bombardment could cave the earth in on the whole nest of them, but the engineer was not optimistic, and the idea of sending troops into those tunnels to try and root an unknown number of Ants, quite possibly many hundreds of the tenacious bastards, was not appealing as a use of either time or materiel. Ants couldn't see in the dark, but their mindlink would give them a good enough picture of their surroundings, built up from a consensus of sound and touch and shared proximity.

Roder let his men celebrate – save for those drawn as sentries, of course – because it was an excuse not to move on while he wrestled with the main problem. He did not want the Eighth to realize that they were not yet done here.

Then, on the dusk of the second day, his visitor arrived. The first he knew of it was a watch sergeant bursting into his tent, as he sat with plans and notes regarding a tentative assault with sappers.

'Sir!' A smart salute. 'Someone here with papers, sir.'

Roder knew what *that* normally meant – some off-the-books Imperial dignitary, Rekef likely as not, come to make his life more complicated. He suppressed his sour look and nodded tiredly. 'Send him in,' he said, clearing up his papers.

'Excuse me, sir, but he's . . . I don't think he wants to come in, sir.'

'But he has papers.'

'The seal of the *Empress*, sir,' the sergeant said, plainly awed by the thought.

Roder stood sharply. 'Show me,' he ordered.

The visitor stood on one of their embankments, looking out at the ruin of the Folly, and Roder's pace slowed as he appreciated just what the wind had blown into his camp. Not a Rekef man, not some Consortium profiteer or Slave Corps major, not a Wasp at all. In all his years of soldiering, he was willing to bet that a figure like this had not graced an Imperial camp, or at least not with official papers.

A man, he could tell, tall and slender, but the rest was just armour – and what armour! Roder knew a little of the collector's trade, and what he was looking on would have driven a half-dozen rich men back in the capital mad with greed. A full set of sentinel plate, enamelled black and gold, but not Imperial crafts-manship. The ancient Inapt smith who had wrought this had worked to an alien aesthetic, crafting something elegant and spined and deadly, producing a carapace more than a suit of armour.

There was a clawed gauntlet on the newcomer's hand, its narrow blade folded back along his arm, where the armour was slit so as to allow the barbs of his Art to jut out. As Roder approached more and more cautiously, fearing some lethal trap set by the Etheryen Mantids, the figure's free arm thrust towards him, with crumpled papers proffered in its gauntleted fingers.

Roder had no intention of getting *that* close, but the sergeant pattered ahead of him and retrieved the documents, handling them as though they were gold dust. Roder glanced down at the seals, and then again. *The Empress's highest recommendations*, he thought. *Her own personal seal.* Nobody so important as to merit all of this would risk themselves by coming out to visit an army in the field. Until now.

One of the Empress's bodyguard, he realized, for he had seen that band of Mantis-kinden at the palace, but were they not all women?

'I give you welcome to the camp of the Eighth Army,' Roder said carefully, watching for the slightest suggestion that this figure was about to turn on him. 'Can I ask your purpose here?' The so-impressive credentials gave no hint of it, simply expressed the Empress's utmost trust and faith in the bearer, who was identified only by the armour he wore. *Could be just about anyone in there . . .*

The armoured Mantis raised an arm and unhinged the metal claw, letting it flick out to point towards the shattered shell of Malkan's Folly.

'You've come to see the result of the battle for the Empress?' Roder hazarded.

For a moment the helm turned towards him. In the failing light there was the suggestion of a ghostly pale face beneath the raised visor, and the man's stare had a cold force that sent Roder back a step.

Then the Mantis was striding forwards, towards the edge of the camp and then beyond it, heading for the fallen fortress, and for its hidden defenders waiting in the darkness below.

That night, some of the sentries reported hearing screams.

Twenty-Two

'She certainly makes a good show,' Colonel Harvang commented. For once he was not eating, although his fleshy lips twitched and moved when he was not speaking, as though still savouring something.

The senior members of General Brugan's conspiracy were meeting in the palace itself, a room buried deep in the cellars, one of a complex of chambers that the Rekef traditionally used for storing useful prisoners and parting them from their secrets with the aid of machinery. It said a great deal about the Empire that such concerns were already in the architects' minds when the edifice was first planned.

General Brugan grunted. He had been with the Empress last night, during another of her debauches. He felt physically drained now, as he always did, and the blood that so obviously fed her seemed only to leach something vital from himself. He had tried, so very hard, to see it all as just the ruler of the Wasps exalting in her power, but he knew that it was more, and that he would never understand.

He shuddered, visibly enough that Harvang raised an eyebrow.

'These tapes . . .' Colonel Vecter was poring over his reports, and had not noticed. 'These cloth things the halfbreed makes . . .' If a machine was not intended for excruciation, he had little time for it. 'They take her voice all over the Empire, inspirational messages to the troops. I have good reports – morale and fighting spirit all kept high. The personal touch.' He tutted. 'General, I was unsure why you were so insistent on keeping her, rather than simply replacing her, but I think I understand. It is a bitter thought but the Empire *does* need her.'

Brugan stared at him. *Oh, you do not understand.* The intrinsic division within him warred constantly. He hated Seda, he feared her: she was unnatural, terrifying, something from the old stories. Yet he could not live without her. The best compromise he could make was to possess her, control her. He could diminish her into a proper example of Wasp-kinden womanhood, and so regain some vestige of control over himself.

They had not brought many of their confederates here; this was Rekef territory after all, and outsiders were seldom welcome. Only Harvang's man, Ostrec, was here to listen in, and that only because the conversation would eventually turn to his orders.

'We have our people mostly in place,' Vecter continued. 'The palace is under our control, and we have Colonel Sherten in the city garrison. There's Major Hasp of the Slavers, and Knowles in the Consortium. No serious inroads into the Engineers, but then they're not a political force yet.' He looked up brightly. 'Time to sound the advance?'

'We still haven't touched her,' Brugan said. The others looked at him blankly, but he knew he was right. Seda seemed to move in another world, a different medium. She had her dubious advisers: the old Woodlouse, passing Moth ambassadors, odd slaves and servants who came and went and disappeared, so that even the Rekef could not keep track of them. The conspirators could control all the soldiers they wanted, but they would not even approach Seda's secret world.

He could not explain this to them. He could barely explain it to himself. He knew, though, that if he was to triumph over her, if he was to become Seda's master, then he must strip her of that orbit of counsellors, those frauds and shysters who whispered mysticism into her ears.

'Ostrec,' he growled, and the major started in surprise. 'Your work.'

'I have been in her presence two or three times, sir,' Ostrec reported. 'I have seen her notice me, perhaps more than notice, but . . . nothing more. I have felt myself on the point of some breakthrough for a tenday or more.'

'Your breakthrough has come,' Brugan told him flatly. 'She has sent for you.'

This was news to everyone and that in itself was a sour point. Ostrec was ostensibly from the Quartermaster Corps, but Seda had given the command to Brugan himself. *So does she know he's Rekef, or not?* And such an offhanded command it had been. 'She said she wants to see more of you. At night.' The words were painful to spit out, and his manner was putting the two colonels on edge. 'The museum, you know it?'

'Yes, sir. I've not visited but I know where it is.'

'You'll go?'

Ostrec frowned, the perfect picture of a dutiful Wasp. 'If you so order it, of course, sir.'

Harvang made a noise, more of hoarse breathing than anything else, but enough to draw their attention. 'Sometimes men go to visit the Empress there and never leave. Just as sometimes slaves – or those of a higher station – are summoned to her at the palace and likewise are not seen again.'

'The servants . . . ?' Ostrec ventured.

'Oh *someone* must be doing it – taking away the bodies, cleaning up the mess, after whatever it is that actually goes on,' Harvang said heavily, and his glance towards the general was keen: *I know that you know more than you let on.* 'There seems to be a hidden cadre within the palace, and we have not been able to infiltrate it – we cannot even see what to infiltrate. Is it just those cursed Mantis bodyguards doing all the work? Who else does she use? She's called you, my boy, and either you'll die of it or you'll find out something useful. You understand?'

'I believe I do, sir,' Ostrec replied calmly.

He was a handsome young man, Brugan thought sourly. Was the Empress motivated by something so commonplace? He thought not, but he could never be certain. *I hope he dies.*

'I feel,' said Seda, 'like a child who has only just learned to read – so very late! – and now they tell me all the libraries burned down before I was born.'

The book beneath her hands was ancient, pages of cracked and tattered vellum on which the faded ink was barely legible, scuffed and rubbed away, and in places there were the tracks of beetle larvae and the blackened edges of old burns. Of the original text perhaps only half remained intact.

'I have come into my inheritance. I have gone to the ancient wardens of the beginning times and exacted tribute from them. I stride into the sunlight to enter into my kingdom and . . . dust and ashes. Where has it *gone?*'

'Five hundred, hm, years, your Imperial Majesty,' came the soft, careful voice of old Gjegevey. Pale in the lamplight, the gaunt and hunchbacked Woodlouse-kinden loomed behind her. Grey-skinned and tall, at least a hundred of the years he spoke of weighed on his shoulders, but his were a long-lived kinden. And even he could not remember the real days of magic that had passed away so long ago, and so completely.

The shutters were drawn, and Seda had ordered servants to nail blankets up across them, sealing out the sun. The fragile Moth-kinden text that she was trying to piece her way through seemed merely blank in daylight. Only guttering flames would reveal the faint scratching of its secrets.

'The Moths themselves,' Seda murmured, 'they come to my court from Tharn, and think to teach me. I would learn, truly I would, but either they are too close-handed with what they know or . . . Gjegevey, they speak mostly politics, no different to any ambassador or courtier. What of their great plans for the world?'

'They are what the times, ah, have made of them,' he ventured. 'And their great magics perhaps come at too great a price, hm? Majesty, you have no doubt heard the same, hrm, rumours from Tharn as I. The magic they raised to, ah, evict your brother's troops, it has, hm, left a stain. Deaths, madness . . . I gain the impression that many of their Skryres did not, hm, survive the experience. And this was the greatest magic our times have seen, undertaken by some of its, hem, most skilled practitioners.'

'So I should think smaller?' she snapped over her shoulder, scathingly. 'I should content myself with their scraps?'

'If that were my, hm, advice, would you follow it, Majesty?'

The look she gave him was answer enough. 'It cannot all be gone.' The book was a history, but the ancient histories of the Inapt made for tortuous reading for one brought up only on lists of battles and generals. Everything was allusion and metaphor, or perhaps it was not metaphor but myth. Or perhaps the myths were being set down as absolute truth. Nothing was plain, or else everything was plain and nothing was believable. 'Were the times so very different back then? Monsters and fires from the sky, and conjuring the bones of the earth? What happened to it all?'

'Theories differ.' When Gjegevey spoke, his voice held more sadness than usual, a reverent and wistful tone. 'My people, hm, these days we mostly believe that it is simply that magic's time has waned, and is still waning, as the turn of the moon leads to darker nights, so some great and, hem, invisible wheel has taken us away from those days when a magician might, ah, hold the world in the palm of his hand. Some day it is to be hoped the, eh, wheel may turn all the way, and magic shall wax once more. For now, though, we are left with only shallows where once the sea rolled.'

'Poetic, but a mixed metaphor,' Seda grumbled. With nobody

else was she so informal as with Gjegevey. He had been one of her earliest supporters but, more than that, he had been some-one who had been willing to associate with her back before her brother's death, when the executioner's shadow hung constantly over her. She was fonder of him than she would admit. 'So tell me some other theory . . . no, I know it. The Apt.'

'The Moth-kinden favour it.'

'The Apt came with their revolutions,' Seda murmured. 'Uprisings in Pathis, in Myna. But it must be more than that. The Masters had already sealed themselves away in Khanaphes long before, and there was never a Commonweal revolution. The Spiders still hold their lands in thrall, but mostly without magic. Perhaps the Apt could take control of their own destiny *because* magic was not what it had once been, even then. And now . . .' She hissed through her teeth. 'But there *are* places where it has clung on, Gjegevey. We know there are. The power of the Darakyon touched me. It set me on this path, but it's gone now, nothing but a stand of twisted trees. I refuse to believe that there is nowhere else.'

'The Darakyon was an evil place, Majesty,' Gjegevey whispered.

She gave him a level look. 'Evil is a word for those we wish our histories to damn. And, besides, where are all the magical places of sweetness and light, old man? Gone, if they were ever there. It would seem that which you term evil has at least one virtue: it abides.' She closed her eyes briefly. 'I have lived most of my life in fear. *You* know that. Now there is some small chance this unlooked for gift will give me control of my own destiny. What is morality against that?'

'And the destiny of the Empire?' he asked cautiously. 'Or just your own?'

'Do you honestly think they are not one and the same? Any other theories, old man?'

She did not expect any, so he surprised her by saying, 'Just the one: that the Inapt, ah, destroyed themselves.'

She stared down at the page before her, with its dense recitals. 'There are a lot of wars in these old histories,' she allowed. 'Or I thought perhaps they were not wars but some other meaning dressed up as war.'

'There were a great many wars,' Gjegevey confirmed, 'but they were wars of a scale and a style that your kinden might not have recognized them as such. Conflicts lasting decades, centuries even. If artifice sends your wars on swift wasps' wings, think of the old days as snails' wars, slow grappling, histories of skirmishes and shifts, no less fierce but utterly alien. One could have lived all one's life within such a war and not known it.'

'Wars for what?'

'For control. In the grand old days of magic, the elite few who understood it all fought wars to control the future, warring ideologies that spawned earthly battlefields. The Moths, they were the greatest, in the end, which is why it is their histories that you read now. By their own claims, they saved the world from a multitude of evils, so, perhaps they used up their magic, weakened themselves so greatly that their slaves could cast them off. But you know all this.'

'I am not sure what I know,' she replied, but his words crystallized a certainty within her. 'Their great wars . . . the Coup of the Assassins, the Purge of the Mosquito-kinden.'

'We record them as true.' Gjegevey ventured a smile. 'Of course we record many, hm, fantastical things as true, but those conflicts were real. There is evidence.'

She remained silent a long time, after that, where he had expected her either to press for more details or to pass on to some other subject. She was not reading, either. The book beneath her hands passed unnoticed.

At last she said, 'Gjegevey . . . there were other conflicts.'

'Many,' he agreed, 'and in all, ehm, probability many that even my people did not record. The past is a deep well, and in those days there were ways to drive an enemy to the very edge

334

of oblivion, even . . .' He stuttered to a halt, for she was staring at him intently.

'Yes . . . ?' she prompted.

He shrugged as if to suggest he had been merely rambling, that she should pay no heed.

Without looking, her quick hands turned pages until she was near the end of the book's legible section. The pages there were water-marked, worm-eaten and frayed. 'What is this, then? For, of all things in this overwritten textbook, this has no legend, no explanation. Just one symbol on a page, and yet I feel . . .'

She stopped, for Gjegevey had drawn away. His face was always pale, and now discoloured by the lamplight, but she would swear that he had become even more ashen, and something leapt within her breast.

'The Seal of the Worm,' he whispered on the edge of hearing, as though against his will. She sensed him struggling with himself, read his mind, almost, seeing him weighing whether he could convince her that it was nothing, just some scholar's idle sketch.

'Yes,' he admitted at last, reluctantly, 'you have found the edges of a hole that the Moths have eaten through history in order to erase an ancient foe. But, Majesty, hear me. If you ever valued my counsel, if you ever thought me wise, look no further in that direction, I beg you.' His voice had changed, lost its vague mannerisms, become like a sword. She actually drew back from him, from this new, changed creature.

On the page before her, the symbol, a crooked spiral hatched with a hundred tiny lines, seemed to writhe.

'I shall consider the matter,' she said, and knew it to be at least a partial acquiescence. She closed the book. She had read enough for one day.

Esmail planned his route carefully so that he had some distance between himself and the Imperial Museum, when he first came in sight of it, viewing it down a long gas-lit avenue lined with grand buildings, factora and offices of the various divisions of the Wasp administration. The museum itself was almost finished, its shape an awkward compromise between aesthetic and functional. The usual ziggurat shape the Wasps preferred – stone copies of the hill forts their ancestors had lived in – had been expanded outward in wings, to allow sufficient space within for all the anticipated exhibits.

A shadow fell on his heart as he saw it. That was the only way he could describe the sensation to himself. He had not seen the building before, his path had not brought him here, but not until now did he realize that some part of him had been avoiding it.

Power. In a city of the Apt, the sense was weak, but someone had been eroding away at the heavy hand of disbelief that held the rest of the city in thrall. Esmail was willing to bet that there would be little of the new to be found, within those walls – no complex artifice in the lighting, no machines, no Imperial efficiency – just hall after hall devoted to the subjugated, and so many of them Inapt. The vast bulk of Capitas's populace would be blind and deaf to it, but Esmail could almost see a brooding cloud hanging over the place. Power indeed, and of no sort that was healthy to be around.

Although, now I consider it, is any of it healthy? The Dragonfly-kinden, perhaps, but is that why their magic has atrophied so much, even by modern standards, until their great and ancient state is nothing but an eggshell ready for crushing? The Moths know: the light of the sun is for the Apt. We cannot bear its touch any more. We need doubt and fear and shadows. That is where the magic endures.

Doubt and fear and shadows practically shrouded the Imperial Museum.

Still, a summons from the Empress could not be ignored. *I must trust to my skills.* Beginning the long walk towards that looming edifice, he shored up the walls of his mind like a lord looking over the defences of his fortress, ensuring that the inner Esmail and the outer Ostrec were in alignment, so that everything he did, everything he thought, would he filtered only through that stolen persona.

If she suspects . . . But he was counting on her not being able to apply her great power with the precision that piercing his mask would require.

All too soon, the great doorway of the museum stood before him. There were no guards, which he knew must be unusual. He guessed that, for nights such as this when the Empress was in residence, the fewer witnesses the better.

He shivered, but it was Ostrec's shiver as well. A little nervousness here would not be out of place, save only that it would not simply be acting.

He went inside.

The entrance hall was devoted to the Wasps' own savage past, which they had contrived to make appear as ancient as the crumbling cities of the Nem. Esmail knew well that three generations back the Wasps had been living that savagery; indeed, they had barely tamed it even now, and the North-Empire still had its share of feuding hill tribes chafing at Capitas's leash. Here were the ranked spears and tattered banners of the tribes that Seda's grandfather had subjugated along the road to Empire. Here was the old armour, just leather and wood and chitin, but the banded construction presaging the shape of things to come. The impression was one of fecund and violent exuberance. The Wasps may have distanced themselves from that past, but they romanticized it as well. Stories set in those days of the fierce and the free were all the rage, just now.

There was no sign of Seda or any other living soul, and he passed on between the serried ranks of barbarism into the next chamber. Here, guttering lamps lit the spoils of the Twelve-year War. The walls were sheathed in screens and tapestries and woven silk depicting idylls of the Commonweal, and now the hill-tribe savagery gave way to simple tragedy: ranks and ranks of enamelled armour, the chitin and fine mail of Dragonfly princes and nobles, their bright colours muted in the dim light. Here were their incomparable bows, their narrow-headed spears, their long-hafted swords. Here – and Esmail paused, despite himself, to study it – was a map of some engagement or other, with tiny wooden soldiers standing in their battalions, demonstrating the invincibility of the Imperial war machine. A plaque explained that every single figure on both sides had been carved by Commonweal slave artisans. Esmail nodded: it fitted what he understood of the Empire and its cruel poetry. It fitted the Commonweal, too, for the slaves had plainly poured into those tiny symbols of their own defeat all the artistry and skill that they would have expended on a tribute to their own lords and ladies. For a moment he had a sudden rending sense of loss, wondering where his wife was, whether their children were safe, whether he would ever see them again.

When he looked up, she was there, the Empress Seda, flanked by two Mantis-kinden women in Imperial colours, clawed gauntlets ready to hand.

'Ah, Estrec,' she said, and the blood froze in his veins. *She knows. She's unmasked me already.* For a moment he was in mad turmoil within his mind, and only the automatic mettle of his long training kept Ostrec's face and form in place. He could not vouch for his expression, but Ostrec himself, discovered unexpectedly by his Empress in that place, would have lost something of his composure too.

She does not know, he insisted to himself. Seda approached him, smiling, her eyes seeming to pierce wherever they rested.

'You must wonder why I show such interest in you, a lowly quartermaster major,' she murmured.

She does not know. He read her expression, as much as he dared, like stealing glimpses at the sun. If she was playing a double game, he could see none of it there. Sweating despite the cool of the night, he forced himself back into his role. *And Ostrec would react how . . . ?*

338

Ostrec would assume she had called him here because he was young and handsome and strong. The real Ostrec saw women as having a simple outlook on the world. He would look at Seda and smile, oblivious to all the occult strength that Esmail could feel radiating from her.

Esmail produced that same smile: lean, a little predatory and horribly out of place. It was the hardest thing he had done.

'You interest me, Ostrec,' she told him, using the right name this time, and he saw that she did not realize how she had misspoken before. It was no simple mistake, though. He was willing to bet that Seda did not make simple mistakes. To his awe and horror, he realized that some deep part of her, some subconscious monitor, really *had* pierced his disguise and seen him, even somehow divined his name. Give Seda another few years and she would learn to listen to that inner voice, and be even more dangerous and indomitable than she already was. For now, though, a lifetime of being deaf and blind to the magical world still chained her. For now.

And this is why the Moths sent me to kill her now.

'I am honoured,' he let Ostrec reply. 'Your Majesty, tell me what I might to do please you.' Esmail was calmer now, feeling out the limits of his situation, feeling three layers of Ostrec rub against one another inside his mind: the man's private thoughts, the pawn in Brugan's covert game and the public face that he was projecting to Seda.

'I collect people who interest me,' she told him, and abruptly turned away, not at all the reaction Ostrec had been expecting, 'if they prove to be truly interesting, if they do not disappoint.' She was striding off, away from the relics of the Twelve-year War, her bodyguards gliding silently along with her. Esmail started Ostrec's feet on the same path, managing the hesitation and little stumble that he knew the man would make after being so wrong-footed.

The Empress paused a moment, gazing into a side-chamber as he caught her up. He risked a glance and saw a work in progress, statues still in open crates and great slabs of stone faced with hundreds of little sigils. *Khanaphes*, he realized. Of course, the Empire had added the ancient city to its holdings recently, and here were the spoils already. This museum was the Empire in miniature, a tally of its conquests.

'What do you see?' Seda asked him. 'What does Khanaphes mean to you, Ostrec?'

'Your latest triumph,' he hazarded, but he felt the ground beneath his feet suddenly uncertain. *If they do not disappoint*, she had said, and he felt on the verge of disappointing her. *We come back to this: Why Ostrec? What has she seen in him, to summon him here?*

'Does Khanaphes speak to you?' she asked him. 'What does it say?'

Again Ostrec's glib answer welled up within him, but he fought it down, very conscious that those would be the wrong words. *She collects people who interest her. What most interests the Empress of the Wasps these days?*

Magic . . .

Esmail felt something lurch within him, his balance momentarily failing. 'I feel power,' he said, conscious that his chance to answer had almost passed. 'Old power, but power nonetheless. I cannot explain it.' It was not what Ostrec would have said. He was improvising, because what Seda had seen within Ostrec was *Esmail.*

His skills hid him well. Even a skilled Skryre, if caught unawares, might not be able to penetrate his guises. Still, there was a taint about him, the inescapable bleedings of magic. Seda had looked on Ostrec and seen a dimension to him that normal Wasp-kinden lacked. He was aware that he was on very dangerous ground now. He had no idea what a woman in her position might *do* with the man she took him for. There must be a few Wasps around with a little of the old blood in them, from half-breedings generations back, or perhaps even survivals from ancient days when the Wasps, too, were Inapt and had some rough type of magician amongst them. From her manner he guessed now that she had gone through this charade before. What had been the outcome? Or had they all disappointed her before? Was all this just some elaborate prequel to a blood-letting?

She led him on, and they continued through all the memora-bilia of the Empire's triumphs, all the detritus of its subject races: tapestries, statues, pottery and art, and always the arms and armour of the defeated, still holed and dented and scorched where the Wasp-kinden had enforced their superiority.

When she stopped he had slowed already, because ahead he sensed what must be her destination. Again he wondered that there could be such power at all, here within the city of the Apt, but he knew it was solely through Seda's own doing, and that she must feed it regularly. The sense of the place ahead was not strong in comparison with the sources of the Moth-kinden power he was used to, but it was flowering in such hostile soil here. Its character was disconcerting and unwholesome, a ming-ling of the shadow-stuff the Moths liked with something even darker. He thought he could scent the faint copper smell of blood upon the air.

Seeing him react, Seda smiled. 'And they said you were cocky,' she murmured.

He had a stab of panic, thinking that he had dropped his mask somehow, but he saw that his hesitation and solemnity here were exactly what she would expect of Ostrec – if Ostrec had been what she took him for. In responding as he was, he was confirming himself as an object of interest rather than a disappointment.

She turned, and stepped into the next hall, past a curtain that one of her guard had drawn aside. For a moment his instincts warred within him: he knew he must not step within, and yet he knew that it was death to turn aside now, a more certain death but perhaps a cleaner one.

But he wanted to know. He wanted to see. He stepped inside.

The walls of the small, windowless chamber had been covered with dead vines and branches, nailed up everywhere to form an ersatz grove, a cage of withered wood. A few dim lanterns hidden amongst the twisted, interlacing boughs provided the only light Seda allowed within.

No arms and armour here, no exhibits, nothing for public edification. Instead there was only one piece of history in the room, and it was not the Empire's. Eight feet tall and formed of rotting, insect-infested wood, it was an effigy, a crude mantis shape: a single warped upright reaching almost to the ceiling, with two crooked arms. Esmail knew the pattern well. Wherever the Mantis-kinden made their homes, somewhere, in the darkest inner glade furthest from foreign eyes, there would be some nasty piece of work like this. Where Seda might have acquired such a ritual figure, he did not know, but he knew that the ancient Mantis traditions fed them with death and blood, and those traditions had not been overly encouraged by that race's Moth masters. It would seem that Seda had resurrected the practice, and from that he guessed that she had probably secured the loyalty of her bodyguards until death and perhaps beyond.

Then there was movement all around. The criss-crossing of the branches, the overwhelming presence of the idol, had blinded him to the fact that the room was already occupied.

Conspirators, he thought immediately, contrasting them with Brugan's fellow plotters, but he knew in a moment there was a better word. There were four of them here, all Wasp-kinden men and nothing special – none of them looked like high-ranking officers, although perhaps not simple soldiers either. He mentally labelled them – slaver, two sergeants and a Consortium clerk – without much justification.

They were waiting for him to step deeper into the room, which would leave the Empress and her guards in the doorway, barring his retreat. It seemed to him, though, that he had already taken too many steps just by coming here. A few more would make no difference.

342

He went in.

'Ostrec, what has your life been to date?' the Empress's soft voice asked him, from over his shoulder. 'Have you found the world empty, unfulfilling. Have you drunk your fill of rank and ambition, and yet remained thirsty? Have you always known that there was more to life, lurking at the edge of vision, in the shadows, on the far side of the mirror?'

And the answer was 'no', of course, as far as the real Ostrec's memories went, but if he had possessed some atavistic spark of the old ways, then no doubt all that *would* have been true. Esmail studied the men around him, and in those Wasps, yes, perhaps there was some taint, some residual sense of discontinuity that hinted at an unsettled heritage. It was pitifully little, but then the Wasps had been an Apt kinden for generation on generation, so it was surprising that even these dregs were left.

He realized that he had nodded, at Seda's words, and there was a scuffle from behind him. He turned quickly, stepping away from the doorway, ending up almost shoulder to shoulder with the slaver. A newcomer had arrived, but not willingly, for two of the Mantis-kinden were manhandling him, his arms bound behind his back. He was a middle-aged Wasp, and Esmail picked out his face from Ostrec's memories, identifying him as a Consortium man in Brugan's pay, just a little cog in the Rekef general's army of informants.

'Ostrec!' the man shouted. 'Help me!'

Esmail glanced at the Empress, whom he realized was observing him closely.

'I will open the doors of your world.' Her voice was gentle, yet the shouting of the bound man could not eclipse it. 'Only follow your instincts, and I will show you what the absence is that has gnawed at your life. I will fill you.'

Could I have killed her in the museum before? He wondered if she had given him the chance to fulfil his mission as they passed through the galleries: to cut her down and then flee her guards, all the way back to the phalanstery near Tharn. *I could even strike now. A moment is all I need, and they are not ready for it. I would die, but perhaps the death of the Empress is worth one killer's blood.*

But they were empty thoughts, because she had already reached him in the way that she intended. Esmail the spy was as caught up in her as she had meant Ostrec to be, for different reasons. *What could she not do, this woman? A Magician-Empress seeking to transform the world.*

The bound man had been forced to his knees in the very shadow of the Mantis icon, and it required no special intuition to see what must now be done. Esmail extended a hand, just as a Wasp should, reaching for Ostrec's Art. To mimic Art was hard, a real test of a spy's skill, and he would not have wanted to try this against a moving target, but the Mantis-kinden were holding their victim very still, with so little apparent effort.

At the last moment he stopped himself, knowing it was wrong. Not mercy, not morality, but wrong by the rules that Seda was playing with. No cauterizing fire here. She wanted blood.

When he held his hand out for the knife, he sensed a change in them all, a measure of acceptance not present a moment before. Only then did he realize that he had passed a test – one he had been on the very brink of failing merely by playing his stolen role too well.

The eyes of his victim beseeched him, and he watched the man's mouth open and shut, calling his borrowed name. One of the Mantids dragged back on the prisoner's head by the hair, baring his throat for Esmail's blade.

A moment's hesitation would pass muster, for Ostrec the quartermaster was not a habitual killer, and Ostrec the Rekef man was still supposed to be a secret. In himself, Esmail found he cared little enough about one more dead Wasp, but a sacrifice in this place, in this company, would unleash a power that he had no say over. He would be doing her will, feeding her fire.

He made it quick, professional – and to the pits with what

344

Ostrec would have done. One of the Mantids caught the first of the blood in a chalice as it spilled. The rest was allowed to run over the floor. He could not help but notice that the stone seemed to suck it up, unnatural and greedy. The reek of blood in the air was sharp as spices, and he felt dizzy and nauseous with it. He could feel the rotten wood of the idol sating its thirst.

The chalice was pressed into his hands, and he now understood. He was a spy, not some great magician. His talents were great within his own narrow field, but this was beyond him. He had not seen the trap until its jaws began closing on him.

'Drink, and be one of my chosen,' Seda told him. 'Cast off all other loyalties; be bound to me, and become greater than you were. *Drink.*'

And they were not empty words. Symbols had power. As a man talented in all manner of evasion and misdirection, he might be able to sidestep the worst, but there would be hooks in him, once he drank. What he yielded to the Empress here could never be fully regained. She would have a hold on him. In some sense, no matter the distance, no matter how he twisted and turned, he would remain hers.

He could refuse, and they would ensure that his blood would be the next offered to the idol. Would such a death be preferably to a life ensnared by this hybrid blood-and-shadow magic that the Empress was building?

But something twisted in him: *Did we not want this? Would the Moths not do this if they could? This is power! Here in the heart of Capitas, in the Empire of the Apt, this is power. If there was ever to be some rebirth of the old days, how else but this way? He looked at the Empress, and saw that she was young and beautiful and strong and bold. Why not her? Where are my loyalties now?*

He drank, and could only trust to his own skills to keep him free – of Seda and the Moths both. The blood was bitter and fierce. It tasted of power.

Twenty-Three

The second air attack on Collegium inflicted considerably more damage than the first. Logistics – which the Beetles had always counted themselves so skilled at – had failed them utterly. There were simply too many jobs to be done, too few pilots to do them.

It had become plain to all that the Wasps had somehow established an airfield within striking distance of the city. Even with the advantage of fixing their wings for additional range, they must still be within a certain radius of Collegium's walls. Whilst the aviation faculty met to draw circles on maps and argue about flight times, Taki and the other pilots were set to searching an ever-increasing span of countryside. It was bare, sparse terrain, and what cover there was consisted of canyons, sunken streambeds, small stands of stubborn trees, nowhere to hide a field of orthopters or all the necessary clutter for keeping them in the air. And yet they found nothing.

At the same time, everyone knew the Imperial machines would be back tomorrow, the next day. The city held its breath, and kept holding it. The same logic that had surmised the hidden airfield knew without doubt those concealed fliers could take wing and attack the city within hours of landing and refuelling. While the Collegium aviators flew over the barren countryside, they also left people on standby at the city airfields, ready to leap to Collegium's defence. At the same time, they were frantically training up the most promising of the student pilots, and *they* were in turn training the less gifted ones, whilst anyone who applied to the faculty was added to a list for beginner's lessons, and the machine shops kept turning out the thousand pieces that made up a Stormreader, fitting them together with a desperate balance of speed and care.

After five days of this without an enemy flier to be seen, the entire system began to become unstuck. The certainty of immediate attack had driven everyone, planners and pilots alike, to ignore human frailties. Aviators remained in the air for hours, then back to rewind their engines for immediate take-off. Nobody was getting much sleep, either pilots or ground crew. There were accidents in the hangars, arguments, fights. One Mynan airman landed while asleep at the controls, nosing his craft into a grounded vessel hard enough to take both orthopters out of the fight. A young Beetle pilot was less lucky. His crashed Stormreader was found by some of the other airfield-hunters, reduced to a folded, splintered wreck where he had rammed it into a hill. There was much excitement, and the searchers redoubled their efforts, in the belief that he had been shot down, which only worsened the underlying problem of fatigue that had done for their fallen comrade.

On the seventh day the Imperials came back and nobody was ready for them. The majority of the Collegium pilots were on the ground by then, and most of them asleep. A mere skeleton flight of a half-dozen machines was actually in the air when a fresh score of enemy were spotted coursing towards the city at top speed.

Taki was shocked into sudden fighting wakefulness by a College functionary standing in the dormitory doorway and ringing a heavy bell over and over, just as though they were all late for class. She tried to kick into the air by instinct, became fouled in her blanket and crashed to the floor. From all around there were demands to know what was going on, loud enough to quite eclipse the answer.

Some of them heard, though. She saw young Pendry Goswell's face turn abruptly ashen, then she was pushing past the bell-ringer, rushing from the room. Franticze, the Mynan's Bee-kinden fanatic, was hot on her heels. Then the warning got through to everyone else at once, and they were all pushing for the door. Taki unlatched one of the high windows, bolting out into the open, her wings slinging her towards the neighbouring airfield, hoping that the news had reached the ground crews, and that they were already wheeling the Stormreaders out for take-off.

As she landed, dropping untidily into the open cockpit of the *Esca Magni*, she looked up and the sight was terrible, already advanced far beyond her fears. There was smoke rising, at least three separate columns of it, and that wheeling, glittering gnat spinning from the sky was surely a damaged Stormreader plummeting to earth. Over the centre of the city a vast airship, a big merchantman freighting supplies in from the Ant cities to the west, was beginning to fall, its airbag ripped open by persistent rotary volleys, a graceful tumble ever accelerating as it vented its gas, the earth reaching for it. It looked as though the doomed vessel would come down somewhere near the Amphiophos.

All around Taki there were pilots stumbling and struggling for their seats, the mechanics throwing themselves clear as the wings were freed to start beating. She dragged her cockpit closed and unleashed the engine, the New Clockwork spring instantly placing all of its power at her fingertips, so that the first tremendous clap of the *Esca*'s wings got her clear of the ground, then she was arrowing away, circling upwards, clawing for height.

She spotted the first neat formation of the enemy, a dozen of their Farsphex cutting a lean curve away from a boiling cloud of smoke, obviously intending to arc back again as tightly as possible and continue work. Twelve to one were not the best odds, but Taki was already committing herself, trusting that her skill would have found refuge in some part of her mind that was not ragged with sleep deprivation.

Before she got in range of them, she was no longer alone. To one side she recognized Franticze, because the mad Bee flew with a fierce attacking fury like nobody else, disdaining all suggestion of formation or order. The Collegiate Stormreader on Taki's left was probably Elser Hardwick, a middle-aged clockwork-maker who had shown a surprising aptitude for flight; and beyond and behind her was surely Taxus, the Tarkesh halfbreed and supposed renegade. Taki was less happy about that, as she had deliberately been keeping the man off any important duties because she didn't entirely trust him. But that meant he was far more fit for active duty than anyone else, and it seemed he had decided to prove himself, whether she wanted him to or not.

All this passed through her mind, in the few fleeting seconds before her rotary piercers opened up. The Imperials had already spotted them – they were seemingly impossible to surprise – and their precise formation broke and parted, individual Farsphex seeming to dart off to solitary freedom before all coming back together, aiming to combine again against the attacking Collegiate craft.

The Wasps were less successful this time, but the reason was hardly to the defenders' credit. A simple failure of cohesion proved to be the Stormreaders' greatest asset. Taki and Hardwick followed the pattern they had drilled with, picking out one enemy and following, with Hardwick hanging back a little to watch for the return of the other Farsphex. Franticze, however, had ideas of her own: bolting through the expanding ring of enemy across the city, skimming the rooftops and off after some other target altogether. Taxus, meanwhile, very nearly got himself shot down by Taki herself, throwing his vessel in front of her, within a hand's span of fouling her attack run. She was close enough to catch a glimpse of the halfbreed gesticulating at her angrily as though *she* was the one doing it wrong.

Her piercers hammered, the stick juddering in her hands with the transmitted force of it. The Farsphex under her sights twisted and turned, shrugging off the shot, odd sparks and flashes showing where she had hit. She was almost there, though. She had the sense again, and very strongly, that the enemy were simply not quite so skilled as pilots, that their larger machines were less nimble in the air. *This should not be so difficult . . .*

She caught a flash of light in the corner of her eye: Hardwick signalling frantically. The others were on her already. A moment later the Beetle pilot peeled off to engage, her weapons glittering the air with bolts.

Just a second more . . . but the Farsphex she was trying to bring down was throwing itself all over the sky, the pilot seeming to have eyes in the back of his head as she tried to predict him, to trick him into cutting across the stream of her bolts. The first enemy shot holed her wing, another striking the engine casing, making her *Esca* shudder. She had already lost sight of Hardwick.

Taxus came back then, trying to draw the enemy away from her, his status as ally changing instantly from dubious to invaluable. Her own target was flying low, almost below the rooftops, taking a straight line down the Pathian Way at an unwise speed, heading straight for the . . .

Refining vats.

The Farsphex had fixed its wings, less agile but faster, outpacing her, and the shots from the however-many enemy still on her were starting to fall like sleet all around her. This single-minded pursuit was making her a target in turn. To her left, two craft spiralled away: Taxus forcing a Wasp from the pack by physically blocking him, matching the Imperial's twists and turns, neither of them getting a shot in. In that glimpse she saw more fliers coming in, without any notion of whose they were.

She had the triggers down still, at an unconscionable cost of ammunition, but she had only this chance to bring the enemy down. She almost felt, rather than saw, her shots impact about the enemy tail, tattering and shredding it, but all without denting the Farsphex's handling. A bolt impacted somewhere behind her, piercing the *Esca*'s casing, canting her entire world to the left as something gave way in one wing.

Too late, too late.

She actually saw the bombs fall, and then her world was smoke and flame, the fuel vats going up like bonfires, gouting thirty feet up as she frantically clawed for height, praying that the silk of her wings would not catch, because that would—

And then she was amongst the enemy. Gaining height had lost her forward momentum, and the Farsphex were all about her without warning, one pulling sharply right to avoid a collision. She had a view of the gaping hatch in its underbelly – was that someone she saw there, crouching at a machine and staring back? Then she had fought her way high enough to find herself in the thick of it.

The Farsphex had regrouped, at least a score of them, and she counted fewer Collegiate pilots than that. The city was pillared with smoke, and she had the sense that the Imperials had already accomplished most of what they had come for.

Again Taxus almost clipped her nose and, though she swore at him, she realized that he somehow thought she would follow him, as though he had signalled her beforehand and she had not noticed, save that he was the slowest heliograph student she had ever seen.

Hold on—

Then she had it – rejoining the pack was a Farsphex that limped a little in the air, a touch blackened and handling badly. *That's mine.* The part of her mind that made such calculations effortlessly told her that its approach was perfect to make it the same bomber that she had lost sight of amidst the smoke. A bloodymindedness came to her, familiar from the old days over Solarno.

You, you bastard, are going down.

She flashed frantically, the brief pattern for *My target!* over and over, hoping that someone was watching and able to follow her lead. Then she was committing herself to a long, shallow dive towards the wounded craft.

It saw her far too soon, and abruptly its wheeling formation was adjusting to take her into account, along with the various Stormreaders that were trying their luck, as detachments of Wasp pilots began changing course to cover each other, opening the jaws of a trap that would snap down exactly where she was headed, while her target sought safety beyond.

She asked the *Esca* for all the speed it could give her, unleashing everything the spring had left, exploiting a design flaw and abusing its engine mercilessly, picking up speed as the entire craft whined and screeched all around her. At the same time, a flurry of Stormreader pilots threw themselves against the Farsphex formation from above and to her right, with Edmon at their head, forcing the enemy to regroup in order to ward them off. Taki bared her teeth: the Collegiate orthopter to Edmon's left had been cut from the air almost instantly, wings freezing to drop it down onto the city. Then she was blurring through the centre of the enemy, too fast for them to catch her, although bolts pattered across the *Esca*'s fuselage, and the unhappy buzz of her right wing was abruptly more pronounced, sounding as if something was working its way loose.

The damaged Farsphex turned across the city, and if it had simply flown straight she might have fallen behind, her motor already flagging, but it was turning back towards its allies, for a moment a slave to its own tactics. Taki opened up.

For the third time she nearly killed Taxus, but this time he held himself back from her line of shot, and then the two of them enjoyed a few seconds of filling the sky around the wounded craft with bolts.

She saw their target lurch and shudder, and suddenly there was a thin line of smoke coming from somewhere around the midsection. Then Taxus peeled off abruptly, again plainly assuming she would simply follow him, and putting himself maddeningly in the wrong place because of it.

Because it's what he's used to—

The sensation was like being punched repeatedly in the back. Three – four – five solid strikes into her *Esca* by the avenging enemy, then her target, though smoking, was getting away—

From the sun, from nowhere, Franticze fell on it, a dive so steep that it was doubtful whether she could even pull out of it before making yet another hole in the city she was supposed to be defending. Taki had a brief sense of her swift descent, and then the damaged Farsphex was at last beyond any help its comrades could give it, virtually breaking in half in the air, with the rear segment exploding savagely before it could reach the ground.

Then the *Esca*'s own engine stuttered, and abruptly she had to focus merely on staying in the air, a task that was increasingly difficult. Taki dragged on the stick again for height, and this time the orthopter could not oblige her, dropping her to street level unexpectedly, so that her left wing clipped some magnate's roof garden and the far half of it disintegrated. Then the cobbles themselves were coming right at her, and she could only back with what wings she had left, and release the landing gear, and hope.

Stenwold stared around the table a little blearily. Nobody had got much sleep since yesterday's attack, and the Collegium War Assembly was looking more like exhumed corpses than the great and the good, just then. To his left was Corog Breaker, ready to report on their aviators. He was pushing them too hard, Stenwold knew, but it was hard to tell him that because Corog was pushing himself hardest of all. He looked ten years more than his real age: a man whose job had been teaching fencing to children, now trying to rise to the challenge of coordinating Collegium's air defence.

Jodry Drillen sat at the table's far end, out of bed with the dawn after a late night with the paperwork. Although the war dominated, the business of the Assembly was more important than ever. Even with everyone nominally pulling in the same direction the paperwork proliferated. He had at least thought ahead about this meeting, if only for his own comfort. He had dragged most of his household staff along to this close, high-windowed room at the Amphiophos, where they circulated with honeybread and spiced tea.

There was a scattering of other Assemblers there, a piecemeal selection of those who were responsible for the logistics of the war: merchants, clerks, academics. No doubt all the questions of the day would be answerable only by those who had not made it to the meeting. Two of the War Assembly were dead, killed in the bombing, and neither had left adequate notes.

Filling out the table were all three commanders of the Merchant Companies: Marteus the Ant sat pale and still as a statue. Elder Padstock sipped at her tea left-handed, her right still bandaged from the burns she had sustained trying to get people out of the wreckage of their homes. Janos Outwright, a plump, moustached Beetle who had never looked this far ahead when setting himself up as a chief officer, gripped the table just to stop his hands trembling. On Outwright's left there was a stocky Beetle College Master named Bola Stormall, one of the two to donate a name to the Collegiate orthopter model, and a leading aviation engineer; next to her was a newcomer, a dun-skinned Ant who had arrived with messages from their allies in Sarn.

Stenwold realized that they had all been sitting here staring dully at one another for far too long, each one willing someone else to speak. 'Corog, tell us about yesterday,' he managed to intervene.

Breaker grunted. 'We lost seven orthopters, four pilots. The chutes are lifesavers, literally, given that most of ours have no Art for flying. If the Empire comes tomorrow, then we're that many craft down. If they leave the same sort of gap then we can repair and replace in order to keep our numbers high – we can have another five or ten maybe, over and above yesterday's numbers, if we call up the next class of pilots – and we've more being trained.' *Untried machines, untried aviators*, were the words he did not say.

'That doesn't sound too bad,' Jodry murmured.

'Because of them and their tactics,' Corog Breaker spat bitterly. 'Jodry, they're not trying to shoot us down. Given the number of armed orthopters up there, it's nothing more than a slapping war for our pilots so far. The enemy . . . their priority is keeping themselves alive. They organize in the air, but it's to defend each other, rallying against any attack so that our people have to break off or else commit suicide. All of our losses have been people caught by surprise or people pushing their luck. The Wasps are prioritizing targets on the ground, and they're being cursed successful with it, too, but they're playing very safe against our fliers. It won't last.'

'What do you mean?' Jodry himself probably understood, Stenwold reckoned, but he asked the question so that everyone was clear.

'They're on the defensive so far. If they turn that discipline into an attack, they'll cut a bloody swathe through us. We'll take more of them than we have so far, for certain, but, if they come three or four days on the trot with the idea of smashing us in the air, they could strip us of every orthopter we've got, for a loss of perhaps half as many of their own, maybe less. They'll do it, too, because if it makes sense to me, it makes sense to them.'

'Assuming they hold their own lives so cheap,' Outwright put in, desperately. Nobody could be bothered to answer him.

'What about Taki?' Stenwold asked softly.

'Conscious now,' Corog said curtly. 'Possibly concussed. Confined to bed under protest while our engineers patch up her machine.'

'Ah, well, then,' Jodry said, with false heartiness. 'To happier matters: what about our prize? Stormall?'

Bola Stormall started on hearing her name. 'Still on fire,' she got out, and took a swallow of tea. 'Willem had it brought to the workshop, but he's letting it burn.'

'A little, ah, wasteful?' Jodry pressed.

'We put most of it out, and I've got a lot of broken pieces to pick over – but Willem has a pack of artificers and chemists who reckon they can get something out of the rest, so we've left it to burn,' Stormall visibly sagged even as she spoke. 'We already know their big trick, the fixed-to-mobile-wing business, from that Taki woman. Which, of course, gives them enough range that we've still not found their airfield, I understand.'

'We're still looking,' Corog growled. 'We think they must move it around.'

'Nobody's criticizing you, Corog,' Jodry said, raising his hands placatingly. 'Next?'

'My men are still holding Banjacs Gripshod under house arrest, which is starting to get tiresome,' Janos Outwright thrust in, before Jodry could continue. 'He says he wants to fight the Wasps, too. Why not let him, rather that than waste people keeping him indoors, especially given the death machine or whatever that takes up half his house?'

Jodry made placating gestures. 'I'll deal with it,' he said. 'I'll speak to him myself. Whatever. Now, next on the agenda – by which I mean the list I have inside my head – news from Sarn.'

Nobody had been given the opportunity to sound out the Sarnesh messenger before the meeting. The young Ant had turned up at the gate only moments before and been ushered into this august company without introductions. It was a misstep that Jodry would not have made under normal circumstances.

The Ant-kinden looked as weary as they all felt, but he stood up stiffly to deliver his report. 'Sarn sends to its allies in Collegium the news that the fortress at Malkan's Folly has fallen to the Imperial Eighth Army, which has now continued its advance towards Sarn. The Empire has deployed various new weapons, the nature of which are not wholly understood. Sarn is not in a position to tender any substantial aid to Collegium in its time of trouble.'

The Collegiates absorbed this.

'New weapons?' Stenwold prompted. 'You mean their orthopters? The artillery and the automotives we saw at Myna?'

'No, Master Maker, we do not,' the Sarnesh told him, and for a moment there was a slight uncertainty in the Ant's level tone. 'Some weapon was used to clear the survivors of the fortress garrison from the underground bunkers. Those that escaped make a . . . disturbing report. A new weapon, its nature unknown.' The Ant spoke the words with his eyes fixed straight ahead, and Stenwold wondered what mental images he had inherited from those who had escaped the doomed fortress.

'Well, the upshot of *that* is clear enough, anyway,' Jodry rumbled. 'We're on our own. What else? Other business?'

'Yes,' Stenwold said flatly, as the Ant sat down. 'Corog, may we take it that the ground damage from yesterday's attack was similarly precise?'

'They knew what they were doing,' Breaker confirmed. 'Several workshops were damaged, all of them contributing to our war preparations in some way. The packing plant on Stoner Street that was turning out rations is gutted entirely. Plus a number of private residences, probably simply bad luck, for the most part. The worst blow was the fuel depot. We're lucky that our fliers are all clockwork, but we were relying on the fuel for our automotives, for when the Second get closer. Nobody knows if we can refine more in time.'

Stenwold nodded because all this was preamble, and he had already put plans in motion to deal with the problem. 'I have sent to certain . . . allies of mine who may be able to procure a supply,' he said carefully, catching Jodry's eye. 'I'm not sure if it's possible, but they have a sample of what we lack and, if they can produce it, they will.' The Sea-kinden, his little secret, had some remarkable Art to produce both raw materials and finished goods, but mineral oil fuels might yet be beyond them.

There were plenty of questions about *that*, of course, but he waved them away. 'Meanwhile we have a more pressing problem. It's plain the Empire has spies aplenty in Collegium, despite all we've done in the past to thin their ranks. They're feeding the Imperial air force information, telling them where to strike. So we need to take action.'

'You've identified these spies?' Stormall asked him hopefully.

Stenwold shook his head. 'We are the victims of our own open society, and the industry that they prey on can hardly be kept a secret. We need to take a sterner line. I want every Wasp-kinden in the city under lock and key by tomorrow evening, first for questioning and then exile.'

There was a pause as the others considered this. Raking the table, Stenwold caught as many eyes as possible. *You know I'm right*, he thought, as though he was an Ant and could place the words in their minds.

'Stenwold, you do know that most of their people will just be Beetle-kinden, or Flies – no shortage of either in the Empire,' Jodry remarked mildly.

Stenwold shrugged. 'The Wasps don't trust "lesser races" as much as you think. Somewhere there will be a Wasp holding their leashes. We can cut the head off the Rekef operation in Collegium by this single step. We need to deny them every advantage we can.'

His gaze was fixed on Jodry now, but the Speaker for the Assembly was not discomfited.

'Oh, no, I don't think so,' the fat Beetle replied, and then managed a wan smile. 'That's not the Collegiate way, Sten.' He looked brightly about the table. 'Any other business?'

'I want a vote,' Stenwold demanded flatly.

Jodry went quite still. 'Now, come on, Sten.'

'We are Collegium, and we are ruled by the vote, so let us vote, those of us here.' Stenwold looked about the table, judging and measuring. 'I say that our city will be safer if we rid it of Wasp-kinden. I say that questioning those same Wasps may even lead us to this cursed airfield. We can't afford to ignore the opportunity. Put it to the vote.'

'Stenwold, we cannot simply have people arrested – some of them citizens, even – without cause.'

'We *have* cause,' Stenwold retorted more sharply. 'The Empire has given us that cause.' He tried to make a sort of ghastly joke of it. 'Are you worried this will cost you at the next Lots?'

'No, Stenwold, I am not,' Jodry snapped. Abruptly he heaved himself to his feet, jowls quivering. 'I do, however, refuse to be the Speaker who opens that door.'

'Then we can take it that you vote against.' Stenwold was standing too, and the rest of the table just stared, seeing these two gears of state, which had run smoothly together for so long, abruptly clashing teeth. 'I vote for.' He turned to Corog Breaker. 'You?'

'For,' Breaker said bluntly.

The merchant beside him looked from Stenwold to Jodry. 'I abstain.'

Several others followed his lead, with one for and one against before the matter came to Bola Stormall, the aviation artificer.

'War Master, I have followed your lead for a long time,' she said, although there was no warmth in her voice. 'I flew against Vek. I crewed on the *Triumph* when the Wasps came here last. I've worked to your plan now and, between me and Willem and Taki, we've got our orthopters off the ground. I will not be part of this.'

'Bola—' Stenwold started, but she held him off with a single gesture.

'Do *not*, Stenwold,' she warned. 'I have relatives in Helleron who told me what life was like there under the Empire, during the last war, the imprisonment and disappearances.'

'Yes,' retorted Stenwold. 'The Wasps torture people and impale them on spears. I'm talking only about arrest and exile. You can't compare—'

'The rule of just law makes us who we are, and I am not the only one who has been wondering if we might have made more ground with the Wasps had we not painted them as irredeemable villains.'

Makerist, Stenwold heard the word, from his memories. 'You've been listening to students too much,' he told her.

'Well, perhaps they're actually learning something useful for a change,' she retorted. 'Besides, you've heard yourself that half the army marching along the coast is Spider-kinden. There are perhaps two dozen Wasps at most within the city, but there are hundreds of Spiders, entire generations of them. Will you round them up as well, adults and old women and children, when the spying doesn't stop? And what then?'

Stenwold stared at her, feeling his will strike hers, hammer to hammer. 'That's not what I'm proposing—'

'—today,' she finished for him. 'Against, Stenwold.'

He took a deep breath. *It doesn't matter*, he told himself, because now there were the three Merchant Company officers. 'Elder?'

'For.' Elder Padstock of the Maker's Own Company, her vote never in question.

'Janos?'

The squat little Assembler looked from Maker to Jodry, his moustache quivering. 'I, in all conscience . . .' He had taken on his current mantle as one of a line of stunts intended to garner the popularity of the masses, and to ensure his own continuing good fortune. Now he looked as though he bitterly regretted it. 'Abstain, I abstain.'

Stenwold nodded equably, because that didn't matter either. 'Marteus?' he asked, with finality.

'There is a Wasp-kinden in my Company,' the renegade Tarkesh said quietly.

Stenwold blinked at him.

'He has lived here for more than ten years. He's a mason,'

Marteus continued, 'and he wants to fight the Empire more than anyone. Of course, I can understand that. If those sancti-monious turds from Tark were at the gates, well, I'd be first in line to throw them back, as you can imagine.' He met Stenwold's eyes readily. 'Of course, by these lights, you'd have locked me up by that point. A man's not his kinden, and a man's not his city-state.'

A delicate span of silence held the room for a few seconds, before Jodry said, quietly and without acrimony, 'Even for and against: the vote is not carried. Stenwold, I'm sure that you will continue to use all *conventional* measures to deal with the spies we undoubtedly have, spotting who's being too nosy, working out how they're exporting this intelligence of theirs. We have all faith in you. Any other business?'

Nobody had any more to say.

That night, Taki woke abruptly out of a dream in which she was being chased through the streets of Collegium by the Tarkesh halfbreed Taxus and, no matter where she flew, he always appeared ahead of her, as preternaturally knowledgeable as the Imperial pilots.

Waking, she gasped, clutching for the sudden understanding that had shocked her out of sleep. One of the medical orderlies, some Beetle-kinden student volunteer, was hurrying over, and she realized that she most have shouted aloud.

She swung her legs out of bed before the Beetle got to her, but a sudden wave of dizziness prevented her making a quick escape.

'Back into bed, please, Mistress Taki,' the young man insisted. 'Not until Doctor Findwell gives you the nod.'

'Get off me!' she snapped. 'I need to speak to Stenwold.' She made to kick off and take to the air, but a moment later realized that she really wasn't ready for that after all, as the world swam and shuddered before her eyes. 'Get me the War Master,' she insisted. 'Or get a message to him. Get me pen and paper, anything. I've worked it out. I know how they're doing it. I know the secret of the Empire's pilots.'

She was already staggering determinedly away, ready to rouse the whole Assembly if need be. 'And get me Taxus!' she shouted over her shoulder. 'I need to shake his cursed hand!'

They told her that Taxus had not come back from his last flight over the city, that the Wasps had caught and killed him in spite of all his idiosyncrasies. It was in a more sober mood that she finally passed on her revelation to Stenwold Maker.

Twenty-Four

'Te Pelle? I didn't know her much,' Pingge said. 'That's two of us dead.'

Kiin nodded. She looked worn out, and had only slept for a handful of hours since her return from the second mission over Collegium. The flight had been a mixed squad, half of them Aarmon's originals, half from the new trainees, but Kiin reported that all the pilots had worked together with the same effortless coordination as before.

Pingge and Gizmer had stolen away from the main body of the bombardiers, now holing up in a store cupboard for a serious discussion of what had happened. It had taken some persuasion for Gizmer to accept *Sergeant* Kiin into their counsels. Since her promotion he had kept a suspicious eye on her, as though expecting her to metamorphose into a Wasp at any moment. Still, the fact that she actually had first-hand knowledge of what had happened was enough to twist his arm. Gossip was always better for a little fresh information.

'The pilot was . . . Bresner, I think. One of the newer ones.'

They considered this information. Te Pelle had been a somewhat haughty girl, not a factory-line worker but an overseer, and of decent family, who had not taken well to being drafted simply for her artificer's skills. Still, the woman had been one of them, and that should be enough.

'Aarmon said something odd,' Kiin added uncertainly.

'He actually spoke?' Pingge asked her. 'Other than to give an order?'

'He said she had done well – no, not like that. He said that Bresner had said that te Pelle had done well. Even when they were getting shot up, she got the bombs away, blew up the fuel store, right on the mark.'

'He said that *Bresner* said?' Pingge frowned.

Kiin nodded, wide-eyed. 'His last message, somehow.'

Gizmer looked from one to the other and grinned, unexpectedly. 'You surprise me, the pair of you. You hadn't worked that out?' He cackled at their expressions. 'Come on, now, look at our lords and masters, eh? Pride of the Air Corps, only not one of them's a pilot by training save for our Captain Aarmon. The rest are just Light Airborne or artificers, Consortium men, all sorts. By basic inclination we're more fit for the job than they are. So didn't you ever wonder *why*?'

'I assumed they'd had some test, some latent gift for it, or . . .' Pingge scowled at him. 'So tell us, big mouth.'

'They have an Art,' Kiin put in, spoiling Gizmer's moment.

He nodded grudgingly. 'Worked it out, then?'

'I'd thought . . . I wasn't sure until you put it that way. They have a mindlink.'

'Don't be ridiculous,' Pingge said, straight away.

'What else then, eh?' Gizmer pressed.

'But the Rekef . . . the generals . . . Who knows?' Pingge's voice had descended to a whisper. Everyone knew that the Wasp-kinden sometimes manifested the same Art that enabled Ants to speak mind to mind, but it was rare. More than that, it was dangerous. Back in the reign of Alvric, First Emperor of the Wasps, there had been troubles, perhaps an attempted coup. The Rekef, then led by the same man who had given the service his name, had flexed its muscles for the first time. Anyone suspected of the mindlink had been hunted down, except for those wretched traitors who had thrown their lot in with the hunters. The Rekef Inlander had chosen its first battlefield: it could not countenance a hidden, unified fifth column within the Empire: the danger to the Emperor's rule was too great to ignore. Hundreds were arrested, tortured for the names of any others they knew, then strung on the crossed pikes. It had been a forging time in the Empire's history. A great many traditions had been born.

After that, anyone who developed the Art kept quiet about it, and tried never to use it in case some fellow pariah betrayed them. Yet it continued to manifest itself, that part of the Wasps' collective soul refusing to be ignored.

'They all know,' Gizmer stated. 'It's a secret but not a conspiracy. Times change. There's a book out there that I snuck a look at – top-secret air tactics and everything. Colonel Varsec's work, all of it. He sets out the Farsphex design in it, but he also sets out the new pilots too. He said they used mindlinked troops to coordinate the taking of Solarno, apparently. So people have been thinking for a while, only it took Varsec to shift the idea over to pilots. No bloody wonder our lot have become the wonders of the air, eh, if they're all inside each other's minds. No wonder we get such a ragbag of recruits, too – women and all. They must have mindlinkers scouting every city in the Empire for more of the same.'

'That's . . .' Pingge shivered. 'So they could be talking to each other all the time, and we'd never know.'

Gizmer gave her a patronizing look. 'They're Wasps, so what does it matter? It's not as though they'd be running everything by us otherwise, eh?'

The door to the store cupboard was abruptly thrown open, and the three of them jumped guiltily, expecting the stern, pale face of Aarmon. Instead it was just one of the newer Fly recruits.

'Sergeant, been looking all over for you!' the girl squeaked. 'Everyone's to assemble. New orders come in.'

The three of them exchanged looks.

'Don't like the sound of that,' Gizmer muttered, and then they set off, half-running, half-flying, to join their fellows.

They met in the barracks common room that Gizmer had dubbed 'the wasteland' because, aside from formal times such as this, neither Fly-kinden nor Wasps spent any time there. A quick head count suggested that just about everyone was there from both camps. Pingge pushed her way into a mob of other Flies, not wanting to be at the back, nor to end up where she might be picked out by Aarmon, who was standing on a table to look them all over. It really was *everyone* here, she realized, including the trainees, because she could spot the female Wasp recruits interspersed amongst the men. That had been an arrangement that everyone had thought would go badly wrong, and in fact there had been one incident, when an engineer – an outsider serving as ground crew – had tried to rape one of the Wasp girls. What happened next only really made sense to Pingge now with the benefit of what Gizmer had told her. The assaulted woman had not even cried out, but Aarmon and another two pilots had appeared almost immediately. They had stung the rapist to death without sparing a moment for his panicky denials.

'Listen up,' Aarmon stated flatly. 'New orders. We're to step up the attacks.'

Everyone waited, but Pingge could sense a stir amongst the Wasps, some additional information passing between them.

'From now on, returning crews get one day of turnaround and then they're out again. The engineers reckon the Farsphex can be repaired and refuelled in time. We'll be rolling missions so, even before one's back, the next shift will be in the air. Collegium's had it too easy, they tell me.'

Collegium's too cursed good at defending itself, Pingge added, thinking of te Pelle. One of the Wasps must have had the same idea, because Aarmon was nodding.

'Yes, the Collegiates are good in the air, better than anyone thought. Yes, we're going to take losses. It's war.' His voice was hard, flat, bleak. 'Do you think that when the land battle starts, none of our soldiers will die? We have a duty to perform. We will look after our own as much as is humanly possible,' and his gaze made no distinction between Wasp or Fly, man or woman, 'but we will do our duty nonetheless. We will make the Empire proud of us.'

There was something behind his words, and Pingge knew enough to understand now: *They culled the mindlinkers once and they can do it again, especially now they're all here and out in the open. If we get it wrong, if we give them cause, then this whole experiment could end up in the Rekef cells.* She shivered. *And it'll be us along with them, sure enough. I know how the Rekef think.*

'We've authority to increase the Chneuma dosing,' Aarmon added. 'Double for pilots, and a single for the bombardiers now.' Seeing the looks on some of the Fly-kinden faces, he added, 'It's something the Engineering Corps alchemists cooked up. We use it to stay awake for the days of the flight. You'll all need it too, now. Sergeant Kiin, see me after, and I'll sort out a supply.'

None of the Flies dared ask what other effects this Chneuma might produce, but it was evident in most expressions there, and no doubt some of the Wasps were posing that silent question, but Aarmon was not being drawn.

'There's one other thing,' he added, 'a change to the operation. We'll be bringing some more of your training into the war.' This time he was looking straight at the Flies and, as he told them what he meant, the idea was both terrifying and strangely attractive.

Yes, Pingge found herself thinking, with a curiously detached feeling of professionalism, *The Collegiates won't know what hit them.*

Laszlo darted between wagons and automotives, flicked up twenty feet for a brief look at the evolving layout of the camp around him, then dropped down again. There were plenty of flying troops in the Grand Army – as even the Imperials were calling it now – but this was still a good way to attract undue attention. The Wasps made it plain that they took full responsibility for the skies above the army, and they were inclined to ask questions.

Progress had slowed over the last few days, though not because of any active resistance. Instead, an order had come from General Tynan that each night everyone would dig in, forming the vehicles into a circle and deploying a remarkable number of ready-made barricades which the Wasps had brought with them. Laszlo understood that Tynan had employed far more complete fortifications the first time he led the Second this way, but the combined force was now simply too large and disunited to protect thoroughly. The Wasps did what they could with what they had, though, and, in addition, every night saw the raising of three skeletal towers within the camp, each with what looked to Laszlo like some enormous sort of lamp.

They had now definitely entered Mantis territory, he understood. The precautions started even as they moved off from the cliffs above Kes, but it was a bitter part of recent Imperial history that the Fourth Army had been destroyed even further out than that, the Mantis-kinden able to travel swiftly by land and water, night and day. Of course, everyone knew that the Second had driven the Mantids out last time, and whether there were any left in the forest was unknown to the Grand Army's leadership, but it was plain that Tynan wasn't taking chances.

Laszlo tried to remember what he knew about the local Mantis-kinden. In fact, he had few fond thoughts of them, because of the actions of one particular individual, but in general he recalled them idling all over Collegium, refugees from their forest domain after Tynan's depredations. Surely those few who might have returned home to rebuild could not pose a threat to the army that was advancing.

He hopped up once again to locate his target, then dropped back quickly. Just now he was in the loose following of Morkaris, the Aldanrael's mercenary adjutant. The lean Spider-kinden was a busy man, constantly meeting with the leaders of various sell-sword companies, settling disputes, disbursing coin and occasionally punching faces. For all his stringy build he seemed to possess a prodigious strength. The demands on his time meant that he could find a use for someone like Laszlo, and just now that meant fetching food from the latest shipment. The Grand Army could never have lived off the land, so there were airships – both Imperial black and gold and smaller many-coloured craft from the Spiderlands – constantly ferrying back and forth with the supplies they needed for the march. When a shipment arrived, the camp cooks descended on it to cook up or preserve everything in danger of going off, and so Laszlo descended on Morkaris with a covered bowl of spiced horsemeat and a jug of soup, which the man grabbed from him the moment he was within arm's reach.

'Good work.' The Spider upended the jug, heedless of the steaming heat of it, and then wiped his mouth on the back of a gauntlet. He was plainly not the kind of mannered Aristos that his counterpart Jadis was, but then the mercenaries obviously appreciated a plain-speaking man as their liaison. The next group with a grievance was approaching him even now: a quartet of hulking Scorpions.

'Watch and learn,' Morkaris remarked, because Laszlo knew how to make himself likeable, and the adjutant had taken a shine to him. The next ten minutes provided a masterclass in Spider–Scorpion relations, and ended with the adjutant sinking an axe into the company leader's skull.

The other three Scorpions had regarded this action with little emotion.

'Fine,' Morkaris had told them. 'You're mine for now, until I say otherwise. Or does someone else want to try their luck?' Nobody had felt that lucky.

Now Laszlo skimmed back over the camp, aiming for home – meaning the wagon that he and Lissart slept in. Running errands for Morkaris had meant a long and busy day, and he would still be hard put to report to Stenwold that he had found any fatal vulnerability in the way the Spider-kinden soldiers operated. The only logical advice would be, *Kill their leaders*, and that would hardly be something Stenwold had not thought of.

He ducked in, and, had he not ducked out again immediately, Lissart would have stabbed him. Hanging in the air outside, his mind was full of the flash of steel, her abrupt, savage movement.

Some part of him found that he was not surprised in the least.

'Laszlo . . . ?' came her quiet voice from under the cloth awning. She sounded shaken, although he felt that he deserved that particular privilege.

A moment later she peered out, and the knife was nowhere to be seen. 'I'm sorry. I didn't realize it was you.'

He descended warily, keeping out of arm's reach, but remembering that she had more weapons than the blade, anyway. She could simply blast him with that fire Art of hers, if she so wished. He reckoned she was certainly strong enough to use it by now.

'Who were you intending to stab?' he asked her, trying to adopt a light tone.

'Laszlo, she's here,' Lissart told him flatly. 'Get under cover, quickly.'

She was frightened, he realized, or at least feigning it, but he made a snap decision, hoping his instincts were being trustworthy, and ducked under the wagon's cover to nestle in beside her. She pressed herself against him and he found she was trembling slightly. The rush of gratitude he felt to the world, that she did not appear to want to kill him just yet, was stronger than he had expected.

Still under her spell, he thought wryly, putting his arms around her. 'Who's here?'

'Garvan,' she said, and he allowed a pause for explanation, but none came.

'Should I know what that means?'

'Garvan, or whatever her real name is,' she persisted, 'the Wasp woman who *stabbed* me. The Rekef one.'

He went quite still, thinking hard. The urge to say, *Are you sure?* was very strong, but she would not have thanked him for doubting her. 'When, where?'

'She must have come in with the supplies. I saw her just walking through the camp, mid-afternoon.'

'Looking for you?'

'I don't *know*,' she snapped, but she was trembling even more now. 'She'll know me, though, and she'll kill me.'

'We can't stay here, then. Can you fly?'

'I don't know.'

There was something in her response that did not quite ring true. 'Are you trying to tell me,' Laszlo pressed gently, 'that you've not experimented while I've been out and about?'

'A short hop, maybe, nothing more,' she whispered. 'We'll leave tonight.' He made a doubting sound, and she twisted her neck to glare at him. 'What?'

'Ever since we got within spit of the Felyal, camp security's right up, especially at night. They have a lot of sharp eyes doing sentry duty now. If you could fly, then I'd say risk it, but . . .'

'But *what*?' she demanded.

'But let me think about it. Stay under cover meanwhile. This Garvan of yours is a Wasp, so no reason for her to poke about the Spider-kinden camp. She won't know me, so I can keep an eye out. Maybe we can stir trouble up against her, especially if she's Rekef. Just . . . wait. Don't do anything we'll regret. Just let me think of something.'

She lay in his arms, facing away from him. In her mind, no doubt, she was reliving the blade going in. *She's crazy*, he told himself. *She's a killer, an enemy agent, the most dangerous woman you've ever got hold of. Just go. Leave her and just go.* But he knew he would not depart without her, even so.

'Think of something quickly,' she said softly. 'I can't hold out forever.'

'Our lack of progress is causing a lot of friction,' Mycella observed. Tynan watched her with grudging admiration, because she was examining her appearance in a mirror while her elaborate tent was raised around her, the one still point in a whirl of carefully orchestrated chaos. Her servants, Spiders and Fly-kinden both, were practically dancing to a common rhythm that allowed them to coordinate with one another to set up poles and guys and embroidered canvas without so much as obstructing their mistress's light, until she stood in a reddening beam of sunset in the midst of an eight-chambered portable palace, with furniture being moved into position as nimbly as though her staff were scene-shifters at the theatre.

'Join me?' she asked him, meeting his eyes in the mirror. A Fly-kinden was already at her elbow with a bottle of dark glass.

'I see your kind's reputation for vanity isn't misplaced,' he observed, although without vitriol.

She raised an eyebrow at him. 'You never feel the need to see your own face, General?'

'Not since I stopped needing a comb,' he told her. It was true, too. Even without his own slaves, he could have shaved himself by touch these days.

'I envy you. Mine holds a grim fascination for me, but it isn't vanity.' She turned towards him at last and collapsed back onto a couch that had not been there a moment before, even as the mirror was spirited away. 'Time, General Tynan . . . I watch it advance on my position, and each day all my armies lose a little ground. I'm older than you, you realize?'

He shrugged, although inwardly he was surprised and then annoyed at letting anything these Spiders did surprise him. 'I've seen less friction than I'd expected.' He found a camp stool placed neatly beside him, standard army issue, and lowered himself into it, accepting a glass of what turned out to be Imperial brandy.

'It's in my camp, mostly, the discontent,' she admitted. 'The mercenaries get paid more for fighting, so they want to start besieging Collegium yesterday, and even our regular soldiers are . . . impatient. Jadis and Morkaris are keeping discipline, but perhaps your scouts have some news that might settle matters a little.'

He gave her an amused look. 'And yours?'

She matched his expression. 'Very well, then. As we skirt the Felyal, it looks increasingly as though there's a fair-sized body of people moving ahead of us – soldiers, not refugees. Much sign of Mantis-kinden, by my trackers' expert opinion, but others as well in fair numbers, certainly hundreds. If they were simply going to join up with the Collegiates, they'd have out-paced us easily, but they're hanging about ahead of our advance, and some of my scouts haven't come back. Some of yours, too, I'd wager? And one of your little airships is late as well, unless you sent it somewhere especially far.'

He nodded grudgingly. 'You're right, of course. Always the bloody Felyal. You weren't here to see the bloodshed last time. You'd think they'd take a hint. But you're correct: it's not just Mantids either. Cherten reckons it's an advance force from the city come to take a poke at us, while they've got the trees to operate from.'

'My intelligence suggests it's unlikely to be directly from Collegium. But what's your plan?'

'Depends how much history repeats itself. So far we've been moving past the Felyal that I burned the last time, but shortly we'll be at the green. If there's going to be trouble, it'll be then, and at night most likely. Or it could be tonight, for that matter, or it might just as easily have been yesterday. Hence our walls and towers and caution – and your friction. My bet is that your mercenaries get to earn their blood money before a tenday's out, though. And if we can break the back of the locals, then we can pick up speed again.'

'You've thought this out, obviously.'

He suspected that she was flattering him rather than being overly sincere, but he could not quite suppress a smile. 'They call my Second Army the Gears, Mycella. We don't stop grinding until there's nothing left but pieces. In order to maintain that reputation, in order to make sure nothing *does* stop us, you have no idea of the amount of forward planning I have to do.'

'Just you? No council of tacticians?'

'Some day I'll get it wrong, and they'll bury me and find another name for my army,' he replied flatly.

'You're grim all of a sudden.'

He felt a jab of annoyance that this smooth, elegant woman should presume to know him – but reminded himself that he had spent quite a few nights sharing a bottle of one thing or another with his co-commander. It was not that he disdained the company of his officers, but they all had their own jobs to do, and she was right – he had nobody to share responsibility with. An army needed a single mind to direct it, and growing too familiar with his subordinates, even Mittoc and Cherten, would take the edge of his orders. Mycella represented a rare opportunity to talk matters over with someone outside his chain of command.

She's up to something. She's using her Art on me, manipulating me somehow. Yet he did not feel manipulated, and he found himself fascinated not by her appearance or her charms, but by the odd glimpse of weakness that she let him see, quite calculatedly: her fear of time, or the past failures that had put her where she was – a battlefield general's role viewed as a spider punishment rather than a Wasp reward.

And she was beautiful, it was true, and all the more so because she was plainly not making the effort she could have done. She faced him instead as soldier to soldier.

This is going to turn out very badly, he knew, and he was too old to play that sort of fool. He should, he was well aware, restrict his meetings with her to daylight business: brief, curt discussions over the running of the army. *Maybe tomorrow I'll do that.*

He was gazing at her, he knew – or almost through her, at the warring ghost of his own mind. He brought his eyes back into focus quickly, expecting to find her eyeing him with a touch of mockery, but she was not looking at him at all, just peering into the growing shadows of her tent, weighing her glass in her hand.

The attack, when it came, justified Tynan's caution. The first Laszlo knew of it was a confused shouting coming from outside, which could have been just about anything. Despite all that the commanders of the Grand Army did to enforce discipline, Spider and Wasp ethics did not rub along easily. Most especially the Wasps had certain views on women, and many of the Spiders, in all fairness, had equally derogatory opinions about men. There had been brawls, rapes, revenge killings, and the wonder of it was that these incidents were isolated and ruthlessly investigated, rather than becoming so widespread as to swallow the entire camp. Imperial discipline and the Spider officers' strength of personality held the entire complex organism together, and pointed in the right direction.

For that reason Laszlo just lay awake listening to the commotion, trying to work out whether it was a diplomatic incident or just some internal Spider dispute. Then Lissart stirred beside him and he realized that the shouting seemed a little too widespread: he could hear voices deep into the camp.

'Get up,' he hissed.

'Get dressed,' Lissart urged him almost at the same moment.

They stared at one another in the darkness, and then they were both scrambling for their clothes, Lissart hissing in pain, as she hunched over the healing scar of her wound.

Laszlo was just pulling his boots on when the first explosion sounded, just a cracking sound, like wood snapping, but he recognized it at once as some sort of grenade.

He buckled on his belt, feeling the comforting weight of his knife against his hip. A bow would have been grand, but his role as camp follower and freelance servant had not warranted it. Lissart, at least, was armed by default.

'We go,' he decided and she nodded with a single, determined jerk of her head. Then they were dropping out of the wagon, as the sleepers around them roused themselves or panicked or hid.

There are thousands of soldiers here, Laszlo was thinking. *You'd be mad to attack an army like this. What can they hope to gain?* It was a rhetorical question, though, for so long as the attackers gained him and Lissart a moment's breathing space to get out of the camp, he could ask for no more.

General Tynan woke instantly as the first alarms were called. Some part of him had been waiting for this for a tenday or more, sleeping lightly in the absolute certain expectation that just this would happen. *The Mantis-kinden are here at last. What kept them?*

There was a plan, of course, and he had made sure that the duty sergeants and lieutenants knew what to do. At this moment his sentries and night watch would be doing everything they could to contain and assess the attack: numbers, direction, intention. They would be fighting for a breathing space in which to take control, just as they had back in the first war. Many of them would even be veterans of that same battle, where the invincible Mantids of the Felyal were taught about the sharp end of progress.

It came as no surprise that a kinden that had unchanged over five hundred years would not have learnt from that defeat either.

He dragged on a banded cuirass, standard Airborne issue,

and snatched up his sword as he strode outside, even as the first officers arrived to report.

'You,' he snapped, picking a captain from the pack of messengers, trusting that senior rank equated to more critical news. Even as the man started to speak, though, there were Mantiskinden amongst them, a handful of warriors just dropping from the sky and laying into whoever was closest. The captain was their first victim.

Tynan had no time to be startled by the attack, for there was a lean, savage-looking woman driving for him with a spear in the next moment, her fluid lunge little more than a suggestion of motion in the fickle lantern light. Long years of soldiering lent him enough instinct to save himself, anticipating her attack before he properly saw it, falling aside from the bright dart of the spearhead and lashing at the woman with his left-hand sting, staggering her. His right arm was already slamming forwards, and if he had been the young, strong major of fifteen years ago he would have killed her with the sword blow. As it was, he felt the blade grate off chitin armour, and she jumped back to get him again at her spear's point, but another of his men blasted her from behind, the fire of his sting landing in the small of her back.

By that time it was over: four Mantis corpses, half a dozen dead Wasps, but the sounds of fighting still came from all directions.

'Get the towers lit, you idiots!' Tynan shouted at his army in general, judging that the time for receiving reports was probably past. In that moment he heard the sharp retort of a grenade, and his mind flipped the scenario it had been devising, turning it on its head. Mantis-kinden were among the Inapt, grenades were not in their arsenal. *Mycella said there were others. Mantis-kinden are insane, and they'd attack a thousand with a dozen, but why would anyone in their right mind go along with them for the ride? What are they after?*

'All of you!' he snapped at the men still present. 'Get men to defend the baggage train – the munitions, fuel stores, automotives, supplies. Go, go!'

A runner came in, and nearly got himself killed by some of the more eager soldiers keen to guard their general now that he had no immediate need of them. Thankfully the long march with the Spider-kinden had given their allies just enough familiarity to slow the Wasps' instinctive responses.

'General, message from the Lady-Martial.' The Spider was a lean, long-limbed youth, presumably picked for his running speed. 'Large force of Mantis-kinden are in the north-camp.' He was breathing heavily, forcing the words out.

'Lieutenant!' Tynan called, on the good officer's principle that there was always a lieutenant within earshot. 'Get me—'

'General, no. We have them contained. I am to say that the flank is secure. My lady urges you to look to the east. Our spotters have seen other movement there.'

East? That's their quickest route to the supplies and vehicles. 'Already being taken care of,' Tynan told him. 'What do you mean "contained"?' Even as he asked it, one of the tower lamps flared up, casting a bright white glare across the camp, Tynan looked about for the other two towers, finding one standing but dark, the last one . . . He blinked, for the easternmost tower was down, somehow. The attack there must be fiercer than he had realized.

'We know about fighting Mantis-kinden, general. We have numbers and we can see in the dark as well as they.' The Spider messenger bowed. 'I must rejoin my lady.'

Tynan waved him away. 'You heard him,' he growled. 'Get men over to the east. Form up and sweep the vermin out of camp – and take some prisoners.'

'But, General, we're to trust these Spiders to hold?' one of his bolder officers demanded.

'We're marching to war alongside them, so we'll have to lean

378

on them eventually. Now's better than before the Collegiate gates,' Tynan snapped. 'Now *move!*'

How close did I just come to dying? a tiny voice said at the back of his mind, but he was a soldier and he fought it down.

All around them, in the maze of alleys and pathways running between the tents of the Spider camp, the fighting twisted and turned. There seemed to be Mantis-kinden everywhere, singly or small packs of them, and wherever the attackers went they met the Spiders, sallying forth to defend their own. That the Mantids wanted nothing more than to shed the blood of their most hated enemies was abundantly clear. This was no line-against-line soldier's engagement, but a mad whirling skirmish, hundreds of individual duels and brawls, small bands of Spiders against smaller number of Mantis-kinden, whilst the more heavily armoured mercenaries formed up into solid units that became reference points for the fluid, unpredictable conflict going on around them. The Mantis-kinden were the deadlier, practically berserk, swifter than sight and utterly intent on blood. The Spiders gave before them, surged in on flanks and from behind, feinted and feigned and lured them into ambushes. The toll on both sides was fearsome.

Laszlo and Lissart dashed from shadow to shadow, tent to tent. The nearest edge of the camp was where the Mantis-kinden were coming *from* – so no escape to that quarter for certain. Instead they were forced further into the camp, looking for some other way out.

Then the tower lamp flared on, and its blinding glare froze the two Flies in their tracks, instantly feeling guilty as though the whole business was aimed only at them. It was an impartial beacon, though, and it stripped away half the hiding places they had been counting on, exposing them under its fierce fire. Above them and before them were Wasp-kinden, the night shift assembling into detachments and deploying, ground or air, wherever the sergeants sent them, the day shift donning their armour as swiftly as they could.

'You! Identify yourselves!' a Wasp sergeant snapped at them, palm forward and plainly keen to remove any further complications the night might offer him.

'Messengers from the Aldanrael,' Lissart shot back at him. 'Which way to the general?'

For a second the man was not buying, but then he nodded briefly, gesturing further into the camp, seeing they had nothing more than knives on them. They passed through the Wasp ranks, constantly jostled and pushed as the soldiers formed ranks.

'We need to get a good look around,' Laszlo stated. 'From down here it's impossible to guess where we can make a break for.' He glanced up, but the sky was busy with Light Airborne and Mantis-kinden both, and flying into that kind of meat-grinder did not appeal to him.

'Head for the tower!' Lissart told him sharply.

'What?'

'Just go!' She shoved him towards the light, her face looking pale and strained. Even as they passed through, utterly beneath the Wasps' notice, a surge of fighters broke away from the fighting about the Spider camps – more Mantids but others, too: Flies, Beetles, Ants, in a ragged but determined mob. They were making for the functioning tower, and the Wasps were instantly on to them, the Airborne taking to the sky whilst stings and snapbows began to rake into the attackers even as they rushed in.

The pair of them ran, or Laszlo ran and buoyed Liss up enough for her to match his pace. Hiding was out of the question now – speed their only friend, which got them to the foot of the tower without challenge.

'Up,' she instructed him. 'See what the blazes is going on, won't you? Find us a way out of this mess.'

Even as he ascended, she turned sharply, jabbing her hand out just as a Wasp would, and he caught a flash of fire from the corner of his eye. *I hope that wasn't one of ours*, came the thought, and then he felt a wrenching sense of dissociation because, of course, nobody out there was one of theirs. There were just two contending groups who might have good cause to kill the pair of them.

He was not the first up the tower, for a dozen Wasp snapbow-men were already perched there, taking long-range potshots at any enemy target that came close enough. They glanced at Laszlo, but he made a grand show of not being up to anything suspect, and apparently he passed muster. Businesslike, with nothing in his pose admitting guilt, he took a good look to all quarters, just as if he were up the topmast back on the *Tidenfree*. There was fighting to the east as well, a vicious melee swirling about the Imperial supply wagons there, and he guessed immediately that everything else was probably just to cover getting *that* strike in place. The Wasps were all over that part of the camp, though, ground and air, and the fighting was dwindling and dwindling, the remaining attackers a diminishing ripple as the Wasps stamped them out.

Then there was a savage roar, and a plume of fire launching high into the air as something exploded. It had come from the very midst of the fighting, and Laszlo flinched despite the distance. The lamp immediately above him was hot enough to slick the back of his neck with sweat, but he almost kidded himself that he could feel an extra wash of boiled air from that eruption to the north.

It's not my business, he had to remind himself, turning his attention elsewhere, because the attack was plainly running out of steam, and the camp would be impossible to get out of once order was restored.

Moments later he had picked his compass direction and he dropped from the tower top, finding Lissart swiftly and pulling her after him. *Freedom or death*, he thought dramatically, though it was probably not too far from the truth.

In the aftermath, Colonel Cherten made his report: a mere hundred Mantis-kinden and around twice as many of various other insurgent kinden had fallen in or near the Spider tents, with perhaps a miscellaneous hundred breaking free and retreating in the direction of the Felyal. They were all from the forest or nearby communities, Cherten believed, who had seen the Empire burn their homes once, and had obviously thought they might make a difference with this sudden strike. Under cover of their noise, a determined band of Mynans had come in from another direction, attacking the towers and then turning towards the supplies. They had been utterly ruthless, fearless, each one selling his life as dearly as possible. As well as the towers, they had managed to ignite one fuel dump, which in itself made a spectacular end to most of the Mynans who had survived to that point, and a painful number of Tynan's soldiers as well. The sabotage only went to prove Colonel Mittoc's wisdom in ensuring that their fuel and munitions were not all kept in one place, as Imperial policy would normally have dictated.

Possibly more serious a loss was the discovery that one of the Sentinels had been left near that fuel store, and the explosion had tipped the machine entirely over and damaged its underside, wrecking several of its legs. Tynan's immediate plans for the Felyal, thankfully, allowed time for repairs.

Casualties had been moderate, the Aldanrael forces bearing the brunt of it as they contained the Mantis offensive. Tynan recorded a formal vote of thanks to their Spider allies.

Regarding two errant Fly-kinden, nobody had the time to spare a thought.

Looking over the Felyal, with the old burn scars of his last visit still plainly visible and the fresh wounds of the night attack in his mind, Tynan gave his orders.

'Burn every home, kill everyone who resists, take prisoner everyone who doesn't. Wherever they make their stand, make it a wasteland of ash. Set the Sentinels on them. Bring explosives, firethrowers, everything we have. They've shown us how they won't learn. Leave nothing behind us that will ever again dare raise a hand against the Empire.'

Twenty-Five

'Well now, about time,' Banjacs Gripshod ground out through gritted teeth. 'I wondered which of you lazy, self-obssessed midgets would finally dare speak to me.'

He had been bearded in his own bedchamber, where house arrest had confined him because the Company men guarding him did not dare let him loose at the machinery that took up so much of his home. The sight of him was not encouraging: skinny, ancient and unwashed, he glowered out at Jodry Drillen as if imprisoned between his fierce eyebrows and wild beard.

'If we can spare the pleasantries—' Jodry began, then stopped. '*Midget?*'

'Intellectual midget,' Banjacs spat. 'I always knew you'd never amount to anything, Drillen, and now you're the man who does the Assembly's dirty work, eh?'

'I am the *Speaker*,' Jodry said, wounded pride replacing his usual composure.

'Who'd vote for *you?*' the old man demanded.

'You know I'm the Speaker, Banjacs, and this sort of behaviour isn't helping your case.'

'Case?' As if Banjacs had never heard the word before.

'You murdered Reyna Pullard,' Jodry reminded him hotly.

'She was a *spy!*' the old artificer hissed.

'She was *my* spy, spying on you because you were doing something that might endanger the city. Did you think all those materials and parts you were buying didn't raise a few eyebrows?'

'Jodry,' a new voice came from outside the room, 'this isn't achieving anything.'

Jodry sagged massively. 'Right, well,' he said, awkwardly. 'I have been asked to at least give you a hearing.'

'Well, isn't that large of you,' Banjacs snarled. 'So you drag your carcass over here past midnight because speaking to me's plainly at the top of your list. Who *interceded* anyway? Who still cares? Why should I deign to speak with you?'

'Banjacs, be quiet.' Another old Beetle man emerged from Jodry's prodigious shadow. He was at least a decade Banjacs's junior, but there was a certain resemblance in their faces, had Banjacs only been clean shaven. His presence chastened the older man instantly, the artificer having the grace to look a little shamefaced.

'Berjek,' he noted.

'Banjacs,' said Berjek Gripshod, his brother. 'Believe me when I say that Master Drillen has very long list these days. However, he has granted me a favour and come to speak with you. Don't waste the time.'

Jodry looked about for a chair, and slumped into it with a creak. 'Right, then, here I am,' he announced. 'The city's fallen down about my ears, the Empire's fliers are expected with the dawn, there's an army that's probably got as far as the Felyal and is now headed right here. What else, Banjacs? What am I supposed to do with you? I'm told you want to help.'

Apparently this was the wrong thing to say. '*Help?*' Banjacs cursed. 'I won't waste my time with whatever wretched plan you have, Drillen. *You* should be helping *me*! Give me command of the city's defences, let me complete my machine, and you'll never worry about anything again, believe me!'

'I fear that may be true,' Jodry managed to keep a level tone. 'As for your machine, well—'

'Did you truly think I didn't see it coming?' Banjacs almost shouted over him, his sudden vehemence rocking Jodry backwards in the chair. 'From the moment that Lial Morless showed us what was possible, this day has been coming . . . has been *inevitable*! But nobody thought it through! Nobody looked ahead! Only me, *me*! You'll give me what I want, Drillen, because there's nobody else. Only I can save the city, but it's men like you, cowardly men without vision, who stand in my way!' He had his hands extended, as though trying to strangle Jodry at a distance.

'Banjacs!' Berjek snapped and, into the silence that followed, added, 'Jodry, do you hear . . . ?'

They felt as much as heard the impact, the rumble of it from outside the window, the shudder beneath their feet.

'They – ah – munitions testing? Over at the College?' Jodry stammered.

A second blast reached them, more distantly. Berjek was at the window. 'Jodry,' he said, his voice abruptly hollow, 'I see flames.'

Jodry shouldered his way to the window, looking out and seeing a red edge to the night, hearing faint cries, shrieks and a familiar – all too familiar – sound: engines over the city, but in darkness, invisible.

'No,' he got out. 'It's not dawn yet – only just midnight – I won't have it!'

But the third booming echo put paid to such illusions, and a moment later he was forcing his bulk out of the room, thundering down the stairs to get out of the mad artificer's house and go . . . who knew where?

Behind him the shrill tones of Banjacs Gripshod followed him down the street, 'Coward! Run, why don't you! You need me! You *need* me!'

Straessa – Subordinate Officer Antspider to her troops – was already on the streets with as many of her followers as she could muster in a minute and a half. Thankfully, Chief Officer Mar-

teus had insisted that the members of the Coldstone Company
sleep in barracks like soldiers. The others, Maker's Own and
Outwright's, went home to their own beds like proper Collegiate
citizens, but the renegade Ant was used to armies, not civilian
militias and, now there was a war on, he expected his followers
to act like an army too.

This meant that, in the moments after the first explosion,
individual members of the other two Companies were still
stumbling out of bed, pulling on their clothes, pausing to see if
they had imagined it, trying to find their armour, then ending
up in the streets and searching for an officer, an armoury, a
purpose. By that time the Coldstone Company, through the
intractability of their leader, was already out in force.

But not to fight, of course. They had their snapbows, their
pikes and most, like the Antspider, had swords at their hip, but
they had nothing that would touch an Imperial orthopter. Their
city was at war, the civilian casualties already in their scores and
Collegium's army had not so much as loosed a shot in anger.

'The airfield. Come on.' The warehouse that Marteus had
co-opted for this division of his Company was sited where they
could at least be on hand to assist the aviators. Straessa and her
two dozen had got halfway down the street towards their
destination when someone called out, 'It's not the airstrip,
Antspider!'

She skidded to a halt. 'Then they'll . . .' The explosion had
been so near, though, and there was nothing else worth bombing
out here. 'Someone get up above and tell me what's going on!'
She was still learning the whole leadership business, but it always
reassured her to know that Marteus used essentially the same
technique of shouting at people until things got done.

One of her Fly-kinden, a tinsmith by trade, sped vertically up
past roof level, high enough that Straessa could only find him
against the night sky with difficulty. He came down a moment
later, looking a little shaken. 'Redlift Way, chief. Going up like a
furnace.'

'But there's nothing on Redlift Way,' someone else objected, and the Fly rounded on him, fists balled at being doubted.

'Enough! Let's go,' the Antspider snapped at them both, and then led by example. Inside her head she was agreeing with the dissenter, though: *Redlift's no use to anyone, just a terrace of houses and that little taverna with the theatre out back. Maybe someone crashed a flier into it.* By that time she had a clear sight down an alley whose far end was limned with the fierce light of flames, and there was a radiance even at roof level from up ahead. *It's on fire, it really is. But what . . . ?*

There had been a few distant *crumps*, and the night air was droning with the sound of Farsphex, but even then she could not quite reconcile it all in her mind until another bomb struck where Redlift Way met Spurn Street, wholly within her view. She saw the flat roof of one house implode with the impact, and a moment later all the windows blew out, fragments of the shutters raking the air like grenade shrapnel, and the angry glare of flames was abruptly leering out at every quarter, bright enough for the next Farsphex passing over to be plainly visible against the dark sky.

For a moment she could only stare, even as Gerethwy began calling for someone to summon the firefighters, to fetch a pumping engine. Then she heard the screams start.

She gave no order, for there was no room in her mind for that. She simply started running towards the stricken house, and some of her people were soon with her, whilst others followed Gerethwy's advice and went to get a pump to turn on the flames.

Pingge let the next bomb fall, concentrating hard on only the science of her new profession. Her current assignment presented her with a range of new challenges, most of them not connected to the night flight. Focus was everything.

As they had neared Collegium, having taken a longer, looped route to come in after dark, she had asked Scain about targets.

She'd had a map of Collegium spread across her knees, written and overwritten with prior strikes, but this time nobody had primed her in advance. 'I mean, I see better in the dark than you, right, but not like a Moth or anything, sir. It's not going to be precise.' Through the open bomb-hatch she could see a couple of the other Farsphex. To give the night attack its maximum impact they had increased the size of the flight by half – thirty machines droning their way towards the Beetle city.

'Don't worry about *precise*,' Scain had called back to her over the noise of the engine. 'Listen, Aarmon has a detail who're going to go after specific targets, so that's not your problem. Ludon has a detail that will attack anything the Collegiates get into the air, if they even do. The rest of you are to let fly anywhere that looks promising.'

'Promising like how, sir?' Pingge had asked him.

'Concentrations of buildings.'

'Yeah, but Collegium's a *city*, right, sir? It's *all* concentrations of buildings.' She had raised the pitch of her voice, thinking that she was not hearing him properly but an uncontrollable yawn mangled the last word. Even after taking a couple of naps, bundled up in a blanket against the encroaching cold, she was still bone weary.

'Take your Chneuma,' Scain had ordered promptly. 'We're close enough.'

Reluctantly, she had chewed the bitter pill, but Scain would not relent until she had swallowed it. Immediately she had felt warmer, although uncomfortably aware that she couldn't really *be* warmer. The drug made her feel as though she could not sit still, as though she should be doing something with her hands.

'Seriously, though, sir, I mean, concentrations of buildings? Most of it's just someone's house or something.'

'That's right.' Glancing back at her, there had been a curious expression on Scain's face. 'Shops, businesses, homes, mostly homes. With the Second getting closer, Aarmon says we're attacking their will to fight. It's the new plan straight from the top. Which means Rekef Outlander, to my thinking.' She had never known Scain to rattle on like this, but then that was probably his own Chneuma talking, the double dose the pilots had taken.

'But sir . . .' she had said. 'I mean, that's not . . . not what we do.'

'We obey orders,' he had snapped over his shoulder, hunching inwards, and had not countenanced the subject being raised again.

Now over Collegium, she let the bombs fall, lining up the reticule carefully on a row of roofs so that the precious cargo of destruction would not be wasted on an open street or square. The first impact had almost paralysed her, her imagination running briefly out of control. This was not soldier work. She had just destroyed someone's *home*. There would be a family, children. The orders had to be wrong. Someone had made a mistake. And, all the while, her hands were working at the reticule, selecting the next target out of the cityscape ahead, so that she had let the second bomb go as thoughtlessly as if it had been a training exercise, even as she still agonized over the first.

And its falling line had been perfect, her aim immaculate.

'The thing is . . . the thing is we're saving lives,' came Scain's voice unexpectedly, as she acquired her next target. 'The Second will be at the gates soon. Breaking the morale of the city will mean fewer of our people die in the attack; fewer of the enemy as well. They just need to be made to understand.'

But Pingge was not listening, merely walking a delicate tightrope in her mind. The worst thing was not the horror and empathy she felt, the trap of knowing that there were actual people below, whom she was hurting and killing. The real difficulty was the opposite: because she was so high up, and so detached, and how easy it was to measure everything against her technical performance, the clinical gauge of accuracy and effect. How easy it would be to assess each explosion on how well she had placed it, how grand the result: *Look, that was a big one –*

must have been a workshop or a brewery, plenty for the incendiary to work on! In just the same way, she imagined, a Rekef interrogator would go about his work, and see the agonies of his subject as merely the proper dues of his craft.

So she concentrated only on the mechanisms and the movements, the calm exercise of her skill, and desperately hoped that the after-effects of the Chneuma would not bring her dreams.

Castre Gorenn dropped from the sky almost into the midst of the Antspider's detachment, nearly getting herself spitted on a pike. The Dragonfly-kinden had turned up at Collegium's gates claiming to be the Commonweal Retaliatory Force, and demanding to sign up with the city's defenders. Marteus had assigned her to the Antspider because Straessa was, to quote, 'Sub-officer in charge of freaks'. Since then Gorenn had refused to use Collegiate weapons or tactics, roving about with her longbow behind the formations of pike and shot. Only her speed and accuracy with the weapon had given the Antspider any hope that this woman would be useful at all.

Now, however, she was proving her worth, if only because Straessa had few Fly-kinden to call on for quick scouting and messaging, and Gorenn could fly as fast and see as well as they could.

'Whole street gone up that way,' the Dragonfly reported. 'Thropters just gone overhead, probably coming back soon.'

'*Which* street?' the Antspider demanded.

'A street. The one over there. Five streets between us and it.' Because to Castre Gorenn the idea of naming streets – of having a city that was big enough to need it – was wholly new. There were no Flies about, though, and Straessa was trying to sort out her mental map of the city even as she and her followers began to run, the pattering of their boots eclipsed as Gerethwy got the pumping engine under way, clack-clacking on its four clockwork legs.

We're on Fen Way, now crossing Parthell, next is Worry Lane, then the Broads, then . . . but the Antspider's mind was already racing ahead, because these were familiar names, not so far from the College. She could name tavernas and chop houses, a music hall she had been to, closer and closer to . . .

She doubled her speed abruptly, heedless of the heft of her Company-issue breastplate, leaving the rest of them behind in a clatter of pikes and snapbows. 'Gerethwy!' she was shouting, as though only he mattered, but he was busy guiding the pumping engine, and surely they'd need the pumping engine . . .

She burst on to Wallender Street, skidding on the uneven paving, a blast of heat striking her as though it were a fist. *No, no, no* – there was the Wall Taverna, tongues of flame roaring from the sockets of its windows, that brightly coloured awning she knew so well already nothing more than floating, embering scraps of cloth, and the chairs and tables like bright skeletons within the crackling interior. That was the tenement next to it, four storeys converted to five, where all the Fly-kinden had lived: the factory workers and the rail-side workers and the musicians who had practised late evenings out on the roof. And now the same little people were frantically darting in and out with whatever possessions they could salvage, or being driven back by the fire and the smoke.

Castre Gorenn was already touching down next to her, a bow in her hand as though she could *fight* any of this. Her long, golden face was cast in ruby by the leaping flames.

There, beyond the tenement, blazing like a pyre, was Raullo Mummers's studio, and the apartments above it, all leaping with gorging fire, the artist's circular window blazing forth like a raging eye. The Antspider tried to yell some order, at who she knew not, but all that came out was a choked sob as she rushed forward, heedless of the heat. Elsewhere in the city, other bombs were falling, and not so far away, but she barely registered them.

The street was clogged with people, hurt and frightened, panicking about those they could not find, milling and screaming and shouting at each other. Straessa passed from face to face, grabbing out to spin people so that the fire could light up their features, shouldering her way through the crowd. She was trying to shout out names, but nothing coherent would emerge. Then she stood before the building itself, and the fire shouted right back at her, roaring and consuming, gutting everything down to the bare stone. The Empire's incendiaries burned as no natural fire could have done.

Can there be anyone inside there? She braced herself, but there couldn't, of course. It was impossible. Nothing could have lived and yet, and yet—

Gorenn grabbed her as she pushed forwards, the roasting air like a physical barrier. For a moment she was wrestling with the Dragonfly, then thrusting her away, not to the ground but upwards, as Gorenn's wings flashed to regain her balance. Then someone else had hold of Straessa, trying to manhandle her away, shouting something meaningless over and over, and the Antspider punched the newcomer in the shoulder, and then had her sword out because she couldn't just stand there – she had to do something, surely, or who else would?

The sound the interfering man uttered resolved itself into 'Straessa!' and his face into Eujen's, smoke-smeared, with a livid bruise at one temple. Heedless of her blade he gripped her by her arms. 'You can't!' he was insisting. 'It's too late!'

'How can you *say* that?' she shrieked at him. 'Raullo . . . he's—'

'He's out, I got him out!' Eujen insisted. 'He's over there, just look!'

At last he got through to her, but she had almost to wrench her eyes off the hungry blaze, hunting the crowd until she spotted the crumpled form. The artist huddled against a wall on the street's far side, shoulders shaking, his hands before him, fingers crooked into claws. There was a small figure beside him, barely a grey shadow – the Fly te Mosca, trying to comfort him.

There was not comfort enough to be had. Raullo's entire world was burning, feeding the flames with his history, the sketches he had layered his walls with.

When Straessa looked away, her detachment were already there at hand, Gerethwy detailing them to start clearing the street. The pumping engine rattled to itself as he directed it – but not at the studio or the taverna or the tenement. The jet of water shot out onto the workshop beside the doomed Wall Taverna, whose shutters were just starting to catch fire. For those buildings already alight, their little engine could do nothing but waste what precious water they had.

'Eujen, help get these people out of here,' she snapped. 'Get them off the streets. Get them into the College cellars.'

She saw the outrage on his face, his eyes taking in her breastplate, her buff coat, all the trappings of her office. Rhetoric welled up inside him, and she wished she had not spoken, but then in an instant his anger was gone.

'I'm deputized, am I?' he asked, and she barely caught the words.

'Please.'

But he was already nodding, heading towards Raullo and te Mosca, waving his arms at them, and at everyone, shooing them as though they were sheep.

Then the next Farsphex barrelled overhead, low enough for its underside to reflect the firelight, and Gorenn had an arrow to her bow, trying to aim even as the flying machine flashed past.

Someone shouted a warning. It might have been Straessa herself.

The bomb hit a building on the side of Wallender Street that was as yet untouched, striking its roof off-centre. Beetles knew how to build solidly in stone, but not even Ants would have made their everyday homes proof against bombardment. The sheer impact cracked the house's facade, and then half the upper storey's front was sloughing away in a great sheet of bricks, into the street, onto the crowd. A moment later the incendiary itself touched off, gouting a broad sheet of searing orange across the sky overhead, dropping flaming chemical gobbets impartially on everything and everyone below.

Raullo was standing now, raising his hands after the orthopter as though he had some Art that would call it back, enact vengeance on it. His mouth was open and screaming, his face contorted by grief and rage, even as te Mosca frantically stripped away his burning tunic. His invective, his howling, whatever sound he made, was lost utterly in the chorus of pain and panic on all sides.

'Get these bloody people off the streets!' Straessa shouted, and it was just as well that her followers were already engaged in just that, because nobody could have heard her.

Another flying machine dashed overhead, but Straessa saw enough of it: the two wings, the more compact frame. *One of ours, thank Providence.*

'Pump's out of water!' Gerethwy communicated by yelling in her ear. 'We're doing nothing here! If there was more wind we'd be dead already!'

People were starting to move at last, the able doing what they could to support the wounded. The faces all around the Ant-spider were marked not with hatred, or even with simple shock, but with incomprehension: men and women and children who could not understand what the world had become.

Taki skipped her refitted *Esca Magni* through the dark air, straining her eyes for the swift movement that would indicate the Farsphex. Had someone told her a tenday ago that she would enter this battle then she would have been exultant. She was no Moth, but her eyes were far better than any Wasp's at night. She would have vaulted into the darkness with the intention of picking every single enemy from the sky.

Now she knew what she knew, now she understood the secret of the Imperial discipline, she recognized that the conflict was going to be horribly uneven the other way. The Sarnesh had proved, in the last war, that a large army could manoeuvre swiftly and quietly in the dark to the fatal surprise of its enemies if it was only linked mind to mind. What one saw, all saw, each man aware of the next in a way that no outsider could appreciate; all at the same pace, nobody stepping on anyone else's feet, perfect coordination making up for any lack of light. Now the Empire had that weapon, too, and it was deployed over the rooftops of Collegium. There would be no surprising any of them, unless Taki could somehow surprise *all* of them, and they would always know which way to turn, and where their allies were. They would find her, too, comparing their mental maps, triangulating, hunting her down.

She had no idea even how many Collegiate orthopters were in the air. The aviators were getting themselves off the ground the moment they could, scattering out across the city in the desperate hope of fending off some of the terror that was raining down.

She saw a trio of Farsphex pass before her, but their formation broke even as she accelerated towards them, and with a chill she guessed some *other* enemy had seen her, someone she had not spotted. She let off a brief spray of rotary shot and was already pulling out of her attack, reaching for height. The attacking Farsphex was a brief, blurred presence to her left, already levelling out in response, and she knew, from years of accrued instinct, that there would be at least one more moving in on her. She was hauling left, coming out on a wingtip and almost directly over the Wasp who had just passed her. The original three were long gone, turning into their next bombing run.

She broke off, scattering in the opposite direction, expecting the enemy to retreat and continue to cover the bombers, but they stayed with her, and she understood. The game had become something more familiar, but no more comforting. The Imperials had changed their tactics, as she knew they would. She was a priority now. She was the target.

Stripping Collegium of its air defences was a necessary preliminary for taking the city, and the Second Army was marching ever closer. It all made perfect tactical sense, textbook stuff. But, of course, Taki *was* the air defences, and abruptly it was all a great deal closer to home.

She spun and danced over Collegium, confident that she was faster and nimbler, but they were working in perfect tandem, driving her between them, taking turns to fix wings for a sudden burst of speed before reverting to orthopter flight when she tried to out-dance them.

Time for desperate measures. She released a chute, but unevenly, the sudden drag slewing her machine about in the air, moments from flipping end over end in a total loss of control, but then she had stabilized, momentarily flying backwards, cutting the chute free to billow off into the night, then letting the *Esca*'s wings stabilize her, trigger down and raking the two oncoming Farsphex with her rotaries, close enough for her to see the sparks as her bolts hit home.

She saw one of the leftmost craft's porthole windows shatter, the brief image of the pilot flinching away. Then she was passing between them, canted right so that their wingtips did not clash, intent on getting some clear air around her.

Even as the first hole was shot through her wing, she was pulling left and up, dragging the *Esca* into a tight turn as another Farsphex stooped towards her from the clouds. She could imagine the other two arcing back towards her, in their minds the precise and exacting picture of where she was relative to their comrade. She fled flat out, putting as much distance between her and them as possible, the new attacker right behind her, keeping up a steady stream of shot that flashed and glittered about her, whichever way she turned.

There was a flash of light ahead of her – a pattern of on and off, and then again. Her mind translated the code automatically: *Evade! Evade!*

Her stomach lurched horribly, taking a fraction of a second

to appreciate just what that meant. She could not go up – that would cut a course right through the scythe of bolts the Farsphex was training on her. Instead she dropped for the streets, skimming roofs and then lower even than that, skittering along a street just above head height, then wrenching the *Esca* into a broad, burning city square, spinning the little orthopter on its wing in the firelight to see the sequel.

Two Stormreaders came blazing in at the Farsphex, their line already taking them through the same air that Taki would have been occupying if she had been a second slower in reacting to their signal, and still on a collision course with the Imperial flier, which was shooting right back at them. She registered Mynans – less by the livery than their flying style – and then the Wasp pilot's nerve broke, or perhaps he had taken too many hits, for he was pulling away.

Taki was already speeding back, and she saw one of the Mynans' nose lift, the Stormreader already seeking for height, looking for the inevitable reinforcements. That was Edmon, she was sure. The other . . .

The other was Franticze, the mad Bee-kinden the Mynans had brought with them, and she had clearly run out of patience with the war as it had been fought to date.

She never adjusted her line, and Taki shouted inside her cockpit, as if the Bee woman could hear, because Franticze was still ploughing straight for the Farsphex, even as it shuddered under her bolts.

At the last, the Bee changed her line – not pulling away, but tilting her orthopter so that, instead of tangling wings, she let the beating vanes of the Wasp vessel crack against her undercarriage and shatter.

There were more coming already, and Taki joined Edmon in raking the skies towards them, but a glance back down gave her more heart than she had known for some days. A second's glimpse showed the Farsphex lurching from the air, its nose striking a roof, flipping the tail up and over, and then the explosion, the fuel tank cracking, catching, one more fire erupting over Collegium.

Then Taki was in the thick of it, and so were they all. Farsphex kept knifing out of the darkness, scattering bolts at her, trying to box her in but never getting in each other's way. She spat and spun, dipping and dancing her *Esca* through the air, feeling the occasional stutter as a shot connected, bullying her way upwards again despite all they could do to pin her to the ground. She lost sight of the two Mynan pilots, then a moment later Franticze was cutting in front of her, rotaries blazing sparks as their firepowder charges ignited, forcing one of the Wasp pilots off – so impelling all of them to readjust their patterns and their plan. Taki could only hope that, between the darkness and the speed that everything over Collegium was moving, their mindlink would miss a few beats, leaving the individual pilots unable to keep track of who was where and what direction they were going.

And they were trying to kill her. The gentleman's war of yesterday was well and truly gone. The Farsphex had new orders, and if abandoning their tight defence would put them at a greater risk, the same would go double for the local aviators.

At last she won free, spiralling up towards the clouds with the great skirmish still weaving its designs beneath her. The Wasps had brought a lot more to the fight this time, and she had no idea how many Stormreaders were even off the ground. As she reached her apex, poised for a dive, the city beneath her was picked out in flames, new eruptions flashing into life even as she watched. The Wasps were maintaining their bombing even as they fought off the city's defenders.

She dropped, arrowing down in a search for targets and for friends. Her keen eyes picked out allies quickly: all over the city, they were fighting alone or in small groups, without reference to each other. Perhaps that was for the best, for it meant the composite enemy mind had to adjust to a dozen separate strategies at once, even if each was a minuscule pinprick.

She found her target, knowing that some Wasp somewhere would have surely spotted her. As she dived she switched suddenly, tailing a flier that crossed her path, the wings of the *Esca* straining at this shift in direction. Sparks flew from the enemy fuselage and it lurched in the air, and immediately she was off again, flashing *Attack here!* in case some other defender was close enough to follow up on her work. Again and again she struck, lightning raids against the larger craft, scattering hits across them, hoping for some narrow strike to hole the fuel tank, or the pilot, and then she was off, skittering across the sky before the enemy formation could close in on her. It was fierce, frustrating work, without a moment for thought, but her little stabs at them were working in other ways, or so she hoped. Each time she made herself a threat, then vanished, she was drawing away their combined concentration, drawing them off her fellows, creating openings.

Or at least I hope that's what I'm doing.

Abruptly she was in the midst of a fierce fight. Some half-dozen Stormreaders were all about her, one of them even punching a few holes in her tail before recognizing the shape of her hull. Edmon was there, and Franticze as well, and she reckoned she spotted Pendry Goswell and Corog Breaker amongst them too. She wheeled with them, and then the Far-sphex were all about them, splitting off into pairs to take them on.

The two flights met like fists. At last there was no dodging away, no escape, and for the moment no reinforcements on either side. The Wasps had greater numbers, two to one, and their cursed linked minds to bring them to bear, but the Collegiates were following Franticze's lead, and the Bee-kinden's berserk fury seemed to have infected them all. Taki saw her Stormreader force one of the enemy almost into the rooftops, sticking to it as though she was about to ram, clinging so close that Wasp bolts were tearing impartially into both craft. Pendry Goswell came to her aid, still leading a pair of enemy, but

Pendry had taken too many strikes to her engine casing, wings seizing in a sudden choke of gears. Even as she must have been pushing at the cockpit to kick her way out, even as her stilled Stormreader's forward motion segued into a dive, the pursuing Farsphex's weapons ripped her open – woman and orthopter both – in a shredding ruin of canvas, brass and blood.

Taki found a target, the two of them passing one another like lancers, her shots spattering across the Farsphex's flank and the Imperial's slamming into her undercarriage, her landing legs springing out in a tangled mess of broken metal. It turned but she was fleeter, even as another enemy orthopter was trying to dive on her. Taki's sudden rush of speed threw off the new attacker's aim, and she managed to catch her original target mid-turn, a brief second's worth of glorious open shooting at its side and belly, a dozen shots punching home, so that the turn became a tilt, the tilt a fall. Even as she was dancing away, enemy bolts ripping the air about her, Franticze descended on the faltering Farsphex Taki had crippled, her rotaries smashing in the cockpit, shattering glass, gutting everything beyond.

More Farsphex were joining the fray, and more Stormreaders too, though fewer. Taki zigzagged her way through the aerial melee, trying both to find a target and to shake her pursuers at the same time. Nobody was free to relieve her, and she felt as though she would be dragging these two killers after her for the rest of her life – or until her springs lost enough tension that she would have to make a landing, which felt more imminent than she would like.

All around her the pride of Collegium's aviation department and the most skilled of the Mynan refugees fought the elite of the Imperial Air Corps, no quarter given. Whirling, fleeting glimpses were all she had of the conflict. She had no idea of its overall shape or structure, simply latching from target to target and letting the enemy behind her continue to waste their ammunition. She saw Corog Breaker go down, with no time to see whether the old man managed to jump clear in time. She saw a

Farsphex, burning, smash into the dome of the College philosophy department. She saw two Stormreaders attack each other, blinded by the night, strung too high on panic and desperation.

Then, at last, the Imperial craft were pulling back, even their discipline left ragged by the night's attrition. Taki was already flashing for *Retreat! Retreat!* but she had no idea who saw or followed her. She had a sense of other orders glittering across the sky, trying to call back some who were still chasing the enemy. Her own engine was dangerously loose now, and she would need all the power and control she could muster to get the *Esca* safely down without its shattered landing legs. She turned for home.

With morning came the count: they had downed all of seven Farsphex, while Collegiate losses stood at seventeen fallen Stormreaders, twelve pilots dead, one missing. Edmon brought her that last news: Franticze had not retreated. Franticze had hated the Wasps too much for that. She had gone after them as they fled across the sky, refusing to give up the fight, oblivious to the orders that Edmon had tried to give her.

The long-range patrols trying to track down the supposed enemy base, who were going out less and less frequently, found her at last: the shattered corpse of her Stormreader intermeshed with the bent frame of a Farsphex – and no survivors.

Twenty-Six

Whenever Seda dreamt, *she* was always there: the other, the twin, her sister and her rival. As she wrestled with her own sleeping mind, trying to recapture the ancient techniques that had allowed the Moth-kinden to parse the future through their nightmares, always there was that presence, sometimes near, sometimes far, but always there. Then the clarity of divination would fragment and crack, the stress of two kindred powers too much for such fragile visions to sustain.

She woke into rage and frustration yet again. *I will destroy you!* But there was a tinge of fear as well. She was the Empress of all the Wasps, and she was crowned the heir to yesterday's lost magic but, so long as she must share the throne, she could not be easy in her mind, and every triumph, every victory would taste like ashes. She had lived in fear most of her life, in the shadow of her vengeful, petty-minded brother, but now she understood the fear that *he* himself had lived in, the power of his office exposing him to threats that would pass over the head of a lesser man.

I will not become Alvdan. And yet one ordinary Beetle-kinden girl, a child of wretched Collegium, was haunting her.

When Seda had been gifted – or cursed – with this inheritance, so too had this Cheerwell Maker. When Seda had gone to the ancient seat of power in Khanaphes and bullied the Masters there into making her their heir, so too had the ignorant, stupid girl also been crowned. Too late Seda had realized what she had created: an equal, an opposite, an enemy. All the power that she had worked so hard for had been divided between her and this witless Beetle. However great Seda had become, so too had Cheerwell Maker, if she only understood it. And Seda knew that the other girl would understand all too soon.

I tried to kill her. She should be dead. Yet the girl lived, and Seda felt her like a thorn, every minute. Worse, the Beetle was even now in the Commonweal, where surely magicians lived who would be teaching her their secrets, and although the Beetle had been made Seda's peer, any new power she coaxed from the Dragonflies would make her *stronger.*

There was only one way out now: Seda must unearth powers that the girl had no claim to. *I would rip out the heart of history if it would but serve me.*

One of the old counterproductive superstitions that could still be found sometimes in some out-of-the-way parts of the Empire was the belief that, when twins were born, their father must kill one soon after the birth or else, when grown, each would destroy the other, neither able to countenance the existence of so close a mirror to themselves. It was a foolish belief, and the practice had been outlawed on pain of death – why deny the Empire its soldiers, after all? – but Seda understood it now. Even if the Beetle girl bore her no ill will, even if she went away and never returned to trouble Seda's ambitions, the simple knowledge that there existed that other self, that counterpart, was to her unbearable.

I will never be free of her unless I destroy her, and to destroy her I must acquire strength.

Where is Gjegevey?

She kicked her way out of bed angrily, shouting for the servants, who entered reluctantly. Being a body servant to Empress Seda was an uncertain prospect. To the cringing women who dared present themselves, Seda shouted, 'Get me

Gjegevey, now!' and they rushed out, grateful for an errand that took them away from their mistress almost immediately.

Seda stood naked in the centre of her bedchamber, quivering slightly from the dregs of the terror and revulsion the dream had left her with.

Something scraped – the husk of a metal sound seeming to come from a greater distance than her bedchamber would allow. When she looked round, an armoured figure stood statue-still in one corner, and she could not have said whether he was there before or not. Certainly, the servants had not noted him, but then Tisamon was very good at passing unseen, and his armour was no hindrance. The armour *was* him, as much the focus of his physical presence as anything else.

'So, you're back,' she said, her tone carefully casual. 'I trust General Roder appreciated your assistance.'

I want to kill him, came the stony rattle of his voice, more felt than heard.

'Of course you do. Sometimes I envy how simple your desires are, how easily satisfied. She stepped towards him like a dancer, feeling the chill of his dead eyes on her bare skin. 'You would kill us all – all of my kinden – I know.' For in life he had hated Wasps, which made her taming of him all the sweeter.

Not you. Never you. She stood well within his reach now, and his bladed gauntlet was donned. A single swift strike, far faster than she could react to, and she would follow her brother and Uctebri into the final dark. She reached out and touched the elegant lines of his mail, following the contours of his carapace. Oh, he was bound to her, and eagerly he followed her commands, but it was not a soldier's loyalty that moved him, nor a slavish obedience, but something stronger and weaker than either. The closest word language had for it was *love*, but what could such a dreadful thing as this revenant make of that idea? She had bound him by holding his blade that was a part of him through the mysteries of the Weaponsmasters. She had bound him by feeding him blood, and she continued to do so, to keep him strong and close. All that was just the foundation, though, preliminaries that had allowed her to open negotiations with his will. She had bound him after that with promises to the heart of his Inapt nature – Inapt by kinden, and Inapt by his very existence now – that she and only she might bring back the old days when magic, and his people, were strong.

Greatest of all, though, she had bound him by understanding the razor edges of his true nature, seeing where they would bend and twist until he was a weapon that would fit her hand only. Passion and death made up the essence of Tisamon. He had been a hero fit for all the old Mantis romances, tragic and doomed and bloody-handed. So it was that what he felt for her was something like love and, if she handled him poorly, if she took a false step in toying with his bitter feelings, he might kill her despite – because of – all the chains of magic that linked them.

And if I take him to my bed? The thought was irresistible. It was possible, she suspected, but the old stories were full of those who had been lured to lie with a ghost, and had found only death. The fools in the tales were all in love themselves, though, and Seda had no such vulnerability. The thought only excited her, and it would bind the revenant to her all the more thoroughly, for good or for ill.

She nearly gave in to the temptation there and then, because *there* was a challenge that she could meet with her eyes open – not like the sly, sneaking threat that the Beetle girl posed. But, no, she had summoned Gjegevey, after all, and if the old man walked in on *that* it might kill him. She smirked at the thought, for a moment just a Wasp girl of good family treasuring a risqué thought. Then her main purpose returned to her, the lurking presence of the *other*, and her need to secure some source of strength that Cheerwell Maker could not touch. Gjegevey was being coy with her, she knew, holding back information because he thought he knew what was best for her. She would have to disabuse him of that notion.

If only she could simply send Tisamon after the wretched Beetle girl, but she knew that would only lose her his services, for the Maker girl had already driven off the revenant before. Unless Seda was close to prevent it, she would do so again, or banish him, or even wrest control of him from Seda's hands. Such tools as the Mantis ghost were best used against more mundane enemies. Any work of magic was vulnerable to a magician, just as (she supposed) any mechanical weapon would fall prey to the enemy's artificers, could they but get hold of it.

There was an almost inaudible scratch at the door, Gjegevey announcing his presence. She shrugged into a robe to spare his stammers, and called for him to enter.

He shuffled in, hunched and grey-skinned, old but sufficiently distant from Wasp-kinden humanity that it was impossible to date him. He wore a robe of Imperial hues today, halved black and gold like an Auxillian's uniform.

'It's time,' she told him, as soon as he had closed the door behind him.

'Ah, Majesty?' Always the vague old man, but she had known him too long to be fooled. He was as keen as a knife behind the wrinkles and the rheumy eyes.

'The Seal of the Worm, you called it,' she told him, 'and to me that said *power*. Something the Moths kept to themselves, all those years ago, almost completely excised from those writings that they let out into the wider world. They didn't think that my people would conquer their roost at Tharn, though, and seize some few of their precious scrolls. The Seal of the Worm, Gjegevey.' Her hand traced the spiral that she remembered, crooking into a claw for the tridentine blot that had formed the centrepiece.

The old man was silent for a moment, still only a step inside the door. 'Majesty,' he said at last, his voice soft and steady, 'you know I am your loyal servant, and have been for perhaps longer than any other. Trust my wisdom on this: you do not want to meddle with it. There is no victory to be had over the Worm. There will be other secrets, but not this one. Trust me, your Majesty.'

Seda nodded as though considering this, and then: 'Kill him,' she said and, without pausing for breath, 'Stop!'

In that eyeblink Tisamon had travelled almost all the way across the room towards Gjegevey, claw upraised. Her last word brought the Mantis to a halt perhaps a foot beyond striking distance. Seda watched Gjegevey's face, the eyes gone wide, the jaw slack, staring at the tip of Tisamon's metal claw glinting in the morning light. *Not so old, then, that death does not hold a little terror for him. Well, it was a lesson he had to learn.*

'I value you, old man,' Seda said lightly. 'You were my friend when I had no friends. You say rightly that you were my first supporter. I treasure your advice and your company, but you must never forget,' and now the steel entered her tone, 'you are my servant, my slave if I decided to enforce that status upon you, and I am the Empress of all the Wasps. I will brook no divided loyalties, even if that other mistress you serve is only your idea of what is best for me. Counsel me, advise me, but do not take me for a child. Do not seek to protect me from the world, and most certainly do not seek to protect it from me. Do you understand?'

He nodded, swallowing. 'I congratulate your Majesty on your, ah, reflexes,' he murmured, just a dry whisper, no doubt calculating what a small fraction of a second's delay in her countermanding order would have accomplished. Tisamon had not moved throughout the exchange.

'There was a war,' she prompted him. 'I have gleaned that much. But there were many wars, and they blur into one another. Mosquitos, Assassin Bugs, Spiders – the Moths were always fighting someone. And they never simply write as historians. Everything is metaphor. Except that I can see the gap, the hole they have made, as they censored their own past. The Seal of the Worm is all that is left.'

'Yes,' Gjegevey agreed heavily. 'The Seal of the Worm is all that is left.' He gave the words such strange weight that Seda paused for a moment, abandoning her rhetoric.

'When we were in Khanaphes together, I saw the embassies there. The ancient Masters had entertained ambassadors from all the great powers of their day, and their Beetle servants had maintained that lost past even to the present day.'

Gjegevey nodded glumly, and his eyes flicked to the uplifted blade again. 'Majesty, may I, ah . . .'

'Stand down, Tisamon.'

There was a notable moment of reluctance before the armoured figure lowered its arm and stood back, freezing once again into that brooding Mantis stillness. She would have to have a slave or a prisoner brought up, she knew, for he hated being denied his ration of blood.

'I saw statues of Moths there,' Seda continued. 'Spiders, Dragonflies, Mantis-kinden even. And your people, Gjegevey, ranked as equals. My own kinden were housed in a building that had two of your cousins displayed in stone at the door, and I was given to understand that this was because, when those likenesses were carved, the lands that would become my Empire were *yours*. Is this true?'

Again that mournful nod and, when her expression hinted at exasperation, he spoke. 'You have guessed it all or, hm, most of it, I think. Yes, my people had their great days. Yes, there was a, mn, a war that came that we could not stay out of. Yes, after that war we were no longer great, nor have we, ah, ever been so again. The will to change the world was gone from us, hm, after that. We had used it all up in the fight against the Worm.'

'Worm-kinden,' she mocked.

'Ah, no, you know better than that, from your stolen Moth

409

scrolls, from your deciphering of their writings. But the term, the insult, was how they were known from the war, for to the Moths there was ever power in names.'

'Gjegevey, the Moths had many enemies,' she told him, and his long face twisted, foreseeing what was coming. 'The Mosquitos were the greatest threat to their power that they write openly of – or at least as openly as they ever do – and I see that conflict was underway before this . . . before whatever it was that resulted in the Seal of the Worm. But your own people . . . ?'

'No,' Gjegevey whispered, 'we took no part.'

'The blood-drinkers, Gjegevey, practitioners of a magic that you yourself have decried. I don't hold the Moths out as paragons of virtue, but surely . . .' She was watching him through narrowed eyes.

'We took no part,' he repeated.

'So what was it that brought your . . . warriors? Did your people even possess such? What brought you into the war against the Worm?'

'Yes, we had warriors,' Gjegevey murmured, so quietly that she could barely hear. 'Our, hm, our Sentinels had mail that was the envy of the world, and we fought. You do not believe me, with only my example before you, but we fought.' Before she could press her questions, he looked up, eyes abruptly sharp. 'Would you see, Majesty?'

She stared at him, and Tisamon quivered slightly, responding to her frustration.

'The Seal of the Worm, Majesty,' Gjegevey went on, a strange tone to his voice. 'Or one of them. I can take you to it.'

To Seda it always seemed that for her to leave Capitas was like having to set in motion an avalanche. Her word was law, her mere whim the driving force behind all the lives around her, but even she could not make these things happen *fast*. The Imperial bureaucracy gathered pace around her, sending advance scouts and guards, forming her entourage, requisitioning vehicles and in all other ways ensuring that her course was as smooth as possible, if not as swift.

At the edge of her notice was the fact that many of the faces – those that shuffled the deck of her staff and set out the new patterns required to get her where she wanted to go – had changed recently. The palace seemed to have suffered some subtle catastrophe, and the men brought in to replace the fallen or lost all had a certain look, almost a taste to them.

But she told herself she would come back to that. She would first see what it was that Gjegevey wished to show her, and she would judge him on it, and if this escapade turned out to be one more attempt merely to turn her aside, then she would deal with the old man once and for all. Not without regret, it was true, but she could not allow herself to be manipulated, not any more. She had lived through enough of that before her brother died.

The salt mine at Coretsy had changed hands a few times in the Empire's history, being sufficiently far north and east from Myna that the Beetle-kinden there had not been able to prevent the Wasps walking in and taking it over when the winds of politics and war had blown that way. Recently the Mynans had reclaimed it as part of their sovereign territory, under the acclaimed Treaty of Gold, but as the Mynans were currently not even holding on to Myna, their control over the mine had also lapsed. Still, it was a surprising and risky move for the Empress, so the number of Wasp soldiers that descended upon the tiny community outnumbered the entire local population several times over.

Alighting from her airship – a small, swift craft that had flown with a half-dozen Spearflights to escort it – Seda saw only a handful of buildings raised in a style that recalled somewhat the low, half-underground dwellings of Bee-kinden, but with rounded roofs, so that from overhead they might be mistaken for little hills. The entry to the mine itself could have swallowed any of the buildings easily, and drew the eye away from such meagre dwellings. The gaping portal was set into a hillside, a maw twelve feet high sloping down into the earth.

Coretsy was thronging with her soldiers, but there was a welcoming committee of locals there too, who stood out by virtue of most of them being twice as tall as the Wasps. Mole Crickets, she saw, and should have expected as much, for they were the best miners, and the Empire shipped them in wherever hard work needed to be done. About waist level to the pitch-skinned giants clustered a knot of others, mostly Beetle-kinden, though they looked subtly different to the sophisticated Capitas breed Seda was used to seeing.

'So, this is who gets condemned to the salt mines, is it?' she asked Gjegevey as she strode out from under the airship's shadow, the old man hobbling after her, with Tisamon's metal silence bringing up the rear.

'Ah, no, your Majesty,' the Woodlouse-kinden corrected her almost urgently. 'They are, hm, not slaves, nor are they sent nor forced, ah . . .' He was losing his breath, unable to keep up with her confident stride, and she found herself suddenly face to face with the delegation of locals. There was a fraction of a pause, very obvious to her, before they knelt, not quite in unison. The Mole Crickets amongst them were still taller than her, even in obeisance.

There was a commonality about them, she noticed, the Beetles and the Crickets. It was as though they had been glazed in the same kiln. A film of white had settled on them, into the creases of their lined faces, in the folds of their clothes. Salt.

'These mines have been worked for . . . a, hm, long time. More than Myna and the, hem, Empire has claimed them over the years. Mosquitos, yes. Moth-kinden, certainly,' Gjegevey huffed, catching up. 'These men are of mining families; their ancestors served the Moths a thousand years ago, hm, no doubt. It is a proud calling. A mystery.'

Seda was about to respond with some flippant rejoinder

calculated to restore her place at the heart of the universe, but another look at these men gave her pause. They had a gravity, a history to them that Gjegevey's words only scratched the surface of. Beetles and Mole Crickets, yes, but there was a scent of the Old Times about them such as she had never known from the Apt. She had thought that working in a salt mine would be a punishing experience, something that destroyed men, but the miners before her seemed hardened, preserved almost, few of them young and yet all of them strong.

'Show me what you have brought me here for,' she ordered, and Gjegevey twitched and bowed, and went shuffling past the kneeling miners, with Seda in his wake and Tisamon following like a steel shadow. As her soldiers moved to accompany her, she held a hand up to halt them.

'No further,' she told them. 'Await my return.'

'But Majesty—' began their captain.

'Should I fear? These are my subjects.' Her gesture encompassed the miners. In truth it was no great risk, for Tisamon would brook no harm to her, and she trusted his reflexes more than all the soldiers of the Empire. Still the captain hovered reluctantly, and she read strange things in the uppermost level of his mind. Not a concern for her wellbeing, not a devotion to his duty, but a need to know so that reports could be made. He was one of the new men, she realized.

Well, your paymaster shall remain ignorant. 'You will stay here,' she ordered, and then turned and followed Gjegevey into the gloom of the mine.

The lights of the Coretsy mine burned with green and blue flames leaping behind glass. Gjegevey had explained that more sophisticated lighting suffered too much from the salt that ate into machinery, so that much of the mine working was still done in ways that the Moth-kinden of old would have recognized. Even so, there were rails set into the floor, and she could hear the deep thump of pumps. Their path took them away from the

413

sounds of machinery and picks. The miners no longer worked the gallery that Gjegevey was leading her to, nor had they for longer than any records showed.

'And I can take it that it was not simply because they ran out of salt,' Seda remarked drily.

'Majesty we are, mn, surrounded by salt: the walls, the ceiling.' He managed a wan smile. 'Taste, if you, ah, do not believe me.'

Two miners were waiting ahead by some manner of device, one of them a Beetle holding a spitting, greenish-purple lantern. The other, standing in his shadow, was a slender creature, pale-skinned, blank eyed: a Moth-kinden. Seda raised an eyebrow at Gjegevey, but he simply stepped onto a platform on the con-traption, and she realized that it must be some manner of lift.

When she had joined him – and reluctantly now, for this sort of travel did not suit her – the lamp was passed to Gjegevey. Once Tisamon was at her shoulder, some unseen signal sent their platform plummeting into darkness.

'Yes, there are, hm, Moths here,' his quiet voice said, as they descended. 'They are the descendants of the overseers, the masters. They dwell entirely within the earth and seldom venture above. This is a place of power, just as you, ah, sought, but I will try to persuade you to look elsewhere. All the, hm, power that the salt and its traditions can muster is committed to what you are about to behold.'

Without warning, the narrow shaft they had been dropping through was gone, the walls opening into a cavern so broad that the lantern light barely scraped its sides, glittering on them, dreamlike, with unnatural colours. Gjegevey held it out at the full length of his thin arm, tilted so that the light fell below them, even as the lift swung and jolted, swinging in a wide spiral as it slowed.

Seda looked down. There, not quite directly beneath them, was what she had come to see. There was no mistaking it, for in the centre of the rock floor – no, the petrified *salt* of the floor –

was a great disc of dark stone, easily ten feet across. It glistened as the light caught it, some peculiarity of its material making it seem wet. She saw the design that had been cut into it: a spiral of beads, each bead crossed through, and at its centre that three-pronged claw, or head.

'The Seal of the Worm,' she breathed.

'None other,' Gjegevey conceded softly. 'Not the first and greatest of them, by any means, for that is lost to record, but a Seal nonetheless. Now, Majesty, your senses far exceed my own, both mundane and magical. You are, I am, mn, sure, quite alive to the invisible world. Would you now descend to step upon the seal?'

Her eyes flashed. 'Do you doubt my courage?'

He shook his head and at that moment the lift touched down onto the greyish stone-like salt of the cavern floor. With a halting step he was out, and another had taken him past the rim of that circular carving, onto the face of the Seal itself. Looking back, he extended a hand. 'Majesty?'

She felt for Tisamon's response and sensed, beyond his usual thorns of suspicion, a thread of fear. But of course Mantis-kinden had been virtually bred to defer to magicians, which was why they had been such valued servants to the Moths, and why the dead man was in her thrall now.

And Gjegevey had dared to walk there, so her choice was either to match him or have him killed. She wondered if he appreciated the position he had put her in.

She was ready for a great deal as she stepped onto that great coin of inscribed stone, reaching out for the lessons in magic that must surely be buried beneath it. But instead she found . . . absence, nothing, a faint aftertaste of power about the edge of the disc, but nothing more. Her reaction must have shown in her face, for Gjegevey was nodding.

'The great war against the Worm was different, as you divined; different enough to draw my people into it. There were two reasons that we took up arms that single time. One was that our own kin, our cousins, were threatened, already in the Worm's shadow, but even for that reason we might not have stirred. We were slow to anger, even when we, ah, possessed the might to make that anger felt. The truth was the nature of our enemy, or so I deduce. The war with the Worm broke us as a power in the world, humbled us and reduced us. Our records from that time and before are, hm, *incomplete*.' His voice betrayed a scholar's horror. 'Our very culture suffered wounds; some records were lost, whilst others, hm . . . our libraries hold the knowledge but will not, ah, disclose it, the pain is still too great.'

'The nature of your enemy?' Seda echoed sceptically. 'They were wicked magicians, like the Mosquitos? Deceivers like the Assassins? Perhaps they were simply a great and conquering empire?' She smiled, but with a touch of steel.

'We wrote that they did not seek to plunder or to conquer, nor to control, nor even achieve such mundane ends as to, ah, kill or to enslave. The Worm had one intent in those days: to make all others like itself in all ways.'

'If this is a thinly veiled attack on some point of Imperial foreign policy, then you are being far too elaborate. I am quite sure your people find our Auxillians and subject cities distasteful. No doubt this is why we have an Empire and they do not.' But Seda's vitriol was automatic, even defensive. Something in Gjegevey's words had struck an uneasy chord within her, some inner understanding that must have accompanied her Inaptitude.

'Your *slave* cities cannot be compared to it,' Gjegevey told her, somehow managing to stress that word without in the least condemning it. 'The Worm killed and enslaved, of course, but our writings say that the Worm's true goal was to simply, mn, overwrite all other cultures, to obliterate all trace of any otherness, and to leave behind nothing but the Worm. I cannot say how this was accomplished, save that it sufficiently provoked my kin that we went to war and paid a great cost: the very future of our kinden as a great people. The Moths and the Mosquitos recovered. We, mn, never did.'

'The Mosquito-kinden fought for the Worm?' Seda queried.

'No, Majesty, they fought alongside us against it.'

That was a sobering thought, and Seda stared down at the great stone Seal beneath her feet. It still made no sense. An age of magic such as she could barely conceive of, and a grand war between magical powers of which this was a relic, and yet . . . nothing but a vacuum, an absence beneath her.

She felt that she was on the very brink of the truth. 'So what happened. What do we stand on?'

'This is all that is left of the Worm. When the Moths had defeated their armies and chased them back to their lairs, there was a, mn, choice. The realm of the Worm was beneath the ground, of course, and extended how far, ahm, no one could say. The Moths had no fear of darkness, but the atrocities that the Worm surely committed within its own halls gave pause to everyone. Whatever obscenity produced that kinden and had made them into the thing we called the Worm lay within that realm, and, hm, in the end the Moths had paid too much already to relish further fight. Instead they fell back on their strengths and devised a ritual.' The old man's gaunt face twisted into a painful smile. 'You know of the great rituals of the Moths, hm? You owe your current status to one of them.'

'The Darakyon,' she reflected, barely breathing the word: the power of a failed ritual that had destroyed a Mantis-kinden hold, twisted an entire forest and liberated her from her former ignorance.

'Bear in mind, then, that the Darakyon was the result of a ritual undertaken *after* the Apt had begun to rise, in the, mm, grey dawn that was bringing an end to the Moth-kinden's world. Back during the War of the Worm, they had real power and, at that war's end, they had the will to use it. They could not simply destroy their enemies, or they would have done so before, and spared us all the war. But with their victories to fuel them, their

417

foot, hm, symbolically on the neck of their enemy, they sealed up the entrances to the Worm's underground domain, and they banished the Worm.'

'There is no such underground domain,' Seda declared, but her voice shook slightly, because, after all, they were some way underground already, and she was acutely aware that Tisamon seemed to be refusing to step on the Seal. 'Any such realm would have been uncovered through some mine or landslip, or this Worm finding some other way out. It cannot be so easy.'

'Banished,' Gjegevey repeated. 'Not buried but banished. All their power, their armed force, even the wretches that they fed on – the other lightless cultures of the under-earth, my own, ah, kin included – all of them, banished and gone. Sent elsewhere, forever. So, no, hem, there is no underground domain of the Worm beneath our feet, but there *was*, once.'

Seda stared at him, as the greenish lantern began to gutter. 'But . . . where?'

'Away,' was all Gjegevey would say. 'Just as there was a world within the Shadow Box, curving away and closed off from the real world that we know, so there is a far greater world where the Worm rules, or perhaps was unthroned there by those other luckless kinden who were exiled with it through no fault of theirs. Perhaps my own, mn, kinden have risen to a greatness there that we have been, hm, denied under the sun. But I fear that, Majesty, if you were to exercise your power and somehow undo the Seal, then you would find the Worm, and nothing but the Worm, patient and bitter, and that is why I ask you to, hm, pursue this no longer, seek this no more. Let the Seal of the Worm lie. Yes, there may be, hm, power to be gleaned there, but the lessons of history are clear. Do not wake it. Do not bring it back.'

She stared at him for a long time, still feeling that absence beneath her. His story was impossible, save that nothing else could account for that inexplicable *lack* that she felt, the echo of what had been. *I will not fear.* But she did fear – not the dread

418

of that Beetle girl usurper or the tedious concerns of state, but a fear of the dark, and of what the dark had once hidden.

'Find me something else, then,' she snapped, and Gjegevey bobbed his head eagerly and gratefully.

'I will, I will,' he assured her. 'Rely on me, Majesty. You shall have what you seek.' His gratitude at having his counsel followed was abject and instant.

Twenty-Seven

Jodry was late, keeping them waiting almost an hour before he heaved his frame into view, sweating from the modest flight of steps leading to this out-of-the-way room in the College. Another meeting, yet another day in the attempts of the Collegiate government of academics and merchants to understand and master the war.

The written rule was still that a full complement of appointed experts and representatives was required to carry any significant motion, but in truth that ideal had barely survived the start of the conflict. The people called to these meetings were also those whose hard work was directing the defence, and by now most simply stayed away, without even the time to read the subsequent minutes. The key decisions were passed on directly by messenger. Collegium was evolving a chain of command, whether it wanted one or not.

So, here was Stenwold Maker, spymaster-turned-spy-hunter. Here was Janos Outwright, Chief Officer of Outwright's Pike and Shot, and nominally in charge of the city gates. Here was Jodry Drillen, the Speaker, even now sinking into his chair, with his man Arvi bustling up behind him with a flask of something restorative. Here was a tall, lean Mantis-kinden woman, a stranger to most of them and looking as though she would rather be slitting throats than talking across a table. That she had sat waiting for an hour showed her to be something more than a savage killer, however, as did the sash she wore, displaying the wheel of Outwright's Merchant Company.

'Jodry,' Stenwold acknowledged his arrival gratefully, then indicated the woman. 'This is Akkestrae, the—'

'She's the spokeswoman for the Collegiate Mantids. Yes, I remember.' Jodry knocked back the contents of the flask, coughed violently, and gasped for breath. 'Where's Dulci Broadster?' referring to one of the College's social history masters.

'Too busy with the refugee business to come and actually talk about it,' Stenwold informed him. It was a complaint more and more familiar as the war escalated. 'It's just us, Jodry. We'll have to do.'

'But what can we . . . ?' Jodry looked at the walls as though expecting more advisers to creep out from between the brick-work. 'Is anything we agree here even valid?'

'I don't know,' Stenwold said tiredly. 'I'm sure your man can round up an extra voice if you think one more would give us any authority. Or we can swear in Akkestrae for the day, if you prefer. Let's just get this done. The Felyal, Jodry . . .'

'Yes.' Jodry took a moment to compose himself. 'So, tell me what happened?'

'From what I hear, they're burning it, all of it,' Stenwold said grimly. 'What Tynan's Second started in the last war, they're finishing up in this. They must be losing I don't know how many days in order to eradicate the place, burning out every hold, killing everyone they can get their hands on, sacking every logging camp and village. Perversely, that's actually bought us time. Tactically, it seems insane, but—'

'But you insist on saying that this Tynan is your enemy,' Akkestrae interrupted. 'The Spiders have done this. Out ancient enemies have had their revenge.'

Normally this would be taken as the usual Mantis rhetoric, but this time her assertion seemed no more than the simple truth. The Felyal had forever been a predator on Spider shipping, a constant thorn in the side of any Spider-kinden that ventured along the Lowlands' south coast. No more, it seemed.

'The refugees are still coming in, and Janos's people are still recording accounts,' Stenwold added. 'There was an attack on the Wasp camp, apparently, by just about everyone from the Felyal who would take up a sword, plus a hundred or so itinerant Mynans who somehow ended up there.' He paused, teeth bared unhappily. 'They were expecting help from us.'

'Then they should have asked for it. How were we supposed to know?' Jodry demanded.

'Well, arguably we should have had people there at the Felyal, because we knew the Second would be marching through there,' Stenwold said wearily. 'However, they *did* ask. Moreover, they were told we were coming. They believed, when they attacked the Wasps, that Collegium would pitch in.'

Jodry stared. 'What?'

'The messengers they sent to Collegium plainly never arrived. The messages of support they received were false. They've been played for fools, and so have we. Our best chance to delay the Second has been lost, and it sounds as though only Spider-kinden grudges have bought us any time at all. For now, we have hundreds of people seeking shelter within our walls – not just Mantids but all those who were making their living around the Felyal, and we're starting to get the first runners from other villages along the way, too.' He gestured to Akkestrae. 'As you see, the Mantis-kinden still want to fight, and we're convincing them to sign up and work with us, rather than just taking off on their own the moment a Spider standard clears the horizon. But, well . . . I've failed the city, Jodry, starting from ten years ago. I've just not been ready for this.'

'What are you talking about?' Jodry asked, although something in his tone suggested he already knew.

'Wasp spies, Jodry. I've been hunting Wasp spies in this city for at least ten years, and I've been good at it,' Stenwold reported tiredly. 'With that mob we cleared out when the Spider fleet was on its way, we probably did just about strip the Rekef of its presence in our city, so I thought I had achieved something. But I was never looking for Spider-kinden, agents of the Aristoi. Even when I knew that the Aldanrael had turned against us, that their agents were watching our merchantmen put out so that they could signal their pirates to attack, I never quite understood what that meant, for a war. The Spiders are subtle, and have had a long time to hide. I am doing what I can, but I don't know if I can unearth their agents in time to do any good.'

'More,' Akkestrae snapped, 'of those refugees you allow within your walls, some will be spies – of the Spiders perhaps, of your Empire, even. If they have no agents in your city, then hiding some Beetles or Flies within those hundreds will be easy. You are compromised by your own kindness.'

Jodry met her glare levelly. 'What do you expect us to do? Take these frightened, dispossessed people and put them in camps outside our walls? Only let in those with family inside the city?'

'Yes,' the Mantis said simply. 'Better that than let your enemy in and welcome her with open arms. Trust none but *my* kinden. Only we can be relied on for our loyalties. Only we will not be in the pay of the enemy.'

'We can't do that.' Jodry gave a shuddering sigh. 'Stenwold, you'll just have to do what you can. Put your own people in amongst the refugees. I think they're all being sent off to the same district, to hostels there. Collegium cannot turn away from those in need, especiaslly not from our own people – but perhaps the genuine refugees can pick out the fakes; I don't know. Just do something, Sten. Make up your lost ground.'

'And do I have your authority, then?' Stenwold asked him flatly. 'Can I have the militia make arrests, wherever there is suspicion, even if it means detaining innocents?'

Jodry regarded him warily. 'What will you do with those innocents?'

'I will question them. I will have logicians from the College take their stories apart. If we find that they are hiding something, if their evidence does not pass muster, then perhaps you would at least let me have them exiled from the city, whether spies or a criminals or perhaps just very unreliable witnesses.'

Jodry opened his mouth a couple of times, his thoughts plain on his face: how far did he trust Stenwold on this? What might Stenwold's interrogation include, what threats, what intimidation? How high would Stenwold set the bar, to catch his spies, and how many others would be cast out unjustly? He met Stenwold's eyes, and a mute entreaty for mutual trust passed between them.

'Do what you must,' the Speaker said at last. 'But, Sten . . . if need be, you'll stand before the Assembly to justify whatever you do.'

'Gladly,' Stenwold confirmed, and sat back. 'Well, then—'

'There's one more thing,' Jodry said, sounding even more wretched. 'We . . . have a prisoner.'

Stenwold stared at him. 'Since when?'

'Since their last air attack. It's one of their aviators.'

'Hand him over,' was Stenwold's prompt response and, at the same time, Akkestrae hissed, 'Give him to us.' Her intentions were absolutely plain in the tone of her voice.

That at last gave Stenwold pause. The Mantids, of course, would not be interested in intelligence or strategic advantage. They wanted nothing but blood and revenge, and yet his voice had echoed hers so perfectly.

'He's been in the infirmary since they dragged him from his vessel, but I'm told he's well enough to face . . . whatever now,' Jodry told them. 'Sten . . .'

'A Wasp-kinden, an enemy combatant. Surely you can't object to my questioning him,' Stenwold protested.

'A *Fly*-kinden,' Jodry corrected. 'But an enemy combatant certainly. And if I'd objected, I'd not have told you just now. But, Sten . . . in Collegium, we are not simply judged by loyalty to our city. That is one of the reasons we fancy ourselves superior to the Wasps, after all. We have a whole faculty of humanists and philosophers who will apply an objective lens to the choices we make in this war. As I said before, do not do anything that you are not happy to account for, afterwards.'

The *Esca Magni* sped over the distant terrain, glimpsed only because the moon was bright tonight: not the cityscape of Collegium but the fields and scrub lying east of it. This was the new battleground that the aviators themselves had chosen.

The Imperials were only coming by night now, squeezing the utmost advantage from the mindlink that Taki had guessed at, but they had been coming more and more often. The Collegium pilots had been used to a couple of days' rest at least, but after the first night attack that had narrowed to a day, and now they came almost every night. Their numbers varied each time, and if the Collegiates did particularly well one night, the next attack would be weaker, the enemy fewer and more cautious, but there always seemed to be more available, just as the Collegiates themselves were putting students into the air the moment that Corog Breaker judged them halfway ready. The one saving grace was that they were not short of volunteers, despite the toll the defence had already taken. To defend Collegium from the skies offered an almost supernatural allure to young ground-bound Beetle-kinden, compared to the dreary work of the Merchant Companies.

At last, the academics Stormall and Reader had cracked all the enemy secrets: as well as having the mindlink, the Wasps had created an engineering marvel in the Farsphex: barely less nimble in the air than the smaller Stormreaders, and carrying a Fly-kinden bombardier as well as the pilot. Beyond that was Willem Reader's report on the fuel the Imperials were using, which had met with the derision and disbelief of his peers until he had shown them his tests. At last the Collegiates had been forced to admit that there was no hidden base nearby, allowing the Farsphex to strike at them. Instead they were casually exceeding the feat of long-distance flight that Taki had been so proud of. They had been flying in from airfields within the Empire itself, fighting over Collegium and then making their way home, all without needing to refuel. Where the miracle fuel oil came from, nobody seemed to know, but its effects were undeniable. Of course, as soon as the Beetles understood this, the Imperials changed their game again. The attacks came more frequently, and at last it was clear that these were not simply successive, overlapping waves. The Second Army, mopping up the last of the Felyal, was close enough for the Wasp aviators to use it as a safe base to refuel from. Taki guessed that they were now overnighting with the Second for two or three raids before taking the long leg back home.

The war had not all gone the Empire's way, however. A few nights ago, Taki and Edmon and a couple of others had taken a flight past the Second Army's camp and brought down two supply airships, which they hoped would set back the ground forces for a few days, putting them on short rations and depriving them of fuel and ammunition. The Farsphex had chased them off soon after, and no doubt there would be a standing force of orthopters running escort from now on, but Taki didn't mind. That meant fewer to attack the city.

After that, one of the College artificers installed the Great Ear atop the loftiest dome of the College roofscape, and the game got really interesting.

The Great Ear – as well as little Ears that all the Stormreaders had been fitting out with – was just one of those branches of artifice that nobody had ever really had much use for previously. This was Collegium's advantage, for academics of sufficient standing had always been allowed to pursue their pet projects, and at times such as these they came out of the woodwork with inventions that their peers had laughed to scorn only tendays before. The Great Ear had been tuned to the drone of the Farsphex engines, and pointed roughly eastward, and when the first far mumble of those machines came to it – long before any human ear could detect them – the Ear began to moan, emitting a distorted, amplified wail that sent people scattering from the streets into cellars and bunkers and the strongest-walled buildings. At the same time, Taki and her fellows went rushing for their machines, casting them off into the night, listening over the clatter of their clockwork for their fliers' own little Ear, which caught the sound of the enemy and allowed the Collegiates to home in and tackle them away from the city, to deny the enemy the chance to drop their bombs.

Sometimes it worked, and they held the enemy off. More often, at least some of the Imperials got through, and Collegium would suffer another night of fire.

Flying off into the vast trackless night to find and engage the enemy had seemed like a fool's errand to Taki, but in practice it had proved more effective than it should have, the Imperial pilots' pinpoint discipline losing its edge during their nocturnal battles, even if some flights of Farsphex were able to break to perform for their bombing run. After the third clash, Taki had realized an extra advantage that the Collegiate tactic had stripped from the enemy. *They have maps, of course, to guide their bombardiers. They use the plan of our own city to coordinate with each other. Out over the open ground, they have only their relative positions in the air to rely on.*

She was not sure when Collegium had become 'our city', but Solarno these days seemed only a distant dream.

The *Esca Magni*'s Ear buzzed louder as Taki searched the skies, looking for moonlight on metal or shapes passing before the stars. There was a stuttering flash from her left – Edmon signalling *Enemy sighted* – and she trusted his judgement and followed as he changed course, passing on the signal to her right as she did so. With luck, most of the Stormreaders would keep up, especially her tyros. For all the excitement, for all the fact that her blood only sang in her veins this way when she was airborne and fighting, these battles *killed*. The Empire had lost its share of Farsphex, but the Collegiate pilots were still bearing more of the brunt, and both sides were surely having to bring up recruits who were not truly ready for the war. Some would be honed by such experience, others would falter, and some of those would die. The Wasps had their own support network, the touch of mind to mind to guide their newcomers. For the Collegiates, each experienced pilot was tailed by a pair of tyros who would do their best to stay with them, following their lead. It was an uncertain business, but it was all the nursemaiding that they could afford.

There. And she caught what Edmon had seen, even as her Ear's buzz changed tone and grew in urgency, a language she had learned within a single night and precise enough to help her aim her weapons. Edmon was climbing, relaying no signals now in an attempt to remain unseen, but she could tell from their shifting formation that the Farsphex had already spotted at least some of the oncoming Collegiate orthopters. They scattered, spaced out in threes and fours, attempting to widen their formation into a trap for their enemies to fly into. Taki reached for height too, hoping to come down from above them. Each side tried to adjust to the adjustments the other was making, and neither had the advantage as their formations were abruptly passing through one another.

Taki let fly with her rotaries, spitting silver bolts into the darkness, trailing one target, then abruptly switching to lead the next, feeling in her gut that she had scored at least a few solid strikes, but with no evidence to back her up. Her tyros clung to her, shooting intermittently, and she only hoped that they wouldn't get too keen and shoot *her* while they were at it. She had lost Edmon and his entourage, but to her right she had a glimpse of a wheeling shape turning too tightly to be the enemy, and she followed that turn, coming in to support whoever it was.

Somewhere up ahead there erupted a flash that hurt her eyes, the accompanying retort of it following a moment later. Then one of the Collegiate craft was on fire, instantly transformed into a blazing wreck and dropping into a steep dive, wings still battering even as they burned. *Some new weapon.* A numb thought: that the Imperial artificers still had more to give. Then something bright lashed past her, a miss by thirty yards but still feeling too close, and she turned towards its origin, opening up with a steady stream of bolts and seeing the Farsphex there trying to pull up above her aim, but too slowly, letting her latch on like a tick and bore away at it. Another bright flare, and she jerked aside instinctively, reflexes saving her as something blazed past her wingtips. *Incendiary ballista set amidships, operated by the bombardier,* registered briefly in her mind, filed for later consideration. *No time now.*

One of her tyros got ahead of her – the Beetle youth with the gap teeth whose name she could not recall. He was swinging hard to keep on the Farsphex's tail, out of reach of its weapons, and she saw sparks fly where his shots hit their mark. Then the other Imperials struck, two of them stooping from the starlit sky. She flashed an urgent message, but fumbled the code, casting gibberish. At the last moment the Beetle pilot dropped away, falling sideways through the sky as he tried to evade the new enemy. They were onto him tight, though, not an inch of give in their manoeuvring as they tried to bring him down. Taki darted in after them, trying to return the favour, desperate to keep the Beetle alive, realizing that she had lost her other tyro somehow, and not even sure when that might have happened.

She was aware of the damaged Farsphex coming back, her mind tracking its most likely approach even as she fought to focus the line of her bolts onto the vessels in front of her. She saw the pursued tyro's Stormreader lurch in the air – how badly hit, she couldn't say. Then shot was dancing past her like raindrops: the original target now trying to fall in behind her. Any moment and she would have to pull up, and then the Beetle was as good as dead.

Almost, almost . . . Trying to pin down at least one of the craft ahead of her, as the entire ensemble flashed through the air with all the speed their combined engines – fuel against clockwork – could give. If she hit one badly enough, it would break off to draw her away, and then she could switch to the other and maybe – maybe—

The Beetle's orthopter abruptly changed direction, and for a moment her mind held only the thought: *I don't think I could have pulled that turn off*, and she was impressed. But then he was dropping, nose down, and she realized that he had lost a wing at least. *So get out, jump, jump!* And impacts began along the length of the *Esca*, the original target coming in from above, a different line to the one that she had guessed at, even as her own bolts finally made a perfect line between her and her target, flaying it down the ridge of its back and then striking – how precise or how lucky? – into the piston chamber, the hammering heart that kept the Farsphex's four wings moving. Abruptly its mechanisms were flying apart with the force of their own impetus, and the enemy was falling, falling . . .

She wrenched at the stick, casting herself sideways into the night, then upwards, feeling the hand of the enemy's aim reaching for her again as she sought that tiny finger's breadth of extra space to make a turn that would remake her from hunted into hunter.

No chance, not this time, for the enemy was on her like a lover, too close for manoeuvre. When Edmon's Stormreader came plunging in, he was diving on both Taki and her enemy, his bolts within a hair of taking her out of the sky even as his piercers ripped across the sky around the enemy cockpit, the effect instantaneous.

The fight was now spread over several miles of open ground, and there had to be a limit to the enemy's mindlink, each successive division and subdivision eating away at the Imperial advantage, even while it would allow some clutches of Farsphex free access to Collegium as they slipped past the blockade.

With Edmon following her up, Taki went hunting in the dark.

The Fly-kinden seemed a frail, small figure, dwarfed even by the small room he was confined to, guards at the door and the shutters locked despite the fact that he could barely walk, and certainly not fly. He had a lean face that spoke of a certain amount of privation even before his injuries had further hollowed his cheeks. His hair had been cut short, close to the skull, and was only just beginning to grow out again.

He had suffered a broken arm, several fractured ribs, a broken ankle. Half his face was one broad bruise. When Stenwold walked in, though, he forced himself to his feet, wincing as the cast took some of his weight, a brief ghost of wings about his shoulders as his Art adjusted his balance.

Outside the room, Stenwold knew, stood two of the Maker's Own Company, Elder Padstock's people, and with them was Akkestrae, newly in Outwright's livery but Mantis to the core. He had only to call out and they would march in and explain to this small man just how some of Collegium's citizens felt right now.

He folded his arms, a luxury not open to the Fly-kinden, but the little man instead put a great deal of work into returning his stare, meeting Stenwold's eyes readily.

'You have a name?' the Beetle asked him.

'Gizmer.' The Fly's light voice came out a little thickly around the bruising.

'Rank?'

'Pissing general. What about you?'

'I'm Stenwold Maker, Master of the College.'

It was evident, beyond any possibility of acting, that the Fly had no idea who *that* was supposed to be. Inwardly Stenwold felt a flash of frustration – not wounded vanity, but at the wider ignorance it probably signalled. What, then, would an Imperial aviator know? What would a Collegiate pilot know, if captured? Precious little of any use to an interrogator.

'You know why I'm here.'

'Yeah, figured that.' Gizmer's gaze dropped at last. 'And you can stuff it.'

'Can I, now?' Stenwold replied ponderously, dragging a chair from the corner of the room and reversing it, leaning against the back as he had seen Tisamon do once, although the wood had not creaked quite so alarmingly on that occasion. 'You're our prisoner now. What do we do with you?'

Gizmer blinked. 'I heard they ran things like a madhouse over here, but shouldn't you already *know* that?'

'Why? We're not used to having enemy soldiers at hand,' Stenwold told him. It was true. When he had dismantled the Rekef presence in Collegium on the eve of the Spider armada's appearance, the spies had been detained for a time, while detailed sketches and descriptions were made, and had then simply been thrown on a rail automotive to Helleron. During the Vekken siege, any enemy still living had been swiftly butchered by the Tarkesh and Spider soldiers – also by some of the residents of Coldstone Street, which had borne the brunt of their incursion, it was true. The Wasps had not got inside the city, and had taken their wounded away with them. 'What would the Empire do, I wonder?' Stenwold added, and then, before Gizmer could respond, 'Interrogation machines and crossed pikes, I know.'

The Fly looked up again, eyes blazing, but said nothing.

'I know you think we're soft here in Collegium. I'm sure it's preached to you by the Wasp-kinden, how they're the superior race, and you're better serving them than living free over here. But, believe me, I can't ignore the likelihood that you possess knowledge that will save Collegiate lives. Knowledge about your masters, their plans, their machines. You're an artificer, I'd guess, if they put you in one of those flying machines.'

'What are you asking?' Gizmer enquired bleakly.

'I'm asking for your help, given willingly,' Stenwold told him. 'Yes, because otherwise I will have to find some other way of securing your help. But that's not our way; it's not what Collegium is built on. Our strength is elsewhere. If you want, I'll get you out into the open air and you can see for yourself the city the Wasps are trying to destroy, see the people who live here. I've seen the Empire myself. Life here may surprise you. There are ways to be strong other than by military force.'

The Fly was nodding, and for a moment Stenwold thought that it might truly be that simple, but then Gizmer's lip curled, and he said, 'Yeah, well I can't help noticing whose city is on *fire* most nights.' When Stenwold made to speak, he butted in, 'Oh, yes, I see what you're after. You're all really *nice* over here, and I should be glad to drop everything and come and be a part of this wonderful thing you've got going on here.'

Stenwold took a breath, adopting a philosophical expression. 'I understand you were *manacled* into your ship. Am I not allowed to draw conclusions?'

'Was to stop me falling out, wasn't it?' Gizmer spat, but this time he couldn't meet Stenwold gaze. 'So that was the Rekef,' he conceded at last. 'They don't trust us, so what? But it was the Rekef, not my people.'

'I don't see that your people were doing much to stop it,' Stenwold remarked mildly, feeling the conversation falling under his control once more. 'But they're the ones who you're protecting.'

Gizmer limped over to the barred shutters, turning his back on the Beetle. 'But even if I had something to say that you could use, it wouldn't be helping you kill the Rekef. It'd be my people.'

'The Fly-kinden.'

'No!' Gizmer rounded on him furiously. 'The aviators. The soldiers. *My* people. So forget it. You know, back there, I grumbled with the rest of them at what we had to put up with, what they made us do. Odd what it takes to make you realize you're loyal after all, ain't it?' And when Stenwold tried to speak,

433

the Fly almost shouted him down. 'And you know what? Stuff your so-bloody-superior Lowlands. You know, I do have something to tell you, and use it how you will. I never told this, not even to my people. I've got a cousin lives with his kin in Helleron, right? He thought the way you seem to reckon I should, went looking for a better life. Every sixmonth or so I hear some word from him, whenever the messengers get through. I hear how it is, how he lives, working in the factories there, just like I did in Capitas before all this. In the Empire my kinden are citizens – not Wasps, but citizens still. We get rights. We get respect. I hear how my cousin lives – they work him like the worst slave in the world, only he has to find food, pay for a roof over his head. He gets nothing from them. When there's no work, he starves. Slaves have it better.'

'Collegium isn't Helleron,' Stenwold snapped, sounding harsh because he had harboured similar thoughts about that other Beetle city himself.

'Lowlands is Lowlands,' Gizmer shot back. 'And what was it you said? I don't see your people doing much to stop it, eh?' He looked Stenwold in the eye, grinning. 'Long live the Empress.'

Stenwold hit him then, clumsily, without plan or purpose, sending the little man flying off his feet and into the wall, wings unable to catch him. A moment later the Beetle was standing over Gizmer as the Fly tried to get away from him, cradling his splinted arm. The surge of violent fury in Stenwold seemed to be the culmination of all the fires, the deaths, the homeless, the grieving – all the scars of his city. He felt the raw edge of the sheer physical pleasure that would come from the use of his fists, his feet, on this tiny outpost of the Empire.

There was a thin thread of civilization that held him back for a moment, and some part of his mind was, even then, playing through what Jodry would say, what the Assembly might do. *Nothing. They would do nothing.* And Drillen might fret, but he was War Master Stenwold Maker and, in the final analysis, they would take what he said and not call him a liar to his face, not over just the death of a Fly.

Abruptly the drive for violence ebbed from him, leaving a sour residue in its wake, and he realized that he did not care about the Assembly, let them censure as they would. It was not fear of public disapproval that stayed his hand, but the personal understanding that he himself might be wrong.

I used to be so certain about things. Where did that go?

He was abruptly aware that the guards had burst in, perhaps somehow assuming that it was Stenwold himself who had been assaulted. He turned to face the two Maker's Own soldiers and Akkestrae, and found not a shred of condemnation on their faces.

'I'm finished here,' he told them.

'What about him?' Akkestrae asked, with a predatory look.

'I can't see that he'd know much, in any event.' That knife-edge of control was still there: another jab, another nudge, and he could see himself lashing out again, seeking some salve for himself by striking at the Empire in any way he could. 'Leave him. Just hold him here.'

'And feed him?' the Mantis asked. 'War Master, there will come a time when food is precious.' The two Merchant Company soldiers stared with loathing at Gizmer as the Fly got to his feet, leaning against the wall for purchase. They would have been out on the streets most nights, Stenwold guessed. They had seen the full horrors of the aerial raids.

'Just . . .' and Stenwold shook his head and pushed past them, his main intent to put distance between himself and Gizmer, and not to reflect too much on what had just happened.

There was a sharp snapping sound that brought him up short.

When he turned, one of the soldiers was slipping a fresh bolt into the breach of his snapbow. The Fly-kinden lay in a crumpled heap against the wall.

435

'He was going for you,' the soldier said, quite matter of factly. 'Rushing you. I thought he had a knife.' The words were spoken as if in rehearsal.

'He . . .' Stenwold looked at the other two, unnameable feelings roiling inside him. The second soldier looked shaken, but was saying nothing. Akkestrae met his gaze with a slight raising of the eyebrows, as though not sure why he was bothering himself about the matter.

'To die in battle is better than to live in chains,' was all she said.

'Would he have thought that?' Stenwold demanded.

'Plainly he did.' There was no getting past her Mantis reserve.

Stenwold turned on the man who had loosed the shot, a Beetle youth who looked barely twenty and wholly unrepentant. 'What's your name?'

'Jons Padstock, War Master,' the soldier reported smartly. '*Maker's* Own Company.'

Padstock . . . and now that the name was out, Stenwold could detect the familiarity in the lad's features. *Her son, of course.* And Elder Padstock, chief officer of the Maker's Own, was his fanatic supporter, and no doubt she had steeped her family in the same doctrine.

But what can I do? He could have the youth arrested. At a time of war, he could have one of his own soldiers hauled before the Assembly for the murder of an enemy combatant, knowing all the while that Jons Padstock had done what he did out of hard loyalty to Collegium, to Stenwold himself. And some traitor part of Stenwold's mind was glad that the decision had been taken from his hands, even pleased with the result. *And this is war. Things happen in war that we would not countenance in peace.*

It was no answer, but he had no answers. He turned away from them and stomped off down the corridor, unwilling to stay there and look his own weakness in the eye.

Twenty-Eight

Helmess Broiler was under scrutiny, he knew.

He was a well-to-do merchant magnate of Collegium, an Assembler, and also an avowed political foe of Stenwold Maker and Jodry Drillen. More than that, he had been taking the pay of the Empire for years, starting way back when nobody but Maker ever imagined that the Wasps would get to this point. And by the time the Imperial Second did come ravening up the coast during the last war, Broiler's existing misdeeds had been enough for the Empire to keep him squarely under its thumb, their man in Collegium.

Stenwold knew all this, as had been brought forcibly to Helmess's attention not so long ago. Helmess himself was only alive and free because Stenwold had a use for him back then, and because it was convenient for Maker to know just who the Empire's current man was, rather than have to hunt down the next one. Since the bombing had started, Helmess had been under observation, with Maker's spies, both hidden and in plain sight, watching for his methods of smuggling information to the city's enemies. It was a waste of time for all concerned because Helmess no longer had any such methods at his disposal. Since the last piece of business, when the Empire's agents had been apprehended neatly before they could take advantage of the oncoming Spider armada – which itself had come to nothing, with the abominable Maker turning them away with apparently nothing more than a harsh word or two – the Empire had ceased to include Helmess Broiler in its plans, squarely blaming him for the failure. Fair enough in a way, because Broiler had given Maker the information that saw the Imperial agents arrested, but it rankled nonetheless because the *Empire* didn't know that.

Right now, Helmess was living a somewhat fraught life. His double loyalties – if he had any loyalties to anything aside from his own best interests – were not public knowledge, but there was an odour about him, nonetheless, of a man in disfavour with those in power. That meant he had few visitors, and fewer opportunities to profit. The Merchant Company soldiers troubled him at his house, tramping through his rooms occasionally for no reason other than to annoy him, and Maker's watchers were looking constantly for heliograph flashes, message-bearing insects and hand signals out of the window, or however they might think he would inform the Empire of whatever knowledge he was supposed to possess. The rare guests at his house were searched aggressively for messages when they left, and probably followed subsequently themselves.

Two nights ago, an Imperial bomb had even landed outside his townhouse during a tense half-hour when the Farsphex seemed to be trying to attack Collegium society from the top down by targeting large houses. He had lost part of his wall, leaving that entire corner of the structure dangerously unsound. Needless to say, nobody was remotely bothered, or called to give their condolences, and he had to send his staff into the city to pay ruinously high prices to secure workmen to impart at least a stopgap stability to his home. By this time, any thought that he might still be on the Empire's books was long gone, and the Empire itself seemed to be rather trying to wipe him out of existence altogether. Certainly his contact – or perhaps his handler – Honory Bellowern had got out of the city without a parting word immediately after the first aerial raid.

When the foreman of the work crew insisted on sorting out payment face to face, Helmess resigned himself to being robbed in broad daylight, possibly to being insulted as well. He received the man in his study, noting a lean Beetle with a badly burned face, the scars looking recent. Of course, that was quite the fashionable look in Collegium just then.

'All right, then, what ludicrous figure–?' he began, and the foreman said, 'Send your servants out, Master Broiler.'

Helmess made another few false starts at the same sentence, feeling the world realign itself around him vertiginously. After a pause, he nodded, waving his retainers away.

'Can I hope, at least, that you've made a genuine job of repairing the house?' he enquired, fighting for calm.

'Oh, the lads are all the real deal, if not exactly masters.' The burn-scarred Beetle sat down across the desk from him, with casual insolence. 'I was lucky. There weren't many people keen to do your dirty work – it was easy to get the contract. I'd probably find a choosier crew to go over the work in a month or so, if I were you. Now, let's get this done with. You've a list?'

'A list?' For a moment, cut off for so long, Helmess didn't know what he meant. Then old conversations came back to him, words shared with the Imperial diplomat Honory Bellowern (when he was still rattling around in the embassy, minus one ambassador, and pointedly not enquiring after Helmess's health). Of course there was a list: the list of the key people, the influential, the anti-Imperial, all those that might serve as rallying points to resistance. In long bitter nights of wondering where it had all gone wrong, adding names to that list had become a mean-spirited joy for Helmess Broiler.

'You came in with the refugees,' Helmess guessed. 'Fake burns from the Felyal rather than from the incendiaries here.'

'I don't do fake,' the man told him. His eyes were very calm, Helmess saw, without in any way being calming. There was a fanatic immobility to those eyes, and he fought away an image of this man applying a blazing branch to his own skin, without so much as a flinch.

'I had thought there was some investigation, quarantine or

something, Maker's work,' Broiler deftly opened the shallow hidden drawer in his desk, and leafed through the few papers there.

'Good thinking that came too late,' the spy told him. 'I'd already got clear of the rest. Now I'm at large in the city, just another Beetle. I helped the fire crews last night.'

'The Rekef—' Helmess started and, when the man raised a cautioning hand, 'If you're worried about being overheard, that ship has sailed.'

'Piss on the Rekef,' the burned agent said levelly. 'They've fallen over their own feet each time they've tackled this city. Army Intelligence gets a go.' He watched for a reaction and saw none. 'We're not so fancy as the Rekef,' went on the man who had crept in pretending to be a refugee and was already establishing himself in the city of his enemies. 'We'll go at this like soldiers.' He looked down at the list Helmess handed to him. 'You don't do this by halves.'

'I assure you, those names—'

'We'll take it under advisement.' There were plenty of names on that list that simply represented Helmess's personal dislikes, and the other man was openly sneering as his eyes flicked down it. 'We have other lists, you can be sure. We'll cross-reference. Your continued loyalty will be noted, I'm sure.'

Helmess raised an eyebrow, still holding to his composure by his fingernails. 'I take it this means bloodshed. May I assume that Stenwold Maker's name will top everybody's list?'

The agent rose abruptly, rolling up the list tightly, then leaning against the chair back to remove his sandal. The crumpled scroll found a new home in its hollow sole. 'You just sit tight, Master Broiler. The Second's on its way, our glorious Gears, and this time they'll chew this city up a treat. I'm to tell you that you'll be remembered when the time comes, and that's straight from my chief here in the city. As for the list, you just keep an ear open and you'll hear the news. Now, we've haggled enough about that slipshod piece of negligence we did on your house, so hand over the coin for my lads and I'll be on my happy way.'

Once the man – *not even a name, this time, see how they regard me?* – had gone, Helmess remained at his desk, staring at the scratched wood of its surface. *You'll be remembered when the time comes*, he considered. As promises went it was not reassuring.

'I trust our intelligence was useful?' The voice of Mycella of the Aldanrael drifted from behind the curtain, along with the steam. General Tynan, who had expected to find her waiting for him, glanced about at the handful of Fly-kinden servants. None of them seemed to find it unusual that their lady was receiving an Imperial general while still in her bath. He was acutely aware of his own appearance – as rough, unshaven and unwashed as any of his soldiers. The Spider-kinden seemed to be able to transport civilization around as though it were a boxable commodity, to be dipped into at need.

'I would have preferred to know more about it beforehand,' he grumbled, just to keep his mind focused.

'And am I to believe the Empire has no secrets from its allies?' came her amused response. 'In matters of espionage, especially, it is best to keep one's cards close.'

Servants – *male* servants – stepped behind the curtain bearing towels and robes. Tynan shook his head. The Imperial line had always been that Spiders were a decadent people, but out there in the dark there were thousands of their warriors living in the same muddy fields as the Wasps, eating the same food, soldiers no more nor less than their Imperial counterparts. They had fought in the Felyal with less discipline but an equal spirit, and they had spilt blood, their own and their enemies', to bring the Mantis-kinden to heel. True, their mercenaries had been in the forefront of the fighting, but the Spiders themselves had not stinted. Many was the Spider-kinden warrior, maid or man, now buried on Mantis soil to prove it.

The friction that had plagued the army since leaving Solarno was mostly gone now, as more and more of the Wasps began to see things the same way. It was awkward, since the Empire had no ready category for free allies – meaning something less than Imperial but more than Auxillian. The men of the Second were having to expand their world view to accommodate the Aldanrael troops. The fighting in the Felyal had cemented it, though, and the two forces had begun to work together, shielding each other's weak points.

Mycella stepped barefoot from behind the curtain, her hair glistening wet and her body swathed in a silk robe of pale green printed with twining white leaves. Tynan felt a tug within him that he fought down. *Her Art, of course.* He told himself it was her Art, at least, because that gave him something to fight against. Beyond that emotional reaction was a purely physical one, a gathering lust that he thought time had extinguished, but was now rising spectacularly from the grave. The look she gave him suggested that she was well aware of it.

'In truth, my intelligence network in Collegium is operating by itself, as intended. I have no convenient way of reaching them with new orders. However, we believe in autonomy in our senior agents. Once they had confirmed the Aldranrael's diplomatic position with the Empire, they have been improvising most successfully, providing you with information for your aerial forces, and infiltrating the Felyal alongside those who were returning there to rebuild. A shame they could not give us warning of the attack on our camp, I know, but I suspect they felt it best not to risk their cover. So, secret from both of us, in a way, but they have sufficed to get your own agents into the enemy city.'

'Let us hope so.' Tynan could not dispute anything she had said, but the speed and elegance of the Spider agents had been daunting. *Let us hope they don't turn on us one day.* 'I trust your people are ready for the next leg of the march?'

'Was that truly what you came here to speak of?' she asked him with an arched eyebrow. 'Some muttering about our spies,

442

and then a question to which you already know the answer?'
Abruptly she had moved almost within arm's reach. 'We are
both too old to waste our time with such matters, General.'

She was mocking him, of course, for she had planted her
barbs in him, by Art or by who knew what other means. She
was now waiting for the venom to drive him to something
further. In truth he could feel the urge within him: an Imperial
soldier's simple response to a woman of a lesser kinden: *Take
her!* And what a piece of diplomacy that would make!

He wanted to say something dismissive and turn away, to
assert himself in some way that would not cripple the war effort,
but part of him was unwilling to take his eyes from her.

'General . . .' came the call from behind him, and he whirled
instantly, the spell broken, becoming once again the stolid old
campaigner. Mittoc, his colonel of Engineers, stood holding
open the tent flap, with a large man looming behind him.

'What is it, Colonel?' It was said with the strong implication
that he, Tynan, was busy with some important military business,
but Mittoc's expression was a full-blown leer as he eyed Mycella,
simple soldier through and through, despite all the artificers'
training in the world.

'Well, General, you said to tell you when the pilots got in.
Got their Major Aarmon here just landed, wants to talk strategy.'

Tynan felt sure that, when he had met this Aarmon a few
days before, the man had been a captain, but then the air force
was expanding at quite a rate. 'Colonel, it's well into the night.
Have Major Aarmon and his crews billeted, and I'll see him at
sun-up.'

'Right you are, sir.' Mittoc stole another rapacious glance at
Mycella, and skulked away.

Tynan turned back to the woman, meeting a complex and
layered expression. Here was the face of the military commander, untouchable and pristine; behind that the temptress
who knew that such a mask on a woman would fire him; behind
that the woman who was too old for such games, mocking

herself for trotting out such worn-out gambits and inviting him to laugh along with her. *We are too old*, she had said and, though she looked so much younger, he felt they were a match in years.

'If I were a younger man . . .' he said, and stopped, because the words had been intended for himself only.

Her expression became transparent, shorn of subterfuge – or of any subterfuge that he could detect – leaving only a worldly fondness settling into near-invisible lines of humour and experience.

'If either of us were younger, we'd not stand here in the same tent without being at each other's throats, Tynan. So surely we're old enough to know when we want something, and not to stand tongue-tied as though we were children of fifteen?'

He laid hands on her. It was the only way he could conceive of it. She was a Spider Aristoi, and her servants were all around, and it was an assault, a declaration of war, to take her by the shoulders and draw her close. His soldier's spirit was up, ready for the fight.

And yet the servants were all gone, slipped out somehow, vanished into the weave of the tent canvas, and it was only her and him, and there was no fight at all.

It was after dark, and Averic made his way cautiously back to his lodgings. Cautiously not through fear of the aerial raids that were an almost nightly occurrence, but because a Wasp alone in Collegium could expect all manner of interesting reactions from people he met, especially soldiers of the Merchant Companies. The Antspider had made sure that the Coldstone Company knew he was no enemy of the city, but the populace at large was proving resistant to the idea. It was always easy to write off an entire kinden as the enemy, after all. If you allowed one of them to become human, that might affect your judgement of the rest. It was a lesson the Wasps themselves had taken to heart generations ago, but Collegium was a city of learning, and hating Wasps was on the modern curriculum.

Ironically, a Beetle on the streets of Capitas would have been safer, at least if he could produce his papers on demand.

Eujen Leadswell had held a meeting at the College, which Averic was returning from. The Beetle student had called together two score or so of his fellows, young men and women of all kinden who had not signed up with the Companies. Some were scared, Averic reckoned, and to him it was a strange world where mere cowardice would suffice to keep you from the war. Others had objections of various kinds, often moral ones like Eujen's own. Still more had work that they could not give up, whether it was assisting the artificers of the College, looking after relatives or helping with the family business in place of others who were already preparing to march out against the Imperial Second. Many of them would not have counted themselves as Eujen's friends, and some had been his avowed critics before the hostilities had commenced. It was hard for them to heckle him now, though: they who had lacked the courage of their convictions and not taken on the sashes of the Companies.

None of them had known what Eujen was going to say. Many probably came expecting some distilled manner of treason, anti-Makerist propaganda at the worst possible time. Some of those who had stayed away had probably not wanted to be implicated in any such talk.

Instead, Eujen had pitched to them the idea of a Student Company.

'Let us hope,' Leadswell had said, 'that the Second is beaten in the field. What I'm proposing is something that we're all better off not needing. But if the Wasps come to the walls, as they did last time, the city will need to rely on all hands. Look at us who, for whatever reason, have not taken up the snapbow and the buff coat. I ask nobody why, I accept all reasons as valid, as I ask you to accept mine, but what will we do when they're at the walls?'

There had been more than a few glances at Averic just then, as he lurked at the back of the room like a shadow of the future.

Averic knew, of course, that this all stemmed from Eujen's arguments with the Antspider, but thankfully nobody at Eujen's meeting had known that this entire venture was essentially to impress a girl.

'We find what arms we can beg or borrow or make,' Eujen had propounded. 'We take up our own sash. While our field army is out of the city, we drill – alongside Outwright's men if we can, as they're staying behind. If the Wasps should come . . .' and his voice faltered slightly because of what that might mean, 'then there will be need of us. And perhaps we can put our scholarship to use, as well. Perhaps the war may benefit from soldiers that do not think like soldiers.'

And of course, someone had stood up to voice the obvious criticism – why was Eujen suddenly advocating the fight, when his voice was normally heard speaking against it? What was going on?

'Do you think,' Eujen had remonstrated, 'that I would not defend our city? Do you think I would not shed my blood for my people? I will take up arms against the Wasps, if they come here. I would do the same against the Vekken or the Spider-kinden or the Sarnesh.' He left a precisely calculated pause. 'I will fight just as hard against those within our city that have guided us towards this war, for I do not believe it was inevitable. I believe that, if we can forge a peace with Vek, then we could have done so with any nation in the world. But now we are at war, and I can't change that. Let us instead work to bring this war to the swiftest close, and seek a true peace thereafter, not merely a period in which to brew up the next conflict.'

He'd had them then, not just by the words but the raw sincerity in his voice, and the first few had come forward to put their names down for his Student Company.

Averic had signed, too. He had not thought he would, and he knew he had done the wrong thing, but he had been carried along on the tide of Eujen's voice. In that moment everything had made so much sense.

His lodgings were not located in the usual student area – at first because he had not known that when choosing them, but later because it was sometimes convenient to escape the attention of his peers. Instead, his neighbours were the poorer class of tradesmen, factory workers and the like, and many of them were out working most of the night and sleeping during the day, especially now, when every workshop was working around the clock. They did not like him, but he had grown adept at avoiding them. Entering the slightly leaning four-storey house, he heard no sound from any living thing, only silence, as if he was the last man in Collegium.

Except someone *was* there, quietly waiting for him, like a spider in its web. When he unlocked his door and pushed it open, a Beetle-halfbreed woman sitting on his bed regarded him with a hard smile.

Instantly he had a hand out, palm towards her, ready to demand some explanation, and in the back of his mind the knowledge that the door had been secured with the lock he himself had installed.

She met him with a similar gesture, and the words, 'I wouldn't.'

For a long time Averic stared at the palm she was training on him, then at her face, the dark skin, something of the features of a Beetle-kinden, but then they were a variable breed, and what other heritage could he discern there . . . ?

He went cold all at once, for she was a Wasp. Not a Beetle at all, not even a little of one, but pure-blood Wasp. He would not have believed it possible. Some sort of dye had been used to colour her skin a deep, rich brown, painstakingly applied so that the palm she showed him was paler, but not as pale as a Wasp's should be. She had padded out her cheeks a little, applied some manner of tape to flatten her nose. She must have walked past hundreds of Collegium citizens to get here, without one of them seeing her as he now did. Who looked closely at halfbreeds, after all?

447

Had she been a man, she could probably not have done it, but everyone knew that the only Wasps for export were men. The idea of a Wasp woman infiltrating the city went against all the carefully hoarded stereotypes that the Collegiate citizens were so fond of.

'Averic, isn't it?' she noted. 'You can call me Gesa. Glad to meet you. You've done a great job here, I'm sure.'

He could not stop staring at her. 'What do you mean?'

'Here you are, in the heart of Collegium, a student at their vaunted College. Have you any idea how hard it's been to get agents entrenched in this city recently, with Stenwold Maker on the war path?'

He felt as though a hammer blow had struck him, inside. 'I'm— I'm not an agent.'

'Of course you are.'

She said the words with such assurance that he needed a moment to regroup his own certainties.

'No.' He was aware that she might kill him – her hand was still up, while his had fallen to his side – but he could not allow her to redefine him in such a way. He could not let her remake him so casually into the thing the Collegiates already muttered that he was.

She was now smiling broadly. 'But, of course, you understand that a deep cover agent must live his cover, Averic. It works best of all if he does not know it himself. Why do you think you were sent here, if not for that?'

The hammer fell once again. 'No, my parents . . .' And the words were damning, treasonous, but he was under attack, with only the truth to defend himself with. 'They sent me here because they believe we can learn from the Collegiates – and more in peace than in war.'

'Is that what they told you?' Her expression was pitying. 'As I say, how better to place you in the bosom of the Beetles?' She shrugged. 'Or perhaps you're right, but then we would have to make sure something happened to your oh-so-prestigious fam-

448

ily, wouldn't we? You won't know this, but the actual truth is always an abstraction in my game. What's important is that you'll do what I want. You don't need to decide whether it's because your people sent you here as an agent, or because they didn't, and they'll suffer for that unless you obey me.'

I'm agreeing to nothing. Just saying the words does not make me theirs. I . . . 'What do you want from me?' *I should kill her now, the moment she turns, loses focus. One sting and she's dead and nobody need know* . . .

Despite his basic army training, Averic had never killed anyone: not an enemy of the Empire, not even a rebellious slave. She was right when she said his family had wealth and power, and as a result he had never been required to use his Art or a blade against a living target. *And, if I killed her I would be a traitor to my people.*

So what am I if I disobey her?

'I want you to be ready, Averic. I want you to get over all your little qualms and become a man at last, and do a man's work when it's asked of you. I'm here now so you can get your angst and agonizing out of the way, and remind yourself what kinden you belong to. When the orders come to you, you'll execute them swiftly and efficiently. And when you report to General Tynan, he'll clap you on the shoulder and tell you that you've done well. Or else you'll die trying to further the Empire's cause – the only death a Wasp-kinden should aspire to.'

He formed the question, *What if I tell them?* but he could not force the words out. Yet she read it on his face as if she was a magician.

'Tell them you're a traitor to them, after all this time? And become a traitor to us at the same time? Oh, Averic, I'm not sure how far you'd have to run to escape the landslide, if you did that.' Her look could almost be construed as kindly. 'Grow up, Averic, and put aside childish things. Remember who you are.' She stood up. Her palm was no longer directed at him but he had no ability to act on that, stepping back like a good subordinate as she walked to the door.

'You'll be hearing from us,' she told him. 'Just be ready.' Then she was gone.

Gesa, who normally went by the name of Garvan, was cautiously satisfied with her work so far. She was playing a dangerous game, and all the more so for the disguise she had chosen. Her great secret, her vulnerability, her own private treason flaunted so openly. It wound her up inside like a clock, tenser and tenser, but the Collegiates did not care, and she made sure not to meet face to face with the other Imperial agents here, simply to leave them messages at the agreed-on drop points. She should have felt freer, here, walking as a woman even if she was forced to hide her kinden, but the habit of secrecy was so deep ingrained in her that she lived every moment on a knife edge, waiting for someone to decry her, not for her race, but for her gender.

Averic would serve, she judged, and he was well placed. The Empire had never tried to infiltrate the College before, but to Gesa that was a grievous omission that had been amended just in time. One could get up to so much mischief in those halls of academe.

The Rekef had been broken against the walls of Collegium more than once. During the brief conflict with the Spider-kinden, an entire Rekef operation had been uncovered and sent home to face disgrace and punitive interrogation, leaving behind barely a trace of Imperial influence in the city. If the Empire had not been able to borrow some intelligence from its new Spider allies, then the war would have been considerably more difficult – and who wanted to have to rely on Spiders?

For that matter, who wanted to have to rely on the Rekef? Army Intelligence was now suddenly at the cutting edge of the agent war. Her heart swelled with pride to think that her mocked and abused corps was suddenly at the core of things, and so was she.

But there was so little time. The insertion of her people had come late in the day, only the influx of refugees from the Felyal giving sufficient cover to accomplish it. She and her fellows now had a great deal of work to do, and precious little time. She was having to allow her subordinates more independence than she liked, as there simply wasn't enough time for her to mastermind everything properly. She had to trust in her peers, and trust was not something that came naturally to her.

It was worth it, though, for this chance to outshine the Rekef. There were Army Intelligence colonels back in Capitas who would salute her with a tear in their eyes, when she came back from winning Collegium for the Empress. Army Intelligence would succeed where the Rekef had only chalked up repeated failure.

And, for one thing, they would kill Stenwold Maker. Of that she was absolutely sure.

Twenty-Nine

'Aerial reconnaissance of the Second Army has become essentially impossible with our resources,' Corog Breaker reported. 'In all honesty it was hit and miss at the best of times, but now there seems to be a substantial aerial strike force accompanying the Second always. We've almost lost several spotters, and we simply don't have the spare Stormreaders.' He did not need to elaborate. Each nocturnal attack on Collegium was resulting in more Farsphex slipping through the fraying net of the defending pilots, more damage to the city, more deaths, more panic. And the Second Army was getting close now. The meeting that Breaker was addressing was specifically to determine the battle tactics of the ground force that would shortly be leaving the city.

'We need to get out there now in order to have a chance of preparing a stand against them,' said Marteus of the Coldstone Company. His face was as blank and closed as always, but there was a tightness in his voice that spoke of stress. 'We're not short of recruits, anyway. Seems like half the fugitives from the Felyal have signed up.'

'Are they ready to fight?' Jodry asked him.

'They have no time left to be made more ready,' Marteus stated flatly.

Jodry was chairing the council. On his left were Marteus and Elder Padstock, the two chief officers who would be taking the fight to the enemy. Corog Breaker slumped on his right, with the Mynan leader Kymene beyond him, head bowed in thought. Across the table from him was Stenwold Maker, no longer the Speaker's great friend and ally. Hardly anyone actually knew what had caused the rift, but tension between them sang in the air like a razor.

'How are the automotives?' Jodry asked. These days that seemed to be his role in life, to stumble around between the people to whom the defence of the city had been delegated, asking them inane questions.

'As ready as anything else,' Elder Padstock confirmed. 'We have quite a fleet of them now, certainly more than the enemy have of the Cyclops machines the War Master told us of, especially with the help from Sarn.'

'Sentinels,' Stenwold reminded her, citing the name that had come in Laszlo's earlier note of warning delivered by the captain of a merchantman. Where Laszlo had got to was just one more worry for Stenwold right now. 'And, armour them how we will, they are not a match for the Imperial vehicles. With the exception of the six Sarnesh automotives, not one of them was even built for war. Bolting some plates and a repeating ballista on won't get us very far.' The aid from Sarn had been an unexpected bonus: a half-dozen boxy, serviceable war automotives – lumbering tracked machines boasting turret-mounted nailbows and paired smallshotters to the fore. They were not Sentinels, but they were considerably more warlike than any of the makeshift contraptions that Collegium was intending to field. Stenwold sighed heavily. 'I have asked some experts to join us,' he told them. 'They're waiting outside. They've put together some idea of how we might win this fight.'

Jodry was too weary for surprise. 'Well, send them in then. Let's hear it.'

They were two more Beetle-kinden: a tall austerely handsome woman in a Master's robes; and man head and shoulders taller than anyone else in the room, vastly broad across the chest, wearing a Company soldier's buff coat that must have been made from two garments of the regular size.

'Mistress Praeda Rakespear of the College faculty of artifice,' Stenwold introduced them, 'and Amnon, former First Soldier of Khanaphes.'

There was a reflective pause from around the table, especially from Jodry, who plainly had not received any forewarning, but then Marteus spoke up: 'Is this a joke? I know this man. He's a good fighter, but his city doesn't even *have* automotives.'

'Chief Officer Marteus,' Praeda snapped, even as Stenwold opened his mouth, 'I would point out that Collegium has no history of fighting wars with automotives either. However, for hundreds of years the Khanaphir have taken chariots to war.'

'*Chariots?*' Marteus demanded.

'Masters,' Amnon rumbled, speaking softly and yet quietening the room. 'It seems to me that your city is about to be attacked by enemies wielding new weapons that you have not faced before, and have no ready defence against. This I can understand.' That reminder that his own city had suffered from the Empire, dragged roughly into the modern age when Wasp leadshotters knocked down its walls, caught their attention. 'It is true your people have many wonderful inventions that mine lack. Every day there seems some new device to lighten the burden of life. However, Praeda has shown me these automotives of yours, and I understand they involve no beasts to fall to arrow or spear, that they are armoured so as to be more durable than our creations of wood but, still, a war with automotives is like a war with chariots, it seems to me. You have prepared your fleet of machines, and the Wasps already have these Sentinels the War Master has spoken of, together with many more vehicles, for the moving of their soldiers and supplies. What use will they put them to, however? What use will you make of yours?'

Marteus shifted restlessly, still less than convinced, and Jodry's expression was doubtful as well, but nobody spoke.

'Chariots – automotives – are in themselves only suited to

454

one thing: attack. They cannot hold, they cannot defend. They must keep moving always to be effective, or they are no more than one more leadshotter, moved swiftly into place. Their strength is in their motion, and in attack.'

'That is convenient given that the Empire will be attacking us,' Marteus pointed out acidly.

'They will not be,' Amnon corrected him patiently, and a look passed between him and Praeda. She set out a long scroll and made some quick marks with a reservoir pen.

'Collegium here,' she noted. 'Second Army's line of approach from the north-east. Now, where is the attack?'

The others leant forward, and Jodry made a vague gesture towards the curved line that was Collegium's wall.

'You haven't been listening to Master Maker, or to me for that matter,' Kymene spoke up, barely glancing at the sketch. 'These automotives did not bring my city's walls down. They were used to break up our positions inside the city only.'

Jodry exchanged a glance with Marteus. 'The artillery.'

'These farshotters, or whatever they're calling them,' Stenwold confirmed. 'Amnon?'

'The Empire will not be attacking. The Empire will be defending,' the Khanaphir explained. 'They need to bring their weapons into range, and then they need to prevent any harm befalling them. It is just as it was with my city. For this they must rely on the sort of makeshift fortification your people say they used around your forest Felyal. They will use their chariots – these automotives – to counter-attack your force, but if you can strike at their leadshotter weapons, you strip them of their chiefest advantage. Now do you see?'

This time Marteus was silent, and everyone else was nodding appreciatively.

'So,' Amnon continued, satisfied. 'The novice chariot commander orders his vehicles straight for the enemy, against their shields. The Empire is yet a novice, so this is most likely what it will do. The wise charioteer brings his forces to the enemy's flanks, even encircling to his rear, using his speed to the fullest, allowing him to strike at his enemy's weakest point. I have seen maps of the land you are most likely to fight on – it is hilly, but flat enough to give you room to move – the path the enemy will attack along means nothing, for you have all the land you need to manoeuvre. You understand?'

After that the discussion became more technical, and Stenwold sat back and watched as the former First Soldier, whose introduction to modern artifice was only a few years old, now tutored those who had lived with it all their lives. This was a part of the war that Stenwold felt himself well rid of. Perhaps in his younger days he would have thrown himself into the planning of it. Now he felt just like the Khanaphir; time and progress moving at a pace that he could not keep up with. He could not do it all. He had to trust to people like Amnon, Marteus and Taki each to hold up their own corner of the war.

Afterwards, he let them drift away, Jodry, Kymene and the others. Night was drawing in. Already the Great Ear would be primed, the airmen and women waiting for the call, their machines wound and ready. Stenwold the historian had a great sense of history, not momentous but merely inexorable. *Could we ever actually defeat the Empire? Should we have mobilized the Lowlands and struck at them while they dealt with their own internal problems, the ink on our treaty still wet? And then what? By the time we finished fighting them all the way across the Empire, what would we create? How many of those freed subject cities would be at each other's throats, and blaming us. Or would we take the Empire's place, forcing them to accept our grand enlightenment down the barrel of a snapbow?*

Where is it going to end?

Someone cleared their throat, and he looked up to see Praeda hovering in the doorway.

'Master Maker, I told Berjek I'd pass on a message for him. As a favour, really.'

'It's about his brother?' Stenwold divined. The problem of

Banjacs Gripshod had not gone away, but just now nobody cared enough to grasp the nettle. 'Jodry went to speak to him a while back, I know.'

'He wants to speak to *you*, Berjek said,' Praeda told him. 'Specifically to *you*. I'm sorry, Stenwold, but Berjek . . . I just said I'd ask. Now I've asked. That's all.'

'If I should somehow ever find a moment spare then perhaps I'll go and see him,' Stenwold told her, 'although I can't honestly think what he might have to say to me.'

'Here they come!' Scain relayed the news for Pingge's benefit, and a moment later their Farsphex fell sideways in the air, breaking formation smoothly even as the Imperial machines broadened their net, ready to take on the Collegiate fliers as they came in. They were still miles from the Beetle city, and the enemy's ability to home in on their attacks was being hotly debated by the engineers back home. Meanwhile intelligence from the spies in Collegium was drying up – either the Beetles were keeping a better watch or they were simply keeping more secrets from each other.

Pingge stared out into the night through her open hatch, watching for the telltale ghosts of movement that would resolve into those vicious, nimble two-winged orthopters the Collegiates built. Before her was the ballista she had recently been saddled with, and if any target presented itself in the small arc of their vessel's left flank that she could actually shoot at, then possibly she might get off a bolt at it. There was a rack of the explosive-tipped ammunition within arm's reach, and it terrified her. One spark, from a stray piercer bolt striking the hull of the Farsphex, say, and they might all go up. For the marginal advantage it gave, the risks seemed ridiculous. The Beetles always seemed to be gaining ground technologically, though, and the Engineering Corps was just as keen to load their vaunted new pilots with every new toy they could devise. *One day we won't get off the ground, for all the advantages they've given us.*

They pitched violently, and she heard Scain curse. A scattering of bolts sprayed them, punching through the outer hull, but none of them making it through the second inner skin that protected the pilot, the bombardier, the engine and the fuel tank. *Just so long as they don't hit the wings or just shoot me directly through this stupid open doorway I've got here.* Then she nearly swallowed her tongue because a Collegiate flier had blurred past, in her sights for a fraction of a second, but gone before she could react, leaving her pointlessly swinging the ballista after it.

She could not remember when she had last slept properly. There was a part of her mind insisting that she should be dropping dead from exhaustion by now. The Chneuma was a merciless mistress, though, goading her on as though it had a handful of hot pokers lodged inside her. The Wasps took far more of the stuff than their Fly-kinden subordinates, too. She didn't want to think about how Scain would be feeling.

They lurched in the air again, and she had a sense that they were pulling further off from the fray. Looking out into a chessboard of cloud and moonlight, she caught sight of orthopters driving at one another, looping and turning, but they were some distance away. *Are they off course, or are we?*

'Hey, sir, what's up?'

Scain was silently concentrating on flying, pulling them ever further away. Pingge risked putting her head and shoulders out, the wings a thunder above her. There were other machines close by, but not fighting. All of them were simply putting as much distance as possible between themselves and the conflict.

And ahead lay geography that had practically written itself on to the back of her eyes: the coast, the harbour . . . Collegium.

'Sir?' she tried again.

'Nishaan's holding them,' Scain rattled back, tensely. 'We're giving the city all we've got before they realize we're mostly past them.'

Pingge reflected drily that the Wasp woman named Nishaana

had mysteriously lost the feminine ending of her name since she had made sergeant. 'New targets, sir?'

'Use your discretion. Industry and residential,' Scain reported to her. 'Attacking their means and their will to fight. You know the drill.'

'Right you are, sir.'

One of the Collegiate pilots had said to Taki, 'I even dream about flying now,' and her immediate thought had been, *I always dreamt of flying, every night – it's just that those used to be good dreams.* All of her life all she had ever wanted was to fly. All her other ambitions – the respect of her aviator peers, her victories in dragon-fights over the Exalsee, her status within the city – remained secondary and inextricably bound up with that one thought. Now she wanted to spend a tenday on the ground, not to touch the control stick of the *Esca Magni*, not to view the world through the glass of her cockpit, not to have her heartbeat fall into step with the beating of her orthopter's wings.

The Great Ear had sounded off early that night, and strongly, and she had already been trying to calculate the enemy force incoming even as her Art wings dropped her into place in her pilot's seat. All about her, the other pilots of her airfield, and her shift, were scrambling for their machines. Around half of them were veterans like Edmon, the other half with only a flight or two to their name, and at least two for whom this would be the acid test, their first combat.

Taki had always thought of herself as young; fighting in the air was a young woman's game, after all. Reflexes decayed like everything else, and eventually experience could no longer offset the loss. She still wondered why Corog Breaker had not been killed yet. The old Master Armsman had a warrior's heart, but she could measure his years in the handling of his machine, that extra second's lapse in time before he reacted. His glider wings had saved his life twice now.

Looking at the new pilots sent to her by the College, she felt old now, as if the gap between her days and Breaker's was slender compared to what separated her from the tyros. Not just raw time, of course, but distance measured in that compressed and saw-edged period she spent in the air, pitting her skills against the enemy and betting her life on it every time. It was a bastard of a way to grow old, but she was beginning to feel it was the only way that she ever would.

The drone of her own craft's Ear increased suddenly, and she spotted the enemy formation as moonbeams darted across them. She held off signalling until she saw them breaking up, splitting off from the pack in readiness, and then sent terse flashes of light towards the fliers on her left and right, the coded orders now coming as naturally as speech. *Left climb, separate off, attack. Right with me, follow, guard.* She had to hope that they had understood her, as she was beginning her attack run even then.

If only I could slow this moment down. For of course she was flying into a chaos of vessels, bringing a wave-front of disorder that seemed to scatter the enemy ahead of her. There must be a point where the onrush of the Collegiate Stormreaders impacting into the widening Farsphex formation was like a stone shattering glass. *Beautiful, it must be beautiful to witness, if only I could.* But, being the stone, she had no such luxury.

She went after three targets, one after the other, loosing a brief burst of shot and then away, imagining the other Wasp pilots out of position – moving in to deflect an attack that was only a feint. Yes, yes, they were in each other's minds, but that didn't mean that she couldn't fool them *all* with an elegant enough deception, and they were still bound by the limits of speed and momentum and mechanical tolerance. Out of position was out of position, and all their mindlink would do was make them fully understand that they had got it wrong.

Now. She had her target, chasing and chasing, and the Farsphex fleeing before her, with a tyro clinging to her back-right quarter, gamely following each twist and turn, and one of the better Collegiate pilots – you know, that boy with the long hair and the smile – guarding from behind and above, waiting ready to fend off the inevitable counterstrike by the Imperials.

And yet she seemed to have out-skipped them for the moment, the reprisal never coming, as she nipped and nipped away at the enemy, and the Farsphex flinging itself about the sky to keep her off it, and it was almost like old times, in a duel over the Exalsee. As her hands threw the *Esca Magni* after her opponent, her mind could step back, admiring the nimbleness of the larger craft in the air, reaching for that brotherhood of flier against flier that she had lived on and thrived on.

She was alive and awake and fierce, and knew joy, because she had forgotten Collegium, the lives at stake, the fires and the fear. *That* was what she missed most from the old days. Back then she had nobody else she need care about. She never cared about her own life, and nobody else's was at stake.

She realized that the pilot watching the skies above *wasn't* that boy with the long hair, because he'd been killed three nights ago, a Wasp pilot's bolt piercing his cockpit even as he tried to cut in front of Taki for a killing shot. She had seen a flash of darkness as his blood sprayed the inside of the glass.

She also realized that she was wide of where she reckoned the main fight must be, and that nobody was coming to save her elusive target. Further realizations followed.

She flashed, *Break off, break off,* to both sides, and then, fumbling with the toggle, *Retreat, retreat,* even before she had wheeled back and scanned a sky that was far too empty. What she could see of the enemy were scattered all over, and so few. Where were the reinforcements that always swooped in to save their fellows? Unless they were above the clouds, there were none to be seen.

No, no no. And she slung her *Esca* past the nearest Collegiate flight, flashing, *Retreat, retreat!* and knowing they must think her mad.

There was no code for 'Gather other pilots', and to spell it out would be too awkward and take too long. She plotted a course that might pass within sight of a few more, but that would see her turned back towards Collegium, in the vain hope she might do some good. Then she was forcing every inch of tension from her engine, flitting through the sky with the ground below a darkened blur.

The streets of Collegium were rushing below them sooner than Pingge had anticipated, lightless now, with even the windows blacked out, as if a single visible candle or lantern would call down a fiery oblivion on the incautious. *And not too far from the truth.* She settled herself by the reticule, glanced into its lens, looked again out of the gaping hatch beside her.

'What the piss is *that*?'

She had a good look at it, in the moment before it opened up on them, for the Farsphex were coming in low to give the bombardiers the best run. Sitting on the roof of a building they were passing was something like a ballista with a big circular magazine positioned behind the arms, set within a frame of steam-pistons that were abruptly thudding into life. Pingge couldn't have asked for a better demonstration of the device, and the only shame was that it was pointing at *them*.

Pull up, but the words died in her throat as the thing loosed, the magazine ratcheting round at a rate of knots, and the air was instantly full of big ten-foot bolts, falling upwards towards the Farsphex in a killing rain, then lighting the night sky with their explosions, a thunder and a roar all around them. Scain cursed and fought the controls, pitching violently right so that Pinggie slammed into the wall and almost ended up dangling out of the hatch.

'Gain height! Gain height!' She knew Scain was not talking to her, but recently his internal conferences with Aarmon and the others had become external ones, the increased Chneuma dose cracking the barriers between the spoken and what was merely thought. Pingge clung on, the reticule forgotten, and hoped and hoped, feeling the craft rock and shudder with each near-miss.

From her viewpoint through the hatch she saw a sudden bonfire in the sky, the blazing shape of a Farsphex leaping out from the blackness for a second before the fuel tank erupted, the rear half of the stricken machine almost disintegrating, leaving the guttering cockpit and wings to plummet.

'Get to work!' Scain snapped, and this time he really was addressing her. They had a little height now, but still low enough for Pingge to pick her targets from the distorted, onrushing view the reticule gave her of the city ahead. There seemed to be quite a few of those repeating ballistae about, the bolts bursting in the air suddenly – *crack-boom!* – at isolated intervals, without pattern or warning.

She forced herself to concentrate on the reticule, trusting to Scain, blinding herself to the dangerous skies. From then on the work was grim and mechanical – spot a target, line up the reticule, release the bomb, all within the few seconds she had between seeing the image and it passing below them. There was never time to look back at the fire in their wake.

Bolts rattled across their hull, one punching a hole within a foot of her, coming in through the open hatch. The Collegiates had put some fresh orthopters in the air. She scrambled for her own little ballista, but Scain snapped at her to leave it alone.

'Just get your job done,' he told her. He sounded sick. For the next few passes, he was throwing their vessel jaggedly about so as to lose whatever was tracking them, or to give Aarmon or one of the others the chance to cut in. She lost her target over and over, and was on the point of shouting at him to hold a level course when she thought that through and decided she would rather he threw them all across the Collegiate sky, after all, and she'd just have to make do.

The minimal air resistance – pilots no doubt woken in a panic, hurling themselves desperately into the sky, in their ones and twos, against an overwhelming force – soon passed, leaving her to get on with her job. That would have been fine, except Scain was talking again.

'It's vile,' he muttered, and she had no idea whether he was talking to her or not. But then: 'When we fly against their machines, *that's* war. What's this?' And she realized she was hearing his side of a mental conversation with the other pilots.

'I know,' he said, and 'I know that, too. They say we're saving lives for the Second, that we're crushing their will to fight. Is that true? Have we seen any evidence that they're losing will, as opposed to machines and pilots and civilian lives?' And: 'I *know*! But what are we, if this is all we're for?' His voice sounded raw, shouting without realizing he was making a sound.

'I want it to end,' he told whoever was on the receiving end of this. He suddenly sounded so lost that Pingge wanted to reach out to him, but she thought that, if he knew he had been heard, he would kill her.

Then they were under attack again, and Scain cut them loose, reaching for height as the city diminished below them. She guessed that the Collegiate attackers that had tried to bottle them up beyond the city's walls had finally realized their error and come back with a vengeance. Then the Farsphex were regrouping, turning to head for the Second Army camp, wherever that had crept to by tonight.

We can't go on like this.

The words were Taki's, and the end of her mumbled report to Stenwold before shunning the grey light of dawn for her bed. The sentiments could have been anyone's of a certain level of seniority within Collegium – those who sat on the right committees and could piece together all the disparate facts.

The foundries of Collegium were still constructing Stormreaders as swiftly as they could, although only as a result of of fresh shipments of raw materials from unexpected quarters – the first ever Vekken trading cog had turned up with a hold full of metal ingots, and the *Tidenfree* had arrived with superior alloys supposedly from across the sea but in reality from beneath it. Still, the pilots that were putting out in those craft were younger and less experienced each time – if the average age of a flying combatant had been plotted by some scholar on a graph, the downward curve would be steep – which meant that the investment in each orthopter was correspondingly riskier. The rooftop artillery was another drain on resources, and had struck down only two enemies, and those in the first salvo. Stenwold had to hope that the simple existence of such a defence might at least complicate matters for the Wasp pilots, putting them off their aim and resulting in fewer bombs dropped, or in bombs dropped less accurately. But of course 'less accurately' meant little consolation to the family whose home was destroyed by a bomb falling wide.

And the Second Army was near. The ground forces – Cold-stone Company and Maker's Own and all the automotives the city had been able to furnish – were marching out any day now, as ready as they would ever be, and another drain on the city, in materiel and in lives.

If the Empire get its artillery set up within range of the walls, then we're done for. And, competing with that, *If the Empire wears down our air defences, then we're done for, too.*

So why am I here?

Ahead of Stenwold rose the imposing edifice of Banjacs Gripshod's townhouse, and it was impossible to know from the facade that the artificer's killing machine had eaten away so much of its innards.

He was here because Praeda had asked him, but, more than that, he was here because there was no need for him anywhere else, which was a bitter realization. Matters had advanced sufficiently that there was no more need for the grand plan. He had sat on his last committee, he knew, and the work was now in the hands of the specialists: Corog Breaker, Taki, Marteus, Kymene, even Amnon. Statesmen such as Stenwold and Jodry Drillen had spoken their piece and taken their final opportunity to adjust the rudder of history. The future would judge them, but their decisions had finally acquired sufficient momentum to break free of the earth and fly, and there would be no calling one word of it back.

The most galling moment had been when he had requested – practically insisted – that he be allowed to accompany the Merchant Companies as they marched out, and Marteus had politely told him that he was 'needed' in Collegium. *He just didn't want me underfoot, questioning his orders, complicating matters.* And Marteus had been right, of course, which was worse.

So he had come here instead, to the home and prison of the madman Banjacs Gripshod, seemingly the one duty left to him.

The man looked even older than Stenwold had imagined: rake-thin, wild-haired and bearded. If the War Master did not know better, he might have imagined that Banjacs had been starved and deprived of all civilized niceties until a minute before Stenwold set eyes on him. When he recognized Stenwold he leapt from his desk and lunged forward so fast that Stenwold instinctively plucked his little snapbow from inside his tunic.

'At last!' Banjacs exclaimed. 'I knew you'd come! Of all the people in this city, Maker, *you* have to understand me.'

Those were depressingly familiar words to hear. Having once been an outspoken maverick in the Assembly, Stenwold had attracted a variety of lunatics over the years, each of them counting on his sympathy just because the same people had laughed at them both. Sadly, in almost every case, they were genuinely laughable.

Stenwold almost turned to go, bitterly aware of the sidelong looks from the two of Outwright's men who had drawn the short straw to guard the door. One thought stopped him for, just once amongst those other deluded babblers, he had turned away an excitable conspiracy-finder only to have the man end up dead at the hands of a very real conspiracy. A flicker of memory tugged at his conscience, and he sighed.

'Master Gripshod, let's make this quick.'

He followed the man back into his room, noting that although

Banjacs was being kept under house arrest, there was no comfort involved. The room was bare of ornament, the furniture unkempt and old: only a bed, a desk, a chair, a few shelves of books. Pale outlines on the walls suggested that it had once been a more congenial place. Apparently, Banjacs had been steadily selling off the family chattels for decades.

'You,' the old man was muttering. 'Of all of them – you look ahead. *I* look ahead, you see. I saw it all, just like you did – but before you were born even! How'd you like that, then, Maker? Before you were ever born I saw where we'd come to!' Without warning he was jabbing an accusing finger at Stenwold. 'Oh, you're the War Master, but I was there first and I warned them.'

'Before I was . . . ?' Stenwold was already regretting not leaving immediately. 'You saw what, Master Gripshod? What did you warn them about?'

'Why, this.' Banjacs's hands embraced some all-encompassing whole. 'What I see from my window every night: the city on fire, death from the air. *This.*'

Ah well, just lunacy after all. 'You foresaw the Wasp Empire's attack before I was born? Of course you did.'

'Don't patronize me, Maker! The Wasps? Who cares about the Wasps? It could have been anyone, you hear me? But I knew from the start that it would come to this. I stood there at Clifftops, barely more than a boy and already with my College accredits. I saw Morless's *Mayfly* over the city, do you under-stand? And what I could never understand was why nobody else grasped it. Once you have *that* then it will lead to *this.*'

'Hold on, slow down.' Stenwold looked the wild old man in the eyes and was about to take advantage of the ensuing pause to dismiss him utterly, when something lodged in his head. 'Clifftops? *Morless?*' Names from the history books, but Banjacs was *old*, and a trip back in time of sixty years would leave him about the age that he claimed, and . . .

Every student knew that Lial Morless had piloted the first heavier-than-air flying machine in the world, right here in

Collegium. Stenwold crossed wordlessly to the window and stared out. Down the street was a house with buckled walls, the upper storey having half-tumbled into the street, courtesy of the Empire's Farsphex.

'Master Gripshod,' he began, and then, 'Banjacs, if I may, tell me what you mean.'

'We were never meant to fly,' Banjacs told him softly, unexpectedly close by his shoulder. 'We were never creatures of the air. We still aren't. The airships were bad enough, but at least they're slow. The orthopters and the like, I *knew* they would bring this on us – it could have been Ants or Wasps or Bees or even our own people, but once the tools were in the world . . . Death from the skies, Maker, it was always going to happen. Since the day I saw Morless fly, I've been trying to find a way . . .'

'A way to what?' Stenwold rounded on him. *Impossible*, was the thought in his mind. *Just a madman*. But these were mad times.

'To defend ourselves. Defend our city. My machine . . .'

'You've shown us what your machine can do, and it was nothing to do with defending the city,' Stenwold pointed out.

'*Listen!* That was just a discharge from the lightning batteries, a side effect. But it needs to be finished. It's not ready. All those years, and I wasn't ready . . .'

Those last words finally struck home, for Stenwold had thought just the same when the Wasps had brought war against them the first time.

'Look at my machine,' Banjacs went on. 'See it for what it is. Let me complete it, Maker. I am so close.'

Impossible, came the familiar old refrain, but Stenwold found it hard to discern what might be impossible these days.

Thirty

There was some attempt at cheering, but Collegium had no grand tradition of military send-offs, nor did Beetle-kinden have any great belief that dying in battle was in some way better than dying in bed. The proud martial heritage of Ants and Mantids was lost on them. They marched to war with the same pragmatism with which they did everything.

Maker's Own Company was already assembled into divisions of two hundred each, Collegium's finest of all kinden moving off along the Pathian Way to reassemble outside the city. Ahead of them, the bulk of the automotives were on the move, deploying left and right of the roadway beyond the walls. Some had been armoured and mounted with weapons for the mechanized attack that was planned, whilst others were little better than livestock carriers to take Collegium's soldiers to the fray.

The Coldstone Company was still assembling, ordering itself by best guess and rough democracy into the smaller fifty-man maniples that Marteus favoured. As sub-officer, the Antspider had one of these to look after, and she marched up and down in front of her soldiers, barking orders at people and pointing with her sword as though she was a lordly Arista and not just a halfbreed given temporary rank. The dignity was feigned, but she felt that running about and shouting was not fitting for her current station.

Her soldiers were all nervous, their mood on a knife-edge

between anticipation and fear. All around them, watching every stumble and jogged elbow, were the crowds, a great mass of Collegium's citizens, yet quiet, eerily quiet. Straessa watched the men and women of Coldstone Company bid farewell to their families and friends before each finding their place: here was gathered a host of wives and husbands, parents and children, all of whom had lived through the last war. This should have been nothing new to them. Many would remember sending these same soldiers off to fight at Malkan's Folly with the Sarnesh, whilst others had stayed at home to hold off this same Imperial army two years before. Now, though, they watched in near-silence, as though draining every last moment from the sight, sucking it dry of memory.

It is because they thought they'd won last time, but here the Empire is, indefatiguable and insatiable. Where will it end?

A new train of automotives ground past, their engines shockingly loud in contrast, the subdued crowd eddying back to give them space. The Antspider caught a glimpse of that absurdly big Khanaphir who suddenly seemed to be in charge of the mechanized assault, standing up to survey the city he was leaving, whilst a woman she knew as Mistress Rakespear of the artifice faculty did the driving. In the next vehicle was a young-ish woman with the blue-grey skin of Myna, whom Straessa knew must be their leader-in-exile, Kymene. There was a sizeable contingent of Mynan soldiers who would be fighting alongside the Merchant Companies, eager to get their teeth into their hated enemy.

'All present and correct, Sub,' the report came to her, dragging her back to the matter in hand. Gerethwy was standing forward from the others. 'We can march out as soon as the Maker's Own are through the gates.'

'Stand ready,' the Antspider confirmed, officer to subordinate. Then she met his eyes directly. Written there for her eyes to translate was the thought, *We are utter fools, aren't we?* and she nodded slowly. 'What's that you've got there?' she enquired, for, carried sloping over his shoulder, was something larger and more complex than a snapbow.

'Foundry-pattern mechanized snapbow,' Gerethwy reported proudly. 'Every squad gets one of these, or else a nailbow, or something like it.'

'How come you get to carry it?' she asked, mock-jealous. Their banter cut at some part of her – so like and yet not like the old days that seemed years ago now, but she clung to it.

'I showed them my accredits as an artificer, didn't I?' the Woodlouse-kinden told her proudly.

'You brought your accredits to a war?'

He shrugged with one shoulder, keeping the fearsome-looking weapon steady. 'That's why I have this lovely toy, Sub.'

'Straessa,' someone interrupted.

She had been expecting the voice, but something lurched inside her when she heard it. She turned to find them: Eujen and Averic, come at last to see her off.

For all the destruction that had happened and the combat that was due, fighting for calm just then proved the hardest part of all. She wanted to run to them, to embarrass herself in front of her squad by venting the feelings that were boiling up inside her. She wanted to quit the army and simply stay here with Eujen, as if that would be any safer for either of them.

Instead she regarded them with affected coolness and a slight smile, her weight cocked on one hip, her arms folded. 'Made it, then?' she observed, and her voice remained steady. 'Purple's a good colour for you,' she added, for they both now wore the sashes of Eujen's Student Company.

'It was the only colour we could get in bulk,' he replied, doing his best to match her reserve, and not quite managing it. 'Straessa . . .'

'How'd you like my soldiers, eh?' Her smile was fragile and brave.

Eujen just stared at her, and in his eyes was the time, ticking down. It looked as though the whole of the Coldstone

Company had milled itself into place now, she reckoned. *And still I can't find the words.* Averic was no help, not even meeting her eyes.

There sounded the tramp of marching feet, altogether too regular for anything under her command, and the Mynan exiles began to pass through: grim, determined men and women, professional in their red and black helms and breastplates. Seeing them, Straessa almost despaired. *And we've got shopkeepers and tailors and artificers' apprentices. Dress them in buff coats, it doesn't make them soldiers.*

Us. It doesn't make us soldiers.

She turned back to Eujen, abruptly fearing that he would be gone, and caught his arm that was held half-out towards her. The casual pose was beginning to hurt, deep inside, but at the same time she could not make herself abandon it.

'Straessa . . .' he began again.

'Gerethwy brought his accredits, can you believe that?' she remarked brightly, inwardly appalled at the trite nonsense she was uttering.

Eujen swallowed, and she felt the moment fray and snap, the weight of an army about to march pulling her away from him. Then someone blundered into them both, making Averic start back, hands momentarily raised, and Raullo Mummers, disenfranchised artist, was hugging them both, tears streaming down his face. 'You hear me? You look after yourself. No more funerals,' he mumbled. 'Come back, come back, that's all.' He was reeling drunk, as he had been for much of the time since his studio burned, hugging Eujen fiercely enough to force the breath out of him.

'*I'm* not going,' Eujen snapped at him.

'No?' Raullo blinked, bewildered, then he goggled at the Antspider. 'You, my favourite model, off to the wars?'

Straessa's gesture managed to indicate all the military motley she wore.

The artist was abruptly transformed into overripe gravitas.

'Then come back, and I shall sketch you. For you alone, I will sketch. And if you don't . . . never, never again.' He lurched, hands out to forestall any help, then slouched into Averic.

A shout went up, from the head of the column, Marteus calling the lead squads to order.

'Come back,' Eujen echoed.

'Do my best,' she promised.

Averic muttered something and took a step back, still encumbered by Raullo's weight.

'Keep the place in one piece until we see it again,' Gerethwy called over to them, one hand raised in salute. 'Come on, Sub, they're starting to move.'

Her calm snapped at that moment, and she lunged forward and threw her arms about Eujen before he could stop her, a brief, fierce embrace. 'See you right here, I swear it,' she hissed, and then she was running back for her own people. 'Come on, ranks, you slipshod bastards! Oi, Gorenn! You, Commonweal Retaliation Army or whatever you call yourself! Just because you've got a bow's no excuse for being out of position!' She put some real fire into it, to burn away the tears that were threatening the corners of her eyes. By the time she had rejoined her maniple, they were in as neat a square as she could have wished, snapbows and pikes shouldered.

'Mind if I march with you, dear?'

The Antspider glanced down to see Sartaea te Mosca, Flykinden associate Master of the Inapt studies department, unarmed but hefting a pack about her shoulders that seemed far too large for her.

'They reckon we might come across some dangerous inscriptions, or something?' Straessa asked her.

'Seconded to the faculty of medicine, dear one,' te Mosca revealed. 'All hands to the pumps, I think, is the Apt phrase for it.'

'You'd better be able to keep up,' Straessa told her mock-sternly, and then there was nothing for it – the squads in front were stuttering into motion, a brief confusion of soldiers trying to find the right foot.

'And off we go!' the Antspider snapped out, and a hundred soldiers heard her words, and set out to war.

Averic watched them go, feeling paralysed, the words of the intelligence officer, Gesa, rattling about in his skull like dice. He was even glad for the wine-reeking burden of Raullo on his arm, because his new knowledge was surely written on his face in letters of shame and guilt, so that even Eujen, idealistic to a fault, would read them there.

Traitor, went the cry, and it seemed to him that the blade was cutting both ways: traitor to Collegium for not telling them what he knew; traitor to his own people for harbouring even these eroding doubts. He had tried to stand with a foot in two worlds, and ended up in neither, merely a halfbreed of the mind.

Then he saw her, marching past in the uniform of a Cold-stone soldier: the same woman, Gesa the Wasp in halfbreed's clothing, undetected and unremarked, seemingly just one more soldier. She was marching to war in Straessa's own Company, one of the rush of recruits that had flocked to the army after the Felyal was burned. Averic felt himself shaking.

There, she's there! Wasp spy! Wasp spy right there! And yet no words came, no accusing finger. He watched Gesa march off, practically holding a knife to Straessa's throat, and yet he teetered on the fence between betrayals, and did nothing and let her go.

And, although he was expected now at the gates along with Jodry and the other prime movers of the war effort, Stenwold stood in Banjacs Gripshod's house and tried to understand.

The machine loomed before him, and he knew that what he could see was only part of it. Beneath his feet the cellar was packed with a battery of glass cells that crackled and roared with stolen lightning, years of painstaking generation hidden down there, lighting up the darkness. The shock that had killed Reyna Pullard had been only an iota of it, the merest spark. Banjacs had indeed been busy. He had enough power down there to wreck more of this city than the Wasp air force already had.

Here, on the ground floor, were the controls: wheels and locks to direct the movement of that primal energy, as if it were something as tame and easily domesticated as steam. Even steam engines exploded once in a while, Stenwold reminded himself. Behind those crude-seeming controls spread the vast mechanical heart of the device, he knew, for Banjacs had shown him the designs, taken from a hidden drawer in the man's desk that nobody had even guessed at. Stenwold himself had not been able to follow the details – his artificing was a decade out of date – but he was willing to bet that the best the College had to offer would have difficulties with Banjacs's close script and his brilliant, cracked mind.

All this time, working on a way out of our current predicament – that's foresight even the Moths wouldn't credit. And Banjacs made no secret that he despised a great deal of what Collegium was, or had become during his long life, most of all because it had not given him due adulation as a genius. Stenwold had steered him away from that topic more than once, for the old man practically foamed at the mouth once he got going. His list of names – the men and women who had held him back, not given him credit, or been preferred over him – was so long that Stenwold had not heard the end of it. Half of the man's rivals and enemies were dead, long dead in some cases, but the old artificer had no intention of forgetting any one of them.

The mechanisms of Banjacs's machine did all that science could do to trap and channel and focus the unleashed lightning, which otherwise would have simply levelled several streets about his house, and probably turned him and his stone walls into some sort of matter that artificers had yet to discover or describe. Above them was a forest of great glass pipes, mirrors, refractors, prisms; a work of art cast in light and bound in

475

bronze; a vast, clear, many-limbed entity frozen in mid-reach and about to burst the roof asunder.

Stenwold surveyed it all, and knew that it was all for *something* – not just a madman's insane assembly of parts, but a working machine, almost finished according to its creator, ready to . . . to do what?

Banjacs claimed it would save the city but, if it was a weapon, there was no suggestion that it could even be aimed. The old man had been desperate to convince, spitting out sincerity and conviction. Stenwold had read no falsehood in him, but Banjacs was plainly partway mad, even if he was telling the truth – perhaps *especially* then – and Stenwold could not rule out the possibility that his machine would be more of a terror than the Wasps to the city Banjacs plainly felt betrayed by.

Stenwold had called therefore for the College's most theoretical artificers to come and take their best guess, but in the end the decision would rest on his shoulders as much as anyone's, and they had so little *time*.

By that evening the artificers' reports were in. Stenwold had them on the table in front of him, sitting in a disused office in the Amphiophos. Words such as 'colossal discharge of lightning energy', 'near-perfect light conductivity' and 'requiring flawless vertical channelling' were underlined, alongside complex calculations comparing volumes of space with assessments of the stored power that Banjacs had accumulated. One artificer had even sketched a plan of the city in profile, lines and arcs above and around, to outline the potential for disaster.

Or for victory.

'Or for victory,' Stenwold murmured, forcing his own thoughts into words, and at that moment Jodry came in, and stopped. Stenwold had not been entirely sure the man would even turn up when asked. Certainly he did not look best pleased to be alone in a room with Stenwold Maker.

'So,' said the Speaker for the Assembly. 'Here you are. You

were looked for, when the Companies departed. You might at least have been there for your Own.'

'I offered to march with them. They turned me down.' Stenwold bit back on his words. 'No, wait, Jodry: this isn't what I wanted to talk about.'

'What then?' Jodry was still standing in the doorway, unwilling to commit to staying. 'Some new way of treating prisoners? Should Spider-kinden and Wasps have to wear—'

'Jodry!' Stenwold snapped. 'Listen, it's nothing of that, I don't want to open that wound right now. Time enough after – drag me before the Assembly, as you said. I'll answer to anything you put before me, I swear. For the good of the city, though, I have something new and I need your help.'

For a moment Jodry looked about to go, and Stenwold said, 'For old times' sake, Jodry, please.'

The fat man gave a sigh every bit as big as himself, and stepped in, hauling a chair out and slumping into it. 'Be quick.'

'I don't know if I can. Read these.'

Jodry glanced down at the reports. 'I'm no artificer.'

'Neither am I, any more. The important parts are written in language plain enough for the Inapt, so just read.'

And for almost twenty minutes, Jodry proceeded to read: first dismissively, then absorbedly, then with wide-eyed alarm. At the end he looked up at Stenwold and said, 'Madness.'

'And yet?'

'Stenwold, what's proposed here . . . Even if we had the time and resources to build something like this, I'm not sure that—'

'We already have one, or as good as,' Stenwold told him. 'It's built, Jodry.'

'But that's ridiculous. Where . . . ?' Jodry's face greyed with sudden realization. 'Founder's Mark, *this?* This is Banjacs Gripshod's device?' At Stenwold's nod, he returned to the reports. 'And it does . . . ?' For a moment he was very still, not seeing anything outside his own head. 'Stenwold, what are you proposing?'

'That we can't go on like this. That was what Taki said to me. We need to win the air war, or we won't be able to win the war at all. And we've tried it all, Jodry – you know we have. We're turning out pilots and orthopters as fast as we can, we've applied every innovation our artificers have come up with, yet we're losing. Losing machines and losing the city.'

'But, Stenwold, you've seen what they've written here. This isn't just a bow to aim at the enemy: this is a bomb. Once we release all that lightning he's got stored away, it's not as though we can keep popping away at them whenever they show themselves.' In the shadow of Banjacs's machine, and all that it implied, Jodry's animosity had drained away.

'I know, Jodry. That's why I need you. I . . .' Stenwold rubbed at his eyes, tired beyond belief, but sick at himself even beyond that. 'You don't like my ideas, I know. Well, I have one more for you to hate, Jodry. The worst one of them all, the most terrible . . . Let's get Taki in here.'

'You scare me, Stenwold,' Jodry said quietly, and he looked as if he meant it.

'Not as much as I frighten myself.'

Taki did not want to be there at all, and she made that plain. She wanted to be in bed or, if that was not an option, she wanted to be in with her fellow pilots waiting for the inevitable sound of the Great Ear amplifying the engine drone of approaching Farsphex.

'We'll be quick,' Stenwold told her, and she glanced between him and Jodry, noting how they were on the same side again, and plainly disliking the idea from base instinct.

'The Wasp orthopters are coming every night now,' Jodry started and, before any sharp retort, 'and I don't need to tell you that, obviously. We all know how the proximity of the Second is allowing them to land and rest up within easy reach of the city. Does that mean we're facing all their airpower every night?'

Stenwold guessed Jodry already knew the answer, but Taki

was plainly relieved to be asked a sensible question. 'No, sieur, in fact I'd guess that we see about a third of their pilots each night. We're getting to recognize a fair number of them by the way they fly – the veterans mostly. They add new blood just like we do. They're taking it easy, rotating their aviators, giving themselves time to rest so that they stay sharp when they fight us. We've bought Collegium that, at least. I think that, when the Second start their artillery assault, we'll get a much more sustained air attack.' She managed the words without a tremor.

'And can we hold that off?' Jodry asked, the patient lecturer.

'No, sieur, we cannot. But we'll try.'

'They're holding back at the moment, though?' Jodry pressed, and a twitch of irritation showed on the Fly-kinden's face.

'That's what I said, sieur.'

'And . . .' Even though he knew the question was coming, Stenwold felt a lurch in his stomach as Jodry spoke the words, 'If our aerial resistance decreased, they'd be in a position to take advantage, I imagine.'

Taki just glanced from Stenwold to Jodry and then back, looking unhappy and uncertain.

'After all, if they committed even two-thirds of their strength, they could cause appalling damage in a single night.' Jodry was almost whispering now.

'Are you . . . you're sending us off to . . . ?' Taki frowned. 'We're going to attack the Second while they're over the city? Sieur – Stenwold, Jodry, listen. We are holding them at bay. We're showing them we can bite, just enough that they're wary of putting their hand into our mouth. You can't take us away from defending the city! Take *advantage*? They'll flatten every building in the place! What have we been fighting and dying for, if not to stop that happening?'

'And yet we *can't* stop that happening,' Stenwold said flatly. 'We can only stave it off.'

'Then we stave it *off*!' she snapped. 'What are you . . . this isn't even my city! What are you thinking?'

479

'Thank you, Mistress Taki,' Jodry said heavily.

'We can hold them!' the little pilot insisted. 'Listen to me: we're doing our best—!'

'Nobody doubts you, any of you. You've worked wonders,' Jodry assured her, but his voice offered no comfort. 'That's all, thank you. You can go.'

When Taki had gone, shaking with bewilderment and injured pride, he gazed at Stenwold across the table.

'We can't do this.'

'What we can't do is tell anyone – *anyone* – what we are going to do. We give the orders to the pilots only on the night itself, and on the day after I will do everything in my power to bottle any word up. Secrecy is paramount, Jodry. The knowledge will be ours to bear,' Stenwold told him. 'Yours and mine. No other.'

'I am not strong enough,' Jodry protested, but then: 'I will try.'

Thirty-One

Gjegevey had been told that the Great College of Collegium, that city of revolution which had thrown off its Moth-kinden overlords almost five and a half centuries earlier, maintained an Inapt studies department where the intrepid could still go to learn about the old ways, the ancient times and magic. The Wasps, of course, had nothing of the sort. To them the past was dead, the present and the future the only prizes worth studying.

Seda herself had gathered a piecemeal library of old Moth and Dragonfly texts, and Gjegevey had sent members of her staff across the city to the collections of veteran officers and Consortium magnates, confiscating anything that might be of use. And he had read, and read. He was looking for anything that the Empress might accept as a substitute for the lure of the Worm. The Lowlands, after all, had a rich history of magic, for all that it was buried under so many years of Aptitude. There must be *some* survival there, some fount of power that the Moths jealously guarded, some other knot of old time, such as the Darakyon forest had been before it was laid to rest.

He would have given anything for even an hour's communion with his own people's great library, where such secrets were certainly held. He had even considered asking Seda for permission to return home for just that. Prudence had warned him off the idea, though. He was not one of his own people any more. For all that he had come to this city as their spy, disguised as a slave, now he was far more Seda's slave, with no disguise needed. He suspected that he would not even be allowed into his people's strongholds, and if he was . . . would the Empire itself be far away? Gjegevey's Woodlouse-kinden lived on the Wasps' very border, only their inhospitable rotting terrain and outsiders' perception that they had nothing worth taking had kept them free from overlords, taxes and levies. If Seda ever found out what a wealth of knowledge they had hoarded in those swamps, then she would indeed have something other than the Worm to aim for.

So he had rooted and grubbed through ancient histories of the Lowlands, cracking, flaking parchments and vellums, dust-laden books and faded scrolls. As Seda had complained, the Moths never wrote anything the simple way, and the Dragonflies were just as bad in their own fashion, but he had bookmarks and notes now, signalling the possibility of survivals and hidden caches. Yet he needed help.

The knock sounded, as expected, for the man would have been too curious to stay away. At Gjegevey's invitation, he entered the cluttered little storeroom that the Woodlouse had made his own, even as Gjegevey turned up the wick on a lamp to let the man see. Up until then, the crooked old Woodlouse had been reading in utter darkness, as comfortable with the pitch black as a Moth.

'Ambassador Tegrec, thank you for, ah, joining me.'

The newcomer was a Wasp-kinden but robed in the Moth style. He had once been an army major who had schemed his way into being made the governor of the Moth city of Tharn which the Wasps had taken over almost as an afterthought, owing to its proximity to Helleron. Covertly, as Gjegevey knew, he had also been a magician, Inapt as Seda was, although Tegrec had been so from birth. In Tharn he had turned his coat and aided the Moths in performing the ritual that had driven out their conquerors, as well as inflicting madness and death upon many of the locals, as Gjegevey understood. Despite his treason,

482

he had been permitted to return to Capitas as the Moths' own ambassador. His position in the Empress's court was an uncertain one, both a diplomat from a neutral power – if the Moths even counted as such – and one of the Inapt who had in recent times found a tenuous new home in the Empress's shadow. He entered the room cautiously, as he did every room in the palace, not sitting down when Gjegevey offered the solitary free chair. In appearance he was a soft man, without a soldier's hard physique, but if he could live alongside the Moths, his mind must be sharp as a dagger.

He would also be as close-mouthed as his Moth-kinden masters, Gjegevey knew, and there was no time to woo him subtly to the cause. Only a direct approach would serve.

'The Empress is seeking to break the Seal of the Worm.'

The words hung between them like a corpse, and Gjegevey left them turning there for a long while before continuing.

'I am, hm, telling this not to the Tharen ambassador, but to a fellow magician who must *know*' – and it was plain from Tegrec's pale face that he did – 'how unwise this might, ahm, turn out to be.'

Tegrec took the offered seat after all. Gjegevey wondered what the man really knew, for surely he had only been allowed to burrow shallowly into the Moth mysteries. Enough to know of the Worm, apparently, and the danger it represented.

'Why would she do that?'

Gjegevey sighed, seeming just the doddering old scholar, his fingers pattering idly on the desktop. 'Oh, well, she is, ah, responsible for her people. She seeks to defend them from all dangers and, hm, now that her eyes have been opened to our wider world, she wishes to be able to protect them from such threats as might be brought by the, hrm, Inapt, even as she does threats from the Apt.' It was a necessary equivocation. 'She sees the Seal as the means to that end. I, hm, have taken it upon myself to find her an alternative.'

Tegrec's look suggested that he did not envy Gjegevey this

role. 'What is this to me, in whatever capacity? What do you ask for?'

'Knowledge,' Gjegevey said simply.

'Not something freely given, anywhere.'

'Then consider me in your, hrm, debt, if that helps. Or perhaps consider just what might be waiting behind the Seal, if she goes ahead with her plans.'

'Perhaps nothing.' Tegrec tried a flippant shrug, and did not quite manage it.

'You don't believe that,' Gjegevey observed. 'I have combed every scrap of old Lowlander lore that I can lay these old, ahm, hands on. I have listed each fount of power, each totemic site, each haunt of, hem, ritual, but we both know that your adopted people are unreliable in what they, hm, commit to paper. Help me, Ambassador: guide my hand.'

For a long moment Tegrec looked at him, his expression as arch and distant as any Moth's, but then he rolled his eyes. 'Let's hear your list,' he said.

And Gjegevey took him through it, some nineteen leads teased from the appendices of history, each one seeming a flower waiting to be plucked by one of sufficient pedigree and will, and each time Tegrec shook his head, sometimes dignifying the suggestion with a terse dismissal, sometimes not even that. The situation was worse than Gjegevey had thought.

The Tharen Moths themselves would have their secret caches of strength, of course, if their ritual against the Imperial occupiers had left them any, but Tegrec was hardly about to assist him in that direction. For the rest . . . the golden history of the pre-revolution Lowlands was merely fool's gold, it seemed nowadays, and he should have known not to trust his sources. The Moths did not set down their losses, as the tide of history turned on them. Oh, *they* would know what to credit and what to discount in their writings, a secret code that must have misled and bewildered a hundred scholars and fortune hunters prior to poor Gjegevey, but, as their influence had shrunk, their glorious

484

places of power grown dim or built over by the Apt, they had simply not updated the maps and gazetteers that showed their world. To put such matters in writing would have been a symbolic concession of a defeat that even now they refused to admit. Tegrec's knowledge might only be limited, but it was enough to snuff out each item on Gjegevey's list in short order, leaving the two men staring glumly at each other.

And then Tegrec said a name: 'Argastos.'

Gjegevey frowned, ill-tempered after constant fruitless searching. 'There is no mention of an Argastos anywhere I've looked.'

'Perhaps not,' Tegrec replied grimly. 'I'll bet there's no mention of the Darakyon, either, but you can't deny that place had power. The Moths do not openly chronicle their failures.' He smiled slightly at the Woodlouse-kinden's expression. 'Oh, you're thinking along the right lines, but against the Worm, what can we do? He was a Moth . . . warlord is perhaps the best word, if you can imagine that. He dwelt amongst the Mantis-kinden of the Etheryon and the Nethyon before they were two separate holds. He was a lord there, and he led the Moth war-host, I think, but he was beholden to nobody.'

'A magician of power?'

'Oh, yes, one of the Great Names, and you know what weight my people place on names.' And if the Moths were not genu-inely "his" people, Gjegevey said nothing of it.

'He left something of his power behind?' the Woodlouse pressed.

'Gjegevey, he's still there, the way they tell it. There is a heart of the wood between Etheryon and Nethyon where the locals don't go, where his stronghold stood, or stands – or his tomb perhaps. They don't write of it, but something happened: either the other Moths came for him, or he himself did something, but now . . . he is still there, in some manner. You understand me.'

For a long while, Gjegevey considered this, and his face clearly indicated the thought, *But better than the Worm, surely.*

485

Then he asked, almost brightly, 'What is the attitude of the, hm, Ancient League and Tharn, regarding this?'

He saw immediately that Tegrec had deliberately steered the conversation this way, and wondered just how much of a Moth the man had become. 'Divided, old man, all of it: Tharn from the League, Tharn within itself, the League within itself, and its attitudes to the Empire likewise not yet finalized. But becoming more united with the progress of the Eighth Army. Every step that General Roder takes is turning them against you.'

'Then . . . ?'

'Are you asking for an intercession from Tharn? Are you asking the Moths of Tharn to assist you in this quest of yours? Then halt the Eighth while we negotiate or, Worm or no, she will not get what she wants.'

Gjegevey regarded him with half-lidded eyes. 'You are well appointed by your masters, Ambassador. They have a shrewd agent in you.'

'I learned more of that right here in Capitas than I ever did in Tharn. So, can you do it?'

'The Empress will trust my advice,' Gjegevey declared, with all the confidence he could muster, before opening the door to usher Tegrec out. A knot of Wasp soldiers was revealed beyond: hard, scowling men in the armour of the Light Airborne.

And Gjegevey thought only, *It's happened at last*, then, *But not now!*

There was an open palm aimed at him, and he retreated back into the study, the soldiers pressing in too, crowding the small room.

'Well, now, two traitors,' said their leader.

'The Empress—' Gjegevey got out, and then the open palm was suddenly in motion, slapping him hard enough to pitch him over the desktop, scattering fragile books and scrolls onto the floor.

'Take them both,' the soldier said. 'Show them the instruments, and then lock them up. Let them reflect on how the Rekef exists to protect the throne from creatures such as them.'

'A toast,' proposed Colonel Harvang, 'to governance guided by strength.' He emptied his goblet, tossing the contents down his gaping throat and spattering his tunic.

General Brugan nodded soberly, his own brandy untouched. All over the palace his men were in motion even now. All suspects were being rounded up for the Rekef cells, all the mongrels and lesser races that the Empress inexplicably chose to associate with, taken to where they could do no more harm, and held ready for disposal later. The list had been surprisingly long, from long-time advisers like doddering old Gjegevey all the way down to dubious servants, Commonwealer slaves. *It's just as well we've stopped the rot here.*

But, of course, that was barely the true reason, in his heart of hearts. He, Harvang and Vecter had just come from a full meeting of the conspirators. His collection of Consortium magnates, army officers and Rekef men were now out doing his bidding, and they all believed that this was simply about building a wall between the Empress and such undesirables, with themselves installed as gatekeepers of course. *But it's not about that.* It was about control. Taking control of *her.* Taking back control of his own life.

She had called him to her, last night. He still felt the shudder inside him, recalling the blood she had offered him, in a goblet finer than the one holding his brandy. Then the sense of something vital being leached from him, as her skin met his . . . and yet he could not stay away from her. He *wanted* her, but he needed to redefine the terms on which he tasted her. He needed to make her *his,* for at the moment he was far more *hers.*

'General?' Harvang prompted, and he knew he had missed something – a bad failing in any high-ranking Wasp, and especially a Rekef general. He glanced from Harvang to neat little Vecter, and tried to recapture the echo of what had been said.

'Ostrec,' he agreed, almost heartily. It was a stab in the dark, but Harvang's expression – a little too much relief for comfort – reassured him. The young major was lurking near the door, looking bland in his Quartermaster Corps uniform. He was quite the favourite with the Empress, Brugan knew, and that knowledge made him grind his teeth. *Someone else for the cells, sooner or later. If only Harvang wasn't so fond of him.* There would be a time, though, when Ostrec slipped out of the greasy orbit of the colonel, and then he would disappear, sinking without trace.

'We owe you a great deal, Major,' Brugan declared, beckoning the younger man to approach. 'You've managed to work up quite a list of names. The Empire thanks you, and so do I.'

'Merely my duty, General,' Ostrec replied smoothly.

Brugan suppressed a scowl. 'All her mystics and hangers-on will be under lock and key before the day is out. The real test will come when we take her bodyguards. Mantis-kinden are too unpredictable. Having them within her presence is asking for trouble. After all, the Eighth is fighting the Mantis-kinden right now.'

'The old Woodlouse was saying that we had to order the Eighth to hold its ground,' Vecter observed, with a raised eyebrow.

Harvang snorted. 'And why? Because the moon was in the wrong phase, or he'd seen a particularly foreboding shadow, no doubt.'

'Something to do with worms.' Vecter dismissed the thought with a flick of his hand.

Ostrec was still standing before Brugan, and for a moment his expression . . . no, not his expression, which was as placid as could be, but there was some shift, as though his face had been momentarily translucent, some other drowned features twitching beneath them. Brugan blinked, feeling ill with the dislocation of it. Nothing was amiss: it was Ostrec, nobody but Ostrec, now looking at him in concern.

'General?'

'That will be all,' Brugan said, too forcefully. *I have to get control before it's too late. She's ruining me,* rattled through his head.

'You, and me,' Scain said, without warning. The Farsphex pilots and their bombardiers had been drawn up in neat ranks beside their machines on the makeshift field that the Second Army had cleared for them that day. Pingge jumped guiltily: there had been quite a long silence and her mind had wandered, and only now did she realize that the Wasps had been conferring.

'What was that, sir?' she whispered.

'Going to talk with the general.'

'*What*, sir?' Heads turned to look and she gritted her teeth.

'We are mounting a delegation to General Tynan. He has some orders for us: a new phase of the war,' Scain murmured. 'We get to go.'

But I don't want *to meet a general,* was a useless comment, and of course she did not say it. Pingge was nervous, though. A ripple of some kind of emotion had passed through the Wasp-kinden, one and all. Aarmon was doing something risky.

'Come on.' Scain stood forward, still just a gangling young Wasp-kinden, for all the flying and fighting experience he had lived through. Pingge saw Kiin pattering forward too, saluting at Aarmon's beckoning gesture, and from further down the ranks came Sergeant Nishaana and her bombardier Tiadro.

'*She's* coming too. Scain . . . I mean, sir?'

Scain looked back at her with a slight smile. 'Aarmon says they can take us as they find us,' he told her.

Six of them: two Wasp men, a Wasp woman, two Fly women and one Fly man, they marched smartly through the great sprawling camp that the Second Army and the Aldanrael forces had established between them. If it had not been for the Spiders, then Pingge guessed fingers would have been pointing from the first moment, but the brightly coloured variety of the Spiderlands troops provided a camouflage that almost anything could have hidden against. Nishaana drew a few glances from soldiers who had not seen a woman of their own kinden for some while who wasn't a whore, but there was none of the comments, jeers and lewd suggestions that Pingge had been expecting. Compared with the Empire's new allies, the aviators were positively normal.

Of course, Aarmon's thunderous glower might have contributed to their reticence, she decided. For most of their way through the camp she could not work out what the man was up to. Only as they were practically at the general's tent did she guess at it: their branch of the Engineers was both new and different, in a society that was suspicious of the first quality and outright hostile towards the second. A division of mind-linked soldiers using experimental machinery and taking on such an unprecedented selection of recruits would already have gathered many enemies back home, for no other reason than just how very new and how very different they were. Faced with that, Aarmon would have had two options: he could work to minimize the outward show, bow his head, hope to be overlooked, or he could look his detractors in the eye and dare them. *And no prizes for guessing which way he's jumped.*

The welcoming committee within the tent was also some way from Imperial standard. General Tynan, nothing more than a bald and ageing Wasp with a fancy rank badge to Pingge's eyes, stood with proper military decorum in the centre of the tent's interior, an easel beside him with maps tacked on and annotated. Beside him, though, an elegant Spider-kinden woman reclined on a couch, attended by a couple of Fly-kinden men, while there were two more Spiders, both men and well armoured, right behind her. On the general's other side were a pair of colonels, a thin one with the badge of the Engineers and a stockier one that she already knew as Cherten of Army Intelligence.

'Major Aarmon.' Tynan received Aarmon's pinpoint salute, even as his eyes flicked over the aviators' delegation. He nodded slightly, and Pingge saw the Spider woman smile a little in acknowledgement of the newcomers' bravado. *But, of course, the Spiders have women soldiers, more of them than the men, and they've been marching with the Second for tendays. This is probably the most receptive audience Aarmon's likely to get.*

'Your people are winning a lot of credit for the Engineers, I understand,' Tynan observed, 'both for your machines and your training. You've made quite an impact. On the enemy as well, I'm sure.' It was not a joke and nobody smiled. 'I'm aware that you're not a standard army detachment.' His eyes made brief reference to the Fly-kinden and Neshaana. 'If you've come here to fight that battle, then take it elsewhere. I don't care. I have a city to capture, and the composition of your force is of no importance to me, so long as you do your job.'

'Yes, sir,' said Aarmon, stiff-backed and outmanoeuvred.

'What you need to know is that there have been developments back home regarding the engineers and your resources.'

'Sir?'

Pingge could almost sense the words passing swiftly between Aarmon and Scain and Neshaana, and the other pilots back at the impromptu airfield.

'Colonel Mittoc?' Tynan prompted his underling.

'Hm.' the skinny engineer nodded rapidly, 'General Lien has finally decided to trust us with a consignment of your fuel. It arrived yesterday, for my personal supervision. All very secret, not to let the enemy get hold of, and so on.' His annoyance at being kept in ignorance was plain on his face. 'However, it's here now, which means no more long hauls to Capitas for you. As of now you're operating from wherever the Second camp, and it's only a hop from here to Collegium, I'm sure. You understand what this means?'

'Yes, sir. Endgame,' Aarmon said coolly.

'Well put, Major.' Tynan took over. 'We will be engaging the ground forces of the Collegiates shortly, and then the battle will move to the walls. Your mission now is twofold: you are to continue your attacks on the city, but you must also target their air power wherever possible, as an absolute priority. And when we begin to take down their walls you must screen the army, and especially the artillery, from air attack. I leave the specifics to you, but the elimination of the enemy air power is paramount. At any cost, you understand?'

There was a second's pause before Aarmon replied, 'I do, sir.' Pingge did not have to be a part of the pilots' communion to understand. *This is it then. This is when they throw us into the fire.* And she thought of the skill and determination of the Collegiate airmen, and wondered how many people she knew would be dead within a tenday.

Thirty-Two

This time, when Averic returned to his meagre lodgings, after a day's drilling with the Student Company and still wearing his purple sash, the lock on his door had simply been smashed.

Thieves, he thought first, but in his heart of hearts he knew otherwise. He had been trying to forget the Wasp woman who had come with her brown-dyed face, and told him he was a traitor, and he had been all along. She had marched away with the army, after all, and the episode had taken on a dreamlike quality, for of course he was *not* a traitor, not to anyone.

Yet he had spent his day drilling with Collegiates who fully intended to kill as many Wasp-kinden as they could, should the fight draw this close and, if he were to subject his position to the philosophical rigour beloved of the academics, he would have to confess that he was surely betraying *someone*. It was just that, so long as he attached his loyalties to the nearest available target, he could pretend that he was unshakably honourable and honest. These were qualities he had always assumed that he possessed, but now he was forcibly reminded that apparently it had all been an act.

Not the woman waiting for him, this time, of course, but a man: a Beetle with burn-scarring about his face. He sat on Averic's bed, wearing the hardwearing patchwork canvas of a tramp artificer, cleaning his nails with a knife and grinning at the Wasp youth standing in the doorway.

'Come on in, why don't you,' he suggested.

Averic directed a palm towards him wordlessly, but his lack of resolution must have shown very plainly in his face, for the man's grin never faltered.

'Very nice, always the posing. Now get over here and take your orders, boy. Stop pissing about.'

By accent, the stranger could have passed for a Collegiate.

'You're Army Intelligence?' Averic asked, in a small voice.

'Right in one. Expecting some sly Rekef bastard, I'll bet. We're ahead of them on this one, and you should be grateful. Rather deal with us than with them, I'll bet. Sit down here beside me, youngster.' He patted the bed with his free hand.

Averic shuddered, unable even to identify the emotions fighting within him, and then he slouched forward and sat down, feeling obscenely like a prostitute before a client. When the man put a heavy arm about his shoulders, he yelped and tried to spring up. The Beetle was strong, though, and the knife was close.

'I hear you're deep cover,' the Beetle gave a smirk that gave onto a world of insinuation. 'Listen, boy, it's all going to come down any day now. We all do our part, the city gets its Imperial governor, and it's commendations all round. This is Intelligence's big chance, before the Rekef boys try to foul things for us. We all pull together, we Imperials.'

'You're no Imperial,' Averic whispered. It was the accent: it was simply too genuine.

'Clever lad. I was in the Empire for almost ten years before coming back here. You Wasps, you know how to run things, and how to look after your own. Flap-mouthed gutbags that run this place – would you trust any one of them? Do you really think they know the first thing about how to make a city go? Piss on them. Sick of this place when I left, I was, and twice as sick of it now I'm back. But that's fine, because it's going to be my sort of place any day now. And yours, too. I've my eyes on a lieutenancy, and I reckon you could scrape sergeant out of this. Could even stay in the College, if there's still enough of it left, and if we let them teach still.' Horribly, inappropriately, he hugged Averic to him. 'Now, boy, our work is all about targets, foci of resistance. The people here will fight – surprised me with that, they have – but we cut off a few heads and they'll fall apart. No chain of command, see.'

'What do you want me to do?' Averic asked dully.

'Cut throats, boy. Burn them. Stick them with a sword. Dead leaders make poor tacticians, as we say. And, as you're here on the inside, you're going to be perfectly placed to catch them off guard. Sure, the Big Men around here, they're out of your range, but you're well placed for some College Masters who won't be suspicious about a student turning up for a little extracurricular, eh?' The Beetle chuckled throatily. 'See here, here's your homework, boy.' He thrust a tattered scroll at Averic.

Averic stared numbly at the list, a meagre handful of Collegiate names, all they would trust him with, set against the grander tapestry of men and women the Empire wanted dead. Treachery seemed to be welling up inside him. *So I was an agent all this time*, he found himself thinking sadly. The Empress expected, apparently, and even at this distance her awful might seemed to weigh on him more than the Beetle's arm. He tried to picture his parents, to review their parting words, parse them for some hint that this had been their plan all along.

He found that he could barely bring their likenesses to mind.

He saw the names of four lecturers who had taught him, three of whom had plainly resented doing so. *Oh how I'll make them twitch when they find out I'm no victim to be slighted. How I shall get even with them.* But there was no fire in that thought. He could not muster the bitterness. Instead he foresaw the acts involved: saw himself stepping through a sequence of patient murders with the same focused attention he had applied to all of his College work. The burned man was right. For all their sneers and insults, they would never expect him to come after them.

He felt full of a venom that had corrupted him without him knowing. Reaching the end of the list, he closed his eyes.

'Bold and swift and bloody,' came the voice of the Beetle-kinden. 'Say it.'

'Bold and swift and bloody,' Averic echoed. He was holding himself deliberately still, because otherwise he would be shaking. He had read to the end of the names, the last addition seeming almost like an afterthought.

The bed lurched as the man stood up suddenly. 'When the army breaks the wall, surrender to the first soldiers you see, ask to be brought to Colonel Cherten for debriefing. They'll spot you for one of their own. I'll have a tougher job, believe me. We won't meet again before then.' He clapped Averic on the shoulder, startling the youth into opening his eyes, staring up into the man's own gaze with a determination tempered like steel.

'Good boy,' the Beetle said, approving, and then he was at the doorway. 'Good luck.' And he was gone.

Still sitting in that dingy, wretched room, Averic stared after him, only now allowing himself to start to shake. *Traitor, I'm a traitor after all this time.* Any doubt had fled him, leaving only a terrible emptiness in its wake. He was going to betray them all.

Eujen Leadswell, was the last name on the list, surely only added after the Student Company had been formed.

In a small study, almost lost in the upper storeys of the Amphiophos, far from the main bustle of governance, Jodry Drillen stared at the desk before him.

'I can't,' he said. 'I've changed my mind.'

'Nothing's changed,' Stenwold told him. 'If we agreed before, we agree now. It's necessary.'

'I didn't have *this* in front of me before,' Jodry whispered. The room was ill lit, neglected, more a storeroom for unwanted records than a place for scholars or Assemblers. 'Stenwold . . . they're never going to forgive me.' The man's pudgy hands were shaking, rattling the Speaker's seal and the reservoir pen.

'Then let me,' Stenwold decided. 'I'm used to the city thinking ill of me. Now that everyone agrees with me, I don't know where to put myself.' He managed tp raise the ghost of a smile, but Jodry merely shook his head.

'It must be *me*,' the Speaker said, 'because it must be obeyed. If we cannot have a full decision of the Assembly – and we can't, I know – then I must put my hand to it.'

'Then do it. And then I'll sign it, too. All the authority we can provide, and the blame can be shared. I'll say I forced you to it, if you want.'

'What will I say to them, Stenwold? The relatives, the homeless. I never thought of this happening, when I put my name forward in the Lots. I never thought that I'd be responsible for . . . that I'd fail them and do so knowingly, eyes open. I thought it would all be trade disputes and paperwork.'

'You're doing well,' Stenwold told him solemnly. 'Better than I'd have thought. But I wouldn't ask this of you, if it wasn't needed.'

Jodry nodded tiredly. 'Banjacs is ready?'

'He will be by tomorrow night.'

The fat man looked up at him, horrified. 'He says that? He'd *better* be ready. I've written him an open pass to the cursed Assembly *Treasury* to get his bloody machine working. If he pisses away the chance we're buying him – at such cost! – I'll strangle the old bastard myself!' A deep breath. 'And their agents?'

'Those that I have identified have been passed the story, by the most indirect channels I could devise. Word should already be heading for the Second, regarding our problems, our weaknesses. And tonight will bear that word out.'

'Will it? And we're gambling on what you think they'll think? Why not, given all the other things we're throwing the dice on? Why not, indeed?'

Stenwold regarded at him without any words of comfort or consolation – and he sensed that Jodry did not want to be

497

comforted, did not believe that he deserved it. They were about a terrible business, a betrayal of their own for reasons of brutal pragmatism, and both of them felt the brand of it burning their skin.

Jodry took the seal, clicked at the top until it welled with red wax, and then stamped it down hard. A shudder went through him, but he took up the pen and signed boldly, with hardly a quiver, before moving on to the next document. Stenwold took out his own pen and added his name to each in turn, the Speaker and the War Master – as much weight as they could give to their conspiracy.

The first order differed from the others, addressed to the Sarse Way airfield, and it read: *By the order of the Assembly of Collegium under the emergency powers granted for the time being the Sarse Way contingent of the Collegiate Air Defence are ordered to: engage the enemy air forces when so prompted by the Great Ear; upon engagement fall back towards the city; upon reaching the skies above the city remain in contact with the enemy for no longer than ten minutes before seeking to land and take shelter; during the course of all contact with the enemy concentrate on preserving yourselves and your machines in priority to attacking the enemy. Further, you are not to return to the defence once you have quit the fight.*

The pilots of Sarse Way would assume that this was some manoeuvre involving a counter-attack by the complements of the other airfields, and would obey dutifully, relieved perhaps to be out of the fighting early and trusting to men such as Jodry and Stenwold to know what was best.

The other missives were all identical and, under the same heading, gave the order: *Do not take wing under any circumstances. You are expressly ordered to keep your machines under cover and out of sight. You are instructed not to participate in any action against the air forces of the Empire on this night, without exception.*

Jodry and Stenwold stared at each other, and at last the fat man folded each order, sealing them one by one with more bloody wax, and reached out to summon Arvi.

'No,' Stenwold told him.

'What? If Arvi's a traitor then anyone is,' Jodry snapped.

'I will take them myself,' Stenwold told him. 'I will instruct the officers not to open them until dark. They will see me and know me. There will be no possibility that this might be an Imperial ploy. We are losing too much, by this, to risk any compromising of our plan.'

'And after that?' Jodry asked him.

'I will go home,' Stenwold explained. 'And I will wait there, and listen, and live with the knowledge.'

The nearest Wasp soldier touched down only yards away from Laszlo's hiding place, stalking through the gnarled, scrubby trees that were barely taller than the man himself: a knotty little grove of stunted olive trees sprouting where some fault in the earth gave them access to water. To a Wasp, only the trees would offer any cover at all, but the ground was loose and crumbling about the roots, and Laszlo had been able to excavate a hollow down beneath one of the trees, digging and digging frantically during the last two hours of the night, bitterly aware that their time was up. Beside him, Liss stirred, biting her lip, and Laszlo could not say whether her shivering was from fear or the fever of her wound.

They had made good time at first, and he thought now that had been their downfall: becoming overconfident, and without a clear idea of how far they would have to go, they had made a clipping pace down the coast, whilst the Second Army stayed back to bludgeon the Felyal into a final submission. They had kept within sight of the sea at first, to aid in navigation and in the hope of spying a ship. There were no sails or funnels to be seen, though. Everything east was black and gold, and no trader trusted the waters.

Lissart had seemed well, in that first rush, or at least she had pretended to be, and they had gone too fast too soon, pressing on into the dark hours so as to increase their lead. Then one night, as they made a sparse but sheltered camp, he had seen her dabbing at her side, and he realized that her wound had reopened. She had done her best to make light of it but, despite everything, he had seen she was terrified of being left behind. The next morning he set a slower pace, but she had not been equal to even that.

She had managed another few days' progress, each slower than the last, and then she had negotiated with him, desperately manoeuvring around her own weakness until he himself suggested a day's pause. Looking into her face, he saw how her cheeks were hollower, her skin almost translucent. She was beautiful still, though, illness giving her an ethereal quality that made her seem almost supernatural.

At first, they had steered clear of the refugees who had fled the ruin of the Felyal, and that had been another mistake. Liss had been suspicious of them, in her eyes every strange face hiding an Imperial agent, or perhaps just a murderer or a rapist. She hated being helpless and raged weakly at herself.

Later, when the last of the refugees had been overtaking them, Laszlo had tried to seek help, but those desperate stragglers had none to offer.

The Second Army had taken its time with the Felyal, but all too soon its work was done, and it began marching westwards at the speed of its laden automotives – faster than Laszlo and poor Liss could manage. The two Flies had covered what ground they could, desperate to stay just another day ahead. Behind them had appeared a distant dust cloud, yet less distant every day.

And, of course, the armies of the Empire did not travel blind. Yesterday Laszlo had seen flitting forms in the sky, as the Light Airborne screened the army's advance. They were far ahead of their main force, a spread of eyes and burning hands searching for any sign of organized resistance, well tutored by the losses suffered by the Imperial forces in the last war, pitted against the bandits and renegades of the Landsarmy.

The soldier so close by shifted position, a few steps forwards, boots crunching on the dry earth. Laszlo guessed there were ten or a dozen that had dropped out of the sky moments ago, seeing the trees as good ground for an ambush and hoping to flush out any threats lurking there. The man was right on the edge of Laszlo's window on the world, which was uncomfortably broad, for he had not been able to dig deep under the tree. There was barely room for the two of them to shelter from the sky. *If we had run, would we still be ahead?*

Could we even have run?

There was a painful stab in his heart that told him that all this effort might be for nothing. Lissart had suffered a terrible wound, and she had been flagging since they left Solarno. She was a fickle, treacherous creature, but Laszlo had gone to such lengths to save her – from the enemy, from herself – surely blind chance would not throw the dice so heavily against them now. *We've come so far.*

In all his days, as pirate, trader and agent, he had assumed at some level that the world was looking out for him. His luck had brought him plenty of good times, and that had always let him ride out the bad times with the understanding that he would still make it through. Now that they had come so far, at such effort, and only lost ground, Laszlo's faith in himself was faltering.

The Wasp took another few steps, shifting fully into the Fly's view now, his back towards the hiding place as he scanned the trees with a snapbow cradled in his arms. His head turned, receiving some gestured signal from a comrade, and he settled down on one knee, watching.

What have they seen? Either the Imperials were setting an ambush themselves, or they were suspicious of encountering one. *Did we leave a trail? Is it us they're looking for?* He had been so hurried, last night. He had done his best to cover their tracks, but still . . .

His hand inched into his tunic, a finger at a time. His one remaining sleevebow was in there, the other little snapbow fallen out unnoticed somewhere along the trail. With excruciating care he began to extract it. Seeing him do so, Liss went tense all over.

The Wasp remained still, weapon held low, merely cautious as yet, and facing the wrong way. Laszlo worked the snapbow free of his clothes, not daring to take his eyes off the man, letting his fingers walk over its chamber, to check that there was a bolt loaded. Then he had the wheel of the air-lock to charge, breathing shallowly, hunching about himself, slowly winding the battery up to strength, his wrists cramping from the awkward angle.

A second soldier crossed into his line of sight, more distant than the first. His wings shimmered briefly, as though he was about to take flight, but something stayed him, and he put his shoulder to a tree, to hide or for cover, and watched keenly. The first man remained motionless, the dusty black and gold of his cuirass blending with the earth tones of the soil and bark and dull leaves.

There came a shout from further off and both men tensed, the closer one fitting his snapbow to his shoulder but not sighting along the barrel, clearly still without a target. The further soldier peered out, half-crouching as he searched for the enemy, then he glanced at his companion to say something, to give a signal, who could know?

His eyes touched Laszlo.

Laszlo tried to jump up but their hollow was too cramped. He kicked forwards into the open air, even as the warning came, bringing his little snapbow to bear not on the man who had seen him, but on the closer soldier, clenching hard on the trigger.

He felt the weapon buck lopsidedly in his hand, jamming

with the charge not yet released. Frantically he shook it, his wings taking him left.

A bolt of fire streaked past from behind him – almost directly through the space he had occupied a moment before – and caught the closer Wasp right in the eyes, sending him backwards, screaming and clawing at his face. A snapbow bolt zipped past Laszlo like an angry insect, and he let his wings spring him high over the trees for a little cover, before coming down close enough for his weapon to do any good, if it would only work.

He loosed, and something struck him on the temple, something else carving a bloody line across his hand and almost up to his elbow. He found himself flat on his back, the world spinning about him. *They got me! Was that a grenade?*

He was being shaken. 'Get up!' Liss was hissing, dragging at his shoulder. 'Get moving!' She held her other arm about her, as though trying to keep her guts in.

Laszlo stumbled to his feet, seeing the soldier lying dead before him, armour holed where the snapbow bolt had gone in. He still clutched the grip of the little weapon, but precious little more of it. Its air battery had exploded, he realized, and there was his luck back again because that could have taken his arm off.

Then more Wasps came pelting through the trees, three at least: two on the ground and one in flight. Pushing Liss ahead of him, Laszlo tried to run, dagger clearing his belt. She made a game try of it but she was slowing already, her breaths coming in gasps of pain. *Cheers, luck, nice knowing you.*

Laszlo brandished his little blade and tried to put fire in his expression, anything to buy Lissart a moment's time. The airborne Wasp was almost on them, snapbow slung and hand extended.

Piss on my luck!

Fine last words for a pirate.

Then there was a flicker and the soldier was down, rolling on the ground with the spine of an arrow standing proud in him. The other Wasps suddenly had more to think about, whipping their snapbows around, but the trees were already echoing to the harsh *snap! snap!* of bolts clipping between the trees too fast to see. The two Wasps were on the ground in moments, and more fighting erupted all around. Laszlo had no eyes for it.

Liss was sitting with her back to a tree, breasts rising and falling as she fought for air, but she gripped his hand when he went to her, her palm still warm from her Art.

The skirmish went on for less than a minute and when a shadow fell over the two of them it was no Wasp but a long-faced Dragonfly-kinden woman wearing the buff coat of the Merchant Companies, a bow as tall as she was in one hand.

Laszlo identified the sash emblem, an Ant-kinden helm in profile.

'Coldstone Company,' he named it. 'Collegium.'

The Dragonfly nodded suspiciously. Others were joining her now, a couple of Beetles, a handful more – Flies, a Moth with a shortbow in a holster at her waist.

'Castre Gorenn, Commonweal Retaliatory Army, currently serving with the Coldstone,' said the Dragonfly archer. 'And what are you?'

'Working for Ma— Stenwold Maker,' Laszlo said, stumbling over the name in his hurry to present his credentials. 'Please – your army's close by?'

'Not so very close,' Castre Gorenn replied, still not trusting either of them an inch. 'We'll get you there sure enough, though. Collegium agents, Imperial agents – don't really care – works either way for me.'

'She's hurt,' Laszlo met Liss's eyes. 'Can you . . .'

Gorenn knelt to study Liss, and for a moment the Dragonfly's easy expression turned grim at the sight of her, making something twist almost to breaking in Laszlo's chest, but then the woman nodded.

'I can fly with her, certainly. Nobody flies like me.' With

surprising delicacy the Dragonfly reached for Liss, who flinched and whimpered, but nevertheless held still as she was picked up like a child. 'You've your own wings, to keep up?'

'Of course.'

'Of course, is it? Well, Master "Of Course", there'll be a couple of these newfangled snappers held on you the whole time, so you better keep your mind on what you're doing.'

Thirty-Three

Eujen Leadswell lodged over a bookbinder's in a well-appointed room that just about scraped a view of the College rooftops, and which he tended to forget was paid for by the stipend he received each moon from his parents, merchants in the beer trade. He was back late tonight, having spent the last hour wrangling with a Master of the social history faculty who had taken issue over his Student Company. Their meeting had not gone well. She had ordered him to dissolve the force, and he had outright refused, and now the matter would apparently go before the head of faculty, or possibly the administrator. Eujen rather suspected that the promised reprimand would arrive some time after the war finished, and at that late point he would be glad to receive it.

He stomped up the stairs to his room – he had his own outside door, more for the convenience of the bookbinder than Eujen's – and shouldered his way in, feeling disgruntled and angry. A moment's fiddling with the gaslamps turned up a rosy glow – and Averic.

Eujen started back with a choked-off cry of alarm, finding his friend standing in the darkness of his own room, unbidden and unlooked for. His first thought, and he was ashamed by it, was *Wasp assassin.*

And Averic's manner, quite aside from this trespass, was not reassuring. The Wasp stared at Eujen as though he had never quite seen him before. The intruder's hands were empty, open, hanging by his side, but Eujen was suddenly aware of the *danger* that Averic represented, simply by virtue of his kinden. *Killing hands.* No wonder, his traitor imagination informed him, they were feared so, having taken the advantage of their Art and become . . .

'Averic?' he asked, his voice creditably calm. For a moment, a silence stretched between them, and then the Great Ear began its monotonous wail outside, and they both looked to the window.

'Here we go again,' Eujen's words came out automatically, disassociated from any part of the awkward space between him and the Wasp. And Averic's followed: 'They're going to kill you.'

Eujen couldn't quite understand what had been said, and just made a questioning grunt.

'The Rekef – or Army Intelligence – the Empire wants to kill you.'

Then Eujen understood that the 'you' was singular, not plural. Not the Beetle-kinden, not the people of Collegium, but *him*.

But why . . . ? But what . . . ? 'But how do you know?'

'Because they told me to do it.'

The moment teetered between them, and every intellectual instinct but one demanded that Eujen flee or fight. The war was here in his room. The war had come to him. The man before him was not Averic. He, Eujen, had been wrong.

'But you're not going to,' he said, and this time his voice finally shook, but he had cast the die. *Live by the sword.* All that time claiming that the Empire – that the Wasps – were redeemable, and he would trust it with his weight now, though the fall would kill him if he was wrong.

'For you,' Averic said simply, 'I betray my people – my family, my kinden – for you.'

The first explosion struck five streets away and still made

the windows rattle, both of them starting at the flash and the roar.

'Eujen,' Averic insisted. 'There are Imperial killers in the city. They are going to be targeting people – we need to tell someone. They gave me some names, but there'll be others. I made a list, everyone I could think of.'

Eujen had opened his mouth, trying to fit all that into his head, when the next bombs struck, one after the other, ten or twelve of them, killing all words, rattling the walls, each slightly quieter than the last as the barrage tracked across the city. Even as Eujen tried to reply, a further bombardment followed, the retorts overlapping so that it was plain that several of the Imperial machines were unleashing their fury all at once.

'Eujen!' Averic repeated, 'We have to tell someone! The Speaker, Corog Breaker, anyone!' The subtext was clear: *Don't let my choice be in vain.*

But Eujen wore a strange expression as he turned from the window. He spoke several times before a gap in the explosions allowed his words out: 'They're not launching.'

'What?'

'None of our machines are in the sky. The Hiram Street airfield is in sight of here, and there's nobody there. It's completely empty. What's going on?'

'Eujen, we have to *tell* somebody. The Empire's people will be working *tonight.*' Averic almost shouted it, and at last the Beetle was with him.

'Yes, yes you're right. We have to . . .' He grimaced. 'Stenwold Maker. We have to find Stenwold Maker.'

When the Great Ear had started to sound, the men and women of Taki's airfield already knew they would not be running straight for their machines. Corog Breaker had passed on the order, and Taki, Edmon and the others assumed that other fields would be launching, hunting out the incoming Farsphex raiders. Nobody asked questions. Everyone *knew* the drill. If –

when – a detachment of the enemy fought past the loose blockade, everyone on duty would go rushing for the airstrip: another night's savage work.

They waited tensely, knowing their moment would come. The Mynans joked, with that hard, calloused humour they had evolved. A couple of the Collegiates were still trying to persevere with their studies, bent close to the lamps with their books.

Then the first bomb hit the city, and they were up on their feet, within moments of each other, looking to Breaker, who stood at the door.

'Not yet,' the old man told them. 'Specific orders tonight. Not our turn.'

The pilots' barracks was sunk low into the earth – using a converted storeroom from when the airfield had serviced only civilian fliers. The small, high-up windows were close to ground level, and Taki had found a perch there, looking out at the dark city with Fly-kinden eyes that could unpick the night.

Who's launching? she wondered, for she knew plenty of the pilots from other fields, and wanted to watch out for them. She had seen machines put out from Sarse Way, no more than a few, but the other airfields were further and she could not expect to spot every Stormreader they put in the air.

Another sequence of explosions rocked them, closer and then further as the Farsphex passed by. In its echo they heard more, further off still, but a constant pounding. One of the Collegiate pilots, a girl of no more than eighteen, swore into the moment's quiet that followed.

'Our turn now, eh?' Edmon suggested, shifting from foot to foot and eyeing the door.

'Not yet. Hold fast,' Corog advised implacably.

Taki was peering up, craning her neck to see the skies. She could pick out the Farsphex clearly, if only for the way they reflected the ground fires they were starting. They seemed to be taking their time tonight, giving the city a virtuoso performance. She blinked into a long bloom of fire that must have taken out that little street three roads away where there had been a taverna and a bakery and a . . . Even as she thought it, another sequence of precise explosions rocked its way closer, so that she saw nearby roofs shudder and crack. A Farsphex passed overhead, almost leisurely. Unopposed.

'Sieur – Master Breaker,' she called down. 'Who's out there for the defence?' And when no answer came: 'I can't see any of ours up there, Corog. We need to put more wings in the air.'

They were all looking at Breaker now, as the rolling thunder of the bombardment went on and on.

'I have orders,' declared Corog Breaker. 'We're not going out.'

'What do you mean, we're not going out?' demanded Edmon, after a pause to digest this statement. A close strike swallowed half his words but his meaning came through.

'Orders,' Corog repeated. 'We're sitting tight. We're not going out tonight at all. Someone else's problem.'

'Corog, there's *none* of ours up there,' Taki insisted. 'Orders don't survive contact with the enemy, Corog. Let's go.' She hopped down and headed for the door, because it was all so obvious. Somebody had tried to be clever in the Amphiophos, and now it was up to the pilots to clear up the mess.

She was half-flying as she reached him, so that Corog's hand, intended just to stop her, almost swatted her to the ground, her feet skidding as they touched down. 'Corog—?'

'What's going on?' Edmon's eyes darted from Corog to the window, red-lit, moment to moment, with the flash of the bombs.

'Orders!' the old Beetle snapped. 'Nobody goes out tonight. Specific orders, right from the top.'

'Then they're the wrong orders!' Edmon shouted into his face. 'It's a Rekef trick. Let me past.' He pushed, but Corog pushed back. Outside the barrack room, the pair of Merchant Company soldiers on guard were paying close attention.

'I got this from Master Maker himself,' Corog snapped. The

next blast was so close that they all ducked, dust filtering from the stonework of the ceiling.

'Then he's mad! *You're* mad!' Edmon's face was sheer bewilderment. 'Let us through, you stupid old man. We want to defend your city, even if *you* don't.'

Probably only Taki saw the tears glinting in Corog's eyes. 'And what the piss do *Mynans* know about actually defending a city?'

Edmon punched him in the face, a furious haymaker that he must have thought would floor Corog straight away. The old man was tough, even for a resilient kinden, and he came swinging straight back . . . and a moment later everyone was brawling. It was Corog and the two soldiers against Edmon's Mynan airmen, and the local pilots pitching in on both sides, apparently at random. Taki staggered back, because being a Fly-kinden in a brawl in an enclosed space was never a good idea, fleeing back to the high window, wondering if she should just squeeze herself through it.

Out on the empty airfield, fire was walking towards her, beautiful and terrible, as an Imperial flier passed overhead.

Taki dropped to the floor, crying 'Watch out!' but nobody could possibly have heard her.

When the tail end of the strike hit, flames erupted through all the windows facing the airfield, and the thunder of it battered every ear, knocking many of them off their feet. The silence that followed made Taki wonder if she had been struck deaf.

Corog was still standing resolutely at the door, one eye already swelling up after Edmon's blow.

'I'm sorry,' Taki heard him say, watching Edmon watch him in turn. 'We don't fly tonight. We watch, and we take it like a whore, but nobody flies.'

Outside, the assault on the city went on and on. It seemed impossible that the Empire had brought so many bombs.

★

'Master Drillen,' Arvi's light voice came from the far side of the door.

Jodry shuddered. 'Go away.' He tried to bellow the words, but they came out merely as a rasp. He was into his third bottle, now, produce of his own family's vineyards that had been growing superior grapes since before the revolution.

'I have made you some tea, Master Drillen,' came those respectful but inexorable tones.

'Don't want tea.' Jodry's first bottle had seen him move out of his offices at the Amphiophos. His initial way of dealing with the knowledge of what tonight must bring had been to remain at his post: Speaker for the city even in the face of annihilation. He had lasted less than an hour, leaving before the bombs had started to fall, and let them all think him a coward for it. Even now there would be a skeleton crew at the heart of Collegium's governance, clerks and servants and a few diligent Assemblers, but Jodry himself could not stay. Every moment he had spent there, once the Great Ear had sounded, he had been clutching at his desk, gritting his teeth, forcibly restraining himself from leaping to his feet and pelting down the corridors of state shouting, 'Get out! Get out of here! Out of the city! Tonight nothing will stay their hands!'

Or something like that. And, once the Imperial fliers began bombarding the city, he knew that he would not be able to restrain himself at all, that it would all come out, and then it would all be in vain.

He had gone home, to add shame to guilt.

'Master—' A particularly close blast rattled the shutters and briefly silenced even Arvi. 'Are you well?'

At last Jodry shambled over and unbolted the door, flinging it open to glower down at the Fly-kinden, his eyes wild and red-rimmed. To Arvi's credit, Jodry's secretary displayed no emotion at all.

'What do you want?' Jodry demanded. 'Have you nothing better to do tonight?'

At that, the Fly did blink. 'There has been a warning that Wasp assassins may be on the prowl, master, targeting our leadership, you included. I took liberties with your name in dispatching some of Outwright's Pike and Shot, just in case. The caution originates in the student body, master, so I suspect it to be nonsense, but even so . . .'

The thought of Wasp assassins tracking him down seemed almost like natural justice. 'Good, whatever,' Jodry grunted. 'Arvi, you're my secretary, so why are you even here? Have you nowhere, nobody, on a night like this?' The crash of the bombs punctuated his words.

'Master?' At last the little man seemed perplexed. 'Alas, I have not been fortunate enough to . . . No, master.'

'Go home, Arvi,' Jodry told him. 'No, bring me more wine, then go home. Another bottle of the Dark Rose 525.'

Arvi's eyes drifted to the cadavers of Jodry's earlier drinking, but he just nodded. 'It seems to be a tumultuous night, master.'

'I shall make you head of the faculty of understatement at the College,' Jodry declared, the humour laboured and failing. 'Go home, find a cellar and hide.'

'There is some filing at your office that requires attention, then—'

'No!' For a moment Jodry and his secretary stared at one another, Arvi patiently waiting for an explanation for his employer's outburst. Jodry wanted to say, *A cellar, a vault, anywhere sheltered from the sky tonight,* but he could not, not even to his secretary, whatever bond of trust existed between them.

Competing shames warred in him then, and one won out. 'Bring the bottle,' he decided. 'Bring the soldiers. We'll go there together. A good night to clear my desk.' And, as Arvi ducked down into the cellar, Jodry looked out of the window at the Imperial air force tearing into the city, and thought about his legacy.

★

Getting from Eujen's lodgings to the College had been easy, although they had not realized it at the time. Collegium was under the hammer, but only the first few tentative beats, like a smith feeling out the flaws in his material. Eujen found people to pass his warning on to, to scribble down the names that Averic had come up with, so as to send word to everyone they could think of: *Beware assassins*. Too late, too early, false alarm? They could not tell. No doubt even assassins would find an aerial bombardment an impediment to easy movement.

When they set off for Stenwold Maker's house, however, they realized that what they had taken for a downpour had only been a shower. Now the skies opened and the bloody deluge came. Looking up into a sky whose occupancy should have been contested by the fragile valour of the Stormreaders, they could see the Imperial orthopters plainly by moonlight, taking their own time over their runs, circling and bombing, and then pulling out to circle again. For a moment the two of them, Wasp and Beetle, just stared up into that blistering sky, at what the war between their kinden had come to.

Then a bomb dropped a street away: the thunderous, glass-breaking sound followed immediately by the killing blossom of an incendiary igniting. Eujen made to run towards the impact, but Averic dragged at his arm, shouting at him.

'Stenwold Maker! We have to get to him!'

'You fly to him, then!' Eujen said desperately, his imagination filling in everything that must be happening just over the rooftops.

'Not without you! I won't leave you,' Averic insisted. 'Besides, he'd probably kill me.'

Almost certainly true, Eujen realized, and wrenched himself free of the grip of his instincts. 'Then let's go!' he decided, as the next close blast savaged them with shards of stone, spraying the street with debris. He caught Averic's eyes, found there a mutual understanding that simply getting across the city was going to kill them, odds-on, and then they were running off down the street. At first they tried to watch the skies, to divine safety and danger by the movement of the Farsphex, but there were too many, and from all angles, and any incoming machine might release its load at any time. Eujen was no more able to make sense of them than he would a Moth prophecy.

In the end, the two of them just ran.

Sometimes soldiers tried to stop them, ordering them off the streets into whatever dubious safety might be found. The home-made sashes of the Student Company let them pass on, as kindred spirits with important business. Nobody seemed to care that they were, by any daylit estimation, merely pretend soldiers. On the streets of Collegium that night, they were just as able to help as the professionals, meaning not at all.

The world seemed to detonate all around them – a determined bombing run coming unlooked-for from behind, smashing houses only two streets away – now one street. They fell into a doorway under a hail of splinters and broken bricks, the fierce wash of fire baking them as an apothecary's workshop across the way erupted into coloured ribbons of flame.

And still the defenders of Collegium were absent, the skies surrendered. *Sabotage? Treachery? Have they murdered all our pilots?* Staring upwards at that hostile sky, Eujen could only think, *Is it the end, right now? Are Straessa and the others dead already, or simply irrelevant? Will the Empire even need to bring its armies, after this?*

It seemed like the city's final night. Certainly it seemed that it could be Eujen's.

When Stenwold returned to his townhouse that evening, before the Ear sounded, he found a letter awaiting him.

He knew it at once, and it must have been delivered by one of the Fly-kinden privateers with whom he had a highly sensitive arrangement, and who represented Collegium's trade contacts with the Sea-kinden, of whose existence the bulk of the Beetle-kinden had yet to learn.

It came on leathery parchment that they wove from seaweed somehow, so it would dry out and fragment within a few days. It would not relate to the closely guarded trade between the land and sea that had given Collegium its improved clockwork. This letter would be strictly personal.

This night of all nights. He dearly needed his mind taken away from what he and Jodry had done, the self-destructive trap they had baited for the Imperial air force – and here it was, just as ordered.

He unfolded the unsealed note, noticing the thick paper start to crack at the seams. The writing within was clumsy and childlike, the letters ill-formed. Just as he himself struggled to create the awkward glyphs that made up the Sea-kinden script, so Paladrya of Hermatyre wrestled determinedly with the alphabet of the land.

She was his Regret. Beetle-kinden were not supposed to have Regrets. Such foibles were for the Inapt in their stories of themselves. Spider-kinden had Regrets, where their webs of loyalties grew tangled. Stenwold's friend, the Mantis Tisamon, had practically lived all his life in one Regret or another. Beetles were supposed to be more prosaic. In the isolation of his own home, though, Stenwold read the Sea-kinden's letter, and relaxed enough to feel that lingering sadness at how the world had managed to separate him from such a remarkable woman.

Stenwold . . . he began to read, although he had to translate each word from the truly outlandish, phonetic spelling that Paladrya was prone to.

I am sending regards of the Edmir to your city
I am sending my own to you also
your letters are much improved
I understand you fight with the colony of the wasps and that
    there is much fear
the fly-kinden send word that blood will be shed soon

I am also afraid for you
stenwold, I would be with you, if I could
perhaps soon the edmir will no longer need any advice
I fear the land
nothing would bring me to it but you
the flies say I should wait until the war is done
that you would not want me with you when you fight
you know you have not left my thoughts since
hermatyre is always open to you.
distance only increases my heart when I think of you, and
   widens my mind.

This would be poetry, he knew, if she had written in her own script, and if he could have read it freely. As it was, it left him bitter at the vagaries of fate, and unsure how much she intended to say, or what was in his reading only.

Maybe, after all this is over and Jodry has me indicted, going back to the sea will be the best option for me. The old fear rose in him of the dark and hungry water, but it seemed less immediate, now, more amenable to negotiation.

For a long time Stenwold stared at the letter, and then he began to work on a reply, less concerned with content than clarity of expression, submerging himself in the scholarly. When the Great Ear sounded, even when the bombs began to fall, he hunkered down and concentrated, as though he was truly an academic again and the sounds outside only the noisy distractions of students. Time and again, he chased away the thoughts, *What if I die tonight; what if Banjacs does? Can this be salvaged, or will the sacrifice of so many come to nothing?* But the queasy feeling grew within him, the uncertainty of the gamble he and Jodry had taken, until he could no longer palm off his mind with Sea-kinden calligraphy, but only stare out of the window and realize that the war hung on tonight and tomorrow, and any misjudgement could lose everything for his people.

There was a knock at the door. He finally put the letter down.

He was not sure who he expected, but Janos Outwright was not the man. The portly little moustachioed Beetle, in pristine uniform with his own wheel of pikes and snapbows proudly displayed, beamed at Stenwold with his usual self-importance. There were two more of Outwright's Pike and Shot standing behind him.

'What's happened?' Stenwold demanded.

'Nothing yet, apparently,' Janos said pleasantly, although the crash and crump of the bombs nearly swallowed up his words. 'Can we come in?'

When he had got under cover, with his men, and when Stenwold grudgingly found some mediocre wine for them, Janos deigned to explain further. 'All very baffling, but there was rumour that the Empire was going to take a poke at some of the great and good, with you as top of the list. Soon as word came, I decided that you merited the finest in guardianship, so here I am.'

'Word from where?'

'Some student,' Janos said airily and then, just as Stenwold was preparing a brusque reply, 'that Wasp one, apparently, though I didn't hear it direct from him.'

'The . . . ?' Stenwold tried to summon the Wasp youth's name to mind, but couldn't. 'Where is he?'

'Running around warning people, like I said.' Janos sipped his wine and made a great show of appreciation. 'You can arrest him tomorrow for it, if you want. Everything seems a bit busy tonight for that sort of thing.' He waggled his eyebrows, as though the detonations so close by outside were just high spirits.

Stenwold did not even hear the next knock, but Janos plainly did. He went strolling over to the door as though he owned the place.

They shot him dead right on Stenwold's doorstep, a snapbow bolt making a ruin of his throat above his gleaming breastplate and scarring the wall beyond, barely slowed. Then they were shouldering in: a half-dozen burly Beetle men, armoured piecemeal with leather and canvas and chitin plate, with knives and swords and two snapbows leading the charge.

Janos saved Stenwold's life even so – both by being the man to answer the door and by bringing two Merchant Company regulars along with him. They were caught off guard, by surprise, and yet both managed to get a shot off, killing a snapbowman and a swordsman, and wounding one of the men behind as the bolt passed right through his comrade.

Then it was blade work. One of the soldiers got his sword clear, receiving a couple of strikes that his mail fended off. The second Merchant Company man had barely dropped his dis-charged snapbow when a dagger was rammed into his groin and he collapsed.

Stenwold had no weapons on him. Shouting for the sole remaining defender to hold, somehow, he rushed for the stairs. A snapbow bolt ploughed past his head into the wall, an oppor-tunistic shot spoiled by the jostle of the melee inside the doorway.

Stenwold usually wore his sword, but not in his own house, and he had left it by the door – as unattainable now as if he had dropped it in the street. Upstairs, though, he had the collected works of a life lived at war with the Empire, if he only had time to deploy them.

There was a choking cry from below, and he guessed that the sole remaining soldier had fallen to superior numbers. Stenwold threw himself into his bedroom, flipping open a drawer of his bedside cabinet, and then hurled himself over the bed, clutching for what was mounted on the wall there. He heard feet thunder-ing up the stairs.

The weight of the piercer fell into his hands, and he checked the weapon every tenday, keeping the monstrous instrument charged and loaded. It had saved his life more than once, a firepowder-charged bolt-thrower with four arm's-length spears in its barrels.

Then the attackers were spilling in, or that was how he read the situation as he pulled the trigger. The first man had time to skid off his feet, falling flat on his back, and the third was still partway up the stairs, recharging his snapbow, so the luckless second man took three of the four bolts dead on, enough to render the bulk of him unrecognizable as human.

The piercer was useless now, and Stenwold leapt for the drawer even as the first man was lunging for him. A shortsword gashed his arm and then he had the little two-barrel snapbow out and tried to bring it to bear. For a moment he and the killer wrestled, each trying to wrench the weapon out of the other's hand, Then there was a shout, and Stenwold's opponent flung himself backwards. The snapbowman in the doorway had his weapon loaded and was frantically charging it.

Stenwold loosed, taking the swordsman in the chest with one barrel, not a tactical decision so much as sheer reflex. He had no time to take the other man, for there was a sizzling flash – a sound and sight odious and familiar to Stenwold from twenty years of personal war.

The third man's snapbow discharged, the snap sounding a moment after the flare, but the wielder was already falling forwards, punched from behind, his weapon's mouth jerking up. Stenwold felt a searing claw rake the side of his face, shooting pain through his head, but he was still standing afterwards, his right ear torn so that he could not tell what of the thunder came from outside, and what from within his head.

A Wasp appeared at the door and Stenwold made a strangled sound and jabbed the little snapbow forwards, There was a flicker of wings as the new arrival fell back, dragging the door closed after him, the bolt holing the wood effortlessly.

Trying to work out what was real, Stenwold stood in his own bedroom, three men in various extremities of death decorating his floor, his own blood flowing freely down the side of his neck and pooling at his collar. His hands, those past masters of necessity, found fresh bolts in the drawer, reloading and recharging the snapbow even as his mind reeled.

From downstairs, an uncertain voice called up, 'Master

Maker?' He felt he should recognize it, but no name sprang to mind.

Stenwold took the bedside cabinet and moved it over to the door, kicking the dead snapbowman clear of its opening arc. His head was still ringing, and the house itself rang, too, the bombardment continuous and close. For a moment Stenwold balanced himself, one foot on the cabinet, a hand on the door, before flinging the door wide and kicking the cabinet out as hard as he could. He heard it reach the stairs, with surprised oaths from below.

Then he went after it, standing at the balcony rail with his snapbow levelled. 'Weapons down!' he yelled, murder in his voice,

There was a Beetle youth below him, also the Wasp, both with their hands held in sight, the Wasps' clenched into fists. They wore some sort of Company sash, and the Beetle looked like a student. They both looked like students.

Eujen Leadswell and Averic, his errant memory recalled, and further reminded him that the snapbowman dead behind him had the charring of a Wasp sting in his back. There was a short-sword at Eujen's feet that had blood on it, too, and that other body at the foot of the stairs had presumably supplied the blood.

For a moment Stenwold simply stood there, trapped in the moment, weapon levelled and listening to the sound of his city being destroyed, until chains of logic fell into place, and he jammed the snapbow in his belt.

Nine dead men downstairs, and Stenwold was shaken now to think how he might have been one more. Step by step, he stomped his way down the stairs. 'What's going on? Why are you here?' he demanded. He could not find it within himself to thank them – not these two.

They exchanged nervous glances, guilty almost. He felt the screw turn within him at the unfairness, given what they had done, but he could not stoop. He found his pride would not let him.

Some consensus was reached, and Eujen spoke first. 'Master Maker, Averic was approached by Imperial agents who tried to recruit him. They had a list of victims to kill tonight. We have passed on details, best guesses as to targets. But you were surely top of the list. We tried to get here sooner. The streets . . .' By the end of his speech he had recognized the corpse of Janos Outwright and was staring at it in horrified fascination.

Thereby saving my life twice over. But still the gracious words would not come. 'I need to know everything they told you,' he snapped at Averic, making the Wasp twitch. 'Come with me, both of you.' He stomped past them, heedless of the blood underfoot, collecting his sword. He was in *command*, he assured himself. The roar and crash from without gave the lie to that thought, but he clung to it, building a self-righteous anger to defend himself, which led on to the words: 'And Master Leadswell, I trust you have reconsidered your stance on the Empire.'

He was so much the mighty engine of state, right then, that he had stepped onto the street outside before realizing that the two students were not simply pattering in his shadow. He looked back, and the flash and gout of the next bomb showed Eujen Leadswell's face all too clearly, standing motionless beside that small fragment of the Empire that had cast its lot in with Collegium this night.

'Master Maker,' Leadswell stated, 'when this is done, I will put myself forward at the Lots and get myself made Assembler, however long it takes. And when I do, I shall fight you at every bloody turn.'

'Let us hope you that have the opportunity. If the Wasps win I don't imagine anyone will be casting Lots any time soon,' Stenwold retorted instantly, even though part of him was listening to his own words and shouting, *Give it a rest! Just unbend and put a hand out to them.* Except that putting a hand out meant friendship only in Collegium. To a Wasp it was a prequel to killing.

Averic's hand was out already, and Stenwold flinched, reaching for his snapbow. The Wasp was pointing, though, his face bloodless and horrified in the ruddy glare of flames.

Stenwold turned, without expectations, and the sight struck him like a blow. There was a colossal conflagration at the centre of the city. The Amphiophos was burning.

Thirty-Four

Reaching the Amphiophos was a nightmare journey through disintegrating streets, encountering the dispossessed, the grieving, the blank-faced Merchant Company soldiers who could not help. The city's familiar landmarks had been picked up and strewn like a child's toys. Collegium was large and the enemy orthopters had been few, relatively speaking. The Beetle-kinden would survive, but still the scale of the damage was daunting. An unopposed incursion finally served to show what the hard work of the Collegiate airmen and women had been achieving as the nightly fruits of their failing defence.

The bombing was tailing off by the time Stenwold reached the first rubble foothills of the Amphiophos, and it was a bitter thought that only a shortage of bombs could be behind their retreat.

They will come in greater numbers tomorrow. That is what this has all been about. If I am wrong about Banjacs's machine, though . . . then I will have invited the end. The thought of that same end being inevitable sooner or later, if Banjacs failed, was not one to comfort him.

Like little ants whose nest has been kicked over. That was the image that came to Stenwold as he set eyes on Collegium's fallen heart of governance. Visible in the light of those fires still blazing, the shell and rubble of the place was crawling with the living, and he knew they were searching for the dead. He saw clerks and Company soldiers, servants, cleaners, concerned citizens, some still in nightshirts, all of them picking over the collapsed grandeur of the sprawling building. The Amphiophos's heart was of ancient Moth construction, and succeeding generations had re-edified it, adding wings and rooms, domes, gardens, spires and suites, but all with surprising taste, preserving the pre-revolution elegance of the original white stone, so that the whole formed a bridge to a distant past that the Beetles had otherwise turned their backs on. From these halls the Moth-kinden had ruled their coastal city of Pathis, and the subject people who would, in the end, overthrow them. From these same white halls the founding parents of Collegium had set their course: embracing not arms and grudges and feuding like their Ant neighbours, but learning and tolerance and thought. The College and the Amphiophos, and the whole of Collegium sprang from that source, mind and heart.

One of the new wings was still standing, its windows just jagged empty sockets, but the interior merely singed rather than gutted. The rest had been laid waste. Domes had cracked like eggshells, often one wall and a section of curved roof still tottering, the rest fallen amidst a devastation of tapestries and murals and mosaics and art, and of lives too. The western end was still on fire, the water crews fighting to beat down the flames. The rest . . . Stenwold had never seen such a wasteland, not even in Myna. The attack on that city had been brutal but swift, but Collegium had been pounded and pounded, night after night, and now . . .

The expressions on the faces of those around him were haggard and gaunt with grief and incredulity, thoughts retreating deep inwards as the hands worked, shifting stones, searching for survivors or for simple confirmation of mortality. There were sobs from a few, but most simply forced themselves to it like automatons, building up a head of grief that would strike them the moment they rested.

In the midst of all this, he found Jodry.

The Speaker for the Assembly came shambling out from between roofless walls, his formal robes torn and soot stained, skin disfigured with bruises. There was a gash on his scalp that had been clumsily, hastily dressed. He stumbled and tripped over the fallen stones, hugging to him a burden that Stenwold could not identify for a moment, and then realized was a mass of papers bundled together awkwardly, charred and ripped and sodden in turn.

Jodry dumped them to the ground, and Stenwold saw that there was already a couple of other similar mounds, a meagre harvest of scrolls and books that were now in too poor a state to be sold in a Helleron street market.

'Jodry,' he called, and the man looked up, eyes bloodshot with the smoke, haunted by knowledge.

'Sten.' The fat man's voice was the ghost of its former self.

'What are you . . . ?' For a moment Stenwold wondered if the Speaker had gone mad.

'The records, Sten. The minutes, laws, Assembly debates . . . our government, Sten.' Jodry gestured helplessly at the ruined papers, even as his secretary, Arvi, staggered out with another pile, looking as battered and begrimed as his master.

'But these . . .' Stenwold crouched to begin leafing through the nearest pile. Loose pages from manifests, transcripts, judgements, accounts, but nothing connecting to its neighbours, nothing complete or whole, each pile almost whimsical in its juxtaposition, books compiled by idiots for illiterates.

'It's all we have. It's Collegium,' Jodry whispered. 'It just needs . . . sorting out and filing, Sten . . .'

'Jodry, for the world's sake, sit down. Get something to drink. Arvi, surely you can . . . ?'

Wearily, the Fly reached into his tunic and produced a flask. Stenwold had the impression that it was not from Jodry's stock, rather for the little man's private consumption, but he passed it to his master without comment. Jodry tipped it back, gagged at whatever was inside, and then choked over it for long enough that, on looking Stenwold in the face again, there was a measure of composure once more in his eyes.

Neither of them said it. Neither of them uttered the words, *We did this*. The thought travelled between them as though they had rented a mindlink from the Ants for the occasion.

Stenwold shook his head. 'It could have been any night, Jodry. It would have come, sometime. The very inevitability of *this*, and all the other variants of *this*, was why we . . . why we made our decision.'

Jodry nodded wearily. 'Banjacs's house still stands,' he said. 'The College lost the Awlbright workshops and machine rooms, and they put a hole through the Prowess Forum roof, though that one didn't go off. And the rest, Sten . . . the list of homes and shops and lives.' He looked up, frowning. 'What happened to your ear?'

In truth, Stenwold had almost forgotten, having just slapped some ointment on the wound – a pain worse than the original – to kill off the animicules before he left the house. 'Assassin,' he explained curtly. His own difficulties seemed trivial by comparison.

'Someone assassinated your ear.' Jodry managed a half-inch worth of weak smile. 'Well that sounds as though the general warning we got was a good one.' The smile was gone. 'More paperwork, then. Who was attacked? Who did they get? I know poor Bola Stormall was shot dead outside her house. We sent soldiers off to guard everyone who seemed likely, but we couldn't protect everyone.'

'And they couldn't attack everyone, either. And the men who came for me won't be moving on down the list, for certain,' Stenwold put in fiercely.

Jodry nodded wearily, unwilling to accept even that meagre victory, and then his eyes lit on something beyond Stenwold. Eujen Leadswell and the Wasp Averic had trailed after him to the devastation of the Amphiophos, and were now standing, humbled and aghast at the sight of the ruin.

'They came to warn you, then,' Jodry noted. 'The Wasp boy guessed you'd be top of their list.' For a moment it seemed that he might gloat, perhaps suggest that Stenwold take Averic off for an interrogation by the soldiers of the Maker's Own. Seeing this diminished man before him, Stenwold would almost have preferred that.

And he could not honestly say to himself that a thorough questioning of Averic, as a potential enemy agent, had not occurred to him. He felt like two men inside: the rational Collegiate and the man who had fought the Empire most of his life. Both of them were eminently logical and consistent within their world views, entirely persuaded by their own arguments, and yet they did not seem to be on speaking terms with each other any more.

'Get some rest,' he told Jodry gruffly. 'All this . . .' A gesture at the scattered, pointless papers.

'I know,' the Speaker for the Assembly agreed miserably. 'But I needed to do something. I couldn't just let it . . .'

'Go,' Stenwold insisted, and then stalked over to his followers.

'Well, you've done a service for the city,' he forced himself to admit. 'You have the thanks of the Assembly, or will have, once it can be assembled.' He overdid his attempt at friendliness, and saw Eujen's gaze cut through it with the cynicism of the young.

'Perhaps you could repay us by answering one question, Master Maker. What happened last night? Where were our orthopters? The Empire raped us from the air.'

'There were defenders.' Stenwold strode past them, aware of them following him, as he knew they would. But he was heading for a stretch of rubble that had been picked over already, with no ears to overhear.

'Where were they? Master Maker, we were on the streets all the way from my lodgings to your townhouse, with a stop at the College on the way, and precious little sign of anyone of ours in the air.'

'Collegium is a large city.' Stenwold turned to face him,

feeling half the warrior, half the statesman, but wholly the combatant.

'This was different,' Eujen insisted, not letting go. 'Different to all the other times. I swear to you I saw barely a Stormreader in the sky.' The boy faced off against him, fists clenched.

'Perhaps our orthopters were engaged elsewhere – on the attack perhaps?'

'*Is* that what happened, Master Maker?'

And at last Stenwold recognized the tone behind the challenge: a plea for reassurance. Not a political opponent, this, but a Collegiate citizen whose home was at stake: a student barely grown, wearing the sash of an invented Company, playing at soldiers in a real war.

But I can't tell him. I certainly can't tell the Wasp. The secrecy is the entire point. He stared at Averic, gaunt and silent at Eujen's shoulder. He would not meet Stenwold's eyes, but there was something there to be confronted nonetheless: the fact that these two, that the Wasp in particular, had saved lives last night – Stenwold's included.

The choices spread before him like a fan opening. Walk away: these two could stir up trouble, but they could force no answers from him. Counter-attack: why not have the Wasp answer some questions – he knew more than he had told, for all that his information had served to the good. Surrender: but Stenwold had spent too much of his life fighting for that, hadn't he?

He stared at the two of them, the spymaster and the soldier in him trying to draw up a harsh word, a put-down that would set the impertinent boy in his place and simplify his own life again. *I don't need this. Haven't I enough to worry about?*

In that second, glowering into Eujen's angry, hurt gaze, he saw himself as Jodry had come to see him: a man going too fast downhill, driven by his obsessions, unwilling to let go of his grudges; *old*, and set in his ways the way old men get. He saw Eujen, too, the young intellectual with a cause that he was willing to fight for no matter what the institution thought. *When did we change places? Wasn't I standing on his side of the line, last time I looked?*

He sat down suddenly, rubble shifting beneath him, sensing Eujen's instinctive lurch forward to assist him. *Have they not earned some answers – even the Wasp? Some small part of the truth, at least?*

'Tomorrow,' he told them. 'I have no answers for you now, but tomorrow . . . I will send for you, and I will take you to where all of this will make sense.' *Or if it does not, then we are lost, and who cares what you think then?*

'We knew something was wrong from about ten minutes in,' Aarmon reported wearily. They were in Tynan's tent, though the general was elsewhere, readying the troops for the first engagement with the Collegiate foot. Instead, the intelligencer Colonel Cherten was taking centre stage, sitting on Tynan's camp stool with borrowed authority, as the same pilot delegation stood before him: Aarmon, Scain, Nishaana, with Kiin, Pingge and Tiadro as their diminutive shadows.

'They met us closer to the city than usual, and with less force, but the efficiency of their first response is variable. We assumed the balance of their machines would come from some unexpected angle. They never came. Instead we broke their formation and chased them all the way to the city. There was some scattered resistance after that, mostly individual orthopters, and their ballistae batteries, of course, but . . .' A small gesture of the hand, barely opening the fingers. 'Where were their machines? Where were their pilots? Colonel, we *know* them by now, the best of them, those that have survived this long fighting against us. No names, but I could identify at least a dozen, maybe a score of their aviators. None of them was in the sky over Collegium last night. I even sent a few machines back—'

'Against orders,' Cherten noted with a crisp smile.

'Sir, when we're in the air, the only orders that count are

mine.' Aarmon was a bigger man than Cherten, and amongst friends, and for a moment the chain of command strained and creaked between them, the intelligence officer off balance for a second before forcing an easy smile to his face, waving the comment off.

'Continue.'

'I had assumed the Collegiates had finally realized that they were losing, night after night, and had committed their air power against the army here, hoping to do enough damage to make taking the city on the ground impossible. I sent machines back to give that warning, and to rouse those who were off shift.' He gestured towards Scain, who had served as the messenger. 'But they never came here. Our entire reserve sat in their Farsphex and waited, but they never came at all. Can I ask about our intelligence operation in Collegium, sir?'

Cherten frowned, because that was a taboo question from anyone outside Army Intelligence. Pingge was well aware that Cherten was reckoned to be a Rekef agent placed within Intelligence, information obtained from some channel of gossip of the pilots most recently out of Capitas. Whatever games the Rekef was playing with its junior cousin right now, the pilots had no idea, save that any such internal division did not bode well.

'And why might that be pertinent, Major?' Cherten asked archly, recovering his superiority.

'If your agents have assassinated a large number of the enemy pilots, that accounts for it, sir,' Aarmon explained bluntly. 'If not, we need another explanation, because something is definitely going on.'

For a long time Cherten just stared at him, holding the impenetrable veil of the intelligence service closed, but then he shrugged. 'We have agents in the city, and they will be liaising with the Aldanrael spies already in place, preparing a kill list and working through it. Viable targets are likely to be their leaders, not the body of their aviators.'

Pingge sensed the slight sense of relief among the pilots, and understood them immediately. They had come to know the enemies who clashed with them night after night, whose faces they never saw but whose technique, individual style and skill were as familiar as a sparring partner's. They had lost friends and comrades to those foes, but there was an honour to that rivalry, and Pingge knew all the pilots believed in it. When the time came, that was how they would go – an endless moment of torn metal and blood, fire and falling. A pilot's death was owed to each of them as the due of their place in the sky's aristocracy. Death by the assassin's blade was a groundsman's death, and their enemies deserved better.

'I have had some reports from our opposite numbers amongst the Spiders, but they're uncertain at best,' Cherten went on. 'Give me your thoughts, Major.'

'Assuming there wasn't some colossal mistake on their part – for instance, sending their machines somewhere way off the mark to counter some attack we didn't make – then it comes down to this: they had machines, however many, that they didn't use. So: either they are saving the remains of their strength for the actual assault, and have decided not to defend their city, or they want us to think them undefended, to make us complacent. It may be that they have amassed a greater force than we are aware of, and want us to bring all our force so that they can challenge it.'

'Are you saying you think this is a trap?' Cherten asked him levelly.

'It might be, sir. We were tearing strips from their city last night. Either they *cannot* defend or they seek a single strike that will cripple our air power. Maybe they have redesigned their machines, or they have reinforcement pilots from Sarn or else-where, or they are simply desperate enough to risk all by committing everything they have. Both sides have understood, from a tenday ago at least, that they are failing to hold us. Each night that their pilots have lessened the impact of our bombs, they have also reduced their ability to defend against us when the army arrives.'

'You know our orders demand commitment now in the air.'

'Sir, what intelligence has come from the city? I can make no suggestion without that.'

Cherten looked uncomfortable. 'It is difficult . . . most of the Spider spies are Inapt, so information regarding technical subjects will always be unreliable. There is a suggestion that Collegium is suffering shortages, to the extent that they are unable to keep their machines airworthy, that they are husbanding their strength against the actual siege. But with the Inapt it's hard to be sure what they think they mean. So, suggestions . . . ?'

'If they have a great force prepared, then anything short of full commitment could see us lose whatever force we send out,' Aarmon said, laying out the options methodically. 'If we hold back on the basis that they may possess some overwhelming force, we lose a night's work, give them more time to repair and rebuild, and we'll only discover the truth of their plan when the army reaches the walls tomorrow.' Aarmon paused for a moment, and Pingge knew that thoughts were flying between him and the others. 'If they are just saving everything they have to throw at us during the siege, then it would be better if we could draw them out tonight. If they truly wish to draw us to one final battle, if they believe that they have a chance to destroy our air strength, then . . . if they have amassed so many additional fliers then our army's chances against the walls are doubtful.'

Colonel Cherten snorted at that, and all six of the aviators – Wasps and Flies, men and women – stared at him.

'I think you overestimate the importance of your machines, Major Aarmon,' the intelligence officer declared, ever so slightly patronizing, and Pingge thought, *Oh, pits, he doesn't understand.*

'Sir, General Tynan must be made aware of all I have said, to make an informed choice,' Aarmon persisted.

'Oh he'll hear it,' Cherten agreed. 'The senior officers will meet with our General and our Lady-Martial, and you will hear of our decision shortly,' he assured them. 'In the meantime, ensure that your orthopters are ready to fly, armed, fuelled and serviced.'

Who'd have thought so much of soldiering was digging holes? Straessa, known as the Antspider, or 'Sub' to her men, watched the earthmovers slugging away at the ground, grinding out trenches that would be five feet deep when they were done, their drivers working to a complex plan laid out back at the camp by a committee of whoever seemed sufficiently interested. Certainly her own chief officer, Marteus, had not been remotely bothered, plainly considering it work not fit for soldiers. So it was that Straessa's detachment were here now, standing about with snapbows on their shoulders watching the machines dig. Three detachments of twenty had come out there to bake in their armour, their automotive transports having slewed to a halt in an untidy clutter behind them. The day was scorching, with not a cloud in the sky. *Weather like that will kill more people than the bows do, if the battle's held in it,* she considered. Sartaea te Mosca was already passing amongst the soldiers, reminding them to drink regularly, taking water bottles back to the automotives for refilling from the barrels they carried. The transformation in the Fly-kinden lecturer fascinated the Antspider. Back at the College she had taught ancient mystical techniques that nobody believed in to students incapable of truly understanding them, and was denied even a full mastership by an institution that was always on the point of obliterating her role entirely. She had pottered about, hosting and socializing, and being both inoffensive and ubiquitous. Meanwhile everybody forgot that she had come to the College from Dorax, where the old Moth ways still held sway. Only her name, Sartaea, was even an echo of her origins, and she otherwise

534

seemed such a mild little creature that she could not possibly carry even a ghost of the Bad Old Days.

Now she was all business, tending to her charges, refusing to take no for an answer. No larger or more obtrusive, but te Mosca seemed to have become almost a force of nature, impossible to argue with. If only she had run her minuscule department with such iron, then she would by now either be a full Master or exiled from Collegium for good.

'Tell me something comforting,' Straessa called out to her, as she passed.

'We can't possibly lose,' te Mosca replied promptly. Her smile was grim and small, but at it least it was still in place. 'The omens have foretold a great victory.'

'Tell me something comforting and true.'

The Fly shrugged, the smile turning bittersweet. 'Ah, well, there you have me.'

The air was laden with dust, a choking morass of it that the earthmovers threw up, gritting the eyes and throat, a smothering blanket that only intensified the heat. *It's just as well I know this is important. Seems like the sort of nonsense they'd give out for punishment detail in other armies.*

The theory was sound, though. When the armies finally clashed – any day now – the Collegiates would make their stand in these earthworks, shielded from enemy shot and shell, defended by a fence of stakes, currently resting on the beds of the automotives, with entrenched artillery to support them. The broken ground of the trenches would trip up even the new Imperial automotives, whilst the Collegiate machines would sally down pre-planned safe paths in order to attack the enemy supply and siege engines.

Straessa pulled down the neckerchief she was using to screen the dust from her lungs, and took a swig of water, more to forestall a telling-off from te Mosca than because she felt the need for it. The Fly-kinden woman veered off, satisfied, and went to berate Gerethwy instead. The lanky Woodlouse youth stared down at her as though he had never seen anything so impertinent in all his life, but within a few moments he too was uncapping his own flask, giving in to the inevitable.

That was when a call went out from on high. They had a few with them who possessed the Art of flight, and there was a rota of lookouts, but Straessa had not expected to need them. After all, the enemy were miles away, according to the scouts.

A Fly-kinden dropped down hard enough to buckle at the knees.

'They're coming!' he shouted.

She fought back all the stupid things she would have said before some Ant had been fool enough to trust her with a rank, however inferior – all the *What?* and *Who?* and *Are you sure?* – and instead just barked out, 'Report!' as she ran over. All around her, soldiers were readying their weapons, charging, loading, not calmly but not panicked either.

'Half-dozen automotives coming along fast, Sub,' the Fly choked out.

'The army?'

'Just the machines, Sub.'

Six automotives? For a moment she felt like laughing. The Collegiate forces could surely defeat them or drive them off. They had sixty soldiers, three armed transports and the earthmovers. The look on the Fly's face brought her up short, though. 'Tell me.'

'Like woodlice, Sub, but they were moving as fast as a horse can gallop, it looked like, and heading straight for us. Sub, these are the ones we've heard of – the ones that did Myna.'

'Sub!' someone else called out to her, pointing. There were dustclouds building rapidly to the north-east, the enemy's machines coming on *fast!*

'Everyone to the automotives!' she shouted. 'Move it, all of you! That means you on the earthmovers too!'

Technically Straessa did not have overall command, for each

detachment was under its own sub-officer. At least one of the other officers was shouting at his men to stand and shoot. *And we should have worked this sort of thing out before.* The Beetle-kinden had no rigorous tradition of giving and obeying orders, though, being a people who loved discussion.

Still, her own people were on the move, and at least some of the others. The bulk of the earthmover drivers were still at work, though, and Straessa pounded over to them, shouting at them to get going.

'We'll never get the machines away in time,' one of them objected. He was a big Beetle of middle years, and plainly did not want to be told what to do by some halfbreed student.

'Sod the machines. Get *yourselves* out!' she snapped at him.

'If I lose this machine—' the Beetle started, plodding to a fault, and then there was a hollow boom nearby, a thunder and a whirling plume of dust, the echo of it almost lifting Straessa from her feet. One of the other earthmovers had been staved in as though an invisible fist had struck it. A moment later its fuel tank exploded with a wretched pop, flames creeping weakly from the burst seams.

The Beetle needed no more encouragement, but was already running for the transports, and then so was almost everyone else. Straessa held on for one moment more, horrified and fascinated, watching the shapes loom out of the dust. Those high-fronted, armoured forms of overlapping armour plates, that single lidded eye that opened only when the machines ground to a skidding halt for a moment, when it flashed and belched as the leadshotter behind it let loose. There was only this half-dozen, but their swift and rushing movement struck a primal fear into Straessa that she had not known she could own to.

A moment later she was pelting towards the transports her-self, aware that she had left her escape surely too late. Even as she thought it, though, one of the rugged wheeled vehicles slewed to an untidy halt next to her, its open back crammed with her soldiers. She saw a young Beetle-kinden girl pedalling the mounted ballista around to face the enemy, while Gerethwy had his mechanized snapbow resting on the back rail.

She leapt up, caught at an outstretched hand and was hauled in, even as the driver kicked the vehicle into motion again, wrestling with the gearings until they were grinding away satisfactorily once more. She heard Gerethwy's weapon discharge with a hammering *snap-snap-snap*. She had already opened her mouth to tell him to stop, that there was no point wasting ammunition at this range, when the first of the enemy automotives had ploughed alongside them, clattering past on its nest of pistoning legs, in pursuit of one of the other transports.

Her mouth remained open.

Gerethwy trained his weapon on it, the snapbow bolts ricocheting hopelessly, without a chance of penetrating those thick armour plates. A moment later, the ballista loosed, the explosive bolt leaping the narrow gap between the vehicles, to bloom and burst against the side of the enemy, knocking it off course a little but leaving only a soot mark and a shallow scar.

'Down!' someone called out, and then their own automotive rocked, veering dangerously towards the enemy machine beside them with its port wheels off the ground. Behind, receding, ascended the plume of a near-miss, and beyond that another of the implacable enemy, getting up speed again.

'Incredible!' Gerethwy shouted. 'Look how fast they accelerate! We couldn't get up speed in twice that time!' He shook his head, the student artificer in him clearly taken by the things, however deadly they were. 'Still, I'll wager we're faster on the flat—'

There was the sound of thunder from ahead and to their right, and they saw one of the other transports abruptly flip sideways, its rear axle and wheels disintegrating as it was caught by a low shot from one of the pursuing enemy, and Gerethwy shut up, long face ashen. There had been bodies flung up in that moment, human ragdoll shapes revolving in the dust. Fellow soldiers, comrades, people they knew.

The ballista was shooting again, loosing bolts back at the machines in their wake, every distraction or deviation winning them a few seconds' grace. *If they did not have to stop to shoot, we'd be done for*, Straessa realized. But Gerethwy had been right: now they had got up to speed they were pulling away, the two transports. Although a few more geysers of dust and dirt fountained up nearby, the enemy was falling behind.

All they had won here was their lives. They had lost the earthmovers, lost the chance of preparing their ground properly, lost a third of their force or more.

And we have seen the enemy. It was an uncertain blessing at best.

A small hand touched her arm, and she looked down to see Sartaea te Mosca. There was blood on the Fly's fingers, and Straessa was surprised to find it was her own, from a shallow line cut into her forearm by some errant shard of metal or broken stone.

'Tell me something comforting,' she said to the Fly, sitting down and letting the little woman smear a stinging ointment on the wound. But Sartaea te Mosca had nothing to say.

Thirty-Five

The woman who called herself Gesa – who had for most of her life borne the name Garvan and dressed like a Wasp-kinden man, but who was currently painted and disguised as a halfbreed Beetle woman – was nothing if not a creature of dutiful field-craft. She had been given the means by which to leave messages for her superiors, and by which to receive orders. She was not to be simply a maverick agent working on her own recognizance.

This she now regretted.

It had been imperative that she entered Collegium as a refugee carrying nothing to mark her as a spy. Once in the city, however, she had been able to buy or steal parts, working to a plan that she had memorized. A little dirigible, its airbag no larger than a human head, was easy enough to arrange, and it seemed almost half the army around her was composed of students and engineers and idle tinkerers. She had assembled her toy within plain sight.

That night she had crept to the camp's perimeter and taken a turn as sentry. The Collegiates were not entirely lax in their security, and indeed their sentries, volunteers mostly, were more diligent and keen than would be the bored, resentful Imperial regulars pressed into such a tedious job. However, they looked only outwards, and were more than happy to be relieved by another. Gesa knew that the Collegiate camp was watched by Spider-kinden agents of the Aldanrael, who had kept pace with

540

the Beetle force's advance. Now she simply sat with her lantern on the ground beside her, and moved her foot in front of it, just a nervous habit to any watcher within camp; but to the dark-adjusted eyes out there, it provided a simple code of bright and dark that told them to expect a message.

At the third repetition, she'd had to hope that the spies had noticed her, for certainly no answering signal would be risked. As she had chosen a camp boundary with the breeze at her back, she had simply let the tiny, dark-ballooned dirigible drift away, her crabbed reports tucked into its little basket.

Two days later, and she had received her orders in response. She had watched the little trench-digging force return in a great hurry, and depleted, all the eyes of the camp watching them. A few hours after that, the camp still reeling from the news of the Imperial automotives, a further body was picked up by the Collegiate scouts. It was one of those who was believed left dead back at the trenchworks, so the assumption was that the man had managed to stagger and crawl back towards his home camp, dying just out of sight of it. Any medical examination would give the lie to that, and Gesa reckoned that very soon someone would be asking why a dead man had been dragged out and left so prominently within a mile of the camp. It was good odds that someone else – perhaps Kymene, the Mynan general, who seemed one of the sharper blades around when it came to mistrusting people – would guess that some manner of message was intended.

By that time, Gesa had already taken her turn carrying the body, and found the folded message hidden in the dead man's boot. By the time anyone started asking difficult questions, there would be no evidence left for them to find.

It had all gone off very smoothly indeed, and she had experienced a flush of pride at being part of Army Intelligence, which had taken the time to devise dozens of such stratagems while the Rekef just bickered and carried out purges and suffered from internal unrest.

Then she had read the orders.

She had reported to them earlier on the structure and the leadership of the Collegium camp, stating that they were divided irregularly, Maker's Own Company into larger units, the Coldstone into smaller, various hangers-on such as the Mynans operating each to their own; that they had no clear chain of command, with decisions being made by a council consisting of the Mynan leader, the big Khanaphir, the two Company chief officers, and whoever they chose to invite along; that their infantry was well armed, armoured and supplied, but that their automotives looked hastily converted for war. She had made plain, in her report, that she was well placed for a variety of mischief within the camp, as well as providing further reports when possible. There was no other Imperial agent within the camp that she was aware of. She had made of herself a prized asset.

And they had thrown it all away. Here then was her order, and it was a kill list of majestic proportions, nothing more sophisticated than the thug's work that her compatriots were tasked with back inside the city. Amongst all the ingenuity they could have set her to, this was the result. All the names she had mentioned were echoed back to her, mocking. *Kill them. Kill them all.*

She was just one woman, and not a trained assassin. Yet here were the orders: kill Kymene, kill Amnon, kill Marteus, kill Elder Padstock, and a half-dozen other names along with them, work enough for a whole team of specialists. Suicide for a single spy.

And that was exactly what these orders were, she realized. They were a death sentence pronounced on her, and finally she understood.

Her service, her beloved Army Intelligence, had overstepped the mark. By virtue of its efficiency, by the way its successes showed up others' past failures, it had come under the red and angry eye of the Rekef, and this was punishment for her and for who could know how many others. Orders that could not be carried out, inviting disobedience or outright failure. Elimination, therefore, of those Intelligence agents who had shown themselves capable servants of the Empire. *I've been sold,* she thought numbly. *After all my work, just sold down the road, cast off.* Cherten, she realized, must be a Rekef man after all, one of many, surely, ensconced within Intelligence ranks. Despite the stakes, despite the battle to come, the Rekef had not changed at all since the last war. It was more concerned with infighting than with the Empire's success.

For a moment the mad thought gripped her – to run, head for Capitas, expose the whole shabby plot to . . . But there was nobody to whom she could go, and Capitas was the haunt of General Brugan, whose vengeful hand lay all over these orders.

She could ignore the commands. She could pretend she had never received them. Unless there *was* another agent, who had seen her take them. Now that the breath of the Rekef was on the back of her neck, she suspected everyone and everything.

Or she could obey, take at least a bite out of that kill list, and surely die in return, unknown and despised by friend and enemy alike.

She crumpled up the orders, then found a fire to consign them to, but she could not burn them out of her mind.

General Brugan had slept well last night, for the first time in months, in fact. The Empress had called him to her bed, but their lovemaking had been markedly different. He could almost persuade himself that all those memories, the nights of terror and helpless desire, had been just a nightmare. Seda had behaved as the demure Imperial wife that befitted a general's station, anxious to please, demure and needful.

He had not gloated, nor mistreated her. What need to, when she was telling him that he had won?

With Vecter and Harvang, and Harvang's man Ostrec, and all the other willing tools who had flocked to Brugan's banner, it had been a simple piece of Rekef machination to isolate the

Empress. Her favourites had been arrested, men such as Gje-gevey now peopling the cells below the palace and waiting for Brugan to decide how best to dispose of them. Palace staff and higher-ranking functionaries of dubious loyalty had been re-deployed, or sometimes just made to disappear. A silent coup had taken place, for the good of the Empire. Seda, who had momentarily escaped from the role that Brugan – and history – had intended for her, was now back in her place.

And the rest of it – the blood, the nights, the queasy, squeamish terror of it all – he could forget. He could write it off as an aberration, the pressure of office overwhelming the woman's mind for a moment, but now put right. Even on his way to meet with Harvang and the others, with a half-dozen men at his back, Brugan paused a moment and shook his head, feeling unsettled.

All done with, he promised himself. *All dealt with. It's over.*

And, of course, with the resumption of the world's ways came the chance to deal with other irritations that had crept up on him while he had been distracted. It was true that the last war had torn some holes in the cloak the Rekef cast over the Empire and beyond, what with Brugan and his two rivals struggling against one another for control. Now it was time to stitch them closed again, to draw down the impenetrable Rekef veil of fear and secrecy, and to cut off whatever might try to crawl through the gaps. Such as Army Intelligence: those upstarts, the second sons, who had always been little more than a mouthpiece for the Rekef's views, hands to undertake the tasks the Rekef disdained, and a source of convenient placements for Rekef agents. They had got above themselves. Without a stern Rekef eye on them, they had begun to imagine that they could actually *do the Rekef's job*.

Brugan knew his proper priorities. The Empire must be protected from its enemies from without, of course – a task that was usually pursued proactively – but more importantly the Empire must be protected from internal strife. The status quo must be defended, and Army Intelligence had begun to make ripples. If they had simply been the clowns they were supposed to be, then no harm would have been done, but they had committed the cardinal error of succeeding, and too many people had been left wondering about the Rekef's power and influence, and questioning the stranglehold it maintained on the Empire. Something had needed to be done, but thankfully there was a longtime Rekef man heading up Intelligence for the Second Army. As soon as Solarno was taken and General Tynan's people took over the westward push, Brugan could ensure that Intelligence had its teeth pulled, firmly and fatally.

'General.'

He acknowledged the salute of the soldier, one of the palace staff. 'Report.'

'Message from Colonel Harvang, sir.'

I'm on my way to meet the fat fool now, Brugan reflected. *What is it that can't wait?*

'He says to tell you, sir, the orders have gone to General Roder and the Eighth.'

Brugan stopped, staring at the man. 'Orders to the Eighth from Harvang? What orders?'

'Forgive me, sir, I don't know.' Receiving the full attention of the general of the Rekef was plainly more than the man was comfortable with.

What is Harvang playing at? The unexpected always put Brugan on the defensive, if only because there should be no room for it in a spymaster's life. He waved the messenger away irritably, and doubled his pace. The possibility that, now the Rekef was firmly holding the reins again, there might be some challenge from the ranks had already occurred to him, and Harvang was certainly the leading contender, especially as he and his little catamite had done so much of the work in putting Seda in her place. *But I had looked for more time to consolidate than this.* Brugan ran a quick mental inventory of assets within the palace – those who were loyal, those who were for hire –

and by his reckoning Harvang possessed nowhere near the support the man would have needed to strike now. Besides, Vecter would never back him, just as Harvang would never back Vecter: a rivalry that Brugan had always encouraged. *So this is perhaps his first ranging shot, to see how I will react. And if it's more, well . . .* The men in formation behind him were a mere formality, of course, but a Rekef general's orders would suffice to have them kill a mere Rekef colonel, of that he was sure.

It was a slightly depressing thought, that he might well have to do away with Harvang's talents. *Although at least I get that vermin Ostrec with him. We'll see how much of a pretty boy he remains after a few rounds with the interrogators.*

Seda always liked this level of the palace, he thought drily, as he mounted a final set of stairs and headed towards sunlight. No dingy Rekef cellars for the conspirators now, but an airy room with a balcony overlooking a muster square. After all, there was no need for secrecy any more.

He stepped through the doorway with the word, 'Harvang . . .' on his lips, and stopped dead.

Colonel Vecter sat on a couch across from the door, or at least he was propped there: his spectacles askew on his nose, eyes wide, his skin deathly pale. Brugan made a sound, just a wordless noise.

The Consortium magnate, Knowles Bellowern, sprawled to his left, lying on his back, dark skin gone an ashen grey. To Brugan's right, as if struck down while rushing for the doorway, was an army major who had been privy to the plot. Only yesterday he had been nagging to receive a reward for his services. Someone had ensured that he had been given it. He lay face down, frozen fingers clawing at the stone floor.

Despite himself, Brugan took another two paces into the room.

There were others, but in the far corner, slouching in a chair, was the vast dead-leviathan bulk of Colonel Harvang, an appalling sack of flesh bleached white like some sea-thing dragged into daylight. Bloodless like them all, his sagging, flaccid face bore an expression of horrified disbelief.

Seda stood beside him, and she was not alone. At one shoulder stood a young Wasp with a faint smile on his face, the one notable absence in the corpse-conspiracy that now surrounded them.

'Ostrec!' Brugan hissed, and then, without pause, 'Kill him! Kill Ostrec now!' for he himself could not raise a hand, not with *her* there.

Something moved very swiftly behind him, and he was spattered by a warm spray. Someone's elbow struck Brugan in the back, staggering him, and there was some small scuffling, no more than that. Reeling back, turning with his palm raised, he found himself facing a figure in full armour of ornate Mantis construction, its only weapon a clawed metal gauntlet on one hand.

His men were dead. All his men were all dead. Brugan's mouth moved, wordlessly. This was one of the Empress's bodyguards, but had they not all been *women*? The faintly glimpsed face within the helm seemed as pale as the drained corpses around them.

He turned, hand directed now at the Empress but shaking so wildly that his true aim would have been unguessable. He could not loose, though. His sting was a prisoner of his hand and her eyes. Her feigning of the night before had been cast aside, as had all his assurances to himself that she was his, that she was just a Wasp woman, that she was in any way *natural*.

'Do you fear, General Brugan?' she asked him sweetly. 'Do not, for you are dear to me, after all. I would not harm you. Come.' She gestured, stepping out onto the balcony, Ostrec a step after her. The presence of the Mantis loomed large behind him, and Brugan felt himself shepherded, driven until he stood out in the open air.

'We have much to celebrate, General,' Seda told him. 'The Empire is to become great in ways you cannot imagine. Drink with me.'

Ostrec held a goblet to him, and Brugan felt keenly aware of all those pale bodies in the room at his back. He knew what the cup would contain.

He saw soldiers out there on the muster field, perhaps a hundred of them in slightly unfamiliar uniforms, the pauldrons and gorgets of gleaming red offsetting the traditional colours of the Empire. Each one of them held a clay beaker, and when Seda lifted her own goblet high, so did they.

'Your Rekef is so prone to plots and divisions,' Seda told him. 'I had hoped when I took the throne that ridding you of your rivals would cure the rot, but it appears that conspiracy is addictive. These men you see before you are *mine*,' and the way she used the word spoke of far more than simple oaths and orders. 'They have been chosen by me for the blood they bear, some last fading touch of a former age that lets me speak to them. They have bound themselves to me and, wherever they go, they shall speak with my voice. They are my Red Watch, and even the Rekef shall obey them. Is that not so, General?'

He could do nothing then, but apparently silence had doomed him to acquiescence, for Seda nodded, satisfied. Perhaps she had read the surrender in his mind. He would believe anything now.

'Drink,' she said, and brought the cup up to her lips, and Brugan felt his own arm move, as if accepting that it had no choice. In the square below, the Red Watch drank too, renewing their pact with the Empress, and all that she represented.

The Eighth Army under General Roder had been making determined but dragging progress towards Sarn, constantly plagued by the attentions of the Mantis-kinden. The forest north of them seemed to throng with inexhaustible numbers of the creatures, and all their unpleasant pets, and every night they would sally forth to plague him in some manner. The army carried its fortress with it, just as General Tynan had pioneered against the Felyal in the last war, constructing it every evening before dark, taking every wall down each morning by dawn. This on its own had slowed progress, but Roder was beginning to wonder if he should not have found a way to lay siege to the forest itself. The Felyal, with its warlike natives, was tiny in comparison, and these two Mantis holds of Etheryon and Nethyon fielded a formidable number of inventive and determined killers.

If they had offered a direct assault, then Roder had no doubt that he would have smashed them. Superior tactics and technology would have sent the savages packing without difficulty. Instead, the Mantids crept in, as ones and twos and small bands, their stealth and their Art evading the eyes of the sentries, however much artificial light the Wasps were able to call upon. They slipped into the camp and killed whoever opportunity put across their path, but they were subtler than mere assassins. In the same way as the Moths of Tharn had plagued the mine owners of Helleron for generations, so the Mantids destroyed everything they could find. Without a shred of the artificer's craft, they were still able to damage vehicles, carts and artillery, to hole water and fuel barrels, and to lay thorny caltrops, snares and spikes for the unwary. During the day, after the army finally got underway, Mantis warbands would shadow them constantly, always on the lookout for an opening to swoop in, loose their deadly arrows and then retreat. They presented Roder with a perfect mathematical challenge. He could defend completely, arraying his men so that the Mantids did not even try an assault, but then the Eighth would proceed at a mere crawl. The faster he advanced, however, the more opportunities he presented to the enemy, and they took them without fail.

He had hoped for howling savages, but the Mantis-kinden here were cunning and patient, and he knew that behind them would be their Moth masters and military advisers from Sarn, which was being given plenty of time to prepare for his assault.

Still, even if he was slowed down, his progress was inexorable, and the casualties and damage had all been within tolerance. He had always known that the Eighth would have to run this gauntlet, even if he had not quite appreciated that they would have to *walk* it.

This morning, though, even as his army was dismantling the previous night's defences, he heard the drone of a flying machine on the air.

The Sarnesh had tried one air attack, a tenday ago. Their machines and pilots were inferior to the Wasp Spearflights that Roder carried with him, but their mindlink made them troublesome opponents, even so. They had not adapted their machines for the sort of ground attacks that Roder knew the Imperial air force was carrying out over Collegium, and so the overall damage was slight, but there was every chance that the Ants would come back with something more effective. He had issued standing orders, so even now a dozen of his own aviators were rushing for their machines.

There was only a single flier incoming, though, and it came from the east, from home. The Spearflights escorted it in, and Roder saw that it was a new long-bodied machine, presumably one of the Farsphex model raiders that were committed to the Collegium offensive.

He knew that these machines carried would carry a passenger, but he did not expect the apparition that unfolded itself awkwardly out of the passenger compartment. Tall, hunched and lanky, grey skin banded with white, and bundled up in a scholar's robe edged with Imperial colours, Roder recognized the Imperial adviser, Gjegevey. If asked to prepare a list of the last men he would expect to see out here, the ancient Woodlouse-kinden would certainly have appeared on it.

Once Gjegevey was tottering on his feet and moving out of the way, the pilot made himself known, and at that point Roder would not have been overly surprised to see the Empress herself. Instead, though, he saw a young man with a captain's rank badge, the uniform of the Light Airborne adorned with red pauldrons and gorget, denoting some unfamiliar unit.

'To what do I owe the pleasure?' Roder asked, though with nothing pleasant in his tone. Men like Gjegevey unsettled him. The old creature had no fixed place in the world, being simultaneously a slave and a great power within the Empire.

'Orders, General. I, mmn, bear the Empress's word.' Gjegevey extracted a somewhat creased scroll from within his robe, and Roder accepted it reluctantly.

When he had broken the seal, checked the signatures and read the contents, his face lost all expression. 'This cannot be,' he said flatly.

'A temporary measure only, General,' Gjegevey assured him, 'but essential. Think of it as part of a greater plan, the, hm, Empress's own.'

'Impossible. I cannot give these orders.'

'They are from the Empress's own hand, sir,' the pilot said, imbuing that 'sir' with precious little respect.

'And who are you?' Roder demanded of the young man, who had the sort of smug confidence he associated only with the Rekef.

'I am of the Red Watch,' the pilot replied. 'I am the voice of the Empress.'

Roder stared at him, and Gjegevey added, in a low voice, 'There have been changes back in Capitas. Believe me, these orders are not negotiable.'

The general sagged slightly, looking about him at his busy army. In a moment he was going to have to tell them, all of them, that they were to withdraw some several miles east and there make camp and wait for further orders. And all the while still within the Mantis-kinden's reach.

Gjegevey, though, who had brought such bad tidings, already seemed to have forgotten him. Instead he was staring north towards the great, engulfing shadow that was the Etheryon–Nethyon forest, with a speculative expression on his face.

Thirty-Six

The tent of Chief Officer Marteus looked spartan, with merely a bedroll slung in one corner and a wooden stand for the man's armour. No map table, for he held his plans in his head, and sharing them with others was not something he was good at. No chair even: he would sit on the floor with his soldiers. Only the fact that he had a tent to himself showed any indication of rank.

Straessa had been called in without warning at first light, and she was not sure whether she had done something wrong. Certainly there had been a fair amount of larking around amongst her troops, which she had hoped was good for morale, or some similar military virtue, for she was not the right officer to quell it.

'Subordinate Officer the Antspider,' Marteus acknowledged her with a nod. The renegade Tarkesh Ant was in full uniform: breastplate and buff coat, even the lobster-tail helm dangling from one hand as though he would don it any moment and charge off to war alone.

'Chief Officer Marteus.' Straessa could not say that she *liked* this man overmuch: he was distant and unsociable, as most Ants were in the company of other kinden. Her respect for him, though, had only grown, for he was so much more the born warrior and logistician than the Collegium locals.

'We'll engage the enemy tomorrow, most likely,' he told her.

'They're keeping a steady progress and, if they chose, they could hit us before dawn, or earlier. They made a fierce pace from Tark to the Felyal. We don't know precisely what time they could manage, if they pushed.'

'I understand, Chief.'

He took a deep breath. 'Battle order, Sub. Bitter as it is to have to spell it out for you, but there's none of you who could work it out for yourself or take it from my mind. It's a simple plan, though. Just keep repeating it to yourself until it sinks in.' He was overdoing the gruff, and that made Straessa nervous. 'The automotives are going to form our wings, flying out left and right to assault the enemy in the flanks. Some will carry light artillery, others just troops. They will do their best not to engage the enemy automotives, for reasons you'll understand full well.'

'Yes, Chief.'

'Their objective is the enemy siege train, specifically anything that looks like a giant leadshotter. That's the word from the Mynans for what took their walls down. From what they say, the Second won't need to get that much closer to Collegium's walls in order to deploy them. As for our centre, you're it.'

Straessa digested all this, standing very still, her face carefully calm, while she played it out in her mind against the backdrop of the desperate retreat from the entrenching works. The more she thought calmly about it, the more her insides churned and twisted, until her mouth came out with, 'Hammer and anvil, Chief?' She did her best to make the words sound casual, because that was how she preferred to think of herself, but the tremor emerged despite her best efforts.

'As you say, Sub.'

'Chief.' *I have fifty comrades who will follow me, and most of them are friends.* 'I can't help noticing,' fighting with each word to keep her voice level, hands clenched into tight fists, 'that their hammer is likely to be their automotives, Chief, And our a-anvil is going to be *us*, Chief, flesh and blood.' And she snapped her mouth shut because to say more than that would be to invite a sundering of her composure.

Marteus nodded briskly. 'That's the plan. You're not to engage their machines, just get out of the way of them if you can, but there will be infantry and airborne coming right after them. They can't take ground with just automotives. Their soldiers you *will* engage, and hold them off with pike and shot.'

'And their . . . their automotives, Chief?' Outside the tent she could hear singing, some of her people, no doubt, some filthy Fly taverna chant.

'I've told you, don't engage.'

But what about when they engage us? She tried to prompt him with her eyes but he was all business, having none of it.

'Go instruct your troops, Sub.'

She just stared at him, and for a moment almost wanted to laugh. It had, she discovered, all been some dreadful mistake. She was not a soldier, after all. She was just a student with delusions of martial prowess – and what set of ridiculous circumstances had conspired to put her here, eh? Where was the department head now, so that she could apply to switch courses?

But Marteus's level gaze had not wavered, and he was plainly expecting her to go and spread the word.

'Chief, I don't think you know what you're . . . What do you think it's going to be like when I tell them – my soldiers, my people – that we're to be where the metal meets? That we're standing at the sharp end?'

His expression – or lack of same – did not alter. 'I know what it's like, Sub. Now get a move on. I've got plenty more of you to see.'

'Tonight you'll understand everything,' said Stenwold. He had kept the two students, Eujen Leadswell and the Wasp Averic, under watch all morning, without them showing any sign of suspicious behaviour. In the afternoon he had sent for them, and he was now heading for Banjacs Gripshod's machine-gutted house, ready for the last act of the drama. Last night they had seen an inexplicable failure or betrayal, as the city was laid bare before the knives of its enemies. Tonight, though . . .

Tonight will go down in history, Stenwold thought unhappily. *One way or another*, and the 'everything' that the boys would understand might leave an altogether more bitter taste. *If they see the reasons behind the sacrifices we have made then, if they understand nothing else, they will understand some of how difficult it is to lead. Let Leadswell choke on that.*

The citizens of Collegium they saw out on the streets were picking their way through the city as though already living in hostile territory. Stenwold had spent the morning with Jodry, pointlessly going over and over each part of the plan, sending unnecessary orders to confirm to every well-briefed individual what he or she already knew. And each of them knew only their own small part, of course. The grand design remained invisible to anyone but Jodry and himself. Everyone in the city must guess that *something* was going on, just as the Empire must, but Jodry and Stenwold had kept their secret safe.

Stenwold thought back to his last look at the Speaker before he set out: the man had been haggard, that great weight of flesh hanging from him like chains, eyes red from drink and tears and lack of sleep. Marching swiftly through Collegium's streets, Stenwold felt a sudden rush of affection for the man. These were hard times to be Collegium's Speaker, all responsibility and no reward, but Jodry had risen to the challenge far better than Stenwold might have expected.

It all comes down, tonight. To win a war in one bold stroke, is that not the tactician's dream? I'll wager no war-leader ever foresaw the battle that we have planned.

'Here,' he snapped back at his two charges, nodding to the two Merchant Company soldiers on the door. They scowled narrowly at Eujen and Averic, but stepped aside to let them all through.

Once inside, Stenwold passed through the entrance hall that was one of the few untouched rooms in Banjacs's house, pushing on until he came to the vast chamber that housed the machine, the mad artificer's ultimate weapon. There were three of the College artificers there, along with Banjacs – the most that Stenwold and Jodry had felt they could trust without hestitation – and they were all hard at work on the machine when he entered.

He had expected that, for Banjacs's life's work was a delicate beast, and they would have no opportunity for a proper testing before they used it. The lightning batteries in the cellars beneath them would take tendays to recharge, according to Banjacs's notes. That was why Stenwold and Jodry had taken the decision they had. That was why so much of Collegium had been laid out as bait for the Farsphex bombs.

Now Banjacs and the artificers tinkered and adjusted, calibrating the machine, testing each individual component of it because they could not test the whole. The three College Masters clambered over the brass and bronze and glass, toolbags slung over their shoulders as if they were just tramp artificers hired in for a construction project. Meanwhile the inventor himself was half-hidden within the works of his machine, metal panels hauled off and discarded on the floor around him. The air in the tall chamber crackled and snapped with errant flecks of power, and from every side there came a hissing and a humming as various parts of the colossal device were powered up for testing. Only when Stenwold called his name a second time did Banjacs push himself backwards out of the monstrous mechanical innards to sit up and glower at him.

'What?'

'How is progress, Banjacs?'

'It will be ready, yes. You doubt me, Maker? I'll show you all just how ready I am once night comes. My life's work, and you come looking to find me wanting now?' When Stenwold indicated the feverish artificers, Banjacs scowled furiously at him.

'Go away. We must tune. We must adjust. Had you not imprisoned me then perhaps we might have time to sit about drinking *wine* like Master the Speaker but, as it is, we must work. We must be perfect. You have no comprehension of the delicacy of my creation.' Beneath wild eyebrows his eyes bored into Stenwold. 'All of Collegium shall know my name,' he said, apparently not as a part of the conversation but just an externalized thought.

'Master Maker,' came Eujen Leadswell's hushed voice, 'what is going on? This is Banjacs Gripshod.'

'So it is.' Stenwold glanced back at him. 'You see, Master Gripshod, how your fame is already spreading.' The humour welled up in lieu of bleaker emotions, tainted by Stenwold's assessment of Banjacs's character and sanity. *What frail things we put our faith in.*

The Wasp, Averic, was staring at Banjacs, perhaps not recognizing the name.

'Master Maker, you said we'd understand. I don't.'

'Tell them what your creation is for, Master Gripshod,' Stenwold suggested.

Banjacs grinning was worse than Banjacs glowering. 'With this, boy, I control the lightning – the greatest engine of its kind the world has ever seen. When active, it shall throw its force straight upwards, charging the very skies over the city. Everything above us will face utter destruction.'

Eujen's expression was familiar to Stenwold, because he himself had worn it when this idea had first been revealed to him. If he had not had artificers go over the plans, he would not have believed it for a moment. He could see the student putting the pieces together steadily, and soon the boy would come to understand the chaos of the previous night, even if Stenwold suspected he would never condone it.

Banjacs was already nodding: the old artificer had fully understood the absence of Stormreaders the previous night, without ever having to be told, and had accepted the decision automatically. After all, it would give his machine a more suitable testing ground. 'When the machines of our enemies have fully gathered over us, we shall annihilate them in a moment.'

Something was dawning on Eujen's face, his mouth opening but the words slow to emerge, but even as he began, 'Master Maker,' in a strangled tone, Banjacs interrupted, hushing him.

'Stop! That sound is wrong! Cease work, you morons!' the old man bellowed at some of the College's most eminent artificers. 'What . . . what is making that sound?' He cast about, as though trying to sniff out the noise.

Stenwold could hear it too, something entirely discordant. *Not now! Don't let the bastard machine go wrong now . . .* It was a great buzzing drone and, in the midst of all this artifice gone mad, it seemed curiously familiar.

'Master Maker,' said Eujen, his face frozen, all condemnation vanished from it. 'It's the Ear.'

Stenwold blinked, his mind taking a moment to catch up on what the boy was saying. The Ear was sounding. The Great Ear, their warning mechanism, was calling out the city's pain, as it had during so many nights before. But outside, the sky was light, the sun still high over the west.

The enemy were coming. The enemy were coming *now*.

'Banjacs!' Stenwold bellowed. 'Get it working – all of it. Get it ready to loose!'

Banjacs goggled at him, hands describing the mess, the missing panels, all the little tasks the artificers were still engaged in.

'Just *work!*' Stenwold almost screamed at him. They were coming, all of them, the air-storm that he had called down upon his people, and he was not *ready*. The Empire had out-thought him, in the end. In his mind he was calculating time and action, plans, orders . . . 'Messenger!'

As if from nowhere, a Fly-kinden in Company sash dropped down beside him, a snapbow seeming over large in his hands.

'Listen carefully: I need this taken to every airfield word for word.' Stenwold felt out of breath, his heart painful in his chest. 'Tell them this: they are to engage the enemy . . .'

The Beetle-kinden man with the burn scar, Army Intelligence's senior man in Collegium, had spent that day counting up the cost of the night's work. That matters had not gone according to plan was an understatement. The modest number of agents under his command had accounted for a mere handful of targets. Some teams had been cut down. Others had found their subjects too well defended.

The aggrieved feeling hung heavy on him that he was labouring under someone else's errors, but he himself had felt that the Wasp boy was securely under the Imperial colours, as had Garvan, his superior. After all, Averic was a Wasp and of good family, and there was a natural order to the world that the burned man had learned long ago. Wasps *were* the Empire. That the boy might have spat in the face of his proud heritage, rejected his own and betrayed his people to Collegium was repugnant to the Beetle with the burn scar. The irony was lost on him.

He still had a small but respectable team working with him, thanks to the prudence that Army Intelligence instilled in its people. Instead of Rekef men raised in a climate of fear and terrified of the consequences of failure, most of his people had simply weighed up the odds and not chanced carrying out attacks. That meant they were still on hand for the night to come.

He had been waiting for contact from the Spider agents in the city, an uncertain prospect, but a lean Fly-kinden man had found them in the early evening in the working man's taverna they were holed up in. The building was missing most of a wall, and all the windows had been smashed, but the landlord was still serving.

They adjourned to an enclosed backroom, after slinging the

landlord a few coins. The burned man expected the Fly to waste time and mince words, weaving a web of allusions and hints, as seemed the Spider way, but instead the report was brutally direct.

'Things have changed. You have a new priority target.'

The Beetle bristled. 'You're not in a position to dictate that.'

'What if we told you that we'd overlooked something until now. Earlier, we'd report that to your general. Now there's no time and we're reporting it to you.'

The burned man sat back, considering. 'What is it?'

'There was a man – he's on your list, but far down it – who's an artificer. There had been some official interest in him recently, but there was a murder; we thought it was just internal Collegiate business carrying on despite the war, you know.' The Fly shrugged. 'We now think it's not that. We think they've played us.'

'Why? Our orders are to kill Stenwold Maker above all others—'

'Good. Fine. He's there now with this man, Banjacs Gripshod. So's your Wasp boy. You need to get out your knives and get moving.'

'What are they doing?'

'We don't *know*,' the Fly hissed, 'but the patterns are all wrong. It's something important, and it's at Gripshod's place it's happening. It's . . .' The difficulty of explaining screwed the little man's face up. 'We have our methods. We look for patterns, feel for the connections between people. But patterns can be deceptive – look at them from a different vantage, you might see something entirely other. That's what's happened here. It wasn't about the murder after all. It's all about the war. Whatever they're doing there in that house is vital, and you need to stop it. I swear on my mistress's honour you do.'

The burn-scarred man stared at him levelly. He had memorized all sorts of places in the city, the dwellings of potential victims amongst them. Part of him was already working out which streets to lead his people down to so as get to Banjacs Gripshod's place as soon as possible. 'And you'll help, will you?'

The Fly spread his hands. 'That is not a part of our mystery,' he said, with a tired smile. 'Besides, surely you won't need us?'

She was gone when Laszlo returned, her sleeping roll disordered, her few personal possessions just smaller absences about her larger one. None of the surgeons or nurses could tell him just when she had slipped out, and he could not know whether she had been feigning her injury, or fooling herself, or whether she had simply been that desperate to be rid of him.

Lissart had vanished, abandoned him after all they had been through. Laszlo could only stare in utter disbelief, and then argue with everyone around him because there were few enough casualties yet for the doctors that surely one of them must have noticed a badly wounded Fly or not-quite-Fly woman pack up her things and *leave*.

But none of them had. Her tradecraft had been her pass in the end. She was gone.

He wasted a great deal of time then, by dashing about the outside of the tent, making sudden rushes in this direction, then in that, as if he would find her just a few paces away, pausing for breath and clutching her wound, *waiting for him*. First, though, before all that furious, undirected, futile action, he just stood and *hurt*. Laszlo the pirate, grinning factor for the *Tidenfree* crew, a girl in every port so long as he had the coin, and he was hurting for her, for his lost te Liss. He had never felt such a tearing before. In its wake, he felt that he would never quite see the world in the same way.

After all that, all the futile battering at the windowpanes of fate, he returned to where she had slept and there found her message.

It was tucked into her discarded bedroll, and anyone could have found it, but nobody else would have understood.

She is here. I can't stay.
She is painted brown and disguised as a Beetle soldier-woman.
Look for me in another place.

Laszlo felt his heart leap at that last line. *We'll meet again. I'll find her or she'll find me.* And then the first two lines took on meaning and his eyes widened.

She could mean only one thing: the Wasp agent who had dealt Lissart such a wound in the first place, she was here in the camp.

He glanced about him. There were Beetle women everywhere, of course there were. But he had already *seen* the Wasp spy – seen her come after Lissart to finish her off. He calmed himself, unhinged his memories, sorting through them for that night that was surely engraved on his mind.

A moment later and he was outside the infirmary tent and peering about him, from face to face. There was a spy in the camp, up to unknowable mischief, and only he could find her.

In her fragmentary and barely remembered dream she was in the air, in a storm, the high winds battering at the framework of the *Esca Volenti* until every part of the loyal machine seemed on the point of coming away from every other. In the midst of wrestling with controls that were suddenly unresponsive in her grip, she was yanked from sleep, shaken into abrupt and uncomprehending wakefulness, unsure of where she was or why.

'Taki! Mistress Taki!' someone was shouting. *Mistress?* But of course, that was how the Collegiates talked, not knowing any better, and what was that dreadful noise?

She sat bolt upright, slapping away the Beetle girl who had woken her. *The Ear!* 'How long did you let me sleep?'

In a moment she was out of her bunk, standing barefoot on the cold floor, in just her shift. She felt leadenly tired, disoriented, as though she had gone to bed only a moment before.

'Mistress Taki, they're coming!' The girl – Taki could not

recall her real name but identified her as 'Still-too-fat-to-be-a-pilot', one of the newer recruits – was a study in wide-eyed panic.

Taki cursed, dragging on her canvas overalls and snagging her chitin and leather helm from the floor. 'You should have woken me an hour ago at least,' she snapped, storming up out of the underground barracks into the common room . . . and stopping.

Broad, glorious daylight sang through the high windows.

'Right,' she said, to nobody in particular. A score of pilots were looking at her expectantly, most of their field's complement.

'Where's Corog? Master Breaker, I mean. Where's everyone else?' she demanded, striving to clear her head.

'Out on the field with their machines,' someone told her, and another put in, 'The Mynans want to take off, but we've no orders . . .'

'*Orders?*' Taki demanded. 'Just go, morons! Get into the air!' And she herself led the charge, wings skimming her up and out to the airfield, darting for the open cockpit of the *Esca Magni*. She saw the rest of the pilots all around, some arguing with ground crew, others already in their machines, wings warming up slowly. Edmon gave her a nod, before bringing his hatch down.

'Hold! Nobody take to the air!' Corog Breaker was rushing across the field, waving his arms like a man trying to catch a departing airship. 'I'll have the hide off anyone that dares fly!'

Edmon rammed his hatch up again, staring at the old man with disgust. 'No,' he shouted back, 'this time we fly. This time we fight the Wasps, even if your people won't. Who's with me, eh?'

There was a lot of shouting then from Mynans and Collegiates both, and Edmon had clearly carried the vote.

'You just listen to me!' Corog Breaker still had a fine old voice, when he needed to use it. 'Yes, we fight! But you listen here, special orders from Stenwold Maker. Nobody gets aloft until they've heard them.'

Edmon scowled belligerently, but waited.

'Just listen, because you have to get this right,' Corog urged them all. 'We're not bearding them beyond the walls this time. We let them come to us.' As the murmur of discontent started up again he raised his arms to quieten them. 'Oh, we fight. When they come over the city, we hold them, but it's more than that. We need to concentrate them, as much as we can. Engage, take the bastards down if you can, but bring all of them over the city's heart.' He glanced back at the scroll he was clutching, breath catching from the run, trying himself to assimilate the instructions. 'Now listen,' he continued. 'The Ear is going to sound again, you understand. You have to listen for it. During the fight, the Ear will sound, and that's your signal.'

'Signal for what, Corog?' Taki asked him.

The old Master Armsman's expression was openly baffled. 'Get out of the sky. Land as soon as you can, on roofs, in the street, crash if you have to. Just get out of the sky. You have to hold them, keep them off the city, until the artificers and Stenwold Maker reckon we've got our best shot. Then you down your machines as soon as the Ear sounds, and . . .'

'And what?' Taki pressed.

'If you're still in the sky right then, you'll find out the hard way,' was all that he would say. 'Now get in your fliers. If your regular machine's with the artificers for the ground-attack refit, get yourself in a spare one. If there's none left, cheer us on.' A proportion of the Stormreaders were being modified following some new requirement from Stenwold Maker or the Speaker or someone: some were still in the workshop being fitted out.

Corog crumpled the scroll and glanced at his own machine. 'We have a little time now, because we're letting them come to us. Make sure your machines are fully wound and ready. Nobody heads off half-sprung. Know this: best guess says that they'll come all together, everything they can put in the air. Ready yourselves for that, as best you can.'

The Ear continued its melancholy drone, and they took to their machines more soberly now – the entire remaining might that Collegium could put in the air. Taki looked around her, thinking about just how many Farsphex the Empire might have to throw at them, and how difficult engaging them for even a short time was going to be without suffering heavy losses. Around her, although she might forget names, she knew every face, as familiar as her old flying comrades from Solarno, most of whom had died in the last war while retaking her city from the Empire. But Solarno now sat under Imperial and Spider colours again, and so what had been the *point*?

She was acutely conscious that this would probably be the last sight she had of many of these people: Mynan airmen, Collegiate student aviators, volunteer academics, merchant pilots turned to war, artificers and tradesmen retrained in the city's time of desperate need. It might equally be their last sight of her.

She was scared, and the sudden fear mingled with the old excitement that an aerial duel had always inspired in her. *I may die, but at least I live first, and show me a better death.*

And, out over the rugged land that separated Collegium from the Second Army, the Farsphex were closing.

General Tynan had listened to every word that Aarmon and Cherten had to say, sitting there with Mycella of the Aldanrael at his right hand, his trusted adviser. With his eyes half-closed, he had heard them both out, taken in every scrap of evidence or supposition, leaping to no conclusions but setting out the facts in his head with the same patient care that had guided his career as an officer.

'You think it's a trap,' he had remarked to Aarmon.

'I think they have husbanded all their strength for tonight, to destroy as many of us as they can, sir. I think they know they must cripple our airpower, for their own to have a chance against your army tomorrow,' the pilot had confirmed.

'And you, Colonel?'

'I think we have our orders, sir,' had come Cherten's response, 'and both my spies and those of the Spiders are reporting that they are simply running out of working machines to put in the air – conserving their strength for the siege.'

'The nature of the trap, Major?'

'New technology or reinforcements for the air,' Aarmon had guessed. 'Better orthopters, perhaps, or Sarnesh machines or pilots to counter our . . . advantage.' For the mindlink was still not a matter to be openly spoken of. 'Their pilots are as good as ours, sir. Their machines are, too. If they could ambush us with twice the number, say, or three times, they could crush our largest raiding party, perhaps stop even one Farsphex escaping.'

Tynan had blinked. 'And if it was more than just a raiding party? You know the Colonel wants a massed bombing raid.'

'Depends on their strength, sir, but, even if they outnumber us, we have the advantage. We fight together in the air.'

For a long time, Tynan had stared at the straight-backed pilot standing to attention before him, and then Mycella had leant in and whispered something to him. Aarmon had felt Colonel Cherten's instant disapproval and frustration – that there were counsels he was being excluded from – but Tynan had simply listened, his eyes flicking up briefly to Aarmon.

Mycella's last words had been loud enough for them all to hear: 'After all, we know about traps, my people.'

And Tynan had looked Aarmon in the eye and said, 'How soon can you be airborne, all of you?'

In the echo of Aarmon's answer, he had then turned to Cherten. 'Double our speed towards Collegium. Their army's out there and they think they have a day at least until we clash. That's a lie. We clash *today*. Abandon the baggage and support here, and move out our soldiers, automotives and the siege train right now. We're going to war.'

Under great protest, Nishaana had been left behind with just four orthopters, a token force to defend the army. If the Collegiates did choose to attack Tynan on the march, even as the Imperial fliers struck their city, then the Second would have to scatter, protect its machines as well as they could, and have one of Nishaana's people make best speed for Collegium to call the fliers back. Aarmon reckoned that the Collegiates were desperate enough to try it, but Cherten had been dismissive.

Pingge knew Aarmon's thoughts, relayed through Scain's murmuring them even as they came to him. Whether or not the Collegiates had reinforcements or some new device, the Wasp aviators knew that Collegiate air power would be the greatest threat to any besieging force, and Collegiate control of the sky would make taking the city near-impossible. War had changed in so few years, but they, the Air Corps and their Collegiate rivals, were at the cutting edge, the masters of the storm.

Their orders were to destroy the enemy air power. Bombing the city was secondary and, for greater speed in the air, they carried a reduced load of explosives, enough for a few hard passes should the chance arise.

'Nearing,' Scain said, loud enough for her to know it was meant for her ears.

Carefully she set to loading and spanning the little ballista they had bolted onto her hatch. A sudden buffet of air sent her lurching her forwards, an explosive-tipped bolt tumbling out into the night. The chain was taut about her ankle, catching her before she needed her wings. Many of the pilots had wanted to forgo the chains, but back in Capitas the engineers had ensured that the stigmatizing protocol was adhered to, and Colonel Cherten proved to be their brother in diligence in the Second Army's camp. For herself, Pingge had felt the benefit of it more than once, when being jolted and rattled about in the heat of an aerial battle. For all her Art, if she had been flung from the Farsphex, she could never have regained her place.

She looked into the reticule, seeing Collegium ahead, landmarks that were as familiar to her now as to a native, it almost seemed, but less so in daylight. 'They didn't launch,' she called, against the rush of air. There had been no Collegiate blockade to meet them halfway to the city, but then halfway to the city was not very far at all this time. The Second Army – the Gears – had made its signature steady progress west, and now its goal was in sight. Pingge was looking at it, even then.

If the Collegiates had attempted such a blockade, they would have been outmanoeuvred. Aarmon had divided his force into three, approaching the city from east, north and south, the latter two to double back west if they met no resistance over the city itself, and thus catch their enemy in the rear. Now it seemed as though all three wings would meet over Collegium, their mindlink allowing them to intermesh effortlessly.

'Light bombing to draw them out,' Scain murmured Aarmon's words, and then his own response, 'Will do, sir,' before pitching his voice up, 'Pick a target, Pings. Wake them up—' and almost immediately, 'No need! They come!'

Thirty-Seven

The Fly-kinden scout attracted some notice by diving out of a clear sky, shrugging off the challenges of sentries, her arms held up to ward of reprisals as she skidded to her feet in the centre of the Collegium camp. By that time enough had seen her Maker's Own sash, and a few more had recognized her face, so she was allowed to pick herself up and take a quick glance to get her bearings. A moment later her wings were skimming her towards the command tent.

Amnon was in conference with her chief officer, the Beetle woman Elder Padstock, when the Fly gasped out her report.

'They're coming!'

'The automotives?' Padstock beckoned a messenger towards her, about to send orders to ready the artillery. The Collegiates had foreseen such a strike, after the disaster at the trenches.

'Their entire army, Chief!' the Fly got out, her chest heaving for breath. 'All of 'em.'

For a second Amnon watched Padstock freeze, expressionless, and then she was rattling off orders. 'Tell the mechanics to have all the automotives readied. Pass word round all the officers and sub-officers to assemble, just like for the drills. You,' and she picked out the exhausted Fly, 'get me the other chief officers right now.'

It seemed forever before they gathered, though in truth it was barely minutes: Marteus of the Coldstone Company, the Mynan commander Kymene and Amnon's lover, Praeda Rakespear. With Padstock and the huge Khanaphir they made up the War Council of Collegium's army, the first such in its history.

'Report,' Padstock prompted the grey-faced Fly, and the diminutive woman straightened up, looking soldierly.

'Saw dust at first, Chief. Got my glass out. Looks like all the fighting bits of the Second are coming our way, double time, right now.' That her mind was fixated on that inexorable advance was very clear. She had been one of the far pickets, a strong-winged flier with a telescope keeping watch for some gambit of the enemy's. Now, it seemed, the Wasps had eschewed gambits.

'Such speed . . .' Praeda said, shaking her head. 'It couldn't be, surely? How clearly did you—?'

'Oh, clear,' the Fly replied belligerently, scowling at the challenge. 'Believe me, all the dust in the world won't hide *that*.'

'What's their battle order?' Marteus snapped.

'Saw maybe ten, maybe a dozen of those woodlouse auto-motives leading the charge, what looked like transports backing 'em, and on either wing too – carting infantry, it looked to me. Heavier transports at back.'

The Collegiate officers exchanged glances.

'That's what we banked on,' Praeda observed.

'Then at least something's going according to plan,' came Marteus's mutter.

Kymene drew herself up, as one of her countrymen began buckling on her breastplate: black with two red arrows, one descending, one ascending, the badge of Myna from before they threw off the Wasps in the last war – *We have fallen, we will rise again.* 'We have to advance to meet them in the field, or else fall back,' she declared, brooking no argument. 'This,' and her gesture took in the whole sprawling Collegiate camp outside the tent, 'cannot be considered a defensive position.'

'We'd not have to retreat far to give our walls over to their artillery,' Praeda pointed out.

There was a moment of exchanged looks, mirrored grim expressions. No general wanted to have his hand forced, but the realities were stark.

'The soldiers are mustering, or already mustered. Let's move them out,' Marteus concluded. For an Ant going to war there was precious little enthusiasm in his voice.

'You must speak to them,' Amnon rumbled, as his first contribution. Kymene was already nodding. After all, the two of them were the only ones present who had actually led an army before.

'They go to fight, perhaps to die,' the Khanaphir First Soldier continued. 'They look to you as their leaders. They trust you to give them the right orders. You must speak to your people, reassure them. Or I will. I have done this many times before. I have the voice for it.'

Padstock and Marteus exchanged glances, but Praeda put a hand on Amnon's arm.

'Do it,' she agreed.

The Collegiate army was still mustering, the last soldiers finding their places as their commanders came out to them, treading the steps of a drill they had practised plenty of times over the last tendays. Amnon glanced about, and then jumped up onto the flat back of a transport automotive, with Marteus and Padstock flanking him. To his left were the cohorts of the Coldstone Company, their motto *In Our Enemy's Robes*, with many of the older soldiers still wearing souvenirs from past battles with the Empire or the Vekken. To the right was the Maker's Own Company, whose words were *Through the Gate*, commemorating the fearless spirit with which Padstock and her fellows had marched out, along with Stenwold Maker, to confront the Second Army at the end of the last war.

Between them Amnon saw the balance of the Collegiate force. Mostly these were Three-city Alliance fugitives, Mynans reinforced by a handful of Szaren Bee-kinden and grim-faced Ants from Maynes. Kymene was already passing amongst them; not

571

for her the grand oration, but a personal valediction: a hand on the shoulder, confirmation to each that she would be with them. Beside these was a handful of Sarnesh drivers and crew for the automotives they had sent in support.

Beyond all of the massed military strength of Collegium, the cooks, servants, mechanics, entertainers and all the other baggage that the army had collected watched on, and no doubt each of them was trying to decide: *Stay, or flee?*

Praeda climbed up beside Amnon and handed him a speaking horn, for even his voice would not carry to so many ears. He took a deep breath, feeling a great weight fall from him, as though he was back in his proper place for the first time since leaving his city and his station. These were not his people, but they were cousins of a sort, and if this battle to come was not his battle, the addition of Khanaphes to the Empire made the wider conflict his war.

'You have heard the call to battle!' he said, voice loud into the horn, and louder still as it rolled like thunder over them. 'The enemy of us all brings his strength against us, and I know full well that each of you feels the worm of fear within you. It is what makes us human. Do not think that I have not felt it, too.' In truth he did not feel it now, but he could dredge up the sense of it from distant memory.

'At your backs is your city. You have not seen my home of Khanaphes, which styles itself the greatest city of the world. For thousands of years has Khanaphes endured, our stones grown old long before your College was ever built. And yet I say to you: if any city is a wonder of the world, it is Collegium. Was ever there a city more fit to take pride in what it has achieved? Was ever there a city whose people were more capable of steering their destinies than you? Where the Wasps have laboured mightily to imprison the minds and bodies of all who fall under their shadow, so have you laboured to set yourselves free.

'Hear me, for these things you take for granted: that you may choose your leaders, that you do not go hungry on a poor harvest, that your surgeons and doctors know all wounds and diseases, that your families live each day without fear of tyranny or oppression.'

He was acutely aware of Praeda standing beside him, and he saw the speaking horn shake as she held it up. He put an arm about her, in front of those thousands, embracing one of their own.

'The Empire will take from you all these things. They know only the chain and the whip and the iron rule of their law which says: *Do as you are told, or suffer.* Do you ask yourselves why they come? Can you imagine the blow you strike against them simply by being as you are? Can you think how many in the Empire must ask, *Why can we not live as they?* The Empire comes to rid you of these freedoms, because those same freedoms will unmake the Empire itself, given time.

'But now, you must march. You must take up the pike and the snapbow, the automotive and the leadshot.' Words that would have been unfamiliar to him not so long ago, and yet he had learned them well. 'For all that you own, for all the comfort and the freedom that your city has gifted you with, you must fight. For all those that you have left behind, friends, family and lovers, you must fight and you must not yield. You are scholars and tradesmen and merchants made into soldiers. Now you must make yourselves heroes!'

And on the last word he thrust his sword high. A Khanaphir army would cheer him immediately, but there was a curious pause, a moment where the Collegiate soldiers made up their own minds rather than being blackmailed into a response, and then a few, and more and then all of them roared their approval at him.

It was all he could do for them, that transplanted fighting spirit. Between that encouragement and their training and the weapons the artificers had crafted for them, they would have to manage.

Praeda raised the speaking horn to her own lips. 'Drivers, to your machines and be ready! Automotives move to the wings, infantry muster in order east of the camp ready for the advance!' She squeezed Amnon's arm and jumped down from the bed of the transporter, running for the automotive that she would drive for him as he led the charge on the left flank, powering towards the enemy siege train.

Amnon climbed down more slowly. It was not that he was weary, but the fierce passion that normally filled him in times of war was waning; perhaps he was too far from his home, too far from any battle his people might recognize. All very well to talk of chariots, but still . . .

There was a brittle crack, and then a thunderous retort, and he felt the very edge of the heatwave as his automotive – Praeda's automotive – exploded.

Amnon stared, unable to put the various pieces of the scene together. The drivers had all rushed to start their machines, spin up their gyroscopes, release their flywheels, fire their engines. Now the two of them either side of her were partly staved in, as though punched by some giant, their sides raked with broken shrapnel, and between them a sort of fiercely burning framework peeling outwards like the petals of a flower. And Amnon bellowed something wordless and rushed towards the flames, arms outstretched, shouting her name, but it was too late, already too late.

People were shouting at each other, soldiers breaking formation. The few drivers whose machines had yet to start were leaping clear of their seats. Cries for surgeons arose from those struck by pieces of Praeda's machine.

Nobody noticed the Wasp woman with the snapbow.

Rigging an automotive to explode – one that relied on a fuel engine – was simpler than Gesa had thought. After all, the thing was almost a bomb already, save that it relied on its explosions to be controlled. Adding all the additional firepowder she could get hold of, and linking the ignition flame to that and to the fuel tank had fallen within the level of artifice that any Army Intelligence agent was trained to. She only regretted that she had not been able to rig more of them, and that the big Khanaphir himself had not been in the machine when it was started.

Now she was stretched out to full length atop one of the big transporters that the army would be leaving behind them, sighting along a Collegiate snapbow at their commanding officers, waiting for a clear shot whilst the tenuous discipline of her enemies disintegrated all around her.

She could feel the sands running out for her. She had decided to fulfil her orders, but that did not mean she could not get out alive as well. She had just killed one of the Collegiate leaders on her list. She would not be able to get them all, but she reckoned that she could make a good enough showing, and then make a stab at escaping too. And wouldn't Colonel Cherten look sour about *that*.

She wanted to take down the Mynan woman, but Kymene was now in the midst of her people, offering no clear shot, so she took the next most dangerous.

A squeeze of the trigger, and abruptly Marteus the Ant was falling backwards, clean kill or just a wound she could not say. She had never been intended as a markswoman.

Next target, now: the other Company chief officer, the woman Padstock. Gesa dropped her spent snapbow onto the transporter cab's roof and took up the other loaded weapon she had left ready. There was a cluster around the downed Marteus, most of them staring about them, but the general panic had obscured the sharp sound of the snapbow.

She sighted up, heart hammering within but all outward calm . . . then there was a scrabbling immediately behind her, and she twisted reflexively, raising the weapon.

Had it not been a Fly-kinden, she would have been able to kill her attacker right then, but the small man was already within the arc of her barrel, elbowing it aside and sweeping something round towards her. She had a glimpse of the knife's blade, and got a knee in his stomach just as it came in, so that it only raked her side, instead of gutting her. He was not even wearing Company colours, just some ragged little renegade.

She kicked him hard in the chest, knowing that she had accomplished all she could and that now was her last chance to get clear. The man was shouting loudly and enough people were taking notice.

She took flight, for already the odd snapbow bolt was heading her way, and there would be enemies in the air, too, at any moment. Her wings cast her over the ridges of tents, through an increasingly busy sky, and then dropped her down amongst the canvas, briefly out of sight. She ducked inside a tent-mouth, pausing to hear the hunt getting nearer. Could she hide here, let them rush past her? No, even the Collegiates were not that incompetent. She backed further in, almost to her knees, and cut a slit down the tent's back to peer out, seeing that the search was organizing itself dangerously fast.

She widened the slit, working swiftly yet patiently until she was holding closed a gap she could push her way through. The first chaotic impetus of the hunt was past her, but those coming after were being more methodical. Timing would be everything.

She took a deep breath, ripped the canvas open and took to the air. Now, only speed would save her.

The snapbow shot hammered into her from *above*, a colossal slap to her shoulder that shocked her more than it hurt, the bolt tearing its way in and then out of her, hurtling her from the air. Landing with breath knocked from her, and the wound abruptly a ball of complaining fire, she saw the self-same Fly descend on her, holding her own second snapbow. He had simply flown up and waited, guessing at her best chance of escape.

He slung the emptied weapon at her as he landed, and she batted it away as an agonizing flurry of her wings hauled her to her feet like a puppet. Then he was on her with his knife, and she stumbled out of reach, hurling her own at him. Even as he

576

flinched back, her hand was open, palm outwards. *One last blow for the Empress.*

Someone punched her hard in the back and abruptly she was lying on her side, and it hurt terribly to breathe. The Fly was standing out of reach – *as if that could have saved him!* – but it seemed that her Art had now deserted her. She had no strength for it any more.

Someone knelt beside her, rolling her over onto her back so that she gasped in pain, blood spattering out of her mouth. She saw the Mynan commander, the woman Kymene, with a snap-bow cradled in one arm.

Just one sting . . .

But all she could do was cough, and the coughing was all blood, and at last she gave up her tenacious hold on life, with the thought, *I have done enough of my duty.*

'What are you all doing, standing around here?' Kymene's high voice cut through the babble of voices as she stormed back through the camp, snapbow in one hand and the blood of the enemy spy on her armour. 'Infantry, muster to the east of the camp as ordered. Automotives – those that have started take your positions, mechanics to check over any yet to start! *Move!* The enemy is still coming! You think *they* will have stopped for this?'

She found Amnon kneeling by the still-burning wreck of the automotive. By then the surgeons had got all of Praeda that was left from the twisted metal, but no science of Collegium nor mystery of the Inapt could do anything for her.

'Come on,' Kymene urged more softly, a woman well acquainted with loss. 'This is no time for grief, Amnon. Not when so many are looking to you. Not when there are Wasps to kill.'

He straightened up slowly. 'Is that it, then? Is that all there is?'

'Until my people are free, I will kill every Wasp and Spider and any other kinden that stands between me and my home. If you must grieve, let your enemy grieve with you. If you want vengeance then they now bring you all the opportunity you need. If you would lose yourself, then lose yourself in duty.'

Amnon glanced around and saw that the armed host of Collegium was finally on the move, assembling in proper battle order east of the camp, ready to advance. The far north-eastern horizon was already dim with the first dust of the Imperial forces.

With a great roar, he leapt for the next automotive to grumble past, swinging himself up beside its artillerist and the smallshotter mounted there.

The *Esca Magni* kicked into the air, that first beat of the orthopter's wings hammering at the ground, throwing the craft straight up, clawing itself away from the yawning pull of the ground. All around Taki, and below her, the rest of Collegium's air power was launching, their Stormreaders ungainly and impossible for that first moment, before transforming into things native to the sky.

She gave the *Esca* its head, let it find its path over the city, her eyes fixed on the eastern sky. The bright sunlight seemed alien to her after so many battles in darkness. Glancing left, she saw a flight of Mynan machines painted in their black and red, whilst a long string of Collegiate pilots trailed off on her far side. She spotted Corog's machine powering ahead, the tip of a great broad arrow that was slowly forming behind him.

Contact! came the flash from one of the locals, and a moment later Taki revised her picture of the sky, for the enemy were far closer than the had anticipated, already diving out of the sun on their first attack run. She cursed herself for falling into useless patterns, for today's fight would owe precious little to any of their previous engagements.

Her lamps stuttered and glowed as she tried to shove a mass

of orders into the minds of her fellows, in a pitiful echoing of the interplay of thought amongst the enemy. *On me; attack full forwards; break off; circle back; drawn them with us.* Knowing, even as she made the attempt, that they would lose the thread of the message before getting halfway through it. In the end she just sent *Follow my lead!* three times, as she made her run.

Piercer bolts flashed and danced about her, the closest Farsphex spotting her – probably they even knew her by now, by her smaller, fleeter craft and her flying style. She jinked left, trusting to the skill of her fellows to adjust, opening up with her own rotaries and scoring a handful of glancing strikes before she and her opponent were past one another, just flashing blurs gleaming in the sun. Her enemy would have to deal with her allies, she with his.

She abandoned her line immediately, because the sky before her was being cut into pieces by shot from both sides. Instead she drove upwards, straight at one of the enemy, forcing him aside because she was feeling madder than he – then she slung the *Esca* right. She found the flank of a Farsphex before her just as she imagined she would, bobbing up ten feet to avoid the bolt the Fly-kinden bombardier loosed at her, then unleashing everything her weapons had to give.

She drew a line of punctures across the top of the enemy's hull before tracking into its open side-hatch. Then she was close enough to discern the red ruin she had just made of the bombardier, a man of her own kinden torn apart by weapons meant to destroy machines. She pulled up hurriedly, sick in her stomach and desperately trying to unsee what she had just witnessed.

But it's war. What did I think would happen? The thought did nothing to erase that bloody image.

Then bolts were falling on her like the patter of rain, and reflexes kicked sentiment aside and slung her, almost upside down, looping out of the way of the oncoming enemy and aside from his friend, who was trying to pinion her – and she was past

579

the two of them, knowing that neither had the angle to get on her tail. Already she was looking for a new target.

Scain swore as the Farsphex rattled about, bouncing Pingge away from the ballista, forcing her to climb uphill towards it one moment, fall past it the next. She was only glad that she was not being ordered to bomb anything right then. The way her aim was being shaken about, the good people of Collegium wouldn't know which was was up.

That thought stuck in her throat, suddenly not funny. Then Scain was cursing again, muttering reports from the other pilots, requests for assistance, attempts to bring their formation together and destroy the enemy. For a moment a Stormreader flashed past the open hatch and she dragged the ballista about, but the target was gone as soon as she had registered it.

Then they were in an abruptly deserted sky, coasting over the silent and seemingly empty city as if this was a dream, and they the only thing in it. Scain was still muttering, and she caught fragments of his constant stream of consciousness: '. . . massing over the centre . . .' 'refusing to engage . . .' 'Aarmon scores a hit . . .' 'Tarsic's down . . .' 'why are they all . . . ?' The pilots were all on extra rations of Chneuma to make up for having had almost no sleep since the night's bombing raid.

There was a rattle, and three points of sky opened up in the hull beside Pingge, making her scream more with shock than with fear. Instantly Scain was hauling the machine into a tight turn, and she expected more damage, the enemy right behind them, but it seemed the Collegiate flier had fled as soon as Scain reacted. A moment later – peering down the narrow neck of the craft and over Scain's shoulder – she saw the sky full of duelling monsters. The entire strength of both sides, practically every orthopter Collegium and the Second Army could muster, was now engaged in a deadly, graceful sparring, vicious and brutal for the men and women within the cockpits, and yet, seeing it from her detached perspective, as they plunged towards it, it seemed a dance where everyone knew the steps, a beautiful interweaving such as the darting shuttles of the looms back in her factory could never have managed.

Scain roared something wordless, and she felt the hammering of the rotaries through the metal floor beneath her. Past his head, in that great populated skyscape, a Stormreader shuddered and lurched, twisting desperately to be rid of him, but he followed its evasions like a Rekef man scenting treason, and abruptly the target's two wings were not beating – were shredding apart under the ferocity of his attack – and then Scain was breaking off and letting his victim make the long fall alone.

A single bolt struck somewhere behind, near the tail, and Scain was already slinging the Farsphex sideways hard enough to make every rivet groan. Another Collegiate machine flashed by, already clutching at the air for an equally tight turn, and Scain thrust their flier forward to put distance between them and their enemy, whilst in his mind he had already summoned help.

Pingge knew she should now be crouching behind her ballista, waiting for that absurd chance that would allow her a shot, but she could not tear her eyes away. Everywhere she looked, the aviators were coming towards the final engagement of their pure and private war, trying to kill each other with every scrap of skill and mechanical genius their respective sides possessed. Stormreaders whirled away with shattered hulls, dead hands still resting on the stick, Farsphex trailed smoke from burning engines or broke up as the convolutions of their pilots and the damage they had taken passed some critical tolerance. It was terrible, it was awe-inspiring. She could not look away.

A fierce flash of flame showed an orthopter consumed, flaming and dropping, either a Stormreader struck by a lucky bolt from a bombardier's ballista, or a Farsphex taken by an even luckier strike from the roof-mounted repeaters the Collegiates were using. Watching the disintegrating, burning thing whirl towards the city below, Pingge could not even tell whether it had been friend or foe.

Thirty-Eight

Standing east of the Collegiate camp, guessing that behind her most of the non-combatants were making their escape already, Straessa recognized a bad idea when she saw it. The last of her people was falling into position, and it seemed the explosion that had killed Praeda Rakespear was still echoing in her ears. She had not even been able to discover if her chief officer was dead or alive.

There was a tug at her sleeve and she glanced down to see Sartaea te Mosca, who should have been with the surgeons. The Fly woman, friend and hostess and occasional lecturer in Inapt studies, looked desperately grave, out of all proportion to her size.

'Keep safe, now.'

'I'll bear it in mind,' Straessa said. 'No promises.'

The hoped-for smile flickered ghostlike over te Mosca's face, then faded. 'There will be stretcher teams following behind the lines, so get your wounded sent back immediately, if you can. Just call out "Stretcher" and, if they hear, they'll come, no matter what.'

'Where did you find them?' Straessa demanded. 'You've learned how to magic people out of thin air, now? Wish you'd taught that in class.'

'Oh, volunteers,' the Fly said casually. 'From the camp, you know: artificers, cooks, prostitutes, whoever we had. I was surprised, really. So many of them wanted to help. It's their Collegium, too, after all.'

Straessa made to reply, but then three clear, shrilling blasts reached her, and she reached for her own whistle, relaying the order even before her mind had decoded it. *Advance. Ah, right.* She squeezed te Mosca's hand, and then the Fly was half-slipping, half-flying away, back to the camp where the surgeons were already preparing themselves for the butchery to come.

Her maniple knew the sign, and for a moment she thought that they would not go with her, would just watch her march off on her own and then quietly slip away. Then they were falling into step, remembering their training in fits and starts. The majority had their snapbows, but about a third – the Inapt or the plain bad shots – had pikes upright and ready. In the second rank, Gerethwy had the considerable weight of his mechanized snapbow shouldered.

To their left and right, other maniples of the Coldstone were making a similar advance, doing their best to keep up with the swiftest of their neighbours – a piecemeal uniformity of move-ment being achieved by army-wide committee, in true Collegiate fashion. Unlike the traditional shield line that Ant-kinden had been so keen on, right up to the invention of the snapbow, each square was loose-knit, and there were gaps between the forma-tions, because to be tight-packed and unable to move would be suicide in this war.

They were the front line – the anvil, as Straessa had said – and that image was foremost in her mind as she led her men out, with a snapbow slung at her side and her rapier at her belt. Ahead was only dust, and then, even as she looked there were shapes smashing their way out of it: the enemy automotives.

She remembered how fast they were, from the trench-works, but here, from on foot, they seemed a good deal faster.

'Ready to disperse!' she yelled out, watching their approach and trying to calculate trajectory. *They really are coming in very fast now.*

This was the Collegiate plan, on facing with the Sentinel automotives: plain avoidance and a stark admission that they had nothing to stop them. On the other hand, there were only around twelve of the machines with the Second, and there was simply a limit to the damage a handful of such monsters could do to an entire army.

The phrase is 'acceptable losses'.

Straessa braced herself, then a moment later she realized that her maniple was to be spared. The unit to her left was breaking, though, the formation disintegrating into fleeing individuals in an undignified muddle as the Sentinel bore down on them, so that, when the armoured machine thundered through, only a luckless pikeman was caught by its charge, abruptly a broken corpse hurled high by the impact. Snapbow bolts rattled uselessly against the machine's metal hide, and she saw some manner of return shot cut down two more soldiers before it was on its way again, rushing into the heart of the Collegiate army, desperate to get its jaws into something more substantial.

They were still advancing, dispersed units reforming and hurrying to catch up, because the enemy airborne and infantry would be following right behind. Straessa risked a look right and left. Towards the trailing edge of the right flank, one maniple had somehow got it completely wrong, spread too late or not at all. She saw a trail of ragged corpses, a gaping hole in their already patchwork line, stretcher-bearers rushing to separate the dead from those who might yet be saved.

'Eyes behind, someone,' she heard herself order. 'I want to know when those bastards decide to come back.'

Beyond the advancing infantry's edge, she saw one wing of the Collegiate automotives start out, overtaking those on foot within moments, dozens of disparate machines converted for war, along with the heavier, slower war engines of the Sarnesh. Each sported some manner of mounted artillery, but they seemed fleeting and frail compared to the Sentinels. *And they're what the Sentinels are after. The plan's working so far.* She guessed that her side's war machines had started off back centre in the formation, so the gaps between the infantry blocks would lead the Imperial scouts to believe that Collegium would be running its automotives through the centre, in order to smash the Empire's ground infantry, just as the Sarnesh had done at the Battle of the Rails. As soon as the infantry had started the advance, though, the automotives had swerved out towards the flanks, and thus the questing Sentinels would not find their prey.

But they'll be right back when they realize it, and that's going to be bloody soon.

'Airborne!' someone shouted, and Straessa looked up to see the sky abruptly busy with shapes that resolved themselves into Wasp soldiers dropping down towards them.

'Pikes up! Snapbows aim and ready. Pick your marks!' All along the line similar orders were being given. The maniple spread out a little, by long training, their sharp spearpoints jutting at slanting angles so that the enemy could not simply drop amongst them with sword and sting, whilst the snapbows were all levelled together, with little precision lost from their time drilling despite the fact that everyone there was surely as terrified as she was.

If it wasn't for them watching me, I'd run, she decided.

'Loose!'

The Wasps were arcing in, already levelling their weapons as they descended, but they had plainly intended touching the ground before shooting, and Straessa's first salvo caught them still in the air. They were moving fast and spread out, so she had not expected much, but of the two score descending towards her people, a good eight or so were abruptly falling rather than flying, and her maniple was already reloading without her having to order it.

'Pick your marks, forward!' Half of her immediate problem was about to drop into the gap between her maniple and the unit to the left of her, because they saw the broken order of the Collegiate troops as a weakness to exploit. The other Wasp squad was coming down in front, ready to stand ground and hold them off until the heavier troops arrived. She could see them quite clearly: lean, rangy men in light armour striped in black and gold, armed with a snapbow, a shortsword and their Art. They had been at the front of every war the Empire had brought to its neighbours, at every expansion of the Imperial borders. She wondered how many thousands had already given their lives for such a fundamentally stupid cause.

'Loose!'

And the snapbows of her maniple's first three ranks raked into the enemy even as they touched down. She saw a good number fall – taken in that moment when landing stripped them of their speed. The rest were shooting back, but they were outnumbered now and, at some word from their sergeant, they took wing and put more distance between themselves and their enemies, waiting for reinforcements that would surely be with them at any second.

The other squad of Airborne had landed mostly intact between the two maniples, intending to take the enemy in the flanks, but those tough little square formations of the Companies had no flanks. Instead, the soldiers on that side were already facing towards them, three ranks deep and shielded by the pikes, and the same reception was waiting for them from the maniple to their other side.

The Collegiate snapbowmen were only given time for a single volley into them, catching the Wasps already returning to the air, recognizing an indefensible position when they saw it. A moment later, Straessa could see that the initial rush of the Airborne was pulling back all the way along the line, and then the three whistle blasts went up again from somewhere, and they were on the move.

General Tynan travelled at the heart of his army, at the apex of a small phalanx of armoured automotives, but in the open back of one so that his messengers could come and go as swiftly as possible. The conflict was widespread, and from the ground he had no clear picture of what was happening. He relied on his Fly-kinden and the swiftest of the Wasps to bring him news.

A Wasp soldier dropped in front of him now, one cheek smeared with blood. 'First contact with the Airborne, sir. Our men driven back. Casualties light to moderate.'

'How do their formations conduct themselves?'

'They can fight on all sides, sir,' the soldier reported – a man who had only moments ago been involved in that same skirmish. 'They're not so packed together as to give the best target, but their spears and their shot make closing with them difficult.'

'Our own spears are closing on them?'

'And they're still advancing towards us. They seem decently armoured – medium infantry at least, and reasonably drilled.'

Tynan glanced across to his guest, Mycella, who likewise kept a flock of airborne spies at her beck and call.

'I need some of your skirmishers,' he told her.

She smiled at him, and he read there fondness and a certain anticipation of bloodshed. Spiders had never held back from the strike, when it counted.

'What orders should I give them?'

'Our medium infantry blocks are about four times as big as theirs, so we'll be engaging several of their squares to each of our own units.' The strategy fell into place in his mind even as he spoke. 'If we can separate them further from each other that will give us a chance to surround them and destroy them individually, but as they are now, the space between each square is a killing ground for them.'

'And you want my skirmishers to step into it?'

'Send your mercenaries, if you want. I'm hoping that these Collegiates won't hold their calm once we have them in a packed melee. Let your people push some of their squares together, break others further apart. Then let our superior order tell.'

He could give her no orders, of course, but she considered the matter and then gave a string of concise commands to one of her people, to be carried to the mercenaries' adjutant, Morkaris.

The Wasp scout returned to the sky, winging back towards the front to report on the clash of lines, whereupon Tynan beckoned another over.

'Send to Colonel Mittoc,' he directed. 'Have him keep a close measure of the range to Collegium's walls. We don't need to reach the city; we only need to be close enough. Have him get the best use out of these greatshotters we've been given.'

The man saluted and was gone, heading for the rear. Even as he did a Fly-kinden took his place.

'Sir, enemy automotives flanking us.'

Tynan stood up, shading his eyes and peering over to where the Fly directed, seeing only flashes of the sun reflecting off metal at the far edge of his force. 'What are they doing?'

'Making inroads, sir. They're a mongrel lot but they're all armed. Our troops there are trying to hold them, but we're taking losses from their artillery and their wheels.'

'Where are the Sentinels?' Tynan growled.

Amnon's automotive bounced and rattled over the scrubby ground in the vanguard of a great straggling wedge of machines that had coursed its way almost unopposed down one side of the Second Army. The enemy had not known what to do with them – and they were gone before any orders could be given. A steady drizzle of opportunistic snapbow bolts and arrows had banged and rattled off the automotives' sides, and at least one machine had slewed to an halt, its driver hit, but Amnon's wing of the mechanized assault was almost untouched so far.

They were turning now, beginning to drive in towards the marching formations, and at the same time the Imperial soldiers were mustering their response. He saw units turning to face the Collegiate machines, kneeling or standing with massed snapbows levelled, but beyond he could see Light Airborne gathering above.

He heard three whistle blasts, keening over the roar of the engines, two short and one long, meaning *Charge*. Beside him, the artificer manning the smallshotter swung the weapon ahead, squinting through the slot in the metal plate someone had bolted onto the engine to cover her. Amnon took up his own snapbow, though his hands itched for his sword hilt.

'Down!' advised the driver, and at the same time they scavenged a burst of speed from somewhere, wheels leaping over the uneven land as they rushed the enemy line. Thus, on both sides, an uneven arrowhead of ramshackle machines were turned into a hammer to crack open then Second Army's flank.

Amnon had been knocked back by the sudden acceleration, and so he was already out of the way when the snapbow lines loosed. In his mind, the sound was like a sudden squall of rain against the metal plates shielding the vehicle. He saw the low-set automotive to his left suddenly swing towards him, its driver dead at the stick, and a moment later it had flipped over entirely, bouncing and jumping enough to fling out the bodies of its crew.

'Watch the skies!' he roared, as loud as he could, but the chances were that nobody heard him over the roar of the machines and the incoming hail of a second snapbow volley. A moment later the Imperial line broke, the soldiers trying to get out of the way of the metal tide. Most had left it too late. They were armoured too heavily to fly, so it became a matter of sheer chance whether they were struck or passed by, buffeted to the ground.

Amnon stood up again, unwisely, but he needed to see what was going on. Over there were the transporters, but they were too far, too deeply buried within the enemy, and the Airborne were coming down. He shot upwards, killing his target neatly, but knowing that he had no time to reload. A moment later his sword was clear of its scabbard, and the Wasp stooping down on him, blade drawn back and off-hand blazing, was cut from the air as soon as he came within reach. All about Amnon, the

Airborne were trying desperately to drop onto the automotives, and some even managed it while others missed, either left behind or – for the luckless – caught in front of the rushing machines.

Nevertheless, they were taking their toll. Taking stock for just a moment, Amnon saw at least four machines had gone off course or halted, falling instant prey to the Wasp landbound infantry.

He hacked at another man that came for him, but the Airborne soldier veered out of reach, only to take a snapbow bolt in the back and tumble away – Amnon never knew whether the shot had come from his own people or the Empire. Nobody was doing well out of a skirmish fought at this speed. Then there was a hollow boom audible well over the engines, and one of the Collegiate machines went from full charge to full stop within a moment, its front staved in by the fist of a leadshotter ball, its stern lifting high with frustrated momentum, until it had turned over completely.

The whistle signal went up again, just two short blasts: *Fall back and regroup.* Amnon ground his teeth as his automotive wheeled around – smallshotter still barking out its answer to the Imperial artillery – and rattled back the way it had come, along with its fellows.

'What's the matter?' he demanded. 'We were reaching them!' That was a lie and he knew it, but the enemy transporters – with their part-assembled greatshotters – had been within sight at least, and to turn away now was maddening.

'Their automotives are coming back, Master,' the driver replied, and a new stillness came over Amnon as he scanned the dust-covered, soldier-cluttered landscape for the Sentinels.

The block of Imperial infantry looming ahead seemed absurdly vast compared to their own modest squares. It came stomping across the plain torwards them in perfect time, the sun glinting on the spearheads and making the gold of their armour flare. In the old days such a unit would have relied entirely on spear and sting, with support from some Auxillian crossbowmen, but some attempt had been made to modernize, and Gerethwy, peering through his glass, now reported that the second rank was armed with snapbows.

'I make out four ranks,' Straessa noted. 'Only the second has 'em, you say?'

'Is what I see,' the tall Woodlouse-kinden confirmed.

A whistle blast was sounded, long then short: *Halt and loose.* Straessa passed it on, hoping very dearly that all these orders were originating from someone who knew what they were doing. She called out, 'Ready!' needlessly, for her soldiers knew the signal and their weapons were charged, each bringing snapbow to shoulder, even as they slowed. And then, 'Loose!'

The maniples to left and right managed to shoot at approximately the same time, catching the Imperial infantry as they were still advancing, and she saw the ranks of the big unit – four hundred soldiers or more in all – rupture and ripple under the impact. They slowed then, and she distantly caught the sound of their officers' voices, eclipsed almost immediately by her own shout of, 'And loose!' She was trusting to her people to have reloaded by now.

They had, their volley ripping into the tight-packed enemy even as they formed up. Straessa was surprised to see just how much damage they had done, the number of sprawled bodies and crawling wounded. *And now they shoot back*, she thought, and her mouth bellowed, 'And loose!' leaving her faintly amazed that her shopkeeper soldiers had got off three complete volleys before the Wasps had managed a reply.

The concerted sound of the Wasp second rank discharging their bows sounded like a great clap of hands, and bolts went whistling past her even as she heard it. The man next to her took one in the eye, a woman in the third rank took one straight through the chest, past breastplate and coat without slowing much. A Mantis-kinden pikeman cursed and dropped with red spreading across his thigh. The call went out for stretchers before Straessa even needed to order it.

She could name all three of the casualties, two of whom were now beyond anything the surgeons could do for them. Yet in her mind was the thought, *Is that it?* and on her lips, 'And loose!' All the while, her eyes kept watching the bludgeoning that her little force – and all the other little bands of Merchant Company soldiers – were inflicting across the front lines of the enemy.

'I reckon it's one in three down, for them.' Gerethwy didn't trust his mechanized bow at this range, so instead he kept his glass on them, unflinching even when a passing bolt plucked at the sleeve of his buff coat.

'And loose! What's going on?' Straessa lowered her own weapon, hands automatically palming a bolt from the box at her waist and slipping it into the breach; then cranking the air battery to charge it, the mechanism smooth and easy as if it was new oiled from the workshops. Even as she asked that question she understood. Wasp infantry was the army's mailed fist, used for breaking the enemy lines by main force, and in close quarters. They were stacked shoulder to shoulder, in contrast to the looser spread of the Collegiates, so that the incoming shot could barely miss them. And the Collegiates had three snapbows per four men, while the Empire had just one.

Sod me, the Antspider thought, slightly awed, *we're winning*.

Then someone shouted, 'Fliers coming in,' and she saw that the Wasp Light Airborne was back to support the infantry. There were a great many of them, a cloud of flying men arching overhead, but this tactic had not worked against the Ants at the Battle of the Rails, and the Collegiates were ready for it. Straessa directed her people to worry about the Imperial infantry, who were plainly realizing that their only hope was a solid charge to get into spear-range. The Collegiate squares behind the front line, mostly unbloodied so far, would be training their snapbows on the incoming Airborne and, though the fliers had the same weapons, shooting on the wing was a challenge for a Fly-kinden marksman, let alone a regular Wasp soldier. And snapbows were quite accurate enough to pick off fast-moving targets.

Straessa saw the Wasp infantry form up to advance – so few of them now compared to just moments ago – but the constant volleys of shot got the better of them, and soon they were pulling back and then disintegrating completely, individual soldiers making their getaway at the best sprint they could manage. For a moment she thought they had broken, but then she saw another unit of them marching in, the runners simply getting out of their way. No doubt these newcomers would have learned some hard lessons from the last minute of fighting, and it was plain that, if allowed to close, their tighter ranks and superior numbers would crush the Collegiate lines.

'And loose!' again and again. No need to tell her soldiers to aim for the invitingly large target that the new formation presented, so that the Wasps were bleeding from the moment they were within range. Despite the distance, they were already running, but still keeping almost shoulder to shoulder, shackled by their out-of-date training. It was a race, then, to see whether simple attrition would turn them aside and snap the spine of their charge before they could arrive. Seeing so many men coming on so fast, Straessa felt her mouth go dry. If they struck, her little band would become like leaves in a storm. The pikemen had their weapons levelled, some straight ahead, others tilted at angles upwards against the Airborne. Bolts were slanting down at them now from the skies above, the Airborne trying to break their firing pattern, but the attention of the squares behind was keeping the bulk of the enemy off the front line.

'Sub! In from the side, Sub!' someone called, and she looked about wildly, until she saw what was meant. From either side of the big Wasp formation, a stream of swifter figures was cascading, no battle order to them, just a swift, loose mob outstripping their allies in their haste to get at the Beetle lines.

'Spider-kinden to our left,' Gerethwy identified calmly. 'And that's, hm, Scorpions to the right.'

Straessa's square was positioned dead centre of the maniples now facing the Wasp unit's charge, so the newcomers were not her problem just yet. If they overwhelmed the Collegiates further down the line, she would know about it quickly enough, but she could do nothing to help or hinder, and she had to trust in her fellows. 'Eyes front! And loose!' Her voice was beginning to give out.

Thirty-Nine

Still the Great Ear had not sounded. In truth, the specifics of Corog's instructions were a distant memory now. Taki guessed that the pitched fighting had taken only minutes so far, but if some scholar could measure sheer *living*, the fear and the fury of it, then lifetimes had been burned.

She dodged about in the air, ramming the stick rapidly through three positions to throw off an enemy, before backing her wings so that the Farsphex went slashing past her. A brief glance about her revealed the ongoing chaos that the battle had become. The Collegiate centre, the idea of holding the enemy to one place, had become impossible almost immediately once the rest of the enemy had come in from north and south. The defenders were abruptly so outnumbered that they surrendered any say over what the enemy might or might not do, or where they might go. Taki guessed that, had the Empire wished to bomb Collegium flat, then she and her fellows could do little even to slow them down.

The Empire didn't want that. The Empire wanted her blood. That great wheeling host of the Imperial air force had new orders, and they were trying to wipe the skies clean of their opponents.

Taki had given up active attack once the new Wasp machines arrived. Since then she had been concentrating on staying alive, leading any number of enemy on a dance around the city's rooftops, being passed from hand to hand as they tried to bring their linked minds to bear on her, never being where they calculated but taking shots at any target that presented itself and moving on. If she had committed herself to the fray, narrowed her possibilities down to those few with offensive potential, they would have second-guessed her and killed her in short order, but she was flying like a madwoman and they could not catch her.

They had not caught her *yet*, anyway. Her dead fellows back in Solarno would scoff if she had told them that this crazed evasion was her finest hour as a pilot, but she knew it to be true.

A brief breath of clear sky and she tried to take stock, half-expecting to find the sky possessed only by the enemy and herself. The sight brought her a swell of hopeless pride, though, for the Collegiate pilots and Mynan airmen were still fighting. Outnumbered and out-coordinated, they still remembered their training and their orders. Just as she was, they were refusing to engage, even the fighting-mad Mynans recognizing the suicidal odds. The Collegiate defence had no cohesion, no pattern or plan, nothing to it but smoke and the swift particles of the Stormreaders as they scattered across the sky. Oh, they were losing – had lost the battle even as it began – but the enemy did not want the sky, and it did not want the city either. It wanted *them*, and now they were running the Wasp pilots ragged in their attempted pursuit.

And it could not last. Even as she watched, she saw another Collegiate machine downed, caught by crossed piercer shot, crumpling and twisting in the air and then falling helplessly away. The Wasps were good, and all the Collegiate pilots were buying for themselves was some few more minutes of time.

And still the Ear – that signal to throw in the fight and down their orthopters – did not sound.

Abruptly a hail of shot strafed along the side of the *Esca Magni*, and Taki slung her craft sideways, cursing herself for the momentary distraction. The enemy kept on her tightly, odd bolts still impacting even as she threw her machine through a series of baffling manoeuvres; down and left, edge on to the roofs, then backing madly, then down a broad street almost at head height, then turning on a wingtip down a sidestreet, only hopping above the roofs to miss an archway that would have stripped her wings clean off.

And the Wasp pilot still tracked her – not following the same course but always returning to her, and this time her madness was not enough and, as she burst back out into the sky, he took his place right behind her as though he had booked it in advance.

She felt she knew this opponent, recognizing and admiring his style even as she did her best to string out her remaining seconds. Her enemy was a pilot she had sparred with before, the veteran of many raids just as she was. She tried her old trick of releasing her winding chute, the silk cloth abruptly billowing away behind her, but the enemy was not so incautious and had kept just enough distance to swing aside, and the lightning sideways twitch she had tried simultaneously somehow just brought her back under his rotaries.

Another scatter of hits, the metal shuddering around her, nothing vital yet, but the next shot could spear the cogs of the engine, or the wing mounts. Or her.

Then he was taking off, rising up and abandoning her, and she wondered wildly if there was some mercy to be given her even now, but then she saw that the Wasp himself had come under attack.

She put the *Esca* into the tightest turn she could manage, hearing a chorus of new creaks and complaints from the abused hull. The Farsphex was rising and dodging, a Stormreader trying to stay with the Wasp but never quite regaining its line of attack.

She recognized the Collegiate craft from the way it flew. It was Corog's ship, unmistakably. She powered in, trying to catch up with them. Too late, too late: in committing himself to the attack, Corog had narrowed all the possible places in the sky that he could occupy down to one desperate, perfect line, the absolute optimum of vectors that would bring him to gut the enemy craft and destroy it. With a lurch of her heart, Taki realized that, even so, it would not be enough. The Imperial machine danced far more nimbly than any craft that size should be able to, so Corog Breaker's attack went wide, and then the other Farsphex, brought there by an unheard summons, clipped off Corog's tail with a scything trail of rotary bolts.

For a moment the Stormreader still maintained its course, still trying to bring its weapons around to its target. Then it slid sideways in the air, the wings wrestling with an element suddenly no longer their friend.

He was spinning. She flung herself closer, looking for the glider wings, imagining the stubborn old man still fighting with the controls. She watched him all the way down to the abrupt, concussive impact with Collegium's streets.

Scain pulled up and away, looking for another target. His monologue rattled on, passing Pingge by with his one-sided commentary on the battle.

'Won't stand and fight ... Arlvec requests permission to bomb ... denied. Orders are to ...' Then a grunt through gritted teeth as he tracked down one of the Collegiate craft to shoot at: a few moments of his silence and the hammering of the rotaries, as he tried to keep the bolts on target, and the expected lurch of the craft around them both as he broke off on another course once he lost the trail.

'Going to try and ... may be grouping up west of centre ... Arlvec requests permission ... denied. Just focus on the job in hand ...' A whole many-handed conversation relayed through his automatic muttering.

Then 'Aarmon!' and they were abruptly dropping from their high vantage and cutting through the sky. Pingge held on to the ballista as their course changed yet again, almost falling from the air, but caught abruptly by a beat of the Farsphex's four wings, then arrowing straight over the rooftops. And all the while Scain's words still came to her: 'I'm coming, I'm coming, almost there, just stave the bastard off. Aarmon . . .'

She clawed her way to where she could see over his shoulder, but the wheeling, whirling view meant nothing to her, and then suddenly there was a Stormreader there, in ferocious pursuit of another Farsphex. Aarmon.

Kiin, she thought, clinging to the wall. *Be safe, Kiin*. For once she could see all the pilot's art laid bare, Scain's hands jockeying the machine into place, matching the Stormreader turn for turn, precisely because it was trying to match Aarmon's own aerobatics, and Aarmon and Scain were linked in perfect tandem, the one telling the other where he would lead their mutual enemy.

And Scain clutched at the trigger, coming in from a little above the Stormreader's line, and clipped its tail off entirely, and Aarmon flew free and unharmed. Pingge grinned fiercely at the sight, but Scain was still reciting.

'See her? No sign of her . . . I know, the one that's not a Stormreader at all . . . like a ghost, that one . . . keep an eye out . . . Arlvec requests permission to commence bombing. Draven seconds it . . . Sir, if we begin on their city, they *have* to take notice and engage . . .'

Then there was a pause, a silence she could detect despite the sound of the engines and the rotary piercers, as Scain tried to pin down another fleeting enemy. She realized that not a single voice was speaking within that shared mindscape, that everyone was now waiting to see what Aarmon would say.

And then Scain was muttering in a different tone, 'No, no, no, come on, no, man, no, we have our orders, come on Aarmon, we don't need to, we don't,' and Pingge realized with shock that these were his own thoughts, unbroadcast and unlinked, the private contents of his head that his traitorous mouth was still churning out.

He slung the Farsphex about for a few mad seconds of chase, loosing a brief salvo of bolts, but his heart was not in it. He was waiting, and so was she, aware that she might soon have more work to do than she could handle, if Aarmon gave the order.

'Do it,' Scain spat. 'Arlvec and Droven and all of your wings, begin work on the ground. Everyone else be ready for the Collegiates to step in and try to stop it.'

The maniple to their left held firm, pikes levelled at the onrushing Spider-kinden skirmishers, and the square's snapbows on that side turning easily to track them, picking off just a scattering of them, but enough that the Spiders faltered, and then lost more of their number as they slowed. Then another square beyond started shooting into the Spiderlands troops as well, whereupon they broke entirely and fled back behind the Wasp lines.

Straessa saw the square on the right crumple like paper. In amidst a swirl of lightly armoured Spider-kinden had come a solid core of Scorpions, heavily mailed and brandishing greatswords and halberds, and led by a rake-thin Spider in dark plate wielding a huge two-handed axe. The snapbow shot flayed away the first rush of Spiders, but by then the Scorpions were up to charging speed, pelting faster than anything so heavily armoured should have been able to. They lost a half-dozen coming in, mostly to the brief stutter of a nailbow, and then the axe of their Spider-kinden leader smashed down two pikes, the man hurling himself shoulder-first into the teeth of his enemies, not to kill but to break up their order just enough. After that, the Scorpions were on them, hacking and smashing at every foe that came in front of their blades. The square disintegrated, and the Ant-spider saw nobody escape the carnage, not from any grand courage in holding to the last man, but because they were not given a chance.

The Collegiate square in the second rank was already trying to move into position, pikes levelled while suffering the attentions of the Light Airborne's bolts and stings. The Scorpions reformed, from bloody butchery to battle order at a shout from their Spider master, and then they were pressing further – Straessa could barely believe it – throwing themselves in the way of the Collegiate reinforcements.

And, of course, the Wasp formation in front of them was advancing now at a run, rushing into the hole punched in the Beetle lines. Straessa supposed the same game must now be being played all the way down the front, with the cohesion of the Collegiate army as the stake.

'Rear rank, get some shot into them!' she rasped, because the Scorpions' backs were broad targets. Then: 'Gerethwy, if you wanted to test your toy, now's your chance.'

Her people were ramming bolts into the approaching Wasps with a desperation that was fraying the edges of their speed, making them fumble with their ammunition and shake their aim. Castre Gorenn, the one-woman Commonweal Retaliatory Army, sent shaft after shaft at the enemy, each a sure hit, but it was just spitting into the tide. A brief glance told Straessa that her left flank was still secure, but if her maniple fell or fled, there would be a great open road leading to the innards of the Collegiate army.

Gerethwy levelled the heavy weapon, a long-barrelled snap-bow with a great mess of clockworks half-exposed, about no fewer than four air batteries. A long strip of tape tailed away into the hands of another soldier, bearing a long rank of bolts. A third soldier rested the barrel on her shoulder, loosing her own snapbow one-handed as she took the weight, while Gerethwy hunched himself against the weapon's stock and pulled the trigger.

There was the brief clatter of tens of gears all working at once, and then the Foundry-pattern mechanized snapbow began its Apt magic. A dozen tightly wound new-metal springs – a quarter of the entire weight of the piece – drove the recharging of each battery as soon as it was emptied, the first ready to loose the moment the fourth was emptied. The tape was dragged through the teeth with a sound like cloth tearing – bolts rattling into the slot on one side, then cast into the enemy at the rate of a handful a second, with the empty strip trailing away, relieved of its burden as abruptly as a conjuror's trick. Gerethwy's job then was to conquer the rebellious shaking and yammering of the machine and keep it aimed, pivoting it on his comrade's shoulder, as she tried to hold the barrel in place.

It would have been useless at long range, for the famous accuracy of the regular snapbows was something this ungainly weapon could never aspire to. This close, though, and with a great mass of men available to bring it to bear on, it was indeed like magic. Even as the individual shots of the rest of the maniple lanced and stung and downed their single targets, so Gerethwy became a maniple to himself. In the twenty seconds of constant metal hammering that he managed, he cored the Wasp charge like an apple, leaving the combatants on both sides appalled by the sight, as though some invisible reaping engine had run through the Wasp lines.

'Out of spring?' Straessa called to him, watching the Imperial formation as it wavered and tried to reform.

'Jammed,' came his terse reply, and she looked round to see Gerethwy already kneeling to prise open the weapon's casing.

A moment later the Scorpions and their leader ploughed back through the gap towards the Wasp lines and safety, the rearmost of them still fighting. Straessa saw a flurry of savage exchanges there, the huge Scorpions turning to fend off their smaller, fleeter antagonists, the Mantis-kinden. Those sons and daughters of the Felyal who had not signed up for the Companies were not to be denied their war and their revenge. Little warbands of them – no more than six or eight in each – were running riot all over the Collegiate front, meeting the enemy skirmishers and taking them on, driving them away and thus giving the battered squares a chance to reform and step up to the line. Straessa saw at least three of the savage Felyen Mantids fall beneath the Scorpions' blades, but soon the enemy had been driven away, and left a handful of their own in the dust behind as well.

The Wasp infantry were falling back now, on seeing that. She heard two long blasts of the whistle from somewhere behind: *Stand and fight.* The advance had now stalled, some would-be tactician weighing the odds and seeing the enemy forces too strong to push against. *Which scares me because, if we're not pushing them, they can push us back.* Straessa wanted to find someone to argue the point with. She wanted to counter the order with her own whistle. Instead she just hovered over Gerethwy as he worked at the mechanism of the Foundry snapbow, and watched the Wasp infantry blocks reform.

Onrushing plumes of dust showed the Sentinels tearing along the flanks of the Collegiate army, shrugging off shot and shell as they followed up the tracks of their automotive rivals.

Amnon stared at them bleakly as the Collegiate train wheeled about him, still exchanging light artillery barrages with the few batteries that the Imperial engineers had set up.

He heard shouting, as someone tried to get a message across over the mutinous thunder of the engines, something too complex for the whistles to communicate. Then one of the big boxy Sarnesh automotives had pulled up, the hatch on top open for a crewman to lean out.

'We'll go after them!' the Ant bellowed. 'You get yours stuck in! We're taking some of yours and going after them!' His jabbing finger made the Sentinels his plain target.

Amnon had no idea of the odds involved, but the Sarnesh machines were designed for war, tracked and armour-plated and mounted with an artillery piece little short of a full leadshotter. The Sarnesh drove on, shouting his message hoarsely to everyone it could reach, and meanwhile the other four Ant-kinden machines formed up with a half-dozen Collegiate automotives, ready to meet the Sentinels, charge for charge.

'You heard him!' Amnon bellowed at his driver. 'Get us moving!' He wished this was a chariot, where he could whip at the beasts himself as need be.

The driver directed an ashen glance at him, and then at the Sarnesh and their allies, who were just moving off, even as the Sentinels' dust rolled fast towards them. For a moment Amnon thought the man's nerve had gone, but their artillerist yelled, 'Come on!' and at last the man turned their machine back towards the Wasp host, and the balance of their machines were following.

Amnon raised his sword high, just as when commanding chariots or cavalry, and the ramshackle wedge of war-adapted machines drove towards the Wasp lines, gaining speed as they went.

The Imperial artillery found them first – larger pieces with a longer range than those the Collegiates had been able to mount – and the machine to the right of Amnon exploded without warning, a leadshot landing directly on it and almost folding it in two. Ballista bolts arced overhead, exploding where they struck, leaving charred craters in the ground but striking nothing. Another automotive towards the back took a leadshot hard on one wheel and spun out of control.

There was some attempt at an infantry line ahead, a wavering wall, but they were clearing out of the way early now, orders or not. Snapbow bolts began to fall amongst the automotives, rattling off metal or driving deep into wooden panels. Behind Amnon, the artillerist woman gave a single bark of surprise, and then she was gone, pitched over the side by the force of the shot that killed her.

Amnon swung himself grimly into her place, behind the weapon, something magical and terrible by his peoples' standards, but simple by the lights of Praeda's instruction. His dead mistress had done her best to equip him for the world he now found himself in, and she had known he would be going to war.

He swung the weapon round to seek out enemy artillery,

finding a leadshotter whose three-man crew was already tilting it to drop a shot towards the back of the automotive column. With sure hands he aimed, and absorbed the thunderous kick of the compact little killer with the great strength of his arms and shoulders. He saw one of the Wasp engineers simply explode as the ball passed through him to punch the artillery piece in the rear, spinning its barrel round to catch at least one of the other crewmen as it did so.

He fumbled with reloading, shoving another fist-sized ball down the barrel and wadding it tight, before prising out the spent firepowder cartridge and replacing it with a new one. Then he spared a glance for the battle with the Sentinels.

It was practically over, and his heart lurched just to see it. There were only three Sentinels there, those great plated mechanical woodlice with their high single-eyed prows, but the wreckage of most of the Collegiate force was strewn around them. As he watched, he saw a Sarnesh machine plough in, smoke gouting as its weapons loosed, and one of the Sentinels rocked under the impact, but no more. A moment later the larger leadshotter within a Sentinel's body spoke out, its eye flashing fire. The side of the Sarnesh machine was staved in, its headlong charge turned into a mad circling as one set of its tracks locked. Then another Sentinel rammed it, aiming for the crumpled side, and tipped the doomed machine over, smashing the Sarnesh automotive onto its side. Amnon saw the third machine lining up carefully to send a leadshot round into the stricken machine's unarmoured undercarriage.

His driver began shouting that something was ahead, and he swung the loaded smallshotter around, hoping to see the great enemy artillery that was their target.

There were three more Sentinels in the way and, even as he watched, smoke exploded from one open eye, and an automotive on his left flank was abruptly flung in the air, fuel tank rupturing in a brief ball of fire.

★

The first bomb had landed close enough for the resounding roar of it to sing through every glass component of Banjacs's machine.

The artificers ceased work a moment as the impact shook the chamber, but Banjacs's own shouting whipped them back to it. The inventor might as well not even have noticed that the city was under attack.

'If you have somewhere to go or people you would be with,' Stenwold addressed the two students with him, 'then go. Nothing's keeping you here.'

Eujen Leadswell's idealistic indignation had retreated into an iron core deep within him. 'No, Master Maker, I'll stay.' And it was plain that the Wasp would stay there with him. Stenwold could not decide whether he would rather have Averic just get out of his sight, or whether remaining where an eye could be kept on him was the best thing.

'Banjacs!' he shouted, as another, more distant explosion ruptured somewhere out beyond the walls. 'How long?'

The old man had been up a stepladder, refitting a rack of metal tubes that looked like miniature organ pipes, after two abortive attempts had so far failed to coax any life out of his machine at all. At Stenwold's words, he jumped down, looking about him wildly.

'Get off the machine, you fools!' he shouted at the artificers, as though they had not been scurrying there to his explicit instructions a moment before. He gave them scant time to scramble clear before fitting the last components back into place and taking a large step back.

Still nothing happened, and Stenwold was about to curse the man furiously, when Eujen pointed upwards. The great glass tubes that formed the lightning engine's main body were now glowing with a pale light, a mere reflection of the enormous storm imprisoned down in Banjacs's cellar.

'It's ready! At last, it's ready!' the inventor whooped, a young man again for just a moment. 'My machine is at your service,

606

Maker.' As he rounded on Stenwold, there was enough passion in those eyes to spark tears, but also a sanity as though the completion of his long-awaited project had given something back to him that he had been missing for many years.

'Messenger!' Stenwold called instantly, and a Fly-kinden who had been watching all this activity with utter vacant bafflement was instantly before him, glad to find himself of some use.

'Go to the Great Ear and tell them to sound,' the War Master ordered. 'Now! Let's get our pilots out of the air.'

The Fly-kinden was off in a moment, wings taking him straight up and through the gaping skylight that would serve as the aperture of Banjacs's great weapon.

'Let us only be in time,' Stenwold added, so quietly that perhaps only the two students overheard him.

There was a shout from the doors, and a moment later they were kicked in. The body of a Company soldier fell through them and, the next second, a band of men came forcing their way in, snapbows and swords in hand, with a burn-scarred Beetle leading the charge.

Forty

There was fighting further down the line. Straessa could see that the troops to her far left were engaged in melee already, and that did not bode well at all. Her own maniple and its neighbours seemed to have fallen into an uneasy stand-off, the Imperial troops still reforming but refusing either to commit to the fray or just to go away. Straessa's people were still shooting bolts at them, letting the Wasps know that they were still within range, but Gerethwy was reporting little harm done.

'Well now,' he said at Straessa's shoulder, studying them again through his glass. 'I think we're about to get the hammer, frankly.'

'Tell me.'

'You can see how they've a mass of Airborne there – and their infantry has formed into smaller detachments, a bit like ours really only rather more of them.' He sounded overly at ease, as if at pains to seem casual. Given his usual effortless calm, she read volumes of emotion into that. 'They have a whole load of Spider-kinden skirmishers too, some sort of Ants and some Scorpions, but they're getting them all in better order this time. I think . . .' he coughed away a little dust, or that was the impression he tried hard to give, 'I think they're ready for us now.'

'I don't reckon we could do all that shifting and changing,' Straessa remarked philosophically. It was dawning on everyone that everything up until now – the Wasp dead, the repulsed charges – had barely bloodied the Second Army: no more than a testing of the waters. Now the Imperial general had determined a suitable response to what was no doubt a slightly novel variation on some textbook tactical problem.

'In fact,' even Gerethwy's careful voice had a quaver in it now, 'I'd say that in three . . . two . . . ah, yes.' And abruptly the milling crowd of Light Airborne redoubled in size, soldiers kicking themselves into the sky with their Art in a great un-ordered mass, whilst below them the ground forces began their advance, the loose screen of skirmishers rushing ahead of the slower blocks of Imperial infantry and shielding them from the snapbow shot that was sleeting down on them.

'Pick your marks. Fire at will,' Straessa ordered, because the oncoming Spiders and their allies were so spread that volley fire would be like punching at mist. The Empire had given up a fair extent of ground when its soldiers fell back, but the skirmish line was coming on fast, rushing to close with the Collegiates and silence their snapbows as swiftly as possible. Around Straessa, the pikemen stirred and braced themselves, watching that oncoming tide.

'Rear ranks, shoot at the Airborne.' *And any moment there'll be an order, and everything will change. Advance, probably, given the record so far.* The Spider-kinden were nearer now and, to the right, a closer-knit band of copper-skinned Ants were loosing their own short-barrelled weapons as they approached, more to spoil their enemies' aim than a serious attempt at killing. *Any moment now.*

She heard the whistles one after each other. *Retreat! Stand and fire!*

'Oh, bollocks,' she said softly, looking about her to see how the other maniples had taken it. As she might have expected, some were already pulling back, either into clear space or pressing against the troops behind them, Others were standing firm, often with both neighbours abruptly stripped from them, and Straessa saw her own leftmost neighbour stand, the wide eyes of its sub-officer show white as the man looked wildly around him. To her right the block was already pulling back.

'Sub, getting real close,' Gerethwy said. Around her, her soldiers were shooting and reloading, shooting and reloading, smooth as a drill because they trusted her ability to make decisions.

And if she stood and fought, she would be supporting her fellows. The pride of Collegium did not enter into it. There were other maniples now depending on her, as they had been relying on their fellows who were already falling back.

And if she retreated, then some of her people might live.

Piss on you, Marteus. Why aren't you here to make the call?

She put her whistle to her lips and blew the signal: *Retreat! Retreat!* She could only hope her neighbours took the hint.

Moving backwards in square formation was not something that could be done at speed, but they were setting new records right then, their order fraying slightly with every step. She saw, to her lasting horror, that the maniple that had been on her left was *not* pulling back along with them, but standing firm, shooting and reloading.

Her people were saving their shot for the Airborne already coursing overhead, and the leading edge of the skirmishers would reach them soon anyway. All around her the Collegiate army was losing its cohesion. She saw the first few soldiers simply start to run, drawing the Airborne after them.

'Hold firm and keep together!' she yelled, but she was still watching that other maniple, its commander either too stupid or too much of a hero to pull back. She saw the skirmishers break over it for a moment like foam on the sea, and then it was overwhelmed, surrounded, the soldiers fighting with shortsword and pike and the weapons of their Art, and fewer and fewer, the opposing numbers and skill at arms eating into their formation and gutting it.

'Steady!' Gerethwy almost snapped. He had the Foundry snapbow levelled again at the onrushing skirmishers, awkwardly feeding the tape himself whilst another soldier steadied the barrel, even as they fell back with increasingly swift and ragged steps. And: 'Now.'

The mechanized weapon hammered out its ugly tune, and this time he just let the mouth swing wildly, ripping across the swiftly approaching skirmishers, cutting down a dozen nimble Spider-kinden, before raking into the band of Ants beyond them. Straessa looked about her, noticing that they were amongst more Collegiates now – the rear maniples that had been held in reserve, unsure of what was happening but now hastily readying themselves for battle.

'Hold now!' she ordered her soldiers. 'Hold and—' and then the skirmishers were just a dozen feet from them and something slapped across her scalp hard enough to send her reeling, and her left ear was ringing with shock. Staggering, she looked about to see that Gerethwy was down, his breastplate and coat dabbled with blood. *Shot?* The truth came to her in the next instant, even as she was hauling her sword from its scabbard. Jagged pieces of the Foundry snapbow lay all about him, the barrel twisted where it had met the mechanism. *Jammed, and then some.*

'Stretcher!' she yelled, her voice shrill above the sounds of battle. The Woodlouse-kinden was curled about his hand, or what the exploding weapon had left of it. *We're going to stand and fight and die now, because we can't pull back fast enough to get clear. But maybe you can get out, Gerethwy. Maybe I can accomplish that much.*

Then the first of the Spider-kinden were upon them, leading with rapiers and short spears, and by old habit she found her swiftly drawn sword falling into a perfect duellist's line, fending aside an oncoming blade and then, even as the attacker tried to pull back, playing her old Prowess Forum trick of flexing her game shoulder forwards for those few critical inches of extra reach, only this time it put the point of her weapon through her surprised opponent's eye.

This experience seemed real in a way that the snapbows had not, but she had no chance to reflect on it just then. Her instincts clamoured at her, *Survive! Just survive!* And the only chance for that was her sword, the slender barrier between her and death.

The *Esca Magni* skipped through the air, zigzagging desperately as Taki felt the little impacts that were the outliers of a stream of piercer bolts trying to close in on her. There were at least two Farsphex behind her now, each taking a turn in following her twists and gyres while the other tried to come at her from below or above. The aerial battlefield wheeled before her, sometimes populated, sometimes not. When it was busy, she saw mostly the enemy, and the friends she did see were engaged in the same fierce flight as she was.

What the blazes is Maker playing at? But it was looking as though she would never find out. Chance and skill and mechanical superiority were eroding around her, moment to moment. The Wasps only needed to get lucky the once.

Abruptly another Stormreader shot across her nose, engaged in furious evasive flight – one of the Mynans from the colours. Something snapped in Taki then, the Exalsee warrior-pilot in her suddenly shouldering aside the cautious air-tactician she had become.

Curse the lot of them, she swore, and wrenched the *Esca* sideways after the Farsphex that was on the Mynan's tail.

She knew she had no time and that she was laying herself open, that the orthopter in her sights would have been warned – was already taking evasive action and drawing her into a line that would see her cut up by her pursuers' shot. *Stupid. Hopeless.* And she dragged all the power she could out of the *Esca*'s springs and leapt forwards, her twinned rotaries blazing bolts, and the cockpit of the Farsphex exploded in broken glass and wood fragments, and the vessel dived purposefully for the earth with the pilot's dead weight against the controls.

There's one for Corog. Then she was flinging herself madly through the air, higher and higher, because the pursuing Wasps were on her, and fighting mad now, their comrade dying in their very minds. *Oh, I went and poked your nest, did I? Well, see how you like it!*

She darted higher, the city spread out like a model beneath her, smouldering where the bombs had struck. She had a brief impression of the battle about her: dozens of circling Farsphex, but so few of Collegium's own. Had the Empire devastated the Collegiate numbers so thoroughly while she was not paying attention?

She tried to dive back down, and for a handful of seconds was engaged in a mad spiralling battle for control with one of the chasing Farsphex. Levelling out for a moment, she saw a couple of Stormreaders, not fighting but dropping – plunging recklessly down into the streets, heedless of the enemy or the bombs or . . .

What's that noise?

It had been sounding for some time, she realized. It was familiar, though she had not heard it from quite this perspective, competing with the rush and clatter of an aerial fight while she was over the city itself. It was the Great Ear.

For a moment she could not think why anyone would be sounding the Ear now, when the enemy had so very plainly already arrived. Then she remembered.

Oh, no, no, no! Because that was the signal, the get-out-of-the-pissing-air signal, which meant Maker or whoever was ready to make something terrible happen.

Still cursing to herself, she rammed her *Esca* towards the ground, because if she was to die, let it be in the air, yes – but let it also be a pilot's death. Whatever Maker had in mind, whatever the artificers of the College had cooked up, she did not want to know. Most particularly she did not want to find out in person.

A staccato rattle of impacts into her undercarriage made her pull the stick back by instinct, heading up again – the second Farsphex had second-guessed her and was trying to drive her into the aim of the first, but most crucially he was driving her away from the ground. How long had the Ear been sounding? How long did she have left? She tried to slip sideways, to lose them just long enough to cut down below the rooftops, but she had gone too high and they were wise to her piloting now, and they would not let her go, would not let her down.

A panicking glance showed her no hope of reprieve. The bulk of the Collegiate machines were down – or downed – and those still in the air were sharing her plight: unable to get out of the fighting without leaving it the hard way.

Frightened as she had not felt for a long time, she threw the *Esca* across the sky, never quite getting free of her pursuers, never quite able to push through the scythe of their shot to land – even to crash. And all around her there were more of the enemy, and they all knew exactly where she was.

Straessa lunged again, spearing a lean Spider – old enough to be her father – in the shoulder, her point piercing between the plates of his chitin mail. Around her, the bulk of her soldiers had resorted to their swords, with a few opportunists behind her still taking potshots with their bows, almost directly into the face of the enemy. The other maniples around them were also locked into the fighting, or else had fled, running back towards the camp and what scant salvation could be found there. Every so often – so incongruous she would have laughed – she heard someone sound the whistle for retreat, but the input of tacticians into this battle had come and gone. It was not even a matter of selling their lives dearly. The flesh wanted to live, and could not be made to understand that this was no longer an option. So they fought, and shed the blood of their enemies just to buy mere minutes more for themselves.

Overhead, the Light Airborne were a constant curse, shooting or diving about the battlefield, but they seemed most concerned about chasing after the runners: whole fistfuls of the black and gold stooping on the backs of fleeing Collegiate soldiers with sword and sting.

Then the Imperial infantry came. They struck over to Straessa's right first, shouldering through the skirmishers and smashing into the already battered maniples with their close order and their years of experience; the Collegiate line simply cracked and fell apart, individual maniples disintegrating within moments of their charge, dying or fleeing. The Wasp soldiers, already bloodied in the initial exchange, were now recapturing their honour, solid, disciplined men in good armour going about their trade.

Straessa risked a glance behind her, because her maniple had now been stripped of a third of its numbers by the skirmishers, and a personal retreat was looking like a good idea, The soldiers behind her, the reserves and the rear squares, had lost formation, most of them milling, some running. She had never much liked trying to rush through a crowd.

'Sub!' someone yelled – possibly a soldier from another maniple calling a different officer altogether, but the cry drew her attention and her heart, already a battered thing, lost what little hope remained in it.

The Imperial infantry had not rushed her people yet, but only because there was a Sentinel on its way and they did not want to end up underneath it.

'Anyone got a grenade?' she shouted, fending off a sword blow, and then the enormous, armour-plated machine surged forwards, absurdly fast for such a weighty thing, and essentially obliterated the maniple to Straessa's left, the force of its impact throwing a few boneless bodies high, crushing far more, and the survivors fell almost instantly as the Sentinel loosed a spray of snapbow shot around it.

Behind it, the Imperial infantry were abruptly in motion, closing the distance.

The Sentinel turned, legs moving in a careful little dance, until its great blind prow was facing Straessa, that covered eye boring into her – specifically her and nobody else, or so it seemed. Then the eye opened, the metal cover sliding up to reveal the gaping barrel of its leadshotter.

One of her people did have a grenade, and also the good sense to wait until that moment before hurling it, the hatched metal sphere arcing overhead towards that gaping hole. The missile was off the mark, though, striking the armour and rebounding, exploding pointlessly in the air. With a desperate war-cry the Dragonfly Castre Gorenn leapt into the air, loosing a final arrow that vanished, without trace or effect, into that gaping eye, her ancient Commonweal skills utterly surpassed by modern artifice, but the silver flecks of snapbow bolts were rebounding from the vehicle's metal hide to no greater effect.

I resign my commission, Straessa decided, *effective immediately.*

Then the Sentinel rocked under a handful of impacts, lurching forwards a few yards, then spinning furiously on the spot to face this new challenge. From behind it, and cutting bloodily through the Wasp lines, a dozen automotives were on the move, the vanguard of the miscellany that Collegium had used for its strike at the enemy artillery.

Does that mean we won? was her first mad thought. But she could see only that dozen or so and, even as she watched, one of the machines at the rear simply exploded, and she saw that there were another handful of Sentinels in hot pursuit.

Oh. But then she saw what the automotives were actually doing – for the line of their charge cut between the Collegiate forces and the bulk of the Wasp army, ploughing into the enemy infantry with brutal abandon, forcing the lines apart.

'Retreat!' Straessa shouted, then she blew the signal on her whistle for all she was worth. After that, she took her own advice, first killing a final Spider skirmisher who was too keen for his own good and then turning to run, keeping pace with her maniple because she was still responsible for them. All around her, the Collegiates were doing the same – some retreating in better order, some simply dropping their weapons and fleeing.

The lead automotive struck the Sentinel at a narrow angle, rocking it back on its legs and rebounding onto a path that churned through the Imperial infantry. The Airborne were already returning to the fray, shooting at the automotives that were causing such havoc to their lines.

They're going to destroy the machine! Stenwold thought, ripping his little snapbow from inside his tunic – the beautiful, vast and yet fragile machine that Banjacs and the artificers had been so frantically tuning, which was even now poised to wipe the skies clear of Collegium's enemies. And now the Rekef had arrived to smash it.

He loosed desperately, because there were almost a dozen of the attackers, and the great vulnerable machine was all around them. There was no way that he could stop them all.

But they were not here for the machine, it seemed. Imperial intelligence extended just so far, informed as it was by Spider agents who were almost entirely Inapt. They began shooting hurriedly, almost wildly, but at the people.

A bolt passed across Stenwold's scalp and he reeled back, but his own quick shot had taken one of the men down, and he was already loosing the second before the tight knot of enemy could break apart.

He saw Banjacs take a bolt in the chest and jerk backwards, a tangle of elbows and knees, blood abruptly appearing bold across his white robes. Almost as valuable as the machine itself was its creator.

The Imperials were not soldiers, and their skill at arms had played second to their intelligence training. After taking the two

617

Company soldiers at the door, they had expected to face only Maker and a handful of scholars. They forgot, or never appreciated, that there were few College men or women who were complete strangers to the Prowess Forum, and that Collegium had been through two sieges over in the last few years.

A heavy workman's hammer, thrown with remarkable skill, took one man full in the face. Another of the artificers had brought a sword, and rushed to meet the attackers blade to blade.

Then the burn-scarred man spotted Averic.

'You little bastard!' he shouted, seeing before him, in the flesh, that fatal miscalculation that had spoiled their operation. What went through the man's mind then, viewing this pure-blooded Wasp-kinden of good family who had inexplicably betrayed all the generations of Empire, was written in ugly lines over the Beetle spy's face. Immediately, he charged the youth, without thought for any aim beyond killing him.

Stenwold was trying to get to Banjacs, but a swordsman was suddenly upon him, a lean Beetle with a knife in his offhand and enough rough skill to force Stenwold on the defensive, driving him further away from his allies.

Behind Stenwold's opponent, the Collegiate swordsman was being forced back by his own adversary, before tripping over the body of another artificer who had fallen to a snapbow bolt. His enemy reared above him, sword drawn back, and then Eujen appeared beside him, face fixed in a horrified expression, and rammed a blade through the spy's ribs.

Stenwold pushed forwards again, realizing, after the initial surprise, that he was the better duellist – perhaps the best swordsman in the room for all that it said about the rest of them. 'Leadswell! Get to Banjacs!' he yelled. The Beetle boy looked at him briefly, and went sprinting over to the old inventor's motionless form.

Averic's wings had carried him up to a gantry, and the burn-scarred man stood below him, raging up at him. 'You traitor! You coward filth! Can't even *fight*? A shame to your own people, curse you!' Abandoning his comrades to the fight, he found a shaking stairway leading up and took it three steps at a time, only to find the Wasp already balanced on the rail, ready to glide down.

Banjacs was plainly gone beyond anything that Eujen could do for him. The old man's ragged form was so thin that it seemed he had died long before, dried out and desiccated until only this husk remained. And yet, as Eujen knelt beside him, those piercing eyes flew open, and the old man took a hacking breath that sprayed more blood over his robes.

'My machine!' he whispered, reaching out for it as if trying to encompass the entire radiant edifice with a clutch of a single hand. 'Take me – take me . . .' And, with the last dregs of a Beetle's bloodyminded endurance, he began lurching across the floor on hands and elbows, a slick red slug's trail behind him and his legs limp and useless.

Eujen caught his rasping plea, 'Help me make it *work*.'

A snapbow in his hand, a second man came at Stenwold, shouting for his fellow to get clear. The weapons were not meant for such close quarters, and the War Master ducked away from a blow to lash his blade at the barrel, knocking it up and away. Then the snapbowman was down, sitting with hands smeared red as they pressed at a stomach wound, and one of the two Company soldiers huddled in the doorway was fumblingly trying to reload her bow even though her breastplate had a puncture hole above her left breast.

And the burn-scarred man looked back towards his people and must have seen almost none of them left now, and that this desperate gambit had failed. 'Traitor,' he repeated, almost a whisper. His expression revealed bitter bewilderment, at why this Wasp had turned so far from his people, and why the boy would not now even finish the job. Looking into Averic's eyes, perhaps he sought some grand answer, some hint of a greater plan, something to justify the waste and the failure.

'I'm sorry,' Averic said, and those two words plainly showed the burned man how Collegium had taken him, body and mind, and corroded all the hard edge of the Empire.

The Beetle spy rushed him, surely without any great hope of achieving anything, because by that time he had nowhere to go and nothing to accomplish. Instead of simply flitting out of reach, Averic's hands came up by instinct and, even as the Wasp kicked back from the railing, his Art flashed and seared, and what fell from the balcony was just a singed corpse.

The swordsman artificer – the only one of the three still living – dropped his blade with a harsh clang. In the doorway, the soldier leant back with a groan, pulling weakly at the straps of her breastplate until Stenwold hurried over to help her.

And, before the lambent majesty of the machine, Eujen propped Banjacs up, the old man's ashen face borrowing a radiance from the great assembly of glass above him. There were no words, but a trembling thrust of the inventor's hands picked out a bronze lever from amidst the chaos of dials and wheels, and Eujen hoisted him higher until he could seize on it.

Banjacs summoned some last strength then, from some inner well or perhaps from the unseen source of all Beetle Art. He shrugged himself free of Eujen's grip, and let his own weight pull down the lever.

Forty-One

What are they doing?

The question flashed at Aarmon from all sides as the battle-field in the air disintegrated. Everywhere the Collegiate orthopters were breaking away, even braving the Imperial shot to ditch in the streets of their city. Aarmon's aviators reported the enemy pilots scrambling from their machines and simply running, leaving the downed Stormreaders as sitting targets for bolt or bomb. Several orthopters were clipped from the sky in their frantic attempts to get clear.

Aarmon put the Farsphex through two more tight turns, swinging wild of the line his target was taking but dragging his craft back on course with a sure hand, pushing his skill and his machine's tolerances to their limits but feeling his quarry start to tire, the panic of the chase in her throat. She was trying to get free, too – she tried to reach the ground again and again, but he was waiting for her each time, as his cohorts hedged her in on either side.

They know they've lost. They're hoping to preserve their air strength for the siege, came the offering from one of his pilots.

They're out of power, their clockwork's run down, from another.

Other speculations kept battering at his mind, when he needed all his concentration to stay with her, his prize.

How he knew it was a *she* he could not say, but this enemy pilot he knew intimately, through a bond as close as that he shared with his comrades. Her orthopter was different, a slighter, nimbler piece of elegance than the admittedly admirable Collegiate standard, and her style was impeccable: a fierce, thrilling blend of excellence and inspiration that took possession of the sky wherever she flew.

She had been responsible for more deaths amongst his fellows than any other Collegiate pilot, her unique ship putting that knowledge beyond doubt. He had sought her out, and sought her out, night after night in the frenzied chaos of their aerial engagements. Now here she was, fleeing him in broad daylight.

It is not revenge; the thought passed through his mind and he knew it had gone out to his fellows, that Scain would be mouthing it even now. It was not hatred that moved him, either, or a desire for conquest. He remembered, when he was a boy, watching the hunting wasps take their prey on the wing, and feeling that *moment* where the destinies of predator and prey intersected, as though by consensus, each to its role. The dream of living that moment had taken him through the Light Airborne, and into the Aviation Corps when that new institution had formed. Not vengeance nor spite, but perfection.

His comrades were still engaging the enemy, of whom fewer and fewer were left to engage. Two-thirds of the surviving Collegiate force had reached the ground, or died trying, and the rest would plainly join them if the Wasps allowed them the opportunity. Still shifting his craft through the impossibly tight and dancing turns that his opponent sped into, he felt a clutching sensation inside him. *A trap. But what?* They had control of the skies, with the Second on its way, and what could Collegium do about it?

Commence bombing as soon as you're free to do so, he ordered. *Let's see if we can't sting them into the air again.*

Then he saw something flash in the heart of the city: a tall house capped with a dome, nothing out of the ordinary save for a circular skylight that—

Lightning leapt and flashed from there, darting and reaching for the vault of sky above. And Aarmon's mind said, *Weapon.*

He had a fraction of a second to realize, out of all his flight, that it was he whose course could be twisted to pass by that sparking roof, and he broke his pursuit off instantly, with only a moment's regret, for sentiment was something he could suddenly not afford to indulge.

'Sergeant!' he snapped back towards Kiin, 'Ready bombs, target domed house dead ahead.'

He hauled the Farsphex about, wings pausing for a moment in their beat, to let it hang and slew in the air, then regaining their pace as he slung his craft towards his mark.

A moment later the first impact rattled against them, and he knew, without needing confirmation, that his former prey had rounded on him; one of those precise dancing-step turns putting her on his tail the moment he abandoned the chase.

Get her off me! He sent to his fellows, because the roof ahead was spitting and flashing like a miniature storm now, and he knew that there could be only one chance.

Taki felt the absence of pursuit as a physical void behind her, freedom from shackles, and her instant thought was to find a place to put down. She was surely in that seconds-long limbo that must come just before whatever storm Stenwold Maker would now unleash on their enemies. And yet . . . and yet . . .

And yet the Collegiate pilots had ceded the skies to the Empire, and nothing had happened. No great stroke of genius from the War Master had manifested itself.

The ground screamed out for her, but she was a thing of the air first and foremost, and she flipped the *Esca* about for one last glance at her erstwhile pursuer.

She picked him out immediately, taking a recklessly straight course so that she found herself following him by sheer fighting pilot's instinct, and ahead she saw a bright flare and spray of pure white light. *A bomb? No, that's something he's aiming for. He's on an attack run.*

She was already flying in his wake and she saw the whole picture, stitched into whole cloth partly from her guesses at Maker's plan, partly just from the Wasp's reaction.

A moment later, she let fly with her rotary piercers, seeing at least a scatter of hits reaching the enemy and knowing that the sky was full of his friends.

The sky was full of her friends, too, those who had not been able to get clear. The sky was about to become a very dangerous place, probably a fatal one. She could only hope that enough of the defenders had managed to touch the ground before now, and that there was someone left who could lead them.

At least I'll end in the air. And she loosed again, her twinned weapons hammering, feeling the vibration coming to her through her feet. Her enemy was trying to dodge her, but at the same time was committed to his own attack. If she could nudge him just a little way, he would lose his chance.

He would have just the one chance, that much she had guessed.

Then she felt the impact of shot punching into her own hull, and she knew that one of the Wasp's friends was on her, and close, so she was abruptly in the same trap as her enemy, caught by her own dedication to her offensive. Her pitiful twists and lurches – all she could allow herself, without losing her line – shrugged off some of the incoming bolts, but she felt a punishing rain against her poor *Esca*'s shell, the tail riddled and shot striking around the gears of the engine, against the pistons of the wings, whose silk spans were instantly peppered with holes, each one a tiny wound bleeding away her machine's grace in the air.

Then there was another Collegiate craft coming in from ahead of her, and she thought, *No! Don't help me! Just take my target!* But she had no mindlink, as the Wasps did, and the

Mynan-painted Stormreader – it was Edmon's own – flashed past the Farsphex she was chasing, two more Imperial orthopters in hot pursuit of him, his rotaries ablaze with bolts as he came to her rescue. For a fragment of a second, Taki saw them all like flies in a web, locked into their individual destinies, each devoted to their chosen attack, and each defenceless as the price of that devotion.

Edmon's shot must have rattled the pilot behind her, at least temporarily, for she felt no further impact on her hull, but she saw a hail of sparks and broken wood and metal as his own machine suffered for it under the weapons of his shadows. She did not know, then, whether the damage to his machine was so great that he could not pull away, or whether Edmon chose his path, simply trusting that, whatever she was about, it *had* to be done and so her pursuer had to be stopped.

Edmon flew so close over her that he blotted out the sky for a blurred second, their wings close to touching, and she neither felt nor heard the impact as he rammed his craft into the vessel behind her, but it echoed in her all the same.

Aarmon cried out in shock in that same instant, a light winking out in his mind. None of his fellows was able to take up the attack, to drag the little Collegiate pilot from his tail, her shot already punching through his craft's hull.

The building ahead, its crown alive with searing argent fire, was in his sights.

'Kiin!' he shouted, and a blistering salvo of shot ripped through the cabin behind him. He heard the Fly-kinden woman shout – not in pain but in rage.

'Reticule's smashed!' the words came to him. 'Sir—!'

'Do it by hand!' he called. 'I have faith in you.'

And their time was up. He was still in the air and over the target, so surely . . .

Bolts scythed through the back and top of his vessel. He felt one wing go still instantly, all connection to the engine severed. He heard Kiin's scream – brief and agonized, cut short almost as as soon as it started.

'*Kiin!*'

The sky was filled with light.

The sky filled with light for Taki, too.

One moment she was in hot pursuit of the Farsphex, and a moment later she was fighting blindly with every part of the *Esca*'s controls, wheeling madly across an unseen roofscape. The gears stuck and stuttered, the wing joints seemed to freeze, falling out of phase, every moving part on the cusp of being welded to its neighbour. And Taki cringed, shrinking into her seat, waiting for the flesh-searing fire that must surely follow.

But the Esca coughed and rattled, and kept on flying, and she could see again, albeit with a great negative blotch before her eyes that was already fading. She nearly died anyway, finding herself pitching downwards in a wild whirl before she could drag the stubborn stick back and get herself level. Then she was still airborne and alive, and as intact as her last skirmish with the enemy had left her.

And all about her the sky was dotted with orthopters, and most of them were the Empire's – all still there. Only the fading skein of sparks crawling about every part of her machine told that anything had happened at all.

Oh, you stupid bastard, Maker. It didn't work.

Then came the first explosion, a Farsphex simply erupting from within, and she stared and stared, as the sky over Collegium played host to a new and fleeting constellation.

And, on the ground, Stenwold Maker and his fellows rushed out of Banjacs's house to stare upwards. The fierce, pale light of the lightning engine behind them was momentarily the god of all shadows, brighter than the sun, and the its charge was gone, hurled impartially into the heavens that were thronging with flying machines.

It was invisible the moment Banjacs's engine discharged it, and yet every sense screamed with it, a moment of monumental wrongness when each hair stood on end, and the sky seemed to bend and boom with energies never meant to have been chained by the hand of man.

In the next breath, it had all been for nothing, and Stenwold felt his heart almost stop with the unfairness, the bitter knowledge of a defeat that his own actions had made so much worse.

Then Eujen was yelling and pointing, and he saw the first explosion: one of his enemies ripping apart as though old Banjacs's ghost was up there tearing the machine asunder with invisible hands.

And another. And more, and Stenwold stared up as the skies caught fire over his city.

Scain screamed.

Pingge could not make out the words. He seemed to have gone mad, wrenching at the stick and yet taking them only in circles. But outside . . .

She saw the sudden bloom of flame as a nearby Farsphex went up, fragments of hull and wing forming momentary silhouettes against the blast.

'Aarmon!' Scain cried out, and Pingge thought, *Kiin!* knowing that her friend of so many years was dead.

Something blew in the engine behind and above her, and she shrieked. Scain was wrestling with his straps, finding them stubborn.

There was no time.

'Scain!' she shrilled, and he was turning back towards her, mad desperation in his tear-streaked face. Even as another shudder rocked them, he had his hand extended back, not seeking help but palm held outwards to sting.

She screamed at him. She saw that he was going to kill her in some Wasp idea of mercy. She felt the searing heat as his Art discharged, and then the fuel tank ruptured and the blast picked her up.

In that last moment, unable to get himself free, the fire of his sting had cracked her chain apart, and she was flung bodily from the Farsphex, out past the ballista – the bolts behind her popping and cracking like fireworks – out into the open air, borne away on the vanguard of the explosion.

Her last sight of Scain was a pale face seen through the cockpit's faceted window, before the flames came.

Taki guided her battered *Esca* through a slow, spiralling descent – in truth the absolute best the machine was capable of just then, while watching the other Collegiate pilots still aloft follow her down. She had, she confessed to herself, no idea what had just happened, and no leap of inspiration could conquer the gap. Apt as she was, it seemed to her as though some great sorcerer of old had waved a hand, invoking an untold power simply to rid the sky of the enemy, leaving herself and her fellows intact.

Only later would she learn that Banjacs's machine had not worked as intended, that the grand obliteration had never come, that even a genius's calculations could harbour errors. Later scholars would suggest that, to fulfil his dream, ten times the charge of raw lightning energy would have been needed, and its backwash would have flash-cooked every living thing in Collegium. As it was, although the Stormreaders that had flown through that particular storm would need refitting, countless small components slightly deformed or melted as the lightning had leapt about them on its way to repatriation with the sky above, they had all landed safely, their pilots shocked and shaky, but alive.

For the Farsphex, however, the residual sparks of that same discharge had, within a varying number of seconds, coursed through the fuel tank and turned all that volatile and devastatingly efficient mineral oil into an instantly detonating bomb.

The Collegiate pilots, those who had reached the ground before then, and those only just now touching down, looked up into a sky that they had won, and around them at a city their path to victory had scarred almost beyond recognition. Even then the messengers were being sent out from Stenwold Maker and Jodry Drillen to tell them their work was not yet done, that the College artificers were waiting for them to complete emergency modifications to the Stormreaders, that the war was still going on.

She had given the order to run once they seemed to have put an acceptable distance between them and the front line – that chaotic tangle of men and vehicles that had given Straessa's maniple the chance to win clear. There were other maniples that had failed to break free, or whose officers had decided on some misguided stand, and she understood she was abandoning them. There was no right answer.

Shortly after she had allowed her people to break formation and just flee, one of the transport automotives rumbled up, the driver vaguely recognizable from amongst the ranks of the camp artificers.

'Get in!' the man said, his face a mask of dust covering goggles and a face scarf.

'Where are you headed?' Straessa demanded. Throughout the mass of retreating Collegiate soldiers, she could see other vehicles performing the same service.

She had a horrible feeling that the driver was about to take them back to the fighting, but he just gestured towards the city, and home.

Straessa did not even need to give the order. By the time she had hauled her aching body on board, most of her maniple were already there, and the nearest stragglers from other units were heading over as well. The driver kept his eye on the churning dust that must be the Imperial forces on the march again. The sky to the east was dark with the Airborne, beginning to range out over the fleeing Beetles to pick them off.

Oh I'm not going to enjoy learning about this in history classes, thought Straessa, because humour had always before been her armour against the world. The following thought was even less funny: *I don't think Collegium's going to be writing the histories.*

When the transport was full, with soldiers hanging off the sides, the driver wrenched it about and headed for the camp at best speed. There were no orders, Straessa understood. Everyone who could was trying to assist with the retreat, to preserve some vestige of armed strength for . . . nobody seemed to be sure for what.

She was the highest-ranking officer on the automotive, which was to say the only one.

'What the blazes is this?' their driver demanded. Ahead of them was a block of soldiers that seemed to be forming up, as though they had arrived late and somehow contrived to overlook what was happening all around them. The sheer idiocy of it offended their driver enough for him to grind the transport to a halt and begin shouting at them.

'What are you doing? Get moving, you fools. They're right behind us!'

There were a fair number of them, Straessa saw – a few hundred at least – and although they were as dust-smothered as everything else she saw that they were mostly all of a piece. These were Mynans, standing in a close block, shoulder to shoulder just as though the snapbow had never been invented, falling back on what they knew.

Someone was approaching the automotive, and Straessa blinked to recognize the Mynan leader, Kymene. The woman looked exhausted, her right arm bandaged up and a sword in her left hand, but a mad fire burned in her eyes.

'We attack!' she snapped. 'What else is there?'

The driver just gaped at her, but Straessa leant past him.

'Commander, we've lost! We have to get back behind our walls before they catch us in the open.'

'They're not trying to catch us in the open, and your walls will not save you,' Kymene declared flatly. She pointed out towards the enemy 'They've halted, Sub-officer.'

Straessa stood, frowning, then stepped on the back of the driver's seat. The trailing mass of fugitive soldiers was still being harried by the Airborne but, now that she looked, the main body of the Imperial army did seem to be holding their ground.

'Well that's . . .' she began uncertainly. 'What does that mean?'

'It means their artillery is in range of the city,' Kymene informe her. 'There is no other reason for them to stop.'

'But they're . . .' She could just about make out what might be Collegium over to the west, although the dust made that uncertain. 'You can't . . . Seriously?' And then came the unwelcome knowledge that, of course, Kymene had been through all this before.

'If we do not act now, the city is lost,' Kymene said, and it was plain that she had no intention of finding herself in this position again, one way or the other. 'We will break into the enemy camp and destroy their engines, just as the automotives were supposed to do. It is the only way. Or else, if you decide to run, just keep running. There's no point stopping once you reach Collegium.'

Coward, was her unspoken implication, just as Straessa's mind was screaming, *Madwoman*. But it stung, that accusation. It stung beyond any veneer of common sense or tactical consideration. And the woman was right, as well, as far as Straessa could weigh the odds.

'Sub?' asked one of her people, or perhaps one of those from another maniple.

'I resign my commission,' said the Antspider, only realizing afterwards that she'd said it aloud. A lot of people were staring at her.

631

'I'm staying,' she called out, pitching her voice to carry. 'I'm giving no orders. Your choice.' With that inspiring speech, she slung herself over the side of the automotive and went to stand by the Mynans.

Perhaps a little under half made the same choice, forming themselves into makeshift, patchwork maniples. Their entire armed strength was just a mote before the great storm that the Empire was bringing.

Punch our way in. Destroy artillery. Get out. Oh, yes, can see all of that happening. Straessa was beginning to hope that Chief Officer Marteus really was dead, because otherwise she was going to kill him for promoting her.

'Let's go,' ordered Kymene, and a moment later the Mynans were moving off: black and red armour and peaked helms, blue-grey faces set in expressions that spoke of being driven to the wall one too many times. After an awkward pause, the rallied Company soldiers followed suit. Straessa shouted at them to spread out, to make themselves more difficult targets, but she barely had the voice for it, nor the heart.

Then there was a buzzing, a murmuring sound that swelled behind them, familiar to them but new to the battlefield, and a moment later the orthopters were racing overhead, wings ablur. The soldiers began to scatter immediately, fearing the worst, but Kymene just stood and stared upwards. Then her sword was pointing high in triumph.

'They're ours!' she cried, to those already with her, and to the others who were still streaming past. 'Collegium to me!'

Amnon hauled himself to his knees, wiping blood from his mouth.

We gave them a chase, though, didn't we?

His surviving automotives had simply not slowed, but rushed like maddened animals back and forth, a mobile barrier of steel to shield the Collegiate retreat, moving swiftly to give the

Imperial artillery – and the Sentinels – a difficult time in bringing their weapons to bear. The Airborne had swooped on them. The infantry had tried to board them. Vehicles had been falling out of the chase from the start, swarmed or smashed. They had failed from the beginning, Amnon understood. They had not been able to get close to the artillery that was even now being erected in the heart of the Imperial camp.

The last wreckage of the Collegiate automotive assault was strewn all around him. His own machine, faithful to the last, had thrown him clear as it turned over, the engine and front axle destroyed by a Sentinel's leadshot, and the driver along with it.

Amnon lurched to his feet. Barely a hundred yards away, well within snapbow range, were the enemy. They had ceased their advance and were putting up slanting barriers of wood and metal about their perimeter, against any Collegiate counter-attack.

Closer, outside that evolving compound, was one of the Sentinels, probably the very one that had finally brought down his automotive. It shifted position minutely as he looked at it. Whatever slots or lenses the driver used to view the world were, he felt, fixed on him. He, who knew the secrets of hunting every living thing in the Jamail delta back home, understood when he had become the quarry.

He found a sword amidst the wreckage – not the leaf-bladed Khanaphir implement he would have preferred, nor even a crescent-guarded Collegium weapon, but a cross-hilted Imperial piece. It would be enough.

The Sentinel came closer, many feet picking a path through the strewn metal. The great blind eye regarded him imperiously.

He was not First Soldier of Khanaphir now, nor was he the partner of Praeda Rakespear, whom he had loved. He was not even an officer of the Collegiate army, given that it was either dead or fled. He was Amnon, though, the warrior and the hunter, and he still had a sword.

He gathered himself with all his strength and then he was running, a handful of swift steps towards the Sentinel and then a leap, even as its rotary piercers started spitting bolts.

The shots almost clipped his heels, then he was grappling with the smooth side of the machine, finding purchase between plates in the moments before those gaps clenched shut. He kept kicking and scrabbling until he was crouched atop the Sentinel, the one place that it could not attack him.

It spun left and right in search of him, then began bucking and lurching, somehow knowing where he was. Amnon clung on, though, hacking at its steel hide until the sword broke, and then slamming his hands down against the metal shell. The first snapbow bolt skipped off the hull nearby, Light Airborne wondering what he thought he could achieve.

Praeda was dead, and Amnon knew he would follow her soon enough, but he had one thing to accomplish first. Getting his fingers underneath one of the great articulated plates of the Sentinel's casing, he planted his feet firmly and heaved. There had never been a beast so fierce that he could not kill it, nor so well armoured that he had not found its weak spot. He *refused* to give in, or admit that his life and skills were obsolete.

Another couple of bolts struck nearby, indicating that the Imperial soldiers were taking more of an interest. Amnon ignored them and continued to strain at the metal, the prodigious strength that had made him the wonder of the age in Khanaphes focusing in the single task of prising the machine's armour up and exposing its innards.

In his mind was Praeda, and his city, and Collegium, all hovering over a solid core of effort, every sinew and every muscle pushed to its limit in seeking the impossible.

It gave an inch in his grip, bolts shearing, and he bellowed, a great anguished yell of loss and defiance, and ripped up the casing in a scream of tortured metal. Triumph flared within him: he was again the First Soldier of Khanaphes and, in that moment, he was the equal of anything this new world could throw at him.

He looked down, and almost laughed at feeling the hope drain out of him. Beneath the armour was just steel, more steel, as invulnerable as the rest.

Then the Wasp soldiers, who had suddenly begun taking him seriously, put a bolt through his leg and another through his shoulder, punching him off his perch atop the machine. He never saw the Stormreaders coming.

Speeding across the bright open sky felt like being in another world: no longer the ravaged city below them, but Collegium's army forming a blurred host, and the enemy ahead.

Oh, now, here we go, Taki thought, because she could see some Farsphex already lurching into the air with unseemly haste, desperate to intercept the oncoming Collegiate fliers. She gritted her teeth, waiting to see whether the Empire had somehow mustered yet another great assembly of orthopters to stop them in their tracks. If they could not carry out their mission here, then the war was lost, despite every price they had paid so far.

A hard, savage smile came to her face. *Five, I see just five.*

Collegium had been able to put thirty-four Stormreaders in the air, twenty-seven of them modified to the latest specification, including this borrowed craft of Taki's. The *Esca Magni* had been too abused to take to the air again with any certainty of it staying there.

Oh, they have heart, she acknowledged, because those five Imperial machines showed no hesitation: in for the kill, their rotaries ablaze with bolts, despite the odds. The modified Stormreaders were handling sluggishly too, due to all that extra weight clasped to their bellies by the modified landing legs. Still, seven of them were as nimble as they ever were, and for once, just this once, Collegium had overwhelming numbers in its favour.

She drew her craft to one side as the lead Farsphex came in, saw the enemy shift sideways, still trying for a kill as it evaded the first jabbing shots of the Collegiates. The Wasp cut up one of the laden Stormreaders badly, making it falter and lose height, before being picked off, a half-dozen different orthopters jockeying for the honour of the strike. The other enemy fared the same, giving a better account of themselves than anyone could have asked in the circumstances, and yet they accomplished nothing.

Then the Imperial army was spread below them, half-ensconced within their walls, and packed close together – just the wrong sort of security.

Some of the others were making their attack runs, but Taki took this chance to pass over and circle back, because they had a mission, and they had to get it right.

Colonel Mittoc looked up into the suddenly busy sky. All around him soldiers were lifting into the air, as though their Art wings or their little stings could make any difference at this point. Behind him were the greatshotters, mostly complete now thanks to the practised skill of his engineers, within range of the Collegiate walls, and ready to bring the city to its knees. He had been looking forward to using them.

The first bomb landed far to his left, tearing open a handful of tents and rather more soldiers. With an artificer's appreciation he noted the way the Collegiates had adapted their vessels' landing gear as a bomb cradle. He estimated that these charges were about half the power of the devices dropped on Collegium itself, the delivery system makeshift, and the small orthopters almost crippled by the weight.

It hardly mattered. The Collegiates had the sky. Not a Farsphex was to be seen.

The Imperial artillery commander knew that this was a time for discretion rather than valour, and that he himself was standing in exactly the wrong place, but Collegiate bombs were spiralling down all over the camp, the pilots still unfamiliar with their new toys, so where exactly was safe?

His men were shouting, and he turned to see a lone Storm-reader coming on a direct line for the greatshotters from behind. Some of his engineers were still working on the siege engines, as though completing them would somehow give the huge weapons the ability to pluck those fleet little orthopters from the sky.

We were close, he thought, and he saw the bomb released even as his wings flared. But he was wearing the heavy armour designed to protect a valuable artificer from harm, and as a result he could barely manage a hop.

General Tynan noted that the Spider-kinden were already on the move, dispersing into individual groups and falling back eastwards – not exactly a rout but not an orderly retreat either. He needed to give the order, but it stuck in his throat. This was the Second Army, the *Gears*, and the Gears did not stop for anything. That was the *point*.

He could observe the walls of Collegium through a glass. For the second time, the city seemed just an inch from his grasp.

He had ordered the Airborne into the sky, to do what they could, but there had been no battle in recent history where flying men had been able to match themselves against flying machines. His own few orthopters had been destroyed within seconds of engaging the enemy.

'Tynan!'

He spun round to see Mycella herself fighting her way through the panicking camp. She had the emaciated mercenary Morkaris and his Scorpions shouldering Wasps out of their way, and her chief of camp, the Melisandyr, strode alongside her in gleaming plate armour, holding a shield aloft as though it would protect anyone from anything.

'What are you still doing here?' Tynan demanded.

'You have to get clear. You have to order a retreat, Tynan!' she shouted to him. To his shock, he detected real concern in her eyes: not for his army, or their chances of winning the war, but solely for him.

And she was right, and he had known that truth for several minutes now, even as his men died.

'Sound the retreat! Head east and regroup with the Spider-kinden!'

Instantly messengers and soldiers began spreading the word, the chain of command reasserting itself. It made him weep with frustration, but there was nothing else for it. He had the superior land force, but half his artillery was smashed and the Collegiates could destroy the rest at their leisure as long as they controlled the air. Under the withering barrage of their bombing, an attempt on the walls did not bear thinking about.

'Come on,' Mycella urged him. He saw she had a sword out as if to fight off the air assault by hand, and the impotence of the gesture touched him.

By degrees, and still under a flagging bombardment from the Collegiate fliers, the Second Army began to retreat from Collegium.

Last to turn round were the Sentinels, which stood before the bombardment unmoved, barely dented even when the bombs fell close. Their blank round eyes stared hungrily westwards, towards Collegium, before they finally turned, with an insolent slowness, and followed after the rest of the Second.

Forty-Two

Returning to their city, the army of Collegium met a hero's welcome. Most of them did not know what to do with it.

There were enough that just accepted what they were given – waving back, kissing the girls or boys that presented themselves, acknowledging the heartfelt thanks of the populace, but Straessa's face remained set tight, and she saw the same look all about her.

This is a sham, she thought. *We lost. If that battle had been an apprentice piece or a student dissertation, they'd have kicked us onto the street. Strong start, lacking discipline in the middle, and chaotic finish failing to prove what you set out to. All in all, shows a lack of preparation.* There was fear in her heart still, from this lesson taught. *They're better soldiers, and they have a better army. We accomplished nothing save get more sons and daughters of Collegium killed.*

Behind the automotive in which she rode marched the Mynans, Kymene at their head. The woman's grim expression mirrored Straessa's thoughts exactly.

So what the pits is everyone cheering for, eh?

And then, as she had got that far in her thoughts, she realized that many of them were not. Those at the front were the enthusiastic ones, but even then she recognized a strain in their eyes, a desperation to make this procession something *worthy* of celebration. They cheered and they waved, trying to find familiar faces in the exhausted ranks, and those that flung themselves forward for an embrace were those that had found one, rather than simply carried away on the tide of victory.

On all sides loomed the buildings of Collegium, the gaps and rubble like missing teeth, as raw and unfamiliar as if they'd come home to some other city altogether.

There were surprisingly few officers left, the individual commands hopelessly intermingled, When her people had formed up raggedly in front of the wreck of the Amphiophos, Straessa sought out Kymene, as did various other officers and sub-officers. She found out then that Marteus had indeed been killed just before the battle, and Elder Padstock wounded during it, though not severely. In the interim, Collegium's army was looking to a Mynan fugitive for leadership.

Kymene appeared as though she had been awake for a tenday, watching her new subordinates through red eyes as a surgeon re-bound her injured arm.

'Go find your people,' she advised. 'Go show them you're alive. Take that opportunity.' She coughed, grimacing as it jarred her injury. 'Keep your weapons to hand, though, and your uniforms. Don't get so drunk you can't fight.' She did not need to say, *They are still out there.*

That evening took Straessa, eventually, to the run-down study from which te Mosca had taught Inapt studies not so long ago. There, she glanced from face to face and realized how lucky she herself had been.

Gerethwy was there, his hand bandaged so heavily that the loss of two fingers was barely noticeable, and his calm due more to the herbal philtres they had given him than to his usual demeanour. In that he matched Raullo Mummers, who had drunk himself comatose before Straessa even arrived. The homeless artist's face was gaunt and ravaged, finding no rest even in sleep.

Sartaea te Mosca herself, the eternal hostess, arrived late,

appearing only after she had done all she could in the infirm-
aries. She turned up at her own door with a bloodied apron
under one arm, ready for washing pending the morrow. Collegium had few Inapt doctors, so she insisted on treating patients
of certain kinden when she could. The regular surgeons muttered and snorted, but her results spoke for themselves. As she
arrived, Straessa found her a drink, and the Fly woman slumped
down on the floor with it.

Eujen and Averic arrived together, wearing the sashes of the
Student Company, having been busy since the army's return.
While the regular soldiers rested, it had been the youthful
Students who had manned the walls and kept watch on the
skies. The aviators had continued to harry the Second Army,
driving it further and further, and even now they were flying out
into the night, showing the Empire all that Collegium had
learned from the Wasps about modern warfare. Still, as each
modified Stormreader could carry only one or two bombs, and
as the city's stocks of munitions were fast drying up, there was
a limit to the amount of pressure they could keep up. An hour
before, though, word had come to the Students that they could
stand down. The Empire's forces were sufficiently far off, and
in sufficient disarray, that no attack could be expected tonight.

The Antspider and Eujen eyed each other, probing the wedge
between them that time and war had hammered in.

'You've been keeping the place tidy while I was gone, then.'
Such flippancy was all she had left to her. Her hand's idle
gesture encompassed the bomb-scarred city outside the shutters.
Seeing his face, noticing the gulf between them only increase
rather than close, she felt a sudden panic, more severe than
anything she had experienced on the field. *What did I say? Why
have the rules changed?*

Then he held his arms out, hugging her to him. 'I know . . .'
she heard him say, 'I know such things.' But he would not
disclose them, the revelations of the last few days: Imperial

641

assassins, Stenwold Maker's ruinous game of chance with the city, Banjacs's death and incidental triumph, all of it sealed in his mind.

Outside, across the city, the citizens of Collegium sat in the shadow of one question: *Will they be back?* Would the Empire – so vast and inexorable and hungry, so often rebuffed and yet seemingly never defeated – would it return for them? They tried to tell themselves that Collegium's freedom was assured; everybody said so, but nobody believed it.

Somewhere else, Laszlo was still trying to find some trace of his vanished Lissart, not knowing whether she was alive or dead, hunting for any rumour that a flame-haired not-quite-Fly girl might have made it safely to the city.

In the College infirmary, lying amongst so many others, Amnon awoke in pain and grief but alive despite it all. They told him that they had found him crawling back towards the Collegium lines, trailing blood, but he remembered none of it.

In his townhouse, the windows boarded up since the glass was blown in, Jodry Drillen slept at his desk, jowl pressed into a half-drafted agenda for the next meeting of the Assembly, wherever that might actually take place. His Fly-kinden secretary, Arvi, glanced in, crept over to remove Jodry's empty bottle and bowl, then tiptoed from the room.

In the hushed chambers allotted to the College librarians, the artificer Willem Reader, co-designer of the Stormreaders that had helped save Collegium, looked in on his sleeping wife and daughter, and thought about the future.

Kymene walked amongst her people with a quiet word here, clasping a shoulder there, giving them heart, giving them hope. Far from home, fighting under another city's flag, they thought only about freedom.

And Stenwold, out on the walls and looking eastwards, brooded on the Empire, as did so many other people.

★

The Second Army was slowly cohering, preparing the most defensible camp that it could after having left its travelling walls behind it, spreading its fires wide to mitigate the next attack. General Tynan was counting his losses.

Between the fighting itself and the disastrous retreat, he had lost some one in six of his soldiers. This engagement, which the more level heads of Collegium were already characterizing as a draw, was the most crushing defeat the Second had ever suffered.

There was a wing of Spearflights on the way to them from Solarno, the reliable old workhorses of the Imperial air force. They were better than nothing but no match for Collegium's machines. There was already a fresh class of the Aviation Corps training in Capitas, with new-built Farsphex and all their other advantages, but nobody knew what had happened to their predecessors. Some catastrophe, some secret Beetle weapon, had swept the sky clear of them, and they were no more.

And General Tynan made fitful plans and growled at his subordinates, or calmed himself in Mycella's company as he waited, always waited, for word from the Empress.

Then, tendays after the battle, and even as fresh Stormreader forays were forcing the Second to move camp further east still, a Fly-kinden woman flew up to the camp's sentries and demanded to be taken to the general himself.

On the southern coast of the Exalsee sat Chasme, the pirate artificing town that had been a thorn in the side of respectable Solarno for generations. Selling its services to all bidders, producing orthopters and pilots, weapons and the men to use them, it had danced a fine line between the other cities that ringed the great lake, useful to each in turn whilst being a venomous annoyance to the others, but never so much to bring about its own destruction.

In recent years, Chasme had changed, though, and while the

people of Solarno might have thought they hated it for its piracy, now they found it all the more loathsome for its honest competition. Chasme was one man's town. He had made it a power on the Exalsee, and was working on making it a power in the wider world. His name was Dariandrephos, known as Drephos to his one confidante and as the Colonel-Auxillian to the Empire, and he commanded the Iron Glove trading cartel.

Here the Sentinels had been born, both their physical frames, their ratiocinator-guided mechanisms and the spun-steel metal-lurgy that made them light enough to move. Here the great-shotters had been built and tested and refined. Drephos and his second-in-command, Totho, were nothing if not prolific in their industry, and such was their reputation for rewarding genius that even proud Solarnese artificers crept cap in hand to them, begging for the chance to serve them.

The Empire had represented a great well of gold to the Iron Glove and, better still, it had given Drephos and Totho the chance to have their inventions *used*, which was worth more than all the riches of the world. Now, unheralded, a new Wasp delegation had come to visit them.

Drephos kept no audience chambers, so he chased appren-tices out of one of the forges and had the great hammers and wheels stilled, and there he awaited his visitors, with Totho standing at his metal shoulder. He wore only his plain robe, and a leather apron over it, as though he had been surprised while working on some personal project. His mottled grey face, its features subtly distorted, held a mocking smile. Totho wore the hardwearing canvas of a Collegiate artificer and the closed expression of any halfbreed who has grown up in a city not enamoured of his kind.

The delegation was small, no great Imperial pomp but a practical-looking Wasp colonel, unusual in his beard and tied-back hair. With him came a handful of soldiers and a Consor-tium factor, and a single Fly-kinden woman in the uniform of the Aviation Corps.

Drephos had gone quite still on seeing the colonel, and the two men studied each other, both of them the Empire's failures and both dealing with the rejection in different ways. Drephos had made himself a new empire here on the Exalsee, whereas this man had fought hard, under the threat of a death sentence, to win himself another chance.

'Varsec, is it not?' Drephos asked.

'That is correct, Colonel-Auxillian.' Imperial colonels were forceful and aggressive and ambitious, but this man – young for a colonel – seemed to have an edge of desperation about him.

'They call you the father of the Imperial Aviation Corps,' Drephos noted. 'Your results speak for themselves. Impressive.'

'You have heard the news from Collegium,' Varsec stated.

'News travels fast, especially when my own people were able to carry it up the coast and past your Second Army, wherever that might be now.' The Colonel-Auxillian was picking his words with care, observing as fine a line as Chasme had ever walked.

'Then you know why I am here.' Varsec spread his hands bitterly. 'I am . . .' He gave a glance back at the other Wasps. The soldiers stood silently, whilst the Consortium man seemed to be making a mental manifest of everything that he saw. 'I am on a knife-edge. My corps has suffered a terrible defeat.'

'However did you convince them not to make an example of you?' Drephos murmured.

'I am still doing so, day to day.' And, without visibly changing at all, the guards behind Varsec assumed a different aspect: not escorts but jailers.

'And you need to fortify your Corps against whatever happened, and you need to do so now – ready for the next engagement of the war. And so you come here, to the Empire's bastard son.' It was not clear whether he meant himself or Chasme and the Iron Glove. 'But I was under the impression that what happened to your Farsphex was not understood.'

'Pingge, step forwards,' Varsec beckoned, and the Fly-kinden woman did so. 'Pingge flew in the assault on Collegium. She is the sole survivor. She saw it all.'

The Fly spoke at length, sometimes faltering with emotion, but pushing herself on. Whatever she had been before, there was a steely determination to her now. It demanded revenge – revenge for all the friends and comrades lost over Collegium. As she made her report, describing Collegium's new weapon, Drephos became more and more focused, his iris-less eyes gleaming, gesturing for Totho to bring him pen and paper.

And, when she had finished, Drephos turned to confer with Totho, his guests utterly forgotten, the two artificers muttering together as excitedly as two young students. The Colonel-Auxillian even got as far as sketching three or four figures, before remembering that he had an audience, and at last he said, 'Why, yes, I believe I see the problem.' He was striving for calm now, but it was plain that Pingge's news had inspired him.

'And your price?' Varsec pressed.

'Can be negotiated with your factor there but' – Drephos's tone made it clear that this was the real prize – 'I will have to see the full schematics for your orthopters, of course.' Varsec's great triumph of mechanics had been denied to Drephos's insatiable curiosity until now.

But Varsec had thought that far ahead. 'Of course. I have them here,' he said, without a pause. 'But it must be soon – even now.' Here was a man in whose future loomed the crossed pikes of the executioner.

Drephos smiled, seldom a pleasant sight. 'It is an invitation I extend to few, Colonel Varsec, but will you join us, then? For I see what must be done, and we had better get to work.'

Glossary

Characters

Aagen – Wasp-kinden, Imperial ambassador to Collegium

Aarmon – Wasp-kinden, leader of the new Imperial Aviation Corps

Aetha – Wasp-kinden, General Tynan's daughter-in-law

Amnon – Beetle-kinden, former First Soldier of Khanaphes

Angved – Wasp-kinden, Imperial artificer

Aradocles – Sea-kinden, Edmir of Hermatyre

Arvi – Fly-kinden, Jodry Drillen's secretary

Averic – Wasp-kinden, student at the College

Axrad – Wasp-kinden pilot

Banjacs Gripshod – Beetle-kinden artificer

Berjek Gripshod – Beetle-kinden diplomat

Bola Stormall – Beetle-kinden aviation artificer

Bordes – Mynan airman

Breighl ('Painful') – halfbreed spy in Solarno

Bresner – Wasp-kinden aviator

Brugan – Wasp-kinden, general of the Rekef

Castre Gorenn – Dragonfly-kinden, exile

Cheerwell Maker – Beetle-kinden, Stenwold's niece

Cherten – Wasp-kinden colonel, Army Intelligence

Chyses – Mynan soldier

Corog Breaker – Beetle-kinden, Master Armsman and pilot

Drephos (Dariandrephos, the Colonel-Auxillian) – halfbreed artificer, leader of the Iron Glove

Dulci Broadster – Beetle-kinden social history Master at the College

Edmon – Mynan airman

Elder Padstock – Beetle-kinden, chief officer of the Maker's Own Company

Elser Hardwick – Beetle-kinden pilot

Erveg – Wasp-kinden, camp colonel for the Eighth Army

Esmail – Bug-kinden assassin and spy

Eujen Leadswell – Beetle-kinden student and agitator

Ferric – Wasp-kinden, engineer with the Eighth Army

Forra – Fly-kinden air crew

Franticze – Bee-kinden pilot flying for Myna

Garvan – *see* Gesa

Gerethwy – Woodlouse-kinden student at the College

Gesa ('Garvan') – female Wasp-kinden major, Army Intelligence

Gizmer – Fly-kinden air crew

Gjegevey – Woodlouse-kinden, slave and adviser to Seda

Greenwise Artector – Beetle-kinden magnate in Helleron

Hallend – Beetle-kinden student

Harvang – Wasp-kinden, Rekef colonel

Hasp – Wasp-kinden major, Slave Corps

Helmess Broiler – Beetle-kinden Assembler in Collegium, Imperial sympathizer

Hokiak – Scorpion-kinden merchant in Myna

Honory Bellowern – Beetle-kinden, Imperial diplomat

Jadis of the Melisandyr – Spider-kinden, Mycella's bodyguard and chief aide

Janos Outwright – Beetle-kinden, chief officer of Outwright's Pike and Shot

Jodry Drillen – Beetle-kinden, Speaker for the Assembly

Jons Padstock – Beetle-kinden soldier, Elder Padstock's son

Kiin – Fly-kinden air crew

Kymene – Mynan leader

Knowles Bellowern – Beetle-kinden, Imperial colonel in the Consortium

Laszlo – Fly-kinden, former pirate and friend of Stenwold Maker

Lien – Wasp-kinden, general of the Engineering Corps

Losel Baldwen – Beetle-kinden scholar

Ludon – Wasp-kinden aviator

Lyren – Wasp-kinden, Tynan's son

Lissart ('te Liss') – Firefly-kinden agent

Malkan – Wasp-kinden, general of the Seventh Army, defeated by the Sarnesh at Malkan's Folly

Marsene – Mynan airwoman

Marteus – Ant-kinden renegade, chief officer of Coldstone Company

Mittoc – Wasp-kinden, colonel of Engineers with Second Army

Morkaris – Spider-kinden, Mycella's mercenary adjutant

Mycella of the Aldanrael – Spider Lady-Martial

Mylus – Ant-kinden, slave to General Tynan

Nishaana – Wasp-kinden aviator

Ostrec – Wasp-kinden, Quartermaster Corps and Rekef

Paladrya – Sea-kinden, advisrr to Aradocles and friend of Stenwold Maker

Parops – Ant-kinden of Tark

Pendry Goswell – Beetle-kinden pilot

Pingge – Fly-kinden air crew

Praeda Rakespear – Beetle-kinden scholar, lover of Amnon

Raullo Mummers – Beetle-kinden artist

Te Remi – Fly-kinden taverner in Solarno

Reyna Pullard – Beetle-kinden, assistant to Banjacs Gripshod

Te Riel – Fly-kinden agent in Solarno

Roder – Wasp-kinden, general of the Eighth Army

Salthric – Wasp-kinden, Broken Sword Father

Sartaea te Mosca – Moth-trained Fly-kinden, lecturer at the College

Scain – Wasp-kinden aviator

Seda I – Empress of the Wasps

Shawmair – Solarnese pilot

Sherten – Wasp-kinden, Rekef agent

Shoel Jhin – Grasshopper-kinden slave

Stenwold Maker – Beetle-kinden, War Master of Collegium

Straessa ('the Antspider') – halfbreed student at the College

Taki (Te Schola Taki-Amre) – Solarnese Fly-kinden aviatrix

Taxus – halfbreed pilot from Tark

Tegrec – Moth-trained Wasp-kinden, Tharen ambassador to the Empire

Tiadro – Fly-kinden air crew

Tisamon – Mantis-kinden Weaponsmaster

Toek – Scorpion camp north of Solarno

Totho – halfbreed artificer, second-in-command of the Iron Glove

Tynan – Wasp-kinden, general of the Second Army

Uctebri – Mosquito-kinden, magician killed by Tisamon

Varsec – Wasp-kinden, aviation artificer

Vecter – Wasp-kinden, colonel of the Rekef

Vorses – Mynan airman

Willem Reader – Beetle-kinden aviation artificer

Xaraea – Moth-kinden agent

Places

Capitas – capital of the Empire

Chasme – city of renegades on the Exalsee

Collegium – Beetle city-state

Commonweal – Dragonfly domain north of the Lowlands

Coretsy – salt mine near Myna

Darakyon – Mantis forest, formerly haunted
Dorax – Moth retreat
Egel – Fly warren
Etheryon – Mantis hold
Everis – Spider island city
Felyal – Mantis hold and forest
Helleron – Beetle city-state
Kes – Ant island city-state
Khanaphes – ancient Beetle city-state
Malkan's Folly – battlefield, now site of Sarnesh fortress
Maynes – Ant city-state, formerly part of the Empire
Merro – Fly warren
Myna – Beetle city-state, formerly part of the Empire
Nethyon – Mantis hold
Princep Salma – city founded by refugees of the last war
Sarn – Ant city-state, ally of Collegium
Seldis – Spider city
Skiel – Imperial town
Solarno – Beetle city on the Exalsee
Sonn – Beetle city in the Empire
Spiderlands – large domain south of the Lowlands
Szar – Bee city-state, formerly part of the Empire
Tark – Ant city-state
Tharn – Moth retreat
Three-city Alliance – Myna, Szar and Maynes
Vek – Ant city-state, recently at peace with Collegium

Organizations and Things

Amphiophos – Collegiate centre of government
Arcanum – Moth secret service
Aristoi – the Spider-kinden ruling class
Army Intelligence – Imperial army corps
Assembly – Collegiate ruling body

Aviation Corps – Imperial army corps, part of the Engineers

Battle of the Rails – battle in which Malkan's Seventh Army defeated the Sarnesh

Broken Sword – pacifist cult within the Empire

Coldstone Company – Collegiate Merchant Company, motto: *In Our Enemies' Robes*

Consensus – Mynan ruling body

Consortium of the Honest – mercantile arm of the Empire

Corta Obscura and **Corta Lucida** – Solarnese ruling bodies

Cranefly – Mynan flying machine

Crystal Standard – Solarnese political party

Eighth Army – commanded by General Roder

Engineering Corps ('the Engineers') – Imperial army corps

Esca Magni – Taki's orthopter

Esca Volenti – Taki's previous orthopter, destroyed in liberation of Myna

Farsphex – new Imperial model of orthopter

Fierce Lady – Mynan flying machine piloted by Marsene

Firebug – new Solarnese model of orthopter

Fourth Army – 'the Barbs', destroyed by Felyen Mantids in the last war

Great College – Collegiate centre of learning

Greatshotter – new Iron Glove-developed artillery

Iron Glove – artificing cartel led by Drephos out of Chasme

Maker's Own – Collegiate Merchant Company, motto: *Through the Gate*

Malkan's Stand/Malkan's Folly – Sarnesh defeat of the Empire, now Sarnesh fortress

Outwright's Pike and Shot – Collegiate Merchant Company, motto: *Outright Victory or Death*

Pacemark – Mynan orthopter piloted by Edmon

Path of Jade – Solarnese political party

Prowess Forum – Collegiate duelling school

Quartermaster Corps – Imperial army corps

Red Anvil – Mynan flying machine

Rekef – Imperial secret service, divided into Inlander and Outlander

Satin Trail – Solarnese political party

Second Army – 'the Gears', commanded by General Tynan

Seventh Army – 'the Winged Furies', Malkan's command, destroyed by Sarnesh in the last war

Slave Corps – Imperial army corps

Sontaken – passenger airship

Spearflight – Imperial model of orthopter

Stonefly – Mynan orthopter piloted by Vorses

Stormreader – Collegiate model of orthopter

Sweet Fire – Mynan fixed-wing flier

Tserinet – Mynan orthopter piloted by Franticze

Twelve-year War – Imperial war against the Commonweal

Wanderer – Mynan orthopter piloted by Bordes